SILVER TALONS GUILD

BOOK ONE

C.L. CARNER

Part One:

The Orb of Dragonkind

ONE

THE SMELL OF FRIED fish and freshly baked bread wafted through the air of The Loose Anchor Tavern as a merry band of musicians played for the enormous crowd. The patrons were mostly sailors making port, passing time as their ships were unloaded. Very few Blackwater residents ventured outside the high stone walls of Blackwater to the dockside tavern that was so often filled with pirates. They gambled, drank, and on occasion, were known to draw a cutlass or two when they disagreed as to the winner of a bet.

Fire from the large stone hearth in the center of the room illuminated the tavern in a deep orange glow dancing shadows throughout the crowd as the flames flickered. The Blackwater flag and the crest of the Silver Talons hung down from the wood beams above, and the head of a dragon-like sea monster stared down from a plaque mounted over the bar. Serving girls maneuvered through the packed tavern with trays of ale and food.

A dirty man, wet with sweat, ale, and the stench of a good long period at sea, grabbed the backside of a young serving girl who brushed past him—a pretty girl with fiery red curls. "Let's see if the carpet matches the drapes," he said as he whirled the girl around to face him. His hot, stinking breath assaulted her nose as he puckered his lips and tried to bring his face to hers while simultaneously trying to get a hand up her dress. The girl groaned with disgust as she shoved away from him, tipping her tray to the side and spilling its contents on the floor. She drew the tray back and smacked him across the face with it. A mixture of saliva and blood flew from his mouth and he looked back at her with furious anger.

"You dirty wench!" he growled as he launched to his feet and drew back his fist to hit her. Before he could make contact, a hand, more powerful than his own, blocked his strike and held his hand in place.

"That would be very unwise of you. I know you probably do not know who this young woman is, but I guarantee, if you lay so much as a finger on her again, your corpse will be hanging from the wooden beam outside this very tavern as a warning and no one in your company will be able to dock here ever again. Now, as the owner of this establishment, I suggest you leave and do not let me see you here again; otherwise, you will be at the mercy of Commander Leon Rend."

His eyes widened at the mention of the name, but the man did not attempt to hide his scowl as he spat more blood and saliva on the floor. He said nothing more as he gathered his things and moved toward the exit. Declan, the owner, watched him go until the tavern doors swung closed behind him.

"Sophie, are you okay?" Declan asked, putting a sympathetic hand on the back of her shoulder.

"Yes, I'm okay," Sophie said, nodding.

"I promised your father you would be safe working here, if you would rather work in the kitchen tonight, I can move you off the floor," Declan offered with concern.

"No, I would prefer to stay out here, I need the tips," Sophie replied brushing off her apron and bending down to pick up the mugs of ale she'd dropped on the floor. Declan returned to the bar and the night carried on as usual.

At closing time, Sophie traded in her coppers for as many silver pieces as she could, and exchanged as many silvers as she could for gold.

"Well, what's the haul tonight, Soph?" Declan asked.

"Eight gold, five silver, and two copper."

"Pirates are lousy tippers." Declan frowned. shaking his head, he reached into a secret pocket inside his vest and pulled out a small leather pouch. "Here, you deserve this, I appreciate you coming in tonight." The bag jingled with coin as he handed it over. Sophie opened it and counted the shiny gold pieces inside.

"Twenty gold? Declan, I know you only pay the other servers half this amount a night. I can't accept this," she argued.

"You can, and you will. You handled yourself pretty well with that pirate, and you deserve this much just for having to deal with him. You not only worked as a server but security too, and on your regular night off. Double duty, double pay." He gave her a pat on the back. "Come on, I will walk you to the gate."

The docks at night could be dangerous for anyone, more so for a young girl traveling alone. Sophie was thankful for Declan's company.

Barely in his thirties, Declan was already a widower. His wife went through a rough pregnancy and an even more difficult childbirth. The midwife did all she could to save the baby, but Katarina did not survive. Their son, Nikolai, was now five years old. Sometimes, Sophie watched him for Declan when the tavern was slow. She enjoyed both jobs equally, even on the worst night.

When they reached the entrance, the guard saw them and immediately signaled for the man on top to raise the gate. The chains crunched between the gigantic stone gears as the man tuned the crank.

"Get home safely, Miss Rend." The guard nodded to Sophie and went back to his post.

"Thank you," she called, then, turned back to Declan, "Thank you for walking me to the gate. I will see you tomorrow evening." She gave him a quick and friendly hug, patting him on the back. He was like family to her, and her father. Declan and his wife used to run the Gilded Lily, the members-only tavern inside the guild hall, but after his wife died, everything within the walls of Blackwater reminded him of her. He made it as far out of town as the Loose Anchor. The old inn closed for a while, a few years back and they had to shut down the docks when the aquahydra took up residence in the bay and destroyed any ship daring to enter. Without patrons, the owner could no longer afford to keep the place.

They thought the monster would eventually move on, but it stayed in the bay for a long time and the town began to suffer, cut off from the supplies they needed to survive. The only path out of town connecting to the rest of the continent was through the Stonehold Mountains. The switchbacks and paths were too narrow for a wagon, horses could make it, but goods and supplies had to be carried through the mountain pass.

Many gladiators from around the realm tried to slay the monster, but none were successful, until Leon Rend came to town with an army from Braidwood. The legend says he gathered every soldier, every magic wielder, and his magical weapon which he'd lovingly named "the Greatsword of Destiny." Together, they made a plan, and Leon bravely led the battle against the creature. The monster claimed a few ships and many lives in the battle, but Leon kept fighting until he struck the final, killing blow.

It was many years ago, Sophie was not yet out of her mother's womb then, but there was no shortage of people to tell her how wonderful, brave, and mighty her father had been. She had lived her whole life so far hearing people tell his story, bards sang songs of his heroism from here to Braidwood. A few months before he got to Blackwater, Leon and his soldiers liberated Braidwood from the tyrant, Orion, and his dragon-riders. He was a true hero, and Sophie bet there wasn't a person on the whole continent who hadn't heard of Leon Rend.

The continent they lived on, was once a kingdom ruled by a man who the stories and folklore say was a good and fair king, but when he passed away without an heir or even a wife, the fighting began. Some wanted the continent to remain a kingdom, others wanted to split the continent into several kingdoms. In the end, three guilds were formed; an eastern, western, and central guild.

Back then, there were dragons, knights, jousting tournaments, and royal balls. Now the dragons have been hunted to extinction and the only ball Sophie had ever been to was the town ball at the Silver Talons Guild Hall. The parties were fun, but it was always the same people from Blackwater. She longed to meet people from other places, such as the kingdom of Ledora. She'd heard so much about their city of gold, lavish masquerades, and their dragon prince—although, she had no idea why they called him that, dragons were extinct as far as she knew.

Stories of dragons and knights, fancy dresses, and royal dinner parties, had always fascinated Sophie, but what interested her more than all of those things combined, was magic. Dragons were not what some stories claimed them to be, yes, they were large, frightening beasts, and were known to get hungry, but they were magical creatures with abilities beyond any human's wildest dreams.

Some legends say the silver dragons could shift into the form of either a human or an elf and could live among the people undetected. Silver dragons used to inhabit the mountains northwest of Blackwater, but the people who feared them, spread their fear to others and led attacks against the beasts until there were none left. The absence of the silver dragons took its toll. The people had not known, but they had been the only thing standing between the neighboring towns and the red dragons inhabiting the island just north of Stonehold Keep. With no peaceful creatures to hold them back, the red beasts attacked, taking children, cattle, and livestock for food and leaving only devastation in their wake.

Stonehold Keep was abandoned after the red dragon attacks. If there were any people left alive, they ran as far and fast as they could. Even though the dragons have been gone for many years, no one has been to the keep since the attack, they're still terrified the red dragons may return. Since then, the people of Blackwater at least, taught their children the silver dragons were our protectors and it was a mistake to attack them. For many years after, people searched the world for a sign of a silver dragon, but if there were any left, they did not wish to be found.

Sophie's thoughts came so quickly, she didn't even realize how far she'd walked until she reached the front stoop of her house. Opening the door to her house quietly, she tried her best not to wake her mother or father. The evening's work and the walk home finally hit her as she crept into her room. She'd barely taken off her boots before collapsing backward onto her bed. The down comforter, and soft furs enveloped her and she drifted off into a dreamless sleep.

The next morning, Sophie came out of her room to find the house empty. Her father was either already at work or had not yet been home. Her mother, Samantha, was probably at the market getting fresh produce for the day, or at her sweet shop. Sophie grabbed her coin pouch, attached it to her belt, then went out to the cellar at the back of the house. The heavy metal doors took some strength to pull open and the force made her stumble backward.

The cellar was dark and musty. The light from outside illuminated only the first few feet and the wooden stairs creaked as she descended. Feeling her way down the wall to the first sconce, Sophie took the torch out of it, lit it using the flint and steel her father kept on the table beneath it. She carried it with her through the main room, which was large and filled with shelf-stable dry goods, spices, flours, and jars of preserved fruits and vegetables. There were three doors off the main room, and she entered the last of them. Sophie placed the torch in a sconce and the dim light illuminated the treasures in the room; trunks and trinkets, men's clothing, and old books about dragons, and about the world before they disappeared. The name Balefire was etched into the front page of some of the tomes, although the name meant nothing to Sophie.

She had been going through the storage room for weeks because of the small leather-bound book she found. It was a wizard's spell book, handwritten with incantations, runes, and recipes for various potions and elixirs. She didn't know any wizards personally, but heard the wizard at the tower in Lapis Highland was looking for an apprentice. The cost of his mentorship was a thousand gold pieces. This was to ensure the safety of his student and to purchase the required focus and components needed for training. A few more weeks working the floor at the tavern and she'd have enough to finally follow her dreams.

Sophie had been practicing for days already and could make a few of the easier spells work, but she needed more components. She continued inspecting the items in the room, going through trunks, and flipping through pages. She pulled a book from the large shelf, and tried to make sense of the strange symbols written inside. It wasn't any language she had ever seen before. Closing it, she put the book in an old satchel she found among the old clothing—she'd ask Gabe to translate it later. After cleaning up a little, Sophie closed the door, and re-locked it the way it had been when she found it.

Nestled in the forest to the west of town, stood an old weeping willow. The stream babbled softly over the rocks just down the bank from the great tree. Birds sang happily in the canopy as other tiny creatures scurried across the forest floor. Sophie always came to this spot when she needed quiet time alone, or when she was sad, it always made her feel better. Making herself comfortable on a patch of moss, she leaned against the trunk of the tree and listened to the birds, the sound of the stream, and then, the crack of a twig behind her. Jumping up, she peered around the trunk of the willow then let out a sigh of relief when she saw it was just her friend heading her way.

"Gabe, you scared me half to death," Sophie scolded.

"Sorry, I thought I might find you here," he said, as he sat down beside the stream and began removing his boots and stockings. Sophie watched as he slid down the bank and into the cool water, which was only ankle-deep.

"Come on, Sophie, wade with me," Gabe called, smiling with child-like wonder. He always took joy in the simple things, the change of seasons, swimming in lakes, wading in streams, and of course, Sophie's company. She didn't know why he always wanted to be around her, she wasn't exactly a ray of sunshine on her best day, but ever since they were little, he was by her side. He never admitted to having feelings for her, which was perfect, because for whatever reason Sophie didn't think of anyone in such a manner.

While the other girls were talking about the boys they liked, Sophie was learning to read and speak other languages. Few girls could speak more than the common tongue here in Blackwater, and they had little interest in learning, but Sophie could not satiate the hunger for knowledge she felt. No matter how many books she had, it was never enough. This alone, usually made people give her a wide berth.

Sophie sat down, resting her back against the tree. She pulled out the small leather book, read the materials needed for the first spell, and then looked around the forest for whatever she could collect. When Gabe saw she was not going to join him in the stream, he climbed up the bank and came over to see what she was so interested in. Sophie showed him the book and the excitement and surprise on his face told her he thought it was the greatest thing he had seen in quite a while.

"Have you tried any spells yet?" he asked.

"I tried a few over the last couple of weeks, but I ran out of components, which is why I came out here. Did you happen to bring your flint and steel?"

"I never leave home without it," Gabe replied with a grin.

Sophie instructed him to build a small fire as she pulled out some components from her bag. She found a cricket by the bank then grabbed a handful of the softest sand and carried both to the fire.

"I'm sorry," Sophie whispered to the cricket as she placed it in the flame. She sprinkled the sand on top of the bug as she whispered, "*somnum penitus*" into the fire. The base of the flame glowed bright green, roared once, and then went out completely. The sand at the base of the fire still had a soft illumination to it. Sophie picked it up in her hand. It was cool to the touch. She spotted a raven hopping along the forest floor nearby and repeated the incantation, blowing the green sand from her hand toward the bird. Immediately, the raven puffed up and settled in for a deep sleep.

"Wow, awesome," Gabe exclaimed staring at the bird Sophie had just magically put to sleep.

Sophie crept close to the raven and apologized before she proceeded to collect her next component; a writing quill plucked from a sleeping bird. She grabbed a few of the raven's long tail feathers, counted to three, apologized to it again, and then pulled as hard and quickly as she could. The raven squawked awake, frantically flapping as it hopped away. Finally, it gained a wind beneath its wings and was able to take off in flight.

"Why'd ya do that to the poor bird?" Gabe asked.

"For these." Sophie looked down at her hand, opening her fist to reveal her prize; five black feathers. "Want to help me try out a new spell?"

"Of course, like you even had to ask. Let's see what you can do," he replied.

"This one will require you to be asleep," Sophie said.

Gabe found a soft patch of moss and made himself comfortable. "Sleep is one of my favorite things to do, I will be your test subject any time as long as I get to take a nap!" he said, as he settled in and closed his eyes.

Sophie waited until he began snoring softly to begin. She focused on the quill in her hand and closed her eyes. She whispered the incantation as the forest disappeared around her. She sat with her legs crossed, focusing on the words. She touched the quill to the palm of her hand and wrote the message she wanted to send to Gabe. *Wake up.* She scrawled the words again, but still Gabe slept.

Maybe I'm not doing it right, she thought as she got up and tapped Gabe on the shoulder.

"What did it do? I don't feel any different." Gabe said, rubbing his eyes.

"It didn't work. I think I need more practice," Sophie replied as she emptied her coin pouch into her hand and stuffed the coins into the pocket of her trousers. Next, she scooped up the remaining sand from the first spell and put it into the small purse. It no longer glowed, but still shined with greenish-blue glitter.

"I have to be heading home. Want to walk with me?" Gabe asked, offering her his hand to help her to her feet. Sophie nodded, accepting his hand. They strolled back through the woods, listening to the birds chirping in the branches, and the bugs trilling in the shade of the budding bushes.

When they reached Gabe's house the goats greeted them at the fence. They bleated loudly as he approached, recognizing him as the one who cares for them.

"I know, you guys are hungry, come on then." Gabe waved goodbye as he led the goats to their feeding trough.

"Hey Gabe, wait," Sophie called, almost forgetting the book she had brought with her. "I don't know what language this is in, but I thought maybe you could find out for me." She handed Gabe the book. He opened it and looked at the strange lettering.

"I have never seen anything like this, but I can ask the other guys at work, there are quite a few older scribes who only write ancient texts because they are the only ones who can read them," he replied.

Sophie thanked him and waved before she continued walking home. The whole way, all she could think about was magic, adventure, dragons, and of course, what it would be like when she became the very first female wizard's apprentice.

TWO

AN OCEAN AWAY, TOWARD the east where the sky met the sea, in the kingdom of Ledora, Prince Dominic wiped the sweat from his forehead using a white handkerchief trimmed with golden thread.

"Again," a voice called out as he stuffed the handkerchief back into the pocket of his trousers. The command came from the great wizard, Alemayehu, as he evaluated the prince's every move. Dominic rolled his wrist in a circle and inside his mind, he recited the incantation; *'mpira wa moto'.* A ball of fire appeared in his hand, hovering only an inch from his skin. He stared at the fireball he'd produced with pride, and in his excitement, Dominic forgot to hurl the flame at the target until the heat began to redden his palm.

"Ow!" Dominic flicked his hand in reaction to the burn and sent the fireball soaring into the anti-magic field surrounding the training yard. As soon as the flame hit the invisible barrier, it fizzled as if it entered the ocean and evaporated into the air around them.

"Again," Alemayehu commanded.

"Are you crazy? My skin is still burning from the last one, can't we practice something else?" Dominic asked. The wizard gave him a stern look.

"How will you ever claim your ancestral powers and rule this land, if you can't take a little heat? Again." The wizard's tone was condescending and short of patience. Dominic turned back to the training target set up one hundred and fifty feet from where he stood. He repeated the spell, producing the ball of flame again. This time, he threw it as quickly and as far as he could. It landed forty feet short of the target and spread out from the area where it hit in a bright flame. Alemayehu waved his hand and the flames disappeared.

"Better, but tomorrow we will continue to work on your range and silent casting. You're throwing from your shoulder when you should be using your arcane energy to propel the fireball." The wizard glanced at the four guards waiting outside the training yard. "We are finished with today's lesson," he said, turning to walk away. His figure became transparent and then disappeared completely after a single step. *When is he going to teach me that trick?* Dominic wondered. The guards surrounded him and moved as a unit, protecting the prince from all sides.

"So, someday, you're going to talk to me right?" Dominic asked, looking back and forth between the men. The guards kept their eyes forward and didn't glance his way.

"Yeah, I thought not." Dominic followed them to his next destination; sword fighting. The weapon's training area was much smaller than the casting yard and tall pillars lined the room on both sides, providing many opportunities to dodge attacks, gain position, or even hide if you needed to. Dominic crossed the room to the weapons rack where his instructor, Master Shujaa stood.

"Why do I have to learn to use a sword when I could just sling fire at our enemies?" he joked, picking up the heavy greatsword Master Shujaa made him practice with. It was made from the heaviest material known to man and then enchanted to add twenty pounds. When Dominic first picked up a sword at the age of five, it was a shortsword weighing only three pounds. As he grew and became stronger, his weapons became heavier, pushing his muscles to their limit with every session.

Dominic was thankful he only had sword training once every two days, it gave his muscles time to recover. On the days he didn't train with a sword, he trained his mind with studies of the ancient dragon texts written hundreds of years before he was born.

This was his life; schedules, classes, training, appointments, and the only people who talked to him were either barking orders or giving instructions. The residents of the kingdom; both noble and base born, spoke of the prince as if he led a wonderous life, always whispering about how lucky he was, and wishing they were in his place. Sometimes, Dominic wished they were too.

Being the heir to the Ledoran throne was a lonely job. Dominic had no friends, only royal advisors and of course his father, King Haki. These days, the king busied himself with the search for a betrothal for his son. As king, Dominic would need to eventually produce an heir of his own to carry on the royal line, but if Dominic had any say at all, it would be a long time before he had to worry about children.

"Are you ready?" Master Shujaa asked, as he held his sword in front of him with one hand, and his other arm folded politely behind his back. Dominic raised his heavy greatsword with two hands and Master Shujaa quickly stepped forward, motioning for Dominic to drop one of his hands.

"One hand only," Master Shujaa told him.

Dominic dropped his left hand, gripping the heavy sword tightly in his right. It already made his bicep sting to hold it at the ready. Master Shujaa circled him, and Dominic countered his steps, paying close attention to the position of his feet.

"Focus only on blocking," the swordmaster instructed as he shuffled in for a strike on Dominic's left side. The Prince swung his sword to meet the opposing steel with a loud clang. He blocked again when a strike came from above, and then from below, once more from the left. A fake to the left again made Dominic react, leaving his right shoulder unprotected. Master Shujaa smacked Dominic's arm with the flat of his blade.

"Always expect your opponent to try and trick you. Don't leave yourself open. Switch hands, let's try it the other way now." Dominic obeyed, gripping the sword with his left hand, which was not his dominant, but he had trained to use it just as much in case his right were ever incapacitated.

They circled around, repeating the dance again and again, switching hands after each set until Dominic was no longer able to hold the sword up.

That night, Dominic tossed and turned, fighting with the covers on his bed as he desperately tried to sleep, his usual dreamless rest was invaded by visions of an island across the sea with four tall mountains, and a vast continent nearby. He saw a girl with strange-colored hair and another with hair as red as fire. The orb of dragon magic his kingdom protected whispered to him in a language he recognized as draconic, but he was not fluent enough to decipher what it was saying. It pulsed with energy and lightning as it swelled. It looked and sounded like it was about to burst. His dream continued in painful flashes of light searing into his mind with the same images repeating over and over; the girls, the mountains, the orb, and the dream ended with a green dragon rising from the mountain. The last thing he saw was the gaping maw of the great green beast as it swallowed him whole.

When he woke up, he was drenched in sweat. The memory of the dragon still haunted him, but he could not stop thinking about the girls he saw at the beginning of his dream. He knew they must be important to the prophecy of the orb, but only the Oracle could tell him where he needed to go and what he needed to do.

THREE

A LOUD, RHYTHMIC KNOCKING startled Laughlin and he jumped as he tried to hang his tunic to dry beside the brick fireplace. The shirt dropped to the floor and he looked between it and the door, unable to decide which was more urgent. He picked up the garment and instead of hanging it on the hook by the hearth, laid it across the back of the wooden dining chair. He crossed the room quickly and opened the door shirtless; beads of perspiration glistening on his chest in the early evening sun. Juniper took in the sight of him and stood speechless for a moment. His dark brown hair hung loosely on his forehead accentuating his deep green eyes. She marveled at her incredible luck that she held the affections of such a man.

Behind Laughlin, a dark gray wolf with ice blue eyes sat patiently waiting to say hello.

"Good Evening, Juniper," Laughlin said with a smile as he moved close and planted a quick peck on her cheek.

"Go ahead, Dusk, say hello." Laughlin moved to the side so Dusk could approach Juniper. The wolf nuzzled her hand and she bent down to give her a proper scratch behind the ear.

"I have planned a hike and a camping trip for us this evening, it's spontaneous, I know, but I hope you will come with me unless you're otherwise engaged with pressing business here?" she asked, rising to meet Laughlin's gaze.

"A hike sounds fantastic, let me get some things together," he replied.

Juniper loved his cabin, it smelled of apples, cinnamon, and the wood stove. She and Laughlin had only been courting for a few cycles of the moon, but Juniper already knew her heart was his. She wandered around the sitting room as Laughlin rummaged around in the back.

"I'm ready," he said, emerging from the bedroom with a pack strapped to his back. His bedroll was secured to the top of the pack and his water skin hung from the side of it, the liquid sloshing with every step. Laughlin had a short sword sheathed on his left hip and when he noticed Juniper's gaze on the weapon he quickly explained.

"Just in case, you never know," he shrugged." It looks like you packed light," Laughlin said, gesturing to the small pack Juniper brought.

"It will make climbing the mountain much easier," she replied. "Come on, Let's go." Laughlin and Dusk followed her out and Laughlin paused to lock up.

Juniper linked her arm through his and they walked up the muddy path together. Along the sides of the path, the first signs of spring were just breaking the surface of the ground. Juniper motioned for Laughlin to wait a moment as she bent down to pick some curled fern.

"These are delicious when you cook them with some herbs and fresh butter," she explained, putting them into a pouch on her belt. When she had foraged as much as she needed, she rejoined Dusk and Laughlin on the path and they made their way out of the forest.

Juniper led them past Blackwater town square, and out the northern gate toward the eastern side of the mountain range, which by far, was the easiest side to climb and the safest. For a few hours, the walk was a gradual incline, with streams and budding plants. Soon there would be berries too, but for now, they would have to settle for fish and fried fern if they got hungry. As they ascended the mountain, the air became cooler and the sun dipped below the western peak, darkening the path. Juniper had no trouble seeing in the dark because of her elven ancestry, but Laughlin's human parentage did not afford him this particular feat.

"Hold on a moment, Juni." Laughlin took off his pack and pulled out a torch and a canister of oil. He dipped the tip of the torch into the oil and struck a piece of flint with a steel ring. The spark took to the fabric and illuminated the area. Laughlin handed Juniper the torch as he packed the things back into his pack, making sure the canister of oil was closed tightly before putting it back into the bag.

"Okay, I'm ready," he said, taking the torch back. Juniper continued leading the way. They had been hiking for close to four hours when Juniper finally told him they were almost there.

The climb became steeper as they reached the switchbacks and the path was soggy from melting snow. The terrain flattened slightly as they reached their destination. Laughlin's legs ached and burned. He hadn't been hiking for quite some time and his muscles reminded him of it with every step. Chopping wood and building his cabin required mostly upper body strength and he hadn't noticed how long it had been since his legs tingled as they did now. He looked around at the camp site Juniper led them to.

Tall pine trees covered in a layer of snow surrounded the clearing where they now stood, and in the center, a steaming hot spring beckoned them to soak their aching muscles. Lanterns were strung from one tree to another and enveloped the area in a soft romantic glow. A large tent sat off to the side of the hot spring, open and lit with the same style of hanging lanterns as the ones strung from the trees. Inside the tent, Laughlin could see the floor lined with warm fur hides and adorned with beautiful pillows. Dusk ran inside and immediately rolled over on her back, snuggling herself on a hide.

"Juniper, this is more beautiful than I ever imagined. You took a lot of effort to plan this, and it looks amazing." He took Juniper in his arms and kissed her deeply. When the kiss ended, she lingered for a moment, eyes closed, letting the sensation fill her with warmth.

They put their packs inside the tent and Juniper took out two bronze chalices and a bottle of wine. She walked outside and sat them on a flat rock beside the hot spring, then stood to undress, draping her over clothes over a low-hanging branch nearby. In only her undergarments, Juniper eased herself down into the steaming water and sighed with relief as the heat loosened all the tension her body held from climbing the mountain twice in one day.

Laughlin watched her as he took off his clothes and slipped into the heated pool. He moved to sit on the underwater ledge next to Juniper and smiled as she poured the wine into the two chalices. She handed him one and raised her cup to his. They clinked softly together and then Laughlin and Juniper relaxed, quietly sipping their wine beneath the starry sky.

"This is so beautiful," Laughlin said, looking around at the decorated clearing. "You're beautiful," he said, taking her wine glass and setting on the flat rock beside his own. Now he was looking into her eyes and she could feel the blush rising to her cheeks as he leaned in and softly brushed his lips against hers, letting his fingers trail down the side of her neck. Despite the warmth of the water, his touch brought out the goose flesh on her skin and she shivered with delight. Juniper rested her head on Laughlin's shoulder and he brushed his fingers up and down her arm as they enjoyed the closeness of each other.

"How did you find your way to Blackwater?" Laughlin asked, finally breaking the silence.

"When I left home, I was with a friend; her name was Maureen. She knew a guy in Northport and she said he would pay us quite well to work in his tavern. I thought it sounded perfect until we got there and we realized his tavern was actually a brothel and the work he wanted us to do was to serve his patrons' twisted desires. I hopped on the next ship out of there but Maureen stayed. The ship brought me to Blackwater. I found work with the guild and decided to remain here and my skills have proved valuable to the guild."

"What skills are those?" Laughlin looked at her with such interest.

"I am a druid of the Forgotten Grove, I can shape-shift at will into many different animal forms. I have a bond with nature allowing me to heal wounds and I draw energy from the moon."

"So, is that why your last name is Moonshadow?" Laughlin asked.

"Not exactly, Moonshadow is the name of our community circle. Every child born in the community is given the name Moon, when a druid is born, there is a solar eclipse and they then are given the name Moonshadow. It is the way we identify those with druidic powers."

"I see. So why did you leave home?" Laughlin asked.

"The reason I left is a much longer story." Juniper sighed and her eyes drifted slightly as she remembered the events of long ago causing her departure from the Forgotten Grove. "My mother and father wanted me to join the order of nature at Moonshadow temple. There, they choose a husband for you; one who matches and compliments your abilities, to strengthen the community circle and produce more powerful druids. I didn't want to disappoint my parents, so I did. I was matched with a husband, and we were given one year to produce a child." Juniper paused to wipe a tear from her cheek. "I wasn't able to do so, and after my second year of failing to get pregnant, they chose a new wife for my husband and I was sent away from the temple. In the years I spent with my husband, I did grow to care for him, and it hurt me to see him with his new wife. They conceived a child so quickly and I know I should have been happy for him, but it broke my heart, so I left." Juniper wiped a tear from her cheek. "I'm sorry, I know no one really wants to hear about the past relationships of their date," Juniper said, pouring her second glass of wine.

"Juni, I'm sorry, I didn't want to bring up pain from the past for you. You have an amazing heart and you are so very thoughtful." Laughlin gestured at the beautiful retreat Juniper made for them. "He was a very lucky man to have you as his wife, even for a short time." Laughlin held Juniper in his arms until they grew tired and then he helped her out of the hot spring and gathered their clothing on the way to the tent.

Dusk was waiting for them, happily lying on a fur hide just inside the entrance. Once they dried off, the three of them snuggled together. Laughlin and Dusk fell asleep right away, but Juniper did not require sleep in the same way they did, she only needed to meditate for a few hours to feel refreshed. Laughlin was still asleep next to Dusk when Juniper heard the sound of feet crunching through the snow north of them.

"Wake up, someone is coming," she said, rolling over to nudge Laughlin awake. "I'm going to check it out." Juniper's body began to glow white and the sound of cracking bones as her shape twisted and shrank startled Dusk, but the wolf remained quiet as Laughlin dressed and grabbed his sword. Laughlin watched in amazement as Juniper's body continued to shrink and her clothes, which were now too large, fell to the floor. Juniper had seemingly disappeared, and in her place, a tiny field mouse nosed its way out of her crumpled clothing.

The little mouse scurried out of the tent and in the direction of the footsteps. Remaining out of sight, Juniper got as close as a field mouse could, to the cloaked figures heading toward their camp.

"Are you sure you know where we are going?" One asked the other in a raspy deep voice.

"Yes, it is here, beyond this mountain, I can feel the orb's power like it's calling to me. The thief is in the city just beyond the pass." The other figure said, pointing toward Blackwater.

"What will we do when we find it?"

"We kill the one who stole it, and take it back, they do not know what they are in possession of."

Juniper ran back to the tent and shifted back into her human form. She quickly grabbed her sleeping shift she'd packed, threw it on, and dug two daggers out of her bag.

"They're going to kill someone in Blackwater. They're looking for an orb of some kind. I have to warn Leon," Juniper said.

"We should take out the threat first," Laughlin suggested, unsheathing his sword.

They waited until the assassins were past the campsite and quietly peered out of the tent. "They'll hear us as soon as our feet make the first sound, I will take the one on the left, can you take the one on the right?" Laughlin asked.

"I think I have enough energy to shift again, I will make it count," she said, dropping her daggers. Juniper began to shift, growing larger and sprouting thick black hair all over her body. She assumed the form of a large black bear and her dress shredded into pieces as she grew. Laughlin gaped at her in her bear form, his face showing slight concern—maybe even fear, hoping Juniper still recognized friend from foe in her predatory form.

"Are you ready? On three. One, two... THREE!" Laughlin shouted and the bear beside him roared as it sprinted toward the assassin on the right. Laughlin charged the man on the left who drew his sword quicker than he thought possible. Their steel clanked together, ringing out through the air.

Juniper bit down with all her force on the appendage nearest her mouth, which happened to be the assassin's left arm. He swung his sword with his right hand and caught her left shoulder with his blade. The animal roared in pain and swiped at the assassin with its massive claw.

Laughlin blocked the strike of the assassin he was engaged in combat with and lunged forward to strike, but his opponent was agile and whirled out of the way, then spun around and tried to make contact again. Laughlin brought his sword up just in time to parry the strike, and with a flick of his wrist, disarmed his opponent. Laughlin glanced over at Juniper just as the other assassin drove his sword through the bear's middle. The beast fell to the ground and slowly, all the hair disappeared and Juniper was left naked and bleeding from her abdomen.

"Drop your weapon, or the girl dies," the assassin commanded, holding his sword to Juniper's neck. Laughlin could see a slight rise and fall of juniper's rib area, but she didn't look like she would last much longer. Laughlin raised his hands and let the sword go.

As his hand opened, Laughlin let out a sharp whistle and before the sword reached his chest, Dusk lunged at the swordsman threatening Juniper, knocking him to the ground. When the hilt of Laughlin's sword reached his waist, he made a quick grab for it and ran it through his unarmed attacker, slicing upward, spilling his insides onto the ground in front of them.

Dusk held the other combatant down. Laughlin kneeled beside the assailant, pulling the red mask down to the man's chin so he could see his whole face. Laughlin noticed the side of his face was covered in what appeared to be scales. Not natural scales, but much like the orc tribes who disfigure themselves by cutting their ears or burning themselves to appear more frightening, he thought it must be for intimidation.

"Hold him there, Dusk," Laughlin said, rushing to Juniper's side. "Juni, can you hear me?" He gently slid his arm under her neck and cradled her to his chest. "Juni, please." The clouds parted and the light of the moon shined down on them. The beams illuminated Juniper's body in an ethereal glow and her wounds began to close, although the bruises remained. "Thank the druids and their power," Laughlin whispered. He left Juniper lying in the moonlight and grabbed the rope from his pack. He tied the assassin's hands and gagged him with a piece of cloth from the man's tunic. Once he was secured, and with Dusk still standing guard, Laughlin moved to help Juniper stand.

She leaned on his strong shoulder as he stood up slowly, guiding her to an upright position.

"Can you walk?" he asked.

"I'm not sure," she replied truthfully. She tried to move toward the tent. Every step sent a shooting pain through her stomach and she sat back down after only three steps. "No, it's okay, get him to Leon, I will be fine here for the night, I will rest, and meet you at your house in the morning," she said.

Laughlin wanted to resist but knew this was urgent and as much as he hated to admit it, Juniper would slow him down.

"Okay," he finally agreed, "Dusk, stay here with Juniper, keep her safe." Laughlin scratched his wolf and kissed Juniper on the forehead. "Can I take you back to the tent at least?" he asked.

"No, I need to stay in the moonlight as long as possible. I will be okay. I have Dusk."

Laughlin turned and grabbed the man by his arm. "On your feet, assassin," he said through gritted teeth.

Juniper watched as Laughlin marched him forward until they disappeared over the switchbacks descending the mountain.

The sun was just beginning to peak over the horizon when Laughlin opened the door to the Silver Talons Guild Hall and guided his prisoner inside. He approached the desk, keeping the prisoner firmly in hand.

"I need to see Leon Rend right away, please, it's urgent," Laughlin spoke quickly, yet respectfully.

"Let me see if he is available." The man behind the desk closed his eyes and was very still for a moment or two and then he opened his eyes. "Commander Rend will be right with you." Laughlin assumed they must be using some form of magical communication as no words were spoken out loud.

"Thank you," Laughlin replied.

While they waited, Laughlin took notice of the beautifully decorated guild hall. The marble floors were pristine and the grand staircase behind the desk was carpeted in a deep greenish-blue fabric accented with silver trimming on each side. A crystal chandelier hung from the vaulted ceiling, with candles flickering light throughout the entrance. The lobby smelled of fresh pine and clean linens. Finally, Laughlin heard the sound of boots coming down the stairs as the Guildmaster, Commander Leon Rend, approached to shake his hand. Several guards followed him and stopped a few paces behind.

"How can we help you?" Leon's voice was deep and gruff. From up close, Laughlin could see the flecks of gray peppering his hair as well as the stubble on his chin.

"I was sent here by Juniper Moonshadow. We were camping on the mountain just northeast of here when this man and his companion passed our campsite. Juniper heard them talking about an orb of some kind and they said the person who stole it was here in Blackwater. They planned to kill the person and take the orb," Laughlin explained.

"Where is his companion?" Leon asked. For a moment it appeared Leon's face had gone pale, but his stone expression did not change.

"When we heard their plan included the murder of a Blackwater resident, we did not hesitate, we attacked. Juniper was injured and is healing at the campsite, the other man did not live to make the journey here," Laughlin replied, leaving out the details of how he had been the one to spill the man's insides.

"Guards, take this man to the dungeon, I will be down to interview him shortly. Hank, will you please send scouts to the mountain to retrieve both Juniper and the body of this man's accomplice?" Leon requested, facing the man behind the desk. Hank nodded and whispered to a nearby squire who ran off to deliver Leon's orders.

The guards moved up, each gripping one of the man's elbows. They moved him swiftly from the hall.

"Thank you, I'm sorry, I don't think I caught your name," Leon said, looking at him as though he were a drifter.

"It's Laughlin, sir. I live in a cabin in the western woods of Blackwater," he explained.

"Oh yes, with the uh... the wolf, right?" Leon asked.

"Yes, sir."

"Well, thank you for bringing this man to me, we will take it from here. If you are ever looking for work, the guild could use more muscle and honorable men." Leon nodded farewell before turning toward the dungeon, the sound of his heavy boots striking the marble floor faded before Laughlin moved from the spot.

Not quite what I expected, he thought, turning to leave. He wasn't sure if he should go back up the mountain to find Juniper or if he should stay out of the way so the scouts could do their job. It was still early, and Juniper did say she would return Dusk to the cabin when she felt rested.

With heavy thoughts and worry, Laughlin returned to his cabin and tried to go back to sleep for a while, but all he saw when he closed his eyes, was the scaly face of the assassin as he thrust his sword through Juniper. He got out of bed and grabbed his tunic, hastily pulling it over his head. He couldn't wait any longer to know if Juniper was okay.

FOUR

Towering over the Kingdom of Ash, a dark castle silhouetted the full moon. Black storm clouds swirled above with frightening menace. The screeching of bats echoed through the empty streets as they tried to flee the storm. A black, horse-drawn carriage moved swiftly over the cobblestones toward the castle. the clopping of the hooves thundered like roaring applause. It didn't matter to Queen Luciana that the townspeople cowered in fear, shutting themselves inside their homes when they heard her carriage approaching. To her, the common people meant less than nothing.

The iron gates creaked unpleasantly as the footmen pushed them open for the Queen's carriage to enter. The footmen jumped back onto the back of the carriage after closing the gates, and the driver steered the horses to the front steps of the castle. The man on the left rushed to open the queen's door, but as he reached for the handle, the door burst open and slamming into his nose.

"Could you have taken any longer?" The Queen snarled as she looked at the footman in disgust as blood dripped from his nose. "Clean yourself up. Someone fetch my daughter and bring her to the throne room." Queen Luciana ordered as she marched forward without a second glance at the help. Her black dress trailed behind her as her heels echoed down the hall. She crossed the grand room and sat rigidly on her throne, tapping her fingers impatiently. Moments later, her daughter, Akiri, stood in front of her with a heavily armored guard on either side.

"I have just come from the Temple of Divination, and guess what the prophecy foretold?" The queen stood and approached her daughter, lifting Akiri's chin with her bony finger. Luciana inspected her face, turning it from one side to the other with a frown.

"I don't know, mother," Akiri replied, adverting her eyes from Luciana's piercing gaze.

"There is an orb of great power in the hands of our enemy, a young prince in the kingdom of Ledora. You need to claim it from him."

"Why me, shouldn't we have an army do such a task?" Akiri asked.

"Because of your bloodline, it is your birthright just as much as it is his, and no one but you, or the young prince can claim it. You must find it before they destroy it, or use the power for themselves. I have a battleship and a crew ready for you. Gather your things and you will leave by nightfall. I want you to bring the orb of power back here to our kingdom." She placed a hand on Akiri's shoulder. This was the closest to motherly affection Akiri had ever experienced. The queen was always so cold and militant in every aspect of her life.

"The ship will be stocked with plenty of gold to cover your travel expenses. You will be captain and the crew will answer to you. Bring the orb of power back here so we can make our kingdom the most powerful in the world." She dismissed her daughter with a wave but held up a finger to one of the guards for him to stay.

"As soon as my daughter gets her hands on the orb, kill her and bring the artifact to me. I cannot wield its power while she lives, but she needs to touch it before she dies to activate its magic."

"Yes, My Queen," he replied with a deep bow, never looking her in the eye. The guard exited the room and Luciana paced from one side of the room to the other. Her black and green dress clung to her slender shape, and the high-collared black cape she wore flowed behind her as she walked and fanned out with every turn. The queen's hair was to her waist, thick, and black as a raven's wing. Her pale skin amplified the dark circles under her eyes. She was tired, but there was no way she was going to be able to sleep any time soon.

Akiri packed the essentials and took another glance around her room to make sure she hadn't forgotten anything important before departing for the ship. She thought about saying goodbye to her mother before she left, but it was a kind of sentiment which had no place in their kingdom, or their relationship.

Akiri's mother taught her to be strong, calculating, cunning, manipulative, and even downright cruel. Nothing else—ever. Motherly advice was not freely given, but a tongue lashing, withholding food, and isolation were common tactics the queen used to make sure Akiri did everything she commanded her to do.

Akiri walked silently from the castle and to the carriage waiting to take her to the docks. She had never captained a crew before, but she had sailed plenty. When your home is an island, traveling to the mainland is sometimes necessary to find what you need, and in some cases, *who* you need. The ride to the docks did not take long and when the footman opened the carriage door, Akiri breathed in the sea air.

When Akiri boarded the ship, the crew was lined up on deck to introduce themselves. She scanned the faces, most of them she already knew. The last person in line caught her eye. She walked down the row, toward the person in the gray cloak. Their hood was drawn and their head down. Akiri approached cautiously.

"Remove your hood please," Akiri said. Two bony, pearl-white hands grabbed the hood and pulled it back, revealing a bald head Akiri was sure had never seen the sun and where her eyes should have been, there was nothing but smooth powder-white skin.

"Who are you?" Akiri asked.

"They call me soothsayer, teller of fortunes, I can see your future and I can guide you to the artifact you seek." The witch's voice was no more than a raspy whisper.

"Right. Okay then, what's our heading?" Akiri asked.

"South-East, until we reach the kingdom with golden peaks, it is there you will find what you seek. A boy, dressed in the armor of gold, the orb of power within his hold." The soothsayer drew her hood once more and walked away toward the stairs leading below deck.

"Okay, men, you heard her, we have our heading, let's shove off." Akiri walked past the sailors and to the captain's quarters. She collapsed onto her bed and stared at the ceiling. Part of her hoped this trip would be short, and the other part wished she could find a new life, somewhere far away from the island of misery; the kingdom called Ash.

FIVE

LEON REND STARED INTO the scale-covered face of the prisoner. Sitting in a chair on the outside of the man's cell, he waited for answers. Leon had left the prisoner locked in the dungeon for almost a full day without food or water, hoping by morning, the breakfast he presented would urge him to talk. Leon sat the tray on the stone floor in front of the cell. The smell of eggs and bacon filled the space and he heard the prisoner's stomach growl.

"Are you ready to talk yet? I don't have all day, I have things to do, so if we don't speak now, it might be a few days before I can make it back here." The man stared at Leon, glanced at the food, then back to Leon with no expression.

"What is your name?" Leon continued, but his question was followed only by more silence. "I will gladly leave you to rot in this dungeon if it means Blackwater is safe from you," he threatened. The man laughed. It was the first sound, and the first emotion Leon had seen from him.

"Please, tell me what is funny about rotting away in a dungeon." Leon rattled the bars of the man's cell.

"It's funny you think this ends with me," the prisoner finally spoke.

"How does this end? I could let you go free, for the right information."

"I will be a dead man either way. I'd rather watch the world burn with me." The corners of his mouth turned upward in a sinister grin.

"Tell me about the orb." Leon gave him a stern look.

"What do you want to know about it?" The way the man looked at him, Leon wondered how much he really knew.

"What is its power? Why do you want it?" Leon asked. The prisoner laughed again and shook his head.

"You know where it is, don't you?" The prisoner's eyes seemed to stare into Leon's soul. "Mark my words, far worse than the likes of me will be coming for it when I don't return." The prisoner moved to the bedroll on the southern wall and without another word, he curled onto the thin foam mat with his back to Leon and just like that, their conversation was over.

Leon slid the tray of food under the bars and into the cell, then left the dungeon with his mind racing. There was so much to do. He sent a messenger with orders for the guards to lock down the gates of Blackwater. No one without proof of residency would be allowed inside and all vendors would be received on the docks. Then he sent the same notice to the town crier so the citizens could be warned against strangers.

"Hank, I'm leaving for the day. Velen Shrike will take care of any Guildmaster duties for the day, but if there is an emergency, please send word to Mrs. Rend," Leon said, removing the pin on his lapel. Hank, the guild receptionist, wore the same pin, a magical item allowing the wearers to communicate telepathically across any distance.

"Deliver this to Velen Shrike," Hank said, handing Leon's pin to the Paige next to him. Hank nodded to Leon. "Safe travels, sir."

Leon didn't want anyone to know where he was going. Stopping at the armory, Leon grabbed a pack of essentials, dry rations, a bedroll, a water skin, and some torches. He packed everything in his leather backpack which bore his initials. He had a day's walk ahead of him and it was best to be prepared. Leon stopped by his office and grabbed his greatsword, a vorpal sword with the power to invoke Hellfire; a sword Leon had affectionately named *Destiny*.

Leon drew up the hood on his cloak and ensured he was not being followed. The temple of Ophay was at the southeastern border of Blackwater. He could have taken his horse, Horatio, but a war horse would draw unnecessary attention. Instead, Leon took the back alleyways where he was less likely to be spotted.

A wonderful artificer Leon knew created a system of underground tunnels connecting to each home's relief chambers. Water trickled into the tunnels throughout the day from the dam they built at the edge of the bay, but it made little difference until the flood gate opened at high tide and washed the waste away. The sewers had four inches of standing wastewater sitting stagnant underground. The stench was almost unbearable, Leon had to pull his tunic up over his nose to breathe, and even doing so did not stop the urge to vomit.

Leon broke into a sprint, gagging as he ran, and when he reached the end of the alley, he released the breath he had been holding. When he got farther away, he took in deep, frantic gasps of the fresh air, thankful no one was around to see him like this; the warrior he was, brought to his knees by the scent of human excrement.

When he regained composure, Leon continued, taking a path through the southern forest, which was was overgrown and still littered with leaves from the previous fall. He thought it wise to stay off the heavier traveled footpaths if he wanted to remain unseen.

In the thick of the forest, it was hard to tell what time of day it was. The sun's position was difficult to see through the thick canopy and the clouds. Leon thought it was at least mid-day because his stomach began to growl. He sat down behind a boulder, using the rock to rest his back, and pulled out a package of rations. The mixture of nuts, dried grapes, dried beef, and mango was strangely satisfying. He hadn't eaten a ration since his days of leading the Blackwater Army. Being the Guildmaster did have its advantages. Leon was never the kind of person to have everything while others went without and he made sure those who lived in Blackwater never went hungry. He might not be able to help the world, but he could help those who lived near him; his friends, and neighbors.

He had to help them now. Leon had to figure out how the small crystal orb he took from Orion and stored in the Temple of Ophay was now calling to people that Leon could only assume were Orion's minions. Leon brushed the dirt from his trousers as he stood and collected his things, packing everything back into the leather backpack before continuing on his way.

Off the path to the left, Leon heard the trickling of water. He hurried toward the sound and found a small but steady stream of water coming down the cliff face. Leon pulled out a handkerchief and laid it over the opening of his water skin to act as a filter. Leon gave the water a taste test, and found it to be clean and refreshing. He filled his water skin to the top after drinking his fill and tied it to his belt. Suddenly, a feeling he was being watched washed over him. He turned around quickly, eyes scanning the forest. He didn't see anyone—he did, however, hear voices heading toward him on the path to his right. The men were talking and laughing. They didn't seem ominous, but Leon did not want to risk it. He ducked down behind a boulder and waited for them to pass. A feeling of dread crept up in Leon's thoughts. *What if they found the temple, and already had the orb?* He wondered. Leon stayed where he was for a while, he did not want to let a cracking branch or a shuffle of forest debris alert the men to his presence.

Panic set in and Leon pushed on, the path became more narrow, and more littered with debris until it didn't look like a path at all. Leon wasn't sure, but it seemed like he had passed that tree before. The forest swirled around him and Leon stumbled, tripping over a root—or his own feet, it was hard to tell, but his head met the ground in a hard thud. Then the nightmare came; a vision of death.

Blackwater was engulfed in flames. Screams erupted from the city as a huge red dragon circled in the sky. Leon's eyes rolled back in his head, and his body seized on the forest floor as the vision intensified.

"Bring me the orb," a voice hissed. Suddenly, he saw Sophie running across the courtyard to her mother's arms. Samantha held their daughter as the large red dragon landed in front of them. With a huff and a thunderous roar, the beast unleashed its fiery breath. Leon screamed in agony as the flames engulfed his whole world—his wife and daughter. "Wake up." Leon looked around at the destruction of Blackwater. "Wake up." Leon thought he heard a voice and searched for it, through tears and desperation. The voice sounded like Sophie's. He called out for her, and then Samantha. "Wake up!" The voice grew louder. "Wake up!" Then he saw it; a great silver dragon dove down from the sky and sank its talons into the neck of the red dragon. "WAKE UP!"

Leon looked around again for Sophie, but saw only a bright shining light. It grew closer and closer until he was inside it and then came a familiar sensation—magical teleportation—a swirling vortex launching him through both time and space, propelled at the speed of light out of the vision and back into the darkness of the forest.

Leon gasped as he came to, first reaching to make sure he still had Destiny, then he grabbed his water skin and greedily gulped the contents until it was empty. He didn't know what the orb had to do with his vision, but he would do anything to keep it from becoming reality. This was not the first time the vision had plagued his dreams. The first time was after the battle of Braidwood when he took the orb from Orion's scepter and wrapped it in his cloak. To Leon, it seemed Orion was controlling the dragons with the magic in the orb. It was a power no one should have again and was the reason he took it and brought it to the temple of Ophay. They had the safest vaults in all the land.

The tomb beneath the temple was deep and the vaults were protected by runes. Leon gave a monthly donation to Ophay to use one. He filled it with random trinkets he had collected over the years, old suits of armor, and old furniture he could not bear to part with; like the wooden cradle Sophie had slept in as an infant.

When it became too dark to continue, Leon laid out his bedroll. He kept everything else packed, his arm through the strap on his backpack, and a firm grip on the hilt of Destiny. He closed his eyes and prayed to the Gods the nightmare would not return.

Leon woke to the sound of birds and the rays of the morning sun peeking through the leaves above. His neck ached from the awkward position in which he had slept and the muscles in his back never felt so tense. Life as the Guildmaster had kept him comfortable over the last sixteen years and he had forgotten what it was like to sleep on the ground beneath the open sky.

Leon rolled his bedroll and secured it to his pack. He wasn't far from the temple now and he wanted to make haste. Leon's stomach growled, but he ignored the hunger and quickened his pace. When he finally saw the temple in the distance, he sighed with relief. The Ophay were working in the gardens. The sun reflecting off of their flowing silver robes made them look like celestials without wings. Leon was astounded by the beauty surrounding him. They were so peaceful and happy. Leon loved the contrast of the golden shimmer across their rich brown skin and the symbol of Ophay painted on their foreheads with glimmering metallic colors. The most astounding feature of all was, each one of them had silver eyes, a curious window to a wise soul.

Leon called out before he approached so he would not startle them. An older woman looked up from the garden and smiled.

"Welcome back, Leon Rend, we have been waiting for you." She glided over to him regally and extended her hand. Leon bowed and kissed her hand as a show of respect.

"Zirri, it has been too long. I hope all has been well," Leon said.

"There has been some... activity," she replied, "Let's go inside to speak." The temple was a small cathedral, with vaulted ceilings, silver sconces, and beautiful painted murals of silver dragons. Leon had never asked, but he assumed the Ophay worshiped these dragons. Zirri led him to the stairwell descending into the catacombs. The corridor, filled with haunting statues; memorials of the dead filled Leon with a sense of unease. Each stone statue was the shape of a dragon with a name and loving inscription carved into it.

As Leon and Zirri grew closer to the vault, a steady hum from inside grew louder as Leon approached. Light seeped into the darkened catacomb from tiny gaps around the door frame. Leon placed his hand on the runes etched into the door; they lit up beneath his touch and it slowly opened. Leon gasped when he saw the orb. It was hovering in the air swirling with magic. Whispers in a strange tongue filled the vault and like a leaf on the wind, the voices floated through the tomb toward the exit.

"Have you been able to understand the whispers?" Leon asked?

"The words sound familiar, but ancient. I haven't been able to place the dialect; it sounds almost draconic, but wrong. When I am near the orb, it calls to me in a sinister way, almost like it's asking me to do something."

Suddenly, an explosion from above rumbled the stone ceiling and the thunderous blast shook everything around them. Leon's gaze jerked toward the exit, then back to the orb.

"You have to go. Take it with you!" Zirri urged as she turned from him and ran from the tomb. Leon wrapped the orb in his cloak. The orb, which was no bigger than a quail egg when Leon took it from Orion, was now the size of the bottom of a tavern mug. It would still fit in his bag, but he'd have to leave his bedroll and some of his supplies. He unloaded what he needed to, then stuffed the orb into his pack and ran back down the corridor. A scream chilled Leon to the bone and it was followed by another blast. He ran as quickly as he could to the end of the hall and up the stairs into the temple.

Leon cracked the door and peered through the gap. It didn't sound safe and he had a feeling he knew why the temple was under attack. Shock took over when he saw the carnage. The hole in the front doors told him whoever stormed the temple blasted their way in. They ransacked the place and overturned all the desks and furniture. His heart twisted into knots as he looked at the lifeless, horror-struck faces of the Ophay scattered across the room and he could still hear the murderers in the altar room, rummaging through the furniture.

Leon tiptoed around the corner carefully, maintaining cover. He inched closer to the door. Glancing into the altar room, he saw a group of men in black cloaks with red scarves over the bottom half of their faces. They were searching bodies, and desk drawers, emptying the contents of chests and boxes. Leon clutched his backpack; he'd not let them get their hands on it.

One of the men turned around and walked back toward him. Leon heard a small gasp from behind the desk next to the one he was crouching behind. He risked peeking around the corner of his cover to see if the noise had given away their position and Leon stifled his sigh of relief when the man turned the corner and descended into the catacombs. Leon made a break for the desk next to him. The young girl looked ready to scream until she saw Leon's face. He put his index finger to his lips and took his pack off and set it next to her.

"I'm going to get you out of here, but I need you to do me a favor," Leon whispered. "Get this pack to Blackwater. It is very important. I am going to lead them away from here so you can get away." Leon opened the bag and reached inside. He unwrapped the orb, and pulled his cloak from the pack rolling it into a ball. The orb still pulsed with magic inside the bag and Leon drew the drawstring tight and pushed it into the girl's hands. Looking into her silver eyes, he whispered; "You will be okay, just take this to the Silver Talons Guild as quickly as you can, wait for the men to follow me out, then go."

Leon jumped up from behind the desk with his cloak balled into his hands and ran to the center of the room.

"Hey!" he shouted, "looking for this?" Leon held up his cloak and the second they turned to look at him, he ran for the exit. He could hear the heavy footfalls of the men behind him as they chased him from the temple.

Their horses were lined up beside the temple. Leon jumped onto the back of one and kicked his heels into the animal's sides. The horse reared back letting out a surprised neigh before it took off in a gallop. Leon looked back, all of the men were following, but one. None of them were doubled up, and Leon had a horse, which meant there was still one man left inside the temple. Then he remembered; *the catacombs.* Leon saw one man go downstairs. Dread filled him and he thought about turning the horse around and going back for the orb and the girl, but surely that would sentence them both to death.

Suddenly, a ball of fire hurled past Leon's head, the flames spread from where the magic hit and the brown leaves from the fall fed the fire. He looked back and through the smoke he saw the man conjuring another ball of fire in one hand, while holding the reigns with the other. Leon guided his horse to a sharp left turn as the other fireball flew wide and struck a tree on their original path. Then he turned the horse to the right, zig-zagging to avoid the attacks.

Leon tried to make the horse go faster, but weaving between the trees, never keeping to a single straight direction, made speed difficult to achieve. The forest thinned as he neared the town of Torzana. Not wanting to lead these murderers toward more innocent people, Leon turned toward the cliff side. The horse would not be able to make it up the steep terrain, but maybe he could circle around and go back toward the temple.

Thundering hooves approached, surrounding Leon before he had time to act. A bolt of lightning flashed from a man's hand and a sharp pain surged throughout his body. Leon fell from the horse and everything went dark.

SIX

THE SCENT OF MENTHOL and cloves filled the front room of Blackwater Apothecary, barely covering the smell of alcohol and ammonia from the back. Sophie and Gabe waited for Delilah to finish scrawling her list. She offered them five gold each to gather the plants and flowers she needed for salves and medicines. Gabe also worked as a scribe, copying books for Blackwater's archives. He copied several books for himself about plants and their many uses over the years and was now a skilled forager.

When Delilah handed Gabe the list, he looked it over then passed it to Sophie. "The cart is around back, you'll find two baskets, the spiles and a mallet in there, with buckets for the sap and birch water. Be sure to cover the bucket with the cloth and tie some twine around it, I don't want bugs in the goods this time, and remember, tap the spile in at the right angle to get a quicker flow, I could use some birch water soon," Delilah reminded him.

"Yes, Miss Delilah," Gabe replied with a smile.

He'd always liked Delilah, she was kind and always paid them for things they were happy to do for free. The forest was Gabe's favorite place to be and Sophie loved foraging for new components from her spell book. Gabe grabbed the handles of the cart and lifted the front of it so they could start walking, but he didn't move yet. He stood contemplating where to begin. The south was the best place to forage for flowers and plants, but the northern forest was the best place to tap trees.

"The trees will take a while, and we are close to the southern forest right now, so I think we should get the flowers and plants first. We can drop them off on our way north. We can also leave the cart until we come back." Gabe picked up two wicker baskets from the wagon and held one out to Sophie.

"Good idea," she agreed. "No need to pull the cart around if we don't have to."

Sophie took out the list and looked at it again. "Wild chamomile, aloe plants with roots, lavender, valerian root, mint, evening prim-rose, beeswax, honey, dandelions, angelica, bay laurel... Do you know what all of these are?" Sophie asked, reading the list with skepticism.

"Most of them, there are a few I might have to look up," Gabe said.

"I could use some of these for my spells."

"You're really serious about this aren't you? You know there aren't any female wizards, women only use magic from the Gods. You would be the first-ever female wizard," Gabe said.

Sophie knew he was right. Women often practiced healing or nature-based magic, but the kind of magic she wanted to do was more, it wasn't divine or even nature-based like Juniper's magic, but Sophie wanted to join the guild and fight alongside them. She didn't have brute fighting skills like the soldiers, but she did have a passion for knowledge which sometimes could prove more powerful than strength alone.

"I don't even know if the wizard in Lapis Highland will train me. He asked for an apprentice, he didn't specify it had to be a boy, so I am hoping if I show up with the gold, and some skill already under my belt, he will accept me anyway."

"How much do you have saved up?" Gabe asked.

"After we get paid today, and after my shift at the tavern tonight, I should have the thousand gold I need." Sophie picked some dande-lions and put them in the basket.

"I'm happy for you, but I'm going to miss you. How long does the training last?" Gabe asked.

"At least a year, maybe more. I guess it depends on how quickly I pick up on the material," Sophie replied with a shrug.

"Well, Soph, I hope you're a fast learner because who will hunt plants and tap trees with me while you're gone?" Gabe asked. The two of them were social outcasts of sorts, Sophie was always reading, and when Gabe wasn't copying books, he was splashing in creeks, searching for pretty rocks, or foraging for plants for Delilah. They only ever had each other, yet Sophie never thought about how hard it would be for Gabe to be alone here while she trained.

"It's only a short ship ride across the bay and maybe a day's walk from Alasia outpost to Highland Tower. Maybe you can come to visit," Sophie suggested. Just then, fast and heavy footfalls came barreling toward them from the forest. They barely had time to turn around to see who was headed their way before someone bumped into Gabe, knocking him to the ground.

A girl with beautiful, shimmering, purple and blue hair, smooth brown skin, and a golden glitter on her cheeks stood up frantically, still looking behind her.

"Are you okay?" Sophie asked Gabe, who was still on the ground.

"I'm fine," he replied pushing himself up from the ground. "Are *you* okay?" Gabe was looking at the girl who had just knocked him down.

"No, I need to get to the Silver Talons Guild right away, the Temple of Ophay has been attacked," she said, clutching the backpack Leon had given her. Sophie recognized the bag displaying her father's initials.

"Who are you, and how did you get my father's bag?" Sophie asked, pointing to the leather backpack.

"My name is Kamara and a man gave it to me, he said I had to get it to the guild," the girl replied.

"Where is he?" Sophie's tone was short and harsh. She didn't mean for it to be, but her father could be in danger.

"He led the attackers away from the temple so I could escape and bring this to the guild." Kamara opened the bag and let her look at the orb. Sophie leaned closer, turning her ear toward the opening. The item was whispering, but she couldn't make out what it was saying.

"Let's go. I will take you to the guild, and then we are going to find my father." Sophie left the basket on the ground and took off, leading the girl toward town square.

"Wait for me!" Gabe called after them, picking up both baskets and running to catch up. As they passed the apothecary, Gabe dropped the baskets in the wagon and kept following the girls. When they reached the guild, Sophie opened the large oak doors to the lobby and ushered Kamara inside. Hank sat behind the reception desk as usual.

"Hank, have you heard from my father?" Sophie asked.

"Not since he left yesterday, why, has something happened?" he asked with concern.

"I'm not sure, can you contact him?"

"I'm afraid he left his com device behind, Miss Rend," Hank told her. Sophie grabbed the backpack and held it up.

"This is my father's backpack. This girl- I'm sorry, I forgot your name," Sophie paused to let the girl answer.

"Kamara," she replied.

"Right, thank you. Kamara told us my father gave her this bag and instructed her to bring it here. He was leading a group of men away so she could escape with this bag. We have to go look for him," Sophie said firmly, handing the backpack to Hank so he could see the artifact for himself. He opened the bag and the room filled with a glow of silver and red light illuminating everything nearby.

"This item contains a lot of magic. I do not know if it is good, or evil magic, but it is very powerful. I will send a group of soldiers to look for your father, and you need to get this to Highland Tower. Maybe the wizard can tell you more about it. I cannot send you alone though, your father would have my head if something happened to you." Hank called for a squire as he handed the bag back to Sophie. "Go into the western woods, about a mile in, and you'll see a cabin. Get Laughlin, and find Juniper. Ask them to accompany Sophie and her companions to Lapis Highland. Also, tell Matthias I need him to visit Temple Ophay and pick up a trail on Commander Rend. Have him assemble a group of soldiers to take with him and expect violence." The squire nodded without a word and gave a slight bow before exiting at a quick pace.

"You guys can wait here," Hank said, gesturing to the chairs in the waiting area. Sophie reluctantly sat down, her leg bouncing wildly as her mind raced. So many thoughts and feelings hit her at once. This was her first guild mission, her father was missing, she didn't know if he was dead or alive, this magical artifact was important to her father but she didn't know why, and she was finally on her way to meet the Wizard of Highland Tower.

Kamara looked more nervous than she did, jumping at every little sound and the turmoil on her face was as though she were having a battle with someone in her mind. Kamara kept glancing at the bag as if at any moment the item inside would jump out and attack them. It made Sophie nervous to hold it, but she didn't know yet if she should trust Kamara.

It seemed hours had passed by the time the young squire came back, with Juniper, Laughlin, and a wolf. Hank filled them in on the situation and looked over toward Sophie, Kamara, and Gabe.

"Get them safely to the wizard and back. Hopefully, he will know more about the item they carry," Hank instructed.

"What about Commander Rend?" Juniper asked.

"I have sent soldiers into the forest to look for signs of him, oh, and uh, it might be safer to take the long way, it sounds like there are some people after this artifact, so you will want to stay as out of sight as possible, no ships, no caravans," Hank warned. Juniper nodded, her brows furrowed with worry.

"Don't worry, we will see this done and hopefully the soldiers will find Commander Rend safe," Juniper said as she turned to face Sophie and the others. "Ready?"

It was late afternoon by the time they'd geared up for their journey. Early spring in the northern mountains was still a very cold time of year, especially at night, so Juniper had them grab warmer cloaks and fur-lined boots.

"I recommend we pack light for our trek through the mountain pass, we can get lighter gear in Northport when we begin to head south on the other side of the bay.

Sophie sent a squire with a message to Samantha letting her know what was going on, and Gabe sent a note to his mother too. By evening, they had reached the base of the northern mountains. Dusk was leading the pack, sniffing for danger as they walked up the path across the western face of the Stonehold Mountains. The air was thin and cold, Sophie was glad she had brought a warm cloak. Kamara did not seem to be phased by the cold at all; in fact, she looked very comfortable, despite the northern wind. Gabe had his cloak wrapped around his arms, bunched at the front, and knotted in his fist. "We should make camp, and start a fire," Sophie suggested. Juniper turned back to look at her. She saw how Gabe was shivering and agreed.

"I was hoping we could at least make it to Northport tonight, but we can camp here," Juniper said. They walked a short distance off the path, to a place where a previous camp had been. A stack of firewood had been left by the previous travelers and Laughlin took some parchment and lamp oil from his pack to start a fire. There wasn't a lot of wood, but it would be enough to get them warm. Juniper began casting a spell, illuminated by the silvery moon as runes appeared in the sky in the shape of a dome around them. The shimmering veil surrounded them, making the entire camp, fire and all, invisible to anyone outside the runes. This spell also did a wonderful job of keeping the heat from the fire inside while dissolving the smoke.

Soon, Gabe was no longer shivering as he warmed himself next to the fire. The others took seats around the fire too, but for several minutes, no one spoke. It was Sophie who broke the silence.

"So, what is the thing in my father's bag?" she asked, looking at Kamara.

"I'm not sure what it is called, but I hear it whispering to me sometimes. I know there is powerful magic inside it—the kind people are willing to kill for. The men in the red masks destroyed everything and everyone at the temple," Kamara said, her eyes filling with tears.

"Including my father?" A knot twisted up in Sophie's chest.

"I don't know, the last time I saw him, he was riding a horse toward Torzana, leading the men away from me so I could escape. He made them think he had the orb so they would follow him. I ran as quickly as I could, fearing there was a stray who might have seen me."

"How did you come to have this artifact at the temple?" Juniper asked.

"Mr. Rend brought it to us one day, about seventeen, maybe eighteen years ago, I am not sure. He asked if we could keep it safe in the tomb of the dead. There are runes there protecting against magic. I guess those protection spells only protected the catacombs though," Kamara lamented.

"Why have people not come for it before now?" Sophie asked.

"I'm not sure, maybe they didn't know where it was."

"How did they find out?" Sophie felt herself getting angry because this girl didn't seem to know anything about the artifact her father might have died for.

"Hey, Soph, it's okay, I am sure our soldiers will find your father," Gabe said, putting an arm around her shoulder. He could always tell what she was thinking, but right now his words brought her little comfort.

"Let's just get some sleep." Sophie pulled away from him and snuggled under the warm wool blanket on her bedroll. The others rustled around to do the same. Sophie sobbed as quietly as she could, not wanting to disturb the others, she stifled her emotions until she finally fell asleep. Juniper kept watch while everyone rested, only waking Laughlin four hours before sunrise so she could meditate. The fire had mostly died out, only red hot coals remained and they were almost out of wood but Laughlin threw another log on, hoping they would have firewood for sale in Northport.

SEVEN

LEON WOKE UP ON a cold stone floor in an unfamiliar dungeon. The swollen lump on his head was tender to the touch and he winced as he tried to assess his wound. They had stripped him to his undergarments and taken everything from him. His sword, Destiny, was no doubt being wielded by the leader of the pack. Magical weapons were rare and a greatsword enchanted to be lightweight *and* invoke the power of fire would no doubt be coveted by all. Every muscle and bone in his body ached. A foul smell filled the dungeon and seemed to be coming from the bucket in the corner—which Leon guessed no one dumped after the last prisoner who occupied the cell.

What became of the prisoner before him; did he escape, did they execute him or simply leave him in the cell to rot and starve? he wondered. From the smell of the bucket, Leon was convinced it was the latter.

He was not alone in the dungeon, from the other cells he could hear moans of pain or mental distress. Even in his current state of undress, Leon wasn't cold—which was strange for a dungeon. He thought they were either very far south; in the Auran Desert, or The Barren. He hoped for the desert. If he was being held in The Barren, even if he did escape, there was no water, plants, or living animals nearby. It would be the perfect place to take prisoners you didn't want anyone to ever find.

Leon hoped his capture was not for nothing and the Ophay girl made it to Blackwater safely. If she did, someone would surely be sending a rescue party soon. Leon wondered how difficult it would be to follow their trail. He didn't know which way the mene took him, he was knocked out almost instantly, but he had woken up mid-journey and could tell they were on a ship. They needed information; otherwise they would have killed him the moment they found out he did not have the orb.

Leon stood up and stretched his body from side to side, listening to his back pop like bubbles all the way up his spine. His mouth was dry and he was hungry. He paced back and forth, impatiently waiting for someone to return, when no one did, he sat down with his back against the wall and tried his best to block negative thoughts from coming through. He had no good thoughts right now, just a bunch of 'what if' scenarios he really didn't want to think about.

Where is everyone? Leon thought. It was very odd; not a single guard had come to talk to him, feed him, or give him water. Leon went through cycles of pacing, sitting, laying down, and banging loudly on the iron bars. Nothing worked, it seemed the only ones who could hear him were in the same predicament he was.

The sudden urge to relieve himself pained Leon, but the thought of using the dirty bucket in the corner made him gag.

"Hey! Can I at least get a clean chamber pot down here?" Leon yelled as loudly as he could. The request was met with laughter from the other prisoners.

"If they can hear us, they pretend not to." The man who spoke was in the cell next to Leon's. They were separated by a stone wall so Leon couldn't see him but he sounded old.

"How long have you been here? If you don't mind my asking."

The prisoner had to think about it. "I suppose it has been a few years, this is the third summer I have spent in this cell. I can tell the change in the season by the temperature, in the winter it gets a little chilly. Never cold, but the temperature is lower than it is now. It makes me wish they at least gave us a blanket," the man said.

"Who are these people?" Leon asked.

"The other prisoners, or our captors?"

"Captors," he replied.

"They call themselves the Order of the Red Dragon. People say they survived for many years drinking only the blood of a red dragon. They cover their faces because the dragon blood has corrupted them, giving them a scaly appearance."

Leon thought back to the scaly man in the Blackwater dungeon. "Are there any red dragons left? How did they get dragon's blood?" Leon asked.

"It's only a rumor, I'm guessin' I never saw a dragon. These people believe the red dragons are trapped; banished from this plane of existence by a powerful magic artifact. They have been searching for it for years; they say the item whispers to them. They've been trying to follow the voices for a long time now."

"You seem to know a lot about them," Leon said suspiciously.

"Well, I used to be a member of their order. Now they consider me a traitor because I refused to follow Orion into the destruction and conquering of the west," the prisoner said.

"That was almost eighteen years ago, have you been here this whole time?"

"No, I left and I traveled, I lived my life happy and free from the order, but something brought me back. My mom had become ill and the order had knowledge of it. They also knew I would come back for her. You see, all those years, they weren't searching for me, they were just waiting. When I came back to be at my mom's side on her deathbed is when they took me. I got to say goodbye, but my mother passed on all alone because I was in here." The prisoner's voice carried such sorrow, Leon almost shed a tear himself. He couldn't imagine how he would feel if his family died while he was locked away in this place.

"Sorry about your mom," Leon said. "I think she knew how much you loved her and you would have been there if you could have."

Leon couldn't hold it anymore, he went to the corner and urinated into the bucket, turning his eyes away from it and holding his breath as his stream made a spattering sound into the half-filled bucket. Boredom took over next, and there was nothing to do except sleep. Leon curled up against the stone wall near the iron bars and closed his eyes.

When he awoke again, someone was finally there to give them food, or whatever passed for it at least. It reminded Leon of the slop they fed to the pigs in Blackwater. There was a muffin; he thought it might be a corn muffin, but it was as hard as a rock. The boy who handed him the tray couldn't be more than fifteen years old. Leon looked into his eyes as he took the food.

"Please, help me. My daughter is about your age, I need to get back to her," Leon pleaded, his voice barely above a whisper. The boy's brows tilted in an empathetic expression and he was about to speak when they heard the sound of boots coming down the stairs. The boy turned away from Leon quickly and moved on to the next prisoner as the footsteps halted in front of Leon's cell.

"Well well well, look who's awake. How's your head?" he asked, laughing. Leon didn't speak. He stood holding his tray of slop, staring at the man in the red mask.

"Tell me what you did with the orb," the man demanded. "If you don't, maybe I will just have to ask your wife... Commander Rend." His tone was mocking, but it sent a chill through Leon. He felt rage boil up inside him. Leon took the tray of slop and threw it at the bars. Some of the food splattered between the gaps and landed all over the man's face.

"You'll regret that," he said, wiping the gelatinous goo from his eyes.

"You might be right, but if you lay a finger on my wife, you'll be the one with regrets," Leon warned. He couldn't see the man's mouth, but his bloodshot eyes squinted as a sinister laugh filled the space and Leon could tell the man's grin was just as wicked.

"I hope you enjoyed your last meal. You won't be getting another one. The echo of his evil laughter followed him up the stairs. Leon picked up his tray from the floor and smelled the slop still clinging to it. His stomach turned instantly. *I'd rather starve than eat this anyway,* he thought.

Samantha Rend joined the search party for her husband. There was absolutely no way she was going to sit around the house waiting for word, she had to find out for herself. She looked like a true warrior in her armor, sitting atop Leon's warhorse, Horatio.

The party was comprised of eleven soldiers, the captain of the guard, and Samantha. Thirteen of them in all. Some would be superstitious and believe the number alone doomed their mission, but not Samantha. She always thought of thirteen as being an incredibly lucky number. Maybe it was her optimism, or maybe it was just her heart's way of telling her brain they were going to find Leon so she didn't spiral.

It had been such a long time since Samantha had been on a horse, not even two hours into their journey, her legs had become saddle sore. She never rode side-saddle like most women, it made her feel weak and if she were completely honest, she felt it was very impractical especially if she needed to get away quickly.

They reached the temple by midday. Samantha looked around at all the destruction, and the bodies of the Ophay littered across their place of worship. Tears slid down her cheeks. The kind of monsters who were capable of this had her husband. No amount of positive thinking or lucky numbers would ease her worry now. She dismounted and approached Matthias Greene, the captain of the guard.

"We need to leave a few soldiers behind to dig graves for these people. We can't leave them like this," she pleaded. Captain Greene nodded. He delegated the task to the nearest three soldiers.

"When you're finished you can head back to Blackwater, we are going to be moving on, no need to try and follow if we don't know where the trail will lead," Matthias said.

They obeyed his command without argument. One began digging graves, and the other two began moving bodies near the burial site.

"Seems like they have done this before," Samantha commented.

"This is not the first time we have seen the slaughter of innocent people. Most of us were a part of the rebellion in Braidwood. Commander Rend saved our lives, and freed an entire city from tyranny and dragons," he told her.

"Thank you for helping to find him, Captain Greene," Samantha said.

"Please, Ma'am, you can just call me Matthias. You are not under my command, you are here as my equal."

"Only if you never call me ma'am again. Just Samantha is preferred." She smiled as best she could manage through the pain and worry she also wore on her face. Matthias bowed to her before excusing himself to search the grounds and the inside of the temple.

Samantha played the scene in her mind like the actors in a summer play. She could see the furniture flying as the temple was stormed, and she could hear the cries of the Ophay as they were cut down either by sword or magic. Tears fell freely now as she looked at the faces of the men, women, and even children. No one was spared—except for one, Leon had saved her life.

"Ma'am- I mean, Samantha, you will want to see this," Matthias called from the catacombs. Samantha descended the stairs and moved down the corridor of dragon statues to the vault. She gasped when she saw all the trinkets and furniture she thought they'd parted with years ago. Leon had kept it all. Samantha walked over and sat down in the rocking chair that used to sit in the corner of the nursery. She remembered many sleepless nights rocking Sophie in her arms as an infant.

She pulled herself out of her memories and closed the vault behind her. "We should get going. It looked like the hoof prints headed toward Torzana, we can head there and ask around.

Matthias agreed and they walked back up the stairs and out to the horses. The other soldiers had pitched in while Matthias was looking around and all the bodies were now by the graves and all eleven men were helping to dig with the small shovels from their pack. It would have gone a lot faster with a full-size shovel, but those were impossible to carry on long journeys. The soldiers were required to have a small shovel in their pack for occasions like this.

Matthias gathered the eight men who were continuing on and they headed west on a path through the woods. There were a lot of tracks in the soft mud, it was impossible to tell, however, if they had anything to do with Leon or the men who captured him.

By late afternoon, they made it to the small farming and fishing village of Torzana. From the looks they were getting, Samantha didn't think outsiders came here often. Surely they would remember seeing strangers two days in a row. Samantha dismounted and approached the nearest house. Outside, in the garden, a woman busied herself with weeding.

"Excuse me, Ma'am," Samantha said softly. The woman looked at her.

"I'm looking for my husband, he was kidnapped, have you seen any strangers in town besides us?" Samantha asked.

The woman nodded and pointed down to the dock where a large fishing boat was being unloaded. Samantha walked back to her horse.

"We should ask down at the dock," she said. Matthias nodded and they made their way through the tiny village. The smell of fish got stronger as they approached the men unloading barrels from the ship. Each one with a different kind of fish.

"We're looking for a man who was kidnapped, he was taken by men on horseback, we don't know how many, have you seen them?" Matthias asked. A man in blue overalls turned to face him. He smelled like the sea and looked like he'd been working in the sun his whole life. The skin on his face looked like dry leather stretched over a skeleton.

"Yeah, saw about five or so yesterday, they had an unconscious fellow on the back of one of their horses. They caught the barge from this dock last night," he replied.

"Where was the ship headed?"

"Usually, when there's livestock such as cows or horses, ships will only go as far as the Auran, longer'n it'd be dangerous for the animals."

"Say we wanted to cross with our horses, when does the barge come back?" Matthias asked.

"Maybe a new moon from now, It will take about a day or so to get to the desert, then the barge goes down around the Barren to pick up things from Braidwood and Ravenhall."

"Thank you for your help," Matthias said, turning back to Samantha. "We have to make it back to Blackwater and have them ready a ship large enough for the horses. I will get the ship and crew together, if you will help these guys get supplies and stock up for a long journey."

Samantha nodded, emotions bubbling beneath the surface. How could they be so close to finding Leon yet still so far away? She hoped he was alive and they would find him before his status changed.

EIGHT

KING HAKI AND THE oracle agreed; Dominic's dream was a glimpse of his destiny. The great green dragon had to be a reference to their kingdom's biggest enemy, the kingdom of Ash.

"It's time to claim your birthright," King Haki said. "No matter what, you cannot let the kingdom of Ash get their hands on the orb."

"You must take the orb to the place in your dream. The four mountains are on the island of Choddrath. It is quite a long journey from here," the oracle told them.

"You can voyage there aboard the flagship of the Royal Navy. I have already given the order. Your personal guards will travel with you to keep you safe," the king said. "I would go with you, but I am needed here. The prophecy says you will be a great and powerful king, with a long line of heirs, so worry not, we will meet again." King Haki hugged his son tightly and then patted his shoulders. The only emotion on his father's face as Dominic walked out of the great hall was pride. It made Dominic feel proud too.

The flagship of the Royal Navy was named for Dominic's mother, the late Queen Zahara. The flag bore the symbol of their kingdom, a dragon silhouetted on a golden sun. The ship was luxurious, the king had spared no expense to make the ship named after his wife the greatest ship any man or woman ever set foot on.

It was the largest vessel anyone had ever seen and took twice the crew to sail. The upper deck had private rooms for the crew and the captain, each furnished the same with the finest hand-crafted furniture. Dominic felt as at home on the ship as he did in Ledora. He thought he might actually like being out to sea more than at home, at least on the ship he didn't have to do magic lessons, or sword fighting lessons, he was free to do what he wanted, although he never quite figured out what his interests were; he never had the time.

He practiced his magic while on the ship, but mostly it was for travel, places he could see, or visualize, he created a kind of wormhole where he entered into one location and exited out of another. He didn't bother walking to the galley anymore, when it was time for chow, he simply appeared at the front of the line, while everyone else had to file from their rooms to the dining area below deck.

On the third day of their journey, something Dominic ate didn't sit right in his stomach. He spent the better half of the morning vomiting over the port-side of the ship. The second half of the day he spent lying in bed, hoping he would not need to use the bucket he had brought from the maintenance closet.

When he woke up the next day, things were even worse than the day before. A massive storm tossed the ship from side to side and a huge wave crashed onto the deck. The crew members were all yelling different commands and frantically pulling ropes and lowering sails. The captain was at the helm trying to steer the ship against the waves in a way that kept them upright. Lightning streaked the sky and thunder rumbled after it in a long low growl like anger from the gods.

The wind howled and a large gust knocked a man overboard. A couple of crew members rushed to throw a rope over the side but the man was lost. Dominic had never been so afraid in his life. He went back to his room on the upper deck, which did nothing to ease his fears, or toss him around less, but at least he was safe from the wind. He grabbed the orb, enclosed it into a leather pouch with drawstrings at the top, and tied it to his belt using a knot he knew would only get tighter when it got wet.

He knew if they went under, his armor would be heavy, but he hoped he would be able to use his magic to get him to dry land. He grabbed as much gold as he could and filled a bag with it, then he took rations, and a flint and steel.

Just as he finished preparing for the worst, it happened. An enormous wave crashed into the ship and it began to capsize. Dominic closed his eyes and summoned all the magic he could, and thought to himself; *nearest dry land, nearest dry land.* Just as the side of the ship crashed into the water, Dominic landed with a thud on the bank.

He checked his personal effects to ensure he still had the orb, and then, his gold and his sword. He sat up on the shore and cried. He was thankful he was safe, but felt terrible he couldn't save everyone else.

When he regained his composure, Dominic stood and looked around, trying to find out where he was. From his location near the shore, Dominic could see the towers of a beautiful, white stone castle. The forest on either side of the castle seemed to have intricately built tree houses, connected to one another with rope bridges.

The forest floor was mostly undisturbed. Nature was free to blossom and grow as Dominic had never seen. A sound floated on the breeze from the direction of the forest; it wasn't an animal it was more like singing. A choir of harmonizing voices started softly and grew louder as Dominic's curiosity led him into the forest.

NINE

Northport was not the sort of place for reputable people. The dealings were often clandestine and the jobs were no better. A shady town filled with either shady people, or those who were trapped. It was in this town, Juniper had last seen her friend Maureen. Juniper had no idea why she'd chosen to stay, and there had been no correspondence between them for years. The last place she saw her was a seedy tavern at the front of the town. It was called The Rusty Mug.

The name had since changed, and the tavern looked brighter, almost cheerful. Now the sign read Blue Lioness Inn. Juniper noticed chickens inside a wooden picket fence on the side of the building, they clucked and walked around happily pecking at the ground and what was left of their morning feed.

"What do you say we stop in for a proper breakfast?" Juniper asked.

The rest of the group heartily agreed. Gabe was still wrapped in his wool blanket from his bedroll and his lips were a slight blue. Juniper chose a table right next to the hearth so Gabe could get warm. It took no time at all for the barkeep to approach with cups of water and when Juniper saw the curly brown hair, and cute, full cheeks her heart leaped for joy.

"Maureen! I am so happy to see you! I didn't think you would still be working here when I saw the name was changed." Juniper stood to embrace her old friend in a hug.

"I own th' place now. I made some pretty good money here, the work was shite but sometimes the coin was worth it. Some of the richer clients would come in, looking for a date to some fancy ball in Ravenhall, and since we get paid by the hour and the trip takes at least a week to get there, and a week back, so you can imagine how much a couple o' those a year'd rake in. When I finally 'ad enough to buy this place an fix it up, I did, and I never looked back. Sure missed you though!" Maureen's face was filled with pride as she looked around at the inn she now owned. "Now, what can I get you for breakfast? It's on the house!"

"Are you sure? Maureen, we can gladly pay!" Juniper argued.

"I insist! It's th' least I can do for an old friend," she replied.

They ordered two loaves of bread, scrambled eggs, bacon, and porridge. When it came, they ate it all, save for the bacon and bread left on Laughlin's plate. Gabe's color returned and he was able to shed the wool blanket. Maureen came back to clear some of the dishes as everyone finished their meal.

"Can I get you anything else?" she asked.

"No thanks, but do you have a general store here in town that might sell lighter cloaks and cooler hiking boots?" Laughlin asked as he scraped his leftovers into a paper bag for Dusk, who was waiting outside.

"We sure do, when you walk out o' here, you'll turn right and it's the third building on the right, a little apparel shop owned by the sweetest old man in Northport."

"Thank you so much, Maureen! I will have to come back and visit when I have longer to stay, but we must be on our way. Thank you for breakfast, and it was so good to see you!" Juniper said.

When Maureen went back to help other patrons, Juniper slipped five gold pieces under the edge of a plate still on the table. Sophie clutched her father's backpack and felt it, to make sure the orb was still in it. It was hard like a crystal ball, but warm and emitting a low hum. You wouldn't really notice it unless you knew what you were listening for.

Kamara and Gabe had been having their own quiet conversations and seemed to be getting to know one another. Sophie didn't know why, but she felt the slight sting of jealousy because she had not been invited into their conversation, after all, she and Gabe had been friends their whole life, and they already knew pretty much everything about each other.

As they walked down the cobblestone path toward the apparel shop, Sophie continued to watch Kamara and Gabe laugh and talk in what seemed to be whispers and she tried to push the feelings of anger aside and averted her eyes, instead, taking in the scenery of Northport. Chimney smoke billowed softly from the tall white and cream-colored buildings and the deep mahogany beams crisscrossed on the front of them gave the building character.

The apparel shop was the only yellow building on the street and instead of mahogany accents, the beams on the yellow building were a light gray oak. It made the whole place look lighthearted and friendly. When they stepped inside, a small man with a slightly hunched back greeted them with a smile.

"Welcome! I have a kettle over here if you would like some hot tea, I will let you look around, and won't bother you, but if you need anything at all, I will be right over there." He pointed a slender and crooked finger to the counter in the front corner of the store, just left of the doorway. He hobbled slowly, his cane clicking slowly as he returned to the counter.

Elegant furs caught juniper's eye, beautiful fox fur in red and white, rabbit furs in white, gray, brown, and black, deep brown buffalo hides, and even coyote furs. Cloaks with fur collars lined the wall, the inside they were made from hide leather, which was thicker and definitely warmer than the ones they could buy in Blackwater, but not what they would need for the journey south. She thought she might like one for the way back though.

Gabe picked out a pair of thin, soft stockings. The material was not itchy and hard like his blanket, rather, the softest he had ever felt.

"What are these made out of?" Gabe asked the owner.

"It comes from my puff plants, I discovered them in the south and since they won't grow up here I have to have the fibers imported. They call it cotton, it's new, and I'm the first to carry it here in the north." The man said proudly.

"How much for these?" Gabe asked. Even though they didn't have a chance to finish gathering herbs for Delilah, Gabe had some coin left from other jobs he had done.

"Thee gold pieces." The man replied. Gabe put the stockings in the crook of his arm to free up his hands to look through the cloaks. Kamara was looking at the trinkets and specialty items in the glass case by the counter. A silver necklace with an opal stone caught her eye. It was a mesmerizing piece, the Ophay never wore jewelry. They opted for a simpler life, with the most elegant things they owned being the temple, and the beautiful silver robes they wore.

Sophie grabbed a lighter cloak and some cotton socks. She wanted to spend as little money as possible because she still intended to try and become the wizard's apprentice. She hoped maybe she could trade him the orb for training. Surely a magical artifact such as this would tempt him, and so far, it seemed to be more trouble than it was worth. Sophie's hand fell to the bulge in the backpack. She didn't know why she had to keep feeling for it, but the anxiety of losing it would not let go of her mind. She wandered through the shop, pausing to look at the statues and artwork around the room. The statue of a warrior princess caught her eye. She took a step back and to the left to admire the detail carved into the wood. When she stepped back, she bumped into Kamara.

Kamara gasped in surprise and Sophie dropped her father's backpack. The orb rolled out of the bag and down the aisle. Kamara dashed after it, securing the artifact as it reached the end of the aisle. Sophie watched, hoping Kamara picked it up before it rolled into the old man's view, but she was too late.

"What is this?" he asked in amazement. "I have never seen anything like it." The crystal ball swirled with a galaxy of magic and inside, the smoke formed two dragons, one red, and one a light bluish silver, they circled after each other but never made contact.

"It's nothing," Sophie said, as she grabbed the orb and shoved it back inside the backpack. She shot a dirty look at Kamara as if she held it out for a little too long on purpose. Sophie turned and rushed for the door, Juniper and Laughlin followed after her.

"What's wrong? Sophie, you're acting strange. I have never seen you this angry," he said with concern.

"I'm fine, just tired. I didn't sleep well last night." The answer seemed to satisfy Laughlin, but Juniper was not convinced. Gabe and Kamara came out just in time, and Sophie was thankful, now they could drop the conversation and continue on their way..

"I paid for your stuff," Gabe said, handing Sophie her cloak and socks.

"Thank you, you didn't have to," she told him.

He shrugged and smiled as she took her items.

They took a few moments to change into their new gear, the weather wouldn't be warmer until they passed Alasia Outpost, a large shipping hold and seller's market on the northern border of Alasia.

The cotton stockings felt just right, and the soft material slid so nicely into their old boots. Gabe now had a light leather cloak buckled by a metal clasp, and of course, his cotton stockings. Sophie's cloak was not as nice as Gabe's but she was being more frugal with her coin. She counted out the total of her items and handed them to Gabe. He tried to refuse, but Sophie insisted he take it, and in the end, he relented.

She was still a little short of a thousand gold- gold she needed to apprentice, but maybe the power of this orb could cover the rest of the fee.

Juniper looked over at Kamara, still wearing the thin silver robes and sandals she had been wearing the whole time.

"Do you want some hiking boots or something, Kamara?" Juniper asked. "I can buy you a pair if you need them."

"I can help too," Gabe said.

"I'm okay, thank you though," Kamara replied.

Sophie could tell Gabe was trying hard to impress this girl. Since they had the orb, she didn't understand why the girl was sticking around when she could go anywhere. Sophie tried to stuff her animosity toward Kamara deep down inside as they started walking again. Dusk walked next to Sophie and occasionally nudged her hand for pets; it brought her some comfort.

Since they were out of the mountains, the wind seemed colder, Gabe and Sophie were bundled up, still freezing, despite the sun shining brightly.

"It looks like it should be warm," Juniper said, seeming to read Sophie's thoughts.

"Maybe we should have waited to change until we got further south," Gabe said. "How long do you think it will take to get to Alasia?"

"We should reach the outpost in a few hours." Laughlin pulled a small sundial out of his bag. It looked like a compass. He set it on the ground and positioned it just right. "Yeah, a few hours should be about right," he said as he placed the tool back in his pack.

The south side of Northport was busy with people in the streets selling their likely stolen goods, gambling booths with sly men beckoning people to play their games of chance, and occasional fights between patrons of those games. Their pace slowed as they weaved through the thick crowds. Gabe positioned himself to walk by Sophie.

"Everything okay Soph?" He asked, looking at her with concern.

"Yeah, I'm okay," she replied, which was only a half-truth.

"Did you bring your spell book with you?" he asked in a hushed whisper.

"Shhh," Sophie scolded, "I haven't told anyone else."

"I was thinking, you could show it to the wizard, and maybe he would know something about the previous owner," Gabe suggested.

"I have it, yes. It's not a bad idea, but I don't want everyone to know," she replied.

Gabe walked silently next to Sophie for a while, stealing occasional glances at Kamara.

"What do you think of her?" Gabe asked, nodding in the girl's direction.

"She's kind of strange, I mean, why did she come with us? She brought us the orb, I don't understand why she is still here," Sophie admitted.

"It sounds as if you don't like her much." Gabe sounded defeated.

"It's not that I don't like her, I don't know her well enough to have an opinion as to whether I like her or not, I just think she's strange is all." Sophie saw the disappointment on Gabe's face. His brows furrowed and his lips were pressed into a thin line as he decided how to respond.

"I've talked to her; she stayed with us because everyone she ever knew was murdered and she is afraid to go back home alone. The only thing waiting for her at Temple Ophay are the bodies of her loved ones. She has nowhere to go and doesn't know anyone else but us. I am not sure what's going on with you, but I don't think I like it. Try having some compassion," Gabe said, quickening his pace to return to Kamara's side.

Sophie had a feeling she couldn't describe, it was anger, but sadness too. She wanted Gabe to be happy, he was her best friend, but there was just something about Kamara that was... off.

By lunchtime, they had reached the outpost. Traders had tents set up in rows, selling hand-made items like goat milk soap, leather works such as armor and saddle bags, and of course, food. The smells were amazing. There were different booths for all kinds of food from around the continent.

They tried a little from several stalls. Sophie wandered around with Dusk, and looked at the crafts and art the vendors were selling. One booth caught her eye in particular; a fortune teller selling her services; scrying, palm reading, rune reading, and crystal gazing. Sophie knew scrying was at least real, the Blackwater oracle used a crystal ball and could see things before they happen, or things happening miles away.

Sophie entered the tent with beautiful tapestries hung like curtains all the way around it. When she entered, the woman closed the front curtain to let other patrons know she was currently in session.

"My dear, I can already tell you have traveled from the Southwest. Yes?" she asked. Sophie nodded, impressed.

"What is it you seek from me?" the woman asked.

"I just want to know if my father is okay," Sophie said. The oracle took her hand and led her to the table with two chairs, one on either side of a large crystal ball. She motioned for Sophie to sit and then she sat down across from her. Sophie dug two pieces of gold out of her coin pouch and handed them to the fortune teller.

"Do you have something of his, so I can make a connection to him?" she asked.

Sophie thought about the bag. She did have something of his, but to hand over her father's bag would risk the security of the orb. She clutched the backpack on her lap as she thought about every possible outcome, and in the end, Sophie finally nodded and presented the leather bag to the clairvoyant.

The woman placed both her hands on the leather satchel and it began to hum. Sophie looked at her nervously, but the woman did not seem to notice. When she took her hands off the bag her crystal ball began to glow and filled with light purple smoke. As she slowly waved her hands around the crystal, the smoke began transforming into figures and shapes.

"I see your father, he is locked away somewhere, the cell he is in is dimly lit. It looks like he is pacing back and forth."

"Can you tell where the dungeon might be?"

The fortune teller circled her hands over the crystal again. Her eyes rolled back in her head and her body jerked forward as if pulled by an imaginary force.

"I see dragons in hiding, men with red masks and black cloaks, I see a great mountain with four peaks, and dragons rising. A battle between good and evil ensues. Fires rage from the dragon's mouth once more, they will rise." The woman collapsed backward into her chair and slumped lifelessly to one side.

"Madame!" Sophie screamed, as she rushed to the woman and tapped the sides of her face. The clairvoyant gasped as she came to and bolted upright in her chair.

"Darling, you are in danger. You have brought the draconic curse upon you, and when they find you, it will not be good." The woman picked up the leather backpack and shoved it into Sophie's chest as she ushered Sophie from the tent.

"But dragons are extinct," Sophie argued.

"They are only sleeping, but they will awaken, and when they do, they're coming for you," she said as she closed the tent flap behind her.

TEN

AKIRI'S SHIP DOCKED AT Ledora's western shore. She walked through town square as if she already owned the place. The guards stopped her as she got to the palace gates.

"State your business," one of the guards commanded.

"My business is my own, and is with the king. You will let me pass." Her words floated across the air like a green wisp of smoke and into the man's ear. His eyes glowed a dark green, and his face became void of expression. He was under Akiri's influence.

"Of course, right this way," he said, opening the gate for her.

"Thank you, you're such a gentleman." Akiri smiled as she entered the courtyard. Strolling through the gardens in her emerald flowing gown, she looked like she belonged there, among the lilies. No one else questioned her presence until she opened the door to the castle and stepped inside.

The foyer alone was as large as the ballroom of her castle and three times as extravagant. White walls trimmed with golden accents made every room seem bigger, and the crystal and gold chandeliers gave the room a touch of arrogance too. Several people turned to look at her as she entered unannounced, and Akiri heard their whispers as she passed by.

"Who are you?" a man in golden half plate armor asked.

"I am Sorceress Akiri, and Her Royal Highness, Princess of Ash. I am seeking audience with your king."

"I'm afraid the king is not available right now, but you might be able to schedule audience with him sometime next week. Now, if you please..." He placed a hand on her back and tried to steer her to the door.

"I don't think you heard me," she said as she reached a hand toward the man and lifted him with an invisible force without even laying a hand on him. His feet dangled beneath him as he gasped for air. "Now that I have your attention, I need to see the king, NOW!" As she shouted the last word, she dropped her hand, and the man she was holding crumpled to the floor coughing and gasping for air.

"Guards!" he manage to shout loudly enough for the guards to start running toward the foyer. Akiri rolled her eyes and let out a great sigh.

"You know, I had really hoped we could be civil about this, but I guess we're doing it the hard way."

The king heard the commotion from the throne room and commanded the guards to barricade the doors to keep the intruder out. They did as commanded, but even the heavy oak board fitted into the steel mounts on the door, were no match for Akiri's magic. King Haki watched as the sorceress melted her way through the barricade with bubbling green acid.

"Sorry about your door, and the guards out front, but they were being completely unreasonable. I know you and I can come to an agreement because I have heard what a fair and gracious king you are." Akiri approached the guards in front of the king. They each held a polearm with a golden morningstar on top and they crossed them to form a large 'X' in front of the throne.

"Have your men stand down, no one else needs to die."

"Do as she asks," the king commanded. "What is it you want?"

"I seek an artifact you've kept for the last seventeen years. My witch says it is here," Akiri told him.

"You're wasting your time. It's no longer on this island—left the kingdom days ago as a matter of fact," he replied with a slight smirk.

"Where is it?" Akiri demanded. Her guards finally caught up to her and filed into the room. They stood in formation behind Akiri as her anger grew.

"It's hard to tell, somewhere out to sea would be my guess. Perhaps it has already been destroyed, or tossed into the ocean depths, it makes no matter to me, as long as you can't get your hands on it. The kingdom of Ash needs no such treasure." King Haki sat back on his throne, wearing a triumphant grin.

"You lie," Akiri said through gritted teeth.

"Well then, by all means, search the kingdom if you like, but you will not find what you seek here."

Akiri screamed with anger, and green streaks of electricity surged from her fingertips as she tried to hit the king right in his lying mouth, but her spell bounced off the invisible barrier surrounding the throne's platform. Akiri saw the waves of magic rippling as the shield reflected her work back at her. Akiri rolled out of the way and gave the king a dirty look as he laughed.

"You're lucky I don't have time for this right now," she growled turning to flee from the room with her guards following behind.

Back on the ship, Akiri stormed into the oracle's cabin.

"You said it was here, it isn't, so where is it?" Akiri demanded angrily. The oracle was silent for longer than Akiri liked. She drew her hand back, and slapped the old woman hard across the face. Akiri's hand print grew bright red on the witch's cheek.

"Even if I knew where it was, I wouldn't tell you now. I hoped you would turn out differently than Queen Luciana because your father was a kind and honorable man, but you are as cruel and heartless as your mother."

"Guard your tongue, witch, or you might just lose it." Akiri turned and walked from the woman's cabin without another word, locking the door from the outside. She didn't know why, but the woman's words stung. She didn't want to be like her mother.

Akiri crossed the deck and addressed the crew. "Set sail for the east, we didn't pass a ship with golden sails, which tells me they did not sail west. We are at least two days behind them, so we need a favorable wind."

"Aye," the men responded and scrambled to the sails to obey her command.

Akiri went into her quarters and closed the double doors behind her.

For the next few days, Akiri took her meals in the captain's quarters. She couldn't stop thinking about what the oracle said about her father. Her mother always told Akiri her father was a coward who left them while Luciana was ill and with child. How could any honorable man do that?

It was true her mother was not the kindest, but she was queen, and sometimes, when people don't respect you, it's best to make them fear you instead. At least, that was what her mother always said.

ELEVEN

LEON COULD FEEL THE hair on his face growing softer, this was not a next-day stubble, it was becoming a full beard. His bangs now hung down into his eyes. He wasn't used to it, his normal style was militant and neat. He had no idea how many days it had been since his capture, he had lost count. The man Leon threw his food at, promised he wouldn't get another meal, and so far, he'd kept to his word.

The day after the incident, Leon's stomach growled, the next day, he felt weak, tired, irritable, and short-tempered. Now, he felt energetic like he got a second wind. His undergarments were loose on him now and he had to keep pulling them up. He didn't know why he bothered, it's not like the other prisoners could see inside his cell, and surely his captors wouldn't care if he wore nothing at all or they would have let him keep his clothing or at the very least, given him a nightshirt. Leon did not like losing weight. From his days as commander of the Braidwood Army, Leon knew a person could go weeks without eating, but typically would only last a few days without water. He had been in the cell for more than a few days now, he was sure of it. If what he learned was true, then it wouldn't be much longer until he shriveled like a sun-dried date.

He paced back and forth, thinking about his family, and hoping more than anything else they were safe. He felt helpless and defeated, something he had never felt before in his life and he hated every moment of it. He was Leon Rend, Commander of the Blackwater Army, Guildmaster of the Silver Talons, Slayer of the Aquahydra, and the Leader of the Braidwood Rebels. So many things were accomplished in his life, only to be bested by some red-masked cultists.

Leon started to get lightheaded from all the pacing and anger, before he realized it was happening, his vision went completely white and his body crumpled to the ground.

The screeching of a dragon overhead drew his attention toward the sky, then he looked around, confused. Leon was back in Blackwater, the dragon's fiery breath was igniting all of the nearby houses. Plumes of black smoke filled the air. This time his vision was different, where was Samantha, where was Sophie? Leon ran, frantically searching for his family, even though this vision always ended with them being engulfed in flames.

Leon pulled Destiny out of the sheath and took up a defensive stance. The red dragon swooped down, the sound of its beating wings was all Leon could hear as he thrust his sword into the air, trying desperately to make contact.

The dragon rolled out of the way ascending back into the sky. Leon raised his hand to his forehead, shielding his eyes from the sun and the brightness of the flames. He caught sight of the dragon, and prepared once more for the creature to dive at him, but before the red dragon could descend, another dragon appeared- flying at a miraculous speed, it collided with the red dragon, pummeling it to the ground. The silver dragon sprayed a cone of freezing wind at the red dragon, paralyzing it. Something was familiar about the way the silver dragon shimmered, the light striking the scales reflected in hues of blue and purple.

Leon came to, his stomach growling again. He thought of the dragon in the vision and tried to remember why the colors blue and purple meant something to him.

Samantha's stomach turned as the large sea vessel bounced across the waves. Samantha had never been on a ship before and she was fairly certain after this time, she never would be again. She leaned over the starboard side and vomited into the water. Seagulls circled overhead, swooping down to pick out the remnants of the last thing Samantha ate. The thought of the seagulls eating her vomit made her stomach turn again and she once more the contents of her stomach spilled over the side of the ship. She rinsed her mouth with water from her water skin and when she felt like there was no more in her stomach to come up, she sat down on the deck with her back against the side of the ship for support. Matthias approached cautiously.

"Here, eat this, it might help." Matthias opened a jar and fished out a piece of yellowish food.

"What is it?" Samantha asked as she took it from him.

"It's ginger root, it will help with the sickness," he replied.

She smelled it and wrinkled her nose. "It doesn't smell like it will make my nausea better." Samantha ate it, but the taste made her gag again. She washed it down with a big gulp of water to quell the urge to retch again.

"How much longer until we dock?" she asked.

"This ship is the fastest in the Blackwater fleet, we might be there by tomorrow evening." Matthias took a seat next to her. He looked as worried as she felt. She didn't bother trying to comfort him with hopes, and he didn't attempt to reassure her either. They both knew time was not on their side and Leon may already be dead, but neither of them dared to speak the thought aloud.

Elevated voices and the pounding of feet across the deck brought them both out of their thoughts. Matthias stood and helped Samantha to her feet then they took off toward the commotion. The crew and the soldiers were all pointing to the surface of the water in the distance.

Samantha's heart was pounding as she surveyed the water for the source of the excitement—or panic—she couldn't tell which. Suddenly, an enormous gray whale breached the surface, forcing a jet of water from its blowhole.

"It is almost the size of the ship!" Samantha shouted gleefully.

"Aye, and she's just a baby!" a sailor chimed in with a smile.

Samantha continued watching in amazement as the whale dove down deep and slapped the surface of the water with its tail. A wave rolled out from the site, and rocked the boat. Samantha lost her balance and fell backward, she would have hit the deck if not for Matthias' quick reaction time. He shot his arms out just in time to catch her and stood her back on her feet.

They both burst out in laughter. As Samantha composed herself, the bell rang for dinner. Everyone began heading below deck.

"You coming?" Matthias asked.

"No, thank you. I'm okay, I'm not sure I should put anything else in this stomach, but maybe save me a piece of bread," Samantha said.

"You got it." Matthias joined the others below the deck. Samantha walked to the side of the ship and looked out over the water which was now calm. The sun was just above the horizon filling the sky with colors Samantha was usually not able to see from the shore. The blue of the water and the deep red of the setting sun created a layer of fuchsia in the sky. The deep orange above, blended into pink and periwinkle as twilight approached.

Please be okay, Leon. I need you. WE need you. Samantha pleaded silently. Samantha wondered if Sophie had reached the wizard tower in Lapis Highland yet. Hank assured her Sophie would be safe with Juniper and Laughlin. Samantha didn't think she would be able to handle it if both Sophie and Leon went missing.

Samantha went below deck, but not to the galley, instead, she went to her hammock in the sleeping quarters. She thought time might go faster if she wasn't thinking about it, and the only way to not think about it was to force sleep.

TWELVE

DOMINIC FOLLOWED THE CHOIR of voices deeper into the most beautiful and greenest forest he had ever seen. The birds whistled merrily among the branches and flowers bloomed all around. Tall mountains with flat tops covered in green shrubbery and trickling waterfalls from mountain springs protected the borders of the western and northern sides of the city. The sky was bright blue with large, fluffy clouds floating lazily from the mountain tops to the hillside across the river in the east.

He knew where he was, there was only one place he had ever heard of like this; The Kingdom of Ravenhall. It was the last-known civilization of elves in the world. Dominic did not learn any history about how the elves felt about trespassers or travelers through their lands, so he proceeded with caution, scanning the trees for the bodies to which the beautiful voices belonged.

There would be no passage out of town on the western or northern side, so Dominic walked east, using the setting sun as his guide. With the light at his back, he walked until he got to the bank of a rushing river. There was no way to cross it there, so he followed the stream north, around the eastern side of the silver castle. Not long into his journey, he saw a group of elves approaching. They didn't look the way he had expected them to, but instead, what he always imagined the ancient ones to look like. The Fae lands were long gone now, and had been since before the battle of Braidwood.

They were taller than any human and more slender than most. Their silver robes and flowing sheer capes made them seem almost transparent in the light of the sun. Their mere presence was a glorious feeling of serenity and happiness.

The leader of the procession carried a white staff, made out of the lightest maple. Tied to the top of it with a thick, shining, silver string, was a crescent moon-shaped crystal adorned with beautiful and fragrant lilacs.

"Greetings, traveler, have you enough provisions for your journey?" she asked. Her voice was as soft as silk and so pleasing to the ear. Dominic found it difficult to find words.

"Yer-yes, I mean, yes, Ma'am," he said with a bow. He had never met elves before, and he had no idea if they were royalty in this kingdom, but he thought it best to bow, just in case.

The elves in the back giggled, but the woman who spoke only smiled kindly as she bowed back to him.

"Is this a custom where you come from?" She sounded generally curious.

"No, er- I mean, only to royalty, mostly my father, no one really bows to me," he stammered.

"Are you royalty?" she asked.

"I am Prince Dominic Ledora, my father is King Haki, our kingdom is named for his great-great-grandfather. I am heir to the throne, but my father is in excellent health and I am relieved to say I think it will be a long time before the responsibility falls to me," Dominic said, regaining his eloquence.

"Well then, allow me to introduce myself, Your Highness, I am Erimaya." She bowed to him and all of the other elves behind her bowed too. "Your Highness, we would be delighted to have you join us this evening for dinner, and you're welcome to stay and get a good night's rest before continuing on your journey."

"Such a kind offer and one I will gladly accept," Dominic replied. He wondered if he would be able to figure out where he needed to go and perhaps he could also find a ride to the next city. He followed the elves to the castle admiring their light-footed, careful steps leaving no trace of their passing. This place was like a dream—not the kind he'd been having lately, but the kind that makes people not want to wake up. There seemed to be no concept of time, the elves didn't hurry or rush about. They were all different in appearance, some were silver-haired while others had hair as black as raven's feathers. Some wore flowing silver robes and others dressed in a combination of leather and leaves.

During his studies, Dominic learned about some of the different groups of elves. The high elves, which ruled the northern court of Aranor, a city which had fallen during the orc wars, and the wood elves of the forgotten grove, a secret realm protected by magic—a realm no outsider had ever set foot in. It was said because the only ones who ever saw it had lived there, it might not have even existed, but Dominic was certain if they went as far as casting warding spells to keep people out, then it was likely they wanted you to think they and their realm were imaginary.

During the times of war when elven cities began to fall, all of the elves left outside of the forgotten grove came together at Ravenhall. The city was bordered by mountains on two sides, a river on one, and the ocean on the last. Since orcs don't swim, and the elves of Ravenhall built no way to traverse the mountain safely, they were able to fortify the kingdom. He was excited to meet the other elves in the castle and hear their stories over dinner.

When they got to the castle, the large stone doors opened without assistance like they could sense their presence. Dominic watched the intricate carvings in the stone alight with a golden glow when the elves came near. One of them made sure to position himself behind Dominic because when the last elf crossed the threshold, the door began to close, and the runes faded.

The grand entrance was white and silver with marble statues lining the walls. Dominic glanced into the rooms as they passed and was amazed by the sight of their library, bookcases stretching from wall to wall, to the cathedral ceiling, filled with handwritten tomes. The centuries of knowledge towered into the colossal room; it was the size of the great hall and ballroom of his father's castle combined.

They went up a grand staircase, then Erimaya led Dominic down a corridor of guest rooms. She opened the door to the third room on the left and took a step back so Dominic could enter first.

"Make yourself comfortable. You're welcome to explore the castle until dinner," Erimaya said. "Will this be okay?" She gestured to the accommodations.

"This is more than okay. It is beautiful; are you sure these are the rooms for your guests?" Dominic asked looking around. The canopy bed was large enough for at least three people and made from the same light wood as Erimaya's staff. Someone intricately carved each piece of furniture in the room. Dominic thought it must have taken years to decorate this room alone.

Erimaya smiled and nodded. "I shall see you at dinner then."

As Dominic walked around the room, he admired the craftsmanship of the furniture. He could even appreciate the architecture of the room. Three identical archways on the eastern wall, opened onto a balcony overlooking the grove; such natural beauty Dominic never got to see in the golden kingdom. In the distance, he thought he heard the rumble of thunder and somehow knew he would sleep well.

He caught himself thinking about how peaceful it was in Ravenhall and how nice it would be if he could ignore his political responsibility and stay there in the elven city forever.

Gathered in the banquet hall, the elves and their guests carried on polite conversations as a trio of musicians played stringed instruments. The food, consisting of crystal bowls filled with crisp apples, leafy green salads, platters of berries, vegetables, freshly baked elven bread, and a rather large plater with some kind of creamy spread made from chickpea, took up three long tables on the western wall. He put a little of everything on his plate and sat down next to Erimaya.

He listened to the beautiful music and the voices of the elves around him. They were all speaking their native tongue, and Dominic now wished he'd learned to speak Elvish.

"I was wondering if you could help me with something, Erimaya," Dominic asked, turning to look at her.

"Of course," she replied.

"I need to get to Choddrath, to the four mountains, have you heard of it?"

"Do you mean Dragon Peak?" Erimaya asked.

"Yes, that sounds like just the place."

"I heard the whole island was nothing more than a lava field. I don't know if the volcano there is still active, and I have never known anyone to go there willingly," she told him.

"Do you know where it is?"

"Not exactly, but our library would be a great place to find out. We have a cartographer, and he has charted most of the high seas and continents." Erimaya placed her embroidered napkin down beside her plate.

"Would you like to go now? These parties can be terribly dull. I prefer the library to the thought of making small talk with those who have had too much wine." She chuckled as she rose from her chair. The feet of the wooden furniture remaining silent as she moved it in to touch the table. They made their way through the great hall and into the enormous library. The tomes were even more impressive close-up. Erimaya pulled a stack of maps from a shelf and handed them to Dominic.

"Here, you look through these, and I'm going to grab another stack," she said. She pointed to the table by the window and Dominic crossed the room to begin searching through the maps. Erimaya joined him a few moments later with a stack of her own. It didn't take long, with her help, to find a map with the island on it. He could go north and maybe catch a boat from somewhere along the northwest.

"Can I take this with me?" Dominic asked.

"I might be able to have someone copy the portion you need," Erimaya replied.

Dominic nodded and pointed out the section of the map showing the north-west region. Erimaya rolled the map up as she walked toward the door then tucked the parchment under her arm.

THIRTEEN

Sophie begged to keep going. Juniper suggested spending the night in Alasia, but after visiting the fortune teller, Sophie wanted to get to the wizard as quickly as possible. She couldn't stop thinking about her father, locked up in a dungeon like a criminal. Sophie's heart ached for Leon, and because of Gabe. With every step they took, Gabe grew closer to Kamara. Sophie did not know why it hurt her heart to see them together, she and Gabe grew up together, and they had only ever been friends, nothing more.

When it got dark, it became hard for Laughlin to see ahead of them, so Juniper took the lead with Dusk scouting fifteen feet ahead of them. Laughlin walked to the back of the group with a lit torch, so the rest of them could see. Traveling at night was more dangerous because the darkness was a perfect shroud for criminals, and the torch was surely a beacon. Laughlin hoped there would be no bandits on the road during their journey.

They moved stealthily, staying alert to the noises around them. Laughlin moved the torchlight back and forth as he scanned the sidelines of the path. There were some trees, but not too many, which made it hard for a group of people to hide. The thought made him feel a little safer.

"Maybe we should have stayed in town," Kamara said softly. Gabe offered her his elbow. Sophie watched them walk arm-in-arm, she politely declined when Gabe offered her his other arm and she forced a slight smile.

Sophie hoped they would reach their destination by morning. She did not like walking at night; at least on the way back, they could take their time. The sounds were stranger at night; nocturnal animals who slept in the day, were stalking their prey. The hoot of an owl, the screech of a bat, and the scurrying of tiny creatures desperate to escape detection were among the sounds Laughlin could identify. It was the noises Laughlin didn't recognize worrying him, though.

They were lucky the trail they took from the outpost to the Highland was a rarely traveled path. When they reached the cliffside, they saw why. The cliff was three hundred feet high and the only way up was a narrow, man-made staircase winding up the face of the cliff.

"I think we should camp here. I don't think we should climb these stairs in the dark." Juniper said. "I'm sorry, Sophie, I know you were hoping to get there by morning, but I promised to keep you safe."

Sophie nodded and unstrapped her bedroll from her pack. Juniper cast the spell for shelter like she did the last time they camped and again, kept watch while everyone else slept. Sophie woke up in the morning to find Laughlin cooking over a fire, and Juniper sitting cross-legged on her bedroll. Juniper's eyes were completely white and her body was as stiff as a marble statue.

"Morning, Sophie, eggs?" Laughlin offered.

"Where did you get those?" she asked.

"I foraged in the forest until I found a bird's nest, and I raided it, we would have had a bird to eat too, but it flew away." Sophie looked offended and started to protest, but Laughlin laughed and revealed the truth.

"I bought them from Maureen before we left the inn. I did gather some wild leeks, baby fern, and sage though. We have to have some greens to stay healthy." Laughlin smiled as he scooped some of the scrambled eggs onto the metal plate from the Blackwater military-issue mess kit. He handed it to Sophie with the matching fork.

Sophie breathed in the fragrance of the herbs. Sophie was hungrier than she knew, because her first bite turned into three, and before she realized it, she gobbled the rest without even looking up from her plate.

When she handed it back, Laughlin scooped some for himself, rinsed the fork with water from his water skin, and finished his breakfast before the others woke up. After everyone was awake and fed, they looked at the climb ahead of them, three hundred feet up, and then it would be only a few more hours until they reached the wizard tower.

They packed up their bedrolls and mess kits and put out the campfire. They were about to have a pretty intense workout, so they shed their cloaks and stuffed them in their packs. The staircase was only wide enough for them to climb single file. Dusk went first, followed by Juniper, Gabe guided Kamara in front of him, and then he turned and asked Sophie to hold onto him if she needed to. Laughlin was the last in line, trying to ensure everyone in front of him stayed safe.

The climb was easy at first, but after the first hundred stairs, Sophie's legs began to burn. She stopped every few steps to massage the aching muscles in her legs. Sweat was dripping down her back, and she could feel it running down her face as well. Juniper stopped them about a third of the way from the top.

"The steps look a little broken up here, we are going to need to step extra carefully," Juniper called back to them. It was easy for Dusk to jump the broken steps, but the others had a more difficult time stretching their legs to skip the broken stairs. Gabe turned around and reached for Sophie's hand to help pull her up. She thought she had a foothold, but the stone beneath her foot crumbled away and she slipped. Gabe was not expecting the sudden jerk of her hand and lost his grip. Sophie screamed as she frantically grabbed for anything solid as she fell, scraping her whole right side down the rock face. Sophie heard a loud crack and knew she had broken her ribs. She managed to grab one of the steps on the way down. As the others rushed back down the steps to her, Gabe pulled a rope out of his bag. He let it unroll and dangled it down to Sophie.

"Grab the rope and tie it around your waist!" He called. Kamara grabbed the slack end of the rope dangling from Gabe's hands and when Sophie had the rope wrapped around her and knotted tightly, they pulled together, Sophie tried to hold onto the rope with her hands and use her feet to brace herself against the mountain, but the rocks kept crumbling beneath her feet and her body would smack against the cliff as they pulled her up. She stopped trying to help so much and just let them pull her up which seemed to work a lot better and finally, Sophie's feet were back on the steps. She collapsed, groaning in pain, she lifted her tunic to reveal her bruised and scraped ribs, it looked like at least two were broken. Sophie's eyes filled with tears and she winced in pain as she pulled her tunic back down to cover her injuries. Then she took Leon's pack off of her back and opened it to check on the orb. She let out a sigh of relief when she found it unharmed.

Juniper squeezed past everyone to get next to her. She spoke an incantation Sophie did not understand and then placed her hands on Sophie's sides. Her ribs popped back into place and the scrapes faded before her eyes.

"Thank you, Juniper," Sophie said, squeezing her hand.

"Do you feel like you can continue? We only have a few hundred steps left," Juniper asked.

"Yes, I'm okay." Sophie turned to Kamara. "Thank you too, I don't think Gabe could have been able to pull me up alone. You saved my life." Sophie stood up and extended her hand to Kamara. When she took her hand, Sophie felt a wind kick up beneath them and some kind of electric charge ran through her body and the orb began to hum. No one but Sophie seemed to notice.

"We need to keep going," Sophie said, still thinking about the fortune teller's warning.

The sun was directly above them when they reached the wizard tower. They didn't know what to expect, none of them had ever met him before. Laughlin grabbed the knocker and banged it against the door three times. It creaked loudly as it opened, swinging inward. Laughlin walked in, looking in every direction for the person who opened the door, but there was no one. The circular room was bare except for the winding staircase on the right-hand side. The light beamed down from the stained glass windows above, funneling into the center of the room and creating a beautiful work of art in the center of the white tile floor.

"Hello?" Laughlin called as the rest of the group began following him into the tower. They started up the stairs. Sophie groaned, she didn't know what she expected in a tower, but more stairs were the last thing she wanted to find. Halfway up the tower, the stairs opened into a beautiful cathedral-style balcony. Custom curved bookshelves took up every wall. Sophie had never seen so many. Gabe got writer's cramps just thinking about how many hours it would take to copy this extensive library by hand. On the other side of the balcony, the staircase continued to a door at the top of the tower.

"Well, this is it. Ready?" Laughlin asked. When the group nodded, Laughlin turned to the door and knocked. A man, who barely looked middle-aged opened the door.

"How can I help you?" he asked in a deep voice.

"We are looking for the wizard, Ryul," Laughlin replied. The man moved to the side and allowed them to enter. The room was beautifully decorated and sectioned into various uses for the room. On one side, there was a study with a desk, and in the center was a summoning circle with a pentagram. There was a fireplace on the far wall with a cauldron suspended over dying embers. In front of the fireplace, there was a large table, covered in assorted herbs, potion bottles, and elixirs.

"Is the wizard here?" Sophie asked.

"I am the wizard, Ryul. Now, what is it I can help you with?" he asked politely. Sophie felt embarrassed. She had heard people talk of the wizard for many years, they said he was over three hundred years old.

"I'm sorry, I just thought..." Sophie began.

"Thought I would look older?" Ryul laughed. "I do hear that one quite a lot. I am descended from the high elves of Aranor. Our lifespan is much longer than any human, and sometimes even other types of elves, I am three hundred fifty-seven years old."

Sophie looked at him in shock. Her father looked older than this man did, and he was centuries older than Leon. She couldn't wait to tell him- if they could find him in time.

"We have brought something, an artifact, and we were hoping you could tell us about it." Sophie removed her father's bag and took out the orb. The light filled the room, A silver dragon and red dragon locked in an endless chase inside the orb cast a prism of colors upon every wall and the floor. The wizard looked carefully at the orb, mesmerized by its gentle hum and beautiful imagery. It almost looked real.

"I think I do know what this is." Ryul glided over to the desk in the study, he pulled a large roll of parchment from the top of a bookshelf and unrolled it onto the table. Sophie had never used a map. Cartographers were few and far between and the ones who could be found were very costly.

"A long time ago- I'm talking about at least a hundred years ago, there were four types of dragons, maybe more, but four which were known about and spotted near this continent. Red, green, silver, and gold. The red and green were the dragons you hear about in story books the ones who destroy villages, eat cattle and sheep, and sometimes, even humans. All of the dragons could shape-shift, but it was mostly the silver and gold dragons who preferred the company of humans and elves over other dragons. They say a shifter could live in your town or village for years, you would see them every day and no one would know the difference." Ryul pointed to the island in the northwest corner of the map. "This is Choddrath, also known as Dragon Peak. Legends say it was the birthplace of all dragons, although hunting practices drove them from the island." He moved his finger to the right, to the island next to Choddrath. "This is where the green dragons migrated when they left Dragon Peak."

Next, he pointed to the Stonehold mountains. "The silver dragons lived here for a time and the red dragons on the island to the north. Ryul walked back over to the orb and held it in his hands. "When humans began hunting dragons for sport, the dragons began retaliating against them, villages were burned, humans were killed, and the ancient silver dragon, who was also a great sorceress, made a pact with the other ancient dragons allowing them to govern each other. The silver and red dragons on the eastern side of the world, and the gold and green on the western side. This orb somehow controlled them and was a system of checks and balances, which would have been fine as long as the orbs stayed in their possession, but they didn't. This one was stolen by a group of humans, cultists of the red dragon. You might have heard of one of these cultists, his name was Orion." Everyone looked at each other as the realization dawned on them.

"So that's how he had control of the red dragons," Juniper said quietly.

"When Orion was killed, my father took the orb and hid it away in the temple, which is why he was there, and why he asked you to bring it to us; but if the dragons are gone, why are they after the orb?" Sophie asked.

"They apparently know something we don't," Juniper replied. "What are we missing?"

Sophie took the orb in her hands and brought it close to her face. Whispers floated from it and she leaned her ear closer to it as she tried to make sense of the words, but she couldn't understand the language it was speaking.

"It's trying to say something," she said, handing the orb to Ryul. He listened carefully as the whispers continued.

"It's Draconic, the language of dragons. I recognize some of the sounds but I don't remember... wait." Ryul handed the orb back to Sophie and blinked out of sight. Everyone looked around for him confused, until a few moments later, he suddenly appeared again with a book in hand. He began leafing through the pages. Sophie recognized what it was, it was a spell book. Compared to hers, this one was massive. It was leather bound and written so neatly there could be no confusion when reading a spell.

"I admit I have been practicing magic a lot today so I am already a little drained, but I might have enough power to cast this once, it will only last for an hour, but you will be able to understand any language you hear. Who wants to listen?" Ryul asked.

"I will," Sophie said, stepping forward with the orb.

Ryul prepared the components and then touched Sophie on the top of her head. Her aura brightened as Ryul spoke the incantation. Instantly, the whispers from the orb began sounding like words.

Born of silver and red, the dragons are coming of age. On the island of Choddrath, the orb and the dragons must merge. Beware the forces seeking destruction, if the orb is destroyed, evil will rise.

Sophie translated the whispers to the group. They looked around at each other, silently processing what they had to do. Their quest was not over, they were not prepared for a journey this long, but going back to restock would take them too long and be too big of a risk with the red masked cultists roaming in search of the orb.

"Why don't we go downstairs to discuss our next move," Gabe suggested. The others began walking toward the door in agreement, but the look Gabe gave Sophie, told her he was trying to buy her a moment alone with Ryul. Sophie followed them toward the door, but once they were outside and on their way down the stairs, Sophie closed the door.

"Ryul, Sir, I heard you were looking for an apprentice, and I know the only wizards until now have been men, but I found this in a trunk of old things in our cellar and was hoping you would allow me to learn from you as soon as I save up the gold. I have already been practicing," Sophie said, holding up the battered old spell book.

Ryul inspected it carefully. He looked at the cover and the handwriting inside. Sophie wasn't sure, but she thought she saw fear in his eyes before he handed the book back to her.

"Did you know him?" Sophie asked.

"I did. His name was Baelfire. He was a fellow wizard. I didn't train him, but we fought in some of the same battles. The last one was the battle of Blackwater Bay," Ryul said. "When I got on the ship going to the right side of the bay, and he got on the ship going to the left side, I never thought it would be the last time I saw him. His ship went down just before the monster was killed and he was one of the men who never made it back to shore."

"I'm sorry, for the loss of your friend," Sophie said.

Ryul gave Sophie a soft smile. "Friend might be too strong of a word. After your journey to Choddrath, if you still wish to apprentice with me, I would be happy to teach you, but it seems at this time, the world needs saving, and your path has aligned with this quest." He motioned Sophie toward the door. "I do have something for you to take with you, consider it your first task," he said, pausing at the desk in the center of the room. He opened a drawer and pulled out a scroll. "This will be of great assistance on your journey," Ryul said as he handed the scroll to Sophie. "Now, your friends are waiting." He opened the door and watched until Sophie was descending the staircase to close the door.

When she reached the bottom, Sophie unrolled the scroll. She read the words with a smile. It would indeed, come in very handy.

"I guess we're off to Choddrath to merge some dragons," Sophie joked as she reached her friends at the bottom of the stairs.

"I think we should go back to Blackwater and see if they have found your father yet. He could help with this," Juniper suggested.

"Every moment we spend with the orb puts us in danger. If we go back to Blackwater and they haven't found Leon, the trip will take us even longer. I think Sophie is right, we should get to Choddrath," Gabe agreed, giving Sophie a trusting nod as they stepped out into the sunlight.

"I feel connected to the orb, I can't explain it, maybe it is just because it was in the temple for so long. My room was right above the vault and I used to fall asleep to the humming sound it makes. I would love to go with you to Choddrath," Kamara said. "If you want me to," Kamara added, looking at Sophie.

"You saved my life. If not for you, I could have fallen off the side of the mountain. I would love for you to come with us," Sophie told her. She wasn't sure if Kamara had sensed her feelings before, or if Kamara's glance in her direction was only coincidence, but Sophie could tell Kamara wanted her approval.

"Okay, it's settled then, we are all going to Choddrath," Laughlin said. Dusk seemed to bark in agreement as she moved in front of Laughlin to take the lead.

Just as they were leaving the wizard's tower, a flash of white light startled them and in the center of the flash, a circle of runes appeared and spread outward, bringing with it a group of men dressed in all black robes with red masks covering the bottom half of their faces.

With instant recognition, Juniper, Laughlin, Sophie, and Gabe all stepped in front of Kamara, hiding her from view. Sophie looked at the man in front as he drew a sword from his back. Not just any sword, a greatsword Sophie would recognize anywhere. It was Destiny, her father's sword. Juniper saw it too, and before another moment passed, roots and vines sprouted out of the earth at the man's feet, wrapping around his ankles. In a moment of surprise and panic, he hacked and slashed at the vines with Leon's sword, trying his best to free himself from the tangle of growth Juniper was creating. The other men drew their weapons as well and began attacking the foliage, trying to free their leader.

Laughlin drew his sword and prepared for attack. Juniper's vines grew quickly, but the enemies were faster at hacking them away. The leader ran forward, meeting Laughlin's weapon with Destiny. Laughlin could hear the slight hum of magic in the blade.

As the man drew back with both hands on the hilt to keep control of the weapon, Laughlin lunged forward to strike his midsection. He barely grazed the skin as the man turned to the side just in time and then swung his weapon back at Laughlin recklessly.

The other men rushed Gabe and Juniper engaging them in battle, and Sophie rushed toward the man who held her father's sword. He was just as surprised as Sophie when the tip of Sophie's weapon came out the front of his abdomen. Destiny fell to the ground and Sophie claimed it, stepping back to stare at the man whose life she had just taken.

"You are not worthy to wield my father's sword," Sophie spat. Even though her anger was prominent, guilt began creeping up on her. She didn't even have time to process how she was feeling before a man grabbed her from behind and dragged her quickly to the teleportation circle. They disappeared in a flash before anyone else could react. Juniper stomped her foot and made the earth beneath their enemies quake. The ground broke apart and a couple of the men fell into the void.

The sound of steel on steel as their swords met over and over again rang out across the highland. Laughlin thought he had gained the upper hand when he backed his opponent toward the edge of the cliff, but what he failed to notice was the teleportation circle he was now standing in. The man laughed as he spoke a word, the circle lit up, and before Laughlin knew what happened, he was being hurtled through space—or time, maybe both—he couldn't tell. It made him nauseous. He became light-headed as a flash of white light surrounded him, and when it went away, they were standing in the middle of a desert.

Laughlin knew deserts were dry and hot, but the sudden atmosphere change left him instantly breathless. There was not a building in sight. The man teleported him to the middle of nowhere.

"Hey, this isn't— before Laughlin could finish his sentence, a rock-hard fist collided with his face. First, a searing pain shot from his nose up to the top of his head. Then a trickle of blood caught him off guard as another blow to the side of his head turned everything black.

"I'm sorry 'bout this, I am, but you should have seen it coming," the man said, spitting on the ground in front of Laughlin as he walked away.

Still outside the wizard's tower, Juniper, Gabe, and Kamara fought off what was left of their attackers. Gabe screamed for Sophie and collapsed to his knees after the last man fell. Gabe only came on this adventure to keep Sophie safe; and he had failed. Kamara tried to comfort him but he shrugged away.

"I just need to feel this right now," he said as he stood and walked back toward the tower for a quiet moment alone. Juniper sat with her head in her hands, crying as Dusk gently nuzzled her.

From the tower, the wizard emerged, appearing frail and tired. He looked older than he had a while ago. Juniper looked up at him as he approached.

"I am sorry I was not more help during the fight. I saw them take your companions and I think this might help. He took a ring from his finger and handed it to Juniper.

"What does it do?" she asked.

"It is of my own design, there isn't another like it. The spell it holds will allow you to see any person who is known to you, reflected on a still, clear surface; a pool of water, a crystal ball, a looking glass, anything with a reflection. You can use it to find your friends."

As Juniper took the ring, the wizard's expression was melancholy. She couldn't find the words to ask why giving up the ring caused him sorrow, but he seemed to sense the question in her mind.

"I used it from time to time so I could see the love I left behind. I moved here to the highland for solitude. The thought of outliving those I loved brought me so much grief for things that hadn't happened yet, but I still wanted to see her. I looked in on her over the years as she married, had children, and lived a good long life for a human. Now that she has passed, I do not need this, but I couldn't bring myself to take it off until now. I hope it will be of use to you."

He placed a sympathetic hand on Juniper's shoulder, then turned and hobbled back to the tower. She could see now why he needed an apprentice; he was dying. *He must have used a glamour spell when they first arrived.* Juniper thought.

Juniper put the ring on her finger and gathered Dusk, Gabe, and Kamara. "We have to get going. We know they will take Sophie to Choddrath with the orb and I would like to at least make it to the lake tonight," Juniper said. She walked to the edge of the cliff and began to cast a spell. The earth grew moist and the dirt turned to mud and began flowing down the side of the cliff.

"Come on, follow me," Juniper called as she sat down in the mud and slid down the slope. Going down by mudslide was much quicker than climbing up the stairs on the other side. The three of them toppled into each other at the base and despite the situation, they each managed to laugh as they stood, covered from head to toe with mud. Dusk came padding down the path after them, still clean in comparison. They were now only a couple of hours away from the lake, but every step they took felt like they had sandpaper between their thighs as the mud dried.

"There is a temple not far from here, they might let us wash up and change our clothes there," Juniper said leading the way. Gabe and Kamara followed Juniper on auto-pilot, lost in their thoughts about Sophie and Laughlin.

FOURTEEN

Leon woke up to the pungent smell of death. He was cold and naked on the stone floor. His muscles were failing and it was hard to stand, or even move. His stomach had stopped growling now, which was both good and bad. It was nice he didn't have the stabbing hunger pangs and auditory reminders of his lack of food, but he was running out of fat stores, and when his body had nothing left, he would be gone.

"Hey, you... prisoner next to me." Leon never asked his name, or at least didn't remember if the man had given it. He waited for a reply and when there was none, he called for him again, this time louder. Still no response. Something told him the man in the cell next to him was dead. He let out a deep wheezing cough as he tried to rise, pushing himself up with shaking arms. It was almost dinner time and he hoped the young boy would be delivering again today and not one of the red masked men.

Leon tried to look down the hall to see any of the other prisoners. He wanted to get someone's attention, someone who could check on the guy next to him. He didn't want to start yelling and draw the wrong kind of attention. He picked up a small piece of rubble from the stone floor and tossed it down the hallway and listened to the clacking sound grow quieter as it bounced further down the hall.

When he heard a stone skipping back toward him, he jumped with excitement. The soft clacking sound reminded him of the wooden box his mother used to have on the piano. She had insisted he learn to play, the box made a ticking sound to the beat of the music. Those times with his mother were some of his favorite memories. She was always calm and patient with him as he tried to learn. Even when the result was the eventual conclusion that he did not possess an aptitude or an ear for music.

"Can you see the guy next to me?" Leon whispered loudly down the hall.

"No, he must be in the back of his cell, hey, Brendan, you awake?" he called to the prisoner next to him. When Brendan groaned in response, he continued talking. "Check on Grandpa."

A few moments of silence followed as Brendan moved to the front of his cell. When he got close to the bars, Leon heard him gag. He wasn't positive, but he had the feeling, it was because of the smell. Brendan yelled for the man they called "Grandpa" a few times, and when he didn't move, Brendan confirmed Leon's suspicion.

"He's dead- his body looks like it is decomposed and he has some kind of blackness spreading through it. Almost

like roots, or... a plague, we shouldn't be breathing this in." Brendan began to panic, and in doing so, woke the other prisoners. Everyone started yelling, trying to attract the attention of the guards upstairs.

"Leon doubled over as a coughing fit overtook him and when he opened his eyes he saw the blackness starting in his foot. He needed a healer, or the sickness would take him too. Leon didn't know how long the man next to him had it, or how quickly it had spread.

"I'm going to die in here," he thought.

The rickety dock on the eastern coast of the Auran Desert creaked under the weight of the horses. It was a floating dock, which meant every time someone stepped on it, the whole dock would sway in one direction or another because there was no support underneath to keep it steady. This spooked the horses and they were extremely hard to control. After the first trial and error, the captain pulled the ship back from the dock and lowered the ramp into the water near the shore.

Samantha was glad to be back on land. The ginger had helped, but her stomach was still in knots. It was hot and there was not a tree in sight. She could see the ripples of the heat in the distance. The horizon looked as though it were dancing in the sweltering afternoon heat.

They thought traveling at night through the desert would be better for the horses, and better for them. It would take them a few hours to reach Auran Oasis, where the horses could drink and they could top off their water skins. They each had two, including the horses.

Matthias and his men unloaded the ship then packed the saddle bags on the horses. Once everything was off the ship, the captain waved to them. "When do you need us to be back?" he asked.

Samantha looked at Matthias, they had never thought about or discussed how long they thought it would take to find Leon, they weren't even sure they were in the right place. They knew the ship had stopped here, but they could have gone anywhere.

"I will send word to Hank when we are headed back to the dock. We aren't sure how long it will take to find Commander Rend," Matthias replied.

"Aye, Sir. Good luck, and we will see you when you've found him." He waved goodbye as the crew prepared the ship for takeoff.

"Ready for this?" Matthias asked, looking at Samantha with a slightly worried look.

"Yes. I hope we are not too late." Samantha mounted her horse and took the reigns in hand.

"Look over here!" one of Matthias' men called. The evidence was faint, but hoof prints were leading away from the docks, toward the oasis they planned to stop at anyway.

"We have no way of knowing if it was them, but it's a start," Matthias said. They took off, following the tracks through the desert. The sun was directly in front of them and Samantha could feel it stinging her face as they rode toward it.

Just as the sun began to dip below the horizon, they reached the oasis. Palm trees, a sparkling pool of water, and a bit of shade put everyone at ease. They made camp there for dinner, taking note of the tracks heading northwest from the camp.

"We will wait for nightfall and then head out. We can use the North Star to help keep us on track. It will be much too hot to travel by day," Matthias told them. "The Auran Desert is vast, this is the last water for days so make sure each water skin is filled." The men all nodded in agreement. "We have enough rations for us each to have two per day, no more than that though." Matthias left his men to their preparations and then walked over to Samantha.

"Now that we are on this side of the continent, I can try once again to use a spell to locate him. It didn't work when I tried in Blackwater, we were too far away, but I will see if I can get a pin on him now." Matthias said. "Keep the faith, we won't stop until we find him," he vowed. Samantha wiped a tear from her eye and nodded in response, gripping his hand tightly.

"Thank you, Matthias, you're a good friend to us and I appreciate it, she said.

Matthias did not eat with everyone else, instead, he went off by himself and worked on his spell. Finding people, enemies, or creatures, was his special skill. Few people knew the skill was magical in nature and were always impressed when he succeeded.

The spell worked, The direction of Leon's location was revealed, but now, he needed to see it. Matthias conjured a hawk and transferred his consciousness into it. His body was meditating, but his mind was free to fly. He flew in the direction the spell had given him, looking for signs of life. Besides a few desert animals, there were none. Matthias kept going, even though the tracks were gone now, covered by the drifting sand. Finally, just before the desert turned into a jungle, Matthias saw a small, but heavily secured camp. There were two towers at the front gates. Two heavily armed and armored soldiers stood guard, and several more patrolled the perimeter.

Matthias flew to the large building in the back and circled it. He tried flying past the windows and peeking in, but he couldn't see anything through them. *This has to be it though, this is where they're keeping him.* Matthias thought. The hawk flew straight up into the sky as he pulled his consciousness back into his own body. The tether was broken and he snapped back into his own mind and saw Samantha staring at him, expectantly.

"Anything?" she asked.

"I think I know where they are keeping him, but it is heavily guarded. It will take us at least two nights to ride there on horseback, but I think once we get close we will need to continue on foot anyway, it's quieter," Matthias said.

"We should leave someone to look after the horses, If I lost Leon's warhorse, I would be afraid to go home with him. I think he loves his horse more than me, he even has a ruby crown. Yes, the *horse* has a ruby crown," Samantha clarified, giving Matthias a serious look.

Matthias laughed. "For a second there, I thought I misheard you," he said. Samantha smiled and shook her head. They walked back to camp to find the soldiers packed and ready to go. Samantha gave Leon's horse a pet on the side of his neck.

"Come on, Horatio, let's go find Leon," Samantha whispered as she touched her forehead to the bridge of Horatio's long nose. She mounted in one swift movement and made a clicking sound as she gently bumped his sides with her heels to get him moving.

The wind had blown sand over the tracks and they were no longer visible, but Matthias knew where to lead them. The wind was still blowing and the sand was hitting their faces like a thousand tiny sewing needles piercing their skin. The sensation made them all stop and take a few moments to make some face coverings from whatever cloth they could tear from their tunics, or find in their bags.

The desert was shockingly cool when the sun was down. The route was not as flat and sandy as Samantha thought it would be, the terrain became rocky and uneven. There were not a lot of plants either, the patches of what Samantha assumed was grass, were dried out and brown. The desert was eerily quiet, except for the sound of their passage through it and the chirping of crickets.

The clouds covering the stars hinted at rain, but Samantha had a feeling they would pass without spilling a drop on the dry cracked earth they currently walked.

After an hour, they stopped to give the horses a break and a drink. Samantha was getting tired and she wondered how they were going to go about getting inside the enemy camp to rescue Leon. She was not a skilled fighter, but she was quiet and could sneak into places undetected if she had to, she had gotten lots of practice when Sophie was a baby because Sophie had been a light sleeper and Samantha always had to tiptoe through the house to avoid waking her.

They didn't rest long, The day would be approaching and then it would be too hot to continue. Matthias hoped there would be a cave or maybe even a large alcove where they could rest during the day, but so far, the only rock formations in sight were too far out of their way.

A little while before sunrise, they stopped to make camp. There were no mountains nearby, but they did have shovels.

"Dig a hole long and wide enough for you to lay in comfortably. Mound the loose dirt and rocks around three sides of it. Use rocks to secure your wool blanket across the top of the opening, leaving the western side uncovered so we will be able to see the sun setting. If we get this done before sunrise, it will keep you cooler, not much, but it's better than nothing," Matthias instructed.

"I will dig a hole for you, Mrs. Rend," he said, pulling the shovel from his pack. Samantha couldn't sit around and do nothing though, so she gathered large rocks and stacked some near the spot each man was digging. Samantha wished they'd brought the tents, but carrying all the extra gear would not help them reach Leon faster.

By the time the sun came up, all the holes were dug and the horses were hitched. Matthias wished there was some shade for them too, he felt bad for the animals, standing in the sun and desert heat.

They tried their best to sleep, but between the heat and the itching of the sand beneath them in what looked like a shallow grave, they got very little rest. By nightfall, they were packing up for the last push. They drank the last of their water and ate a ration. Samantha only ate half of hers. She wanted to save some food for Leon. With any luck, they would reach him by the next dawn.

Samantha wiped the sweat from her forehead. They had ridden all night, and now they were so close to finding Leon—they had to push on through the day. The sun, although it was rising and shining on their backs, made the sand bright and it hurt Samantha's eyes. Even the blue sky was almost blinding. The flat cracked desert earth was now a series of mounds and hills of sand, the horses' hooves sank into it and they walked slower than before. They were now riding next to a mesa which was, unfortunately, on the north side and did nothing to offer them shade or shelter.

Silent buzzards circled something up ahead. Samantha felt like they would be circling her soon too if she didn't get some water and cool down. As they rode closer to the buzzards overhead, Matthias spotted what it was the birds were interested in.

"It's a body!" he called to the others. Matthias ran over to the figure and crouched beside him. As he rolled the man over, his black curls matted to his face with a mixture of blood and sand.

"Is he dead?" Samantha asked, alarmed.

"Not yet, but he's not far from it." Matthias pulled his waterskin from his belt. He didn't have much water left, but it might be just enough. Matthias sat the man up and gently squished his cheeks together forcing his lips open. Matthias poured a little water into the man's mouth.

A low, almost inaudible groan escaped the man as he began to awaken. Matthias helped him sit up and told him to cup his hands. When he did, Matthias filled them with water so he could wash the blood and sand from his face.

"Laughlin?" Samantha asked in a confused voice when he looked up at them. "I thought you were with Sophie, are they okay?"

"The guys in the red masks caught up to us at Lapis Highland. One of them took Sophie. They're using teleportation circles to get around," Laughlin explained wincing in pain as he touched his bruises and the bridge of his nose. It had to be broken. He had never felt this much pain in his life.

"What about the artifact?" Samantha asked.

"Sophie had it in her bag, so I assume they have it now, but don't worry, we know where they will be going and Juniper and Gabe won't stop until they find her."

"Where are they headed?" Matthias asked.

"Choddrath," Laughlin replied. "The wizard gave Sophie the ability to understand what the orb was saying, and it said the dragon and the orb must merge in Choddrath or something," Laughlin recalled as he tried to stand. Matthias walked around the spot searching for tracks they could follow.

"So how did you end up here?" Samantha asked.

"As I was sword fighting one of the cultists, he led me into the teleportation circle. I think he hit me too." Laughlin looked around on the ground.

"Over here!" Matthias called. "There are footprints in the sand."

"Okay, get on," Samantha said to Laughlin, sliding forward to make room for him on the horse with her.

"You, ride back to the dock as quickly as you can and wait there for the ship, tell them we need all guild members and all available soldiers on the next ship to Choddrath as quickly as possible. Sophie needs help," Matthias told one of the soldiers.

"Yes, sir," he replied and he turned and rode away as quickly as the horse would run.

"Okay, Let's go," Matthias said, turning back to the rest of them.

Matthias rode in front, following the footprints as far as he cold before they disappeared in the sand. He kept them on course using the position of the sun until the camp was in sight. On their way, he'd thought of a plan.

"Okay, so here's what we are going to do, we might not be close enough for them to see us yet, but when we are close enough we are going to make camp."

"Wait, you *want* them to see us?" Samantha asked.

"Yes, here's why; when they see us camping, not attacking, and minding our business, they're going to get curious, they might send out a scout, someone to come and see who we are and what our business is out here in the desert. We can lure him this way, around the bend of the mesa where half our men will be waiting. The other half will come up behind him, to block his retreat. Then we are going to knock him out, take his clothes, and one of us can pretend to be him to infiltrate the base. There's a building toward the back, the only solid structure in the camp. I imagine it's where the dungeon is. We make our way there and find the holding cells and there too we will find Leon. The rest of you will ride past the camp like you're moving on, and when it gets dark again we can break him out," Matthias said, looking very proud of his plan.

"What if they send more than one and we can't overpower them all?" Samantha asked.

"We can tell them we are looking for a medicinal flower from the desert cacti and just stopped here because it was too hot. Then when it gets dark we can continue the plan." Matthias said.

Samantha didn't want to stop, she didn't want to wait another day to find Leon and know if he was okay, but Matthias was right, it would be better, and easier to wait for the cover of darkness.

They waited for evening in the valley between two mounds. Laughlin foraged for some fishhook barrel cacti to eat since they were not near a source of water, he thought the cactus could serve a dual purpose.

Matthias conjured the hawk again and flew around the compound looking through its eyes.

"One guard at the gate, the perimeter is a wooden fence with sharpened branches facing outward. There is a spot in the back right corner of the fence that looks vulnerable. There are several long tents with cots set up inside, looks like sleeping quarters. A few patrols are walking around—looks like they follow the same pattern so if we time it just right, we can sneak past them. They are carrying some bodies out of the only building in the camp. They're burning them on a pyre." The hawk perched on a nearby stump to look at the faces of the people they were throwing onto the fire. One of the men snapped his head toward the bird and made eye contact. Matthias gasped as he was forced out of the bird and back into himself.

"They know," he said.

"Know what?" Samantha asked.

"The bird, one of them looked at it, made eye contact like he knew he was being watched. They might not actually know anything. Didn't mean to alarm you." Matthias seemed confused and disoriented. Samantha wondered if it was perhaps the heat getting to him.

Evening approached, and darkness loomed minutes away as Matthias led the troop out into the open. With the suspicion at least one of the red masked men knew they were being watched, it might be harder to convince them they were just passing through.

Half the men stayed back, around the edge of the mesa and out of the sight of the enemy camp. The other half moved into sight and built a fire. They wanted to be seen. Laughlin waited with the men around the edge of the mesa, four of the eight of them.

Matthias, Samantha, and the other four waited for a man in a red mask to come and inquire about their intent. He tried not to continually look in the direction of the enemy, hoping it would not look obvious they were trying to draw one of them out.

They sat and waited for quite some time, about to give up hope when they saw a torch light in the distance. A man on horseback was headed their way. Samantha signaled to Laughlin and they prepared to carry out the plan.

The man who approached them was wearing all black with a red mask covering his mouth and nose. *Perfect.* Matthias thought to himself as he suppressed a smile.

"Can I ask why you guys are out here in the middle of the desert?" The man asked.

"We are foraging for a rare desert flower said to heal the deepest wounds and cure a feeble mind," Samantha said.

"Ain't no flowers here, best be on your way," he said.

Just then, Laughlin replicated the call of a wolf. The man's attention snapped to the area beyond the mesa. He looked at Samantha and Matthias and then back toward the mesa once more.

"What was that?" he asked suspiciously when no one else seemed alarmed by the sound of a wild animal. He got off his horse, taking slow, cautious steps around the edge of the mesa. He barely had time to recognize the trap before the soldiers closed in on him from all sides. Matthias's men gave him no time to raise alarm, he was unconscious before he could even produce a gasp.

Since Matthias had already scoped out the camp, he volunteered to wear the uniform and find Leon. He dressed in the man's black robes and red mask, tucking his own clothes into the waistband of his pants for Leon to change into. Samantha and Laughlin led the rest of the men north, and into the cover of the jungle. They waited in the tree line, ducked down like a lion stalking its prey. The soldiers hitched all of their horses to the trees farther back in the foliage to obscure them from view.

Matthias rode into the camp as if he'd done it a million times, no one questioned him as they watched the outsiders ride north. Matthias took the horse back to the stable and entered the building in the center of camp. The man who sat guard nodded to Matthias as he entered and stood up, gathering his personal effects.

"It's about time, I was falling asleep at the desk. Thank goodness for shift change!" He stretched and yawned before clapping Matthias on the back and motioning for him to take his seat. He took the key ring off his belt and laid it on the desk.

"Not that you'll need 'em, we already cleared out the dead. Any more of 'em die tonight and they can wait til morning," he said, walking toward the door. "Try to stay awake," the guard joked as he stepped out into the fresh night air.

Matthias waited until the man was well on his way to the sleeping quarters before quickly grabbing the keys and finding the rickety wooden staircase leading to the dungeon.

"Leon!" he whispered moving down the stairs and toward the hall of cells. He heard a groan coming from the first cell. "Leon?" he called again. Pulling his mask down so Leon could recognize him, Matthias unlocked the cell and helped him to his feet.

Commander Rend was skin and bone, dirty, and smelled of urine. Matthias recalled seeing a barrel of water by the stairs which looked clean enough and it had a stack of metal buckets beside it. He first, tasted it to make sure it was drinkable, then he filled one bucket for Leon to drink from and another for him to wash with.

"We have to work fast," Matthias said, pulling the spare clothes from the waistband of his pants. Leon rinsed his body with the clean water, sighing with relief at the mere hint of cleanliness. Once he finished rinsing and had dripped as dry as he had time to get, Leon quickly dressed as Matthias filled two water skins. His clothes were big on Leon, so

Matthias ripped a long strip of fabric from the black robes he had on to make a belt to hold Leon's pants up as they ran.

He led Leon up the stairs, walking ahead of him to check for enemies. They moved through the back door of the building and ducked behind crates and carts or whatever else they could find to shield them from enemy view. Matthias and Leon made it to the back of the sleeping tent without being detected. They could see the gap in the fence in the back corner, but to get to it, they had to pass the open flap of the sleeping tent and make it across the back side of the camp, where there were not a lot of items to provide cover.

Matthias heard voices coming from inside, and through the tent, he saw the flicker of lantern light and the shadows of at least two men awake inside, but he couldn't tell which way they were facing. There was no other way, though, they were going to have to pass the tent. Laughlin and Samantha would be waiting right outside the fence with the Blackwater soldiers, they were just going to have to run.

"Okay, on three, we're going to make a break for the back right corner, to the gap in the fence," Matthias explained. Leon nodded his under-standing and Matthias counted. "One... two...three!" They sprinted out from behind the tent, ignoring the shouts coming from behind them as the red masked men gave chase.

"Keep going Leon, get to the gap," Matthias yelled as he stopped and turned to face the men. He hadn't brought any weapons with him, but he saw some hanging on a rack next to the sleeping tent. He ran back toward the tent and grabbed a sword and dagger from the rack as he passed by it, and then with a swift movement, he turned and hurled the dagger at the man chasing Leon. The knife met its mark with ease as it pierced the back of the man's head. He fell forward with a thud as another man turned to face Matthias.

Leon made it out, it was the only thing that mattered now. The man walked toward Matthias, who stood his ground, gripping the hilt of the sword as he moved around him in a defensive position. The man surprised him though, instead of attacking, he moved to a large pole, and pulled a lever. An alarm bell rang out across the camp and it wasn't long at all before an arrow whistled through the air and squelched through

Matthias's chest. A thunder of feet pounding the ground came from all directions and in a matter of moments, a dozen blades were aimed at his chest. Matthias gave one good swing with all his might, meeting nothing but the air in front of him as his vision blurred and he fell forward, blood pooling around him.

Leon watched in horror from the other side of the fence as one of the men plunged his sword into Matthias' abdomen to be sure the job was finished. When he turned to see Samantha, he knew they had no time for the reunion he had been dreaming of, they had to get to the cover of the jungle before the men came after them all.

The Blackwater soldiers formed a line at the trees, bows, and arrows drawn as Leon and Samantha retreated into the jungle. The few men who jumped the gap in the fence met with only arrows.

They rode all night; north through the thick jungle, to the abandoned temple, a sanctuary for good. Protected with runes and wards against evil, the temple was the safest place they could be. Those who used to worship there, traded the life of foraging, and facing the dangers of the jungle, for the safety of cities and towns. Over the years, the jungle temple became a holy place, visited only when one needed to find their connection to the goddess. Most of the furniture was gone now though, so it would not be as comfortable as it once had been many years before.

They laid out their bedrolls on the stone floor, but didn't bother making a fire. They lit a few torches and put them into the sconces on the walls around them. Samantha pulled out a ration and gave it to Leon. He ate the canned meat with his fingers and swallowed each wad without even chewing. When Samantha saw he had almost finished everything, she handed him the leftovers from her ration as well. She wanted to hug him, but something about him seemed different; almost afraid. She decided it might be best to give him some time.

The soldiers took shifts keeping watch, two at a time, standing inside the only entrance of the temple they didn't barricade. Samantha tried to sleep, but she couldn't, she kept looking at Leon like any moment she would awaken and he would be gone again.

FIFTEEN

By sunrise, Dominic was packed and already on his way out of Ravenhall. The evening before, Dominic made a rough copy of the map to take with him. He planned to head north through the jungle, camp at Aerulean Lake, then head west to either Braidwood or Ashenport where he could board a ship to Choddrath.

The elves walked everywhere, so his hopes of finding a ride were gone, at least until he got to the lake. Walking before the sunrise was always his favorite time to be out; watching it turn from darkness to light made him feel like he was accomplishing great things. Erimaya made him a travel basket filled with apples and fresh bread. Dominic did not want to carry the basket, so he packed the contents into his backpack. He tried to get Erimaya to let him pay for the room, but she insisted it was no trouble and he was her guest.

The birds began to wake and sang happily in the trees as Dominic walked through the forest, and when he reached the bridge, he spied a couple of beavers trying to build a dam in the narrow part of the stream. When he was ready to have breakfast, he walked to the bank of the river and spread his blanket over the ground. He had an apple, and a piece of bread as he listened to the beautiful sounds of nature. The quiet of the seclusion, the sound of the water flowing downstream, birds whistling their good morning song in the branches, and the hush of the breeze blowing through the leaves made him feel sleepy. Dominic was certain he could sleep for another hour- at least, if only he had the time.

Since he had places to be though, he forced himself to get up. He took the time to dig a small hole and he buried his apple core in it. He hoped the next time he came through, he would see a green sprout coming out of the earth in that very same spot, and he would know he had given back to the earth, and the elves for their kindness.

Across the bridge, in the town of Hillside, Dominic felt very tall. There were ponies pulling wagons seemingly child-sized compared to him, and all the buildings, houses, and gardens were very small as well. The people there, although they looked like children varied in age from very young, to very old and were all roughly the same height except for the babies.

No one there wore shoes and their feet were exceptionally wide and covered in the earth-just the way they liked them. Their ears were pointed like the elves, but they did not conduct themselves the way elves did. The people did not make much effort to speak to Dominic, but they all watched him as he walked through town. There was music, dancing, lots of food, and the drinking of ale.

"Yer mighty tall fer an elfling- hic!" A jolly fellow said as he bumped into Dominic during a lavish twirl from his latest dance move.

"I'm sorry, a what?" Dominic asked.

"You know, an elfling, wee folk, like us!" he told him, as he continued dancing to the jovial tune.

"Oh, I see, I am not an elfling, but I think I would quite like to be, this seems like a fun party." Dominic said with a smile.

"This isn't a-hic- party, it's just another day-hic!" The elfling took another gulp of his ale and then filled his cheeks with air, trying to hold his breath to rid himself of the hiccups. His face began to turn red, his eyes crossed, and finally, the sound of a whistling teapot came out of his mouth as he released the breath he was holding.

Dominic chuckled softly as the elfling twirled back into the crowd. He kept walking north, now with the river to his left, and by late afternoon, he reached the thick, humid forest of the Auran Jungle. The jungle floor was much softer than in the forest of Ravenhall; It was also wet and sticky, as if there had just been a heavy rain. Within the first few minutes of walking, Dominic dripped with sweat and was thirstier than he had ever been.

He drank the contents of his water skin and then filled it up with the clearest water he could find. It tasted earthy and full of minerals from the rocks over which it flowed, but it quenched his thirst, which was all he needed it to do.

He marched on, trudging through the muck and thickets. When the path became less worn, and reclaimed by nature, he spent the journey ducking branches and using his sword to cut away foliage too thick for passing. The sound of a monkey screeching somewhere in the trees above startled him, he couldn't see the monkey, but it definitely knew he was there. As he walked deeper and deeper into the jungle, the screeching grew louder and more frequent. Once he made his way into the clearing, he saw why; the screeching was a warning for the rest of the troop.

On one side of the clearing, the monkeys hung from the branches, and stood together along the treeline. The second Dominic left the tree line, they were all staring at him. One wrong movement could startle them and then he was sure they would attack together. Dominic wouldn't stand a chance against all of them. He moved very slowly, laying down his sword at his feet. Next, he took off his pack just as slowly, and opened it to reveal the food inside.

He emptied the contents, taking the non-food items out of the pile. Then he stepped back into the treeline and watched as the first little monkey came forward and took and apple. Once he began eating it, the others started grabbing what they could too. He watched as one of the monkeys tasted the bread, threw it aside, and snatched an apple instead.

When all the apples were gone, the monkeys disappeared into the trees, eating their fruit quietly and paying Dominic no mind as he picked up his things. The bread was a little dirty now, but if he got hungry enough, it would serve its purpose. He stuffed the loaf, minus the bite the monkey took, back into his pack.

By the time he made it out of the jungle it was dark again, it had taken him all day, from dawn, until well after dusk. He was thankful to have only encountered monkeys on his journey. The lake looked like a beautiful spot. There were cabins, and tents set up around the lake. People were cooking on fires, playing games, and fishing.

Dominic thought he might like to stay there and rest tomorrow, catch and cook some fish, and maybe wash and dry his clothes before continuing his journey to Choddrath. Lanterns were flickering outside the main cabin. A sign on top of the building read: Camp Rentals. Movement from the window told Dominic there was someone inside, he wasn't sure if this place operated like an inn, but if so, no matter what time of night it was, there was usually someone to take your coin. Dominic knocked on the door and waited for the voice from inside.

"It's open." Dominic peeked his head inside, before stepping in.

"I'm sorry, I didn't mean to arrive so late, but I was hoping I could rent a cabin for tonight, and tomorrow night."

"It's your lucky night, we have one left. It's five gold a night, but it doesn't look like it will be a problem for you." He said, eyeing Dominic's golden armor.

The way he was looking at him made Dominic uncomfortable. He fished out the ten gold, careful not to jingle his coin too much, and handed it to the man. He took the coin and put it in a chest under the counter and slid a key back across the counter to Dominic. This made Dominic feel a little better, at least he would be able to lock his door.

SIXTEEN

During the night, dark clouds rolled in over the jungle canopy. The sky let loose with streaks of lightning and furious thunder. Rain poured heavily on the temple roof and the wind blew the storm inside the columned windows lining the southern wall. Puddles gathered around the broken front door and along the windows. The shutters were all in various states of disrepair and useless against the force of the storm they currently faced.

Samantha thought about lighting a fire in the hearth, but she had not yet found a single log that wasn't soaked through. The Blackwater soldiers were looking in other parts of the temple for dry wood. The jungle, which was usually alive with the sounds of monkeys, and birds, was eerily quiet.

Laughlin brought the horses into the temple. There was no other choice, he couldn't leave them out in the storm with no shelter. Luckily, the temple was accommodating and he found a room lined with tall stone pillars with an hourglass shape, perfect for hitching a horse at the smallest circumference. Laughlin found their nosebags and strapped one to each horse so they could eat.

In what was once one of many day rooms, or common areas of the temple, Leon moved some empty bookshelves and lined them side by side to partition off a section of the room near the archway to the garden for privacy. He undressed behind the shelves and went outside

113

to wash himself off in the rain. The Blackwater mission packs always had a hygiene kit and Leon was never happier to see soap. He found a spot where the rainwater rolled off the roof in a steady stream and stood under it, letting the water wash away all the dirt from top to bottom. The hygiene kit unfortunately did not have a straight razor, so his beard would have to stay. Leon came back into the temple through the archway behind his partition and dried himself by using the web of his hands to push the excess water off his body then he wrapped himself in the wool blanket from Matthias' bedroll until he was dry enough to get dressed.

Leon put on a spare change of clothes from one of the smaller soldiers. He was sure within a few weeks he would be back to his normal weight. He had been kept in awful conditions for more than a week without so much as a scrap of food or a cup of water. He didn't know how he had survived so long with no water. His weight loss was probably attributed more to dehydration than the lack of food.

Before putting on his socks, Leon looked at the black, inky, lines creeping up his foot. It had started between his big toe and his second, at first, it was only an inch or two long, but now, it had spread up the top of his foot almost to his ankle. The top of his foot was turning slightly purple and it was almost double its normal size. He promised himself he would go see Delilah when he got back to Blackwater to see if she could help. Once his boots were on, Leon joined the others.

"Sir, we found an old barrel in the back, we put it outside to collect rainwater, there is a cauldron in the mess hall we can use to boil it. The cellar is filled with chopped wood, I have a few men bringing some up now." A soldier reported to Leon.

"Thank you, I'm going to wander around the temple a little, and see if I can find anything else we might find useful. I think there used to be a library upstairs, although I am guessing anything worth having was cleaned out long ago," Leon said. The soldier snapped to attention, gave Leon a salute, and waited for Leon to return it- which excused him from Leon's presence. It was strange to be in control of a troop again.

Leon couldn't help thinking of Matthias. He was a wonderful Captain, although he hated to be addressed as such. He would have made an amazing commander too. Leon knew the reason Matthias did not wish to be formally addressed. Matthias and his father did not see eye to eye, and he did not wish to be called by his father's last name.

"Can I get you anything?" Samantha asked, as she gently caressed her husband's cheek.

"I'm okay for right now, I do want to find the library and I would love to have your company." The wrinkles under his eyes indicated he was smiling, but Samantha couldn't tell what was behind his beard. She looped her arm through Leon's and walked beside him as they ascended the winding staircase. The library was a loft overlooking the entrance below. Rows of shelves took up the center of the loft, and comfortable reading chairs and writing desks sat at the end of each row. Each desk had a lantern light, but no oil from what Leon saw. The sconces were all missing torches and the storm allowed for no light from the windows.

Samantha picked up a lantern and whispered a word to it and the lantern started to glow, illuminating the area. The very few spells Samantha could do often came in handy. Although Leon did not mind women using magic, it made the nobles and other Guildmasters nervous.

Once a year the guilds held a summit where the leaders would discuss rules every guild would be expected to follow. At one of these summits, a majority decided women could only use magic to heal. Most men thought females were too emotional to be trusted with offensive magic. It was also decided those women who do practice magic must be blessed with their magical ability by a deity.

Leon never enforced such laws in Blackwater, deeming them unfair and unjust to women, who he viewed as valued members of the social structure and society. His blind eye could not help those who traveled outside Blackwater and into another guild's territory, but he promised all women within the walls of his city would be safe. Samantha had always admired him for that, among many other things.

She watched her husband as he browsed through the books. His brow furrowed as he scanned shelf after shelf.

"Looking for something in particular? Perhaps I could help?" Samantha asked. Leon looked at her and shook his head.

"Nothing in particular, but anything useful." He continued looking, taking a book off the shelf now and then to leaf through a couple of pages before putting it back.

When he had checked more than half the library, Leon felt tired and had to sit down. A layer of dust puffed out of the cushion as Leon sat down in one of the reading chairs between the rows. He coughed as the cloud dispersed throughout the room. His foot was throbbing. He wanted to look at it but didn't want to alarm anyone, especially his wife. He just needed to make it back to Blackwater and then everything would be okay.

The rain continued through the night, the fire was now roaring in the hearth, and the rainwater was boiled. The soldiers used a funnel from the kitchen to make a filter using cloth, gravel, sand, and rocks. Leon was impressed with how intelligent these men were, they set up an elaborate filtration system with whatever they could find in the kitchen. They were siphoning the water from the cauldron, slowly into the filter, which was now dripping at a steady pace back into the barrel they had used to collect the rainwater. By morning, they would all be able to fill their water skins with fresh, filtered water.

When nightfall came, they all arranged their bedrolls around the fire. The rain had caused the temperature to drop and they thought it was safer to stay in one room anyway.

"Now since we are all here and settled in for the evening by the fire, I thought it would be nice to get to know you all. Until now we haven't had the opportunity to talk. You all know me as Mrs. Rend or the commander's wife, but I also run a little sweet shop in town called Samantha's Sweets. I make chocolates, cookies, cakes, and candies. Our daughter, Sophie, works at the Loose Anchor Tavern and plays several instruments. Now, tell us a little about yourselves, you go first," Samantha said, nodding to the soldier next to her.

"My name is Jacob. My father was a rebel in Braidwood. We came over with Leon when he freed us from Orion. I was maybe four or five at the time. I have a girlfriend named Sara, she is the armorer's daughter in Blackwater. We plan to get married when the weather cools again," Jacob said with a shrug. He looked at the person next to him to indicate he was finished.

"I'm Tybard, most of these guys call me 'Tibbs' though. I have always wanted to be a soldier, ever since I was little and I would see the soldiers marching by on their way to the formation, or during the ceremonies. Their uniforms, and the way every movement was so precise and synchronized. I wanted perfection. My dad was one of the first Blackwater soldiers, he died defending the city during the battle of Blackwater Bay."

"I'm sorry to hear it, I lost someone in the battle. I had a very hard time with the loss and was thankful for Leon's help in getting through it. He checked on me every day. I honestly don't know where I or Sophie would be without him." She smiled at her husband and gave Tybard a sympathetic smile as well.

"My name's Charlie, I'm 'sposed to be retirin' this year so me an' the wife can travel, she has always wanted to see the world. I promised her I'd take her someday. I grew up in Blackwater 'fore it was even called Blackwater. I did my adventurin' in my early days before there was a guild to pay me for it. I took a job with the city guard to stay close to my wife." When he stopped talking everyone's eyes instinctively moved on to the next in the line.

"My name is Octavian, this is Percy," he said, introducing the man next to him. "Percy was captured by bandits on a guild mission and by the time we rescued him, they had cut out his tongue. We live and work together in Blackwater, so we can look out for each other." Octavian took Percy's hand and looked at him with a smile. There was love between them and Samantha found it endearing. Without noticeable pause, the next man spoke.

"My name is Malcolm, my mum and dad have lived in Blackwater their whole life. My family runs a dairy farm. My dad was upset with me when I decided to join the city guard instead of taking over the farm, but I have five brothers, and a sister still living at home. I just don't like farm life, I knew I wanted more, besides, soldiering is sometimes more money and less work," he joked.

Malcolm tried to tap Maximus, who had been sitting beside him, but when he turned to look at him, his spot was empty. When he looked around and didn't see him, Malcolm looked at the others. "I'll go find him," he said. "Please, continue without me." He tapped Laughlin on the shoulder as he got up and moved toward the hallway.

"Well, some of you already know me, I'm Laughlin. I am a lumberjack. I plant and cut trees in the forest for building and woodworking. I plant three trees for each one I cut to sustain the forest. I have a cabin in Blackwater I built, and I am dating Juniper who is a druid and a veteran guild member. Oh, and I have an animal companion, her name is Dusk and she is a wolf."

"Thank you, everyone, for sharing." Samantha smiled as Leon squeezed her a little and planted a kiss on the top of her head.

Maximus was in the kitchen when Malcolm found him, he was sitting near the dying fire in the stone pit where they had boiled the water.

"Hey, Max, you okay?" Malcolm asked in a hushed voice.

Max nodded but didn't look up from the fire. He watched as the glowing hot coals cracked and whistled. He picked up the iron poker next to him and stoked the fire, watching the sparks float up into the air as the embers broke apart.

"Something is bothering you, what's going on?" Malcolm sat down beside the other soldier.

"Matthias was like a father to me, I didn't have my dad growing up so when I joined the guard, Matthias took me under his wing and taught me a lot. Hell, I didn't even know how to fight when I showed up. All I knew was I had to help Mama. She got sick and couldn't work anymore. Arthritis in her hands became too much and what use was a seamstress who couldn't sew? Matthias made sure I didn't give up, and always made sure Mama was taken care of, even while I was in training and not making any coin. I can't believe he didn't make it out of there. He was such a good man and it feels wrong to go back without him. It also feels strange having Commander Rend back, he seems different now, don't you think?"

"I think anyone who has just been held hostage and starved for weeks and left without water might act a little different. We might just have to give him some time," Malcolm explained.

"Maybe you're right. I still don't feel like sharing though, so If you don't mind, I will just sit here a little while longer and I will come out to go to sleep when everything is quiet."

Malcolm stood and turned to leave the room. He glanced back to Maximus momentarily before he went back down the hall and into the room with everyone else.

Leon leaned his back against the wall and Samantha sat between his legs, resting her back against his body. Leon wrapped his arms around his wife and intertwined his fingers with hers. They looked like teenagers in love rather than a couple who had been married for seventeen years.

Some of the soldiers were already sleeping as the rain fell softly outside. Samantha hoped tomorrow the rain would be over, otherwise, they might just have to continue despite the rain, and being wet would make for a miserable trip.

SEVENTEEN

AKIRI AND HER CREW had been at sea for days when someone spotted debris from a recent shipwreck floating in the water. The golden sun on the flag they found told Akiri they were on the right track, but there was no way to know if the prince made it to shore, or if he went down with the ship, unless...

"Bring me the witch," Akiri commanded. Two men went below deck and appeared a few moments later, one on each side of the woman. They gripped her arms tightly so she could not escape them.

"Tell me, seer, is the orb of power at the bottom of the ocean or did it make it to shore?" Akiri asked. The old woman spat at her. Akiri drew back her hand and slapped the seer across the face, her cheek reddened again.

"Tell me now," Akiri said, "or I will make you regret it."

"Why don't you swim down there and find out for yourself?" The woman asked.

"Maybe I would rather find a way to get you to do your blasted job, and tell me what I need to know." Akiri went to the side of the ship and grabbed the bucket they used for swabbing the deck, lowered it into the water and used the rope to pull it back up. She soaked her handkerchief in the salty water and walked back over to the seer. Akiri pulled out her dagger and grabbed the old lady's hand, slicing open the woman's palm. The seer winced but did not cry out.

"Where is the orb?" she asked again.

"I will not tell you a thing," The old woman said through gritted teeth and a clenched jaw.

Akiri squeezed the handkerchief over the wound. The ocean water burned as it ran though the trench of the cut.

"Tell me," Akiri demanded. The woman shook her head, refusing to cooperate.

"Why must you be so stubborn?" Akiri hissed a word and swirling green smoke encircled the woman's head, as Akiri's eyes turned a glowing green.

"Now, I will ask you once more, where can I find the orb?" No words came out of the woman's mouth, but the information Akiri needed flooded the seer's thoughts and she was able to read them like a storybook. The seer tried to block Akiri from her mind, but the invasion was stronger than the walls she built. Akiri patted the woman on her red cheek.

"That wasn't so hard was it?" Akiri's voice sounded soft and sweet, but it bit like razor blades in the woman's ears. "The orb is on it's way to an island north-west of this location. Adjust the sails to turn around and we will meet up with them on the island. Take her to the brig and lock her up." Akiri said, waving a dismissive hand toward the old woman.

The crew moved about the deck, unwinding ropes and moving the sails to adjust course. Akiri went back to her room, closed the double doors and drew the curtains. She couldn't stop thinking about the orb of power. *Maybe I should keep it for myself.* She thought. *Why shouldn't I? After all, I am doing all the work to find it, why should I take it back to my mother?*

EIGHTEEN

SOPHIE AWOKE TO THE smell of smoke. She must have been knocked out during the battle. It wasn't the same as a campfire, but instead, the scent of burning flesh. Her heart thudded in her chest as she looked around for the source. A piercing scream cut through the air like a vorpal sword through fresh cream butter. Sophie's head snapped toward the sound. A thunderous rumble shook the earth as a huge figure moved toward them.

"Guys, wake up! wake up!" she screamed, but her companions didn't move. Fear grabbed her and made her skin go cold. She ran to Gabe's side and tried to shake him awake. Blood flew from his mouth as he coughed and went limp in Sophie's grasp. "No, no, no, please, no," Sophie cried as she ran over to Juniper who sat cross-legged on her mat with her eyes closed. Sophie tapped her on the shoulder and Juniper's lifeless body toppled over. Next, Sophie tried to wake Kamara, but her eyes were wide open with nothing but the whites visible. Her body began to rise, hovering above the camp in a catatonic state. Then the whispers began, swirling around them. These were not normal whispers, the frequency of them hurt Sophie's ears, they were screeching inside her mind.

"Trust no one. The dragon will rise. Evil will rise." She watched Kamara's body transform. First, her fingers elongated and became sharp like talons, then her body grew larger and changed shape as a tail extended from her tailbone and two large leathery wings poked through the skin on her back.

When the transformation was done, Sophie was looking into the face of a silver dragon.

One last shriek shattered the world as the highland, the wizard tower, and everything surrounding Sophie cracked and fell away piece by piece.

Sophie woke up in her bed- no, not *her* bed, a bed. She looked around for any hint of familiarity but found none, except for her father's sword, and bag, both placed neatly in the corner of the room. A tray of food awaited her, grapes and berries, fresh bread, and smoked, dried meat. *Where am I?* She wondered.

The last thing she remembered was... *The orb!* Sophie jumped out of the bed and ran to the backpack, her heart pounding out of her chest as she fiddled with the drawstrings. She opened it as quickly as she could and a lump jumped into her throat when she peered into the bag. It was gone. She collapsed to the ground with her head in her hands and cried.

She cried for her father, Juniper, Gabe, and Laughlin. She even felt bad for Kamara and all the trouble this orb had brought her way, all for nothing.

The room she was in had no windows, just two heavy oak doors. She had no way of knowing what she would find on the other side, but she had to try. She ran to the door and grasped the two large brass handles, one in each hand, and pulled. The doors didn't budge. She pulled again and again, when her attempts failed, she pushed them, knowing even that was hopeless.

When she heard footsteps outside the door, Sophie jumped to her feet and backed away toward the corner of the room. A man in black robes entered. He looked to be about the same age as Sophie's parents, with bright green eyes, a kind smile, and clean auburn hair hanging loosely to his shoulders.

"I am so happy to see you are awake. How are you feeling?" he asked.

"Where am I? Where are my friends?" Sophie demanded.

"Your friends are fine, I made certain to tell my men not to harm them."

"Wait- the men in the red masks, those are your men?"

"They are."

"Why am I here?"

"I wanted to meet you, of course. I am sorry it has taken me this long to make myself known to you, but we are in a very delicate situation," he explained.

"What situation?"

"The world is in danger, and only we can save it. I am a very powerful wizard, more powerful even than the wizard Ryul in Lapis Highland. I found this in your bag when we recovered the orb." He held up the battered old spell book and handed it back to Sophie.

"Did you know him?" she asked.

"I'm afraid not, but what this book tells me, is you are eager to learn magic. I want to teach you because I feel a great power in you. I saw you in a dream, wielding the ancient magic of our people. You are to be our queen," he said, bowing to her. Sophie was confused. She was not even a leader, let alone a queen.

"Where is the orb?" she asked.

"Your Majesty, it is safe, I will take you to see it when you are ready. Have you had a chance to eat?" He gestured to the buffet.

"I would like to see the orb first."

"Very well, right this way." He turned and walked from the room and waited just across the threshold for her to follow. Sophie thought it was strange there were no windows in the hall either. Iron sconces with lit torches lined the stone walls. The stones were not squared and built like bricks or even formed like old stone castles, it looked as if the walls had been carved out, or mined. The stone was black and shiny, but at the same time, jagged with deep grooves from the pickaxes used to shape them.

"You never introduced yourself," Sophie said as she walked a few paces behind him.

"Forgive me, Your Majesty, my name is not important, everyone here just calls me Sir, and I call them the same. But you can call me what you wish, My Queen." He didn't need to constantly look behind him to figure out if she was still following, because there was nowhere else for her to go.

Sophie followed him through the dimly lit corridors opening into a great hall with a large rune circle in the middle. When she entered, all of the men dressed in their black robes and red masks took a knee and in unison declared "My Queen!"

Sophie didn't know what to think, did these people really believe she was their queen? She wasn't completely convinced this wasn't a dream. The man led her to the rune circle and as he spoke an incantation, a bright white light filled the area. Sophie felt weightless, like when she was swimming in the lake on summer vacation, but a few seconds later, she landed with a thud on a hard stone floor. when the light faded, and her vision returned to normal, she saw they were standing in the center of another rune circle on the flat top between the four mountain peaks of Choddrath. Each peak had a door leading down into the mountain keep from which they had come.

On the right side of the rune circle, there were four stone dragons. They faced two podiums shaped like a dragon's claw. In one of the claws, Sophie saw the orb. When she moved closer to one of the four stone dragons, she could see they were no ordinary statues, but thrones—one silver, one green, one red, and one gold. The red and the silver throne were illuminated by the magic from the orb hovering above the podium between them.

"This is the throne of our ancestors. The red dragon throne," the man explained.

"What do you mean *our* ancestors?" Sophie asked.

"Oh...a tale for another time." He seemed to be deep in thought, with a look of pride on his face Sophie found strange. He walked over to the throne and held out his hand, motioning for Sophie to sit on it. She approached with caution and could feel the low hum of the orb's power vibrating through the stone seat.

A wind picked up as she sat down, and an aura of red light surrounded her. She felt the magic coursing through her veins. *What is happening? This can't be right, it's not me, I'm not the dragon.* She thought to herself. She could hear the orb whispering in the same language it always did, and even though the wizard's spell had long since worn off, Sophie still understood what it was saying.

"The time is near, gather the heirs."

"What does it mean to *gather the heirs*?" Sophie asked.

"It means all four dragon heirs need to sit upon their throne to release the powers." He looked defeated. "I thought it might work with only one, but it seems I was wrong."

"How am I the dragon's heir? I'm just a girl from Blackwater, I don't understand."

"We have a lot of work to do. I say we start with some casting lessons. If it's okay with you, Your Majesty," he said. "The rest will be learned when the time is right."

NINETEEN

Juniper, Gabe, Kamara, and Dusk reached Aerulean Lake by late afternoon. Juniper paid for a campsite down by the water, on the western side of the lake. She rented a tent at the general store and set it up on their designated lot. Gabe gathered wood for the fire and Kamara gathered long, thin branches from the nearby woods so Juniper could carve spears for fishing.

Once everything was set up and the fire was burning well, the four of them made their way down to the lake. Dusk lay on the dock, happily chewing on one of the branches not needed for fishing.

Juniper showed Gabe and Kamara how to hold their spears and what stance to take. "You have to be still so the fish think you belong there. Let them get used to you," she said.

"I've done this before, but not with a spear, I used rocks in the stream back in Blackwater. Of course, there all I could get was trout though." Gabe said.

"Same idea, you want to aim just in front of the fish because if you aim at its middle it will swim away before your spear hits the water." Juniper stood very still, her eyes followed her target. She drew back the spear and then very suddenly plunged it into the water. When she lifted it out of the water, the fish was skewered right through the gill and out the mouth. "Now you guys try, when you have caught your dinner bring it up and I will fry it, I'm going to prepare a cooking space," Juniper said, leaving Gabe and Kamara to fish.

Gabe plunged his spear into the water and pulled it out empty. He resumed his statuesque position, not moving, barely breathing, and not talking. He waited for the fish to circle his feet again and then struck again, down into the water. When his spear came up empty again he threw it onto the bank and plopped down beside it.

Kamara sat down next to him. "We will find her," she said. "I can see how much she means to you and your determination. I have no doubt you will not stop until you find her safe."

Kamara meant for her pep talk to cheer him up, so she felt horrible when she heard him sobbing softly. He hid his eyes from her as he wiped them on the sleeve of his tunic. "You're in love with her, aren't you?" she asked.

"Is it so obvious? And here I thought I was hiding it so well," Gabe joked wiping away the tears and trying to recover his composure. "I know she isn't interested in being more than friends, I would have seen the signs, but she means everything to me and I would do anything to keep her in my life. Even if it means keeping my feelings for her a secret."

"I understand how you feel, and I think she loves you too, maybe not in the same way, but she would do anything for you too," Kamara said.

"What about you? Were there any love interests in your past?" Gabe asked.

"I was in love once, I think. I was too afraid to say anything. She was a sea nymph and could control the tide, she often went to Torzana to help the fishermen have a bountiful day at sea. She brought home coin and dinner on those days."

"She sounds like a druid, almost like Juniper in a way," Gabe commented.

"Kind of, except her magic comes from a bloodline of nereids, or sea-nymphs."

"Like a mermaid?" Gabe asked.

"I mean, she didn't have a tail or anything; not from what I saw at least. So not really like a mermaid because she lived on land, but she was a really fast swimmer and could hold her breath for a long time."

"So what happened to her?" Gabe asked. It was too late to take the question back, but the second it passed his lips he thought it might be insensitive to ask. "I'm sorry if it's too personal or-"

"No, it's fine," Kamara said. "She was called away to travel with the captain of some royal navy or something. It was her duty." Kamara stared across the lake.

"So what is your duty?" he asked.

"My duty is to help you and Juniper find Sophie and Laughlin, and to destroy whatever evil comes out of the orb," she replied with a smile.

"Thanks for talking me down, I needed this. I felt like I was about to spiral out of control."

"Did you guys catch anything yet?" They turned to see Juniper walking toward them from the campsite.

"No, sorry, we got distracted," Gabe said.

"Don't worry, I can help." A male's voice surprised them and they looked toward the source, expecting to see Laughlin, but instead, they saw a boy, their age, dressed in a fine white and gold tunic and black trousers. He wore his hair in braids, bunched together in the back "I have been spearfishing my whole life," he said. "May I?" He reached out, gesturing to the spears lying on the bank.

"Sure, help yourself," Gabe said.

Dominic picked up a spear and walked a few feet away from the rest of them. Wading in the lake just far enough for the water to almost reach his knees, Dominic watched a fish swim close and then dart away. He stood still and waited for it to swim back, took aim just in front of the fish's head then quickly plunged the spear into the water and through the fish's gills. He pulled it out of the water turning around to show them his prize. He took the fish off the spear and threw it to Gabe, who would have caught it if the fish hadn't started flopping wildly as it flew through the air.

Dominic turned back to the water and continued fishing. Before long, they had a feast of fish on the bank. Juniper gutted and cleaned them in the lake water. "Would you like to have dinner with us? You caught us the fish after all," Juniper asked.

"I am quite good at catching fish, but I am afraid I am horrible at cooking them, so it would be my honor to join you for dinner," Dominic said. He looked at Kamara and the way the evening sun lit up the flecks of gold on her dark skin. Her hair was light purple and blue with shining silver strands. She was even more beautiful in person than she had been in his dream.

"Hi, I'm Dominic," he said, holding his hand out to Kamara. She introduced herself as she shook his hand and as their hands touched a low hum rang out from the pouch on his belt. He cupped the pouch nervously as she looked at him strangely. They both heard the whispers. He knew it.

"What do you have in the pouch?" Kamara asked suspiciously.

"It's nothing," Dominic said, backing away.

"I have heard those whispers before. How did you get the orb and where is Sophie?" Kamara shouted.

"Whoa, I don't know Sophie, never met her. How do you know about the orb?" Dominic asked.

"Sophie had it in her bag, we were taking it to Choddrath, but she was kidnapped by a man in a red mask. So why do you have it?"

"This orb has been in my kingdom since before I was born," Dominic said. He pulled out the artifact so they could see it. A golden dragon and a green dragon inside it circled each other just as the red and silver dragons did in the orb they brought from the Temple of Ophay.

"This one is different. What are you doing with it?"

"I was taking it to Choddrath, the same place you were taking yours," Dominic said.

"The whispers said the orb and the dragon had to merge and if the orb was destroyed then–" Kamara stopped mid-sentence, thinking of how to say the next part delicately.

"Evil will rise," Dominic finished. "I saw it in a dream. A huge green dragon." Dominic put the orb back in his pouch.

"We will help you finish this. Chances are, the men who have Sophie took her to Choddrath. We can have dinner tonight, get some rest, and then leave for Ashenport at first light," Juniper said.

They sat down around the campfire, each of them with haunting thoughts floating through their minds. Juniper wondered if Laughlin was okay, Gabe couldn't stop thinking about Sophie and how those men might be treating her. Was she locked up in a dungeon? Were they hitting her, or worse? Dominic worried about the crew aboard the ship as it went under. The screams haunted him as he tried to eat, he took a few bites of his fillet and then offered the rest to dusk, who happily took it from him.

"I have a cabin for the night if you guys would like to sleep in there, sadly there's only one bed, but the floor won't be any worse than the ground out here," Dominic offered.

"It's okay, I already rented the tent and I prefer to meditate under the moon. I find it helps me recharge," Juniper replied. Dominic looked over at Gabe and Kamara.

"Sorry, I don't want to leave Juniper out here alone," Kamara said.

"I want to stay with them," Gabe said gesturing to Kamara and Juniper.

"It seems you guys are all pretty close," Dominic said, with a tone of disappointment.

Suddenly, Kamara felt bad for him. She placed her hand on his. "You're welcome to stay with us too, you don't have to go back to your cabin alone," she said.

When he looked at her, Kamara's silver eyes sparkled in the setting sun and it took her a few moments to realize she was still holding his hand. She quickly let go, putting her hands back into her lap.

"I'm sorry," she said quickly.

"I don't mind." Dominic smiled as Kamara's cheeks flushed and she looked down at her plate.

"It's okay, I was liking having a place to myself, which so rarely happens at home."

"Why not? Lots of brothers and sisters, or a girlfriend?"

"No, just a lot of authoritative figures and a strict schedule."

"No friends?" Kamara asked.

"Not really, being heir to the throne does have its drawbacks, it's all work and no play all the time," Dominic said.

"You're the *prince*?" Kamara sounded mortified. "I am so sorry, Your Highness." She stood up and curtsied the way she was taught to at the temple when they would have royal visitors.

"No, please, just call me Dominic, and no fuss or fanfare, I just want to be normal for a while. I am no prince here." He reached out his hand for Kamara to help her sit back down.

"Where are you guys from?" Dominic asked.

"We are mostly from Blackwater, it's on the east coast. Sophie's father is the Guildmaster of the Silver Talons," Juniper said.

"Is 'Guildmaster' what you call the lawmaker of your country?"

"Not of the country, just our city," Juniper said. "The laws are made by the guild council though, the leaders of each guild meet once a year to discuss how things are going and if any changes need to be made."

"Sounds a lot better than putting all the pressure on one person," Dominic said.

"I am from the Temple of Ophay. I rarely left home so I only had sisters, not sure how many of them were my actual friends," Kamara said.

"Well, we can be friends, and solve both of our 'not having friends' problems." Dominic smiled as Kamara nodded in agreement.

The fire began to die down and the sun dipped below the horizon. "I should probably get some sleep." Dominic got up and stretched.

"Would you like me to walk with you?" Kamara offered as she stood up as well.

"I would love to, but then who would walk you back?" Dominic asked.

"I'll go too," Gabe said, joining them. "So you won't have to walk back alone," he said, looking at Kamara.

Once they were gone, Juniper took out the ring she got from the Wizard and slipped it onto her finger. She felt the transference of energy and focused on letting the ring know her mind. She walked to the edge of the lake and looked down at the water. She thought of Laughlin. It was like the ring could hear her thoughts, on the surface of the water, images began to come into focus. She saw him, lying in a bedroll in front of a fire, there were soldiers around him, and then she saw Samantha and Leon, they were safe, and together, that was enough.

Then she thought of Sophie and couldn't believe what she saw. *This can't be right.* Juniper thought. She saw Sophie, sitting on a dragon throne, and the men in red masks were bowing to her. *Oh no, what has she done?*

TWENTY

THE SOUNDS OF THE jungle awoke Laughlin from his slumber before the others. He wasn't sure if it was the sound of the parrots squawking, or the screaming of monkeys in the distance that roused him, but whatever the reason, it was the sound of human voices he found most concerning. Thinking the men from The Barren camp had finally caught up with them, Laughlin got up and walked to the old stone entry way. He peered through the trees as far as he could looking for signs of human passage.

When he was satisfied there was no one nearby, he ventured outside and into the forest, looking closely for tracks or hoof prints. The forest floor was mostly deep, squishy, mud and with every step he cringed at the wet, sucking sound his boots made as he pulled it out of the sludge.

Laughlin was certain there had been no one but them in the area for at least a couple days, the only prints in the mud were their own. He didn't desire to go any further, at least until the sun had time to come up and dry out some of the muck, but the thick canopy above would make it impossible for the sun to reach them and they were a bit too close to the enemy camp for his liking.

He walked back inside, removing his muddy boots before continuing into the temple. The others were awake now and packing up, eager to put more distance between them and the masked cultists.

"It's very wet and muddy, traveling will be loud and slow, but I have scouted around and your way East seems to be clear," Laughlin reported to Samantha.

"Wait- you're not coming with us?" she asked.

"No, I'm going to continue to Choddrath in hopes of finding Sophie and the others. Once I make it out of this jungle, I should be able to follow the river North and book passage on a ship from Braidwood or Ashenport," he replied.

"We have an extra horse, Leon and I can double on Matthias' horse, you can take Horatio. You'll reach the docks much faster on horseback," Samantha offered.

"Are you sure?"

"Positive. Please bring Sophie home safe, I have already sent what's left of the Blackwater forces and the Silver Soldiers to Choddrath so I am sure by the time you get there, you will have all the help you need." Samantha wrapped her arms around Laughlin and squeezed him tightly.

When she released him, Laughlin gathered his bedroll and whatever supplies could be spared, then walked through the temple and out the back to the pillars where the horses were hitched.

All the horses were bare and the tack was organized neatly along the northern wall. Leon's horse was by far the biggest, so Laughlin looked for the biggest saddle. He was thankful when the other soldiers began filing into the room to prepare their horses.

"Do any of you know which saddle is for Commander Rend's horse?" Laughlin asked.

"This one here," Charlie said, exchanging Laughlin for the correct tack.

"Thanks," he replied.

"No problem," he paused. "Hey, I heard you talking to Mrs. Rend earlier about Choddrath, what's going on there?" Charlie asked.

"Oh, uh... just this thing I have to do." Laughlin was pretty sure he couldn't disclose the real reason he was going to the island, he doubted Commander Rend would want to panic everyone with the thought of dragon worshiping cultists and magical artifacts that these men would kill for.

"The only thing I have ever heard about Choddrath is that it's the last place in the realm where there are still dragons. I can't imagine anything on that island is worth your life," Charlie said with concern.

"Have you ever seen a dragon?" Laughlin asked.

"A long time ago when I was just a boy. They were flying around the Stonehold Mountains north of Blackwater. I was playing outside and the loudest screech I ever heard rang out from the mountain peaks. I ran to the edge of our yard, intrigued. My mother, who had been hanging the wash on the line, heard it too and when she saw it flying toward the city she grabbed me by the ear and dragged me inside like our little wooden house would protect us from a dragon's fiery breath," he said with a chuckle.

"I have never seen a dragon, I imagine it would be terrifying, yet exhilarating at the same time," Laughlin said as he buckled the saddle around Horatio.

"Here, take this," Charlie pulled a pendant out of his tunic and held it out to Laughlin, "it's a little something to keep you safe. I'm headed home for good so I won't need it anymore." He placed the chain over Laughlin's head and the amulet dangled down the front of his leather armor. "It's an amulet of health, you're not invincible while you wear it, but you might feel like you are so be careful," he warned.

"Thank you, Charlie," Laughlin said as he admired the golden amulet covered in ancient runes.

Samantha and Leon were the last ones out. Leon drank as much water as he could and then filled his water skin again before mounting Matthias' horse.

"We should ride through until we get to Northport. It will be a hard push for the horses, but we will be able to sleep in a real bed and have a hot meal. They'll have a stable for the horses and we can let then rest there for a day before we finish the journey home," Samantha suggested.

She looked at her husband. His eyes were vacant and he put up no protest to her order. The others nodded their agreement.

"I'll ride with you as far as Aerulean Lake, then I'll head west," Laughlin said.

"Okay, let's move out," Samantha replied.

They made their way through the muddy jungle at a slower pace than expected because the horses' hooves kept sinking into the soft earth and squelched with every step.

Samantha held on to her husband's waist as they rode and she could feel the heat radiating off him even through his clothing which was already soaked with sweat. "Are you alright?" she asked.

"I'm fine," Leon snapped.

Samantha had never heard him sound so angry with her. His mood paired with sweat and fever worried her, she knew this was not normal for Leon, but it was also not the time to to push the conversation further. She accepted his answer and adjusted herself on the horse, putting some space between them so the air could hit Leon's back and cool him down.

It took several hours to reach the northern edge of the jungle and when they moved from beneath the canopy the sunlight was almost blinding. At the bottom of the campground, Laughlin waved farewell and steered Horatio to the west and leaned forward to pick up speed. He was going to find them, or die trying.

TWENTY-ONE

IT WAS STILL DARK when Juniper woke everyone so they could get packed and on the road before sunrise. Dominic met them at the campsite just in time to help them finish packing the last few things.

"Where do you think it would be easier to find a ship? Braidwood, or Ashenport," Juniper asked.

"Choddrath is closer to Ashenport, but their docks are smaller, as in, there's not room for many ships. Braidwood has a lot more ships coming and going so it might be easier to find passage there," Gabe replied.

Juniper led them west, and then south along the river toward Braidwood. They stopped for breakfast at sunrise just before the crossing point. There were no nearby plants, herbs, or berries to forage; it was still too early in the season for most, so they made the best of their dry rations. When they finished eating, they continued on their way.

"Halfway across the bridge, Juniper spotted a few of the red mask cultists, they seemed to be looking for someone. Juniper had a feeling she knew who and what they were looking for.

"We have to go back. We can't cross here." Juniper pointed out the men to everyone else.

"Do you think they will be watching the bridge to Ashenport as well?" Kamara asked.

"If I were them, I would be," Juniper said.

"What if we don't use a bridge? Maybe we find the lowest part of the river and cross there? We will be wet and uncomfortable for a bit but they won't expect us to cross in the water and we might be able to slip past them," Gabe suggested.

"Perhaps you're right," Juniper said. "Let's go north again and see if we can find a suitable crossing point."

They turned around on the bridge slowly so as not to draw attention to themselves. Juniper was relieved Laughlin had trained Dusk as well as he had. The wolf followed wherever Juniper went, and although Dusk did draw the attention of passersby, they did not get close enough to the men in red masks for them to notice.

Just before midday, they reached a bend in the river where the water was low. It looked to be ankle deep for most of the way, and probably waist deep at its highest. Juniper whispered a spell surrounding everyone in a shimmering veil.

When they waded into the water, Kamara saw what the spell did, it was as if the water was flowing right through them, there was no disturbance or ripple in the flow of water from their passing; no way for those downstream to know anyone was crossing the river north of them.

Dusk swam all the way across with no trouble. It took the others a little longer and a bit more effort with all of their gear, but once everyone was across the river, they took a few moments to rest.

"Are we in Ashenport now?" Kamara asked.

"No, we're too far north, we are in Viridia plains, but the gate to Ashenport isn't far. They will not expect us to be coming from the north and they will be watching the bridge, so we should be able to get past them easily," Juniper said as she twisted her clothing between her hands to wring the water from it. "Let's camp here for the day, lay our things out to dry, we can sleep through the night, and enter the city tomorrow morning when it's busy. We will be easier to spot at night with a group our size, it would be best to blend in with the crowds during the day." Juniper began removing the wet things from her pack and the others followed her lead.

The plains were flat and grassy but offered no cover for privacy; not that they had any dry clothes to change into. Juniper gathered everyone into a circle and cast a spell, a strong gust of wind swirled around them, drying their clothes and hair. Kamara's curls were less curl and more frizz after the wind dried them, so she pulled her hair back and secured it tightly with a ribbon.

Juniper and Gabe went out to hunt. They needed to make a fire, but trees were scarce and Juniper did not have an ax. Laughlin would have one were he there with them. Some way off in the distance they came upon a couple of apple trees. The tree was of course bare and only beginning to bud. The only apples to be found were rotting on the ground from the fall harvest.

"I can fix this," Juniper said. She spoke the incantation in Elvish as she waved her hand over the branches of the tree. The buds opened, and the apple blossoms turned from pink and fragrant, to white with yellow stamens. Soon, the petals began to wilt away and then where the buds had been, the plants began to swell. Juniper kept concentrating, growing the apples nice and plump. When she stopped and dropped her hand, Gabe helped her collect all the apples. Gabe took off his cloak and put the apples into the middle of it, then gathered the edges of the cloak and carried it on his back like a traveler's sack.

"Wow- what you did with the apples. I have never seen fruit grow so fast," Gabe commented.

"It is very handy when you're in a bad spot, but the plant has to already be there to make it bloom, I can't make things grow from nothing."

"Good thing these trees were here then," he said.

When they got back to camp, Kamara and Dominic had found a way to get the fire going. Dominic cleared the grass from a large area around the fire ring so they could lay out their bedrolls to dry before they went to sleep

"Thanks to you both for getting camp set up, we brought back apples," Juniper said. Gabe put his cloak on the ground and dropped the sides of it he had gathered in his hand. The cloak opened as the cloth fell revealing the pile of apples.

"Wow, where did you find apples this time of year?" Kamara asked.

"Juniper made them grow. I watched them go from buds to blossoms, to apples in minutes, it was pretty amazing," Gabe explained.

They feasted on the apples and sat by the fire talking and sharing stories as the afternoon sun moved lower in the sky too slowly to notice. Juniper got up and asked the group to carry on for a few minutes without her. She took a walk by herself to the river and sat down on a rock near the water.

She closed her eyes and thought of Laughlin while turning the ring on her finger. She peered down into the water and waited for his reflection to appear. She saw him, riding a horse. She couldn't tell where he was, but he was near a river. He could be on his way to Braidwood or Ashenport. She hoped he would be elusive enough to avoid a second capture and would find his way to her.

Next, she thought of Sophie, instead of the fiery-haired girl she had known since birth, she saw a flaming red dragon roaring from the mountain top on the island of Choddrath. As she stared into the water, she saw their future, it was clear now. Laughlin would be waiting for them in Ashenport. She'd find a way to get them there and together, they'd travel to Choddrath to save Sophie.

TWENTY-TWO

EVEN AS SHE SAT on the same horse with him, Samantha had never felt farther from her husband. On the ride past Aerulean Lake, Leon had become increasingly irritable. Every time she tried to talk to him, he shut her out. Leon's disposition was never sunny, or bubbly, but now he just seemed angry all the time and Samantha had no idea why. They were almost to Northport now and would be able to get a room and an actual meal, maybe then she and Leon would talk. It was well after midday already and they had ridden through the night so tensions were heightened among the men. Most of the soldiers decided to continue pushing through and were would probably be on their way down the mountain toward Blackwater by dinner time. Charlie and Jacob remained with Leon and Samantha to ensure their safety.

The air in Northport was cooler and Samantha was thankful for the breeze from the Icewind Channel. She knew Leon had a fever, but if she brought it up he would surely be cross with her. She thought about trying to convince him to see a cleric in Northport but he was always stubborn about when it came to asking for help. They stabled the horses and went to The Blue Lioness Inn to pay for their lodging. Samantha kept looking at Leon who was getting paler by the minute. While Jacob paid for the rooms, Leon sat down at the bar and ordered a whiskey double. While he was drinking, Samantha took his things to the room so when he was ready, he could sleep. As she was walking back down to the bar, she saw Charlie leaving his room.

"Hey, Charlie, I know you have known Leon a long time, and maybe what he needs is a gentle nudge from a peer and not his wife. I'm worried about him, he is feverish and pale and he is still having those coughing fits from time to time. He should probably see a cleric, but if I bring it up he might get upset. Do you think you could try to convince him?" Samantha asked.

"Sure thing, Ma'am, I will see what I can do. Noticed myself he wasn't lookin' too good."

"Thanks, Charlie," she said. The two went their separate ways and Samantha hopes Charlie would be successful in his talk with Leon.

After they were settled for the evening, Samantha went to dinner alone. Leon had gone to sleep and she tried to wake him but he just groaned and his eyes remained closed. Samantha ordered soup for him and had it sent to their room so he would have something when he woke up.

Samantha saw Jacob sitting in the dining room and walked over to his table.

"Mind If I join you? I hate eating alone and I'm afraid Leon is a little under the weather," she explained.

"Sure, Mrs. Rend." He jumped up to pull out the chair for her.

"Thank you, but it is not necessary, and please, call me Samantha. She sat down across from him and looked at the menu. There were not a lot of choices for dinner, but Samantha still couldn't decide between the salmon and potatoes, or the beef stew.

"What are you going to get?" She asked, looking up at Jacob.

"I think I'm going to have the stew, never really liked fish much," he said.

"I think I will have the stew as well then I'll have to have a bowl sent up for Leon as well," She said decidedly, placing her menu down on the table so the server knew she was ready to order.

Leon woke up drenched in sweat and gasping for air from the nightmare which had seemed so real. His family hated him. No longer willing to deal with his nightmares and his constant work schedule, he dreamed he'd heard them whispering, plotting to kill him, poison his food with nightshade, or belladonna. Then he saw the soup on the nightstand beside the bed. It was cold but the spoon was in the bowl like someone had been eating it. *Did Samantha feed this to me?* He thought. Leon smelled it and instantly recoiled from it, swiping it off the nightstand tray and all. He watched it clatter to the floor; the thick liquid from the stew dripped into the cracks in the wood floor.

He walked over to the wash basin and sat down on the wooden chair by the vanity and removed his sweat drenched stockings, leaving them on the floor in a pile along with his pants and shirt. Grabbing a wash cloth, Leon poured water from the pitcher into the wash basin. The cool liquid felt nice as he splashed it over his skin, which was swollen, red, and beginning to blister. The blackness in his veins almost reached his hips now and the swelling was moving along with it too. Soon he wouldn't be able to walk. He needed to see a healer. He threw on a robe and walked out of the door barefoot with his vision blurring and pulsing. His head was pounding and swirling with thoughts and voices jumbling together making it sound like the crowded tavern was inside his head.

He walked through the lobby, pausing only for a moment to see his wife smiling, and enjoying herself, having dinner with another man while he lay sick in bed. This was why the soup was poisoned. She wanted to be with someone else, but now it made sense. Leon thought about barreling through the dining room and flipping the table over on both of them, but what would it solve?

No, no, stop it, you know it's not true, your wife loves you, she is loyal, she would never... Finally, the voice of reason crept inside his mind and he rushed out the door before the other voice had a chance to change his mind again.

Leon needed to get to the temple. He did not know what gods they served, and at this point, as long as their gods granted them the power to heal him, he didn't care. The temple wasn't far from the inn, but there were more people out and about than he expected to see at this time of night. Leon avoided their gaze as he clutched his bathrobe closed and ran toward the temple. His bare feet padded up the steps and the edges of his vision turned bright and radiated outward. Shaking it away, he pounded on the large oak door of the temple, the cold ground beneath his feet felt amazing, he just wanted to lie down on the front step and go to sleep.

The door opened, and on the other side of it stood a woman dressed in a white gown with long sleeves and a collar fanning out like a golden peacock behind her head. She also wore a winged coif, a white apron with deep pockets, and a golden pendant of an eight-pointed star. Her face was plain, with no notable features drawing the eye to any partic-ular part. Leon thought about how strange it was; the light came from behind her, and became so intense it blocked her out completely until everything went black. He collapsed into her arms as even her shadow faded.

"Sister Ladia! I need help!" Giani cried. The other women rushed to her side, each scooping their hands under Leon's limp body. They moved him to one of the stone altars along the eastern side of the temple. Each altar was surrounded by three walls, each of which had a mounted lantern burning brightly. The walls separated the altars from each other, providing just the right amount of privacy. The sisters had covered each altar with soft padding and white sheet, and a comfortable-looking chair sat next to each altar for either a family member or a sister, to watch over the patient. The ceiling was made of stained glass in the shape of the same eight-pointed star the women wore around their necks. Leon saw flashes of it as he moved in and out of consciousness.

"Sister Giani, please bring me a pail of water, a sponge, another pillow and sheet, the willow bark extract, and the poppy extract," Ladia said as she opened Leon's robe to see the black spidery veins spreading throughout his lower body. His feet were so red and swollen they looked as if they were about to explode.

When Giani returned with the requested items, Ladia began washing Leon's body. She muttered a prayer quietly while she worked. She picked up the willow bark extract and put a few drops on each foot, then worked the oil into Leon's feet and up his legs. Then she brought the poppy extract to his lips, parting them slightly, she deposited two drops of the extract into his mouth. When she was finished, she covered him with the other sheet and propped his feet up on the extra pillow to elevate them.

"He will sleep comfortably for a while, I have never seen this affliction before. I tried to cure his illness with the power of the Goddess Divine, but this might be a curse rather than a disease. I will be in my study, researching a way to help him. Watch over him through the night, take shifts, if he wakes up in pain you can give him another drop of the poppy extract, no more than a drop per shift, and only if he wakes. Continue using the willow bark every couple hours, a few drops on each foot and rub it into the skin on his feet and up his legs." Ladia turned and swiftly moved toward the staircase ascending to her study, which was a large loft on the second floor.

"You ladies can get some sleep, I will take the first shift," Giani said. Her sisters each bowed to her before leaving the altar. Giani sat in the chair next to Leon. He looked so peaceful now with his affliction hidden beneath the white sheet. Giani wondered if the man had a family, she didn't even have a chance to ask his name before he collapsed, but she worried someone might be out there looking for him. When Sister Matilda arrived to relieve her, Giani stood up and stretched, yawning.

"Thank you, Sister, I was getting sleepy. Our patient slept the entire time, I applied the willow bark oil again just a few minutes ago, so it won't need to be given until the end of your shift. If he wakes, please try to find out his name, and if he has any family he wants us to notify."

When Samantha excused herself after dinner, she went to her room to check on Leon. She found his clothing piled in the middle of the room and the remnants of his dinner soaking into the crevices of the old wood floor. Samantha called for Leon, knowing she would get no answer, and then she noticed one of the robes from the washroom door was gone. Samantha ran down the stairs to the lobby.

"Have you seen a man in a bathing robe?" Samantha realized how strange those words were as soon as they passed her lips, but when the man's eyes widened she didn't even need his confirmation.

"Yes, he left a little while ago, I tried to stop him because he was wearing one of our robes, but he was in a hurry," The barkeep told her.

"Thank you!" Samantha yelled as she rushed out the door and down the street. If there had been people out and about when Leon left, they were gone now. There was no one to ask where he might have gone. Samantha looked around frantically for any clues. Only one thought entered her mind, *The temple.* Samantha ran as quickly as she could to the temple and knocked on the door loudly. *Please let him be okay.* She pleaded to the Gods. Samantha raised her hand to knock again, but before she made contact with the door, it opened.

"Please, I am looking for my husband, he was wearing a bathing robe and he's not well, did he come here?" Samantha asked.

"Yes Ma'am, he's not in great shape though, we have given him poppy extract and he is sleeping at the moment, but you are welcome to come sit with him." Matilda invited Samantha in.

"Thank you," Samantha said as the woman closed the door and led Samantha to the altar where her husband was resting.

"Have you seen his affliction?" Matilda asked.

"Affliction?"

Matilda lifted the sheet, revealing the black veins. Samantha gasped, taking a few steps backward as she stared at her husband's feet and legs.

"What is it?" she asked.

"We aren't sure, it's not like anything we have ever seen. Where has he been? If we pinpoint a region we can search for diseases known in the area and it might help us."

"He was imprisoned in a dungeon in the Auran Desert. The conditions of the dungeon were terrible. He was left without food or water for several days, and the chamber pot in his cell was already full when he got there."

"Those are indeed some very unsanitary conditions, I will let Sister La-dia know immediately." Matilda turned from the room, leaving Samantha with Leon. She stood by his bed and reached down to find his hand.

"Leon, I'm here," she whispered, clutching his hand in hers. She felt a small response from his fingers as she moved her fingertips across his palm. She moved the chair closer to his bed so she could sit beside him. At some point, she fell asleep. She woke up to the light shining down from the golden star in the stained glass above. She looked at Leon who was still sleeping. Giani stopped by to see how he was doing. She was so glad he now had someone here for him. She looked at his feet and legs, rubbing more of the willow bark extract onto them. As she touched the bottom of his foot this time, he twitched and his eyes opened.

"Where am I?" he asked.

"You are at the Temple of Sol. We are trying to heal you, Sir."

"How did I get here?" he asked.

"You don't remember?" Giani handed him a cup of water.

"No." Leon lifted his head just enough to meet the cup and gulped the contents.

"You collapsed at the door, wearing nothing but a dressing robe," Giani told him. "We are trying to figure out what is going on with your feet and legs. The redness and swelling have gone down a considerable amount but the other affliction is resistant to the medications we have."

Leon began coughing. Giani rushed to get him more water and a handkerchief. He took a sip, hoping to relieve his throat from the itch, but no luck. He coughed harder and more frequently until he coughed up the same inky blackness filling his veins. Giani gasped.

She pulled back the sheet from Leon's chest revealing the further spread of his ailment. It was up to his rib cage now, looking like tiny twisted roots of death gripping him from the inside.

"We are running out of time, I have to go see Sister Ladia now. Are you in pain?" Giani looked at Leon.

"Every second," Leon said, only half joking.

Giani gave him a couple of drops of poppy extract and refilled his cup with the last of the water, taking the empty pitcher with her.

"I'll bring you some more water too," she said as she exited the altar room. Leon looked over at Samantha.

"I'm glad you're here. I didn't want to worry you, I should have told you sooner. I was just trying to make it back to Blackwater and then I was going to go see Delilah," he explained.

"I'm worried about you, I do wish you had told me sooner, although I am not sure there was anything I could have done about it where we were, but I'd have loved to be looped in," Samantha said.

"The older man in the cell next to me died. I saw the guards carry his body out. His body was black and rotting, it looked like it had been burned in a fire." Leon coughed into his handkerchief and looked at the black substance he had expelled from his lungs.

"I think I'm going to die." He looked far off in the distance, thinking about all the things he would have done if he knew how little time was left. "Tell Sophie how we met. Tell her about her father. She is old enough to hear it now. I don't want her to find out on her own one day and hate me and resent you because we never told her the truth." Samantha sobbed, denying his words.

"No, you're not going to die, we will find a way and we will save you. I won't give up on you. We can tell Sophie together when we get home." Samantha held Leon's hand tightly and caressed his hair with her other hand, looking into his eyes as they began to roll backward in his head as his eyelids closed. His chest still held a steady rise and fall so Samantha knew she hadn't lost him yet. She did something then, she hadn't done in years, she prayed. She prayed to all the Gods and Goddesses she knew. She would praise the name of the one who spared her husband for all eternity for more time with him.

TWENTY-THREE

BEFORE SUNRISE, LAUGHLIN STEPPED off the boat onto the shore of the island of Choddrath. Turning around, he extended his hand to Juniper and steadied her as she stepped onto land. He did the same for Kamara. Laughlin left Dusk with the stable master in Ashenport, it was strange being here without her, but he knew she was safe at least.

The overpowering stench of sulfur greeted them, accompanied by the sound of a thick boiling substance. From the water, to the shore, the temperature rose at least twenty degrees. The air was humid; sweat trickled down their backs. Laughlin could feel his perspiration gathering at the dip in the base of his spine. "So... I think I know why no one comes to this island," he said, wiping his forehead.

Kamara's natural curls had already expanded to three times the normal size. She pulled the wild mass of hair into a ponytail, twisted it around to make a bun, and tied her handkerchief around it. With her hair out of her face, the sparkle on Kamara's dark skin shimmered, and Dominic caught himself staring. He didn't think he had ever seen someone so beautiful, but he had no time to dwell on such thoughts.

They began walking inland; the terrain was uneven and covered in thick, black rock. A low rumbling from under their feet vibrated the earth, and a large pillar of smoke steadily rose from behind the four mountains.

"This volcano is active; we need to be careful," Juniper said.

"Any chance you know where we are supposed to go?" Laughlin asked, looking out over the vast lava field. "I thought these mountains were closer."

"Hold on," Dominic called as he stopped to open his pack. He pulled out the orb and peered into it. He could feel the orb's magic pulling him toward the mountains.

"We need to go up there." Dominic pointed to the peak of the tallest mountain.

"How?" Laughlin asked, looking at the formation. "There are no hand-holds or anything."

"I'm not sure," Dominic said. They continued walking toward the mountain, hoping the answer would reveal itself. As the sun began to rise behind them, the heat became even more unbearable. They stopped frequently for drinks to stave off the heat until their water skins were empty. By the time they reached the base of the four mountains, they were drained of energy and soaking wet with perspiration, but at least there was a little shade. Juniper tried to use a spell to create water, but it was like the heat drank it all first, evaporating it into the air. A soft rain fell for only a moment and the drops hit the black earth below and sizzled away on contact.

"We have to go all the way around the mountain, if this is where we need to go, there has to be a way," Gabe suggested. He climbed out of the valley between two slopes, trying to get a better view and suddenly an arrow whistled next to his ear and shattered against the mountainside. Shouts rang out from the northern shore.

"I think we have company," Gabe shouted.

There would be no resting here. Dominic groaned in frustration as he shoved the orb back into his bag. The rest of the group made similar sounds as they stood to prepare for the fight ahead of them. For the first time since the trip began, Gabe was afraid he might not make it back. Fatigue had taken over each of them and now this.

Laughlin rushed forward with his sword, making contact with the enemy's blade. Gabe pulled out his bow and drew an arrow from the quiver, nocking it. He aimed slowly and carefully, then loosed his arrow. It zipped through the air, close to Laughlin, so close in fact, Laughlin heard the squelch as the arrow found its mark and a soldier to his left fell lifelessly to the ground.

Dominic's arms were stronger now, wielding his heavy greatsword was less difficult than it had been even a few short months ago. He still had to use two hands to control it, but he could swing it with little effort now. He didn't have to swing, one of the men rushed him with a sword at their shoulder. When it was too late for the person to change course, Dominic lined up his sword with the horizon, pointing the tip at his attacker's chest. He saw the man's eyes go wide as the point of the greatsword pierced his leather armor and cut deep. Dominic twisted the sword back and forth to loosen it enough to withdraw it from the man's wound. This caused him agony and he screamed as the sword came out and collapsed at Dominic's feet in a pool of blood. He stared down in disbelief as the man took his last breath. He'd never killed anyone before.

Juniper caused the earth to shake and crack as thick, thorny bushes and vines sprouted right in front of the incoming enemies. They hacked and sliced their way through, which gave Dominic time to prepare a spell. Juniper ran forward, grabbing one of the vines from the bush and cracked it through the air like a whip. She pulled a dagger off her leather belt and held it tightly in the other hand. Just as she was about to lash the whip toward the man in front of her, Juniper felt the heat from a trail of fire sizzle past her. Entangled in the vines, unable move, the soldier screamed in agony as the fire claimed him.

The man Juniper had set her sights on, saw the difficult terrain emerge before them and changed direction, turning Juniper's attention away from the men struggling to hack away at the thorny bushes. Juniper swirled the end of her vine whip in the air and flicked her wrist effortlessly toward the man. The vine wrapped around his neck and Juniper pulled back on the whip, dragging her enemy in close. She drove the dagger downward into his side, right in between two ribs, pushing it deep into his lung.

"Juniper, watch out!" Dominic's voice rang out over the sounds of battle, quickly pulled her dagger out of the corpse, and whirled around to meet her next opponent. The man grabbed her by the throat as she turned. Juniper frantically sliced his wrist with her dagger, spilling his blood onto her clothes. The man shouted, pulling his arm back, he clutched it with the other hand, closing the wound as best he could.

Gabe aimed his bow, carefully choosing another mark, he took a deep breath, drew back as far as he could, and then sent an arrow flying. It struck a man with hardly any armor at all. He fell forward, arrow meeting the ground, pushing it deeper inside the wound and out the man's back.

Gabe saw Dominic's backpack sitting on the ground. Grabbing it, he sprinted to Dominic, shoving the pack outward to him. "We can handle these guys, you and Kamara need to get to the top."

"How?" Kamara asked.

"I don't know, circle the mountain, look for a way up. We will buy you as much time as we can!" Gabe called as he ran back toward the battle.

Dominic and Kamara ran to the base of the mountain, searching for a staircase, switchbacks on the northern face, or any other way to get to the top. She heard the orb pulse in Dominic's bag as they rounded the bend and the path revealed itself to her. The mountain seemed to open before her eyes, and a shining glamour dissipated to reveal a tunnel behind the magical veil.

"This way!" Kamara shouted. Dominic turned around to see which direction Kamara was suggesting, but instead watched her disappear into the mountain. He followed, making it into the secret tunnel just before it regenerated the glamour.

TWENTY-FOUR

IN THE OBSIDIAN KEEP, beneath the dragon throne, the man called Sir taught Sophie magic. She had learned more from him in three days than she could decipher from Baelfire's spellbook in months. Sophie liked being queen. It felt good to have the power to make decisions and to be in charge. The Red Order was still out searching for the other heirs, and the other orb. Sophie's orb was already in place.

Sophie heard the movement of heavy armor behind her and she turned to find one of the Red Order guards standing in the doorway.

"I'm so sorry to interrupt, Your Majesty, but there are three armies that just docked on the island, they have already begun fighting. Should I send more soldiers down?" he asked.

"No, stand guard by the thrones, I will make sure the heirs are in place, I have already unglamored the entrance so they can find it." Sophie said. The man bowed as well as he could in plate armor and left to give the orders to his men.

"My Queen, It is time you learned the truth." The man called Sir approached. "I wished your mother would tell you." He held up the spell book from Sophie's bag. "Do you know how this came to be in your possession?"

"Yes, of course, I found it in the cellar, I already told you."

"But *why* was it in your cellar?"

Sophie thought for a moment, but couldn't think of a reason her parents would have a secret room in the cellar filled with the old junk of some guy named Baelfire.

"Your mother was married before she married Leon. His name was Baelfire.

"You lie."

"My Queen, I would never *lie.*"

"But- Leon..."

"Leon did what he could, but he is not your father, this-" he held up the book. "-the man who wrote this, is your father. That's why his things were in your cellar, and how you came to have his spell book."

Why would they lie to me? Sophie wondered. *This can't be true, can it? They would have told me, why...*Sophie retreated to be alone with her thoughts. She wandered through the corridors and then up the stairs to her throne. The guards stepped aside for her to do as she pleased. Sophie felt the hum of the power- her power- trapped inside her. As she neared the stone seat of the red dragon, she dragged her fingers across the rough surface, feeling the steady surge of electricity between her and it. Sir appeared in the center of the rune circle, drawing her attention from the throne.

"My Queen, I know this news is weighing heavy on your mind, but there is a battle on our shores which we must address."

"I have taken care of it, the heirs should be finding their way up here any minute now, no one else will be able to enter. Gather what we need for the ceremony." Sophie said with authority.

"You continue to surprise me, My Queen." He bowed to her as she dismissed him to gather things they needed for the coronation.

Sophie could hear the sounds of clanging metal against metal and the grunts and battle cries from below. She wondered if Gabe was down there fighting, and Kamara, Juniper, and Laughlin. She wondered if they found her father- no, not her father, *Leon.* She still didn't want to believe it, and what reason could they have had to keep it from her?

TWENTY-FIVE

THE SOLDIERS WHO HAD remained with Samantha and Leon awaited word at the inn. When Samantha arrived, it was not the news they expected.

"You are all dismissed from this mission and free to return home. Leon and I will be staying at the temple until he is well enough to travel. I ask you to inform the guild of Leon's whereabouts, and if our daughter Sophie should return before I do, please have her go to the temple right away."

"Is Commander Rend going to be okay?" Jacob asked.

"He is very ill, I will not lie to you. The healers at the temple of Sol are doing all they can to help him," she said with a grim expression.

"Let me stay with him, you can go to find your daughter," Charlie offered.

"That is very kind of you, but your wife is expecting you home, your retirement awaits. I should stay here with my husband. I have arranged for another team of soldiers to sail to Choddrath to help Laughlin and Juniper get Sophie back, Besides, I could never make it to Choddrath in time." Samantha placed a hand on Charlie's shoulder. When the moment ended, Charlie nodded a quick farewell and excused himself to pack.

Samantha turned and walked back toward the temple. She was more worried about Leon, and Sophie than she wanted people to believe. She knew Juniper and Laughlin would do everything in their power to bring

Sophie home safe, so for now, her focus had to be on finding a cure for Leon.

When she got back to Leon's altar room, Samantha poured him a cup of water and helped him to sit up. She gave him the cup, but his hands were too weak to hold it. His fingers were almost completely black and withered as if he had aged a hundred and forty years overnight.

Samantha had to choke back tears when she heard his raspy voice and strained breaths. She didn't even want to think about what she would do without him. Samantha wiped her tears as Leon drifted off to sleep. Her thoughts trailed to Sophie and the difficult conversation yet to come. Leon spoke of telling Sophie the truth, the real truth, not the lie the citizens of Blackwater were told of the mysterious disappearance of Samantha's first husband. They all believed he was on one of the ships dragged to the depths at the battle of Blackwater Bay. No one found it odd his body was never recovered because no one kept a roster of who was on each ship.

Samantha had loved him once upon a time; the year of courtship before they wed, and for the first year after, but when his love of power grew greater than his love for her, things deteriorated quickly. When learning magic wasn't enough, he made a pact with a monster. Samantha was never quite clear who or what the monster was, but everything about him changed rapidly, the more evil deeds he did, the more power his patron granted him.

"Ma'am," A voice abruptly ended Samantha's thoughts as she looked up. "I'm sorry it took me so long, but this condition is rare. He is infected with Barren blight. This disease was a plague spreading through the part of the desert known as The Barren, it killed all of the plant life and animals, and now, nothing can grow and no one can live there," Ladia explained.

"Sounds grim, can it be cured?" Samantha couldn't hide the worry on her face.

"To an extent, what is dead will stay dead, but we can fight back the blight with a blessing ritual. It will take a while to prepare, but then in a week or so, he might be well enough to travel home. The herbs we burn in the temple will keep the blight from spreading to the rest of us, so don't worry, it is safe to hold his hands and to make him comfortable in the meantime."

"Thank you, Ladia," Samantha said, holding her husband's hand as he slept. Ladia excused herself from the room. The other sisters busied themselves with their daily tasks, cleaning, praying, and studying. Each hour, one of the sisters came by to check on Leon. He slept through each visit. Samantha began to worry whether or not he would wake at all.

At one point, his eyelids began to move rapidly and Samantha wondered if he was having a nightmare, one he was stuck in, and couldn't wake from. He'd long suffered vivid nightmares but she could usually pull him out of them and bring him back to the real world. She shook him gently, calling his name quietly, not expecting it to work this time.

His eyes never opened, but they settled and Samantha was at least relieved he was no longer being tortured by his dream. She sat in the chair beside him, resting her head on the stone altar. Sister Ladia had given her a bedroll, but Samantha preferred to stay where Leon could feel her presence.

A knock on the altar room doorway woke her. She didn't know how long she had been asleep, but her guess was not long because when she turned to the doorway, she saw Charlie standing there.

"M'lady, I have something that might help you. The wizard in Lapis Highland owes me a favor. Give him this coin, and he can open a portal to anywhere you need to go—even Choddrath I'm willing to bet." He held out a large gold coin to her. When she inspected it, her eyes widened.

"This is—"

"Yep, It is- one of only three pieces. It was my good luck charm. I won it off of him in a drunken bet one night. I told him if I ever needed a huge favor, I would get it back to him. Go, Mrs. Rend. I will stay here with Leon while you go get Sophie. My wife will understand."

Samantha threw her arms around him and hugged him tightly. "Thank you, Charlie, this means the world to me. Tell Leon I love him, and I am bringing our daughter home."

"Will do Mrs. Rend," he said with a warm smile.

TWENTY-SIX

SSAMANTHA RUSHED TO THE wizard as quickly as her horse would carry her. A recent landslide had flattened the side of the cliff, making an easy path to the tower. Samantha knocked on the door as loudly as she could, knowing the wizard would likely be at the top of the tower.

The door opened for her, although there was no one on the first floor to open it, there was just a circular room with a staircase on the right side, winding up the tower walls. Samantha took the stairs two at a time, desperate to get to her daughter before it was too late. At the top, the door to the wizard's study was open, and she saw him, hovering over a large book at his desk.

"What is it I can help you with?" he asked, looking up from his work.

"I know who you are. A young girl was here, just a few days ago with red hair and freckles just like yours. You must be her mother, yes? " Ryul asked the question, but he was already positive about the answer.

"Yes, and she is in trouble. A friend of mine told me to give you this," she showed him the golden coin. "He said you would help me get to her."

"I have not been to Choddrath for a very long time, but I do still recall a permanent rune circle on the top of the four peaks. I can teleport you there, but it requires a component I will need to have replenished. Since time is of the essence, I will do this for you, but you have to arrange payment first. I have a spell that will allow you to send a telepathic message to the person of your choice. Once we receive confirmation the component is on its way, I can begin." He handed Samantha a strip of parchment, a quill, and ink. "Write your message on this strip, and it will be sent to the person you choose. I need three hundred gold to replace the items I am about to use."

Samantha took the quill and wrote;

Hank,

Please send 300 gold pieces to the Wizard in Lapis Highland as soon as possible.

~Mrs. Rend

She fanned the parchment until the ink was dry, then handed the message to Ryul. Instantly, more writing began to appear beneath Samantha's.

Mrs. Rend,

I have withdrawn the requested amount from the guild account and given it to Sir Edwin Jace to deliver to the Wizard in Lapis Highland. ETA 2 days.

Hank

"Very well, let's get to work then." Ryul walked over to his bookshelf and pulled out an old leather-bound book and leafed through it until he found the page he needed. Gathering various chalks and inks, candles, and crystals, Ryul made his way to the center of the room.

He began drawing runes on the floor. Samantha couldn't read them, or tell what they meant, but the chalk he used sparkled in the light like thousands of tiny stars. Ryul continued looking from the page to the floor as he copied the circle from his spell book. When completed, the chalk lit up a glittering bright blue. Then he used ink and a rather large quill to write words around the inner rim of the circle. Once the layers were connected, the circle glowed a beautiful sea green.

Samantha waited as he worked, pacing the floor, hoping every second, she would make it to her daughter in time. Ryul got up, and Samantha turned to him, ready to go, but instead, Ryul walked back to a cabinet filled with potions and liquids, powders, gems, feathers, and what looked like preserved animal parts. Ryul grabbed three or four bottles from the cabinet and returned to the circle.

Samantha wasn't sure what time it was when he finally finished, but the rune circle was now glowing gold.

"This is it? This will take me to Sophie?" Samantha asked.

"Many years ago, I copied the rune circle from Dragon Peak, if the runes have not been destroyed, it should teleport you there." Samantha stepped inside the rune circle and Ryul spoke the words to activate the teleportation magic.

"Best of luck Mrs. Rend."

TWENTY-SEVEN

AKIRI AND HER CREW had been waiting off the shore of Choddrath for days, watching the island for activity. When the fighting began on the southern shore, the crew looked to Akiri for direction.

"Wait it out, let them kill each other, roll the bodies when it's over, take anything of value. I'm going to find a way to the top of the mountain. I have a feeling that is where the orbs are going."

Akiri got into the rowboat on the side of the ship and the crew helped lower it into the water. Akiri rowed to the northern shore and pulled the boat onto the beach. There was no one on this side of the mountain, which was perfect because she was not here for the fight, just the orb.

The mountains were jagged and tall. Akiri knew climbing to the top would be impossible. She could hear whispering in the wind, it seemed to be coming from the base of the mountain. She hurried in the direction of the sound, pausing to listen for the whispers now and again. When she reached the northwestern side of the mountain, a hidden archway revealed itself to her.

Through the shimmering veil of illusion magic, Akiri saw a staircase winding up the inside of the hollowed mountain. She had never seen anything like it, it was as though the mountains themselves were not even real. She saw a doorway to the left, and stairs to her right.

Akiri tried the door first, it was locked as she suspected it might be. She looked at the stairs. *Well, I guess there is no other way than up.* She thought as she began to climb.

She took the stairs two at a time at first, until she looked down and saw how high she was off the ground. There was no railing, only the carved stone steps. She hugged the wall as she continued, slower now, and her muscles had already begun to ache. *Mother is crazy if she thinks I'm bringing this orb back to her after all this.* Akiri thought. She paused to rub out a cramp in her leg. She was nearly halfway up. *At this rate, I will never make it.* She sat down on the step to catch her breath and rub the pain from all the muscles in her lower body. Then she heard the hum. The undeniable sound of magic. She got a second wind and ran up the stairs as quickly as she could.

Dominic and Kamara glanced around the mountain entrance. She'd prefer to not have to climb more stairs, so Kamara turned to the door and pulled on the handle. Locked. *It figures,* she thought.

"Well, we do need to get up top right?" Dominic asked. He pointed to the staircase. Kamara groaned. "I know, I wish there was an easier way too."

They started climbing together. Dominic tried making small talk, anything to take their mind off of the stairs.

"What did you do at the temple? Did you have a job or school?" he asked.

"I had studies, and then we worked in the garden. We grew all of our own food, except for meat, we got fish from Torzana and beef from Blackwater."

"This Sophie girl, did you know her well?"

"Not really, I met her the day her father handed me the orb and told me to get it to the guild in Blackwater."

"What about Gabe? Were you guys friends before?"

"No, he is Sophie's friend, he lives in Blackwater."

"So this might be a bold question to ask, but, when this is all over, assuming we make it out alive, would you want to come back to Ledora with me? It doesn't sound like you have to stay at the temple, and if you came with me, at least we would both always have a friend." Kamara turned around on the step to look at him.

"Where would I stay?" she asked.

"You could stay with me, at the castle- I mean, you would have your own room, of course, and you'd be allowed to come to court. It wouldn't be so boring if you were there with me."

"I'll think about it." Kamara smiled then turned back around to finish the climb. When they reached the last round of stairs, they both heard the familiar hum of the orb.

"We're close, let's go," Dominic said.

Everything after happened in a flash. Sophie was sitting on her throne, feeling the magic humming through her entire body when two of the four doors in the mountain peaks burst open.

"It's the heirs, My Queen," Sir said. Then a blinding light from the center of the runes caused Sophie to look away. When the light was gone, she saw her mother standing in the center of the circle.

"Sophie!" she screamed and started to move toward her daughter, but an invisible force field blocked her path. Sir stepped out from behind Sophie's dragon throne. Samantha gasped.

"Baelfire? You're dead... I mean, you died. How are you...?" Samantha stammered. Sophie looked at the man called Sir—not Sir, Baelfire. She could see it now; the resemblance. He was her father.

"How nice of you to join our little family reunion, Samantha." He raised his hand toward her but didn't touch her. Still, she choked and struggled against his magic. Samantha grasped at her throat feeling nothing but her skin as Baelfire lifted her off the ground.

"You know, I should have killed you and taken Sophie when she was a baby, instead of letting you raise her with that dirty rat, Leon."

"How... was he... a rat?" Samantha choked out.

"At the battle of Blackwater, he didn't defeat the monster, although he had no problem telling everyone he did. Just as I was about to cast a spell to banish the creature from this realm, he saw me casting and knocked me overboard. He stole my victory, my glory, my rise to power, it all should have been mine, guild leader, commander of the Blackwater Army, access to the guild bank, everything. Now, it will all be Sophie's. You shouldn't have lied to her about who her father was for all these years. She will never forgive you." Baelfire's eyes were filled with flames as he let Samantha go. She tried to run, but the barrier kept her inside the circle.

"You get to watch the transformation happen. Everyone is here! Please, heirs, go sit upon your throne and claim your power." Baelfire motioned to the stone seats. Each dragon was marked with the color of its heir.

Akiri wasted no time, she moved to the throne and sat down. The orb in the center glowed green as she lowered herself into the seat. Next, Dominic sat on his throne and the orb balanced out, once again two dragons encircled each other in an endless chase, one green, and one gold. Kamara was the last to join them. She took cautious steps in the direction of the silver throne and stopped to glance at Sophie.

"Sophie, we don't have to do this," she pleaded.

For a moment, Sophie felt sorry for Kamara, she was so sweet and naive, she had not yet been hurt by those she trusted most.

"We do though. If we don't, someone else will." Sophie said.

Both of the orbs began to hum loudly and the thrones surged with power. The magic held them to their seats, and the stone wings began to move. They wrapped around each heir like chrysalis as the magic from the orbs was absorbed into the statues.

Samantha felt the earth beneath her rumbling and growing warmer. She screamed for Sophie. Samantha picked up whatever rubble she could find on the old stone floor beneath her and threw it into the force field. Baelfire felt the rumbling too and he rushed to the center of the rune circle and disappeared in a flash. The force field dropped, just as a hole in the floor opened revealing a lava forge beneath. The four dragon thrones were now shaped like dragon eggs, moved closer to the center and hovered just above the forge. The rumbling grew louder and Samantha could feel the heat from the lava as the stone eggs began to change color from the bottom.

"Sophie!" Samantha screamed. She ran up behind Sophie's throne and searched for a way to open it. It cracked from the heat, but Samantha could not get it to open before the temperature became too much to bear. Samantha backed away, watching helplessly as her daughter was lowered into the boiling lava.

She screamed in agony and cried for her daughter. "I'm sorry I never told you, I'm sorry you found out this way, I love you and I only wanted what was best for you. Leon was a good man and a great father. You deserved to have a great father."

Samantha crawled on her hands and knees to the edge of the mountain, she had lost Sophie, and might even lose Leon. She sat on the edge of the flat top, looking at the ground hundreds, maybe thousands of miles beneath her. A high-pitched screeching sound made Samantha turn away from the edge. She looked back toward the enormous hole in the flat top.

From the lava, the first dragon emerged. A silver dragon with light blue and purple iridescent scales. The silver dragon flew right for Samantha and scooped her up in its very large talons. Samantha screamed as the dragon swooped off of the mountain and did a nose-dive toward the ground below. The dragon slowed before they reached the ground and sat Samantha down gently then flew back toward the top of the mountain.

"Mrs. Rend?" Laughlin's voice caught her attention and she saw Juniper, Laughlin, and Gabe running across the fields of black in her direction. Laughlin looked up.

"What do you think will happen?" Laughlin asked, staring at the Mountain.

"I'm not sure," Samantha replied.

TWENTY-EIGHT

LEON WAS STUCK IN his nightmares. Over and over again, the same dream haunted him. He tried to wake himself up but nothing worked. In all of his dreams, his family was attacked by dragons, he watched as everyone he loved was either burned by the dragon's breath or swallowed whole. While Leon tried to fight his way back to the waking world, Charlie sat at his bedside, just as he told Samantha he would. He hoped if his wife were ever in this position that someone would do the same for them.

Sister Giani had invited Charlie to eat with them in the dining hall, but he politely declined, preferring to be at Leon's side when he woke up. Like clockwork, the clerics came in and gave him the same treatments at the top of every hour. On the second day, Charlie heard Leon whimpering in his sleep like he was having a bad dream, he tried to nudge him awake, but he was unsuccessful. "Have you ever seen someone come back from this?" Charlie asked Sister Giani when she came for Leon's next treatment.

"I have never seen anyone with this particular illness, so it is hard to say. Although, we once had a guy here once who slept for an entire year, we watched all four seasons come and go, yet still, he slept. We didn't think he would ever wake. Then one day, all of a sudden, he woke up. He was asking for his wife, but she left after two seasons and never came back. I don't know if she moved on, or if she just couldn't bear to see her husband in perpetual slumber any longer. I never heard from him after he left to know if they ever found each other again, but I hope they did." Giani smiled thoughtfully as she cleaned up the debris from Leon's new wound dressings.

Charlie thought about his wife. He had given up this life of adventuring to be with her, and took a job with the city guard so he could provide a nice life for her. He wondered if he slept, and she did not expect him to wake up, whether or not she would move on. He wondered whether or not he would want her to.

"Charlie?" Leon's voice came out in a raspy whisper. Charlie jumped because the voice startled him.

"Yeah, it's me I'm here with you buddy," Charlie said, patting Leon's shoulder.

"Water." Leon didn't have the moisture in his throat to say more. Charlie handed him the pint mug of water one of the sisters had brought in during their rounds. Charlie sat Leon up and helped him drink. Leon gulped the entire mug of water and had to catch his breath. When he was finished. Charlie refilled it for him and Leon drank another half a mug.

"Thank you, where's Samantha? I thought she was here," Leon asked.

"She was, but Sophie has run into trouble on Choddrath and she had to go to the wizard for help. I told her I would stay with you-" Charlie cut off mid-sentence when Leon tried to stand. "Whoa, where do ya think yer going there? Doc ain't said yer ready for travelin' yet, we don't even know if you should be getting up." Charlie put his hand out toward Leon's chest. "Just wait, I'll find one of the nice ladies and see what they say."

Charlie left the room and Leon took the opportunity to look for his clothes, but all he saw was a white bathrobe. *Surely I wore clothes here... didn't I?* Leon wondered.

"Mr. Rend, I am so glad to see you're feeling better," Sister Ladia said. "It looks like the tonic has been working to stop the spread of your blight too. Let me get you some medicine to go home with and you can be on your way." Sister Ladia went over to the temple apothecary, just across the hall, and requested a few things. Leon wrapped himself in his bath robe.

"Have you got any coin on you? I can't go to Choddrath like this," Leon asked Charlie.

"How are you even going to get there? Do you have any idea how far it is from here?" Charlie asked as he handed over his coin pouch.

"If the Wizard got Samantha there, surely he can get me there too."

Sister Ladia came back into the altar room and handed Leon his medication. "I wrote down the instructions for you, just in case, but come back if it gets worse, or see your local cleric."

"Will do, thanks for all your help, Sister." As she left the room he turned to Charlie. "Thank you too, for everything. You take care of yourself." Leon patted him on the shoulder with a smile.

"Pardon my sayin' so, but yer crazy if you think yer going alone. I'm going too," Charlie said.

TWENTY-NINE

ON THE SOUTHERN SHORE of Choddrath, the battle continued between Akiri's soldiers and the Ledoran soldiers, The red order retreated inside their mountain keep. Gabe and Laughlin were dripping with sweat and exhaustion, but the adrenaline coursing through their veins kept them pushing forward.

More ships arrived, two flying sails with the golden sun of Ledora, and three from Blackwater. What was left of Akiri's soldiers ran for the rowboats, knowing there were too few of them left to crew the ship, they abandoned the vessel off the northwestern shore.

Gabe hurried to meet the Blackwater soldiers as they got off the ship. The soldiers watched the sky, sensing something was off about the island and the ominous storm now gathering overhead.

"It seems the Red Order has retreated, and neither of these armies seem to be concerned with us. Please have at least one ship ready to go. Our objective is to secure Mrs. Rend, and Sophie, as well as Juniper and Laughlin and get them safely home. Please leave enough men back to crew Mrs. Rend's ship, the rest of you, let's go get Sophie," Gabe said. He had no power, or authority to command the troops, but they rallied behind him anyway, knowing everything he said was the reason they were there.

"Come on, Mrs. Rend, we have to get you out of here." Juniper tried to get Samantha to follow her toward the Blackwater ships.

"No, I can't leave without Sophie." Samantha turned and ran back toward the mountain but the beating sound of very large wings stopped her in her tracks as an enormous black dragon landed in front of her. It roared; its breath like the shockwave after an explosion. The sound forced her to cover her ears and she closed her eyes in anticipation of the dragon's breath, instead, the beast grabbed her and flew back to the top of the mountain. When her feet were firmly on the ground again, the dragon released its grip. Samantha heard the cracking of bones and an awful screeching sound as the dragon shifted, shrank, and returned to human form.

"You're not going to want to miss this," Baelfire said. He cast a spell paralyzing Samantha where she stood as if her body were submerged in quicksand up to her shoulders. The lava started bubbling and spilling onto the platform. A red dragon emerged from the pool of boiling magma, as the stone flat top disappeared in the spillage. The rune circle where Samantha first appeared was now melted.

The red dragon looked at her, Samantha was trapped in the path of the pending volcanic eruption.

"Make your choice, Sophie. Me and this infinite power, or her and Leon. "Remember who has never lied to you, I might have waited to reveal all the details, but I told you the truth," Baelfire said.

The red dragon made a swift dive for Baelfire.

"Sophie! No!" Samantha screamed, as Sophie picked Baelfire up in her talons. She flew up high, hovering over the boiling mixture of lava and molten rock, and dropped him in.

Just before he reached the lava, he shifted into his dragon form and his black leathery wings carried him away from the searing liquid. The change took his concentration off of the spell he was using to hold Samantha in place and Sophie landed long enough for her mother to climb onto her back. With a thunderous roar, Sophie unleashed her fiery breath at Baelfire. The black dragon rolled out of the way.

Sophie flew around the mountain, to the unoccupied Northern shore. She landed long enough for Samantha to dismount. Sophie flew into the clouds and the roaring of two dragons as they engaged each other in battle kept Samantha's eyes fixed on the last place she saw her daughter's dragon form.

A green beast swooped down from the clouds, followed by a golden one of similar size. The green fled the island, flying off toward the horizon, carrying someone in its talons. The gold dragon started to follow but then changed course. The clouds parted, then, Samantha could see what was happening. The gold, the silver, and Sophie were teaming up against Baelfire The Black.

The silver combated Baelfire's flame with a beam of frost. The hot and cold combined and turned into rain. The lava began spilling over the sides of the mountain and running down into the crevices left behind from the last eruption.

An explosion from the volcano shook the entire island. Hundreds of men in red masks came running out of the northern side of the mountain keep to commandeer the ship waiting off-shore. Lava exploded from the top of the volcano and a huge wave of the molten rock came right for Samantha. Just as she turned to run, the silver dragon flew by and doused the heat with her frosty breath. A flash of lightning struck the ground next to Samantha and when the light dimmed, Leon and Charlie were lying in a heap, like they had been dropped there due to some magical mishap.

"Leon!" Samantha shouted as she ran to her husband. She helped Leon and Charlie to their feet and hugged her husband tightly. I am so glad you're awake!" she said as she clung to him, not ever wanting to let him go again. An ear-piercing scream from the sky broke up the reunion.

"Where's Sophie?" Leon asked.

Just then, Sophie emerged from the base of the mountain, in human form, carrying Leon's bag and Destiny. She saw Leon and was overcome with joy. He ran toward her, yearning to hug the child he had raised, the daughter he loved more than anything. Just before they could make contact with each other, The black dragon flew into them at full speed, knocking them both to the ground, and then ascended back into the sky. Destiny flew from Sophie's hand as the gust of wind from the beating of the dragon's giant wings sent her toppling backward. The second Charlie laid eyes on the black dragon he fainted, falling to the ground with a thud. Juniper tried to tend to him, but she could not cure his fright. He was conscious, but backing as far away from the dragon as he could.

Gabe rushed to Sophie's side and picked her up off the ground. He stood in front of her as if his body would shield her from the enormous beast.

Leon grabbed the sword and searched the sky for the black dragon. When he saw it diving down to make another strike, Leon readied his weapon, determined to not allow the visions and nightmares that plagued him over the years to come to fruition. Baelfire swiped at Leon with his claw as he flew past, but Leon ducked out of the way and thrust his sword up. The tip of the sword stuck into the dragon's claw like a splinter, it was enough to make him roar, but not enough to stop the assault.

Sophie tried to shift back into dragon form to protect her family, but she was hot and exhausted and the magic wouldn't work. Juniper ran to Sophie and cast a spell into her water skin, she watched the water skin swell as it filled with liquid.

"Hurry, drink before it bursts, this spell was meant to be cast on a larger container."

Sophie gulped the water down quickly and drank until her thirst was quenched. The water skin broke open, spilling the contents all over her, but she relished in the refreshment. Juniper tried to cast a spell on the dragon as it propelled itself forward to dive down at them, but Baelfire hit her in the head with his tail as he passed over them. Juniper lost consciousness as she crumpled to the ground.

Leon took another swipe at Baelfire as the black dragon landed and stomped toward him, releasing his breath weapon. Leon Dodged the inky black sludge from the dragon's mouth just in time. It was thick like the tar pits, and sizzled through the rock it landed on.

The gold dragon descended over the top of Baelfire and sunk his claws into his back. The black dragon roared in pain and turned to slash at his attacker while batting Leon across the battlefield and into the side of the mountain with his tail. The gold dragon flew back up above the clouds to gain momentum for another strike. Leon struggled to get back on his feet, and Baelfire set his sights on Sophie. As the black dragon stomped toward her, Leon let out a massive battle cry as he ran toward the dragon with his sword pointed out, ready for the kill.

Sophie tried once more to shift, it was difficult, but she could feel herself starting to change just as Leon took a stab at the dragon's neck. Black sludge sprayed out of the wound and the dragon yelped in pain. Baelfire swung his head up and crashed it down on top of Leon, then with an enormous talon, he pierced Leon's heart. Sophie's shift abruptly ended as she saw Baelfire's attack.

Both Sophie and Samantha screamed as they watched the dragon withdraw his talon, which was now covered in Leon's blood. Satisfied with himself, Baelfire turned and started moving toward Sophie. Out of nowhere, a silver dragon landed between them and roared its icy breath at Baelfire. The black dragon shook off the shards of ice and took flight, soaring into the clouds. Sophie was angrier than she had ever been and screamed as she forced the shift once more and gave chase to Baelfire. She searched the sky, looking for the black dragon who had taken her father from her.

When she spotted him, he was going after the gold dragon. Sophie and the gold dragon flanked Baelfire The Black from either side and just as he dove down to get away from them, the silver dragon blocked his path. All three of them used their breath weapons against him at the same time. Baelfire let out an agonizing screech as his dragon form melted away. An obsidian rock was all that was left behind, and it fell, hurling toward the ground.

Sophie dove down to catch the black, shiny stone and then landed on the ground beside Samantha and Leon. The gold and the silver dragons joined her, all shifting back to their human forms. "Sophie!" Samantha cried as she threw her arms around her daughter and pulled her into a hug. Tears flowed freely as they held each other. Sophie knelt beside

Leon and took his hand in hers. She wept for her father, as her mother did. Leon coughed and spit up blood as he tried to choke out words.

"I love you, Sophie, You have always been my daughter, and will always be," he said.

Juniper ran over, still rubbing the bump on her head. She summoned all the power she could, and then placed her hands on Leon's wound. A flash of silver light filled the hole in Leon's chest and it began to close. As the beam of light got smaller, so did the gaping wound, until there was no wound left at all. Juniper slumped to the side, exhausted, but Leon gasped and sat up. Sophie wrapped her arms around him and sobbed into his shoulder, Samantha hugged them both and cried tears of relief and joy.

Laughlin lifted Juniper off the ground and held her in his arms. She groaned softly as he adjusted her position to give her more comfort. Juniper rested her head on his shoulder and slept deeply.

"This way, I had them keep a ship ready," Gabe said as he slid his arm under Leon's, and helped him to his feet. Samantha and Sophie followed. Sophie looked at Gabe, her unwavering friend, her rock, and her protector.

THIRTY

IN THE WEEKS AFTER the event on the island of Choddrath, Leon healed and then returned to work. His first order of business was to call an emergency meeting of the guild council. When the other two guild leaders arrived, Leon led them to the conference room in the Silver Talon's Guild Hall, where Kamara, Dominic, and Sophie were already seated.

"What is this?" Leon heard one of them grumble as they walked in.

"I am so sorry I had to call this emergency meeting, but I hope your travels went smoothly," Leon said as they all took their seats around the heavy wooden table.

"We were 'sposta meet on th' next new moon anyway, don't see what couldn't wait til then." A gruff voice came from the far end of the table. Farris Ungar, Guilmaster of the Stonehold Keep Miner's Guild, was barely tall enough to see over the table, and his bushy red beard was almost as long as he was tall.

"Well, Mr. Ungar, let me waste no time, I don't know how many of you are aware of the recent activity on the island of Choddrath to the north-west, but-"

"A volcano erupted, that's hardly cause to call an emergency council meeting." Johann Stromhelm interrupted.

"Well, that is the story being told by those who weren't there, but I was, and I saw the return of dragons to this realm. I witnessed a fight between a rather large, black dragon, a red, silver, and a gold. I was told there was also a green dragon. Its current location is unknown, but we suspect the green dragon to be from Ash," Leon said. He walked around the table as he continued. "Dominic is the crowned prince of Ledora, Kamara is the sole survivor of the massacre of the Temple of Ophay, and my daughter, Sophie is Queen of the Red Order of Choddrath, whose members are currently displaced. I called this meeting because I believe we require a new council, one to ally with us to keep us safe from further attack should more dragons rise."

"And I suppose you want these... children to be appointed to these positions? Why even consult us at all? You can do as you please with your guild the same as we can with ours." Johann said dismissively.

"It's because this position is bigger than us, it's bigger than our guilds. They should be the high council and we would do well to heed their advice."

"You mean t'say they should rule over *us*?" Farris Ungar stood on his chair to look Leon in the eye.

"Come with me, please. I will show you exactly why we, as guild leaders should allow these *children*, as Mr. Stromhelm so delicately put it, to have a seat above us on the high council."

Leon led them down the corridors of the guild hall and out the back door to a newly excavated pit arena. Leon led the council members to the stadium seats on the top level.

"If we're gonna watch 'em fight, we should sit closer, so we can really see the punches," Farris said.

"No one will be fighting today. Let's just watch." Leon said. They took their seats as Dominic, Kamara, and Sophie walked down the steps and into the large oval floor of the arena. They lined up, standing several feet apart from each other.

The council members leaned forward in their seats, looking closely at the three tiny figures below them. With great roars, the three dragons shifted, extended their wings, and then turned toward the western side of the arena where Leon had placed two training dummies. Sophie went first.

Her target was a dummy made of straw with a scarecrow's hat. When Sophie's breath collided with the target. The fire engulfed the dummy, sending plumes of dark smoke billowing into the clouds.

Kamara breathed a cone of frost onto the flames, instantly dousing it and leaving behind falling snow which melted as it hit the ground.

Next, Juniper walked out onto the arena floor and used her magic to turn Dominic's dummy into a grizzly bear. Then juniper ran. The bear gave chase, and just before he caught up to Juniper, Dominic unleashed a cloud of gas. As soon as the odor hit the bear's snout, his muscles started failing and he could no longer stand.

"Three dragons! I thought they were all dead." Farris was still staring at the dragons wide-eyed and with his mouth hanging open from shock.

"I thought red dragons were horrible creatures that burned villages to the ground and now you are saying we should trust one to be in the highest seat of power this realm has ever known?"

"I have raised this girl as my own, she has my name, and the blood of her mother, who is the kindest, most gentle woman I have ever met. There is no one I would trust more to lead any other red dragons we may not yet know about. They will rule their own kind and offer advice to this council and it will benefit us all. This is a pact we must form between human and dragonkind for the preservation of the realm." The other men nodded and shook Leon's hand.

"I hope we never see the day when we have to regret this decision, but for now, it is what is best for all parties," Johann said.

"What about the green dragon?" Farris asked.

"She might be something the Council of Dragonkind has to deal with in the future, but for now, let's take comfort in the protection of our new ruling council."

They all looked back down at the three dragons who were now circling each other in flight around the arena.

Gabe waited under the willow, throwing rocks into the creek when he heard footsteps approaching. He jumped to his feet and turned to see Sophie walking toward him. It was like a dream, seeing her here, in the forest just like always—just like when they were kids. Gabe missed the feeling of childhood, and his ability to control his feelings for Sophie. He loved her then too, but now, it made his heart ache to think of not being with her.

He searched for the right words to tell her. He still didn't have them, he was too afraid of losing her so he said nothing. She was wearing a dress. In all the time he had known her, Gabe had never seen her in a dress of her own free will. Gabe didn't say a word, he just watched her as she walked over to the bank of the stream, took off her sandals, lifted the skirt of her dress to her knees, and stepped into the water.

"Come and wade with me," She called, reaching out for him.

He rapidly took his boots and stockings off to join her. She always thought he was silly for playing in the creek. How many times had he asked her to wade with him? He couldn't recall.

Gabe took her hand as he stepped into the water and when he looked into her green eyes, his heart was bursting, he couldn't hold it in anymore.

"Sophie, I-" She pressed her lips to his before he could even finish his sentence. Was he dreaming? Was he dead? What was happening? His head swirled for a moment until he lost all train of thought and just kissed her back, tangling his fingers in her fiery curls.

"Me too," she said when they finally parted. "Me too."

THIRTY-ONE

Upon her return to The Kingdom of Ash, Akiri carried her mother's guard in her talons. When she landed on the outskirts of the city and returned to her human form, she stood him up keeping his hands firmly bound. His eyes wandered briefly to her exposed body and Akiri forcefully turned him around, keeping a tight grip on the back of his elbow as she marched him through the city, ignoring the stares and fingers pointed in her direction.

When she burst through the double doors, her mother startled and a small gasp escaped her lips. Akiri shoved the prisoner toward her mother.

The look on Queen Luciana's face angered Akiri. It was both a look of surprise and disappointment at once.

"This man had a very interesting tale to tell. He told me when I found the artifact, his order from *you* was to kill me and steal the orb."

"That's just absurd, you are my only daughter, surely you don't believe him?" Queen Luciana tried to move toward her but Akiri shot out her hand. She tried to further convince her daughter she was on her side, but Akiri would hear none of it.

"I have brought the artifact home, Don't you want it?"

"I am so happy to hear it! I would love to see it." Her mother tried to move toward her again but Akiri warned her to stop. Queen Luciana obeyed, desperate to see the source of untold power.

Akiri shoved the bound man to the side to make room in the grand throne room, and she sifted, taking her dragon form. All her fury and anger came out in a loud, terrible screech as a thick green sludge sprayed over Queen Luciana.

By the time the guards reached the great hall, Akiri shifted back and watched as the acid sludge melted Queen Luciana into a puddle as black as her heart. Akiri walked up to the throne and took a seat.

"Queen Luciana is dead. I am now your queen," she declared, looking down at the guards with authority.

The men looked around in shock. The sizzling puddle of dark green sludge where the queen previously stood made them gag, and the girl who now sat upon the throne stared at them remorselessly. They looked at Akiri with fear in their eyes. No one except the queen, and the man in the corner, saw what happened in the throne room. They had all heard the roaring of a great beast, though, so it seemed to them; they had no choice.

Akiri looked down at the guards, all of them kneeling for her. She would make a name for herself during her reign. Her kingdom would rise from the ashes like a phoenix; the rest of the world would cower in their presence. She sat on the throne with a smug expression thinking of the possibilities her new power would bring. She could feel it. This was only the beginning.

Part Two:

Ascent From Ash

PROLOGUE

A GENERATION BEFORE THE kingdom of ASH was known as such, it was known by another name. It was called Adesh. Like many of the kingdoms across the sea, Adesh was named for its Queen, Anu Adesh. Her father, King Viraj, became sick with fever before her birth, and crossed into the afterlife just weeks before her arrival. Shortly after her birth, the same fever took her mother too. For many years, the Regent sat the throne in Anu's stead, until she came of age.

On the fourteenth anniversary of her birth, Anu was crowned Queen and sat upon the throne for the very first time. For seven years, the kingdom struggled and commoners had to choose between paying their taxes or feeding their families. Angry villagers stormed the castle gates daily, those who made it past the stationary guards, were often caught trying to steal whatever they could carry by sentries in the castle gardens.

Queen Anu ordered her men to expand the dungeon to make room for the thieves who would dare steal from the royal gardens. The miner's families received a month's compensation for the miner's absence in advance and then they started to dig. The hammering of pickaxes and the chipping and cracking of stone echoed through the castle for days, until they were well beneath the old stone floor.

The miners discovered coal, and sparkling white diamonds in the depths of the dungeon, and when the Queen's captain of the guard saw what they had found he ordered them to keep digging and extracting the gemstones. The miners had no concept of day or night, they lost track of how long they had been digging. Their families came to the Queen often to ask when the men would be able to come home, and her response was always the same. Queen Anu would put two gold pieces in their hand and say; "soon." The truth of it was, there were too few of them. To get the work done faster, Anu needed more men.

She asked the nearby kingdom of Ledora to send help. In return, she promised to send each miner back with his weight in gold—after she sold the diamonds, of course. The King of Ledora happily sent willing miners to earn their riches, but one day, A wall of the mine collapsed, weakened by the striking of their tools and barraged by rushing water from the ocean. The ceiling caved in and buried most of the men alive. Those who weren't buried, drowned when the mine filled with water.

The townspeople heard the commotion and the rumbling from underground. They gathered around the castle awaiting news and hoping to see their loved ones emerge. When they found out the miners were lost in the collapse and would not be returning, they went mad. Mobs of people stormed the castle. When news traveled back to Ledora, the King sent a group of his soldiers to demand the payment promised, each man returned *with* his weight in gold. The king felt it was the very least Queen Anu could do for the many families who were now grieving because of her greed.

William Lazar, a local sugar cane farmer, and rum runner, led a group of Adeshi men inside the castle; they found the queen and delivered swift justice as the mobs outside burned the kingdom to the ground in protest. William ascended the steps to the throne and sat upon it.

"Adesh will henceforth be known as The Kingdom of Ash, to remind us all of how we suffer under a tyrant's hand. I will do my duty to the realm and build a kingdom from the ashes like no one has ever seen!" The soldiers in the throne room all took a knee and bowed to their new king.

"All hail, King William, of Ash!"

Three years into his reign, at the urging of the King's Counsel, William took a wife and had three children; Theo, Natalia, and Anca. His wife, Queen Clarice, passed during childbirth, but their youngest child was born healthy and William thanked the Gods every day he did not lose them both.

As king, William grew the sugar cane fields and expanded the rum-making warehouses. Soon, the kingdom of Ash was the leading producer of rum in the world. King William was well-loved by the people of Ash because he always paid them fairly, took care of the families of his workers, and took the kingdom from squalor to riches. Despite his popularity, the king was unhappy. He longed to sail the seas again. The memories of his time with the rum runners in the years before he took the throne were second only to the memories of his children being born. He vowed to prepare Theo to take his crown, and when he stepped down, then he would retire to the sea.

In an effort to restore peace between Ash and Ledora, King William wrote to the Ledoran king and offered a betrothal of his eldest daughter, Natalia to Prince Haki, who would take the Ledoran throne after his father.

The King of Ledora saw this offer as a great insult and he refused to wed his son, Prince of Ledora to the second in line for the throne of Ash. In the years following this failed betrothal, many men and women came to court. There was a banquet, and a ball every full moon. Theo met a raven-haired beauty named Luciana and became enchanted. They courted for a few years before they married. Luciana was the youngest of four children. She had three brothers in line for the throne in her own kingdom, and there were whispers in the beginning that it was for this very reason she set her sights on Theo.

Anca, the youngest, and by far the bravest of King William's children, disappeared one day. It was rumored she disguised herself as a boy and left with the rum runners, although it was never confirmed. William was overcome with grief. His interest in ruling diminished more every day.

Natalia married a noble she met at court from Immernacht, a kingdom far east. After they wed, she went with him back to his kingdom as wives were expected to do. William knew his time had come. He held a coronation for Theo and named him King of Ash. Two weeks later, William was at sea once more.

Shortly after King Theo announced his wife was to give birth to their first child, he became ill. During the time King Theo spent bedridden, a dragon attacked the kingdom and burned the sugar cane fields to the ground. It had been the first sighting in a decade, and it had been a black dragon. No one knew much about them, the black dragons were rarely spotted, even in the days before the age of Kings when dragons were everywhere. No one knew if it was because there were fewer of them, or if they were just smarter than the others; smart enough to avoid humans most of the time.

Theo tried to get news to the rum runners and his father, but word came back saying their ship had been destroyed by a monstrous sea creature in Blackwater Bay. Theo grew weaker every day, and his dear, pregnant wife Luciana sat at his bedside quietly praying to the gods for his recovery. The sickness took him in the night; the next morning, Luciana was crowned Queen. With the rum runners out of business, and the sugar cane fields now barren, Luciana began taxing for imports and taxing the businesses within the kingdom.

No one liked giving up their hard-earned coin, especially when it was barely enough to feed their families as it was without the sugar cane income. Families who could afford it bought passage to other kingdoms and only those who were too poor to leave remained in Ash.

By the time her daughter was born, Luciana was finished being abandoned, because of this, she never bonded with her child. Akiri was nourished by the wet nurses and looked after by the castle staff. Akiri learned magic, and how to crew a ship, but she never learned what love was, not even from her mother.

ONE

THE CLICKING OF AKIRI'S heels on the stone floor echoed through the council chamber as she paced back and forth across the room. Six men sat at the long rectangular table, three on each side, looking at her expectantly.

"How many gladiators have signed up for the tournament?" she asked, pausing to look at her council.

"Forty, Your Grace." The answer came from a thin weasel-faced man who sat in the middle seat on the left side of the table.

"What is the entry fee?" she asked.

"One hundred gold pieces."

"How about we require an entry fee for each event instead of the whole tournament? We can lower the entry fee to fifty gold, but then it will be fifty for the joust, fifty for beast taming, another fifty for hand-to-hand combat, and yet another fifty for weapons combat. Assuming the knight or gladiator wanted to participate in all the events, that would be two hundred gold pieces each."

"Then would the prize be increased as well?" the weasel-faced man, Timothy Ackerman inquired.

"Instead of one prize, each event could have its own purse. The winner will get thirty percent of the pool and the kingdom would make double that at least on the bets." Akiri shrugged her shoulders and widened her eyes as if to ask them what they thought of the idea. They mulled it over for a moment or two then they each began nodding in agreement.

"Now that the tourney is sorted out, My Queen, we must discuss diplomacy." The man seated next to Akiri on the right side of the table stood up.

"Okay, what have you today, Ser William?" Akiri asked.

"You have a proposal from a Ser Archibald Wentworth of Braidwood. Next, another proposal, this time from a man named Dmitri who claims to be immortal. He has offered his gift of immortality for your hand."

Akiri nodded and rolled her eyes. "He wishes to be king, and even if he *is* immortal, that just means we would be stuck with the same king, and queen forever. I wake up some days not sure if I want to do this job at all, let alone *forever*. What else do you have?"

"Your lair is almost complete. According to all the tomes we have requested from Ravenhall, you will be able to produce a clutch of eggs soon, they will only produce dragons if..." The man cleared his throat and gave Akiri an uneasy look. "If they are fertilized, Your Grace." He darted his eyes away from her."

"I only know of one male dragon, and there is no way he would help me produce a clutch, he is the son of King Haki of Ledora. The other two dragons were female, and I am pretty sure they killed the black dragon. How are we going to find another male dragon?" Akiri asked.

"Perhaps we do not need another *dragon*. My Queen." The man bowed to her and then took his seat once more. Akiri pondered his meaning and wondered if a human lover could help her produce a clutch of dragon eggs. Shifters are half-human anyway.

"Does anyone else have anything to add?" Akiri asked. The silence followed, so Akiri adjourned the meeting. As she rolled Ser William's words over in her mind, her head became heavy, she felt the need for fresh air. Akiri didn't wait for the men to get out of their seats, she pushed past the table and hurried out the back door and across the western courtyard to the newly constructed arena. Akiri stopped, closing her eyes, she relished the wind on her face, letting the breeze wash over her. After removing her robes, she began to shift into her dragon form. It was easier now, It used to hurt, but now it felt like a good stretch, the pain made her feel alive. Akiri's large green talons dug into the sand as she prepared to run the length of the jousting arena. The sidelines became a blur as her feet moved faster, propelling her forward. A cloud of dust expanded out from beneath her wings as she took flight. The air was cool on her face and little droplets of condensation from the clouds clung to her body as she ascended into the sky. She always flew above the clouds, trying to remain out of sight. She read of dragon hunters in the ancient texts and feared she would one day be hunted too.

Akiri soared across the kingdom, and to the western sea. When there was no land nearby, Akiri dipped down to the edge of the water, dragging her feet lightly across the surface. When she ascended again, she rolled to one side, and then the other, and then went upside-down as she rolled, dancing in the sky to a tune only she could hear.

Akiri thought about the council meeting and Ser William's words. What would she even do with a clutch of dragon eggs if she had them? She knew they could teach the dragons to defend the kingdom, but beyond that, she had no idea who would be responsible for raising them, or more importantly, feeding them. Would the dragons share the ability to shift into human form, or would they only be dragons? Akiri couldn't stop thinking about all the questions, flying was sup-posed to help her clear her mind, but she found it was not working in her current situation. Akiri's council brought up the subject of her marriage quite often as of late. She knew it was a royal's duty to marry and have children so the kingdom would always have a ruler, but Akiri never wanted children when she was younger and the thought of being a mother used to make her feel ill, but dragons sounded nice. She wondered if she was cut out to rule the kingdom after all.

When Akiri landed back in the jousting arena she saw someone in the stands. A frail-looking figure wearing all black. The person's hood was drawn, obscuring their face in darkness. As Akiri picked up her robe and hastily pulled it on, she hurried further toward the arena's exit. Akiri saw the figure turn to follow her, so she quickened her pace.

Akiri broke into a sprint and ran from the arena to the castle doors, then up the grand staircase, and down the left-side corridor to her chamber. She only let out a sigh of relief when she closed and barred the heavy oak door behind her.

Akiri leaned her back against the door with her eyes closed until her breathing slowed; but the second she opened her eyes, the figure was standing right in front of her. She could see the face clearly now, smooth pale skin, no hair, and no holes where the eyes should be; only skin. It was the seer, the oracle her mother had sent with her to Choddrath. Akiri felt the air leave her lungs as she tried to scream.

The woman pointed her long bony finger and pressed it right in the middle of Akiri's forehead. Everything around her went black and she felt herself falling into nothingness, a large black void where no life existed. *Is this what it feels like to die?* Akiri wondered.

TWO

AN OMINOUS DARK CLOUD loomed above Highland Tower. Sophie drew in
the power of the wind and swirled her right hand clockwise, pulling the
clouds down into a funnel with her mind. A bolt of lightning, followed
by a deafening clap of thunder broke her concentration and the cloud
bounced back into its former shape.

"You have to maintain, no matter the distraction, don't lose your focus,"
Ryul instructed. "Try again, this time, I want you to make the cyclone
touch down." The wizard stood there, examining her every movement.
She wanted to impress him. Mastering control of the elements was a
difficult lesson and she'd already spent two full moons practicing with
wind and rain to create a storm, now she had to learn to control its path
and intensity.

Sophie took a deep breath and turned toward the storm cloud. She
fixed her gaze on the bottom of it and envisioned in her mind what she
wanted to happen. Sophie swirled her hand again and it started to mimic
the motion of her hand as if her fingers were holding onto the bottom of
the cloud. The lightning struck again, this time, Sophie anticipated the
thunder that followed and kept her eyes intently on the cloud.

Swirling her hand faster, she pulled the cloud down into a point,
creating a cyclone. It was now spinning and holding its shape, so she
didn't need to keep moving her hand in a circle, but now she had to pull it
down. Focusing on the point, she saw exactly what she wanted to happen

inside her mind, but couldn't get it to touch down. She almost had it, but was becoming exhausted and wasn't sure how much longer she would be able to keep going.

"Sophie!" Gabe's voice called out to her from the side of the tower. She turned to look, forgetting about her work, but it was not Gabe she saw. It was the Wizard Ryul projecting her friend's voice.

"Your enemies will use any tactic they can to destroy your spells, they will use not only the voices of your loved ones, but sometimes they will take those you care about most and bend you to their will. It is best to have no attachments. We can be done for the day, rest up and we will start again in the morning." Ryul turned and went back inside the tower, the dark cloud departed with him as it evaporated back into the sky.

Sophie stepped to the edge of the cliff and watched the waterfall cascade down the rocky form. She sat at a picnic table under a tall poplar tree. It wasn't like the forest, or the weeping willow where she and Gabe spent much of their childhood, and the waterfall was nothing like the stream in which Gabe always tried to get her to wade.

Since Sophie's first day at the tower, the full moon had come and gone three times already. It was the end of summer when she'd arrived and now it was harvest. Sophie would be going home after harvest to spend Solstice with her family, and then she would come back to the tower to continue training. Sophie almost changed her mind and decided not to go after she and Gabe kissed, but being a wizard was her dream, and there was no one telling her she couldn't do it. Partly was because she was a dragon shifter, and the other reason was because her father was still in charge of the Silver Talons Guild.

The Red Order, those who were loyalists to the red dragon, set up a temple in Alasia so they could be close to Sophie; their queen. Some of the men were not happy when Sophie took the throne. The men who craved power for themselves and refused to bow to their new queen were shunned from the order and left without a home to wander the world. Those who stayed were tasked with doing good deeds and helping those in need. Sophie was determined her reign would not be remembered as a reign of terror.

The sun dipped below the horizon and a cool sea breeze brought out goose flesh on Sophie's arms. With a shiver, she hugged herself, rubbing her hands up and down her arms to warm them as she walked back to the tower. Her room was cozy; there was a low, crackling fire in the hearth. Sophie walked over to it and held her palms out to the flames as she watched them dance. Ryul must have lit the fire when he came inside. He was not what she had expected. When first they met, he had been younger in appearance than her father, now he looked more like a great, maybe even a great-great-grandfather. He used glamour when he had surprise visitors because he didn't want to appear broken or frail. He was neither of those things when his magic was strong, but proving it used more energy than he cared to put into it on any given day. Sophie helped him in the evenings when his magic waned for the day and had come to see him as her grandfather. Sophie never knew her real grandparents, so Ryul was the closest she would ever have.

When it was time for dinner, Sophie helped Ryul to his seat and poured him some water. She looked at the table, which was bare, except for two plates, two cups, and a pitcher of water. Sophie closed her eyes and pointed to a spot on the table. She thought of a whole chicken, and imagined it in her mind; the crispy golden skin covered in fresh herbs and the aroma of a perfectly roasted bird. Next, she thought of freshly baked rolls with fresh butter from the dairy farm in Blackwater. Sophie imagined a large garden salad with mixed greens, carrots, tomatoes, peppers, and a light ginger dressing. Finally, Sophie pictured the fruit pastries from her mother's sweet shop. When she opened her eyes, the very feast she imagined lay before them on the table. Ryul smiled at her.

"Well done Sophie, conjuration is a difficult thing to master," Ryul clapped his hands together as he looked at the feast Sophie's magic had given them. They filled their plates and ate until they were full. When they finished, Sophie waved her hand over the top of the table and the surface cleared as if it had all been an illusion.

"You are learning so quickly. I am so proud to have such a wonderful student. I can feel the elves of Aranor calling me home. It will soon be time for you to take my place. Tomorrow will be for copying spells, copy as many as you can so you will continue to learn even after I am gone." Ryul placed a wrinkled hand on top of Sophie's.

A tear slid from Sophie's eye as she placed her other hand on top of his. "We do not need to talk of such things now, you still have time, I know it." She stood up, helping him to his feet then walked him to the rune circle at the base of the stairs. Sophie pictured the wizard's study in her mind. A moment later they were standing in the matching circle in his room at the top of the tower.

She helped him to bed. He would change his robes in the morning when his energy was restored, she was certain. Sophie bid him goodnight and quietly retreated to her room downstairs.

THREE

Electricity coursed through the golden dragon as it flew across the sky. The people of Ledora had always known one day the golden dragon would return, and now that it had finally happened, the streets were filled with Ledoran men, women, and children, gathered to see The Dragon Prince fly. Dominic dipped down low and made a quick glide over the cheering crowd before soaring back up into the clouds. He let out a deep and throaty roar as he unleashed his breath weapon into the air. The popping of a large electrical spark rang out as lightning streaked from Dominic's mouth, illuminating the clouds with flashed of light. The only thunder to follow was deafening applause from the crowd below.

King Haki watched his son with pride from the balcony of the King's Keep. When Dominic finished his flight, he landed on the beach south of the castle to resume his human form. As he dressed, his gaze drifted to the old wooden boardwalk and the docks where the flagship of the royal fleet used to drop anchor. The beach always reminded Dominic of the day the Crown Jewel, Zahara, capsized in the storm. Luckily, most of the crew had been rescued and returned to Ledora aboard another ship. Dominic knew his father had worried when the surviving crew returned home without him. Dominic hadn't realized how long he'd been gone. It seemed like only days to him, but in reality, it had been several months between the day he left and his return to Ledora. Upon his return, King

Haki hugged him, scolded him, then hugged him again and he didn't let go for what seemed like hours.

The days since Dominic's return were busy, every waking hour had been scheduled much like it was before. After waking and eating breakfast, Dominic began the day with studies of lore, not only dragon lore, but also the histories and stories from all around the world. After lore, he studied Draconic, the ancient language of dragons. After Draconic, he practiced casting, and then he had lunch. The afternoons were spent flying and fighting in dragon form. Before dinner, Dominic sat on his mother's throne while King Haki listened to the concerns of the Ledoran people. The King allowed Dominic to handle some things, to prepare him for the decisions he would face as king someday. The King was also more insistent than ever for Dominic to choose a wife.

After granting an audience to the subjects, King Haki turned to Dominic. "My son, at week's end, we have planned a royal ball, we have invited all of the noble ladies from Ledora, as well as Queen Sophie, and Kamara. I know you have expressed your desire to choose a match in your own time, but-" The King's voice dropped off and he closed his eyes and took a deep breath before continuing, and Dominic could tell whatever he had to say was difficult for him.

"I'm not well. I have been sick since before you left. I didn't tell you, because I didn't want you to worry, but my illness is progressing and the shaman believes I will join our ancestors soon. I should like to meet your wife, and perhaps my grandchild before I leave this world." He placed a hand on Dominic's shoulder and when the prince looked up from the floor, his face was streaked with tears.

"Father, I am so sorry. I never would have left had I known." Dominic choked back sobs as he threw his arms around his father.

"I know, son, but if you had not, the legacy of the dragon would be gone. The magic was sealed away in that orb for too long with no one to carry it. Just, promise me you will be open to your options."

He nodded. "I will, father."

Dominic spent the rest of the evening thinking about what the king had told him. He wasn't ready to be king, he wasn't ready to get married, or have children, but most of all, he wasn't ready to lose his father. Emotions came in waves and he fought back the tears for as long as he could, and when he was unable to hold his emotions together any longer, he ran to the beach, where the dragon within him took over. Letting loose a mournful screech, Dominic took flight. The golden dragon blended into the sunset as he did a barrel roll and changed direction to fly North. There was only one person he wanted to see.

He flew up high, above the clouds to obscure him from the view of people on the islands below. Dominic knew about the islands below from his days on the flagship of Ledora, Zahara, which was named after his mother. Pirates ruled a cluster of islands in this area and normal sailors dared not to stop there if they had a choice, for they would surely sail out a lot lighter than they came in, and that was if they were lucky.

The next island below him, Dominic flew around rather than over. The island of Immernacht was always covered by a dark and ominous cloud. He didn't know why it was always storming there, but in Ledora, he'd heard a lot of whispers about an evil there that despised the sun and fed on the blood of others. He gave Immernacht a wide berth and then finally, after hours of flying, he reached The Cliffside Coast which rose to the right of Torzana and looked over the Southern forest of Blackwater.

He landed at the edge of the forest and resumed his human form. He hurried through the trees, to the beautiful silver temple, the Temple of Ophay. It was late at night and he didn't know if Kamara would be awake, but the temple was always open to those who were friendly. Thankfully, now it was warded against evil thanks to Sophie and the wizard, Ryul. Dominic walked inside and down a corridor on the left. He found the room he often stayed in when he visited. Kamara had made up his bed and left a clean tunic and a pair of trousers hanging in the closet. He walked to the chest of drawers and opened the top drawer.

She thought of everything, he thought with a smile as he pulled undergarments from the drawer and put them on. There were two very unfortunate things about being able to turn into a dragon, the transformation always destroyed your clothes; unless you thought to remove them first, and in dragon form, you had no pockets, so even if you did remove your clothes, you couldn't take them with you unless you carried them in your mouth. Then again, showing up places completely naked could be amusing. Once he was dressed, Dominic tiptoed down the hall to Kamara's room and opened her door softly. He tiptoed to her bedside, kneeled beside her, and brushed his fingers lightly up and down her cheek. She stirred at his gentle caress, the corners of her lips lifting into a sleepy smile.

"Kamara," he whispered. She brushed her hair out of her face as she drew a deep breath.

"Dominic?" Kamara whispered without opening her eyes.

"Yes, It's me."

Kamara lifted the silk sheet and down-filled comforter, then patted the bed in front of her. She moved back toward the wall so Dominic could crawl into the bed in front of her. As he laid down with his back to her, Kamara covered him with the bedding and put her arm around his middle. He felt so safe with her arms around him, as if she could take away all the hurt he'd ever felt with the softest touch.

Dominic didn't remember closing his eyes, but when he woke up, despite there being no windows in the room where they had slept, he could tell it was morning. Kamara was already up and Dominic had no idea how she got out of bed without him noticing. He hurried back to his room and dressed in the tunic and trousers Kamara had left for him. He found Kamara in the breakfast nook; she was reading a book as she absentmindedly stirred her morning tea. She glanced up from her book when she noticed him standing in the archway watching her.

"The water in the kettle is still hot if you would like some tea." she said.

Dominic nodded, crossing the room to the wood stove. He took a jar of tea leaves from the shelf, pulled out a cloth pouch for the loose leaves, and poured a mug of hot water from the kettle. He carried his mug to the table and sat down across from Kamara.

"How was your flight?" she asked, placing her book face down on the table to save her page.

"It was fine, it gave me time to have a good cry before I got here," he admitted.

"Cry? What's bothering you?" Kamara's eyebrows turned up at the inside corner and Dominic could see her concern was genuine.

"My father is ill, he told me yesterday, he might have a couple of years left." Dominic removed the tea bag from his mug and squeezed the rest of the liquid out before discarding it. Dominic thought if he met her gaze at that moment, he might cry again, so instead, he sipped his tea, which was still much too hot.

"I am so sorry about your father. I got his invitation to the ball just two days past. It said you intend to choose a wife so the Kingdom of Ledora will continue the royal line. I didn't know these plans were so urgent." She placed her hand on his. Dominic couldn't hide his thoughts from her. She sensed his apprehension about ruling a kingdom without his father's wisdom.

"If I have to choose a wife, I want to choose someone who means a great deal to me. Someone I know will be caring and kind. Kamara, I can't think of anyone else I want to spend my life with; when I got the news from my father, I only longed to be comforted by you. I can feel my feelings without fear of judgment when I am with you. Kamara, will you please, come to the royal ball so I can ask you this officially?" He moved from the table and bent down to one knee. "Kamara, you are my best friend; I want to spend the rest of my life with your guidance and love. Will you please do me the honor of accepting me as your husband?"

Kamara looked at him in shock, and tears welled up in her eyes. She nodded her head, unable to make words come out. She accepted with her whole heart.

FOUR

THE BLACK VOID SWALLOWED her whole. She could feel herself falling through the nothingness until she hit the solid ground with a THUD! Akiri sat up and looked around for the woman, the exit, or even a weapon she could use. There was nothing there but darkness. Then a flash of light attracted her attention. Akiri whirled around to see a massive black dragon breathing its fiery breath across the Kingdom of Ash. She heard the screams as the subjects fled their homes and ran out into the open, into a trap. The dragon breathed a wall of fire down every cobblestone street, engulfing the houses and livelihoods of her people. When the entire city was on fire, the dragon turned its attention to the castle. The city looked older and Akiri wondered if the seer was showing her the past.

The lights went out again. *Am I inside the seer's mind? Is this her vision?* Akiri's thoughts raced as whispers swirled around her.

"Ash will fall again, you cannot trust your council; one of them will betray you," the whispers warned.

"Who is this betrayer?" Akiri asked, looking in every direction for the source of the whispers.

"I can't see who, it's best to not trust anyone."

A flash of white light as bright as the day star. When everything went dark again, Akiri opened her eyes; she was in her bed. She looked around her room for the woman, but there was no sign of her. *Was it all a dream?* Akiri wondered.

It was dark outside and the breeze carried the smell of wood fire stoves in through the window, which was pleasant, but the scent was overpowered by the not-so-pleasant smell of the muckrakers cleaning the latrines, and the armorers tanning their leather. Akiri walked to the window and closed it. There was a small fire in her hearth and it had enough flame left to light some incense.

Akiri noticed a letter on her writing desk; it hadn't been there yesterday. She crossed the room to pick it up and inspected the golden sun of Ledora stamped into the wax seal. She opened it, pulling out the elegant invitation card inside.

The last time she saw the King of Ledora, she had blown a hole in his throne room doors, tried to melt His Majesty with an acid ball, and stormed out of his kingdom on a mission to kill his only child and take the orb of power for herself. When she thought about it now, it all seemed so juvenile, yet as sick as the gladiators when they fight to the death. She was so angry, at people she had never met, and for reasons only implanted in her mind by her mother. She regretted everything, but it was too late to take anything back.

She set the invitation on the table beside her bed as a visual reminder to take it to the council meeting first thing in the morning. Akiri tried to sleep, and she might have- for a little while at least. Tossing and turning all night, she kept seeing the black dragon as it burned the kingdom and the faceless old woman in her dreams warning her she would be betrayed.

When the first light beamed through her bedroom window, Akiri dragged herself out of bed. Her shoulder blades ached and her neck was stiff. Walking over to the looking glass beside her wardrobe, she turned her backside to the mirror. A dark purple bruise covered her left hip and her normally porcelain complexion was reddened across her buttocks and lower back. She winced in pain as she touched the bruise to test the tenderness. She definitely had not been dreaming when she fell.

Akiri dressed and brushed her long black hair, put on her crown, and grabbed the Invitation from Ledora. A cool rush of air made Akiri shiver as she stepped into the hallway on her way to the council chamber.

"One of them will betray you. Trust no one." the seer's words echoed in her mind as she saw the six men gathered around the table. They stood as she walked past them to her seat at the head of the table and they didn't sit down until she did.

"Before we begin, I received this invitation in my bed chamber. Do any of you know who delivered it there?" Akiri asked. The men looked from one to the other with confusion, none of them knew anything about the invitation. *Who left it in my bedchamber then?* she thought.

"What is it for, My Queen?" Ser William asked. He was a heavy-set man with only a horseshoe of gray hair around his head. He was a former Knight and had served on the city guard for many years. Akiri slid the invitation over to him and watched his expression as he read it.

"The last time I saw the King, I tried to kill him. If it had not been for his anti-magic barrier, I might have succeeded. Now he is inviting me to a royal ball? It doesn't make sense. As my Master of Diplomacy, Ser William, tell me, should I go, or does this seem like a trap?"

"Your Grace, You have the power to turn into a mighty dragon at will. It would not be in their best interest to try to lead you into a trap. There is no doubt in my mind they want to make peace so they will not have you as an enemy."

"If he has an anti-magic field, it could prevent Queen Akiri from shifting into her dragon form, they could imprison her-or worse," the young captain of the city guard, Nohan Arach, interrupted. "I don't think it is a safe idea for Her Majesty to attend."

Akiri gave him a serious look. "What if this Prince wants to choose another dragon for a wife, and *this* is the reason they invited me. Perhaps they crave strength, and having two powerful dragons is better than one. In this case, Don't you think it would be a good move, diplo-matically, of course, to merge our kingdoms and our Draconic line?"

Nohan looked as if Akiri had beaten him in combat. He hung his head and muttered; "Yes, Your Grace."

"Now, the tournament is days away, and the arena is nearly set up, how are the accommodations coming along?" Akiri asked the castle Steward, Roland Koffery.

"The chambers are ready and the kitchen staff has begun preparing for the opening feast."

"Very well, Thank you, Mr. Koffery." Next, Akiri looked to the weasel-faced man, Timothy Ackerman. Before she could speak, the voice inside her head whispered again, *One of them will betray you, don't trust anyone.* Akiri shook the thoughts away and continued, but the uneasiness she felt when she looked at him clung to her.

"How is our budget for the tournament?" Mr. Ackerman looked at his ledger, the numbers were orderly and detailed, outlining how the crown spent every copper.

"Our budget looks good. The fees for the contests will cover the cost of the tournament; we should come out a few thousand gold pieces ahead when all is said and done." Mr. Ackerman said.

Next, Akiri looked at the leader of the builder's guild. "Are the new stables ready for our guests?"

"Yes, Your Grace, the construction was completed two days ago and the stalls will be stocked and ready to go this afternoon before guests start arriving."

"I assume if there were any threats or concerns for the security of the castle or your Queen, you would have already acted, right, Ser Stewart?" Horace Stewart silently nodded to his queen. "Okay, then this concludes today's meeting, Mr. Koffery, if you would, please, tell my chambermaids I would like to have a bath drawn," Akiri said as she stood up. The council members stood as well and waited for their queen to exit the council chamber.

As Akiri walked down the hall, she heard the voice of the woman in her head again. *One of them will betray you,* the voice whispered. Akiri turned back to look at the door. Horace Stewart and the guard who stood outside the chamber door were only a few feet away from her as they usually were, protecting her, yet still giving her space. The other men filed out of the room and scattered in all directions to attend to their other duties.

"Ser Stewart, may I ask you something?" Akiri looked at the man in his silver half-plate armor and green cloak.

"Yes, My Queen."

"You are sworn to me, by the oath of your life to the sword, yes?"

"Yes, My Queen." Akiri moved in close to the Captain of the Queen's Guard and whispered her next words.

"If one of the men on my council would betray me, who would you think it would be?"

"Your Grace, I could not say, but if you like, I have eyes and ears all over the city ready at my command, would you have me utilize them?"

"Yes, please. I received a grave warning from the seer and we must be vigilant, she said someone on my council would betray me."

"The seer? She was presumed dead after you returned without her and the ship."

"She is not dead, I can tell you for certain. It does seem very strange she would want to warn me of anything. I was not very kind to her when she sailed with me to Choddrath."

"Perhaps the betrayer is her, and sowing these seeds of mistrust within your counsel is her way of isolating you from your protectors. I will send word to all of my informants and see what they can find out."

"Thank you." Akiri turned around and walked toward her bedchamber. As she entered, her guards remained at the door, facing outward with their hands folded in front of them. Akiri crossed the room and put the invitation back on the writing desk where she'd found it.

She stepped out of her shoes and undressed before heading to the bath. Steam rose from the tub in slow but steady wisps. Akiri dipped a toe in to make sure it wasn't too hot and then eased herself into the water. Her muscles relaxed and all the tension in her lower back and shoulders slowly eased away as the hot water enveloped her. She closed her eyes, relishing in the comfort of weightlessness. She leaned back in the water, floating on her back, ears fully submerged; the sounds of the old castle melted away.

When Akiri opened her eyes, the water was cold. She stepped out of the bath and grabbed her robe, quickly rapping it around her wet body and securing the belt, she tiptoed across the stone floor, leaving small puddles of water beneath her feet as she moved from her bed chamber, into the hall. Everyone was gone, the guards, the lady's maids, servants—everyone. The castle was too quiet. There was no light coming in through the windows, and no lanterns to light. Akiri held the stone banister as she descended the stairs. Reaching the bottom, she looked at her hand; it was covered in a layer of thick, gray dust from the railing.

The room started to spin and everything became a blur. When the world stopped moving around her, Akiri could see she was in her lair. An underground cave built for her dragon form. The council wanted her to lay eggs to produce more dragons to protect the kingdom. Akiri wondered if it was really to protect the Kingdom, or if it was to have more power than the other kingdoms or cities. From the back of the lair, Akiri heard a small snuffling sound. She walked back to the nest in the back of her lair and she saw the tiniest baby dragon.

It wasn't green like her, it was as dark as the night sky, and it looked up at her with such big bluish-green eyes. She knelt beside the dragon and put her hands out in front of it. With little hesitation, the tiny dragon crawled into her hands. It snuggled against the warmth of her skin and curled into a ball. It trusted her like a child trusts a mother. Akiri watched the dragon sleep in her palms, admiring each bump of its skin. She felt connected to it. This was her child, her dragon.

Akiri knew it was a dream-she knew it, but she didn't want to wake up. This new, indescribable feeling overwhelmed her. She had never been so happy. The little creature in her hand started to fade, and the lair around her began to disappear. "No! I'm not ready!" She screamed, but the dream melted away and she startled awake in her cold bathwater.

Akiri knew what it was— feeling—it was love. She would do anything to feel it again. It meant she would have to produce a clutch, she wanted to raise a dragon.

FIVE

RYUL DID NOT COME down for breakfast, Nor did he send any messages. By lunch, Sophie began to worry. The teleportation circle was not working. Ryul usually erased or changed one of the runes at night so no one could teleport in and disturb his slumber so this didn't particularly bother her, but the fact he had been so silent and had not eaten caused her to worry. She took a tray of lunch up the stairs. She'd forgotten how many steps there were, two hundred to get to the library alone, then probably another hundred steps to get to the top, where Ryul's room was. By the time she reached his door, she was out of breath.

Sophie knocked quietly and waited for any sound from the other side. When she heard none, she opened the door slowly and peeked in. The hinges on the door creaked loudly, giving her away. *No point in trying to be stealthy now,* Sophie thought. She walked across the dark and musty room to the desk and set down the tray of food. She glided to the window, parting the heavy curtains, and opened the shutters to let in some fresh air. Sophie called for Ryul as she walked around his room. He had already made his bed, and was nowhere to be found. On the nightstand beside his bed, she saw it- the letter addressed to her.

Sophie-

I wish I could have stayed to teach you more, but I am afraid my illness is getting worse. Although the lives of my ancestors are long, we are not immortal. I have gone to the elven city of Ravenhall to be with what is left

213

of my family. I wanted to spare you seeing me like this. You have a special gift and have already learned so much. You are ready to take the torch and lead the way. You are the last red dragon, Queen of the Red Order, and you are becoming a powerful wizard. I have left you the tower and all of its contents. The wards and protections will expire upon my death, so practice what we have been working on and set up your own defenses. Most of all, Don't be like me, enjoy your family and friends and live life to the fullest.

All my best,

-Ryul

Tears rolled down her cheeks and she made no effort to wipe them away. They dripped from her face onto the paper, smearing the ink in small circles. She had known this day was coming, he had told her as much, but she didn't think it would be so soon. Sophie couldn't tell if she was sad or angry, probably both. *Why did he not say goodbye in person? Did he not value our friendship more than this?* Sophie crumpled the letter and threw it to the floor, leaving the tray of food where it was, she ran from the room. Taking the stairs two at a time, she descended the tower and kept running out the the front door and across the yard. Before she got to the edge of the cliff, her wings emerged. The rest of her dragon form followed and in one swift transformation and she was no longer a girl, but a mighty red dragon, flying over Blackwater Bay toward her home, her family, and Gabe.

She flew north, to the training arena so she would not have to land in the forest. When her talons touched the ground below, the momentum from her flight propelled her forward. She slowed herself with every step until she was finally able to come to a complete stop. Transforming back into her human form, she cast a quick illusion spell to make herself appear dressed. *This will work well enough until I get home,* she thought.

From the arena behind the Silver Talons Guild Hall, Sophie walked around the building and through the western side of Blackwater. Her family's home was not extravagant, but just as plain as all the other houses in town, although, it was a little larger than the others, as befitting a Guildmaster's station. Sophie opened the door and looked around. Samantha leaned around the corner to see who had come in and called to Sophie from the kitchen where she was hanging herbs to dry. Sophie turned and wiped her face and eyes to clean up any evidence of her distress and hurried to her mother. A few bundles of sage and rosemary remained on the counter as Samantha hung the last of the lavender.

"Hi Sophie, it's so good to see you, how's training going?" Samantha asked, opening her arms. Sophie melted into the comfort of her mother's embrace and her chest heaved as she tried to stifle sobs . Samantha didn't force her to talk, she just held her tightly. It had been so long since Sophie had been home, she'd let her mother hold her forever if she could.

"Ryul left, he's dying. He left me a letter and I didn't even get to say goodbye, I just thought..." Her words trailed off as she buried her face in Samantha's shoulder.

"Shh, I'm here, my sweet, my little Sophie Sweet." Samantha brushed her hand up and down her daughter's back as she held her close. Sophie Sweet was the nickname her mother called her when she was little. It always made her feel safe and happy. Sophie pulled away slowly and forced a sad smile then began helping Samantha hang the herbs. They tied string around five or six stems to make a bunch, then hung them upside down from the flower drying rack hanging above the counter. When The herbs were finished, Sophie thought of Gabe.

"Mama, I'm going to stop by and see Gabe," Sophie said. Samantha offered a nod and smiled, indicating her approval. Sophie went to her room to change into real clothes, her spell would only last an hour and it had almost been that long already since she'd arrived. Her room was just as she had left it, not a thing was out of place. On her desk, three of the five feathers she had plucked from a sleeping raven, called to her like a muse. She picked up the longest of the three and suddenly felt the urge to write. She thought of Gabe and grabbed a piece of parchment. For this spell, she didn't need ink. She had practiced this with Ryul many times during her training. Sophie wrote:

Meet me at the willow tree. -S

The words showed up on the parchment lightly, as if she had written them with water. Then they disappeared. If it worked, Gabe would be at the tree by the time she got there. Sophie dressed quickly, putting on a pair of her most comfortable trousers, a fitted tunic tapered at the waist, and a pair of brown sandals. She pulled her bouncy red curls into a bunch, separated her hair into three sections, and braided it to one side. When she was finished, the braid almost reached her waist.

The thought of seeing Gabe made her nervous, although she didn't know why. They had spent their whole childhood together, he knew her better than anyone else, yet still her anxiety rose as she walked across town. The Blackwater market was bustling with shoppers going from cart to cart for vegetables, fruits, jewelry, eggs, and various cooked foods. The air smelled of roasted meat and exotic spices and herbs. Sophie hurried past, trying to resist. She hadn't brought her coin pouch with her and if she lingered, hunger would take over the urgency to make it to the forest, and seeing Gabe was more important to her.

Sophie took the same path through the trees she always took, only now, it was overgrown and untrodden. It made her wonder if her spell had worked, but as soon as she made it past the first set of trees, the willow came into view, and Gabe as well. He was a man now, not the boy she remembered him being not even a year ago. His shoulders had broadened; he looked stronger; more muscular. His face now had a light stubble on it which made him seem older. She stood still for a moment watching him, taking notice of all the vast differences a year had made. She could feel her chest fluttering and stirring as she gazed at him. She regretted the timing of their kiss and how she'd left to learn magic with the wizard.

Sophie would have stood there frozen for even longer, but he glanced up from the stream and saw her. She moved out of the thicket and into the clearing under the willow. She expected him to run to her, but he didn't. He smiled, but there was a pain he couldn't hide behind it. She walked up to embrace him, but anxiety made her pause. She saw moisture welling in Gabe's eyes.

"I'm sorry I—

"No, Soph, it's okay, I know why you went to the tower, it's just…" Gabe's voice caught in his throat and his turmoil grew more evident. "My father passed," he said.

"I'm so sorry. I didn't know." Sophie tried to reach out to caress his cheek, but Gabe backed away.

"My mom drank her feelings every night down at the Loose Anchor, she gambled away every last copper we had and when the coin ran out, she gave up the deed to the house. I couldn't let them take my mother's home and kick her out to the cobblestones like a rat, but let's face it, Soph, scribes don't get paid well enough to cover that kind of debt." Gabe wiped a tear from his face. Sophie had no idea what he was about to say next, but she knew it was painful for him. "I'm sorry, Sophie... I accepted a position with the guild to pay off my mother's debt. The house is free and clear, and the deed belongs to me so no one can ever take it from her, but I am leaving for a new post in two days' time.

"They're sending you on an assignment alone, without a team of guild members?" Sophie asked, confused. "They wouldn't, my father wouldn't..."

"Not exactly. It's a top-secret assignment, so I can't say more. I just want to tell you: I will always love you, but you have to move on," Gabe said.

"You say that like you're not coming back." Sophie couldn't hide the fear in her voice. "You're coming back, right?"

Gabe shook his head, "I'm sorry." He turned away from Sophie quickly, before she could see his tears. She stood there as he walked away, crying under the willow where she and Gabe had so many memories, where they had played as children, read stories from around the world as teens, played in the creek, and collected components for Sophie's spells. It was there, under the willow, where they had shared their first kiss, and now, it was there, under the willow, where Gabe broke Sophie's heart.

SIX

THE SUN WAS BRIGHT and hot, shining down on the packed arena. Akiri regretted her wardrobe choice not even one match into the tournament; black was not a good color to wear on a day like this. Sweat ran down her back, dampening the fabric of her dress. Akiri held her hand to her brow, shielding her eyes from the harsh sunlight as she looked down at the two competitors on horseback, charging each other with sticks. She'd always found such sports dreadfully boring but as the Queen of Ash, she had to at least feign interest in the tournament. After the joust, was archery, then hand-to-hand combat, weapons combat, and finally, the last competition of the day: magical combat. She at least found one event to be worth watching.

When the day was finally over and she was back in her chamber, Akiri undressed with haste, never more satisfied to be unlaced. Even though she had a layer of cloth beneath her corset, it still clung to her and was completely soaked through. The whale bones inside the garment left indentations on her skin, and even though she was no longer wearing it, the hourglass shape remained. She admired her curves in the looking glass; no longer seeing the child she once was; rather a woman, with a narrow waist, thick hips—perfect for child-bearing, or so she'd heard the men on her council whisper when they thought no one could hear.

Akiri cleaned herself up and dressed quickly in her flying robes. First she'd attend the post-event council meeting, make her announcement, then she would fly to clear her mind and free her from the day's responsibilities. She walked down the hall, her guards following closely behind her until she reached the council chamber. Pausing in front of the room, she allowed her guards to step forward to open the doors for her. The men were already seated around the table and all stood up as she entered. She motioned for them all to sit down and walked swiftly to her seat.

"I called you here because I have urgent news. Through private correspondence and political outreach, I have chosen a husband. We will meet at Prince Dominic's Royal ball and travel back here together to be married within a week of our arrival. I think a clutch of eggs, and an heir or two were both sound suggestions. I will need you, Mr. Koffery, and Mr. Ackerman, to set up, and decorate for a royal wedding. I want a private ceremony, but afterward, gather the entire kingdom in the front courtyard for our first public appearance and King and Queen."

"Yes, My Queen," they said in unison.

A pain shot through Akiri's abdomen, she tried her best to hide her discomfort, pressing a hand to her stomach and she forced herself to continue the meeting.

"Mr. Ackerman, did we come out ahead from the tournament?"

"Yes, Your Grace, we are several platinum richer after the settlements," he replied, wiggling his nose back and forth as if it itched, but he dared not to scratch in front of her. This movement only made him appear more rodent-like than he already did. Akiri always thought perhaps this was the reason she favored him. She'd befriended a small mouse in her childhood and he reminded her of that.

"Good, apply the extra coin to the wedding. Meeting adjourned." Akiri gave no one time to question her further, she was Queen after all, she didn't have to adhere to the demands of the men seated around her table, and she had no parents to arrange a marriage for her. It could be her choice. She'd marry now for political reasons and perhaps love would follow. She hoped it would, anyway.

Akiri left the council room with as much poise and grace as she could muster, but as soon as she was out of their sight, she made an expeditious retreat from the castle to her lair. The lower right side of her stomach cramped, and pain ripped through her from front to back. She experienced cramps like these every month, they usually hit a day or two before her month's blood, but this time it was different. They felt stronger and lasted longer. Akiri took off her robe and shifted into her dragon form. She curled onto her nest and tried to breathe through it. Her dragon form absorbed some of the pain of which her human body could not. What would have been a groan in her human form came out as a thunderous roar and she was certain everyone in on the castle grounds probably heard her. She spent the whole night in the lair, curled in her nest. By morning, the pain had dulled and she was energized enough to take a flight.

When she returned to the castle, everyone was busy with wedding preparations, cleaning and decorating. Her betrothed would arrive in a couple more days, and she had to prepare herself as well. Akiri soaked in a tub of milk and lavender to soften her skin and give it a fragrant scent. She washed her hair with rice water. It was just her luck; her month's blood would come soon- just as her future husband was to arrive. She didn't know if others could tell, but her Draconic blood heightened her senses and she thought during this time of the month, she had a very distinct smell, like old coppers that had been rolling around in the trouser pockets of a thousand villagers, or like the smell of the miners after a long day of extracting iron.

After her bath, she put on a pair of snug-fitted undergarments and lined them with a folded absorbent cloth. Next, she put on a pair of sheepskin bloomers to prevent leaking during the night. While she dressed, her chamber maids turned down her bed and put a warming pan under her sheets at the foot. They also had a blanket warming by the fire to cover her after she crawled into bed. The warm blanket eased her muscles as the ladies tucked her in. She didn't even hear them creep out of the room before she drifted off comfortably to sleep.

The next day, Akiri did not feel like going to the council chambers, so she had her maids set up seven chairs around the hearth in her room. They assured her, preparations for her intended's arrival were on track and they had put coins into the pocket of every local shop owner in the kingdom as per her wishes. Of course, they were all interested to know which suitor she had chosen, but Akiri liked feeling in control of her choices and gave nothing away. She did not need a council of men telling her who to marry. She was Queen and had made this match for herself.

After the meeting, Akiri asked for some warm tea and a pain relief tonic. The maids brought it to her and warmed her blanket again. She thought about the kingdom under her mother's rule, and how much happier the subjects were now since the crown was no longer imposing harsh collections on their businesses. The tournament and gladiator arena not only provided income for the kingdom but entertainment to the subjects. She was making a difference, and soon, she would secure her line of succession and have a family of dragons to guard their homeland.

SEVEN

Leon Rend sat behind his mahogany desk with his hands folded in front of him. The furnishings in his office were all matching in a carved wood décor and had a very sophisticated style which Gabe was not used to. He fidgeted in his chair, across the desk from the Guildmaster, who looked at him with a stone expression. Gabe was waiting for him to say something about Sophie, certain Commander Rend had already gotten an earful from her after hearing the news of Gabe's new guild posting.

"We need to talk about your assignment, Gabe," Leon said. A twinge of hope lodged in his chest. *Is he calling the whole thing off?* Gabe wondered.

"When you get there, and it's done, I will need you to be able to get messages back here secretly. What I am about to teach you, cannot leave this room. We need a telepathic link to each other, but it cannot be an item, just in case you are stripped of your possessions and searched for magical items, so we need to create a link in a more dangerous way, but it is undetectable. The only way someone would know is if they are reading your mind while you send the message, so you have to make sure you are alone when you transmit your thoughts." Leon said.

Gabe was not sure what he meant by all of this, but his hopes of getting out of this disappeared as quickly as they'd come.

"Sir, I had hoped we might talk about Sophie, is she okay?" Gabe asked.

"You didn't tell her the details of the assignment did you?" Leon's stone expression turned to alarm.

"Only that I was leaving, not what I was leaving to do," Gabe replied.

"Good, the less she knows the better. She will be fine, in my teens, I suffered more than a few broken hearts and still ended up a happily married man, I am sure Sophie will be no different."

Leon's words brought no comfort. The thought of Sophie married to someone other than him, weighed on his chest as if a boulder were crushing his heart. He could not hide his pained expression from Leon's perceptive gaze.

"I know this is hard for you too. I know you love my daughter. I am sorry, If we had a better option, I want you to know, I would have given you my blessing for you to marry Sophie." Leon paused and his face softened. "It doesn't have to be forever, but we really need a young man on the inside, and it might take a long time to earn their trust and influence their council members." Leon looked back down at the paperwork in front of him bearing his signature and seal. Knowing he would have had Commander Rend's blessing made leaving Sophie even harder. In another life, they could have been together. In another life, they could have been happy. Gabe choked back his emotions and buried them deep, clearing his throat before continuing.

"So, how do we form the telepathic link?" he asked.

"With this." Leon opened his top desk drawer and pulled out a small wooden container. The inside of the box was lined with ice, it had to be a spell, there was no other way to get ice in summer, except in the Icewind Channel above the city of Northport, and it would be melted by the time it reached Blackwater in this weather. Gabe looked at the two pieces of gray matter inside, they seemed to be pulsing with electricity and beating like a heart.

"What is it?" Gabe asked.

"This is the neural pathway of a mensmonstrum," Leon said as he picked up a piece and slid the box over to Gabe.

"Wait- those things are *real*? I thought those were an old fable told by parents to get their children to be honest."

"No, they are very real. They live in a world deep beneath ours, where no sunlight ever shines, and only evil thrives. If we share this piece of elder brain, it will create a neural link between us and our minds will be able to send messages to each other. This is a closely guarded secret, not many people know about this ability. Luckily, our necromancer is infinitely wise and forever advancing knowledge of our bodies, as well as those of our enemies. This link will only last a few weeks or so, long enough for you to carry out phase one and report," he paused, holding up the piece of brain. "Well, no time like the present." Leon popped the fleshy tissue into his mouth and swallowed it whole.

"I thought you said this was dangerous?" Gabe asked as he ate his piece apprehensively. Unable to swallow it whole as Leon had, Gabe had to chew it to make it smaller. It was nearly the same as a fatty steak; gelatinous and a little stringy. The texture activated Gabe's gag reflex and he almost threw up before he could swallow the last bit.

"It can be, sometimes the host brain tries to reject the neural link and they will hear whispers forever, or sounds which pain them physically as well as mentally-it can drive a person mad," Leon said. "It could take up to a day to complete the fusion of our minds, but let me know right away if you hear whispers, screeching, or anything like that, okay?" Leon stood up and rounded the desk to Gabe as he got up and headed for the door.

"I will, Sir," Gabe said, stepping into the hall. Leon nodded and closed the door behind him.

That night, Gabe had trouble sleeping. A million thoughts ran through his mind, but the most recurring one, was the sight of Sophie as he turned away from her. The memory was sure to haunt him until he returned if the day ever came. Gabe rolled over and cried into his pillow until he fell asleep.

In the morning, he heard Leon's unexpected voice in his mind.

"*This is a test, Gabe can you hear me?*"

"Yes," Gabe answered aloud.

"*Don't speak your answer, imagine me standing there in front of you and just think what you want to say.*"

"*Oh, okay, like this?*" Gabe thought.

"Yes exactly," Leon said.

"*Can you hear my thoughts all the time?*" Gabe asked.

"*No, only when you mean for me to hear,*" Leon replied.

Gabe really hoped Leon was telling the truth. He didn't want anyone to know the anguish he felt at the thought of leaving Sophie behind. It would only make what he had to do much more difficult.

EIGHT

Kamara and Dominic flew to Ledora together. Dominic did not want to break the news to his father until the ball. He was sure guests were already arriving, so Kamara's presence would not necessarily give them away. Before they left The Temple of Ophay, Dominic made a special bag he could carry in dragon form so they could bring a change of clothes with them. They dressed on the beach, the moon was nearly full—tomorrow night it would be. If Dominic believed such things, he might have warned his father against having a royal ball on the night of a full moon. He didn't believe such things though, people behaving oddly had less to do with the moon, and more to do with the person themselves.

Before heading into the city, Dominic embraced Kamara and pressed his lips to hers already counting the moments until he would get the chance to hold her in his arms again. The moonlight danced on her skin, illuminating the tiny hairs on her neck, and her arms, which now stood on end. She wrapped her arms around his neck and kissed him back, deeply. If circumstances were different and his father's health were not failing, Dominic would have gladly stayed at the temple with Kamara for as long as possible.

"We should split up, if we walk in together, they may suspect something. My father took a lot of time to plan the ball, and I would like for him to think it was through his efforts we were matched," Dominic said.

"I understand. I will go into the city to go shopping for a new dress before I come to the castle, May I have my coin pouch please?" Kamara gave him a sly smile as he dug into his bag to pull out the last item in it. The pouch jingled with gold dragons, the Ledoran currency. She had exchanged the generic gold pieces they used on the mainland the last time she visited Ledora and Dominic had thankfully reminded her to grab the pouch before they left Ophay.

"Thanks. I will see you soon." She blew him a kiss as she walked toward the entrance to the golden city as he turned in the opposite direction, shuffling toward the castle. missing her already.

"Prince Dominic, there you are!" The King's jovial voice rang out through the foyer as Dominic entered. He was standing with two elegantly dressed, older women. "I want to introduce you to a couple of our guests. This is Lady Harlow, of Ellsworth, and a proxy of Lady Delacroix of Immernacht who was unable to attend herself, they have both brought their daughters to meet you at the ball tomorrow night." King Haki stepped back to let the ladies engage with the prince.

"It's so lovely to meet you both," Dominic said as he suavely swept each woman's hand to his lips and placed a gentle, courteous kiss just above the knuckle of their middle finger.

"King Haki, you said he was handsome, but I am afraid you did not do him justice." Lady Harlow said.

"My lady, you are too kind." Dominic put on his best diplomatic voice. "I am terribly sorry, but I just got back from my travels and I am afraid I need to freshen up. I look forward to seeing you and meeting your daughters tomorrow night." The ladies bowed to him as he left and went up the stairs to his chamber. He did not bother calling for the castle staff, Dominic waved his hands around a cauldron on the floor beside the hearth. Blue wisps of light encircled the pot, swirling as his hands moved. The cauldron began to fill with water. When it was full, he lifted it and hung it on the iron tripod inside the fireplace. He produced a bolt of flame launching it from his hand, onto logs beneath the black iron pot.

Dominic walked to the balcony of his room. It overlooked the courtyard and he could see more guests arriving. He hoped he would see Kamara returning from her shopping trip, but he heard the low rolling sound of boiling. Dominic used a spell to levitate the cauldron to the tub and pour the water into it, and then he used another incantation to double the amount of hot water in his bath. He draped his arm over the side of the tub and ran his fingers across the surface of the water, his fingers turned blue and steam rose from the bath until Dominic pulled his hand away from the water. He touched his hair, fingering the rows of braids which had grown out almost a fingertip's length since it had been braided last.

When the temperature was just right, Dominic stepped into the bath and eased himself down into the heat. scrubbed his body with a cloth and a bar of soap, then unbraided his hair so he could wash it as well. He would have it re-done in the morning. When he finished his bath, Dominic massaged mineral oil onto his skin, paying extra-close attention to his hands, elbows, and knees. He pulled his hair back into a silk cap and secured it tightly so it would not move during the night. The festivities would begin at lunchtime and continue throughout the day, so he needed to get some sleep. As soon as his head rested on his pillow, Dominic was in a deep, dreamless, slumber.

NINE

AN EARLY SUMMER BREEZE blew through the window and rustled the papers on Sophie's desk. She rushed over to the scene and placed a book on top of the invitation to secure it in place while she packed. Sophie looked at her bed and Leon's old leather backpack, the one she'd carried with her to Choddrath only a year ago. She had piles of clothing folded and laid out across the bed, not everything was going to fit into the backpack, so she would have to make some choices. If she left within the next hour or two, Sophie would be in Ledora by late afternoon and would have plenty of time to shop for a new ball gown.

She grabbed her coin pouch and put it into the bag first, then her spell book. Next, she added a stack of sleeping clothes and a stack of plain day clothes. Sophie crossed the room and grabbed her hair comb, a box of hair pins, and her lavender pomade from the top of her chest of drawers. She made it half-way back to the bed, but turned back abruptly, adding a bottle of perfume to her already filled arms and crossed back to the bed. She dropped everything into her bag and closed up the backpack.

Okay, coin purse, spell book, sleep clothes, day clothes, hair things, perfume... It seems like I'm forgetting something, Sophie thought. She looked around the room, but couldn't think of anything she'd forgotten. Sophie removed her dressing robe, hung it on the back of her bedroom door, and then cast the illusion spell to make herself appear dressed.

Downstairs, her mother was in the kitchen baking pastries for her sweet shop. Samantha smiled as Sophie entered the room and offered her a pastry.

"Thanks, Mama," he said, taking a bite of the soft, freshly baked treat. "I'm heading out to Ledora today for Prince Dominic's ball."

"I'm so happy you decided to go anyway. I know you would have invited Gabe if things had been different. I hope you will still be friends when he comes home, and you won't be angry with him for long." Samantha said.

"We'll see, Mama. I love you." Sophie kissed her mother's cheek and waved as she walked toward the door.

"I love you too, Sophie. Be careful!" Samantha called.

Sophie nearly ran to the arena. She was sure Gabe already left, but just in case she was wrong, she made haste to avoid running into him, she couldn't handle a second goodbye. When she made it to the center of the arena, she laid her backpack on the ground in front of her, took a few steps back from it, and stretched, pushing her appendages outward. Bones cracked and contorted as her body grew and transformed into a red dragon. She gently hooked a tooth under one of the straps of her backpack, so she could use her talons to get a running start.

The beating of her wings kicked up the dust covering the arena floor and left a cloud beneath her as she lifted from the ground and toward the clouds. Sophie ascended until she could see nothing but the sky. She felt so free above the clouds, like nothing mattered, not her broken heart, not Ryul joining his ancestors, not her father sending Gabe away, and least of all, where she was going to choose to live when she returned. Lapis Highland was hers now, and she did still have a group of red dragon enthusiasts who called her Queen and were loyal to her. Lapis Highland could be her own kingdom, but her family was in Blackwater.

Sophie flew for hours to get to Ledora, the sunlight made it difficult for her to see but her calculations were correct, it was late afternoon when she touched down on the eastern beach of The Golden Kingdom. As she resumed her human form, Sophie noticed the tracks of two other dragons in the sand. *How strange, the green dragon would surely land on the western beach given the location of Ash,* Sophie thought. She'd never even learned the name of the green dragon. She hadn't thought much about her at all since the day her father told the guild council she declined the invitation to join the Dragon Alliance. Sophie wasn't even sure what they were calling themselves these days, Dragon Council, assembly, committee, union... nothing much had changed; only one new law had been made, and it was proposed by Leon- killing a dragon was now punishable by death.

Sophie dressed on the beach and then walked toward the castle. She wanted to find her room and drop off her bag before going shopping. As she approached the gates in front of the castle, two heavily armored guards blocked her path.

"State your business," one said.

"I'm here to attend the royal ball," Sophie told them.

"Present your invitation," said the other guard.

Sophie took off her pack and reached inside, feeling for the stiff parchment on which the invitation had been written. She dug to the bottom of the bag before her mind thought back to the window and the breeze that almost blew the invite away. She saw it plainly under the book on her desk.

"I accidentally left it," Sophie said. "But, I am Queen Sophie, of Lapis Highland and Blackwater."

"Come back when you have an invitation or an escort." The guard did not even look her in the eye, he kept his gaze fixed forward on nothing at all in particular.

"It will take me hours to fly home and back!" Sophie protested. Their eyes widened with surprise when she said "fly", but they stood firm.

"An invitation, or an escort, Miss Sophie."

She huffed at them as she walked away. *Great*, she thought. Instead of arguing further when it was obvious it would get her nowhere, Sophie walked toward the city. She could find a dress and then go through her spell book to see if she could get a message to Prince Dominic.

Ledora was beautiful; tall white archways trimmed in gold marked the entrance to every street. The city guards wore golden half-plate and white cloaks trimmed in gold embroidery. The buildings were all pristine, not a single broken shutter or stone out of place. Instead of the clapboard houses they had in Blackwater, these buildings were all made from white clay. The trim sparkled with a golden shimmer, and each door bore the symbol of the golden sun with a dragon silhouette.

Sophie wandered around, looking at all the shops and taverns in amazement. Ledora made Blackwater seem like a remote village, growing up there it had always seemed so big when she had nothing to compare it to. Sophie walked into the first dress shop she saw. The inside was lavishly decorated with a formal sitting area, beautiful antique looking glasses, several changing areas, and plenty of staff to help patrons get into their formal wear. There were rows and rows of dresses hanging from horizontal poles. At the front of each row, a mannequin modeled a dress which could be found on the corresponding rack. The dresses came in all sizes and each one was just a little different in style but the racks were sorted by color. Sophie had never shopped in a place like this, she rarely wore dresses before becoming Queen, and in those days, when she did, they were made for her by the guild seamstress.

"Looking for a gown to wear to the ball?" A woman's voice interrupted Sophie's thoughts and she looked up from the dressed to greet her.

"Yes Ma'am, but I'm afraid I don't know what size to get."

"I can help you, dear," she said. "My name is Adelaide, but you can call me Addie, and what's yours, dear?" she asked.

"Sophie Rend."

"Oh, Sophie, what a beautiful name, and what beautiful red hair you have. I think I know just the dress for you, but we will have to get your measurements first." Addie walked over to the counter and grabbed a ribbon with strange markings on it like the ones on the sticks the builders used to measure materials. Addie wrapped the ribbon around Sophie's waist, and then her chest, hips, the length of her torso from her belly button to the curve of her waist and then from her breast bone to her belly button, and finally, the length of her arm. She wrote the measurements on a piece of paper and then led Sophie to one of the privacy screens.

"This is Margaret, and Henrietta, they will help you dress. Do you need an underbodice?"

"I'm sorry a what?" Sophie asked.

"It's okay, dear, I will bring you one, go ahead and undress."

Sophie did as instructed and Addie started bringing pieces of clothing to Margaret. The first was a white cotton tube with drawstrings on both ends. Margaret instructed Sophie to put her arms up and then slipped the fabric over her head. She pulled the first drawstring so the garment was snug beneath Sophie's breasts and tied it in the back. Then she tightened the bottom, which went down to Sophie's hip.

Then Addie handed Henrietta a cream-colored corset with metal clasps on the front. Henrietta fitted it around Sophie's waist and lined up the hourglass shape of the corset with the natural curve of Sophie's waist and then she hooked the busk. Margaret had Sophie put her hands on the wall as she began tightening her corset, hooking a finger under the intersections of string and pulling each one, from the bottom to the top, until she came to the middle. Sophie was surprised at how comfortable the corset was, she was prepared to feel pain, or to have trouble breathing, but she found the garment took the pressure off of her lower back and improved her posture-which at times, could be pretty atrocious.

Next, they dressed her in a petticoat with sewn-in hip pads. Then came the dress. It was a beautiful dark green silk dress with a golden pattern on the bodice and skirt which Addie called *damask*, except for the triangle which started at a point in the middle and fanned out to the outsides of her feet. That section of the dress was a shimmering emerald green. The sleeves belled out at the elbow and were layered in the green damask and black to match the front of the dress. When Sophie saw her reflection, she did not see a girl who longed to be a wizard or the mighty dragon, she saw a woman suited for life at court. Sophie expected to hate it, but she didn't. It made her feel more beautiful than she'd ever felt before, she was a Queen, but now she looked the part.

"What do you think?" Addie asked her.

"I love it. How much is it?"

"Everything you have on is a total of one hundred gold dragons," Addie replied.

"Oh." Sophie pulled some gold out of her coin pouch. "All I have are these," she said. Sophie hadn't even thought Ledora might use their own currency, Everywhere she had been previously all used the same gold, but she was across the ocean now.

"Okay, let me weigh it." Addie put a piece of Sophie's gold into the bowl of a scale and put a piece of Ledoran gold on the other side. The side with the Ledoran gold was slightly heavier. Addie added another of Sophie's gold and it tipped the scale the other way.

"Throw in twenty more of these, and we have a deal because I like you," Addie said.

"Sophie counted out one hundred and eighteen more gold and added it to the other two on the counter.

"You will be sure to win the Prince's heart in this dress," Addie commented.

"No, but I-" Sophie began to tell her she wasn't here to win Dominic's heart but stopped short.

"Sophie?" A familiar voice startled her and she turned toward the doorway.

"Kamara!" Sophie exclaimed.

"You look amazing!" Kamara gushed. "Is this what you're wearing tonight?"

"Yes, I was thinking about changing back into my day clothes but I'm not sure how I would get back into this dress," Sophie admitted.

"We can get ready together! Addie, would you please have this dress sent to the castle with mine?" Kamara asked.

"It would be my pleasure, Miss Kamara," Addie replied.

"I saw you through the window and had to say hi. Get changed, I'll wait for you, we have a lot to catch up on!" Kamara said with a grin nearly stretching from ear to ear.

Sophie excused herself to go back behind the dressing screen to change. Margaret and Henrietta helped her remove all of the pieces of her ball gown. They hung and packed the pieces neatly together and marked the cover with Sophie's name.

When Sophie was dressed she stepped out from behind the screen to see Kamara was still waiting for her as promised.

"Are you heading to the castle now? We can walk together."

"I do need an escort. I forgot my invitation at home," Sophie explained.

"No problem, I can get us in." Kamara pulled out her invitation.

They left the shop together, strolling toward the castle leisurely. Sophie noticed a shop called The White Raven. The window display showcased crystals and pendulums, tapestries of mystical elements, and herbs and other components for spells. She made a mental note to return there someday.

When they got back to the castle, Kamara presented her invitation and the guards moved aside allowing them both to enter without question.

"When did you get here?" Sophie asked.

"I arrived yesterday," Kamara replied. Sophie remembered the dragon tracks from the beach.

"Did you land on the eastern beach?"

"Yeah, why do you ask?"

"I saw two sets of dragon prints on the beach when I landed, I thought maybe you were here, but I wondered who the other set belonged to."

"Shh, I have much to tell you, but let's get up to my chamber first." Kamara smiled as she thought about whatever it was she wanted to tell her, and Sophie couldn't tell for sure, but she thought Kamara was blushing.

The inside of the castle was more beautiful than the outside. The floor was made of dark gray marble and had a path of white tiles, edged with gold down the center of every hallway and leading to the throne. Beautiful archways much like the ones in the city lined both the eastern and western sides of the throne room. On their way to Kamara's chamber, they ran into Prince Dominic. They curtsied and greeted the Prince according to the customs of the court.

"Please, we are friends," Dominic said as he motioned for them to stand. "Sophie, it's so good to see you, where is Gabe? I thought he would be here with you?" Dominic asked.

Sophie's smile faded and she looked forlorn. "He left for assignment with the guild," Sophie explained.

"Ah well, next time then?" Dominic asked.

"Sure, next time," she said.

"There will be no shortage of noble young men here tonight, I would say fill your dance card with as many of them as possible and save one for me," Dominic said. He gave both Sophie and Kamara a quick hug. Sophie noticed the way Dominic embraced Kamara a moment longer than her and the pieces began to fit together. Sophie was certain she already knew what Kamara had to tell her, but she would not spoil her friend's joy by pointing it out. When Dominic walked away the two women hurried to Kamara's chamber like school girls ready to gossip.

When they reached Kamara's room they closed the door and made their way to the bed, hopping onto it and sitting with their legs crossed.

"What is your news? What has you smiling so wide... or should I ask *who*?" Sophie asked.

"No, you first, it seemed like you were sad when Dominic brought up Gabe, did something happen?"

"He told me he was leaving on assignment with the guild and I needed to move on." Sophie's eyes welled with tears. "It took me all this time to finally admit there was anything more than friendship between us, then I left to train with Ryul. I took everything for granted. I thought Gabe would always be there, and now, I think I have lost him."

Kamara scooted closer to Sophie on the large canopy bed. She reached out and wiped the tears from her cheek.

"I'm so sorry, Sophie. I know how much he cared about you, I don't understand why he would just leave." Kamara put her arm around Sophie's shoulder.

"Whatever, I want to try not to think about it tonight, there are plenty of attractive nobles here tonight to help me forget." Sophie forced a smile. "What about you? You said you had so much to tell me earlier and I am dying to know."

"Well, it's about the other set of tracks you saw on the beach. They were Dominic's," Kamara said.

"What were you two doing out there?" Sophie asked. "Wait- were you..."

"Shh!" Kamara covered Sophie's mouth with her hand. "He came to visit me at the temple. We flew back together."

"Are you guys courting?" Sophie asked. Before Kamara could answer the question there was a knock on her chamber door.

"I have a delivery for Kamara and Sophie from Adelaide's." Kamara opened the door and took the dresses from the servant. She thanked him and hurried back to the bed to lay out their dresses.

"It's time for us to get ready!" Kamara squealed excitedly. Sophie couldn't tell if the change in subject was deliberate, or a well-timed coincidence, but Kamara was already taking the pieces of their dresses from their packages.

Sophie helped Kamara with her corset, and then she did the same for her. When they were dressed, they did each other's hair and sprayed a little of Sophie's perfume on the inside of their wrists. The perfume was a symbol of status, not everyone could afford the fragrances, for each was hand-made by a perfumer. This skill was not a common one, so supply was very short and the demand was high. Perfumes were expensive, and only royalty could usually afford them. Sophie's had been a gift from Leon and she used it very sparingly.

"Are you ready? You look gorgeous!" Sophie said, admiring the gold ball gown Kamara had chosen.

"I'm ready, you?" Sophie nodded. "Don't think about *him* tonight; enjoy yourself," Kamara said as she took Sophie by the hand.

"I plan to," she replied.

TEN

Queen Akiri admired her form in the looking glass; the black lace dress she wore hugged every curve and her porcelain skin peeked through in the most strategic places. There was no way her new intended would not fall to his knees at the sight of her in this gown. She picked up the finishing touch; a crown made of silver and onyx. She watched it glimmer in the mirror as she placed it delicately on her head. A knock on the door startled her and made her jump. The crown fell and she fumbled to keep it from hitting the stone floor. Akiri let out a heavy sigh, secured the crown to her head once more, pressing it down for a tighter hold.

She paced the room, clutching a handkerchief in her hand. "Hello, it's lovely to meet you," she said, practicing aloud. Akiri gave a quick curtsy, until she remembered she was no longer a princess, but a queen, and queens didn't bow to anyone. She extended her hand for a shake then pulled it back with a jerk. No, *not like that*, she thought, then tried again, this time fingertips down daintily offering it for her imaginary partner to kiss.

She startled when the knock on her chamber door signaled the time. "Your Majesty, we are ready for you," the Ledoran ambassador called from the hall.

"Thank you, Sir." Akiri quickly brushed her hands down the front of her gown and tucked a few flyaway strands of hair behind her ears as the doors opened.

The Ledoran ambassador led toward the end of the hall to the grand ballroom and when they reached the staircase, he directed her to the wing on her left. "We are going to announce the new royal couples, ladies will wait in this line, gentlemen in the other," he said as he pointed to the other hall. "When we call your names you will meet at the top of the stairs, bow to each other, and descend the stairs for your first public appearance together," he explained.

Akiri nodded and joined the other women in line. She was too far back to see into the other hallway, but it didn't stop her from craning her neck to try. She thought about all the letters she'd gotten from potential suitors and how smug most of them had seemed. A lot of them were royalty—princes who were fourth or tenth in line for their own thrones and longed for a crown, but the letter from "Suitor number twelve" was different. He wasn't looking for a crown, but an escape. He didn't come right out and say it in his letter, but Akiri guessed he'd had his heart broken and the daily reminders were too much to bear. He seemed sweet and had a sense of humor which was more than she could say for most of the men who wrote to her.

The line moved up as the announcer called the first name. Akiri stepped forward and tried to see past the line again with no success. She wondered if he would be tall, or as handsome as his portrait. She crossed her fingers for luck as the line inched forward again. Tapping her fingers on her thighs, Akiri grew closer to the front with each announcement. When the last girl in front of her moved out of the way, she could see him waiting in the opposite angled hall. His brown hair was neatly groomed and when their eyes met, he smiled. His teeth shined like the whitest pearls and her heart fluttered, he was even more beautiful in person.

ELEVEN

Sophie grabbed a small bunch of grapes and placed it on her plate next to chunks of pineapple and coconut shavings. Kamara's plate looked similar and Sophie knew it was because they rarely got fresh tropical fruit in Blackwater and Ophay. The announcer's voice rang out across the ballroom as if he were projecting it.

"Introducing, the newest royal engagements of the season; Princess Juliette and her betrothed, Sir Andrew Lee." Sophie glanced at the top of the stairs as a young woman came from the right and a man from the left. They paused together at the top of the stairs before descending into the ballroom. "Next, Prince Stephan, and his betrothed, Miss Angela Flores." Sophie poured another glass of punch from the large bowl and took a few sips. After each announcement, the ballroom erupted with applause. Sophie was only half listening as she popped another grape into her mouth.

"Queen Akiri Of Ash and her betrothed, Gabriel Taylor." Sophie gasped and the grape rolled into her throat, she coughed, trying to force the fruit back up. *It can't be, no... it can't.* Sophie thought as Kamara hit her on the back until the grape launched out of her throat and rolled across the ballroom floor. All sound faded away for a moment as her heart seemingly plummeted from her chest. She thought she heard Kamara's voice asking if she was okay, but it faded away too until all she could hear was the beating of her heart. Sophie kept her eyes fixed to the top of the stairs and sure enough, it was Gabe. *Her* Gabe, here, with Akiri. Not just *with* Akiri, but *engaged to* her. Sophie turned to face the table and gulped down her punch. She thought about escaping, but just as she turned to look for the nearest exit, the first dance began. She had already promised her first three dances. The first gentleman approached her, bowed, and extended his hand politely.

"Are you okay?" He asked her as she placed her hands where they needed to be. He twirled her softly into the center of the dance floor. He glided so effortlessly it was as if her feet barely touched the marble below.

"I just had a bit of a shock is all. I'm sorry," Sophie said trying to shake off her feelings of anger and rejection.

"What is your name?" he asked.

"Sophie," she responded, but her eyes were searching the ballroom, darting from face to face as they swayed.

"A beautiful name, for a beautiful woman. I am Bastian, it is a pleasure to meet you."

"The pleasure is all mine," she replied dutifully. Finally, she spotted Gabe and Akiri dancing. He didn't even glance in her direction, his eyes were fixed on his new fiancée.

"I see, was he an old flame?" The question startled Sophie, she hadn't realized her staring had been so obvious.

"Days old," Sophie admitted bitterly. "Apologies, I just found out, normally I would not be this rude when a handsome gentleman asks me to dance."

"I am sorry your heart has been broken, but if I may be so bold to say, it is *his* loss, truly." Bastian smiled and she looked up at him for the first time. He was handsome, polite, kind, and understanding, yet she could not tear her attention away from Gabe.

"Thank you for saying so, you're too kind." Sophie tried to enjoy Bastian's company, but she hadn't even had time to process the shock before the dance began, and then, it was over much too soon. The music ended and the couples moved back to the sides of the room.

"I would love to dance again later if you wish, or we could take a walk onto the terrace and just get to know each other. Until then, Sophie."

He bowed to her and disappeared into the crowd. Why would he be interested in dancing with her again? She'd given him very little attention and it had been clear to him her heart already belonged to another.

Sophie looked at her card. She did not see the man who had signed his name under the second dance. Kamara was dancing with someone already, and she had lost sight of Gabe and Akiri, which was probably for the best.

"May I have this dance?" Sophie turned to see Dominic extending his hand to her. She nodded and followed him to the floor. He held her close as they began their dance.

"I'm sorry, Sophie. I had no idea. I never would have asked you about him had I known." Dominic spoke close to her ear so she could hear him over the music.

"It's okay, I didn't know either. It was a total shock to see him here." The crowd parted just enough for Gabe and Akiri to come back into her view and she couldn't stop a tear from rolling down her cheek. Dominic wiped it away with his thumb as he held her close to comfort her.

"I have an idea," he said, stealthily guiding them closer to Gabe and Akiri. "Put on your brave face Sophie, and try to look like you're into me, just a little." Dominic chuckled as he slid his hand up Sophie's back and dipped her, when she rose to face him again his lips were less than an inch from hers, she could feel his warm breath on her lips as he caressed her cheek with the back of his knuckles and then trailed his breath down her neck and to her cleavage as he leaned her back in his arms once more. Sophie could feel Gabe's gaze on them, but she didn't even look his way. She was staring at the prince who so willingly chose to show Gabe what he was missing.

In the middle of the song, Dominic felt a tap on his shoulder. His smile indicated he had expected this to happen and he turned to face Gabe.

"May I cut in?" he asked.

"I am sorry, I do not wish to give up my time with Sophie. Perhaps you can find her later," Dominic replied as he moved his forehead to touch Sophie's again. He looked into her eyes and held her full attention. Gabe huffed as he walked away. When the dance ended, Dominic leaned in to whisper in her ear. "Let me know if you need a rescue later," he winked as he backed away, allowing her next dance partner to offer his hand.

After her third partner, there was an intermission for the band, and a chance for the dancers to get a drink. Sophie grabbed two chalices of wine from a passing tray and hastily drank both.

"Hey, Sophie!" Kamara called. "That was quite a dance huh?" She smiled at her friend.

"Yes, Prince Dominic is a wonderful dancer, the closeness, I assure you was just to spite Gabe," Sophie explained, afraid Kamara would get the wrong idea about her and the Prince.

"I know, it's fine. Honestly, I thought it was kind of...hot." Kamara raised her eyebrows and pursed her lips slightly. Sophie grinned as she let out a gasp of shock.

"Kamara!" she scolded playfully.

"What? Can you blame me? Look at you both!" She fanned herself and then giggled nervously.

"Excuse me, would you like to dance with me next?" A man asked as he offered his hand to Kamara.

"I would be delighted," she said, handing him her dance card.

"I will meet you over by the refreshments. I think I need another drink," Kamara said as he finished signing his name.

"I could use another drink too," Sophie said. They crossed the room together and by the time they reached the table, Kamara's next dance partner already had two glasses of punch poured.

"You got over here quickly," Kamara commented. He held the cups out to both her and Sophie.

"Thank you, sir, Kamara replied, taking both from him and passing one to her friend.

As Sophie sipped her punch, Bastian approached her again. He was dressed in a white suit with a blue tunic underneath and his wardrobe went strikingly well with his shoulder-length blond hair.

"Sophie, It would honor me greatly to dance with you again," he said.

"It would be my pleasure," she replied, handing him her ballspende. "This time I promise to be more attentive."

Of all the men she danced with, Bastian was her favorite. Not because he was the best dancer, that was definitely Dominic, but because he was interested in getting to know her and didn't only talk about himself like a lot of the other men did. He asked her questions about her life, hopes, and dreams, her friends and as she went on an on about these things, his attention never strayed.

In between dances, Sophie pounded back glasses of wine, until eventually, she was numb to the pain. Most of her senses were dulled by the alcohol, but the sensation she felt at another's touch was heightened. She especially loved the way Bastian's hands held her as they danced, and the way he glided his fingertips up and down her arms. She wasn't sure how it happened, but she found herself kissing him. Bastian was surprised by her sudden desire but eagerly kissed her back and they moved slowly out of the crowd until Sophie's back was against the wall and Bastian was so close she could feel the heat from his body even through the layers of their clothing. His lips crashed into hers desperately and Sophie had forgotten there was anyone else in the room until Bastian groggily tore his lips away from hers and turned to see Gabe standing behind him.

"Can I cut in, please?" he asked with disdain in his voice.

Bastian was too disoriented from their heavy public display of affection to refuse, he moved aside, allowing Gabe to sweep Sophie back to the dance floor.

"What are you doing?" Gabe asked angrily.

"What do you mean? I'm enjoying myself like you should be doing," Sophie fired back.

"First, you let Prince Dominic all but publicly claim you as his mistress on the dance floor, and now this... Are you trying to punish me?" Gabe gestured to Bastian who had retreated to the refreshment table.

"Prince Dominic didn't clai—"

"His hands and lips were all over you, Sophie! In front of everyone, what are people supposed to think?"

"At least I didn't show up engaged." Sophie could not hide the bitterness in her voice.

"I know how it looks. It's not what you think."

"So, you're not engaged then?" she demanded. When Gabe did not confirm, she nodded at him, her lips pressed into a tight line as she searched for words.

"That's what I thought." She tried to pull away from him but he held her hand and twirled her back in so his lips were next to her ear.

"I never stopped loving you. My engagement is business, not pleasure. Do you really think this is what I wanted?"

"How am I supposed to know what you want any more, Gabe?"

"It will always be you." Gabe made a quick retreat, leaving her standing there desperate for him to stay but at the same time, unable to bear the sight of him. She watched as Akiri found him and wrapped her arms around his waist. She whispered something in his ear and they disappeared from the ballroom.

The ringing of a bell caught her attention and the King spoke.

"My son, Prince Dominic, has chosen his future bride!" Cheering and applause broke out across the grand room. When Prince Dominic joined him on the stage, many of the girls he had danced with throughout the evening screamed at the sight of him, hoping he was about to call one of their names.

"Lady Kamara of Ophay, would you join me please?" Dominic waited for her to come up onto the throne platform with him. He took her hand and got down on one knee.

"You are the light in my darkness, and more beautiful than all the stars in the night sky, will you please make me the happiest man alive and give me the honor of being your husband?"

"Yes," she whispered through tears as he slid a beautiful opal ring onto her finger.

Dominic stood and kissed her. The crowd cheered again but not in the excited way they had before.

"Now, the final dance is for the future King and his future Queen!" King Haki announced. The ballroom cleared as Dominic and Kamara walked down the steps and onto the dance floor. They looked at each other like they were the only two people in the room. Sophie wanted that too someday. She downed another glass of wine as she watched them sway to the music. They danced alone for the first minute of the song, until others were allowed to join them on the dance floor.

Bastian appeared with a soft and empathetic smile, holding his hand out to Sophie. She never noticed how his blue eyes sparkled until now. She placed her hand in his and followed him into the dancing crowd.

TWELVE

WHEN THE BALL WAS finally over, Dominic and Kamara disappeared from the crowd and made their way to the beach. Soon, they were in the sky, the two dragons raced through the clouds. Dominic sent a flash of lightning from his mouth across the endless night. Kamara's breath blew cold and each droplet formed into crystals and fell softly through the sky. Each snowflake turned to rain before it reached the ground. *It must look like a thunderstorm to the people down there,* Kamara thought. The dragons tangled themselves together as they danced through the stars, savoring the freedom while they had it.

By the time they reached the Temple of Ophay, the sun was just beginning to peek over the horizon. Kamara's home was their own private getaway; the best place for a newly engaged couple to celebrate. Very few people knew about the temple, those in Blackwater, and of course, Dominic's father.

Kamara led him around the side of the temple and through the gardens. The cliff-face standing before them now had a large tunnel leading into an enormous cavern. They walked inside the entrance and took in the natural splendor. Turquoise hot springs bubbled softly in a large deep pool reflecting the speleothems descending from the rocks above like icicles made of stone.

"I only wanted a small lair, but when the builders opened the entrance to this by accident, they were done. It was perfect and made by the Goddess—mother of the land. It's like it was meant to be".

"Wow, this place is incredible," Dominic said. He strolled to the back of the cavern to the largest nest he'd ever seen. Turquoise hot springs bubbled softly in a large deep pool reflecting the stalactites descending from the rocks above like icicles made of stone.

"What's this for?" he asked, walking around the large bed of twigs, moss, flowers and furs.

"It's for our eggs. I have done a lot of research while here. Dragon couples have the highest chance of producing viable dragon eggs. Those who mate with humans have a lower chance, but it isn't impossible. Our children could also become shifters themselves at the end of their seventeenth year as we did. Dragons who mate with humans have less of a chance of their child being a shifter, but their offspring can be just as powerful as they inherit draconic sorcery from the bloodline."

"So, you've been thinking of having kids already huh?" Dominic flashed a mischievous grin at Kamara with a raised brow as he slid his arm around her waist, pulling her close to him. She gave him a playful shove, but melted into his embrace. His lips brushed hers gently and made every part of her body tingle with excitement. Holding both of her hands in his, Dominic stepped backward into the shallow end of the hot spring. Kamara followed him into the bubbling water. Finding a perfect, seat-shaped rock, Dominic sat down, guiding Kamara to his lap. She pressed her lips to his softly as his hands roamed her body. He hardened from her touch, throbbing with desire. Kamara shifted to straddle him, positioning him at her entrance. He groaned as her sex brushed against his. He cupped her breast, moving his thumb back and forth across the peak of her nipple. She moaned with pleasure as she rolled her hips to envelop his length.

His eyes widened and without meaning to, he abruptly floated her away from him. Breathing hard, he bent forward, the pain of his own denial of pleasure almost too much to bear. Kamara looked at him with concern and a bit of shock, having no understanding of what happened. "I'm sorry. I want to... trust me, I have never wanted anything or anyone as much as I want this, but we must wait until after the wedding. If you had a child before we wed, you'd be unfit to take the throne. I need you, there is no way I can do this without you." His voice came out a little more than a whisper and he winced in discomfort.

"I understand, but there are ways to find release which could not possibly result in reproduction. Let me help you." She moved closer to him, caressing his face as he met her gaze.

Kamara and Dominic spent hours in the cavern, taking turns pleasuring each other and when they could no longer evade sleep, went back inside the temple to a new room Kamara had the builders construct as an engagement gift; a royal chamber fit for a King and Queen. A four-poster canopy bed with heavy curtains to block out the morning light sat upon a raised platform.

"I know we will be spending most of our time in Ledora, but I thought we could keep the temple as a home away from home, somewhere we can visit when the pressures of court become too much."

"It's perfect. We don't have to live in Ledora; not until I have to assume the throne. We could live here until then. We could raise our children here, away from court and the weight of responsibility. Here they will be safe. I will see to it. We can invite some staff and security here and turn this place into our little village, just for us."

"It sounds amazing," Kamara replied dreamily.

They fell asleep snuggled together in the middle of the enormous bed. Kamara's dreams played out their life together, the children they might have, and the dragons they could become.

The next morning, Dominic and Kamara made the trek north through the forest to Blackwater. They spoke to the Guildmaster, Leon Rend, about contracting help from the guild to make improvements on the temple, and about buying some horses. Leon sent them to the stable master with a letter of importance. Sometimes the wait list for a horse was long, mares carry their foal for almost a full year and only give birth to one. It takes three years before a horse is of breeding age, and two years before most breeders will sell.

Kamara gave the letter to the stable master and he led them to the horses.

"I only 'ave two colts right now, they're two and a half years old, or thereabout. If you're lookin' to breed 'em, you can come back next spring and this gal here will be ready t' go." He pointed to a mare across the stable.

"It's okay, Sir. We'll take the two Colts, we are going to ride them ourselves, or hitch them to a cart when needed."

"Okie Dokie then." The man said as he began preparing the horses. When he was finished, Kamara paid him and they took the horses with a lead and a feed bag. Next, they went to the saddle maker. She measured their horses and wrote everything down.

"Give me about a week and I will have them done for you," she said. Kamara and Dominic noticed the several saddles she and her three apprentices were already working on and simply nodded to her.

"Thank you very much," Kamara said as they left.

"Anything else you want to do while in town?" Dominic asked Kamara. She thought about it, and suddenly, her face lit up.

"We should stop by and visit Juniper and Laughlin," she said.

They led their horses through the eastern forest. Kamara took in her favorite sights and sounds, green foliage guiding winding pathways through the forest, trees older than time itself, and birds singing in the canopy above. It all brought her great joy.

When Laughlin and Juniper's cabin finally came into view, Dominic hitched the horses to a nearby oak so he and Kamara could go to the door together. As they took the first step onto the porch, Dusk let out a loud bark from behind the door and startled them. Dominic knocked and waited for someone inside to answer. Laughlin opened the door a few moments alter and a smile spread across his face at the sight of them. Dusk sniffed the air from behind him and when she realized there was no threat, the wolf returned to the round rug in front of the fireplace and laid down.

"Hey, how are you guys? Long time no see," Laughlin said as he moved aside and gestured for them to come in.

"Is Juniper here? We were hoping to share our news with both of you." Kamara looked around and then at Laughlin.

"Uh, no, she went out to gather herbs and said she needed the fresh air. She should be back soon though if you want to wait, I'll put on some tea." Laughlin said grabbing his kettle from the wood stove. He filled it up from a pipe above his kitchen wash basin. Kamara looked at it in astonishment.

"How?" she asked, still staring at the faucet.

"I made a special rain collection system. Come, I'll show you." Laughlin led them out the patio door and pointed to a barrel he had mounted to the side of his house. "Inside the bottom of this barrel, I layered different materials used for filtration, I covered the top of the filter with a thin white cloth. I attached this bit of hose, it's a new bendable material, which makes my life easier. When I lift this handle, the pressure on the hose releases, allowing the water to flow, and when I push it down like this, it puts pressure on the hose and stops the flow of water."

"Wow, nice! We need a setup like this for our place." Dominic said to Kamara.

"Oh, is this your news? You're moving in together?" Laughlin asked. "We have news too, but I need to let Juni tell you herself."

"It's a little more than moving in together," Kamara told him.

Just then the kettle started whistling and Laughlin rushed over to pull it off of the wood stove and pour the hot liquid into teacups. Just as they took their seats around the table, Juniper came in. Right away, Kamara and Dominic could see what news Juniper had to tell them. She had a perfectly round and swollen belly.

"Juniper! Are you..." Kamara began. Juniper nodded and grinned from ear to ear. She hugged her friends tightly and they took turns putting their hands on her belly to see if they could feel the life growing inside her.

"I am so happy for you guys!" Kamara squealed.

"Me too," Dominic said.

"What was your news?" Laughlin asked.

"We are engaged, and talking about making the temple of Ophay our home until we are needed in Ledora to rule."

"How wonderful! When is the wedding?" Juniper asked.

"We didn't talk about it yet," Kamara said as she looked at Dominic.

"Soon, I hope," Dominic said, he looked at Kamara with starry eyes. She smiled and leaned over to rest her head on his shoulder.

"Good news all around. This deserves a celebration, a housewarming, and an engagement party. I can plan it if Kamara will handle the guest list, and Dominic, you, and Laughlin can help with decorating. We will meet you at the temple tomorrow morning to get started." Juniper couldn't hide her excitement. The four of them talked for more than an hour, until hunger set it. They said their farewells and departed.

Kamara and Dominic rode the horses bareback to the temple. Dominic gave them a bale of hay to distract them while casting a spell. He raised both hands with his palms facing the horses, moving them in a circle as blue runes rose from the ground and spread like lightning across the dome. He turned to see Kamara watching him.

"This will protect them from the weather until we get the stable built," he explained.

"I'm thinking about naming mine Phoenix. How about you?" Kamara said.

"I'm not sure, I'm going to sleep on it. Maybe you could think of a name for mine tonight." Dominic replied. They turned from the horses and walked back inside to settle in for the evening.

THIRTEEN

The morning air was no cooler than the day before had been, the southern heat was just as he'd always heard it was. Akiri led Gabe through the courtyard and past the city toward the western coast. "How are we getting back to Ash?" he asked.

"We're going to fly, of course, but don't worry, I had a special saddle made to strap a rider to my back," she replied.

"Oh," Gabe managed to choke out. Anxiety crept up inside him and stuck in his throat like a crabapple. He wiped his palms on his trousers as they continued walking across the beach. The saddle was larger than he thought it would be and the closer they got, the larger it seemed to grow. He'd never flown on dragon back before and to be honest, he'd hoped never to have to.

"So, what was going on in there between you and the red dragon?" Akiri asked as she packed her things into the saddle bags and positioned the straps where she needed them to be.

"Huh?" Gabe looked up, abandoning his thoughts and meeting her glare. "What do you mean?"

"The girl you danced with last night with curly red hair. I know you traveled to Choddrath together, but you seemed worried about her last night, so I was wondering if you used to court her?"

"Not exactly. We grew up together is all, we were just friends," Gabe said.

"Were? Meaning you aren't anymore?" Akiri's face reflected concern and Gabe wasn't sure if it was for him, or for the state of his relationship status.

"We had an argument a few days ago and we just hadn't talked since, I didn't want to leave without apologizing is all," he told her. Akiri turned back to the saddle, seemingly satisfied with his answer.

"When I take shape, you have to buckle the harness around me. Make sure the belts are tight." Akiri went under the saddle, which looked more like a cave compared to her human form. Gabe could hear her bones cracking as she changed shape and when her dragon form emerged, her shining green scales shimmered in the moonlight. Gabe watched in amazement as her body continued to grow into the underside of the saddle perfectly and when the leather was snug around her body, Gabe pulled the belts tight and buckled them.

A large saddle bag hung from each side and Akiri had packed their clothes in them. Beside the saddle bag on the dragon's right side was a ladder to climb up into the seat. Gabe strapped his legs into the leather sleeves which buckled just above his knees. The backrest had a belt to wear across his chest as well and by the time he was all strapped in, he felt surprisingly safe.

When Akiri started to run, the momentum pushed Gabe's body back against the saddle and when she lifted off the ground, he closed his eyes. His heart was pounding so hard and fast, he thought it might beat out of his chest. His palms were damp with sweat so he wrapped the reins around his hands to maintain his grip. He didn't know how high off the ground they were, but he was sure if he opened his eyes to look he would pass out.

When Akiri was finally gliding smoothly in a straight line, Gabe found the courage to open his eyes. Stretching on forever, as far as his eyes could see, the night sky glittered with millions of stars. His heart thumped faster as he dared to look down. He was thankful for the clouds, which obscured the truth of how high up they actually were.

Flying wasn't as bad as Gabe had expected. Before the end, he thought he might even like it, but as they neared The Kingdom of Ash, Akiri pointed her nose down and Gabe's stomach dropped. He felt like he might be sick as they descended. The wind pounded into his face, stinging like tiny needles poking his skin and he found it hard to breathe. Leaning forward, Gabe positioned his face behind Akiri's head to block the wind.

She landed in the arena and waited for Gabe to unbuckle and dismount before returning to human form. Gabe looked away as Akiri grabbed a dress out of the saddle bag, slipped it on, then detached her luggage from the saddle and threw the strap over her shoulder like a soldier's duffel. She went to the other side, unhooked the other bag, and gave it to Gabe to carry.

"I told my council we wanted privacy tonight so we will have to carry our things. Come on, I'll show you to your chamber. I have a council meeting after I get you settled and I am sure they will all want to meet you before the wedding tomorrow night, but you can rest for now and I will let them know you will accompany me to the council chamber tomorrow morning." Akiri was no longer the girl he had spent the night dancing with, she was now Queen Akiri; a monarch with duties, and responsibilities. Gabe thought about his mission here, so far he had nothing to report. He was listening for plans and plots against the Dragons Guild, which was the new governing body of the northern continent. Akiri's refusal to join the guild was viewed as a seed of mistrust. The Silver Talons Guild, mostly Leon, wanted to know more about the Queen of Ash. He specifically wanted to know what her plans were, and how she was using her dragon powers, and he wanted Gabe to make friends with someone on her council. He wasn't ready to get married-especially to someone he met only hours ago, but if he didn't go through with it he would blow his cover which might mean death, and if he did, he would lose Sophie forever. He wasn't sure which was worse.

The outside of the castle was dark; a collection of black, towering, spires silhouetted the full moon. The decorations for the wedding made it look festive and welcoming though. Lilies of every color and bright blue roses lined the walkway to the castle doors. Strings of small oil lanterns illuminated the flower gardens, making the dark fortress seem almost inviting.

The interior of the castle was dimly lit. Black iron sconces held torches and illuminated the hallways in soft flickering light. The shadows moved like ghosts and followed them down the hall. Akiri opened a door to a large bedchamber. Despite the look of the rest of the castle, this room was brighter. The bedding was royal blue with black velvet buttons sewn into the comforter where the material gathered together to make it look like a royal cushion. An abstract painting above the hearth looked like a stained glass window. The top of the canvas was even curved into a semi-circle to enhance the illusion of a window. Had it been on the wall, and not the fireplace, Gabe might have mistaken it for a real stained glass window. A large Chandelier with unlit candles hung from the center of the ceiling and gave the room a touch more elegance. The fire in the hearth was new, the three logs were barely burned and would last the night at least.

"You can have the servants draw you a bath if you like. This will eventually be our room, but until you're comfortable and we know each other a little better, I will stay in my old room just down the hall." Akiri smiled and nodded as she turned toward the door. She paused in the doorway, "Sleep well, I'll see you in the morning."

Akiri was not what he'd expected. When they met on Choddrath, he had been too preoccupied with trying to save Sophie to pay her much attention except when she was slinging spells at him during the battle. He expected her to be cruel, much like all the stories he heard about her mother, the late Queen Luciana, but so far, she seemed kind. Gabe wondered if it was just to make him feel comfortable until the wedding. They didn't have much time to get to know each other. She was in a hurry to be married for some reason, and it wasn't about wealth, because he didn't have any of that.

Gabe didn't bother having the servants draw him a bath, he would have to bathe before the wedding anyway. He changed into his sleeping clothes and snuggled between the sheets which were smooth as silk but as soft and warm as his cotton stockings. He was about to close his eyes when a knock on the door startled him.

"Yes?" he answered. Two servants walked in, both boys and younger than Gabe. He guessed them to have seen no more than the thirteenth anniversary of their birth. Gabe stayed under the covers in his half-dressed state as they busied themselves about the room. They picked up the clothes he had just taken off and put them into a basket for washing. One of the boys had red hair and Gabe caught himself thinking about Sophie and if someday her son would have the same look about him.

"Would you like a bed warmer, Sir?" The dark-haired boy asked. Gabe nodded and the kid grabbed a metal pan with a long handle. Gabe watched him scoop hot coals from the bottom of the hearth to fill it. The lid had holes in it to vent the heat and he fitted it over the bottom lip of the pan perfectly. The boy lifted the comforter and the sheets at the foot of the bed and slid the warmer in. Gabe hadn't realized before how cold his toes had been, but the coals in the pan made them feel toasty; the warmth spread throughout his body and he shivered as the last bit of cold left him. Gabe was more comfortable than he had ever been before, but still, he could not fall asleep.

FOURTEEN

THE MEN SEATED AROUND the table in the council chamber rose from their chairs when Akiri entered the room. She waved at them to sit back down making her way to the head of the table. "I won't take much of your time, just a quick announcement from Ledora; Prince Dominic chose Kamara, the silver dragon, to be his bride. I met my betrothed and we traveled back together as planned. There were no other events of significance to report. Thank you for making yourselves scarce as requested for our return." Akiri settled into her seat.

"My Queen, this is most unorthodox. Are you really going to trust this man you've known only for a day to rule at your side?" The captain of the city guard objected.

"I have not met any of the other men who requested my hand either, so are you upset I am engaged and the six of you did not get to choose my future husband or are you upset that you yourself weren't considered?" Akiri looked at each of them and when no one said another word, she continued. "Well? If anyone has anything to say about their queen's decision, it's best to get it out now." Some of the men looked down at the table, and others shifted uncomfortably in their chairs, but none of them spoke another word.

"Okay, good. Meeting adjourned, be back here in the morning for introductions, and please have a chair placed at the other end of the table for your future king." Akiri gestured to the spot directly across from her.

"Yes, My Queen," the council replied.

Akiri left the room as quickly as she'd come in and made her way back to her bedchamber. It was the same space she had been in since childhood. She could have moved to the Queen's quarters when she was crowned, but she found it hard to leave behind the memories her sanctuary had provided her all these years. Her mother had not been the sentimental type, so Akiri never really had toys to play with or even human friends. She hoped now, with Gabe, she could fill the emptiness and she would never feel lonely again.

She removed her dress and hung it on the outside of the wardrobe to wear again another day. She hadn't had it on long so it did not yet need to be taken for cleaning. Akiri crawled into bed, snuggling beneath the covers, but sleep evaded her. This time tomorrow she would be married. She wondered if they would share a bed on their wedding night. Akiri tossed and turned for what seemed like hours before finally giving up. Getting out of bed, she slipped on a long robe, pulling it over her shoulders and tying it in the front. Walking the castle at night always helped ease her mind on sleepless nights. Her guards stood outside the bedchamber door and when she passed, she motioned for them to stay. Reluctantly, they obeyed as she walked away. The torches in the long hall were no longer lit so she grabbed one and cast a light spell on it. The end of the torch glowed, but there were no flames. She carried it with her through the darkened halls and made her way to the kitchen. Placing the torch in the sconce just above the breakfast nook, Akiri opened the store room for the wine and ale. She did not need the torch in there, she knew exactly where her favorite wine was. She grabbed a bottle and turned around to see Gabe standing in the doorway.

"You couldn't sleep either?" he asked. Akiri shook her head. She had planned to drink the bottle of wine herself and force sleep to come, but since Gabe was here now, she thought it might be rude not to offer him some. She grabbed two silver chalices and they walked over to the table. She poured the fragrant liquid into both cups and slid one across the table to Gabe.

"Thank you," he replied, taking the chalice in hand.

"You're welcome. Are you nervous about tomorrow?" Akiri asked, drawing her cup to her lips and taking a long sip.

"I would be lying if I said I wasn't," Gabe admitted. "What about you?"

"Extremely." She gulped down her first cup of wine and poured another.

"How about while we drink, we get to know each other? It might ease some of our trepidations," Gabe suggested.

"Sure. You go first, ask me anything," Akiri told him. Gabe looked at her and thought about what to ask. He took a long drink of his wine as he studied her facial features and expression.

"What is your biggest fear?" he asked, finally.

"Oh, we're jumping right into the deep stuff. Okay, um... I guess the thing I am most afraid of is never knowing what love feels like." She didn't look at him, instead, Akiri took a drink before asking him a question. "What are your parents like?"

"When I was little, things were great, My dad was a jack of all trades, and my mom was a seamstress. I didn't grow up wealthy, but we weren't poor either. When my dad got injured and could no longer swing a hammer, or a sword, he became angry and was not a nice man anymore, maybe he never was, perhaps it just went beyond my notice because he was always working. My mom drank to deal with him, and then it spiraled downward from there. My dad passed away, and mom drank and gambled away any coin she had left. It was then I knew I would have to take care of myself." Akiri could see the pain in his eyes as he thought about his parents. *This was what he'd been trying to escape, the memories of a difficult childhood, like me,* she thought. "What were your parents like?" he asked.

"I don't remember my father. Mother never talked about him much either. Mother was cruel and only wanted what was best for her. She never cared about me." Akiri tipped her head back and finished off another drink.

"I'm sorry, I know it must have been a lonely life to grow up with a mother like her," Gabe replied, reaching across the table to place his hand on top of hers. Akiri looked up at him and his rich brown eyes stared into hers. Her face tingled as she admired his warm brown skin and the shape of his jawline. Pulling her hand away, Akiri poured another cup of wine.

"Yeah. Okay, next question, Have you ever been in love?" Akiri asked.

Gabe paused. He knew if he lied, his face would betray him, and honesty was important in a marriage, even an arranged one, so he answered with the truth. "Yes."

Akiri studied his face. "Are you still in love?" she asked.

"You don't get to go again, it's my turn." Gabe smiled, pretending to scold her, wagging his finger back and forth with a "tsk tsk" as she feigned surprise.

"Let's see here, I have to make my next question good." He thought for what seemed longer than a few moments to Akiri before he spoke. "When you think of the future of this Kingdom, what do you see?" He looked at her intently. She sipped her wine and a drop of the red liquid spilled out of the corner of her mouth and rolled to her chin. She wiped it away with the back of her hand. The answer was easy, she had been dreaming about it since she was a little girl.

"I see a Queen and King with many heirs living happily and doing everything they can to help the kingdom and all of its residents flourish."

"That's quite an answer. I like it," he said, pouring his second cup.

"My turn. The same question; are you in love right now?" Gabe had hoped she would forget her previous inquiry, but now he had to answer.

"Yes," he admitted. Akiri nodded, thinking quietly before continuing.

"The red dragon?" Akiri asked. She knew it was Gabe's turn, but she couldn't help it, the words came out involuntarily.

"Her name is Sophie, but yes. I fell in love with her, but she didn't choose me, so I decided to move on with my life far away from Blackwater, which is why I sent my proposal to you. I am glad you accepted and in time I could see myself falling in love with you too. We can help each other fill the loneliness in our hearts."

Akiri saw a pain in his eyes mirroring her own, she knew they were the same; craving love they never received. She couldn't resist any longer. Maybe it was the alcohol, or perhaps it was truly a connection. She laced her fingers through Gabe's, stood up and moved toward him. His eyes drifted over her face as he rose from his chair. She guided his hands to her waist and lightly grazed his neck with her fingertips. Gabe followed her lead as she moved her face toward his, pulling him closer. Her kiss was hungry and needful. She walked backward slowly, pulling him with her until her backside was against the table. She sat on the edge of it and wrapped her legs around him as they unleashed years of repressed passion. He trailed his hands up her robe and squeezed her outer thighs. The ties of her robe loosened and the shoulder fell to one side, exposing her breast to him. Gabe groaned and pressed his body against hers as they kissed. She could feel his bulge pressed against her inner thigh and she wanted nothing more at that moment than for him to ravage her right there on the kitchen table. She pushed her hands up the front of his tunic and felt his smooth abdomen and twirled her fingers in the tiny patch of hair on his chest. Her fingers trailed back down to the tie of his trousers, she pulled one of the strings and felt the knot pop as his trousers loosened. She was about to claim her prize when a noise from behind startled them.

"Ahem."

Akiri gasped and frantically adjusted her robe to cover herself as she spotted Roland Koffery, the castle steward, standing in the doorway.

"My apologies Your Majesty, I heard a commotion and came to investigate." Mister Koffery averted his gaze until Akiri was decent.

"It's alright, Mister Koffery, This is Gabriel Taylor of Blackwater, my intended."

"It is a pleasure to meet you, sir. I look forward to the wedding, which is another reason I was on my way to the kitchen; I have to begin the preparations for dinner tomorrow."

"We'll get out of your way. Akiri grabbed the chalices and crossed the room to get another bottle of wine from the store room. "Care for a nightcap?" She gently moved the bottle back and forth, holding it up to Gabe. He nodded as he tied his trouser strings and followed Akiri from the kitchen.

When they got to her room, she poured them each a glass. Akiri raised her cup to him.

"To the start of a marriage filled with adventure." Akiri's cheeks were bright pink as she smiled and touched her cup to Gabe's. Mister Koffery might have ruined the mood, but Gabe found he still craved satisfaction; the feel of her skin against his. He wondered what it was about her that had effected him so strongly. He was certain his chance with Sophie was gone, so moving on was really what was best for everyone. Akiri was beautiful, there was no denying, and it seemed they had a connection deeper than duty. He was there to do a job, but he saw no reason why he shouldn't enjoy it.

"Thank you for an enjoyable late night, but I should try to get some sleep now," Akiri said as she stood up from the chair beside the fireplace. "I will see you in the morning at the council meeting, but then not until the wedding. I hear it's terrible luck." She kissed him on the cheek before walking him to the door.

Gabe watched her with a longing gaze as she closed her bedroom door and left him standing in the hallway. He wandered back to his room and collapsed onto his bed with a groan. The soft cushion of the comforter enveloped him as if he were laying on a cloud. He slept deeply for a few hours until the servants came knocking once more.

FIFTEEN

MORNING LIGHT ROUSED SOPHIE from a deep sleep. She was still in Ledora, but this was not her bed. She lifted the sheet and comforter to reveal her naked body, then turned her head to see Bastian still asleep beside her. Sophie groaned quietly as she slid out of bed, sure she would die of embarrassment if he woke and then they'd have to have the awkward *'it's not you, it's me. I'm not ready for anything serious,'* conversation. Trying to piece together the events of the evening before, Sophie remembered Bastian asking her to dance, but she'd convinced him to drink with her instead. She was pretty sure they talked about Gabe, and she wondered if she'd given Bastian the chance to say anything about himself. Sophie knew she had not been good company last night, and would likely not be good company today either, but her sour mood hadn't stopped Bastian from taking her to his bed. She was certain at the time she had been willing to ease her pain with him, the handsome distraction he was, but now she was dressed, and it was time to go.

She tiptoed to the door and opened it slowly, hoping it wouldn't creak and wake him. She slipped into the hallway undetected, closing the door behind her. Sophie walked with hurried steps back to her room and gathered her things into Leon's pack. Taking off the clothes she had on and stuffing them in the bag as well, she cast illusion on herself to make it appear as though she had on a full set of fine clothing. Leaving her guest room with her bag in hand, Sophie made her way down the hall to the grand staircase. She couldn't wait to get back to Lapis Highland. *Perhaps there is a spell for mending a broken heart,* she thought. The comfort of her mother's arms never failed her though, so she decided to fly home first. She hated flying during the day, the sun was bright and always shined directly into her eyes, making it difficult to see where she was going. She knew the way back home though and was confident she could make it back to Blackwater by late afternoon. She just had to fly north.

When Sophie arrived in Blackwater, she landed in the arena to transform back into her human form. She pulled some clothing out of her bag and quickly dressed. When she was finished, she slung her father's leather backpack over her shoulder and headed toward her childhood home. The door was unlocked, so she pushed it open to see her father preparing to return to work.

"Hey kiddo," he said, wrapping her in a hug. "How are you doing?"

"Dad, can I talk to you?" Sophie asked. She hadn't had a chance to talk to him since she found out what Gabe's assignment was and she just needed to know why. Leon and Sophie walked out back to the garden and sat on a bench in the clearing of lilac bushes and peonies. It smelled so nice in the garden, she could see why her mother loved it so much.

"I think I know what this is about, and I can tell you, it's not what you think," Leon began.

"So Gabe isn't going to marry Akiri?" Sophie asked. She already knew the answer, but needed to let Leon know it was exactly what she thought.

"He is going to marry her, but it will give us a spy on the inside. We will know her plans and be warned if she ever decides to attack." Leon said.

"You're paranoid, why would she ever attack us?" Sophie couldn't control the anger in her voice.

"There are things you are still too young to understand. I have seen what power does to people, it makes them hungry. They always want more no matter how much they have, and how long do you think she will be happy being Queen of that hunk of rock where the only thing growing is sugar cane from hundreds of years of making rum?"

"You think she is planning an invasion." It was a statement, not a question, but Leon answered anyway.

"Yes, I think she will invade if given a chance, if not here, then Braidwood, or even Hillside, or Aerulean Lake. She did not join the Dragon Alliance, so she is not bound to any rules or guidelines we have put in place to protect the cities and the villagers across the continent."

"Why Gabe, though? I thought you liked him." Sophie was almost in tears now.

"Akiri sent out a request for suitors. She made a list of qualifications, he had to be around her age, taller than her, never married, and so on. Gabe was the only one in the guild who met all of the requirements so we had his portrait painted and sent to her with an offer letter. We didn't know she would accept so quickly, but apparently, she is in a hurry to get married—which is another cause for concern; why does she need to marry so quickly? With Gabe on her council and at her side, we will know her every move." Sophie leaned against Leon's shoulder and sniffled. "I'm sorry, again. I know how much he meant to you, but in time you will meet someone just as great as you are, I know it." Sophie wiped a tear from her cheek as she stood up.

"I should be getting back to the tower, I have to clean up and get some practice in," Sophie said.

"Okay, kiddo. I love you." Leon stood up and brushed the seat of his trousers.

"Love you too, Dad."

Sophie returned to the kitchen where her mom was sitting at the table drinking coffee. Sophie walked up behind Samantha and hugged her.

"I will see you soon, I have a lot of work to do at the tower," Sophie said.

"I can come over and help you later this week if you want, sweetie," Samantha replied, setting down her cup. She turned to face her and Samantha's eyes roamed Sophie's face, no doubt making a mental note of the redness around her eyes. She could hold it together until she got outside, at least that's what she kept telling herself. Whether or not she believed it was the real question.

"It's okay mom, I think I just need to be alone for a while to process everything."

"Okay, if you're sure," Samantha said. Sophie nodded and kissed her mother's cheek.

SIXTEEN

THE MAIN ROOM OFF the the foyer of Temple Ophay which was once used as the gathering place for worship now stood empty. Light filtered in through the enormous windows and cast shadows of the panes across the marble floor. Kamara had her sleeves rolled up and her hair tied back with a ribbon. She had already done so much to transform the temple into a home. The worship room seemed larger now and Kamara thought it would make a beautiful parlor for when they had company.

Dominic ordered furniture from the Silver Talons builders weeks ago and it was scheduled to be delivered by mid-day. He kept peeking out the front doors, waiting for the wagon to arrive. Kamara had a list of staff positions she needed to fill. She wrote them on two scrolls, one for the job board in Torzana, and one for the crier in Blackwater.

"I'm going to go deliver these, I will be back in about an hour," Kamara said, planting a kiss on Dominic's cheek.

"Okay, my love. I'll stay and wait for the furniture and hopefully when you get back this place will look like home." Kamara could see the joy on his face as he said the word 'home' and it made her heart soar. She couldn't wait to become his wife, and not just because he was a prince, or because he was destined to rule Ledora, not because he was rich, or handsome—incredibly handsome—nor was it because marrying him meant she would be Queen. None of it mattered half as much as the thought of spending the rest of her life with her best friend.

Kamara rode West to Torzana first because she knew it would take no time at all to post the parchment on the cork board at the tavern. Torzana had one road with about twenty homes, and it had always been a good place to find people in need of jobs. Torzana had one dock and their only export was fish. The market was open every day, and in addition to gold and silver, Torzana was open to bartering. Unfortunately for the teenagers of Torzana, there was not enough work to go around so many took jobs in Blackwater and even as far as Northport sometimes. Kamara rode straight to the tavern and dismounted, hitching her horse to the post. She pushed through the swinging saloon doors and headed for the billboard. Flies buzzed about and she swatted them away. It was hotter inside the tavern than it was outside despite the shade. A burley man behind the counter looked at her and offered a polite nod.

"Can I get you a drink? We have ale and uh..." his voice trailed off as he opened the cabinet behind him and peered into emptiness. Spider webs stretched from one corner half-way down the cabinet. "...and ale. Sorry miss, it's all we got 'til our caravanner gets back from Blackwater."

"Oh, thank you, but I really must be on my way, I have a lot of work to get done," she replied.

"Alrighty, good luck with it," he called as she made her way back to the exit. She thanked him and waved as the doors , whipped back and forth a couple times before settling in their closed position. She didn't stop to talk to anyone else, she had to hurry. Laughlin and Juniper were supposed to join them for tea in the afternoon. She rode on to Blackwater and went to the center of town where the crier usually stood, but he wasn't there. She continued through town toward the guild, if she couldn't track down the crier, at least she could deliver her request to Commander Rend, surely he could help get the word out. Kamara got off her horse and hitched him up. A young boy caught her attention. He was staring at the building in front of them with a sad expression.

"Waiting for someone?" she asked keeling down to be face-to face with him.

"No, what makes you ask that?" the boy answered.

"The way you keep watching the door, like any minute someone you know is going to open it."

"I tried t' get a job there, but they said I's too young." He shuffled his foot back and forth in the dirt.

"How old are you?" Kamara asked assessing his features. His face was gaunt and he was quite thin. He and his clothing were dirty, but he did not yet have the odor of a teenager.

"I'm ten," he answered.

"Where are your parents?"

"My dad left when I was just a baby, Mama never talked about him much, Mama got sick a while back and went to lay down, she went to sleep but never woke up. I told a cleric to see if she could heal her, but she said Mama's soul had already passed on. They took Mama, buried her, and then they took the house."

Kamara couldn't believe Commander Rend would leave a child homeless. It didn't seem like him. Leon was a good man, with a kind heart. He'd rescued her from the temple and put himself at risk doing it.

"Are you from Blackwater?"

"No, Ma'am, I'm from Northport, I stowed away on a ship because they tried to send me to the mines. I'm scared of the dark so I didn't want to, but a man hit me and said I would do what I was told. That's why I ran away."

"I'm sorry to hear it. It sounds like you've had an awful time. What's your name?"

"Johne," the boy answered.

"A good strong name, I'll make you a deal, Johne, if you can do a favor for me, I will give you a job."

"What d' I gotta do?" he asked.

"All you have to do is tell everyone you know about my temple, it just south through those woods. Tell them I am hiring staff and I can pay them well. I am to marry the prince of Ledora after all.

"Really? You're a real-life princess?" the boy's eyes widened.

"Not yet, but I will be, and you could come and work for me."

"That sounds nice, I wish more people were like you," he said.

"Well, I always heard good deeds have a way of coming back around, and so do bad ones, which is why I always try my hardest to do the right thing."

The boy smiled and took off with the scroll reading Kamara's words out loud. She got back on her horse and headed south toward home. She couldn't wait to get back, and hoped she would have time for a bath before Juniper and Laughlin arrived. The return trip didn't seem to take as long , perhaps because she didn't have to return to Torzana. Dominic was helping to unload the wagon of furniture when she approached the front entrance.

"Do you need my help?" Kamara asked.

"No, we can finish up here, you can relax and I'll take care of everything." Dominic kissed her on the forehead and her cheeks tingled. Kamara went to her bath chamber and plugged the tub. She pumped the handle up and down, and finally, water began pouring out of the spout. When the tub was full she took a cauldron and filled it. She carried it to the fire and hung it on the hook. While her bathwater heated, she went to the wardrobe to choose an outfit to wear for company.

The sound of a rolling boil came from the cauldron and Kamara took it off the fire with an iron. She carried it carefully to the bath tub and lowered it to the side, using the edge of the tub to tip the scorching bowl of hot water into the tub. The boiling water mixed with the now room temperature water produced a cloud of steam. Kamara set the empty cauldron on the bricks beside the fireplace and finally lowered herself into a nice warm bath.

As promised, by the time she got out of the bath and back downstairs, Dominic had the parlor furniture positioned and the room decorated. Three couches sat around a large table which they could use to serve coffee, tea, and appetizers to their guests. Hand-crafted book shelves stood empty along the northern and eastern corners of the room. She couldn't wait to fill them with tomes and stories of adventure, love, and friendship.

"Wow, it looks beautiful, and just in time for company!" Kamara exclaimed as they heard a knock on the door. Kamara hurried to the door and invited their guests inside. Juniper was glowing with her golden hair, rosy cheeks, and a perfectly round belly. Laughlin's proud smile beamed from ear to ear.

"Juniper, you look radiant." Kamara complimented as she hugged her. "Laughlin, it's so good to see you again. Please, come in and sit."

"Your home looks lovely," Juniper said as she sat down on one of the sofas.

"Thank you, we just got the furniture today, I will do more decorating as we go. Would you like some tea or water?" Kamara asked.

"Oh, no thank you," Juniper said. Laughlin declined as well as they got comfortable in the sitting room.

"I noticed the horses out there, are you looking to have a stable built? I would be happy to help." Laughlin offered.

"Yes, I was planning to build one here in the next few days so whenever you're available to help I would be happy to have a hand with it," Dominic said.

"Have you guys seen Sophie?" Juniper asked. "Leon mentioned we might want to check in on her, is everything okay?"

"I guess you heard about Gabe?" Kamara asked.

"No, what happened to Gabe, is he okay?"

"He's fine, but he showed up to the Ledoran Ball with Akiri and they were announced as one of the newly engaged royal couples," Dominic told them.

"Oh no, how did Sophie take it?" Juniper asked.

"She was shocked and angry. We all were, to be honest." Kamara said.

"She seemed friendly with one of the other guests though, so I asked him to check in on her before Kamara and I left. Is Sophie home now?" Dominic asked.

"Home and gone again, Leon said she stopped in to say quick goodbyes to him and her mom, and then she was off to Lapis Highland again," Juniper said.

"Maybe I should go tomorrow morning and see if she needs a friend." Kamara thought out loud.

"I am sure Sophie would be happy to have another girl there to talk to. Maybe you and Juniper could go, take the boat from Torzana, and Laughlin and I could work on the stables?" Dominic suggested.

"Are you okay to travel?" Kamara asked, looking at Juniper's baby bump.

"I still have plenty of time before the baby is due, it would be nice to see Sophie," Juniper said.

"Okay, I will make up the guest room for you and Laughlin and we can leave in the morning."

After they sat and talked for a while, Kamara showed them around the temple, pointing out the various things she'd changed about it since the last time Juniper had visited, all the wile thinking about Sophie and feeling guilty for leaving her after the ball. Kamara hoped her friend would not be angry with her. The thought weighed heavily on her the rest of the night, making sleep difficult. She tossed and turned, paced the floor, and finally used some valerian root extract. When she crawled back into bed beside Dominic, she snuggled into his arm and fell into a deep dreamless sleep.

SEVENTEEN

THE SIX COUNCILMEN WERE already standing when Akiri and Gabe entered the chamber. Akiri introduced Gabe to them and then hastily got on with the meeting. The arena was earning a lot with the new food vendors and contests. The entry fee to watch the daily joust was only two silver pieces and the stands were filled every day. Knights from other countries who came to compete would rent a horse from the stable master, stay at one of the four local inns, and buy their food and ale from one of the many taverns.

"It sounds like things are going very well, and the people are happy?" Akiri asked.

"Yes, My Queen, they are very happy we are no longer taxing them, and they love the entertainment we are providing with the arena," Nohan said.

"Nohan, you and your soldiers come in contact with the people more than anyone else in the castle, what would you say the rate of joblessness is among the subjects?" Akiri asked.

"I would say there's a good five percent of the population who can work, who don't have jobs currently," Nohan answered.

"Gabriel will be needing his own guards. I would like to take some men you have already trained and employ them here, which will open up new positions with the city guard. Timothy, see to it Nohan is fairly compensated for his trained men."

"Yes, My Queen," Timothy said.

"Your Grace, how many of my men will The King Consort require?" Nohan asked.

"At least three, four if you can spare them," Akiri answered. "And please address him as His Majesty, or King Gabriel, not consort."

"Forgive me, and I hope His Majesty will also forgive my error. I will assign the guards at once, Your Grace," he replied.

"If there is nothing else, I will see you at the wedding. Meeting adjourned."

Akiri and Gabe stood first, then everyone else followed suit. They waited for Akiri to take Gabe's arm and exit before they began shuffling about. Gabe heard Nohan grumbling under his breath as they left, he looked at Akiri and knew she heard it too, but chose to ignore it. When they were back in the privacy of their corridor, Gabe stopped and looked at his bride-to-be.

"If it means the city guard will be left untrained, I am fine with not having a personal guard detail. It seems your captain wasn't too happy about giving up three or four of his trained men." Gabe said.

"There are thirty-six men currently working for the city guard, they can spare four and still have plenty. He's only angry because I asked him to train new men to replace them. He doesn't understand; jobless people are the biggest threat to the crown. If I had my way about it, everyone would have a job and be able to take care of their families, but that isn't the way it is." Gabe looked into Akiri's face, he could see she cared a lot more for other people than anyone knew. He felt ashamed he had believed the rumors about her before anyone took the time to get to know her. Gabe leaned forward and kissed her cheek.

"I'll see you in a little while," he whispered in her ear. His hot breath sent a chill down Akiri's neck and she smiled.

The wedding took place in the garden courtyard in front of a beautiful stone fountain and the wedding arch was covered in trailing clematis blooms. The ceremony was private, only the castle staff was invited, but the subjects of Ash all gathered at the front of the castle for the first glance at their queen and her new king. Akiri's dress was white trimmed in teal and made of silk. It clung to her curves and accentuated her waist and hips. Gabe's suit jacket was black with teal trim and his undershirt had ruffles at the center of his chest which made him think of the nobles at the Solstice Ball.

They recited their vows and kissed before the witnesses as the castle staff applauded. Akiri and Gabe made their way back down the aisle and up to the second-floor balcony. They waved to the people of Ash for the first time as King and Queen.

Akiri looked up at Gabe and he leaned down to kiss her. The crowd erupted in cheers once more. As the noise from the people continued, a strange kind of static filled Gabe's head.

"Is it done? Can you hear me?" Gabe heard Leon's voice cutting in through the white noise filling his head, the cheers of the crowd and the static blended and made Gabe's head hurt. He winced from the sharp, high-pitched tone ringing in his ear.

"Are you okay? What's wrong, Gabe?"

"My head, sorry. Yes, I'm okay. I think maybe it was just too much wine last night, my head hurts." Akiri helped Gabe back inside. As soon as they were away from the cheering crowd, the static faded, and Gabe's mind was clear again.

"I need to get some water, and rest for a bit, could you come to wake me up for dinner? In the meantime, maybe you could pack up your things from your old room to move into our room?"

"Really?" Akiri's eyes lit up and she grinned. "Are you sure?"

"Positive, we are married after all." Gabe kissed her softly on the lips. Akiri let out a squeal of delight as she took off down the hall toward her old chamber.

Once Gabe was alone, he contacted Leon. It made his head hurt, like something inside his mind was tearing.

"It's done, we are married." Gabe pictured Leon in his mind. He could see his face as they talked through their thoughts.

"Have you befriended anyone on the council yet?" Leon asked.

"I haven't had time, we got back here after the ball and the wedding was today, it all moved very quickly."

"What was her hurry to get married?" Leon asked.

"Other than being lonely, I'm not sure. She is just a normal.. well, not *normal*, you know what I mean. She is just alone here, ruling a kingdom. I am sure she fears her council may want to unseat her. She has six men on it, they probably pushed her to marry so they wouldn't have to take orders from a woman," Gabe said.

"Perhaps, but don't underestimate her, she is very dangerous when she's angry. You all saw her the day on Choddrath," Leon warned. Gabe was sure what happened on the shores of Choddrath a year ago was a misunderstanding.

"Yes, Sir. I will endear myself to the council and find out their plans. I will report back when I have some intel. Until then, I'm going to mend my broken heart by getting to know my new wife."

"Understood. I will wait for your report, just know we don't have much more time, this connection will only last a few months at best." Just like that, Leon was out of his head, and the sharp pains turned to a dull ache, and finally, as he laid on his bed with his eyes closed, the headache eased too. Gabe wished it were that easy to cure his heartache.

When Akiri woke Gabe for dinner, her maids were with her, their arms filled with things from Akiri's room. They filed into the royal chamber, going about their tasks. Gabe noticed the smile on Akiri's face and he smiled too. They left the staff to work, hanging clothes, and placing Akiri's items and furniture around the room the way she liked them. The kitchen staff had prepared a hearty stew with lots of potatoes, carrots, and beef.

Gabe wondered where they got the cow but then thought maybe he didn't want to know the answer after all, at least not until he ate his fill.

After dinner, Akiri and Gabe walked around the gardens, and then to the beach. It wasn't a nice, sandy beach like the one on Ledora's shore, this one was rocky and covered in shells. Gabe started sorting through the shells. He picked out quite a few he liked and put them in the pocket of his trousers for later.

"Do you like to read?" Akiri asked.

"I do. I used to be a scribe at the citadel in Blackwater. I will admit I like reading, but I don't want to copy any more books," Gabe said with a chuckle.

"I don't have many books. My mother never liked to read. She was only ever concerned with power."

"Is it true..." Gabe stopped as he looked at Akiri. He wanted to ask if she had killed her mother. It was the rumor that made its way to Blackwater, but Gabe knew how rumors could get out of control.

"Is what true? That I killed my mother?" Akiri lost the cool tone she had before and her voice sounded a little more hostile now.

"I'm sorry, it's just what I heard." Gabe pleaded with his eyes. He didn't want her to be mad at him already.

"Yes, it's true. People ask me if I regret it sometimes, and I know I should, but she was an evil woman, who was planning to kill me so she could take the dragon powers for herself. She was going to have her hired guard kill her only daughter. I just beat her to the punch is all."

"I'm sorry. Akiri, growing up with a mother like her must have been difficult."

"The kingdom is better off for it as well. My mother taxed the local businesses so much they couldn't afford to stay open. They all hated her, and honestly, she didn't even think enough of them to hate them. To her, the subjects were specs of dust too small to even notice."

"It seems they like you though." Gabe nudged her with his elbow.

"I gave them entertainment, and let them spend their money willingly. I don't tax the people at all, and most of them are healthy and happy. There are still quite a few people who can't provide for themselves or their families and I am working on figuring out what I can do for them."

"You are a good Queen. Ash is lucky to have you." Gabe paused. "*I'm lucky to have you.*"

Akiri looked up at him, and he ran his fingertips through her hair to sweep it away from her face. He brought his lips to hers. She melted into his arms as they kissed under the starry sky.

When their lips parted, Akiri shivered. "Let's go get you warmed up," Gabe said as he gently took her hand, interlacing her fingers between his own. They walked back to the castle and to their room in a comfortable quiet.

They warmed themselves in front of the fireplace until the chill was gone from their fingers and then Gabe began to undress. He took off his tunic and laid it over the back of the chair, then turned it to face the fire. "This way it will be warm in the morning," he explained.

"Good idea," Akiri replied as she did the same, only taking her eyes away from Gabe's as she drew the garment over her head. His skin under the light of the fire was the most beautiful color Akiri had ever seen. Gabe looked at her in surprise. He did not expect her to undress too. She was bold and daring. It was one of the things he liked most about her. She moved closer to him and lightly moved her hands up his chest to his neck, luring him into a slow and passionate kiss. He picked her up and carried her to the bed, unable to pull his lips away from hers.

Gabe's hands roamed down her body until his fingertips grazed the waistband of her trousers. He tugged at them gently as she playfully bit his lower lip. Gabe groaned as he hooked his fingers into her waistband and slid her pants down. She lifted her bottom off the bed so he could easily pull them off. He stood for a moment to remove his own trousers, noticing the way Akiri's pupils dilated as he stood before her. He crawled onto the bed, straddling her.

"Let me know if this is too fast," Gabe whispered as he looked into her eyes. "We don't have to do this tonight if you're not-"

Akiri pressed her lips to Gabe's and reached her hand between them, wrapping her delicate fingers around his sex. She moved her hand up and down, caressing his rock-hard shaft. He groaned into her mouth as Akiri guided his erection into her wet entrance. A moan escaped Gabe's lips as she lifted and pumped her hips to match his speed. Gabe closed his eyes and as he moved his hips back and forth slowly, he didn't know why, but he imagined Sophie and her red curls flowing softly over the pillow, and the freckles lightly speckling her skin, he imagined it was Sophie's soft lips on his, and the thought of being inside her was enough to bring him to a quick climax. He pushed himself deep inside his wife and gave her every bit of his seed. He didn't pull out until the throbbing stopped.

When he opened his eyes and saw Akiri looking up at him, he felt ashamed. He had always imagined his first time would be with Sophie, but he didn't want to have to imagine her when he made love to his wife. Gabe got up and walked to the vanity to get a cloth. There was still water in the wash basin so he dampened a cloth and cleaned himself up. Then he dampened another and took it to Akiri, he was startled when he saw the blood.

"Are you okay? I didn't hurt you did I?" Gabe asked, concerned.

"It hurt a little at first, but it's okay. I have been told this happens your first time," she said. Gabe relaxed a little.

"It was my first time too," he admitted.

"I'm glad it was with you," Akiri said as she cleaned herself and wiped up the spot on the bed.

"Me too," Gabe lied, feeling even worse now for thinking about someone else.

Their first time left a stain on the sheets and Akiri stood to strip the bed. She pulled another fitted sheet from the linen wardrobe and Gabe helped her put it on the mattress. They crawled into bed and Akiri laid her head on Gabe's chest. He combed his fingers through her hair until she was sleeping soundly and Gabe stared silently at the ceiling, thinking about Sophie until sleep came for him as well.

EIGHTEEN

LAUGHLIN AND DOMINIC BEGAN working on the barn at first light. When Kamara woke and made her way to the kitchen, She found Juniper making tea. She walked in, greeted her and sat down at the table, still not fully awake. Juniper looked refreshed and full of energy. Kamara wondered what her secret was.

"Would you like a cup of tea?" Juniper asked.

"Yes, please," Kamara replied with a sleepy nod.

"Here ya go." Juniper slid one of the mugs across the table. Kamara got up to retrieve a spoon and some sugar from the cabinet. She didn't like how bitter tea was without it.

"Did you sleep well?" Juniper asked.

"I slept fine, it's just waking up that's difficult, what about you?" Kamara asked.

"I meditated in the garden out back for a few hours in the moonlight. It's so beautiful out there," she replied.

"The garden? I thought it was overgrown and dead, I haven't touched it since before..." Kamara didn't have to finish the sentence, Juniper knew she meant; before Baelfire's men came looking for the orb and Kamara was the only survivor.

"I did some weeding last night and uncovered some plants that were still good, and a few that needed some help. You have tomatoes, potatoes, onions, and a bed or two of flowers. I couldn't save the rest of the garden, but we can plant more next spring, or we could plant some hearty winter vegetables," juniper suggested.

"Thank you, you didn't have to do all that," Kamara said.

"I know, but working in the soil under the light of the moon recharges me, so thank you."

A commotion outside caught their attention, and they both ran to the door just in time to see Sophie land in the only spot not covered by the canopy of treetops. They waited as she took her human form, emerging from her dragon shape with clothes on. Kamara looked at her in confusion, wondering how, but still ran out to greet her.

"Sophie! We were just getting ready to come to the tower for a visit. This is a nice surprise!" Kamara said. Sophie hugged Kamara and then looked at Juniper. Her eyes were drawn to her rounded belly.

"Juniper, you're going to have a baby? I'm so happy for you!" Sophie wrapped her arms around her friend, careful not to squeeze her too tightly. Dominic and Laughlin waved from the frame of the barn they were working on, but they couldn't stop until the frame was complete.

"Juniper just made some tea if you would like to have some. We can let these guys finish up while we chat inside. Will you be staying the night?" Kamara asked as she noticed the bag Sophie had brought with her.

"Well, I was hoping I could stay with you for a little while. I have builders constructing a ground-level castle instead of the tower and it might take a while to complete the construction, if not, I can stay with my parents, I just really needed a friend right now, Ryul left and didn't even say goodbye, Gabe got engaged to the Queen of Ash, and I just had a drunken rebound with some guy whose last name I don't even remember," Sophie explained.

"You can stay as long as you would like, you are always welcome here, but you know I'm going to need all the details about this new rebound guy!" Kamara looped her arm through Sophie's and followed Juniper back to the kitchen.

"You changed a lot in here, it's nice. It feels more like a home than a temple now." Sophie said.

"Dominic and I thought we might live here until he is needed in Ledora. Sorry, we left after the ball, we came here and had a little engagement celebration, just the two of us." Kamara said.

"It's okay." Sophie smiled as her thoughts trailed back to that night.

"So, this mystery guy... Is he who you're thinking about now?" Kamara asked, gesturing to Sophie's expression. "Tell me, how did it happen?"

"After I found out about Gabe's engagement, I started throwing back chalices of wine. I just wanted to numb the pain. Bastian asked me to dance a few times and before the end of the night, I kissed him. Gabe saw the whole thing and that's the last thing I remember before waking up in Bastian's bed."

"You didn't!" Kamara exclaimed. Sophie nodded and sipped her tea.

"I wonder what Bastian thought when he woke up." Juniper raised her eyebrows at Sophie.

"I bet he thought it had all been a dream," Kamara said. "Whenever you're finished with your tea, I will show you around." She walked over to the counter and poured water from a pitcher into her cup to rinse it.

"I'm going to go see if the guys need any help, be sure to take a look a the garden," Juniper said as she filled two cups with water for Laughlin and Dominic.

"I will," Kamara replied.

Kamara led Sophie down the hall where the guest rooms were and showed her the room that would be hers. Sophie put her bag on the bed before they continued the tour so she didn't have to carry it with her. Kamara showed her the sitting room, and the patio leading to the garden, and then she showed Sophie to the lair.

"Do you think we can produce more dragons?" Sophie asked when she saw the nest.

"I don't see why we couldn't. I don't know how to do it though, if we need to be in dragon shape, or if our human shape will just create dragonshifters like us. We will use trial and error until we get it right, but we are preparing for every possible outcome," Kamara replied.

Suddenly, Sophie felt very lonely. Kamara had Dominic, Juniper had Laughlin and a baby on the way, and even Akiri had Gabe. Kamara noticed Sophie's sullen appearance and she wrapped her arms around her.

"I'm sorry," she said. "I would ask if you're okay, but I can see you're not. How can I help?" Kamara asked.

"I don't know. I just miss Gabe. He was in love with me for longer than I knew and I took him for granted. Now he's gone, married to Akiri. I will likely never even get to see him again. Everything changed when I went to the tower to train with Ryul. I thought Gabe would wait for me, I thought I could learn magic, become a wizard and then Gabe and I would have the life we always dreamed of," Sophie told her.

"We could always invite Bastian over for tea," Kamara joked. "Awe, I saw you smile!" Sophie rolled her eyes, but Kamara was right, she was smiling. Sophie was thankful Kamara had tried to make her laugh about Bastian instead of urging her to talk more about Gabe. Sophie's eyes migrated to the hot spring. She could feel the heat from it and longed to ease her muscles.

"Want to get in?" Kamara asked as if reading her mind. "I do all the time. It's like a bath, but it never gets cold, and the water bubbles up from the underground spring so it's not stagnant and it's always clean."

"It sounds lovely," Sophie replied.

Kamara took off her dress and laid it on a dry rock. She stepped into the pool in her undergarments. Sophie let her illusion spell drop momentarily, and then re-cast the illusion of a black bodysuit.

"I wondered how you did that," Kamara said as Sophie eased her body down into the pool of water.

"Did what?"

"Shifted back to human form without appearing naked," Kamara said.

"Oh, yes, the illusion was one of the first spells I worked on with Ryul, basically, I just think about what I want others to see and concentrate my energy on it," Sophie told her. "I could try to teach you."

"I'm afraid I don't have any magical ability, other than being able to shift. Dominic tried to teach me some magic too and I just do not have the aptitude for it." Kamara said laying her head back against a warm rock. They relaxed quietly in the spring for quite some time, and when their muscles were relaxed and their fingers were pruned, Kamara and Sophie got out of the hot spring and walked back to the temple to dry off. Sophie went to her room and put on some actual clothes so she could rest her mind. Keeping up the illusion spell for long periods required a lot of mental focus and she learned it tired her out quickly.

Sophie stretched out on her bed and fell asleep. Kamara and Juniper rode into town to get meat from the butcher, and pick up some things from the market. When they returned to the temple, the barn was half finished.

"You guys have done such great work today. It looks wonderful," Kamara complimented. "I will let you guys know when dinner is ready." Kamara and Juniper carried the groceries into the kitchen. Sophie was already awake and when she saw Kamara and Juniper come in with their arms full she hurried over to pitch in and help.

The three of them peeled and cut potatoes, celery, carrots, garlic, onions, and beef. Sophie sautéed the vegetables while Kamara cooked the beef with the bones to make a hearty broth. Using some of the broth, Sophie made a roux with the vegetables and some flour, adding it to the soup. They covered it and let the stew cook for a few hours. Juniper added some more seasoning, tasting it between pinches of salt and pepper. She used a mortar and pestle to grind up dried rosemary, oregano, and some dried peppers and threw in a few bay leaves and some fresh basil.

The smell filled the kitchen and made it feel warm and inviting, It smelled like home to Sophie. When everyone was washed up and gathered at the table, Kamara served the stew in large bowls with fresh dinner rolls and butter from the market.

"This is amazing, thank you for cooking," Dominic said as he tasted his stew.

"It was a joint effort, Sophie and Juniper helped," she said.

"It's delicious," Laughlin said.

After dinner, Sophie washed the dishes and Kamara dried and put them away. The rest of the evening, they sat by the fire talking, playing games, and forgetting all of the tough times they had been through in the last year. Despite all their struggles, they had each other, which made Sophie especially happy.

The next morning, Sophie helped Laughlin, Dominic, and Kamara finish the barn while Juniper worked in the garden. By midday, Sophie slipped away into the house and conjured a feast for lunch. She didn't take credit for it when everyone came inside to see it, but they all suspected it had been her. By evening, the barn was finished, and the horses were happy and safe from the elements inside their stalls.

"Thanks for all your help, I couldn't have gotten it finished without you," Dominic said to Laughlin.

"No problem, It was nice to have your help too. If you want to earn some coin, I would gladly split the profits of my next job with you if you wanted to work with me in town."

"I would love to," Dominic replied. He was so much happier now than he had been growing up in Ledora. It had been lonely not having friends and never knowing if people were being nice because they had to be or because they liked you. Here, he was just Dominic. He wasn't a prince or even a future king. It made him wonder how long he would get to live life this way before his father or the king's council called him home to assume the throne.

NINETEEN

THE NEXT MORNING WHEN he woke up, Gabe stretched and reached out across the bed. Akiri's side was cold. He got up, stretched again, and dressed for the day. The early morning light had just started to peek in through the balcony archway, and Gabe knew there was a council meeting every morning. He didn't know why Akiri didn't wake him up, but he thought perhaps he should find out.

When he reached the chamber, the doors were closed and two guards stood beside the entrance- Akiri's guards. As soon as they noticed Gabe, they shuffled apart and opened the doors for him. Everyone at the table looked up at Gabe as he entered the room and the six men stood up until Gabe took his seat.

"Continue," Akiri said. Ser William Robert looked from Gabe back to Akiri. She nodded at him and finally, he continued.

"As I was saying, No one here has ever seen a dragon egg so we do not know how long they will take to hatch, we don't know if they have to stay at a certain temperature, or what other husbandry their habitat requires. We will have to use trial and error until we get it right."

"Wait, do you have dragon eggs now?" Gabe asked, confused.

"Assuming your marriage was consummated, Queen Akiri should be able to take her dragon form now, and by the new moon she should be able to produce a clutch of fertilized eggs."

"So you're saying she has to stay in dragon shape until she lays?" Gabe looked at Akiri to see if she was considering this.

"The other option is having a human child who may or may not inherit the gift of dragon shape. As far as we know, The Queen and the other dragons she saw on Choddrath are the only ones left." Ser William said.

"What do you want? Do you want to stay in dragon form for weeks to produce eggs that may or may not be viable?" Gabe asked. He didn't know why, but the thought of having a human child appealed to him. He thought about teaching his son or daughter to hunt and fish. He thought about chasing them around the castle and hearing them giggling as they ran from him. He dreamed of one day taking them to Blackwater and showing them the stream where he used to play as a kid, and watching them climb in the branches of the willow tree. He pushed the thoughts away as Akiri started to speak.

"I- I want to try to produce a clutch first, just to see if it can be done. If we have dragons protecting our kingdom no one would dare try to take it from us or try to harm any children we have in the future."

"Is someone making threats?" Gabe asked.

"No, but the history of Ash indicates when the people become unhappy, they revolt and take the throne by force. I'm ashamed to say, even I took the throne from my mother by force. I don't want anyone to take it from our family. I want to protect us, and our future children by giving them dragons." Akiri pleaded. Gabe relented.

"If this is what you want, I will support you, My Queen."

When the meeting was over, Gabe and Akiri walked out together as they usually did. Akiri kept looking up at Gabe as they walked in silence back to their chamber. A million thoughts ran through his mind and his heart felt conflicted. This was an assignment. He was here to monitor the kingdom and ensure they were not planning hostile actions against the other dragons, Ledora, or anywhere else. He made a promise to Akiri though, it was a promise which in the eyes of the Gods could only be made to one other person, and then you were bound forever. It had not been his choice and he could have refused, but then his childhood home would be gone and his mother would have to resort to selling herself to the pirates at the Loose Anchor Tavern.

Family really was everything to Gabe, and maybe it was why he wanted a human child—a real family, not a flock of dragons. *Compromise is important in a marriage, right?* Gabe thought.

"Are you angry with me?" Akiri asked. Gabe let out a heavy sigh.

"No, I'm not angry with you, I'm a little hurt. I just wish we had talked about these plans first, just between us, before involving the council. When you are in the council room, I am not your equal. You are the ruler of this kingdom and I am here to support *your* decisions. Here in this room, I am your husband and your friend, someone you can lean on and talk to, someone to share your burdens with, but I can't be those things for you if you make all your decisions alone," Gabe said.

"You're right. I'm sorry. I should have included you in the plan from the beginning."

"Is this why you were so eager to get married? Was this the plan all along?"

"Yes. The plan was—is— to lay a successful clutch of eggs, and hatch baby dragons to secure the throne and the kingdom, and then produce heirs to the throne. Don't think for one second I chose you at random though. We have been planning this for almost a year, and I have been searching for a mate ever since. I had so many offers- men looking for dragon power, or a throne, but you were the only one who seemed uninterested in those things. You were wholesome and kind, devoted and determined. I know how you traveled to Choddrath for Sophie. I didn't know what happened between you two that caused you to offer marriage, but I couldn't let the opportunity pass by."

"You knew about Sophie and me the whole time?" Gabe asked.

"I saw you, and the way you looked at her when the black dragon was holding her captive at the top of Dragon Peak. I knew then. I was only interested in claiming my power to end my mother's tyranny here in Ash though, so I left as soon as I saw the threat was handled."

"Why didn't you join the dragon council?" Gabe asked.

"I'm not interested in the affairs of other kingdoms or living by other people's set of rules. I just want to worry about my kingdom and the people in it."

"I heard you were unkind. I was afraid at first, but I wanted to get away from all the memories I had in Blackwater."

"I was unkind. My mother was cruel and she was the only example I had to learn from. When I was chasing the orb, I did terrible things, I hurt people, and I let my anger get the better of me. All I wanted was to end my mother's rule. I was going to just force her to give up the throne and exile her, but when her guard told me she had asked him to kill me and steal the orb the second I got my hands on it, well, I blacked out in a rage and confronted her. I shifted in front of her to show her my power and then I tried to roar, for intimidation, only, it wasn't just sound that came out and I killed her. I didn't mean to, but once it happened and it was too late to take it back, I couldn't let anyone else know it was an accident. If they feared me and what I could do, there was no way they would try to usurp my family's throne." A tear slid down her cheek and Gabe pulled her into his arms, gently wiping it from her face. "The worst part was; I didn't feel bad about it. I watched her guard cower in the corner as I shifted back and walked right up to the throne and sat down. I was mad with power and I dreamed about making our enemies pay, but then I had a dream or a premonition of what my life *could* be instead. A life without war, a life with baby dragons, a family, and love. I think this dream was sent to me by the oracle so I would not end up like my mother; bitter and evil."

"Akiri, I had no idea you had been through so much. I am glad you have opened your heart and didn't continue down the same path as your mother." Gabe said as he held her tighter.

"So am I," she replied.

"When do you have to... you know, change?"

"The sooner, the better, if it takes as long as they say."

"Let's have one more night before you do. I want to hold you." Gabe leaned forward, pressed his forehead to hers and looked into her eyes. He caressed her cheek and as he brought his lips to hers. Every real conversation they had made him feel closer to her, but every step he took toward a life with Akiri felt like a betrayal when he thought of his feelings for Sophie. He wondered if his heart could belong to more than one.

"Let's get out of the castle today, and get some fresh air. We could go to the joust," Akiri suggested.

"That sounds fun, let's do it."

Akiri crossed the room, opened the door, and asked one of the guards to have their carriage brought around. He quickly agreed and left to do as his queen asked. Akiri changed into a white silk dress with twisted green rope trim. She braided her long black hair to one side and then put on her most comfortable sandals. The sight of her took Gabe's breath.

"Gods, you're beautiful," he whispered. Akiri's cheeks turned rosy pink, but she smiled.

"You are too kind, Sir," Akiri said in a playful tone. Before the wedding, Roland Koffery had tasked the maids with measuring Gabe and then purchasing a wardrobe for him. All of his clothing was now fit for a king, even his undergarments and sleeping robes were the finest he had ever seen. Gabe picked a tunic to match the green in Akiri's dress.

When the Queen and King were ready, their guards, two of Akiri's and two of Gabe's, walked them to their carriage. The men followed them to the arena on horses. When they arrived, the carriage doors remained closed until all of their guards were in position. They walked them to their seats in the tower. The villagers stood up as the royal procession walked by and cheered as Akiri and Gabe waved to them before sitting down.

"Have you ever been to a joust before?" Akiri asked.

"No, how does it work?"

"Two knights on horseback try to unseat each other with a lance. You win if you knock the other person off their horse, otherwise, you earn points by either striking your opponent or breaking your lance."

"Why do you get points for breaking your lance?" Gabe asked.

"You know, I'm not sure. I guess because if you hit them hard enough to break your lance, but don't unseat your opponent, you get points for a good hit at least." They watched as the first two knights were announced.

"Ser Finn Marquee of Hagen against Ser Jarett Weiss of Portage." The announcer's voice boomed throughout the arena and Gabe wondered how he had done it. *It has to be a magic spell*, he thought. The two knights ran at each other at full speed and Ser Jarrett got the first hit on his opponent's shoulder. They took up their positions at the end of the run, their squires checked their armor quickly and they were off again. This time, Ser Jarett shattered the tip of his lance on Finn's shield, but Finn stayed on his horse. In the third attempt, Ser Finn lowered his lance just before striking and it shattered on Ser Jarett's armored abdomen. The blow knocked Jarett backward and he fell to the ground. The announcer walked out into the middle of the arena again as the squires cleared the field.

"Next, we have Ser Boris Madder of Braidwood, and Ser Colby Ricard of Ash."

"One from my continent against one of yours. This should be interesting," Gabe said.

"Care to make a wager?" Akiri asked, playfully.

"I don't gamble, but I am sure one of my guards will take your bet." Gabe looked at the guard closest to him.

"Absolutely, My Queen," the guard said.

"Okay, Jack, I got two gold on Colby," Akiri said. She handed her two gold pieces to Gabe.

"I'll match, Your Grace." Jack pulled out two gold and handed them to Gabe as well.

"Good Luck, Jack," Akiri said.

"You too, My Queen."

The knights took position and ran at each other, Boris got the first hit and almost unseated Colby, who dropped his lance, but squeezed the horse with his legs and managed to stay in the saddle. He rode to the end of the list and his squires quickly put another lance in his hand. The second strike went to Colby as he raised his lance and struck Boris in the shoulder.

"Third time's a charm?" Gabe asked.

"Maybe," Akiri said. This time, Colby raised his lance even higher, and not wanting to get hit in the face, Boris got startled and pulled back on the reins the horse made a sharp turn toward the stands then bucked. Boris fell off his horse with a loud clank as his armor hit the ground.

"Does that count?" Gabe asked.

"No, I don't think so. Wait- what is he doing?" Akiri leaned forward to see what was going on, Boris stomped over to the referee and threw his hands up. He was shouting something at the man but Akiri couldn't hear because of the shouts from the crowd.

"Ser Boris Madder has yielded!" The announcer said. The crowd went wild.

"So, technically you won?" Gabe handed the gold to Akiri.

"No, no one won, Boris got mad and quit it's not the same." Akiri tried to hand Jack his coins back.

"No, My Queen, you keep it. You clearly picked the better knight." Jack said with a smile. Akiri put the coins in her purse.

They refrained from betting throughout the rest of the joust and when it was over, the guards walked Gabe and Akiri to their carriage.

"I had a great time. Thank you for bringing me," Gabe said.

"My pleasure."

When they were back at the castle and had retreated to the privacy of their chamber, Gabe began undressing. He took off his tunic first and tossed it in the laundry bin. He started to take off his trousers, but he felt Akiri's eyes on him. He turned to look at her. She was standing by the chair in front of the fireplace still wearing the silk dress. Gabe moved over to his wife and took her in his arms. He loved the way her body felt against his; her soft warm skin, and the way her nipples peaked beneath the silk when he touched her. He pulled the pin from her hair, letting it fall in a cascading black waterfall. Her lips parted as she gazed into his eyes, piercing his soul with her beauty. She reached down, pulling the laces of his trousers. They slid off his hips with little effort and Akiri pressed her body against him. The heat of her sex, even through the silk of her dress, made his cock pulse. Gabe gripped her hips and a soft groan escaped him as she trailed kisses across his chest. He lifted the silk of her dress, discovering she was already without undergarments. He slid his hand from her hip and slipped it between her thighs, dipping two fingers into her core. She was dripping wet and Gabe could think of nothing he wanted more than to taste her.

Guiding her to the bed, Gabe laid her down and slid the silk gown all the way up her belly. He kissed his way down Akiri's abdomen until his face was between her thighs. Using his thumb and first finger, he spread open her lips and glided his tongue from her entrance to her clit. He flicked his tongue and Akiri's back arched as she gripped the bed sheets in her fists. Moaning as he pleasured her in ways she'd never experienced. Just before she reached climax, Gabe inserted his fingers once more, moving them both back and forth, and slightly curling the tips forward. She cried out his name as she every nerve in her body ignited, fluid spilling from her and dripping down Gabe's hand. She motioned for him to rise. His lips crashed against hers as she tangled her fingers into his dark, wavy locks.

"Make love to me," she requested breathlessly. Her eyes sparkled with want. He gazed at her as he moved his hips back and forth letting his shaft caress up and down her sex. She lifted her hips in response and he slid into her gently. Her mouth fell open at the sensation and her beautiful brown eyes rolled back as she closed them, savoring every inch of him. Pumping back and forth, slowly, Gabe admired his wife's body and the way her breasts bounced ever so slightly, and the way her lower belly swelled to his shape every time he thrusted into her. Her hips were perfect; not too thin and just soft enough for him to grip. He pulled out of her, rolling onto his back and pulling her on top of him.

"I've never done this before," she admitted self-consciously.

"Nor have I, but I'm happy for us to learn together," Gabe replied.

She straddled him and he guided his cock back into her. She moaned with pleasure as she slid down his length. With his hands on her hips he guided her movements, mesmerized by the pleasure on her face and the response of her body to his. She rode him faster, rolling her hips forward with every pump. The sound of her voice crying out for the gods sent him over the edge. He couldn't contain it anymore, his orgasm filled her and her walls squeezed his cock just right as she too reached climax. He held her on his lap until the throbbing stopped, then she rolled off of him, both satisfied and exhausted.

TWENTY

TIME SEEMED TO MOVE so quickly. The first day, turned into three, then before Sophie knew how it happened, she had been with Kamara and Dominic for more than two weeks. They settled into a routine. During the week, Sophie and Kamara would spend their morning gardening while Dominic worked on various building projects. The horses now had a fence spanning the entire left side of the property, which included a fresh spring to drink from and plenty of pasture to roam. They also obtained goats for milk, and pigs for bacon, ham, and sausage, of course, it would be at least a year before any of the pigs were ready for the slaughterhouse- which Dominic had yet to build.

On the weekends, they flew to Ledora and spent time with the king during the day and enjoyed court life at night. As the Princess, had been trained in diplomacy and knew almost everyone now. She often introduced Sophie to people she thought she might like. Sophie became quite popular with the noblemen at court, but the whispers she over- heard were contrary. It was usually the women who spoke ill of her behind her back. She knew they were talking about her because when she approached, they all stopped talking and stared at her without saying a word until she walked away.

On more than one occasion, a woman engaged her in polite conversa- tion only to dig up gossip to spread to her flock of hens. The questions were always the same. Why did she turn down every proposal? Wasn't she worried about protecting her virtue? How did she plan to find a husband if she didn't remain chaste? It had been a week since the last occasion and already a new rumor was circulating the court. Sophie overheard the whisper this time in the powder room.

"I know why she turns down every man who tries to court her, she's Prince Dominic's mistress. She even lives with them in their new castle, If you can even call it that," one girl said to another.

"They have a new castle?" a third asked with a bit of jealousy in her tone.

"Well, not *new, and technically not a castle*. They just fixed up the old temple where all those religious people were murdered outside Blackwater."

"I swear Blackwater is a curse," the other woman remarked.

"I know! Positively a curse, you know that's where Sophie is *from*, no wonder she's so weird." The girls giggled, obviously in agreement.

Sophie had heard enough, she opened the door to the privy and stomped over to the girl starting the rumors. When they spotted Sophie all they all fell silent, knowing she'd heard every word. "What's your name?" Sophie asked as she reached up to touch the brooch of the girl's family crest pinned on her dress. The girl remained quiet. "This is such a pretty pin." Sophie gave it a quick tug and the back of the pin popped open and the pin came off in Sophie's hand.

"Since you ladies want all the juicy gossip, let *me* be the one to give it to you. The reason I haven't accepted a proposal because I like to sample everything at the buffet. I get bored of the same old thing all the time and unlike you, I run my own Kingdom and am not forced to choose a husband just for the sake of being married. Secondly, I am sure Prince Dominic would love to hear how you're implying-no-flat out *telling* people he has taken a mistress and broken his vow to Kamara before they have even wed. How would the king feel about these rumors you're spreading about his only son and heir? If I were you, I would take more care with your tongue, before you lose it. Oh, and I'm keeping this." She held up the brooch. "Let me hear you say another word about me or my friends and they will be the last words you speak."

Sophie didn't wait for any of them to respond, she twirled around and stomped out of the powder room with her head held high. She could feel all their eyes on her as she left. She rounded the corner quickly, in a hurry to find Kamara and tell her what happened. In her haste, she bumped right into someone. She almost fell but he caught her. "Woah, careful. Sophie, it's so good to see you," he said, helping her to her feet. She knew his voice before she even looked up to see his face.

"Bastian, I- uh... hello." Sophie stumbled on her words. She hadn't expected to see him again after their drunken night together at Dominic and Kamara's engagement. His blue eyes sparkled like sapphires and his blond hair, which was now long enough to pull into a ponytail was tied back with a black ribbon. To the right of them, Sophie saw a maiden with her fan drawn up to her chin. She looked at Sophie with envy and then batted her lashes as she gazed back at Bastian.

"Would you please dance with me?" he asked, extending his hand to Sophie, ignoring the other girl. She nodded and gently placed her hand in his as he suavely guided her into the ballroom. Moving in close to her, he ran his fingers up the sensitive part of her arms as she raised them above her head. Sophie brought one hand down slowly, caressing the side of his face. The moment before their lips touched, he twirled her out, just beyond the edge of his reach. She glided away from him as his steps lightly followed her. She paused, looking away from him, and he put his arm around her from behind, resting his hand on her abdomen. He slowly turned her chin toward him with his other hand, and as she gazed up at him, their lips grew closer. He dipped her smoothly, staying so close she could feel his breath trail all the way from her lips to her breasts as she leaned back in his arms. When he guided her back up, his hands roamed her body and his face was nearly touching hers. She wanted to kiss him, but he controlled their every move as he led the seductive dance. Everyone watched them as their bodies told a story of desire and longing. The crowd gathered around the ballroom to watch and burst into applause when the song was over. Bastian's lips still never even brushed hers.

He had a strong effect on her. She desired to claim him, and be claimed by him. This time, she was completely sober and the magnetic draw she felt was undeniable. He bowed to her and kissed her hand, letting his lips linger against her skin for a moment.

"Thank you, Sophie. I hope I see you again."

"What do you mean? Are you leaving?"

"I am, I was already on my way out when I ran into you, but-" His words cut off, but Sophie could tell there was more he wanted to say. "I couldn't resist you, I had to hold you close if only for one dance. It was really good to see you again," he said, then quickly turned to make his way back through the crowd toward the exit.

Sophie stood there in shock as he disappeared into the sea of people. *Wait, that's it? Really?* Sophie thought. Their dance had left her almost breathless and needful. She tried to follow him through the crowd, but by the time she made it across the room and through the doors leading outside, he was gone. *How did he disappear so quickly?* Sophie thought.

She stood outside for a while, looking off into the distance, trying to calm her racing thoughts, and let the feeling of arousal pass. She had spent the night with Bastian when first they met, and this time it seemed that the second things started heating up between them, he was in a hurry to leave. She wondered if he regretted their night together. Sophie was about to head back inside when the doors behind her opened and Kamara came out to join her.

"Did you just need some fresh air? I would, after that dance. Sss ow!" Kamara touched Sophie's shoulder with her fingertip and pretended it sizzled and burned, her sound effects did make Sophie smile.

"Bastian left. He was already gone by the time I made it to the door like he just disappeared. I don't understand how he vanished so quickly." Sophie told her.

"That's strange. I don't know him other than from the ball so I am afraid I won't be much help in finding him, but we could go back in and dance." Kamara smiled and took Sophie's hand. "I mean- I doubt I'm as seductive a dancer as Bastian, but I will try my best." She winked and Sophie moved the thoughts of Bastian to the back of her mind and she followed Kamara back inside and onto the dance floor.

As Sophie slept, strange dreams overtook her thoughts. The night sky was filled with heavy, dark, rain clouds and the air was cool. Sophie didn't know where she was, the town was strange-looking with twisted alleyways lined with wooden houses, all shuttered up. Not even a lantern illuminated her way. The full moon shined down through a part in the clouds. Sophie watched the sky to see if she could tell which way the storm was going, but the clouds didn't move. It was like they were magical in nature and used to engulf the city in shadows.

Sophie walked down the narrow cobblestone path toward the sound of a cawing raven. She saw the bird perched on an old stone wall beside an iron gate. When the bird noticed her drawing closer, it cawed again and flew away. She ran after the sound of flapping wings, into a graveyard. She tripped over a small headstone and fell to the ground. She stood up and ran through the cemetery until she reached the other end of it. The raven perched on the wall again and it seemed to look at her as she approached. Sophie reached out her hand to touch the bird and it squawked angrily. It darted toward her face and she reacted too late, the bird's talon scratched her on the side of her neck as it swooped past, it swooped like a bat-not a bird. *How odd.* she thought.

Just then, Bastian stepped out of the shadows and he seemed to float to where she stood holding her neck. She looked at her hand and saw blood. He didn't say a word, instead, stared at her with his piercing eyes. Sophie felt irresistibly drawn to him and in an instant, she closed the gap between them and kissed him. He pulled back only a little as he brushed his lips against hers in the most teasing way, then kissed the corner of her mouth, her cheek, her jaw, and then her neck. She moaned softly as she felt his tongue glide gently up the scratch, and just as abruptly as he had disappeared from court, the dream was over and Sophie woke up. She groaned loudly in the frustration of her empty bed and tried to remember what had happened between them the night of Kamara and Dominic's engagement. Why couldn't she remember anything besides waking up next to him and why did she need him so badly now?

Damn it, Sophie, pull yourself together. She scolded herself. She tried as hard as she could to fall back asleep, but it evaded her. When she tried to think back on her dream she found it was gone from her memory. She knew it had been about Bastian, and it had made her crave him more than ever, but the details beyond that were gone.

She was usually not even attracted to Bastian's type, really, she had only ever been attracted to one other person, and that was Gabe. The two men could not be more opposite. Gabe was a little shorter and outdoorsy with a dark brown complexion and dark hair. He liked to wade in the creek, skip rocks, fish, and gather herbs in the forest. Sophie only reached Bastian's shoulder, he was poised and proper, well-dressed, and well-mannered most of the time. His hair was long, blonde, and he had piercing blue eyes. He was the very embodiment of the social elite, a great dancer, diplomatic, and yet there was something so mysterious about him.

Hours passed and Sophie still couldn't sleep, so she stopped trying. Instead, she took a walk; wandering aimlessly through the gardens, stopping now and again to smell the flowers. She couldn't see the moon, it was cloudy now, so the only light came from the flickering oil lanterns hung on shepherd hooks at the end of every flower bed.

Sophie sat down on a bench beside a bed of stargazer lilies. Even in the dark, the bright pink flower stood out against the stems and leaves of green filling the rest of the flower bed. The wind whispered softly through her hair and chilled her arms. She shivered once but quickly recovered as she rubbed the back of her arms with her palms.

"Couldn't sleep?" Sophie looked up to see Dominic.

She smiled and shook her head. "No, what about you?"

"I always take a night flight before I go to sleep, it helps me relax."

"Where's Kamara?" Sophie looked around, but she didn't see her.

"She fell asleep already and I didn't want to wake her. So, what's on your mind? Why can't you sleep? Is it Gabe?" Dominic took a seat on the bench beside Sophie.

"Surprisingly, it's not Gabe, but Bastian. The night you and Kamara got engaged, I somehow ended up in his room-in his *bed*. I don't remember leaving the ballroom with him, but when we danced tonight it felt like a spark, like a magnet pulling us together and a heat between our bodies that could melt steel. Then he disappeared and I don't know why," Sophie told him. Dominic's eyes widened. He looked like he had seen a ghost.

"What?" Sophie asked. He knew something about him, she could tell.

"Nothing, I mean, I thought you were out here pining over Gabe, I'm just surprised you moved on and I didn't hear about it sooner." He managed a smile. "Bastian seems nice, I know him from court, and we are friendly enough, but now that I think about it, I don't know anything about him other than his first name. It's strange."

"Well, I should be getting back inside, I need to try to get a little sleep before tomorrow evening when we fly back," Sophie said.

"I'll walk you to your room." Dominic rose to his feet first and offered his hand to Sophie. She took his hand until she was on her feet and then she pulled away quickly. She hadn't meant to and hoped he wouldn't notice the abrupt movement, but he did.

"What's wrong?" he asked.

"There were some girls in the powder room today, gossiping, normally I wouldn't listen to other girls, but I it put your honor in question. They thought I was your mistress and the reason I was staying with you and Kamara was so we could continue our affair. I set them straight though and believe me, they were scared, but If someone saw us holding hands, I'm afraid the rumors might get worse.

"Since when do you care what anyone thinks? You are Queen Sophie Rend of Lapis Highland, Wizard of the North, and one of my very best friends. They can think what they want, however, let them speak badly of you in front of me and I will hand you their tongue." Dominic nudged her with his shoulder.

When they got to Sophie's room, Dominic embraced her warmly. "Sleep well, Soph. I will see you in the morning for breakfast." She closed the door as he walked down the hall toward his room. As soon as her head touched the pillow, Sophie drifted into a deep dreamless sleep and didn't wake until the morning light peeked in through the curtains.

TWENTY-ONE

THE CASTLE WAS LONELY without Akiri. She'd left Gabe in charge of handling the council meetings and requested he only visit once a week, right after her feeding. She didn't know how staying in dragon shape would affect her or her mind, and the last thing she wanted was to see Gabe as a tasty snack. Alone in his chamber, Gabe brought the image of Leon into the front of his mind.

"Commander Rend, it's me, Gabe," he thought. His head began to ache, it was dull this time, but he could feel the neural link stretching and connecting across the distance. It wasn't as strong as before, and Gabe thought the connection might be nearing its end.

"Yes, Gabe, what's the report?" Leon asked. His voice sounded far off and static-filled.

"Akiri is currently in dragon shape, she will be for at least the next four weeks while she tries to produce a clutch of eggs."

"What does she plan to do with the eggs?"

"She told me she wants to raise the dragons to protect her family and kingdom."

"Hopefully she doesn't decide to conquer other kingdoms, we are in a treaty with Ledora, and we have to honor the call for aid should Akiri plan an attack, Dragons for Ash could mean war for the rest of us, be careful. Keep me posted. How are you holding up?"

"Better now," he thought. "I will message back when Akiri has made progress with a clutch." Gabe didn't want to give Leon the chance to bring up Sophie, so he dropped the connection on the link for the time being so his thoughts could be his own.

As the weeks passed, the daily routine became easier. He didn't give himself a lot of free time, between sword fighting lessons, archery, ballroom dancing, and diplomacy classes. There was a lot to learn, even a King Consort needed to know who their noble lords were and who ruled the other countries. Gabe spent his evenings reading by the fireplace in his room, mostly books about dragons, what they ate, how they grew, and how to train them. He did as Akiri requested and only visited after she had eaten. On his third visit, Akiri moved away from the nest to show him a clutch of five green eggs. The shells were covered in scales.

"Do you have to stay in dragon shape for them to hatch?" Gabe asked.

Akiri didn't answer, he didn't know if she was even capable of speaking in dragon form. She couldn't lay on top of them because her size would crush them, instead, she curled up beside the nest and wrapped her tail around them. Gabe sat down beside her and placed his hand on one of the eggs. He could feel movement beneath the scales; the steady beating pulse of new life.

"What if we sent two of our guards down here to keep an eye on the eggs, they could switch out every twelve hours. Then you could come inside." Gabe looked into Akiri's eyes; they were different in her dragon form. The pupil was thinner and came to a point at the top and bottom, the iris was bright gold in the middle and turned a darker golden red on the outer rim.

Akiri uncurled from the nest and shifted back into her human form. She bent down to pick up one of the eggs, lovingly stroking the scales with her fingertips as the creature inside responded to her touch.

"We created these. Every one of these eggs has a baby dragon inside. Do you know how much people would pay for these? Dominic, Kamara, me, and Sophie are the last known dragons in this world, and we have the ability to create more. I fear money and power would cloud the judgment of men. I am not sure I can trust anyone enough to not be tempted to take one of our children for themselves."

"I understand, but do you even know how long they will take to hatch? How long are you willing to live in this underground tomb? What if it takes years?"

Akiri looked back at the nest and then to Gabe. With a heavy sigh, she relented, knowing he was right. "We need a heavy steel door," she said, finally. "It will need to be locked and protected with magic. Then I might feel safe enough to leave them with guards at the door," she replied, gently placing the egg back in the nest.

"No problem, I will see it done today, my Queen." Gabe took her hand in his and kissed it as he bowed to her. Goose flesh rose on her arm and spread across her body. The way he said "my queen" made her melt. When others said it, their words blended together and it sounded more like m'lady, but when Gabe said those words it felt like he was telling her she meant more to him than anything else and she was his *Queen*. Not just in title, but in his heart.

The local Blacksmith stared at the entrance to the lair. "The openin' is a little bigger'n what I thought it was gonna be, to be honest, carrying that much steel up here whole will be impossible. I'd need a forge here to do a job this big."

"Whatever you need, we will set you up. Go ahead and gather your supplies and tell this guy what you need and he will get it for you." Gabe told the blacksmith as he gestured to the guard nearest him. The blacksmith agreed an bowed to Gabe before following his escort back toward the castle.

Gabe still had to find a wizard to protect the door when it was finished. He'd had no luck finding someone during his trip into the city of Ash and the only other thing he could think of was to reach out to Commander Rend. He walked back to his chamber and closed the doors behind him. He thought of Leon and waited for the link to connect their minds.

"I need a wizard who can do protection spells for the lair," Gabe told him, getting right to business.

"Hello to you too, Gabe. I take it Akiri was successful in producing a clutch, but now doesn't want to leave the nest?" Leon asked.

"Yes, there are five eggs in total and they are all moving. We could have five dragons soon, although none of the texts I got from Ravenhall say anything about how long it takes a dragon egg to hatch."

"I will reach out to a contact in Northport, I am assuming Sophie is out of the question," Leon said. It was a statement, not an inquiry because he already knew the answer.

"Yes, sir. We didn't part on the best of terms last time." Gabe replied as he thought back to his last interaction with Sophie.

"I'm sorry, but the information you have given us already is proving very valuable. The fact humans and dragonshifters can produce eggs- is truly fascinating. Keep up the good work, Gabe." Leon said.

"Thank you, let me know when the spell caster is on their way." Gabe disconnected their mental link before Leon could continue. Gabe disliked being reminded of Sophie every time they talked. He wanted to move on. Forcing the conversation and Sophie from his mind, he went to the storage closet and gathered two bedrolls and pillows. Then grabbed two robes and arranged for Mister Koffery to bring him and Akiri dinner in the lair.

The blacksmith was working diligently as Gabe approached. The dirt box forge the builders crafted was working perfectly, Akiri's dragon fire had helped bring it to temperature and the large steel door was already almost complete. It was not solid, but rather, the top of the door looked more like cell doors in a dungeon. If they put a solid door on the lair, he worried the eggs might not survive if cut off from fresh air.

Gabe walked down the stairs, and around the corner to where Akiri sat beside the nest, humming to the eggs. He laid out the two bedrolls and pillows side by side. Akiri looked at him curiously.

"What's this?" She asked.

"Until the door is finished, I thought I would stay down here with you, to help you watch over our babies," Gabe said as he placed a hand gently on one of the eggs. "I have already arranged for Mister Koffery to bring us dinner, and I brought our robes, so we can be comfy." Gabe watched Akiri's face turn from surprise to awe. She stood up and walked over to him as a tear ran down her cheek.

Gabe took her in his arms and held her close as he reached up and wiped the tear from her cheek with his thumb. "Please, don't cry."

"I'm sorry." She said.

"What do you have to be sorry for?"

"I just don't understand my feelings. You are so sweet and you make me so happy, but then the thought of possibly losing you makes me feel like a piece of me is gone. When I think this must have been the way Sophie felt about you, and the way you felt about her, I am ashamed I took that from you both."

"No, the situation with me and Sophie was beyond anyone's control, it was her choices and mine that led me to you and I don't regret a single thing. This feeling you're talking about, that's love, this is what love feels like. I don't want to lose you either, not for anything in the world. I'm not going anywhere. I'm yours, Akiri. I love you." His voice was deep and soft in her ear and it sent a shiver down her spine. Her skin prickled as Gabe ran his fingertips up her bare back and in what seemed like an instant, but forever at the same time, he kissed her. It was slow and soft.

Gabe ran his fingers through her long black hair as he deepened the kiss. The room felt like it was spinning to Akiri, she felt woozy like she had the very first time she had wine. Gabe's fingertips explored the curves of her body as he trailed kisses down her neck. They forgot anyone else in the world existed until they heard someone behind them loudly clear their throat.

They jumped, startled by the sudden noise and Gabe rushed to grab the robe he brought for Akiri. Gabe's guard, Jack turned his back while he waited for Akiri to slip the robe on and tie it at the front.

"Yes?" Akiri asked as she adjusted her robe and brushed the hair out of her face.

"Sorry to interrupt, My Queen, I just wanted to let you know the door is finished. This is the key and it is the only copy. Keep it with you, we can't open the door without it." Jack said as he handed it to Akiri. Jack bowed, then turned and left the lair.

Akiri glanced at Gabe. She saw the obvious sign of frustration about the interruption and smiled as she stood on her tiptoes to wrap her arms around his shoulders.

"What do you say we lock up here, and go finish what we started in our bedchamber?" she whispered.

Gabe agreed enthusiastically.

TWENTY-TWO

GABE AND AKIRI JOLTED awake to the sound of a dragon screeching as it passed by their bedroom window. Akiri jumped out of bed with her heart pounding and threw on a dressing gown. She was already out of the room and down the hall before Gabe could even get out of bed. Loud clanging from the bell tower put the entire castle on alert. Akiri ran out the back doors and across the southern courtyard. Her heart dropped and she screamed as she surveyed the scene.

Smoke billowed from the door of the lair and Akiri bolted from the back of the courtyard to the steel door. Disregarding the heat of the steel door, she grabbed the handle and pulled with all her might. She screamed for Gabe as she cried frantically trying to open the steel door but it was stuck and her hand sizzled as she gripped the handle until she could no longer stand the pain. Her palm was now missing the top layer of skin and she wailed, holding the injured hand close to her chest. Gabe had not been close enough to prevent her burn, but as he ran to her, he grabbed a bucket of water from the garden well. She plunged her hand down into the liquid and muffled a scream as the water took the heat from her wound.

Another ear-piercing roar rang out as a large, dark shadow passed over them. Gabe and Akiri searched the sky for the source to see a large black dragon flying south with a bag hanging from its mouth.

"It can't be. I thought he was dead?" Gabe wondered aloud.

"The eggs! The eggs!" Akiri screamed.

Gabe ran to the training yard on the western side of the courtyard and grabbed two swords from the rack. When he got them back to the door, he ran both of them through the handle of the door in opposite directions. He took off his tunic and ripped it in half, he wrapped both of his hands in the fabric to protect them from the blades. He grabbed the handle and blade of each sword and pulled back as hard as he could.

"Can you cast any water spells?" Gabe asked as the door flew open. A wall of heat and smoke poured from the opening, causing Gabe to recoil as he felt every hair on his body singe.

Akiri was still frantic, crying as she looked at the entrance to the lair. She carried the bucket to the doorway and emptied it, throwing the water as far into the lair as it would go. It made little difference to the flames burning at the bottom of the stairs. She put her hand in the empty bucket and tried to cast a water spell but the bucket would not fill. Her casting hand was injured. She screamed again and threw the bucket down the stairs. The thin metal pail clank down the stairs until it too reached the bottom and disappeared in the flames.

"This is your fault," Akiri screamed at Gabe. "I wanted to stay with the nest, I wanted to stay with our babies, but you... you," she couldn't finish her sentence, she fell to the ground and cried. It was the most mournful sound Gabe had ever heard. She knew it wasn't his fault- not entirely, but she still felt like he had clouded her judgment.

"How could this even happen? Weren't the guards supposed to be here?" Gabe asked.

With no way to fight the flames, Gabe sat down on the ground next to Akiri and tried to comfort her. He had no words to cheer her up so he placed his hand on her shoulder. She was curled in the fetal position, sobbing and shrugged away from his touch.

"Akiri, I'm sorry. I didn't know something like this could even happen. I promise I will get to the bottom of it." Gabe said.

Akiri got up from the ground and shifted into her dragon form. She braved the flames and went down into the lair. Her breath weapon was an acidic sludge, which would do no good. She pushed her way through the flame; her scales protecting her from the heat. Akiri heard a *crunch* as she stepped on something she couldn't see through the fire and smoke. She backed up and kneeled down beneath the cloud of gray to see she had crushed a human skull. The skin was melted off of the corpse, but she would recognize the armor anywhere, this was one of her guards. *He must have died trying to protect the nest,* she thought.

Akiri made it to where the eggs should have been and found only broken shells in the remains of the nest. There seemed to be fewer shells than she expected for five eggs. *Some of them must have turned to ash in the flames.* She thought, *either that or the black dragon took what he wanted and burned the rest.*

Akiri ran up the steps and took flight, leaving Gabe on the ground below. The castle staff had gathered and formed a chain from the well to the lair as they filled bucket after bucket of water and tried to put out the fire.

Akiri flew until she reached Ledora. She landed on the western beach and walked to the castle gates without care that she had arrived naked; better than showing up in dragon form, which after the way she treated King Haki last year, could be perceived as a threat. A coughing fit took over her as she approached the gates, she caught the attention of the two castle guards standing on either side.

They both rushed to help her. One of them took off his cape and wrapped it around her while checking her face for bruises, cuts, or any other sign of violence.

"Who are you running from, Miss?" he asked with concern.

"I need help, I need to see Prince Dominic and Princess Kamara please," Akiri said. One guard took off toward the castle while the other tried to keep Akiri engaged in conversation.

"Have you been hurt?" He noticed her hand and the soot on her face. "Of course you have—a silly question, what I meant was, *who* hurt you?"

"I'm not sure. I- uh…" She didn't know if she should tell the guard about her lair or not. Prince Dominic and Kamara would probably try to have children soon, so she needed to warn them about the egg thief, but not everyone needed to know.

"Can you tell me what happened? We want to help you. Did it happen here in the city?" Akiri shook her head.

"No, it happened at my castle in Ash, but I would rather wait for Prince Dominic and Princess Kamara, it's a personal matter."

Just then, the other guard returned with the Prince and Princess. When they saw Akiri in the state she was in, Dominic rushed to her and offered his hand to help her up.

"It's okay, we have her from here. Thank you for coming to get me," Dominic told the guards.

They led Akiri through the front doors of the castle and into one of the guest rooms located on the second floor. Kamara asked one of the maids to find Akiri some clothes and Dominic heated some water for a bath. Akiri was seated in the chair beside the hearth, still wrapped in the guard's cloak. Kamara grabbed her a dressing robe and sent the guard's cloak with one of the castle maids.

"What happened, Akiri?" Kamara asked as she pulled the other chair closer to Akiri's.

"He's back. The black dragon I mean- he destroyed my nest and my clutch of eggs." Akiri sobbed.

"Are you talking about Baelfire? We killed him, it can't be him, can it?" Kamara asked.

"I don't know, but he was very much alive when he destroyed my babies and then flew off toward the south with a bag of something hanging from his mouth, My guess would be he stole an egg."

Kamara looked at Dominic, "We should tell Sophie."

"Would you mind if we asked Sophie to join us?" Dominic asked Akiri.

"I- I'm not sure she will want to see me, given the history she has with King Gabriel."

It was strange hearing her call Gabe by his full name, he never used his full name, not in Blackwater, or during their journey to Choddrath last year.

"I can ask her if you want, but we don't have to."

"I don't mind, I just want to find the bastard who hurt my babies, and I can't do it alone," Akiri said.

Kamara nodded and got up. "Dominic and I can go talk to Sophie and in the meantime, you can clean up and get dressed. Meet us in the kitchen when you're ready, we will leave a guard outside your door to show you the way when you're finished." Kamara placed a friendly hand on Akiri's shoulder.

"I know we have never been friends, nor have we ever really worked together, but I would like to," Kamara said softly. She smiled at Akiri before she turned to follow Dominic into the hall.

Akiri went to the bath and slipped the robe off. She stepped into the large tub cautiously. The water was still quite warm and it stung her skin as she eased herself down into it. She did not put her burned hand into the water, instead, she used a cloth to gently clean around the wound as best she could. When she finished washing her body, she stood up, the water was black with soot from the fire and smoke. She pulled down on the handle and the stopper popped up from the drain. She watched the black water get lower and lower until it swirled around in a circle at the mouth of the drain.

She found herself wondering where the water goes as the tub emptied. Her maids still had to empty her bath by hand. She felt a lot better, except for her hand which had begun to blister. When she was dressed, Akiri opened the door to find the guard standing beside it as Kamara told her he would be.

"I'm ready, Sir," she said.

"Right this way." He turned and walked down the hallway. Akiri loved the way the golden trim brightened up the castle walls, it made it not as dark and scary looking as the dark halls of her castle. The guard led her to a set of double doors which opened into a large kitchen with several workstations. The pots and pans dangled from the rack above the kitchen island. Sophie, Kamara, and Dominic were sitting at a small table in the corner of the kitchen and there was a chair left for her. They had heated a kettle of water for tea and waited for her before they began.

"Please, join us," Dominic said, as he gestured to the empty chair. As she sat down, he poured water from the kettle into their cups.

"We want to help you, but we need to come to an agreement first," Sophie said.

"What kind of agreement?" Akiri asked. She fearing it might have something to do with Gabe.

"A year ago, we formed the dragon alliance between us and The Silver Talons Guild. It is our job to protect the interest of dragons, by assuring peace with humankind. If humans fear us, they will hunt us, and we would be forced to defend ourselves. No one wants war. Humans who commit acts of violence or threaten dragonkind will be brought to justice. My father is the leader of the guild, so believe me, the punishment will fit the crime. We will only help you if you join the alliance with the Silver Talons Guild and agree to follow these rules." Sophie slid a handwritten book bound in leather across the table to Akiri.

"Okay, I agree," Akiri said without hesitation or even opening the book. She wanted to find who was responsible and bring them to justice, she would do anything to see that happen, even join a guild.

"Great, it looks like we are heading to Ash. We can wait until sundown and then leave, if you need to rest up or eat, do it while we have time to spare. We will meet on the western beach at sunset." Dominic said. Sophie started to stand up, but Akiri put her uninjured hand on top of Sophie's.

"I hope we can become friends," Akiri said. She had wanted to say she was sorry about Gabe, but knew hearing his name from her lips would cause Sophie pain so she didn't. Sophie pulled her hand away.

"Just take care of Gabe and we will have no problems," Sophie said. She walked away, not offering any expression or other hint as to her thoughts. Akiri looked at Kamara and Dominic. *She said they'd have no problems, but made no mention of whether or not a friendship could ever be possible.*

"She needs more time, Gabe was her best friend since they were children, and she is helping you as part of the dragon alliance code, if you want anything more, you will have to earn her trust," Dominic said.

"Gods know I don't deserve yours after Choddrath, and what I did to your father last year," Akiri replied.

"Lucky for you, I believe in second chances. I don't want enemies when I take the throne, I would much rather have friends and allies."

Akiri winced in pain as she tried to rise from the table, she had accidentally placed her hand, palm down on the table to push up from the chair and instant regret filled her as she collapsed back into her seat.

"Let me take a look at your injury." Dominic held out his hand to her. She turned her hand over and showed him her palm. It was blistered and red and still looked dirty. Dominic waved his free hand over the wound and whispered an incantation. As his hand encircled hers, a blue crackling of lightning surrounded them like a bubble. The particles of dirt and smudges of soot lifted from her hand and floated away into the magical sphere.

"All I can do is clean it out, you need to see Clarice in the infirmary. Come on, I'll take you."

Dominic stood and reached for Akiri's good hand to help her up.

"While you show her to the infirmary, I'm going to go talk to Sophie," Kamara said. Dominic kissed her softly. And whispered something in her ear. She leaned in, placing her hand on his chest as she listened, and smiled.

"I love you too," she said back to him as he led Akiri out the door.

The infirmary smelled like every herb all at once. The wall to their right was lined with shelves of tinctures, potions, salves, and the wall to the left was lined with beds. An older woman with gray hair and an apron stood to greet them as they came in.

"How Can I help you, My Prince?" she asked with a curtsy.

"She has a pretty bad burn on her hand, she needs healing, please." Clarice looked at Akiri's palm. She closed her eyes and began to chant in a language Akiri had never heard. As she spoke, new skin began to form and covered the burn in soft pale flesh.

Akiri glanced at her hand in amazement, she opened and closed her fist, turned her hand upside-down, and inspected the back of it as well.

"I've never seen magic like this, it's like it never happened. Thank you."

"Yes, of course, this is my purpose. The Goddess gifted me with this power so I could help others." Clarice explained.

"You should get some rest before we go, It has been a traumatic day for you," Dominic said.

Akiri nodded, although, traumatic did not even begin to describe it.

TWENTY-THREE

Sophie paced back and forth across her room biting her nails. The coppery tang of blood hit her tongue before the pain signal made it to her brain and she looked down at her fingertips to see two of them had started to bleed.

"Sophie, can I come in?" Kamara's voice came from the other side of the door. Sophie rushed over to open it and invite Kamara in.

"I don't understand, we *killed* Baelfire. I saw him turn to dust, he can't be back." Sophie began pacing again as Kamara closed the door and walked over to join her.

"Maybe there was another black dragon. We thought we were the only four until Baelfire emerged, so maybe he wasn't the only other one." Kamara suggested, crossing the room to sit on the edge of the bed.

"How can we find him? It's not like we're going to see an enormous sign pointing us to his lair."

"Sophie, stop, come sit down before you pace trenches into the floorboards." Kamara patted the end of the bed next to her. Sophie joined her but continued biting her nails, and her leg bounced rapidly.

"I'm worried for Gabe, Akiri left him there alone, what if the black dragon comes back before we get there?" Sophie asked.

"I hope he can fortify himself somewhere safe. We can leave as soon as the sun sets. We will be flying west, so we won't be able to see until twilight at least," Kamara said.

"I'm going to get some rest, you should too; try at least," Kamara said as she walked toward the door.

"I will," Sophie promised.

When Kamara was gone and sleep still evaded her, Sophie pulled out her spell book and practiced some incantations, without the hand movements, the spells were ineffective, but her pronunciation needed work. She could cast fire in a bolt or an area, simple illusions such as the appearance of clothing, and she could create food and drink, and she could even turn invisible for a short time, but only in human form. She was unable to cast at all in dragon form.

When Sophie was finished practicing, she kept to her promise and tried to rest. She closed her eyes and tried to force sleep, but it would not come. Instead, thoughts of Gabe and Bastian mingled in her mind and kept her awake. *Why can't I get him out of my head?* Sophie thought. She tried to think of the day under the willow when she and Gabe had kissed. She thought of his soft lips on hers, and her skin tingled. She closed her eyes, but then it was Bastian's face she saw before her.

No matter how hard she tried, she could not remember what happened between them the night of the engagement ball. She remembered kissing him, Gabe interrupting, and then she woke up next to Bastian. She didn't remember walking to his room, undressing, or getting into his bed, let alone whatever happened between them after those events.

Ugh, this is useless. Sophie thought as she threw back the covers and sat up. The wood floor beneath her feet was cold, she looked toward the hearth and noticed the fire was out. She put on her robe and crossed the room to put a few pieces of wood in the fireplace. As soon as she stood, there was a knock on the door.

"You couldn't rest either?" Sophie called. She expected to see Kamara again, but when she opened the door, Bastian stood before her. Sophie looked at him in surprise but moved back so he could enter. He looked at her so intensely it made her heart flutter and her face flush. Sophie closed the door and locked it.

"When I heard you were here..." his voice trailed off.

Bastian moved closer to her, his blue eyes staring deep into her soul. He didn't hesitate any longer, in an instant, his lips were on hers and her robe slipped off her shoulders and fell to the floor. He picked her up pressing her back gently against the wall as his lips explored her. She could feel his arousal. He carried her to the bed, their lips only parting long enough to take in a breath. He laid her down gently, carefully placing her long hair to the side of the pillow. Trailing kisses down her body, he cupped her breast and caressed his thumb across her nipple. He slowed down and gazed into her eyes as he ran his fingertips down her sides, and then her hips.

"Is this real, or am I dreaming again?" Sophie managed to ask.

Bastian smiled, "You've been dreaming of me?" he asked, kissing her stomach, her belly button, and then lower, until his mouth found its prize. His steamy breath warmed her as he flicked his tongue on the secret spot that made Sophie moan his name. She gripped the bed sheet in each hand with a white-knuckle grasp and arched her back. He kissed his way back up her body until he reached her breast and then he took her nipple in his mouth and sucked gently elongating and hardening it. He played with her nipples and teased them with his tongue until Sophie's desire was too strong and she could bear it no longer. She reached between them and took his length in her hand, gripping as much of him as she could in one palm, and positioned him at her entrance.

Bastian watched her face as he slowly pushed inside her. She gasped and no words came, but she moaned softly as he moved his hips back and forth slowly, sliding himself deep inside her and pulling out to the very tip before inserting his length again. Bastian lifted her hips, pulling her body toward him as he thrust faster and harder until he felt her contracting. They reached climax together and he buried himself deep within her, and stayed inside until the contraction of her orgasm forced him out. He looked down at her soft red lips and her eyes which reminded him of a doe. Bastian rolled over onto his side, still admiring her face. Her rosy pink skin glistened with perspiration and he traced constellations in the freckles speckling her shoulders and chest. Bastian curled a lock of her hair around his finger and then let it bounce back into place, *a perfect ringlet on a perfect girl,* he thought.

Sophie rolled over and kissed him. Bastian held her body to his as she accepted his tongue into her mouth. His body responded to her passion and she felt him harden again as his erection pressed against her inner thigh. Bastian turned her onto her back and positioned his face between her legs. He licked up and down her sex as his arms wrapped around her thighs and held her in place. He could feel her trying to squirm as he swirled his tongue around her clit and sucked it into his mouth, flicking his tongue back and forth. She moaned his name and begged for him to enter her again.

He sat up, pulling Sophie onto his lap. She straddled him as he kissed her passionately and tangled his fingers in her hair, pulling gently to tilt her head back. He kissed her chest and her neck as she moved back and forth, sliding his cock between her lower lips. Her wetness enveloped his sex and he bucked his hips as Sophie moved her hips forward and he thrust inside of her.

"Oh goddess, you feel so good," Sophie told him. Bastian gripped her ass, lifted her up, and slid her back down giving her every inch of his passion. She loved the way he filled her, and how he hit every right spot. Fluid dripped from her sex. She moaned as her pleasure mounted and called out his name as she reached orgasm. He felt her walls pulsing around his cock and he let himself climax with her again.

Sleep came easily then for both of them and when Sophie woke up, the sky was deep orange. She sat up quickly and this time, her movement woke Bastian. He tried to coax her to lie back down with him, and if the threat of great danger weren't looming over them, she might have considered it.

"I'm sorry, I have to go, but I will see you here next weekend, I hope," Sophie told him.

"Maybe I could come to visit you before then?"

She couldn't resist him, although she tried. "My castle isn't complete yet, I am staying with Prince Dominic and Princess Kamara."

"Your castle? Are you a Princess?" Bastian asked as he got out of bed and closed the distance she'd put between them.

"No," she replied. Bastian looked at her confused. "I'm a Queen, actually," she said with a smirk.

He pulled her in close and growled softly in her ear, "A *Queen*. I guess that makes me the Queen's Consort."

"Or the Queen's Plaything." Sophie teased. "If I married, my husband's official title would be King Consort though, not Queen's consort."

"I can't say I'm disappointed by either title." He kissed her softly, pulling her body against his. She made a deep, inarticulate sound filled with desire and regret as she swiftly took a step back and cast the clothing illusion.

"I'm sorry, I have to go. I'll be here next week, and I want to see you again," Sophie said with a commanding tone.

"Yes, *My Queen*." The way he said those words; a half-whisper and half-lust-filled groan, drove Sophie crazy, if she weren't so worried about Gabe, she might be tempted to stay longer and have her way with him again, but she gathered all her strength, and her bag, then headed for the beach.

The flight to Ash was shorter than Sophie expected, but the landscape was exactly what she heard it was; flat farmland for miles and a small town near a dark, looming castle carved from the stone of the only mountain on the island. Sophie instantly felt sorry for Gabe, this dreary place was now his home. She thought he must miss the forest and the streams. She wondered if he might even miss his job at the citadel.

They landed on a rocky beach, it was dark and everyone else had to get dressed. Sophie picked up a rock and whispered an incantation to it. The stone lit up like a full moon and they had to shield their eyes from it as Sophie tossed it a few feet down the beach. The area where they stood was now dimly lit and everyone could see to get dressed.

"Thanks, Sophie. Magic sure comes in handy doesn't it?" Dominic asked. Sophie chuckled and nodded.

"Sometimes."

When everyone was dressed and ready to continue, they took a dirt path leading away from the beach and between the neglected fields. It was a longer walk than it appeared, and when they finally got to town, everything was already closed. They walked up the cobblestone street toward the castle in silence. Akiri led them through the front door, around the left corridor, and through the back doors overlooking the southern courtyard. She picked up an oil lantern on the way so they could see.

Sophie could smell the ash and smoldering remains as soon as they stepped out the back door. The scent intensified the closer they got to the entrance to the lair. The three of them followed Akiri down the steps into the underground cave which had been carved out by hand tools, much like the rest of her castle, and the mountain keep on Choddrath. Remnants of metal armor and weapons remained, but not much else.

"This is where my nest was, I laid five eggs. They all had movement inside. I would have had children, but they were murdered, or perhaps even stolen. There were broken eggshells down here, but it didn't look like enough to be all five eggs." Akiri turned to face them with tears streaming down her cheeks. Sophie didn't know how to feel. A year ago she would have thought Akiri was incapable of feeling. The way she had claimed her power and left the rest of them to take care of Baelfire alone.

Now here she was, crying and broken because someone had taken everything she loved away from her. Sophie knew she had a habit of harshly judging others in the past. She once thought Kamara was too naive to survive the real world, and she had not been hurt by it enough to be cautious in her actions. She had been wrong to think this though, because Kamara had been hurt by the world more than any of them when Baelfire's men stormed her temple and killed everyone she knew. She had been lucky to escape, and smart to stay with the guild even after delivering the orb.

"Sophie." Kamara's voice brought her back from her thoughts of the past and she looked up to see them all standing at the base of the stairs. "Ready to go?" Kamara asked.

"Oh, yeah. Sorry." Sophie followed them back through the courtyard and into the castle. Gabe was waiting for them just inside the door. When their eyes met, Sophie wanted to run to him and throw her arms around his neck, but it seemed inappropriate now, with him being married and all.

"How are you, Sophie?" Gabe asked.

"I'm okay. I would ask how you are, but it seems like a silly question given the circumstance." she replied. Gabe nodded and turned toward the guard standing to the left of the entrance.

"Jack, would you please ask Mr. Koffery to make some tea and bring it to the dining hall?"

"Yes, Your Grace," he replied with a quick bow and hurried off to do as Gabe asked.

"You have adjusted to royal life well," Sophie said.

Akiri put her arm through Gabe's and the two of them led the way to the dining room. The table was modest with only eight chairs. Akiri sat at one end, and Gabe at the other.

"Please, sit wherever you would like," Akiri said. Sophie chose a seat in the middle and Kamara sat next to her, closest to Gabe so Dominic walked to the other side of the table and sat in the middle across from Sophie.

Kitchen maids served them tea and brought in a tray of sugar and milk. The teacups were made of some kind of smooth black stone. It held in the heat, even after the fresh milk was added. They waited for everyone else to leave the room, and when they were gone Akiri cast a magical dome around them.

"Don't worry, this is just magical soundproofing. Only those of us sitting at this table will be able to hear our conversation." She finished the incantation and paused before speaking again. "I saw the black dragon fly south from here with something hanging from his teeth like it was carrying a bag. I suspect they might have taken an egg or two before they destroyed my lair." Akiri said as she sipped her tea.

"It can't be Baelfire, we turned him to dust," Dominic said.

"There's more. A seer told me someone on my council would betray me. She didn't say how, or who, but she knew it was going to happen. I haven't seen her since she made the prophecy."

"You think it might be her?" Kamara asked.

"No, but she knew someone would betray me and she is now missing. I have looked for her in the city and turned up nothing, I have had the city guard looking for her, as well as the sailors down at the port and so far, everyone has come up empty-handed."

"What's her name?" Sophie asked.

"Agatha Stone, although, She was often called Madame Stone," Akiri told them. She left out the part about how she only used to call her 'witch' or worse.

"So where do we go from here? We could fly south and look for clues, or we could re-create the situation, and tell everyone you have a new lair, and this time you are not telling anyone where your lair is. Next, you can confide in each council member privately and give them each a different location. Then we watch those locations, and if the dragon shows up at one of them, whoever you gave that particular location to is the betrayer. Does this make sense? I know I kind of rambled for a minute." Sophie said.

"I think it might work, Sophie, you're a genius!" Akiri said.

"Yeah, good idea, Sophie." Gabe smiled as he glanced at her, but then quickly looked away. She knew he was trying to keep things friendly between them.

"This plan will take months to execute, It will also require me to be away from Ash, and away from the council during my ovulation period. I hate to ask, but would you know of somewhere I can stay, where I can remain hidden during this time?" Akiri asked. Kamara looked at Sophie, and she nodded back to her.

"You can stay in one of the guest rooms at the castle Ophay with me. Dominic will return to Ledora, Sophie will return to Lapis Highland, and Gabe will remain here in Ash. We will still need two more locations and people to watch over them." Kamara said.

"I can ask Juniper and Laughlin to go to Northport, and my dad can send men to Stonehold Keep," Sophie suggested.

"It sounds like a plan. You can all sleep here tonight and we will fly northeast tomorrow afternoon. I will let Gabe show you to your rooms, I'm going to let the kitchen staff know to prepare extra breakfast," Akiri said. The shimmering veil surrounding them dissipated and became no more than specs of dust as Akiri dropped the spell.

Gabe stood up and waited for the others to join him. "Right this way," he said as he turned to lead them from the dining hall. The castle seemed eerie. Sophie wondered if it was this lonely during the day too, or if it was just because they arrived at night. Gabe stopped and opened the door to a guest room.

"Kamara and Dominic, this room is yours," Gabe said. "If you need anything, my room is just across the hall," Gabe said. He returned to the hall and looked at Sophie. "Your room is a little farther down." They walked to the end of the hallway and around the corner to the left. He stopped at the first door. The rooms were all on the right because the left was an open balcony overlooking the central courtyard.

Gabe walked into the room and Sophie followed. She could see the sadness in his eyes when he turned to face her. She had to turn her eyes away, she hated seeing him like this.

"I'm sorry about the eggs," Sophie said.

"Thanks." Gabe stood there in silence as if looking for the right words. She wanted to say so much to him, apologize for leaving him to learn magic, and go back to the way things were when they'd kissed, but it was too late. He'd never be hers and she had to accept it. She had no one to blame but herself.

"My room is around the corner at the end of the hall if you need anything," he said. Sophie nodded, and watched as Gabe forced his feet to move back to the door. She closed it behind him and listened to the sound of his footsteps receding. She hated this. Gabe was miserable. She knew him better than anyone and she could tell. Sophie longed to have back those days beneath the willow now more than ever.

Sophie cried herself to sleep, and in the morning, her head ached. She rolled over to get out of bed and noticed a tray on the bedside table that had not been there when she went to sleep. It had toasted bread, berries, a small bowl of oatmeal, a pitcher of water, and a cup. She poured a cup of water and when she lifted it to take a sip she saw a note. She recognized Gabe's handwriting right away.

The rose is beautiful and sweet. It was almost a line from Sophie's favorite poem. The line actually said; the rose *was* beautiful and sweet. It was a poem about a metaphorical flower given as a symbol of love, losing all of its petals because it was neglected by the person it was given to. Sophie wasn't sure what he meant by this. *Is he trying to tell me he is happy?* Sophie wondered. She was touched by the fact he remembered her favorite poem. She'd first read it in a book of poetry Gabe had copied from the citadel. Most of the poems were anonymously written, but they were all beautiful and filled with so much emotion. It was one of the greatest books Sophie ever read. She thought she might ask him about it today if she could find a moment alone with him before they left.

TWENTY-FOUR

THE NEXT MORNING, GABE sat in the council meeting, studying the mannerisms and words of each man intently as Akiri questioned them about what happened to her lair. Had he known from the start Akiri suspected one of them might betray her, he would have been watching them closely the whole time. Most of the men at the table, not counting Gabe were well into their fifties, except for two. Nohan Arach was perhaps in his twenties, and Timothy Ackerman had just celebrated his thirtieth day of birth.

"My guard, Michael Roman is dead, burned alive in my lair. My eggs were destroyed. I want to know where all of you were while this was happening." Akiri demanded. They all began speaking at once, denying their involvement or knowledge of the event.

"Stop. You first, Ser William. Where were you when the black dragon came and destroyed my lair?"

"Your Grace, I was in town, doing the weekly shopping, by the time I got back to the castle, you were gone and King Gabriel was fighting the fire, one bucket of water at a time so I gathered the household staff and all the buckets we could find and we created a chain from the well to the lair to put the fire out," William said.

"Mister Ackerman, what about you?" Akiri asked.

"I was not feeling well the night before, something I ate didn't agree with me and I was finally asleep after spending all night in the privy." Timothy looked embarrassed as he admitted his whereabouts.

"Can anyone vouch for this?"

"Perhaps the maid staff, I asked for some ginger tea and honey around sunrise," he replied.

"Very well, Nohan, what about you?" Akiri continued questioning around the table.

"Your Grace, I had the night off, so I visited the brothel and spent the whole night there, several girls can account for my whereabouts." He looked particularly proud of himself, but Akiri wore an expression of disgust.

"Mister Koffery."

"When the fire broke out, I was holding the staff meeting I hold every morning just after council. It is my time to plan out the day and delegate tasks. As soon as I heard the commotion, I ran out to help," he said.

"Very well, Bertram?"

"I was repairing a broken stall door at the arena, and then I went to check how far along construction was on the new town square. I didn't arrive home until the evening."

"Was anyone a witness to your presence there?" Akiri asked.

"I suppose the locals were all aware I was there, but if they will remember seeing me I cannot say, Your Grace." He looked nervous and let out an inaudible sigh of relief when Akiri moved on.

"Mister Stewart?" Akiri nodded to her guard.

"Your Grace, I was outside your room when I smelled the smoke. I investigated the source of the smell and when I saw where the smoke was coming from, I ran to the bell tower to ring it."

"I do remember hearing the bell as soon as I saw the smoke coming from the lair. Thank you, your quick action helped extinguish the flames, but unfortunately, we did not act fast enough to save my eggs. I want you all to be extra vigilant. Bertram, can you stay behind? I would like to speak with you privately. Everyone else, you're dismissed." Akiri watched as everyone else got up from the table. When Bertram and Gabe were the only ones left in the room, Akiri closed the doors and returned to her seat.

"Bertram, I asked for privacy because I want this to stay between us. You are the leader of the builder's guild and I know you have some engineers within your company. I was hoping you could design and have them build a weapon capable of shooting a dragon from the sky. I'm thinking something *like* a bow and arrow, but bigger and made of something strong enough to pierce a dragon's skin." Akiri said.

"I will see what I can do, Your Grace," Bertram said.

"Thank you. I'm also going to be gone for a while and will be leaving Gabe in charge, I'm not telling anyone else, so please keep this to yourself, but I am making a new lair far away from here, but in case you need to reach me, and I do mean *only* you, I will be going to Stonehold Keep. It's been abandoned for years, it's the perfect place for a lair." Akiri said.

"I'll not tell a soul, My Queen," Bertram said.

"Thank you, when you have a prototype of the weapon let either me or King Gabriel know immediately. I would like for it to be built on top of the castle."

"Absolutely, Your Grace." Bertram waited to be dismissed and when he was, he bowed to them before exiting.

"First seed is planted. I think I need to take a rest already, I'm still a little tired from the stress of the last couple of days." Akiri said.

"Me too. Would you like for me to lay with you for a while?" Gabe offered.

"I would like that very much."

On the way back to their room, they saw Sophie walking down the hall. She seemed deep in thought and eager to get somewhere.

"Is everything okay, Sophie?" Gabe asked.

"Yeah, fine. I'm just going to go out for some fresh air, maybe walk around town for a bit before we go later this afternoon."

"Okay, will I see you before you leave?" Gabe asked.

"I- uh, if I make it back in time. I'll try," Sophie replied.

Gabe couldn't hide his disappointment. He'd lost his best friend, and blamed himself. His mother couldn't help her situation, she'd been overcome with both grief and elation at her husband's death, and guilt not only for what she'd done, but the happiness of being free of him. Those emotions ravaged her, so she quieted them with drink. If there had been any other way to save his mother from becoming homeless, or worse; killed for her gambling debts he would have. Fate was cruel sometimes. He turned his head to watch Sophie walk away. She didn't even look back at him.

"Come on," Akiri gently pulled on Gabe's arm as she led him into their bedroom. She directed him to the bed and told him firmly to sit down. "It's not fair," she said. "I want you to look at me the same way you look at her. I want to know what it feels like. Akiri's fingers started to glow with a green light. Gabe was nervous. He hadn't meant to make his wife feel this way.

Akiri whispered an incantation and as she waved her hands over her body and morphed into Sophie's likeness. Every detail was the same, down to the very last freckle. She sauntered over and straddled him as she pressed her lips against his. He pulled away.

"What's wrong? Isn't this what you want?" she asked.

"Not like this, I don't need you to become *her*." He said the words, but they held no weight against his desire as he looked back at this woman who was Sophie in almost every way. Akiri knew, too because she felt his arousal beneath her as she stared down at him. Gabe swept her fiery red curls behind her shoulders as he kissed her lips. She stood up and slid the straps of her dress off her shoulders and let it pool to the floor around her feet.

"I want you, Gabe. Take off your clothes," she commanded. He couldn't resist. He undressed faster than he ever had before and when he was finished, Akiri walked over to him and pushed him down on the bed. She walked her fingers up his stomach, to his chest as she mounted him. She hadn't even needed her hand to guide him inside her. He was more aroused than he had ever been before and Akiri knew why. She rolled her hips forward and back as she watched her husband admire every inch of her. She moaned with pleasure as he held her hips with his hands and pushed deeper inside her. In a swift movement, he rolled Akiri over and positioned himself between her legs. He lifted her hips as he thrust himself inside of her again. Gabe stared down at her as he slowed his pace. He leaned down and kissed her gently as his free hand cupped her breast.

"I love you, Sophie," he whispered. He hadn't meant to say it, but after the words left his mouth he couldn't take them back. Akiri dropped the illusion and looked at Gabe angrily. He tried to apologize but she cut him off.

"I knew you were still in love with her."

"This is on you. If you knew how I felt why did you turn yourself into her visage? I told you I didn't need you to become her."

"Your lips might have said the words, but your body told a very different story," she countered.

"Do you not think it possible for me to care for you both? Godsdamn it, Akiri, I'm trying here. I was in love with Sophie since childhood, and that doesn't just go away, but it also doesn't mean I can't grow to love you too. The real you, not you trying to be her." Gabe got up and started dressing.

"Where are you going?" Akiri asked. Her face was stone. Gabe had expected some emotion other than anger, but if she felt any, they didn't show.

"I don't know, right now, just away from you." He slammed the chamber door as he left. Gabe walked out the front door of the castle with his guard following behind. Gabe turned to face him and put his hand up.

"I'm fine, I don't need an escort, I need to be alone," he said. The guard paused and looked as if he were considering following anyway. "That's an order, stay here," Gabe told him.

"As you wish, Your Grace."

Gabe watched him walk back to the castle and Gabe went toward town. He had not spent a lot of time in the village, he doubted if the subjects would even recognize him without his royal armor.

He walked down the cobblestone streets past the shops and when he came to a tavern in the center of town, he was drawn in by the music. They never had music at the castle and Gabe had not realized how much he missed it. He walked in and sat down at the bar. When the barkeep asked him what he would like, Gabe ordered the best ale they had. He had never tried ale before, but the way everyone talked about it, he thought it might be good.

The barkeep handed him a mug of dark brown liquid with a thin layer of white foam on top. Gabe took a big gulp and started coughing as soon as the ale slid down his throat. It tasted bitter and robust, like coffee, but with a strong flavor of copper and herb. As he choked on the ale, the other patrons at the tavern laughed at him.

"First time eh? Yea that'll put th' hair on ye chest won' it?" Gabe turned toward the voice speaking to him.

"It will do something, for sure," Gabe replied.

"Ya get used to it after a bit. It ain't the taste ya drink it for, it's to forget, and it looks like you got some'n you wanna forget."

"I do."

"Don't we all?" The man gestured around the tavern to the other patrons.

"M' name's Kendrick, but mostly people call me Ken. I got the cow farm o'er there by those old sugar cane fields," Ken explained.

"I see, I'm Gabe."

"Gabe, the King?" Ken's eyes widened and he jumped from his seat ready to take a knee, but Gabe stopped him.

"Shh, keep it down, I don't want anyone making a fuss."

"So what's my king drinkin' to forget?" Ken asked.

"It's personal, I had an argument with someone today and I feel bad about it, but I also feel like I'm not wrong."

"Well I don't know much about diplomacy, but it sounds like you could patch things up with a little communication, but you'll never fix anything if you look for all your solutions at the bottom of a pint glass."

"Thanks, Ken, that's not bad advice." Gabe sighed as he pushed the ale back toward the barkeep to signal he was finished with it. Drinking hadn't worked out for his family and he didn't know why he even thought getting a drink would make him feel better.

"Hey, if yer not gonna drink it, I will, no point in wastin' it," Ken said.

"What about all that 'don't look for solutions in a pint glass' talk?" Gabe joked.

"I'm not looking for solutions, just numbness. It's too late to get back what I lost, but it sounds like you still have time." Ken chugged the last half of Gabe's ale and slid the mug back across the bar when he was done.

"Hey, thanks for the talk, I'm going to go see if I can't patch things up." Gabe managed a smile as he pushed in his bar stool and started back toward the castle. Before he made it out of town, Sophie spotted him from across the street.

"Gabe!" she called. He turned to see her already on her way across the street to him.

"Hey Sophie, how are you?"

"I'm fine. I got your note this morning. What did you mean by it?" Sophie asked, getting right to the point.

"I knew you liked that poem is all," he replied.

"You know I can always tell when you're lying." Sophie playfully nudged his shoulder.

"I was just saying you look happy and I hope you are," he said.

"Do you want me to be honest, or do you want to feel good?"

"Please, be honest. Always."

"When I came back to Blackwater, I came back to tell you how I felt. I was finally ready for us to be together. When you said you were leaving and didn't know if you would be coming back, I was devastated. Then when I saw you and Akiri among the newly engaged royal couples I was heartbroken. Now, I know I should stay away, and I know being your friend is infinitely harder with my feelings being what they are, but I can't lose you again."

"I should have told you from the start how I felt about you, but I was afraid you didn't feel the same, and I would lose even your friendship. Then all this happened with my mom and the guild. I messed everything up and I'm sorry," Gabe said.

"It's okay, I could never stay mad at you. Even if you are a complete bonehead."

"I have to get going now, there are a few things I have to take care of before you guys leave. I will be there this afternoon when you go," Gabe said.

Sophie nodded and hugged him tightly, not knowing if she would be able to later when his wife was on the beach with them.

TWENTY-FIVE

THE EVENING SUN WAS beginning to dip below the horizon as they said their goodbyes on the beach. Kamara and Akiri were going back to the temple Ophay, Dominic was going back to Ledora, and Sophie would be returning to Lapis Highland. She hoped the castle was finished, or at least her bed chamber. Gabe was there to see them off, just as he said he would be.

"I made these for us." Sophie handed each of them a quill. And a notebook. "They are all connected by the same magical spell. When you write in the notebook, the ink appears, then disappears like this," she demonstrated by writing her name into her notebook. All the other notebooks began to glow. "Go ahead, open them," Sophie said. When they opened the notebook they saw Sophie's name written in their notebooks. "When you close the book again, the messages disappear, so make sure you only open the book when you have time to read it, but this way we can quickly get messages to each other from anywhere. If you want to message only certain people, just write their name first and underline it, like this," she wrote Kamara's name, underlined it, and then wrote a little note. Only Kamara's notebook lit up. When Kamara read the note she giggled. They all packed their notebooks and quills into their bags. For Sophie, it was her father's backpack, which was beginning to show signs of wear on the straps from being carried in her teeth.

"This is a great gift, Sophie. Very thoughtful." Kamara said as she packed it.

"I agree, thank you." Gabe and Sophie's eyes met and his gaze lingered a moment too long and he heard Akiri huff. He quickly looked away. "Safe travels, everyone. Hope to see you soon."

When he moved forward to kiss Akiri goodbye, she turned her face and his kiss landed on her cheek. Sophie looked away quickly, not wanting to insert herself in the obvious spat they had going on. They shifted into their dragon forms, Dominic, the majestic gold dragon with the power to exhale lightning, Sophie, the fierce red dragon with fiery breath, Kamara, the silver with the ability to bring ice and frost upon the land, and Akiri, the dark green dragon who could spit acidic sludge and melt metal with it. Sophie knew if the four of them were on the same team, there would be no force strong enough to take them on, not even the black dragon would stand a chance.

Gabe watched as they took off into the sky. He thought it must be so freeing to be able to fly wherever you wanted to go in no time at all. Traveling by ship sometimes took weeks compared to the trip from Ledora to Ash on dragonback, which only took a couple of hours.

Sophie felt weightless in the sky, which was quite a feat for a dragon. She loved soaring through the clouds and beside the birds. She felt so free of everything when she was flying and most of the time, she wished she never had to come back down.

Even though she loved staying at the Temple Ophay, with Akiri there now, she was glad to be going back home. It was dark when she landed, but she could see Highland Castle was now complete. When the guards saw her, they bowed immediately.

"Welcome back, My Queen." Sophie heard as she approached the castle doors.

"Thank you," she said as she continued inside.

"I would like to call an emergency meeting. If the throne room is completed gather the Highlanders and have them wait in there. I'm going to make myself presentable." Sophie turned to the other guard, "would you mind showing me to my chamber?"

"Right this way, My Queen." He led her up the grand staircase, which opened into a small library and sitting room. Comfortable-looking chairs stood in front of large windows with bookshelves in between them. They turned right down a hallway and the guard stopped.

"This entire wing is yours. You have your chamber here," he pointed to the first door on the left, "and then you have your study. All of your magical items and components have been stocked and are in your study for you. There is a secret passage leading from your bedchamber to the lair and from the lair to your study. I will leave you to explore, but please, My Queen, if there is anything you need, I will be right here." He pointed to the corner of the hall and the library. "I have been assigned to be your guard unless you choose another, Your Grace."

"I feel like if we are to be working so closely together, I should know your name," Sophie said.

"My name is Thomas, Your Grace," he said. The boy was no older than Sophie, but he was muscular and looked like he could win a fight.

"Thomas, do you know how to use your sword?" Sophie gestured to the short sword sheathed at his hip.

"Yes, My Queen, I have trained every day since I could hold a blade."

"Then you will make a wonderful queen's guard, Thomas." Sophie smiled and retreated to her chamber, taking notice of the boy's prideful expression as she left.

Her bed chamber was beautifully decorated with a carved mahogany canopy bed with red and black curtains, a matching chest of drawers, and matching bedside tables. A silver chandelier illuminated the room with flickering candlelight. The nightstands each held a beautiful oil lamp, as well as the vanity and the writing desk. The bath chamber was the most surprising, She didn't know how they did it, but the marble tub had a metal spout and handle to pump hot water into the tub. The water drained from a hole in the base, no one would have to carry buckets of water to fill or empty her tub.

Even with all of her magic, this was one of the greatest things she had ever seen, at least that was what she thought until she saw the privy. There was a tank of water on the back and a chain connecting the tank to a handle. When Sophie pulled it, the water drained from the tank into the bowl and the bowl filled momentarily and then washed down the large drain. *Wow*, Sophie thought.

She quickly cleansed herself in the bath and dressed in a lavish gown. She put on her obsidian crown which was made for her on the island of Choddrath, inside the mountain keep. She exited her room and approached the guard.

"Would you please, escort me to the throne room?"

"Of course, My Queen." Without another word, he did as he was asked and led her to a set of carved double doors. When he opened them he walked in before her.

"Please stand for Queen Sophia Rend, The Red Dragon," Thomas announced. Everyone stood and turned toward the center aisle to watch Sophie enter. She walked confidently to the throne and when she sat down, everyone else did as well.

"I know you might not be aware of recent events, but A black dragon has attacked the kingdom of Ash. This dragon destroyed something very important and irreplaceable to the Queen. If you see the black dragon, you are to report it immediately. Anyone caught knowingly concealing the dragon's identity or human form will be sentenced to death. I do not know if this black dragon is Baelfire, I thought for sure he was dead, but know I am your rightful Queen and anyone who does not swear fealty to me, here and now can leave the Highland and never return." Sophie stood and walked to the edge of the platform.

"If you are true to your Queen, take a knee at this time and promise to defend Lapis Highland and the Red Dragon from all enemies." Sophie had never seen an entire room of people kneel so quickly. There was not a single person left standing.

"My Queen!" They all declared.

Over the next few weeks, Sophie settled into a routine. She chose a small council and found a way to make money selling potions and magical items created in her study. She was becoming more practiced in wizardry and her new shop in Alasia Outpost, the shopping district of Alasia, did very well on its grand opening. The shopkeeper, a Highlander by the name of Gladys was an experienced caravan operator and she sent her people out in all directions selling Sophie's enchanted items to people in every town they traveled to.

By her third week back at Highland Castle, Sophie began feeling ill. She was throwing up like she had a stomach bug and was tired all the time. The healer brought her things like plain toast and ginger, but nothing seemed to help. Everything she ate or drank came back up. When another week passed and she did not get her blood with the new moon, she thought of Bastian. *Oh no, what have I done?* Sophie thought of the last day they spent together and a tear rolled down her cheek as her hands protectively felt her stomach for signs of movement. There weren't any yet, but the bottom of her stomach felt hard and just a little bloated. It was not much bigger than normal, maybe the same as it was after a large meal. *I need to keep this to myself for now,* she thought.

TWENTY-SIX

KAMARA WAS A GRACIOUS host. Temple Ophay was beautiful and homey. It wasn't large like a castle, but it did have plenty of guest rooms and Akiri's favorite part, a gorgeous lair with bubbling hot springs. Akiri liked the forest, it was a lot better than the dry island of Ash. She thought of Gabe and hoped he was doing well.

Before she left, Akiri had already given three of her council members false locations, and Gabe was feeding the other three information. He was also in charge of watching the councilmen making sure they weren't discussing the locations with each other and uncovering their lies. The plan counted on them not finding out they each had a different location. Weeks passed and Kamara and Akiri spent much of the time talking and getting to know each other. Akiri had been good at concealing her sadness in the first few days, but her thoughts weighed on her until they became too much. Kamara saw her expression and couldn't stand it any longer.

"Akiri, would you like some tea?" Kamara asked.

"No thank you, I just need someone to talk to." Akiri was in the sitting room on the end of a sofa nearest the fireplace. Kamara walked over and sat down beside her.

"What's wrong?" Kamara asked. Akiri's eyes were red and she clutched her handkerchief tightly.

"Gabriel is still in love with Sophie. I tried to overlook it because I wanted a clutch of eggs, I wanted children, but now I realize, more than anything, what I want is love-*his* love. The way he looks at her... he'll never look at me that way." Akiri wiped a tear from her cheek.

"The situation you are in sounds difficult, I can't imagine how hard it is for you. Is he at least trying?"

Akiri nodded, unable to speak for fear she might start sobbing again. She touched the cloth in her hand to her eyes and sniffled.

"Perhaps in time, he will come to love you just as much," Kamara added.

"Maybe, I don't deserve his love. Honestly, the only reason I accepted his proposal was because he was a Silver Talons Guild member. I thought having him in Ash would gain me leverage. I thought he might be able to call the Guild Army to his back should Ash need to defend itself. Then when I got to know him... I just wanted him to like me as much as I liked him, but I blew it."

"Maybe not. Gabe is honorable and determined. He made a promise to you and I don't see him breaking it, he will try to work things out when you get back, I know it." Kamara was trying to comfort her, but it was hard to shake the feeling she had messed everything up.

"I have another cloak with a hood here somewhere, we could go into town and find something to do. I don't think anyone here would recognize you."

"I can do better than a cloak." Akiri used her magic and turned her hair blonde, and changed the shape of her face. She looked like a completely different person.

"Wow, impressive!" Kamara said as she looked at the girl in front of her who looked nothing like Akiri. "What should we call you?"

"My nanny when I was young, her name was Margaret, She was my favorite, I think I will go by 'Maggie' in her honor," she replied.

"Maggie, it's nice to meet you, are you ready to go to town? I know just the place to wash those blues away!" Kamara said.

They took the horses and a short ride later, they rode out the western Blackwater gate toward the docks. When they reached the Loose Anchor Tavern, Kamara hitched the horses out front and pulled their oat bags over their snouts.

Jovial music and the pounding of heels against the wooden floorboards greeted them before they even opened the door. Akiri had never been to a Tavern like this. The one in Ash was quieter, more like a place of lament than celebration.

"Come on, Maggie!" Kamara called as she danced her way through the crowd to the bar.

"Two honey ales please!" Akiri heard Kamara say when the barkeep approached her. "I normally don't like ale, but their honey ale is delicious!" Kamara was talking very loudly so Akiri could hear her over the sound of the music and dancing.

When the barkeep slid their drinks across the counter, Kamara handed him a silver piece and then waited for Akiri to try the ale. "It's good huh? I told you!" Kamara smiled and took a big gulp. When they finished their drink, Kamara pulled Akiri out onto the dance floor. They blended in with the crowd and were as invisible as they had hoped to be. They had a few more drinks until they felt tired and like it was hard to hold their eyes open. A few times, Akiri felt like the room was spinning, or maybe she was spinning.

"I need to sit down, in the fresh air," she said, stumbling to the exit.

Her heart was pounding, and so was her head, she'd only made it a few steps out the door when all the ale came back up. She did at least manage to turn away from the footpath and vomited into the bushes instead. Kamara walked out of the tavern right behind Akiri in time to see the aftermath of her honey ale.

"Oh, I'm sorry, I guess we had a little too much. What do you say we get back home? You might want to put your hood up, I think your spell has dropped, you look like yourself again." Kamara said. Akiri's hair was once again raven black, and her skin was ghostly pale. Akiri drew her hood and mounted the horse as best she could. Kamara helped her and strapped her feet into the stirrups. She hooked the horses together as if they would be pulling a cart and then mounted her horse.

"You know, When we first got these horses, I did name one of them, but I forget now what I chose. What are some good horse names you think?" Kamara asked. If Akiri weren't completely drunk, she might have recognized Kamara was just trying to keep her awake.

"Umm, Ale and Rum," she said, pointing from Kamara's horse to the one she was riding.

"Because you like rum?"

"Nah, it's 'cause Ash was... its history... the uh, rum runners and um... What was I talking about?" Akiri wasn't used to her mind working so slowly, and not being able to think of the words to say what she meant.

"The names for the horses, Ale, and Rum," Kamara chuckled.

"That's right! I forgot. Ale for yours, and Rum for this one." Akiri said. There was a long period of silence between them as they listened to the birds in the trees and the shuffling of the horses' hooves through the debris on the forest floor.

"I think a nice long soak in the hot spring sounds lovely when we get back," Akiri said longingly.

"You're right, that does sound nice, If you can put the horses in the pasture, I will make us some tea and meet you in the lair. The silvery temple had just come into view and they both sighed in relief at the thought of spending the rest of the evening relaxing.

When they dismounted, Kamara handed the reigns of her horse to Akiri and they went about their separate tasks. Kamara started a fire in the hearth and heated the kettle on the hook over the fire. When the water was hot she made a cup of tea, both for herself and Akiri.

Kamara strolled through the back garden with a cup in each hand. She wasn't close enough to see inside the lair, but she had a feeling something was wrong. She called for Akiri as she got to the mouth of the cavern but received no response. Then she saw them, boot prints too wide and long to be from Akiri's small foot. Someone had been in her lair. Kamara set the tea down quickly. She rushed to the hot spring and looked around the empty lair. *Oh no, oh no, what's happened?* Kamara thought as she ran back out to the entrance of the cavern. Then she saw it, it was the tiniest bit of evidence, but it was evidence nonetheless, a blood-stained rock discarded carelessly to the side. The boot prints seemed to go no further than the entrance.

TWENTY-SEVEN

THE KING WAS HAPPY to have his son home again, but of course wondered why his son had not brought his Princess with him. Dominic had said she was feeling under the weather and chose to stay at the Temple Ophay. He told his father he had come to practice his royal duties, this made the King very happy and of course, he had commanded a banquet in his son's honor. He set the date of the event three weeks in advance to give all of the guests enough travel time.

On the night of the banquet, Dominic wore his royal uniform the coat was a royal blue with gold embroidery along the buttons, and his collar was an elegant white lace ruffle covering the top half of his vest which matched the coat and trousers. Dominic's father was not the only one to notice his wife-to-be, Princess Kamara had not accompanied him, and as they usually do, the whispers began to spread.

"Prince Dominic!" The Prince whirled around to see Bastian approaching him with outstretched arms and a smile. "It's been too long," he said as Dominic took his hand in a firm shake and clapped his other hand on Bastian's shoulder.

"How are you?" Dominic asked politely.

"Honestly, I've been better. I'm lovesick. I was hoping Sophie would be here but I haven't seen her." It was more of a question than a statement, Dominic could tell he was hoping he would offer up some information as to her whereabouts.

"I haven't seen her either, not for a few weeks," Dominic said. Bastian looked forlorn. "But hey, there are plenty of ladies here tonight, perhaps you can find one to help you forget?" Sophie had never confided in Dominic her true feelings for Bastian, but he thought if she wanted to be with him then she would have invited him to travel with her.

"I don't want to forget. Sophie is the one I want. I think I'm in love with her," he said dreamily.

"Has she told you how she feels about you?"

"Not with words, but I know she feels the connection we have."

"I'm sorry, I wish I could help you, but my father is calling for me. I wish you and Sophie the best of luck!" Dominic called as he maneuvered his way through the crowded banquet hall. He stopped at the series of buffet tables along the wall on which, sat beautifully arranged and delicious delicacies for snacking. He picked up a plate and selected some strawberry tarts, pineapple chunks, a couple of samosas, and some kofta made with ground beef and lamb, mixed with herbs and spices, skewered, and grilled over the fire. When his plate was full, he took his place beside his father at the center of the banquet table. The King raised a chalice and toasted to Dominic and the Kingdom of Ledora. The crowd cheered as they all took their seats at the table. The servants brought course after course while musicians played music on stringed instruments.

When the banquet was over and most of the castle had retired for the evening, Dominic found himself thinking of Kamara. He thought about going back to the temple to see how things were going, but he couldn't tell anyone in Ledora about the black dragon.

"My son, why do you look so glum?" Dominic hadn't heard his father approach and he startled slightly at his voice.

"Oh, sorry, I'm just missing Kamara."

"What's going on? Why has she not joined you? You have been away for weeks now and to my knowledge have not even received a messenger from her." King Haki sat down beside Dominic and prepared to listen to his woes. Dominic did not tell him of the magic notebook he and Kamara used to talk regularly.

"Honestly, things between us were great, we were setting up a home at the temple. It's easier for us to work with the guild this way, but truthfully,

I am here, and she is there because we are on assignment. We are trying to lure out a rat," he confided.

"I see, it's such a demanding assignment, to be away from the one you love." The King showed empathy.

"I think I am going to take a walk and get some fresh air," Dominic said.

"Should you need to talk again, you can always come to me, no matter the time." The King rose to his feet and hugged his son before they parted ways.

The night-time air in Ledora was cool, a blessed reprieve from the scorching sun of the daytime hours. Dominic walked from the castle through the Golden City, then out the eastern gate toward the beach where he and Kamara always landed. The moon, although not full, still cast the beach in a soft white glow. A low, rumbling sound stopped Dominic in his tracks. He tiptoed up behind the dunes and peeked out across the crest. He saw a cloaked figure shift into the form of a black dragon.

Dominic gasped and then, afraid the dragon might have heard, clasped his hands over his mouth and ducked down behind the dune. He waited, anticipating the sound of the dragon's footsteps in his direction, but instead, he heard the beating of two large, leathery wings as the dragon took flight to the northwest. He had to get back and use the notebook from Sophie, he had to let all of them know the dragon was leaving Ledora.

Dominic ran across the beach toward the western gates of the Golden City. His feet sank into the sand as he ran and slowed him down. By the time he reached the steps of the castle, he was gasping for breath. He rushed to his bedchamber and bolted the door behind him.

The notebook was in his bag, he grabbed it and dumped it on the bed. He opened the notebook and scribbled; *The Black Dragon was just spotted leaving the beach in Ledora.*

Not long after he wrote the message, his notebook lit up. *I know who it was, it was Akiri's guard, Horace Stewart. I will handle it on my end. Meet here as soon as possible. -Gabe*

Right after the message from Gabe, another message appeared. *Akiri is gone, they've taken her. I'm headed to Ash right now.* It was from Kamara.

TWENTY-EIGHT

Sophie was in a deep slumber when the sound of heavy armored boots marching down the corridor roused her. The footsteps stopped at her chamber door. She was already up and on her way over when the metal armor clanged against the wood.

"Your Grace, I am so sorry to disturb you at this hour, but there is a gentleman at the front entrance who is very insistent upon seeing you," the guard explained through the door.

"Did he give you his name?"

"Bastian, Your Grace." Sophie's heart leaped. She was so happy he had found her. After Sophie left Ledora to go to Ash she wondered how long it would be before she got to see him again. Sophie tied her dressing robe around her waist and ran to the stairs taking them two at a time to get down them faster. When she reached the front entrance, she was out of breath but threw her arms around Bastian's neck at once. The guards averted their eyes as this stranger handled their queen in such a familiar way, grasping her backside as he lifted her off the ground and kissed her deeply. One of the guards cleared his throat. Remembering they were not alone, Sophie led Bastian up the stairs to her room. He tried to kiss her again as soon as they crossed the threshold, but Sophie stopped him.

"I want to see you undress," She commanded. Bastian began quickly untying his tunic, but again she stopped him. "Slowly." Sophie sat down on the edge of the bed and watched him intently as he pulled at one string very slowly and the knot came untied with an almost inaudible pop. He slid his fingertips under his tunic, letting his hands showcase his abs and chest as he lifted his tunic over his head. He walked up to Sophie, positioning the tie to his trousers close to her mouth. She touched him, running her palms from his chest to his hips.

She kissed the sensitive skin between his belly button and his trousers and then took the end of the string in her teeth and pulled the bow loose and then quickly pushed him backward. He hooked his thumbs into the waist of his trousers and then slid them down. Sophie watched with anticipation as his body was revealed. He was perfectly sculpted, not over-muscular, but defined.

Sophie stood up, untied her robe, and pulled the silk belt from the loops. As she glided over to where Bastian was standing she could tell he was imagining her shape beneath the robe which hung open, barely obscuring her breasts. Sophie put the silk belt around the back of Bastian's neck and used it like reins to guide him to the bed.

She pushed him backward onto the bed and then slipped out of her robe as she crawled onto the bed after him. "Put your arms up," she commanded.

"As you wish, My Queen." His eyes never left her as she used the silk belt of her robe to tie his arms to the headboard of the wooden canopy bed. She trailed kisses from his lips, to his neck and down his chest, then his inner thighs. He writhed beneath her, as she paid attention to every part of his body except his sex which was throbbing with desire. He moaned as her breasts grazed his skin as she kissed her way back up his thigh and then took him into her mouth, swirling her tongue around the tip which was already salty with the first drippings of his seed. She stopped then, leaving him wanting more as she crossed the room for no other reason than to let him desire her as she stood out of his reach.

"Sophie, please," he begged.

"I didn't say you could speak," Sophie said quietly. She stared at him intently as he continued to squirm, and move his hips in an attempt to relieve the pressure. She smiled as he moaned and begged for her without daring to utter another word. She crawled onto the bed again, this time she straddled him, leaning over to kiss his lips as she let him slide into her. He groaned as she rolled her hips slowly, arching her back as she rode him. He longed to touch her body, fondle her breasts, and thrust into her deeply, but she was in complete control.

When she was satisfied, she reached up to untie him. In an instant, his hands were all over her, one hand squeezed her buttocks while the other grasped her breast. He gently flicked her nipple back and forth with his thumb which caused her to cry out. She then turned around on her hands and knees facing the foot of the bed. Bastian quickly rose to his knees and entered her from behind. He grabbed her hips and pulled her toward him as he thrust into her. He moaned as he felt her muscles contract around him and it made him thrust harder and faster. He pulled her toward him slightly so he could run his hands up her belly to squeeze her breasts and his right hand went further still as he held her throat gently. He loved the way her curly hair grazed the small of her back as she rose from all fours to her knees with him still inside her.

"Turn around, I want to look at you. Please," Bastian requested breathlessly. She did as he asked, staring into his blue eyes as he positioned himself between her legs. He pushed into her again, slowly this time, teasing her with the tip and then finally giving her a good deep thrust. He watched her face as he did this, noticing the way her mouth fell open when he was deep inside her and the way her eyes rolled back when he only gave her the shallow, quick thrusts, and how her nipples hardened and lengthened at his touch. He moaned her name as he reached climax and pumped inside her until he slid out soft and satisfied.

"I love you, Sophie," he said as he gazed down at her.

"I-" She started to speak but a faint light from the desk caught her eye. It was the notebook. *Oh no, how long had it been lit up?* she wondered.

"Hold that thought," Sophie said as she scrambled up off the bed. She opened the notebook and read the messages from Dominic and Kamara. "I'm sorry, I have to go." Sophie didn't bother packing a bag, she used the illusion spell to dress in the bath chamber and then ran out to the side of the castle, She prepared her body to shift but it wouldn't work. She tried again, this time, focusing on her hands, stretching her fingers to make them grow into talons. It was no use. She couldn't shift. A fluttering in her lower stomach told her why. The sudden fear of having to tell people why she couldn't shift took over her mind and she began to cry, but dried her eyes as best she could before returning to her room to face Bastian.

"Is everything okay, should I leave?" he asked as he tied his tunic.

"Everything is okay, don't leave. We need to talk." All the joy left his face at those words.

"Oh, is this the 'it's not you, it's me' talk, or the 'we need to see other people' talk?" he asked.

"This is the 'I'm pregnant, what are we going to do about it?' talk," she replied.

Bastian sat back down on the edge of the bed, his eyes wide, and his hand over his mouth.

"I mean, I had no idea it was possible, so we didn't exactly do anything to prevent it. How do you feel about it?" Bastian looked at her.

"I'm not sure." Sophie thought about shifting, she couldn't get to Ash, if she sailed, it would take her weeks to get there because she would have to sail around The Barren. She went to the desk and grabbed the notebook and the quill and wrote;

Can't make it; I will explain later, handle the guard and then let's meet here.

Sophie closed the notebook, placed it in the desk drawer, and then sat on the bed beside Bastian.

"I thought you were leaving, I didn't know if I should stay with you not here," he said. Bastian had his boot in his hand but put it down when Sophie came over to sit beside him.

"You don't have to leave. I would prefer you stayed." Sophie leaned her head on his shoulder. Moisture began to gather in the wells of her eyes. She didn't know why she was suddenly overwhelmed with sadness, but Bastian put his arm around her and softly kissed the top of her head. He rested his head on hers.

"Would you like to lie down? Maybe you need to rest?" he suggested.

"Perhaps you are right." Sophie dropped the illusion spell and crawled beneath the covers of her bed.

"Would you like for me to stay in a guest room?" Bastian asked.

"No, I want you to hold me and tell me everything is going to be okay," she replied.

Sophie was finally able to sleep when the last of her energy was cried out. Bastian held her most of the night. She didn't feel him slip out of bed, but he was gone when she woke. Sophie pulled on a robe and walked about the castle looking for him. The guards stood in their places and nodded as Sophie walked by.

"Did Bastian say where he was going?" Sophie asked the guard standing at the front doors.

"Yes, My Queen. He said he was going to go into town to go shopping."

"How long ago did he leave?"

"He left before the sun came up, Your Grace."

"Thank you," Sophie didn't remember the guard's name. The castle staff had been hired by Ezra. He ran the underground keep for Baelfire but swore fealty to Sophie when Baelfire was killed. He gave Sophie no reason not to trust him and she knew it was because of him, and his rallying, she now had this castle. Ezra was a good man. Giles too, he'd been the first to declare for Sophie when the keep fell. He had whispered to her in secret: if anyone could free them from Baelfire it was her. Giles was a yes man, he was too afraid of punishment to outright disobey, so he always did as Baelfire commanded without question. In the time Sophie spent in the mountain keep of Choddrath, she witnessed Baelfire's mistreatment of those he felt were beneath him. He treated her like a princess, of course, his daughter- the heir to follow in his footsteps and carry out his plans. Too bad for him Sophie's plans included her family- her real family- Leon, and Samantha.

Sophie wandered to the kitchen and put on a kettle for tea, she loved being able to get water from the pipe over a large basin. Even with all of her magic, this still seemed like sorcery to her. She sipped her tea while she wanted to wait for Bastian, until Dominic and the others arrived.

TWENTY-NINE

THE THRONE ROOM WAS dark; black slate floors, dark gray stone walls, and southern-facing windows shaded by large trees. Gabe walked around lighting the torches in the sconces around the room. The only light coming in from outside, shined down from a round skylight over the throne.

Gabe walked onto the platform and behind the throne to the rope hanging from the bell tower. He pulled the rope at least eight times, the clanging vibrated through the rope. He took a seat on the throne as everyone in the castle began filing in. They sat on long benches lined up on both the left and right of the center aisle. It reminded him of a wedding, but no one would be getting married today. He waited for the guards and the small council to be present, and when most of the castle staff had taken their seats, he let them know the reason for the meeting.

"It has come to our attention, the incident which happened last month with the Queen's lair and her eggs, was an inside job. One of you knows something, one of you knows the black dragon who killed our children. I intend to reveal this traitor to the crown, and they will be dealt with accordingly, before I call the guards upon this individual, I want to give them the chance to step forward, admit their wrongdoing and beg our Queen's forgiveness."

"The Queen isn't here though, where is she? She left us here with this outsider sitting on the throne, ruling *our* kingdom while the Queen herself hides," said a gruff man with long greasy hair. He stood in the back with his arms crossed.

"I hear your frustration, and believe me, I did not intend to be ruling without Queen Akiri, but the attack on her children can not be forgiven, and it is our goal to protect her until the guilty party is brought to justice. It's evident the guilty party has chosen not to come forward, so without further delay, guards, please arrest Horace Stewart." Angry outbursts erupted from the crowd. The guards moved up behind Horace and seized him by each arm. They brought him in front of Gabe and put him on his knees. Horace's face was filled with shock and confusion. "We have evidence to believe you gave sensitive intel to the black dragon so he might find the Queen's new lair. Have you anything to say for yourself?" Gabe asked.

"My King, I have only ever served Queen Akiri loyally, I am not the betrayer. The burden of proof may not be on my side, so I would ask your mercy and that I might stay locked in the dungeon until you find this black dragon and dispatch him. It be the Queen herself to decide my fate." He bowed to Gabe so deeply that all he could see was the tip of his boot.

"Very well, guards. Lock him in the dungeon, we will let Queen Akiri decide what to do with him when she returns. You all are dismissed." Gabe sat down on the throne as everyone exited.

When the throne room was empty, Kamara and Dominic approached Gabe. He looked at them, confused for a moment. "Where's Akiri, and Sophie?" Dominic and Kamara looked at each other.

"You haven't read the last couple of messages, have you?" Dominic asked.

"No, I went to sleep last night after I sent my message and I left the notebook in my desk drawer this morning, why, what's happened?"

"Akiri has been taken, we aren't sure how, or who, but there were boot prints in the lair, which means her kidnapper was human. Even if they were a dragon, when they shift in and out of human form they're naked, they wouldn't have boots on."

"How did this happen? You were supposed to be watching her!" Gabe shouted at Kamara.

"This isn't her fault." Dominic put his hand up to prevent Gabe from getting any closer to Kamara.

"I was making us tea and we were going to soak in the hot spring." Gabe took a breath and thought about what this meant.

"If the dragon was in Ledora, and the Temple, there has to be more than one traitor among Akiri's councilmen. I will try my best to get someone to slip here, you guys go to Sophie and make sure she is okay. Please, don't let anything happen to her." Gabe said.

"We will do our best," Dominic promised. He wrapped Gabe in a quick hug to comfort him and then looked at Kamara. "Can you lead the way? I have never been to Lapis Highland before." Kamara nodded.

"I can lead us there, but we wait until the evening sun is gone, otherwise we will be flying blind," Kamara said.

When evening, after Dominic and Kamara left, Gabe called an emergency council meeting, expecting all five councilmen in attendance, minus Horace Stewart, who was in the dungeon. Gabe was seated in Akiri's chair at the head of the table. He waited fifteen minutes past the time he commanded them to be there, and one of the men was still missing.

"Where is Nohan Arach?" Gabe asked. The men looked at each other. "Bertram, send guards to the city watch barracks and see if he is there. He is to be brought here by any means necessary, we will continue without him for now." Gabe waited for Bertram to come back inside the room and take his seat. "Is the weapon finished, Bertram?"

"Yes, we have placed it on top of the northeastern tower. We have plenty of bolts already made and even more in production."

"Good. Inform everyone, if the black dragon is spotted flying over Ash, the triggerman should fire immediately. Do we have a plan of defense should there be an attack? What will we do with the women and children?" Gabe asked.

"We have turned the old dungeon into an underground stronghold. We are stocked with supplies enough for the city to survive for a year at least without the need to go above ground. We have a mushroom farm down there for protein and an entire storeroom of fifty-pound bags of rice.

There is a mountain spring running fresh water down there, and only one entrance so it is easy to defend." Roland Koffery said.

"Perfect, Alert the villagers, have them ready to run at the first sign of trouble."

"Yes, My King," he replied.

"Okay, if anyone sees Nohan Arach, he is to be taken directly to the dungeon and come get me immediately. Dismissed." Gabe thought about Nohan, Gabe was sure the captain of the city guard was the same age as he was, if he was older, it couldn't be more than by a year or two. Akiri had told Horace Stewart herself that her Lair would be in Ledora and the black dragon was spotted there. But Gabe had told Nohan the lair was at the Temple Ophay, and Akiri was taken from the temple. *What am I missing? It has to be one of them if not both, doesn't it?* Gabe thought.

THIRTY

WHEN SHE OPENED HER eyes, she saw only darkness. Akiri lifted her hand to the back of her head and felt the lump that had formed there while she was out. It was painful to the touch and the size of a plum. Her hair was sticky and matted with what she could only assume was blood. The floor was made of stone and seemed to be swept clean, there was no debris or dirt beneath her—at least none she could feel. Akiri tried to cast a spell for light, but as she tried to cast, the manacles around her writs glowed a faint green and absorbed the magic from her hands. Her ankles were chained as well, she could get up and walk around, but when she got a few feet away from the wall, the cuffs around her ankles pulled her back and almost tripped her.

She was naked, but she didn't remember undressing. She searched her memory for what had happened. *We got back from the tavern, I stalled the horses, and closed up the barn; Kamara went to make tea. I went to the lair...* All she could remember after that was darkness. It seemed like hours before she finally heard footsteps approaching and could see a lantern in the distance. Akiri moved back toward the wall as the figure grew closer. She could now see the outline of their shape, a hooded figure in dark robes, and a dragon mask hiding their face and made it impossible for Akiri to recognize her captor.

"Please, why am I here? What do you want from me?" she demanded. As they approached, her captor hung the lantern on a hook on the wall.

"This is your new lair, what do you think?" Akiri tried to place the voice, but it sounded distorted as if some magical interference carried it from somewhere else entirely. She couldn't even tell if the voice was male or female.

"Who are you?" she asked.

"It doesn't matter who I am, I am no one. I am here to make sure you are taken care of." With a whisper and a wave, a few small berries appeared in the captor's hand. "Eat one," they said. Akiri backed away, shaking her head.

"Girl, don't be a fool. You cannot escape, no one knows where you are, and even if you did manage to make it out of this cell, I assure you, there a single morsel to eat on this island. Oh, and I forgot to mention, don't bother trying to shift, or use magic, those fancy bracelets you're wearing won't allow it."

"I don't understand, why are you doing this?" Akiri asked. "I just want to go home."

"Our master needs a mate. He cannot produce eggs, but you can. You have been wasting your birthright with the human boy, creating abominations that are half dragon, half human without the ability to shift."

"How do you know- You took one, I knew the dragon took one." Akiri reveled in her realization.

"You will never get what you want if you continue to mate with the human boy, he is not special. I would show you the result of your union with the human, but we already disposed of it."

"You're monsters, those were my children," Akiri spat.

"No- those were monsters who would have been chased from the villages with torches and pitchforks. No one would have trusted them, or loved them. What kind of life would that be? One where you are hated by everyone, everywhere, for your whole life. We are offering you better children, dragons to be feared by all and make your kingdoms the strongest in the realm."

"You can't just kill my children and then expect me to..."

"It's your choice, you can stay here forever, unable to get back to those you love, or you could do this one simple thing, and produce a clutch of eggs for us and then you can take half and go free," the captor said.

"I will never let him touch me."

"Then you will remain here until you die." The captor left a single berry on the floor in front of Akiri. "You'll want it when you get hungry." They left it just out of Akiri's reach and grabbed the lantern from the wall. Akiri listened to the footsteps retreat. Her magic was useless with the manacles , there were no rocks, weapons, or anything else she could use to break the chains. Kamara and the others were her only hope. They had to be looking for her by now. She curled in the fetal position and cried herself to sleep. She hoped for dreams, but even those seemed to abandon her.

When she woke up it was still completely dark, she had no indication as to what time of day it was. No light came in from outside, and the temperature was always the same. She hated to admit her captor was right, but since she had slept, now she was hungry. Akiri held out as long as she could and when the pain became too great she stretched and reached for the berry. She wiggled her fingertips and lengthened both her arms and legs as much as the chains would allow until finally, she was able to reach her breakfast.

She rolled it in her fingers, and she remembered from seeing it in the lantern light it had been a red berry, smooth and round like a blueberry, but deep red. She put it into her mouth and chewed it up. The taste was dry but strong; it was tart and bitter at the same time and not as soft as she had expected it to be, but it was also not crunchy like some dried fruit. Once she swallowed it, she felt full; like she had eaten a whole meal. She also was not thirsty anymore-which she didn't understand since the berry had been dried.

A little while after, the captor returned. Akiri watched the lantern swing back and forth as the captor walked closer. "I see you've eaten, good girl," they said. "Have you given any more thought to our request?"

"It wasn't a request, was it? You say that word like I was given a choice, but the only choice is to do what you want, or die." Akiri said bitterly.

"I never said it was a good choice, but you do have one," the captor replied.

"I have another question, this black dragon is your master, yes?" The captor looked confused. "Is he Baelfire?" Akiri asked.

"No, not even close. First of all, Master is dark green, not black, and second, Baelfire? No one follows him anymore, he is dead."

"So then how does this green dragon still have his powers? I thought all the power was given up when the ancients contained the magic in the orbs?"

"The island of Immernacht where Master was born holds many secrets. Magic affecting the rest of the realm does not penetrate the barrier protecting Immernacht. When all the other dragons lost their power, It was a fate Master was lucky enough to escape. He and his brothers, although his younger brother left Immernacht well before the age of seventeen to squire for some noble family, as you know, the power of the dragon lays dormant in a shifter until they are seventeen. It's because the body is too weak before then to handle the shift. When we realized Master still had his power, he promised he would restore dragons to our kingdom so we could finally see the sun again."

Akiri thought about the darkness in the room where she was, and how she had seen no light at all since she got there, not even remnants of light from the opening of the tunnel. "Are we in Immernacht now?" she asked.

"Our time is up, no more questions. Master will be back in a few days, you should think about the offer. I think he is being pretty generous," the captor said.

THIRTY-ONE

T HE MORNING SUN WAS just peeking over the horizon when Kamara and Dominic arrived at Highland Castle. Sophie met them in what would eventually be the western courtyard with robes for them to wear.

"I'm going to have changing stalls built here, and in the eastern courtyard as well, so when you come to visit you don't have to walk very far without clothing, or worry about where you can get dressed. I didn't know if you brought clothes with you, so I brought you these," she said as she handed them the robes. She had brought three robes out with her, but Gabe had not come with them.

"Gabe had to stay in Ash, with Akiri gone, he is the King there and he can't leave, there is no one he trusts enough to rule," Dominic said. "Otherwise, you know he would have come."

"Are you okay, Sophie? Why can't you shift?" Kamara asked.

"I'm pregnant," Sophie said. She felt it was better to just rip the bandage off.

"Oh my goodness, Sophie... Who-"

"Bastian."

"That's wonderful, Sophie! Isn't it?" Kamara saw the apprehension on Sophie's face and then wasn't so sure she was ready to celebrate the news. Dominic looked even more shocked than Sophie.

"I just saw Bastian in Ledora, he was looking for you."

"He found me. He's here now," Sophie said.

Dominic looked confused. He was trying to process through the shock how Bastian could be in Lapis Highland already, but he thought it best to continue thinking for a while. He didn't want to alarm Sophie. She guided them from the unfinished courtyard to the stone walkway leading to the front doors of Highland Castle.

"I'm sorry, I know it's not much yet, but after some landscaping and gardening, it will be as beautiful a castle as I ever dreamed." Sophie smiled.

They entered the grand foyer and saw the staircase which opened into a small sitting library, but Sophie led them to a meeting chamber with comfortable chairs and a large round table. She sat down and waited for Dominic and Kamara to take their seats too.

"Do either of you have a plan or any leads as to where they might have taken Akiri?" Sophie asked.

"No, but there were very few footprints near the lair or inside it, so either the kidnapper is extremely light-footed, or they can fly," Kamara said.

"Do you think it was the black dragon who took her?" Sophie asked.

"It's possible. I think our focus now should be, finding out who this black dragon is." Dominic looked at Sophie. "I saw Bastian, just the other night in Ledora, by ship the trip from Ledora to Blackwater Bay takes at least four days on a direct route, then from Northport, it's another half a day's walk... How is he here so fast? Did you see him arrive?" Dominic asked softly. Sophie looked horrified as her mind came to the same conclusion as Dominic's.

"You don't think Bastian is the black dragon do you?" Sophie looked as if she were about to cry. "It can't be true, there has to be some other explanation, teleportation circles, or maybe even a polymorph spell that could turn him into a bird, something..." Sophie clutched her stomach as the salty tears roll down her cheeks. "How could I have been so stupid, I never should have-"

"Sophie, none of this is your fault. We will find her. We just have to figure out where he might have taken her. Did he tell you where he was from?"

"We never really talked about his past, at least I don't remember if he mentioned it."

"What did you guys talk about?" Dominic asked.

Sophie tried to remember actual conversations, but all she could think about was how he made her feel when they were together in her bed. She didn't recall having any meaningful conversations about him, or even about herself. She looked ashamed as she shrugged at Dominic. Kamara put her arm around Sophie's shoulder.

"Don't worry Sophie, everything will work out," Kamara said. "In the meantime, we can give you a ride back to Ash if you want, so you can see Gabe."

"I have to deal with Bastian first, we can't just leave him here, and we can't expect my castle staff to stop a dragon, I have an idea, we will take him with us, but I need to brew a pretty strong sleeping potion first."

Dominic and Kamara followed Sophie upstairs and to the room across from her bedchamber. "Wow, this is a pretty amazing study," Kamara commented.

"Thank you, it's not finished yet though, I have more things in storage I don't have shelves for yet," Sophie said as she grabbed some ingredients from a cabinet. She began mixing herbs and powders in a miniature cauldron hanging over a candle flame. She added some water from a jar with an amethyst tied around the mouth of it. She put in a scoop of glowing teal powder and a deep blue smoke rose from the cauldron as the contents started to boil.

Dominic and Kamara watched her with amazement as she created the potion. When she was finished, she strained the liquid into several small vials. The potion inside was a shimmering dark blue. It looked like the night sky filled with millions of shimmering stars.

"Will it work?" Kamara asked.

"If we can get him to drink it, he should sleep for a few hours. We might have to give him another dose mid-flight, depending on how long it takes."

"From Ash to here it was about seven or eight hours, We left in the evening, and arrived at sunrise," Dominic said.

"I will give him a little extra, hopefully, it will last until we can get to Ash." Sophie stuffed the vials into the pocket of the robe she was still wearing just as Thomas, her guard stepped into the room.

"Bastian has returned, Your Grace," he said.

"Thank you, Thomas, these are my friends, Dominic and Kamara, they are free to roam the castle as if they live here, with no restrictions."

"As you wish, Your Grace."

Sophie looked at Kamara and Dominic. "Perfect timing, give me an hour and then meet me in the western courtyard." Sophie walked toward the door and Thomas moved out of the doorway so Sophie could exit. She went downstairs and greeted Bastian in the foyer. He held out a bouquet of bright pink lilies and kissed her cheek as she took them.

"They're beautiful. I should get these in some water, and I was just about to make some tea, do you want a cup?" Bastian nodded and Sophie looked at him the way she always had, but was nervous he might sense something had changed. Sophie and Bastian walked to the kitchen, with Thomas following a few feet behind to guard the door. Thomas stood with his back to the kitchen to give them the semblance of privacy.

Sophie found a vase for the flowers and then put the kettle back on the wood stove, the fire was burning low so she placed another piece of wood onto the hot coals and stoked it to get the flames going again. She took one of the vials out of her pocket and held it tightly in her hand.

"Would you mind asking Ezra for some milk from the cold storage? Thomas can direct you to him, it's just a few doors down." Bastian smiled and got up from the table. He kissed her before going about his task. As soon as he was gone Sophie uncorked the vial and poured the contents into his cup. She cast an illusion spell on it to make it appear empty and then carried both cups, spoons, and sugar to the table. She lifted the strainer from the kettle to check the color of the tea inside, it was dark, just like she wanted it.

When Bastian returned with milk, they both sat down at the table. She offered the milk to Bastian first, which he refused. Sophie was relieved, the color of the tea might be slightly off with milk in it and then he might know something was strange. She poured her cup first, and then as she poured Bastian's cup she dropped the illusion spell as the dark liquid mixed and covered the potion. Bastian put some sugar into his tea and stirred it.

Sophie sipped her tea eagerly, since it had been poured from the same kettle into two seemingly empty cups, Bastian would have no reason to distrust her and refuse the tea. Finally, he raised the cup to his lips and sipped it.

"This tea is really good, where did you get it?" Bastian blew onto the surface of his drink to cool it.

"I bought it in Alasia from the tea shop, it's a special blend of elven tea from Ravenhall," Sophie said as she took another drink. "I think after we finish our tea, we should take a walk in the courtyard, maybe pack a basket and have brunch beside the ocean," Sophie suggested. Bastian's eyes were filled with nothing but stars for her as he enthusiastically agreed. They finished their tea, and Sophie conjured a basket of delicious treats to take to the cliffside. Sophie dressed quickly and made sure to stash the extra vials of sleeping potion into the pocket of her trousers.

"Ready?" She asked Bastian when she came back downstairs.

"I'm feeling kind of sleepy all of a sudden, maybe we should take a nap first." Bastian yawned.

"I'm sure you'll get your energy back once you eat something," Sophie said.

"You're right, I am a little hungry." He carried the basket for her with one hand and held her hand with the other. Sophie couldn't help the overwhelming sadness she felt, not only because of the deceit but because of the way things could be if Bastian were not suspected of treachery.

As they reached the back of the western courtyard, Bastian began to stumble. "What the-" Sophie gasped and tried to help him sit down, but he pushed her hand away. "What was in the tea you gave me?" He looked at her in a daze.

"Nothing, I feel fine, it must be something else, did you eat or drink anything while you were in town?" Sophie dropped to her knees at his side. Bastian was sitting on the grass near the edge of the cliff.

"Everything is spinning, I don't... I think I need to lie down." Bastian fell backward and Sophie caught his head in her hands and lowered it gently to the ground.

"Bastian!" She called his name a few more times and when she was sure he was sleeping soundly, Sophie called to Kamara and Dominic who were waiting around the corner of the castle out of sight with a large coil of rope.

"Let's hurry," Dominic said as he shifted. The sun illuminated his golden scales and he had never looked so magnificent before. The golden dragon bowed down to accept his rider. Sophie called for help from the castle guards and asked them to hoist Bastian onto Dominic's back.

The guards were apprehensive about the dragon at first, and with good reason, since they had all been at the battle of Choddrath, but they did as Sophie commanded because she was their Queen. Kamara and Sophie tied Bastian to Dominic's back with the rope and then Kamara shifted as well. Sophie climbed onto Kamara's back and found a couple of handholds near the silver dragon's neck.

They took flight into the sky, even though the sun was just above them, they knew the way now, and there was no time to waste. They flew below the clouds because at least the clouds gave them a little coverage from the sun and they could see well enough to know they were on course. Sophie had never flown on dragonback before and she decided it was not her favorite mode of transportation. She loved to fly, but she needed to have control. She kept watching Dominic. He flew straight and steady, but despite the smooth flight, it looked like the ropes were loosening, and Bastian was slipping. She hoped it was only a trick of the light, but when Bastian slipped to the other side of Dominic's back, the golden dragon rolled sharply to try to keep his rider on, but despite his best effort, Bastian began to fall. Dominic tried to turn around and dive down beneath him, but he was not fast enough, his enormous dragon body would not allow him to turn as quickly as he needed and Sophie screamed as Bastian plunged into the ocean below.

"No! He's in a magical sleep, he'll drown!" She screamed. Dominic had never dove into the ocean in his dragon form, he wasn't sure if he could swim, but he went after Bastian who was sinking beneath the waves as his lungs filled with the salty water. Dominic needed to breathe. He breached the surface, took a breath, and then tried to dive down again, but Bastian was now too deep for Dominic to see, the darkness claimed him.

When Dominic flew up out of the water without Bastian again, Sophie let out a wail. It was a sorrowful sound, Kamara and Dominic knew despite their revelation that Bastian might be the dragon who kidnapped Akiri and destroyed her lair, Sophie was in love with him. Dominic was about to dive down again when a loud rumbling sound came from beneath him, he flew up out of the way and watched as a dark dragon emerged from the water. He spotted Sophie on Kamara's back and flew straight for them. Dominic got in between them and swung his tail at the beast. His tail caught Bastian in the neck and the dragon tumbled backward through the air.

"Go!" Dominic shouted to Kamara. Sophie heard Kamara's voice inside her head tell her to hold on tightly as Kamara accelerated quickly. Sophie screamed and held onto Kamara's scales as tightly as she could. Sophie leaned forward, almost laying down completely against the back of Kamara's neck, but she wanted to look back, she had to know if Bastian was okay. Dominic flew toward them, but stayed a safe distance away, as he waited for Bastian to attack again.

Kamara flew as quickly as she could, she was not able to look back without slowing their progress, but Sophie kept trying to turn around and search the sky while still trying desperately to maintain her grip. She hoped Dominic was okay, but she also secretly hoped Bastian was too. Her heart was shattered. How could he do these things, destroy Akiri's lair, crush her eggs, kidnap her... no, this didn't sound like him at all. There was no denying he had been keeping his dragon a secret from everyone, including Sophie.

They heard nothing but the beating of wings, roaring, electricity, and screeching behind them as the wind battered their faces, but Kamara didn't stop until she reached the rocky shore of Ash. Kamara laid as flat as she could so Sophie could climb down. When she backed away, Kamara looked at her and knew Kamara wasn't going to stay with her, she was going back to help Dominic.

"Be careful!" Sophie called, as Kamara ascended into the sky once more.

THIRTY-TWO

BASTIAN ROARED AT DOMINIC as a cone of fire erupted from his mouth and stopped short just before it reached him. Dominic kept his eyes fixed on the figure in front of him. They hovered in the air, and the beating of their wings began to turn the clouds into a funnel as they faced off against each other. Bastian darted forward and then suddenly rolled right. Dominic was expecting some kind of trickery and rolled left to head him off. Dominic's body crashed into Bastian's. The bright light of day made it hard for Dominic to see much of anything and in dragon form, he couldn't even squint to shield his eyes from the sun. He relied on his other senses, he could hear Bastian's wings beating to his left so Dominic again, darted to the left and rammed into Bastian's body with his own.

Bastian screeched as he tried to blow past Dominic to chase after Sophie and Kamara. Dominic drew in all the air he could hold and used all of his might to strike Bastian with his lightning breath. Dominic saw the smoke rising from Bastian's back as the black dragon spiraled out of control and fell beneath the clouds. Dominic flew toward Ash as quickly as he could, there was no way he was going to leave Kamara and Sophie unprotected.

Dominic kept listening for the sound of beating wings, or Bastian roaring after him, but the sky stayed quiet which was both unsettling and suspicious, but there was no time to stop, he had to get to Ash. When he finally did hear the beating of wings, Dominic drew in a breath and prepared for a fight, but it was a silver dragon that emerged from the clouds. He let out a sigh of relief which came out sounding like a sorrowful roar. Once she saw Dominic was okay, Kamara turned around and led him back to where she had left Sophie. They landed on the rocks and shifted back to their human forms.

"Sophie!" Kamara yelled. She scanned the beach, tall rocks towered like jagged spires from the earth and it occurred to Kamara Sophie could be hiding behind one of them. Kamara took off running across the beach, calling for Sophie as she passed each rock. Dominic ran to the beach in the opposite direction, calling Sophie's name as he searched. When Kamara and Dominic reached the opposite ends of the beach with no luck in finding Sophie, they ran back to each other.

"Maybe she already started making her way to the castle, we have to go, I don't want to be the one to tell Gabe if she didn't make it there though," Kamara said. Dominic and Kamara exchanged a glance and looked away. Dominic knew she felt it too. The same nagging guilt he felt. They promised to keep Sophie safe and now they had no idea where she was. They started walking toward the castle. It loomed in the distance like a dark cloud of despair. Kamara was silent as they walked and Dominic knew she was fighting back tears. He took her hand and gripped it tightly. He couldn't reassure her the situation would turn out fine, but he could reassure her of his love and support.

By the time they reached the castle steps, their feet were bleeding and sore from the broken shells and sharp rocks on the beach and the walk to the gates with no shoes. When the guards spotted them, they knew immediately to fetch buckets of water for their feet, gowns to cover their bodies and the healer from the infirmary.

"Please, we need to see King Gabriel, It's important." Kamara pleaded.

"We will have him come out to you, Princess." The guard said as he placed a pail under each of Kamara's feet and then slid the next two buckets under Dominic's. The water stung as their feet soaked. Kamara winced.

"I know, Princess, but the herbs in the water will clean your wounds and save you from infection." He gave each of them a white dressing gown to slip on, and just as they covered themselves Gabe entered the guard post.

"What happened? Where's Sophie?" His heart sank. Dominic could see the pain in his face already. He was hoping Sophie had already made it to the castle and this conversation would not be as grim as he expected it to be.

"We found out who the dragon is, we drugged him with a sleeping potion and tied him to my back in his human form. We were going to bring him here, but as we were flying over the ocean he began to slip off. He fell into the ocean, but he emerged as a dragon and tried to go after Sophie. Kamara flew here as quickly as she could with Sophie on her back, while I headed off the black dragon and impeded his progress, I hit him with my lightning breath. Kamara left Sophie on the beach to come back to help me take care of him, but we didn't see him anymore, so we rushed back to the beach and by the time we got back, Sophie was gone, we hoped she had come straight here." Dominic explained.

"I'm sorry, Gabe, I know I shouldn't have left her, but I thought she would be safe and Dominic was the one who seemed to be in danger. I was only trying to protect them both."

Gabe's face twisted in anger. His eyes welled with tears. He opened his mouth to speak several times, and Dominic could see him working through what he wanted to say to them. They were friends, but Dominic knew how betrayed Gabe felt. Gabe turned and walked back toward the castle without saying anything at all. Kamara looked at Dominic.

"Maybe we should keep looking. I mean, where would they have gone? They didn't fly past us, and Sophie can't shift so there is no way she would go with him unless she wanted to, they have to still be here on Ash."

"Maybe," Dominic said.

THIRTY-THREE

AKIRI DIDN'T KNOW HOW long it had been now, three days, four? It was always dark inside the lair. The person in the dragon mask had come to check on her every day and each day they left her a single berry. When Akiri ate the first one, it had given her the sensation of being full as if she had eaten a large meal. It also quenched her thirst. She knew the berry would be the only source of food, and with no other options, she accepted it daily.

When the captor arrived today, their interaction was different. They didn't offer her a berry, instead, they inspected her body. "You look healthy. Today, you will shift. This lair was designed to disable your dragon's breath, so don't get any ideas. Also, the tunnel is too small for you to escape in dragon form, and once you shift, you will not be able to shift back until we drop the spell. If you perform your duty for us today, you will be rewarded. If you do not, you will be punished. Do you understand?" Akiri nodded, but a tear rolled down her cheek.

"Turn around and face the back wall and don't look anywhere else but the wall." The captor commanded. Akiri did as she was told. She heard another set of footsteps enter the lair behind her, and then the cracking of bones and the roaring of a dragon.

"You may turn and look on the face of your mate." The captor said.

Akiri turned to face the dragon. He was large, possibly a year or two older than she was judging by his size. His scales were dark, almost black, but the captor had said he was dark green, not black. Akiri was afraid.

"Turn back around." The captor commanded. When Akiri faced the wall again, the captor removed her manacles. The chains clanked to the floor in a pile. "Now shift." Akiri did as she was commanded to do. She wanted to go home. If this was her only way to go free, she would do it. She shifted, her fingers stretched first, bending into long and sharp talons, then her arms bent and cracked as her bones grew and changed shape. She felt her face elongate and her back stretch into the shape of her dragon body. She felt her tailbone grow into the length of her tail and then the scales became hard and more defined, like armor.

The dragon wasted no time in mounting her, rubbing her tail with his back leg until she lifted her own to accept him. His front legs wrapped around hers and she was pinned to the floor, unable to move her upper body. She lifted her tail by rolling her bottom half slightly to the right. He entered her sideways, holding her to him as he drilled into her again and again. His roar was a low rumble shaking the earth beneath them which would have resembled the groan of a climax if they were in human form. She remained silent and unsatisfied by the captor's pet. Before he got off of her, the captor placed one of the manacles around her back talon, above the knuckle so it could not come off without damaging her talon.

"Within a few weeks, hopefully, you will be able to lay eggs, if not, we will have to repeat this until you can produce. Now, keep facing the wall." the captor commanded. Akiri heard the dragon shifting back into human form so he could leave through the tunnel. Akiri knew she was risking everything, but she had to know who it was. She turned her head and she saw him wiping himself off. The captor was facing him, but they saw Akiri move out of the corner of their eyes. Akiri roared in anger and tried to shift, but she couldn't. She didn't know if it was the manacle, or a spell placed on the lair, either way, she was stuck.

"I told you to face the wall and not to look back," the captor hissed. "Now I have to punish you."

"No need, so she has seen my face, what does it matter if we get what we want?" Akiri looked at him, Nohan Arach, Captain of the City Guard of Ash, and member of her council. It was him all along. Akiri felt so stupid for not seeing his ambition before. She wanted to cover them both in her acid breath, but of course, she couldn't do that either.

"If she produces a clutch for us, we can just kill her and no one will ever know," Nohan said coldly as he walked around to look her in the eye. "Then we will kill her human husband in Ash, and I will finally take the throne as I was always meant to do with a thunder of dragons at my back." Nohan looked at her and laughed. Smoke flared from her nostrils, and she swiped at him. He backed away, but not quickly enough to escape her talon and a red gash opened on his chest. It wasn't deep enough to cause him real harm, which Akiri felt was unfortunate. He looked down at his chest and the scratch which was now beading with droplets of blood from his left collarbone to his right pectoral. Nohan turned and left without another word and the captor followed him, leaving her alone. Now since they were gone, she realized she was hungry, and her outburst and disobedience were surely the reason the captor had not left a berry.

Akiri inspected the manacle on her back talon. Her body was too long, and she couldn't get the talon to her mouth, no matter how she tried, it would be the equivalent of trying to lick your elbow in human form, such things were impossible due to physical limitations, yet it did not stop children from daring each other to do it and laughing at them when they tried.

Akiri rolled over onto her back and tried to get one of the talons from her free leg under the manacle. She would rip off her talon at the knuckle if she had to if it meant she could escape and get back to Ash to warn Gabe, but it was tight to her skin, and her thick talon could not even get under the iron. She cried until she fell asleep.

The next morning, the captor brought her a berry. They looked at her. Akiri could see their eyes, but the mask still obscured their face. Akiri wanted to ask them what their name was, but no words came out when she tried to speak, only low rumbling roars. She didn't understand how dragons had their own language if they couldn't speak, or maybe it was something they had to be taught to do and Akiri just never had anyone to teach her.

She waited for the captor to leave, and then Akiri flicked the berry across the room. She would not eat another bite. Maybe after a week of starving herself, she would be able to slip her talon out of the manacle. Akiri paced as much as the manacle would allow and flapped her wings as much as the size of the lair would accommodate. She worked out all day until she was too tired and sore to move, then it was time to go to sleep so she could do this all over again when she woke up.

Akiri dreamed of returning to Ash, preparing for war, and hatching a clutch of dragons to protect the kingdom for generations. She dreamed of Gabe and his soft brown skin, and brown eyes. She missed the feeling of his arms around her, and his lips on hers. She wondered if Nohan was still sitting in the council chambers, pretending to serve the kingdom, pretending to serve Gabe, biding his time until he could have an army of dragons to steal her throne and destroy everything she loved.

It was hard for her to sleep, even when she cried for hours at a time. Her head pounded and her eyes felt puffy even under the tight reptilian skin of her dragon form. She tried for hours to sleep, but it would not come to her. She paced the lair some more until finally, the captor returned with a berry, which told Akiri another day had passed. She realized she could keep track of how many days she was there by counting the berries. The one she flung across the room and the one the captor gave her today made two, and guessed she had been there at least three days before receiving her first berry, although, it was difficult to know for sure. *About five days total so far.* Akiri thought.

Akiri placed the berry along the wall and scraped dirt over it. When she first got here, the floor had been clean, but her exercise and the beating of her wings stirred up the dust and dirt from the walls and the corners. The berry looked like a small pebble covered in dirt, but she would know what it was. *It's been two days since my last meal.* Akiri thought. She tried to slide her talon out of the manacle, it was looser now, and it was almost loose enough to get a talon from her free claw under the metal. *A few more days should do it,* Akiri thought. She continued exercising, ignoring the pain in her abdomen and the loud growl of her stomach.

THIRTY-FOUR

SOPHIE TRIED TO SCREAM as she watched her friends separate from each other on the beach, she couldn't hear them, but it was obvious they were searching for her. She tried to scream to get their attention, but they couldn't hear her either. Bastian had grabbed her and then it was like they blinked out of existence, but the world around them went on. *Why can't they see me?* Sophie wondered.

"Sophie, I'm sorry. I wanted to tell you, I—" Bastian started to explain, but Sophie cut him off.

"No. You don't get to say; *Sophie, I'm the bad guy, sorry I didn't fucking tell you.*" She was sure her face was red, and couldn't remember a time when she wanted to punch someone's face more than she wanted to punch his right now, but as angry as she was, she could never be the one to bring harm to him.

"I'm NOT though, this is what I'm trying to tell you. I'm just a dragon-shifter, like you. We were raised to never tell anyone our secret because the humans would hunt us to extinction, but the problem is, we are going to go extinct anyway, because the only dragonshifters who survived on the island of Immernacht, were male. A couple of them tried to mate with humans, hoping their mates would birth more shifters, but instead, the babies were born with a human shape, but the scales of a dragon, destined to live their lives as outcasts from both human and dragon-shifter societies because how could we keep our secret with half dragon children?" The subject seemed like a painful one for Bastian to talk about, but Sophie needed to hear the rest of it.

"What happened to the children?" Sophie asked.

"Baelfire took them years ago, they tried to scrape off their scales to look more human but resorted to wearing masks in the end. Baelfire said he found a way to restore dragons to the earth. He told us we had to stay on Immernacht until we heard of the dragon's return, and then we must leave and find a dragon mate."

"When you say we, how many of you were there, and how did you get there? You're not Baelfire's *son*... are you?" Sophie tried to hold back the urge to vomit, but her stomach turned and she put her hands on it. She felt the fluttering of life inside her.

"No, but our mothers were all taken to Immernacht before the ancients took power away from the remaining dragons. We were spared the curse on Immernacht because of the wardings over the island. I lived there, in the dark for eighteen years, never seeing the sun, green grass, or blue skies. Then last year, we finally heard it was safe to leave the island and I went to Ledora. I read about the Golden City, and the lavish balls King Haki liked to throw. I knew I had to see it for myself. Six months after my first trip to Ledora, I came back, and I met you. It was the best night of my life, and when I woke up in the morning and you were gone, I felt broken. I thought maybe I could stay away, but I couldn't. When I came back and we danced, I felt myself being drawn to you like a magnet, and I knew if we continued on, I would wake up alone again, so I left. I flew out of there to clear my head. Sophie, I love you. I can't explain it, but it feels like there's a huge hole in my chest when I'm away from you. I *need* you." Bastian embraced her and kissed her forehead. Sophie cried into his chest. It made his skin warm and wet with her tears.

"Who was it then?" Sophie asked.

"What?"

"Who destroyed Akiri's lair, and kidnapped Akiri?"

"I don't know, I have only been interested in seeing you again, this is my first time ever seeing this island." Bastian said.

"How many black dragons are there?"

"I'm the only black dragon, but Nohan is dark green and often is mistaken for black, the other dragons are brown and gray," Bastian told her.

"We have to get to the castle. We have to tell them. It has to be this Nohan guy, I have heard his name before, I think he might be on the staff at the castle." Sophie's voice was urgent.

"They will kill me. I can't go."

"Not if we talk to them, and tell them what you told me, if you help them stop Nohan and find Akiri, I promise we can show them you are not what they thought." Sophie pleaded. She didn't want to go alone, and she cared about Bastian, she didn't want to leave him again. He finally nodded and dropped the spell shrouding them from the outside world.

Sophie cast the illusion spell on Bastian so he would appear dressed. He looked down at himself and even he could see the cream-colored tunic which tied in a pattern of x's at his chest and ruffled at the bottom of the sleeve. His trousers were black and well-fitted and the boots were nicer than the formal shoes he wore to the ball. He followed Sophie to the castle gates and when the guards approached them, they looked shocked.

"Queen Sophia, the King, Prince Dominic, and Princess Kamara have been looking for you. I will announce you at once. He led them to the front doors of the castle and the door guards directed them to the council chamber. When the doors opened, Gabe got up from his seat and stared with his mouth open like he was seeing her ghost. He ran to Sophie and took her in his arms. Gabe held onto her until Bastian cleared his throat.

"What is he doing here?" Gabe demanded. "Sophie, did he harm you?"

"What? No. We came to tell you he is not the one responsible for the attack, we know who it was, it was-"

"Nohan Arach." Gabe said.

"You already knew?" Sophie looked at Gabe and anger flashed in her eyes, but she stuffed it down, she didn't want to be angry at Gabe, she missed him too much. He was her best friend after all.

"We suspected, but this just confirmed it. If Bastian were responsible, there is no way you could have convinced him to come here. Bastian, where would Nohan have taken Akiri?"

"Nohan was one of Baelfire's loyalists. I would guess he would have made a lair in the last place he knew Baelfire to be..."

"Choddrath," they all said in unison.

"Okay, we know where we need to go, all we need is a plan. Why don't we get some sleep and meet here in the morning, we can discuss a plan then. Jack, can you show Bastian to a guest room? Dominic and Kamara already know where their rooms are, I need to talk to Queen Sophie, I will show her to her room myself." Gabe said to his guard. Bastian looked like he wanted to protest, but he didn't.

"Yes, Your Grace." Gabe's guard gestured to the door and waited for Bastian to exit, then led him down the eastern wing and left around the corner to the third room in the hall next to the central courtyard.

When they were alone in the doorway of Sophie's room, Gabe stepped in close to her. He didn't want their conversation to be overheard. "Sophie, I missed you so much. If he hurt you, you would tell me right?" Gabe asked.

"Of course, and no, he hasn't," Sophie replied.

"So what's going on, why can't you shift?"

"I- uh..." The words were harder to form than she had anticipated. Why did she have a feeling this news would hurt him? Was it because his chance at having children died in Akiri's lair, or was it because she knew, deep down Gabe was still in love with her? Mostly, she thought it might be because even though she tried not to be, she was still very much in love with him.

"Sophie, you can tell me anything," he coaxed. They crossed the room to the chairs by the hearth.

"I'm pregnant," she couldn't hold it in, the words fell out of her mouth like crumbs.

"I see. I assume, Bastian is the father?" Gabe's voice was cool and even. "I mean, I see the way you look at him. The way you looked at me the day we kissed under the willow, do you remember?" Gabe pulled the chair back a little for Sophie so she could sit down. He sat beside her and held her hand.

"Of course, I remember, it seems like a lifetime ago, you got married and I did what I could to ease the pain. At first, Bastian was just a distraction, but the more time I spent with him, the closer we became." Sophie said.

"It was the same with Akiri and me. It was a duty at first, a way to fulfill my debt to the guild, but then I saw her, I *really* saw her for who she was, not who she wanted to appear to be. Everyone thought she was evil, and yes, she did do some of the horrible things she was accused of, but she told me the reasons and showed remorse for the ones she couldn't justify. I soon found out my heart was capable of loving two people at the same time."

Sophie smiled, he was right, because she also loved two people at the same time. Bastian, and him. She looked into his deep brown eyes, they were kind and soft, and his hands were gentle and loving. Why could she not have them both? She felt sometimes, life was cruel to give her a soul mate who was always just out of reach.

"I should get some rest," Sophie said.

"Would you like to stay here, or would you like me to take you to Bastian?" Gabe asked. Sophie noted his voice sounded different, almost sad to have to ask her about him, so she asked to stay in the room where she was.

"Bastian's room is two doors down from yours, just in case. If you need anything... Above all else, I just want you to be happy, Sophie." Gabe kissed her cheek and left her there at the door to the guest room. When the sound of his footsteps was gone, Sophie closed the door softly. She would have gone to Bastian, but it would not be fair to him when all she could think about was Gabe.

She stared at the ceiling for a long time before she finally fell asleep. She saw the willow tree in Blackwater, and dreamed of the kiss she and Gabe shared. The life they could have built together, if only she had chosen him over her ambition to train with Ryul at Lapis Highland ran through her mind like a play. They were married and had two children, a boy, and a girl. Neither of them had the power to shift as far as she knew.

Sophie worked with Delilah at the infirmary and made healing potions, tonics, and salves. Gabe still worked for the guild, but he got a job training recruits to fight with a sword, which meant he got to come home every night. There was something just so mundane about it though, there was no action, no adventure, just working, and raising children.

She woke up to the sound of someone knocking on her door. She opened it to see Bastian's face filled with worry. "Are you okay? It sounded like you were having a nightmare."

"You could hear me through the room between us?" she asked.

"Yes, it's why I'm here, to make sure you're okay," he said. Sophie pulled him inside, closing the door behind him and threw her arms around his neck. He held her firmly like he never wanted to let go. She pulled him into a kiss and he eagerly kissed her back. She pulled away suddenly, eyes wide as if she couldn't believe what she was doing.

"What's wrong?" he asked.

"Bastian, I..." Her voice trailed off as she considered telling him about her feelings for Gabe and the guilt eating her up inside at the thought of this betrayal. She didn't want to hurt him though, and it's not like anything would—or could—happen between her and Gabe, he was married to Akiri, and she was pregnant with Bastian's child. "Being friends with Gabe is harder than I thought it would be, seeing him brings back the pain of his engagement as if the wound were fresh. I know it's not fair to you and I only hope you can forgive me."

"There is nothing to forgive, I love you, Sophie, and I don't want to live another day without you. My Queen, my mate, my love." He closed his eyes and pressed his lips to her forehead. "I am yours from this day, until we leave this world," he vowed.

THIRTY-FIVE

SHE DIDN'T REMEMBER FALLING asleep, but Akiri woke to the sound of the captor's voice. They brought her another berry. *I've not eaten in four days.* Akiri thought. When the captor was gone, Akiri hid the berry along the wall with the other three and tried again to slip her talon under the iron. It worked! She was overjoyed, but now she had to perform the hard part. Breaking the talon of her back leg would be like breaking her toes all at once. It was going to be painful, not only right now, but painful to walk out of the lair, and that was assuming she could shift after the manacle was removed.

Akiri decided to do it quickly, she hooked her talon under the manacle, counted to three, and then pulled it as hard and fast as she could. Her strength surprised her as she looked at the aftermath, her whole back claw was covered in blood and the back talon was laying across the room with the manacle still attached to it. She wanted to scream in pain, but adrenaline coursed through her and she could think of nothing else but escape. She rushed over to the wall and looked at the berries, they were covered in dirt, but she thought she might find a place to rinse them on her way out. *Okay, the moment of truth...* Akiri closed her eyes and thought of her human body, two legs, two arms, smooth skin, no tail, and she shifted. *Thank the Goddess.* Akiri sighed, pleased to be back in her own body and that the anti-magic spell was only on the manacles and not the lair itself. She cast a disguise, giving herself the appearance of blond hair, blue eyes, clothes, and shoes.

Her foot was in excruciating pain as she knew it would be, but she still ran through the winding tunnel until finally, she saw a light, the bright light of the sun, beckoning her to soak up the rays. She walked cautiously to the mouth of the cave, shielding her eyes from the light she had been deprived of for days. Akiri recognized the ruins of the volcano, and the black obsidian fields of Choddrath and the scene brought back the fear and anger she felt the last time she was there. Her mother had sent a guard to kill her and steal the orb for herself, and at the time, Akiri had no one loyal to her.

Across the black stone earth, Akiri saw a new keep. It wasn't large, or fancy, but she knew it was where her captor, and possibly, the black dragon were staying. She hesitated for a moment, the urge to fight and attack them while they weren't expecting it sounded almost like a good plan, but getting as far away as she could, sounded better. She popped one of the berries into her mouth and dropped the rest, the only water around was the salty ocean, not suitable for drinking. It would only take her a few hours to get back if she just flew South, she made this trip once before while carrying a prisoner, and she was sure this trip would be even quicker.

Without looking back again, Akiri soared through the sky and flew as fast as her wings would carry her. She needed to make it to Ash before sunset, it was hard to see, but luckily, Akiri knew the way. She was hungry, and thirsty, but determined to make it back to Ash and gather all the power of the dragon alliance, and the city guard. Akiri hoped they wouldn't realize she was gone at least until morning.

The sun was directly above her when Akiri reached the Northern shore of Ash, but she didn't land until she reached the castle. She heard screams and people scattering as her enormous shadow darkened the landscape. As soon as she was close enough to the ground, she shifted and limped as quickly as she could to the castle doors.

"Gabe!" Akiri screamed through the hall, the room started to spin, and then a bright white light took over. She heard the guards and Gabe as they approached her body, but they sounded far away like they were in a tunnel, or perhaps she was in a tunnel.

Akiri was in the infirmary when she came to. Her foot was cleaned up and she sat up to inspect the damage. Her big toe and her middle toe were missing. The last three were still there and she wiggled them slowly. It was more difficult without her other toes. She sat up and slid to the edge of the infirmary bed. She planted her unscathed foot on the floor first and then pushed herself up off the bed. She was surprised when she stood, it didn't hurt, but she had no grip on the floor with her injured foot, and her first steps were shaky as she wobbled to the infirmary door.

"Woah, hold on there, Your Grace." A woman wearing a blue dress with a white apron brought Akiri a walking stick. It wasn't a staff, but more like a Noble Lord's cane. "Lean on this," she said as she placed a gentle hand on Akiri's back to steady her.

"Who are you?" Akiri asked softly. When she was here last, Ash did not have a cleric, or a healer and the infirmary was an empty room with a few bandages on a shelf. Now the room was stocked with shelves of potions, salves, medical tools, and this kind woman.

"I'm Nadine Garrison, I came from Blackwater. King Gabriel said Ash needed a healer. I was trained by Delilah, the cleric in Blackwater, I am not a cleric, but I can perform first aid and know many herbal treatments for pain and warding off infection." Nadine walked with Akiri down the hall from the infirmary to the council chamber.

"Will I always need the cane?" Akiri asked.

"When you are in your human form, you might always need it for added stability, but I don't think it should affect your flight at all," Nadine said.

"Thank you so much. It's a pleasure to have you here, but I fear we don't have much time, I need to call a meeting, I would like for you to be here too," Akiri said.

"Yes, Your Grace, I will have Mister Koffery ring the bell." Nadine quickly walked down the hall and Akiri hobbled to her seat at the head of the table. The bell rang moments later and it took no time at all for what was left of the council, Gabe, Dominic, Sophie, Kamara, and some new person to join Akiri in the council room.

"Who is this?" Akiri asked.

"I an Bastian Delacroix, of Immernacht, Your Grace." He bowed to her.

"What is your purpose at this council meeting?"

"I am a dragonshifter and I am here to offer my service to the Kingdom of Ash and its Queen." Bastian did not rise until Akiri told him he could. He was respectful, which she appreciated.

"Where is Horace Stewart?" Akiri asked as she looked at Gabe.

"I am having him brought up from the dungeon, We have only just learned the dragon we saw on the beach of Ledora was Bastian, and not the dragon responsible for the attack on your lair, or your abduction. Since he was the keeper of Ledora, we assumed he had sent the dragon there looking for you." Akiri knew by 'keeper' Gabe meant he had told Horace Akiri's new lair was in Ledora.

"I understand your confusion in the situation and you did the right thing. Here's the deal, I know you do not know what happened to me because I have not had time to fill you in, nor do I have time to go over all the details right now, but Nohan Arach is our enemy. He is currently staying on Choddrath and when he notices I am gone, I am sure he will attack Ash. Gabe, I would like for you to alert the city guard and the royal fleet. Have them prepare the ships to evacuate the city. I want women, children, elderly, and disabled people shipped out, possibly to Ledora if it is okay with you, Prince Dominic?" Akiri paused for him to nod his confirmation and then continued. "Every able-bodied man will be given a sword or a bow and whatever armor we can find. We also need to man the large bow on the Eastern tower and have it ready to fire. That's all I have for you right now, let's prepare for war, dismissed." Akiri had to lean on her cane as she stood. She motioned for Nadine to wait for her as everyone else started filing out of the chamber to fulfill their tasks.

"Nadine, I want you to be safe, but I also know we will require your services if things don't go as planned. We have a storage room beneath the castle where I would like for you to set up your supplies. I will have some of the staff help you move everything down there, the trapdoor is under the rug in the kitchen. After the supplies are down there, I will give you a choice, you can board the ship, or you can stay."

"It will be my honor to stay with you and help the people of Ash, Your Grace." Nadine bent to one knee and swore service to Akiri.

"I appreciate your service. Thank you, Nadine."

As the afternoon turned to evening, Akiri walked outside, the city had been evacuated in record time, the last ship was about to set sail within the hour and the Kingdom was eerily quiet. It was almost peaceful, she would have enjoyed the quiet if not for the sense of impending doom weighing on her chest.

"Hey. How are you?" Gabe asked as he came up behind his wife.

"I've been better, but I've also been worse," she let out a halfhearted chuckle as Gabe wrapped his arms around her.

"What happened? Did he hurt you?" Gabe asked. Akiri didn't want to answer. She thought about being in the dark cave, and what she had to do to get home. She didn't want Gabe to be angry or put himself in danger on her behalf. Gabe wasn't a dragon, he didn't practice magic, he *was*, however, an excellent swordsman, but what good was a sword against the breath or weight of a dragon?

"No," she finally answered. "I'm okay." Her eyes gave her away, Gabe could tell she was holding back, but he didn't press the matter, to her relief.

"Let's go inside, I want to lay in our bed and hold you. I missed you." Gabe let her lean on him, rather than the cane. She had missed him too. He was a good man and every day she became more thankful to have chosen him over the other suitors.

THIRTY-SIX

"Please, get on the ship, Sophie," Bastian begged. "I couldn't bear it if anything happened to you and you can't shift right now."

"I can still hold a sword. I wielded Destiny, my father's magical greatsword, and I can also use magic. I can still fight," Sophie argued.

"Think about our baby, it's not just you I am trying to protect, it's both of you." He embraced her and placed one hand on her stomach. And pressed his forehead to hers. "You are my whole world and the thought of losing you shatters my heart, please, get on the ship," he whispered. Hot tears fell from his eyes and onto Sophie's cheeks. She felt the tugging of his heart on hers. She hated it, but he was right.

"What about you? What if something happens to you? Come with me." Sophie urged.

"You know I can't, I vowed my assistance to the crown and I am nothing if not a man of my word."

"I know, I *know*. I just wish we had more time together, we have not spent more than one night at a time together since we met and now I need you more than ever. Please, be careful. I will go, but only if you promise to meet me in Ledora when it's over."

"I promise, I will see you again." Bastian pressed his lips to Sophie's and stroked her cheek with his thumb. He didn't know if he was wiping Sophie's tears from her face or his own.

"I love you, Bastian."

"I love you more," he replied.

The ship was packed, hot, and smelly below deck already. It would take two days to get to Ledora by ship, and that was if they happened to have favorable wind. The bouncing of the ship over the crests of the waves made Sophie nauseous but she held back the urge to vomit. Dinner was just rice and beans, it didn't offer much in the way of flavor, but Sophie was sure it was because rice and beans were cheap, shelf-stable, and could feed a lot of people. She was given a bedroll and slept on the deck of the ship the first night, under the starry sky. A crescent moon hung just over the starboard side of the ship and Sophie gazed at it until she drifted into the land of dreams, lulled by the gentle rocking and hushed lapping sound of the waves.

She didn't wake up until sunrise, and what a glorious sunrise it was, the sky was still dark blue at the top, then it was purple, pink, and finally, red just above the horizon. She wished she could paint so she might capture the beauty of the sky reflected on the surface of the still ocean, but art as such was a skill she never learned. Below deck, Sophie heard infants crying, and young children yelling for chamber pots. Soon, the ship was bustling with life, and the peaceful sunrise was over.

Breakfast was rice and beans with the leftovers from the night before mixed in. Sophie gave her portion to a young boy who was complaining to his mother about still being hungry, his mother had eaten almost half of her own breakfast and was ready to give him the rest when Sophie approached. "Here, take mine," she said. "I'm still full from last night." Sophie handed the boy her bowl. The mother looked thankful she would get to finish eating and silently nodded her thanks.

"What's your name?" Sophie asked the boy as she sat down beside them on the steps between the upper and lower deck of the ship.

"Patrick," the boy said with a mouthful of beans and rice.

"Patrick, don't talk with your mouth full," his mother scolded.

"Sorry," he swallowed and then asked; "What's yours?"

"I'm Sophie." The boy's eyes widened.

"You mean Queen Sophie? Is it true you're a dragon?" He was so excited he forgot about his breakfast for a moment.

"I'm a dragonshifter, I can turn into a dragon," she explained.

"So why didn't you fly to Ledora?" he asked.

"Well, I can't shift right now."

"You sick 'er somethin'?" he asked as he took another bite.

"What did I say about talking with your mouth full? Show Queen Sophie some respect, son. I am so sorry, Your Grace." Patrick's mother seemed mortified.

"He's just a boy, it's quite alright," Sophie told her.

"I'm not sick, I'm going to be a mother," she smiled at the boy and his mom.

"If you have a boy, you should name him Sam." The boy said.

"Why did you choose Sam?"

"I had a puppy named Sam, but Mama said we couldn't bring him with us."

"My mother's name is Samantha, I think Sam is a wonderful name, sometimes people call my mom that when they're in a hurry because it's faster than saying, Samantha." Sophie could tell the boy was trying not to worry about his pet. "I hope Sam will be happy to see you when you get back," Sophie told him.

"Me too." The boy smiled at her.

"Take care, Patrick, and listen to your Mama."

Sophie walked to the bow of the ship and looked across the water. Ash was already a day behind her and all she could see was the ocean and sky. She was worried about her friends and Bastian, she had never really been the religious type; so many deities and none of them had ever sent her a calling, but at the moment she could think of no better Goddess to ask for her favor than Freyja, Goddess of love, fertility, and battle.

Please Freyja, protect those in the Kingdom of Ash and guide their swords, arrows, and bodies in battle. Protect my child and my body, the vessel in which my baby grows. Protect the love between us all and leave none of my friends brokenhearted. Sophie wiped a tear from her cheek as she ended her request to the Goddess. Sophie decided when she got to Ledora, she would make an altar and light a candle. She hoped the goddess would accept her offering and give them all her divine favor.

THIRTY-SEVEN

AKIRI FELT THE RISE and fall of Gabe's chest and listened to the rhythmic thumping of his heart, his skin was warm and soft against hers. He was still awake, neither of them could sleep on what might very well be the eve of battle. He turned over on his side, looking deep into Akiri's eyes. He gently stroked her long black hair away from her face.

"You are so beautiful, I want to remember this moment for the rest of my life." His eyes surveyed every inch of her face as if engraving it into his memory.

"I don't think I will be able to sleep tonight, I'm scared. I know Nohan is going to be angry when they realize I am gone, and I have no idea what kind of followers he has amassed, the one other person he had with him, called him Master, like he was a God or something," Akiri admitted.

"Maybe they are the only followers he has, and this will be easy if he even shows up at all." Gabe hoped he was right, but he had a feeling there was going to be nothing easy about this fight. Akiri's mind wandered to her lair and the eggs Nohan had destroyed. She knew it wouldn't be tonight, but she wondered if she might lay another clutch soon. She decided she would shift in the morning, in preparation for an attack, they all would, and she would stay in dragon form until the new moon came again, if she had not laid a clutch by then, she would give up her dream of having baby dragons, and she would give Gabe the human children his heart desired. He deserved to have a family, he was kind and strong, loving and patient. She knew he would make a great father.

They might have gotten an hour of sleep between the two of them, and when Akiri tired of trying, she got out of bed and stood on the balcony overlooking the front courtyard. The stars began to fade away as the first light of morning chased away the shadows of the night. "Gabe, it's time, I'm going to shift and head to the front courtyard. Have Dominic, Kamara, and Bastian meet me there, please," Akiri requested. Gabe nodded and kissed her before she left him to dress for battle.

Akiri shifted in the courtyard and kept her eyes fixed on the sky to the North. The others joined her, shifting into their dragon forms and taking defensive positions in front of the castle. The bell did not ring. It could be heard from miles away, and they did not want to let their enemy know they were prepared to fight.

The lanterns were all snuffed out and other than the light from the sky, which wasn't much yet, the castle remained dark. The triggerman was locked and loaded on the large bow at the top of the castle and waiting for the dragon to make an appearance. The city guard and combat-trained civilians gathered in formation around the front gates of the courtyard and stood with their weapons at the ready.

Every moment seemed like an eternity. Akiri was almost relieved and thought maybe Nohan wouldn't pursue her after all, but the relief was short-lived because, at the same moment, an ear-piercing screech echoed through the sky. Akiri kept watch in the direction the sound came from and soon realized it was not an echo after all, but a battle cry from multiple dragons. They flew in formation across Ash and breathed fire onto every wooden house in the kingdom. Akiri was glad she'd expected this and evacuated the city, but the dragons circled the area, she knew they were expecting screams of fear and panic.

The dark green dragon, Nohan, bellowed a guttural, angry-sounding roar and flew straight for the castle, leading the others in an angular formation. An enormous arrow flew through the sky toward him, he performed a barrel roll out of the way, and the bolt struck one of the dragons behind him. It screamed in pain as it spiraled and fell from the sky. Akiri heard it land with a crash on what sounded like the stables. Lucky for the horses they had been moved.

Akiri roared, letting the others know it was time to attack. They took flight, Bastian flew straight for the gray dragon, and surprised it by swinging his tail like a club. He hit the gray dragon right in the chest which hurt, but it seemed to only make him angry. The gray dragon flew at Bastian and breathed a dark cloud of smoke at him. Bastian dipped below it, quickly flew behind the gray dragon, and sank his teeth deep into his scale-covered tail. The dragon wailed in pain and flicked his tail toward his front claw and hooked Bastian's cheek.

Akiri rushed straight for Nohan and shot her dark green acidic sludge at him. He dodged it easily and seemed to laugh as he circled to face her again. He rushed her and slammed his body into hers. He tried to wrap his tail around hers and tried to lift it. She roared in anger and disgust, even now, he was trying to mate with her. She slapped her tail across his face and turned around as quickly as she could. She bit his neck, but her teeth barely punctured his scales. He pushed her off of him, and she heard him laugh again. *Impossible, how?* Akiri thought.

"I don't want to hurt you, I just want you to fulfill your duty to our kind, to dragonkind." She wasn't crazy, she heard him speak in her mind.

"Then come down and talk to me, face to face." Akiri thought about the words she wanted to say to him, she didn't know if the technique would work, but she had to try.

"Maybe, in a minute." Nohan did a nose dive and then lifted just before hitting the ground, he barreled through the armored men with swords in the front line of the formation. A few brave members of the city guard stabbed him with their swords, barely breaking through the dragon's thick skin. He knew these men, and they knew him, or thought they had.

Some of the men in the back witnessed the front row get taken out like ants and a few of them dropped their weapons and were now cowering at the castle doors, trying to get back inside. Akiri had to get him back into the sky so the triggerman could have another shot at him. Akiri flew over him and let out a roar as she passed. He looked up and followed her. She circled the tower, trying to get Nohan in a position to reveal his less armored underbelly to the bolt.

She heard the weapon fire and listened as it whistled through the wind. It found its mark and embedded deep into the soft tissue of Nohan's underarm. He howled, but not in pain, in frustration. The bolt seemed to be no more than a thorn in his very large side. He tried to pull it out, but the barbs on the tip of the arrow were made to open. What he didn't notice until it was too late, was the chain attached to the end of the bolt. It jerked him toward the tower as they began rolling the chain in with a hand crank.

Nohan tried to resist, but the more he tried to fight against it, the more the barb ripped into the fleshy unarmored part of his body. He had no other choice, he shifted. His body released the bolt and he fell from the sky at an alarming rate, his first attempt to shift back failed and the ground grew closer by the second. Humans have one major flaw; they're squishy. Nohan gave one more desperate attempt to shift and his wings lifted him back into the sky just before he hit the ground. He drew in a deep breath as arrows flew at him from every direction.

He blasted half of the archers from the parapet with one breath and then flew toward Akiri with a screech, but before he could reach her, Dominic crashed into his body and sent him rolling backward. Kamara tried to attack Nohan from behind, but a cone of fiery breath shot between them. Kamara pulled back, drew in a deep breath, and unleashed an icy cold which dropped the dragon to the ground, she watched as he transformed back into the shape of a human. His skin was a light blue as he lay shivering on the ground, unable to feel the warmth. Kamara landed and shifted so she could get a closer look, she didn't want to kill anyone if she could help it. When she saw he was starting to regain mobility in his hands and feet Kamara called to the remaining soldiers waiting on the front line.

"Seize him," Kamara commanded, and two of the city guards took the shivering man into custody and carried him by the arms to the dungeon.

Two gray dragons, a red, another brown, and Nohan, a very dark green, remained, although, Kamara could only see two of them. The sound of a horn blasted from every direction but south where the castle stood and in moments, the castle gates were surrounded. The dragons weren't alone, they brought an army with them. Kamara looked up, she couldn't see anyone. If they didn't knock back some of the ground forces, the battle would be lost.

Kamara shifted and flew straight up into the sky letting out a wail akin to a banshee. The soldiers on the ground dropped their weapons, and the other dragons fell from the sky to escape the sound, she held the high-pitched note until she spotted Dominic, Akiri, and Bastian. She rushed to them in her human form and waited for them to shift as well.

"Kamara, what was *that*?" Dominic asked.

"I'm not sure, I was just trying to get your attention." She pointed to the heavily armored forces standing ominously, waiting for the command of their officer. There must have been five hundred in all. Ash's Army was less than half the size of theirs. They looked at each other in defeat. Gabe emerged from the formation behind them.

"I've taken all of the injured to the kitchen, there's no room in the infirmary, Nadine is working as fast as she can to keep them all alive, but we have lost a lot of men." Akiri ran to him and hugged him, thankful to see him alive.

"I'm so sorry, I should have stayed, I should have stayed in the lair and given Nohan what he wanted and none of this would be happening." Her face was streaked with tears.

"I only wanted what was mine." Nohan appeared in front of his troops.

"What do you mean?" Gabe asked.

"My children, of course. Didn't your wife tell you?"

"Tell me what? Akiri, what happened?"

"I–" Akiri choked on her words and couldn't bring herself to break Gabe's heart. Nohan walked closer, but Gabe's eyes were fixed on his wife.

"She didn't tell you, because the truth is; she knows I'm right, she is only wasting her time with you. We are mated, and the eggs she will lay will be dragons, not some half-human-dragon outcast with no chance in this world." Nohan smirked as Gabe's face contorted in anger. He loved how his words affected the King of Ash.

"What are you talking about, *mated*?" Gabe asked clenching his fists. He was staring directly at Nohan, but it was Akiri who spoke.

"When they captured me, he told me if I produced a clutch of eggs with him, they would allow me to come home, but I couldn't wait that long so I escaped."

"But not before we made love in our dragon forms, you should have heard her roar for me, Gabe, it was like... well, nothing like you will ever experience, ohh it makes me hard just thinking about it." Nohan reached out his hand and fondled Akiri's breast. She slapped his hand away and covered herself as she stepped behind Gabe for cover.

"Shut your mouth, I swear to the Gods, I will end you right here if you touch her again." Gabe pointed his sword at Nohan.

Nohan held out his hand to the soldiers behind him and without a word, they passed him a sword. "Let's see what you got, loverboy," Nohan said with a sick grin. "If anyone interferes, I will give the command to my troops to waste you all."

"And If I win?" Gabe asked.

"Unlikely, but sure, if I die, my troops and the other dragons will return to Choddrath and leave what's left of this dump to its Queen. It has to be a fair fight though, lose the armor, and the clothes." Nohan pointed to Gabe and moved the tip of his sword up and down, gesturing for Gabe to remove everything. When he was naked and armed with his sword, the two rushed into battle. The clanking and scraping of metal against metal rang in everyone's ears as they watched the two men block strike after strike. They whirled, and ducked, then parried, like they were performing a choreographed dance with swords. Gabe ducked low and swung his foot behind Nohan's and hooked him by the ankle. The move swept him off his feet and his back hit the ground with a smack. Gabe pointed his sword at him and cheers erupted from the people and friends of Ash, but Nohan was far from finished, he flicked his wrist and hooked Gabe's sword by the hilt. He pulled back with a quick flourish and sent the sword flying from his hand. Gabe backed away, then ducked, rolling toward his weapon. He slashed his sword just as Nohan rushed him, opening a shallow gash across Nohan's stomach. Bright red blood started to bead up inside the cut and in a rage, Nohan rushed forward, grabbing Gabe by the back of the head, and drove his sword through his middle.

"I told you it was unlikely," Nohan whispered as he pulled up sharply on his sword.

"You're still going to die, I poisoned my blade." Gabe laughed, coughing as blood splattered from his mouth. Nohan's vision blurred and he felt dizzy. His blood grew thicker, slowing its flow as it congealed and coagulated beneath his skin. The beads of red fluid in the gash on his abdomen turned black and festered as the same dark liquid began leaking from his eyes, nose, and ears. He fell to his knees as he coughed up the black sludge.

When the gurgling stopped, Nohan collapsed in front of Gabe who still had Nohan's sword through his abdomen. Akiri ran to Gabe's side to support him.

"You heard him, he's dead! Leave my kingdom, and never return," Akiri shouted. The sound of heavy armor retreating was all Gabe heard before his vision tunneled and his body collapsed in Akiri's arms.

"Help me please!" she screamed as Gabe's light faded away. Kamara and Dominic cradled his shoulders, as Bastian supported his legs. They carried him inside and straight to the kitchen.

"Nadine, help him, please," Akiri pleaded. The healer hurried over to them and her eyes fell to the sword in Gabe's middle.

"I am sorry, Your Grace, his wounds are too great. I told you I am not a cleric, I can't heal his severed organs." Nadine's face streamed with tears as Akiri's scream of anguish filled the room. They laid Gabe on an empty bedroll, his breaths were shallow and his heartbeat had slowed. There was a trail of blood droplets from the front door to the bedroll where he now rested. Akiri curled up beside him with her head on the bedroll next to his. She kissed his face as she sobbed and he reached for her hand. His grip was weak, but she held onto it firmly.

"My love for you will never die." Gabe's raspy voice whispered in Akiri's ear.

"I will love you forever. I am so sorry, Gabe." She held him even after his breathing stopped, and his heart was still, she lay beside her husband until his body went cold and Dominic finally helped her to her feet.

"My Queen, would you like something for the pain?" Nadine asked. Akiri didn't know if there was anything that could take away the pain of a broken heart, but she was willing to try anything.

"Would you please get her cleaned up and settled in bed? I will bring her some tea." Nadine asked. The two chambermaids nodded and helped Akiri to her room. It wasn't her room- it was Gabe's. Her sorrow overcame her again as the chamber maids scrubbed Akiri's body clean of the blood and dirt from battle. They dressed her in a loose-fitting gown and helped her to bed. One of them grabbed a warming pan and slid in under the covers at Akiri's feet, and the other girl knelt at Akiri's bedside and stroked her hair as she mourned her husband.

"Here you go, this will help you get some sleep." Nadine came in carrying a cup of tea. Akiri sat up and took the cup from her.

"Uggh, this smells like sweaty stockings, what is this?" Akiri asked with a look of disgust.

"It's tea made from the root of valerian, a wonderful flower with powerful medicinal properties," Nadine explained. "It has honey in it too, so I promise it won't taste as bad as it smells."

Akiri held her breath and drank it down. She was right about the honey making it palatable. Akiri handed the cup back to Nadine with her thanks and then snuggled back down into her comforter. Nadine left the room quietly, but one of the chambermaids stayed behind to keep watch over The Queen.

THIRTY-EIGHT

THE ENTIRE CASTLE WAS in mourning. The damages from the battle had been catastrophic, not only to Akiri, who lost her husband but to every citizen of Ash who lost their homes and their livelihoods. The city had been burned to the ground, and not a single structure stood unscathed, not even the castle. The Western tower was crumbling, and the dragon-sized crossbow had been ripped from the East tower and now lay on the ground beneath it like a pile of old junk, broken and beyond repair. The men who survived the battle cradled their sons, friends, fathers, or neighbors who didn't make it through the battle alive.

Sorrow hung like a heavy cloud over all of them. Kamara, Dominic, and Bastian all sat in the council chamber at the long table. They were silent for a long time, contemplating their next move. "I checked on Her Grace this morning, she was still sleeping. She didn't touch her breakfast. I'm worried about her," Kamara said.

"Me too, but we still have to tell Sophie." Dominic replied as they exchanged glances around the table.

"I know, he was her best friend, she loved him. I knew the first night we met when he asked to cut in during our dance. The way she looked at him... I'd be lying if I said I wasn't a little jealous." Bastian looked away from them with shame in his eyes.

"What are we going to do about all these people and Akiri? I mean, they can't stay here, this place is nothing but...*ash*." Kamara asked. They all realized how ironic it was, like the name of the Kingdom had been prophesied from the start.

"We could offer to take her back to Temple Ophay. We will leave there one day to rule Ledora anyway, and it will be good for Akiri to have friends in her court." Dominic suggested.

"Do you think she will go for it? I mean, leaving your home after you've lost everything else seems like a kick while you're down."

"Why don't you talk to her about it, I will fly to Ledora and break the news to Sophie, Bastian, do you want to come with me?" Dominic asked. Bastian agreed but thought the news would be easier to hear coming from someone who knew them well.

"I'll let you do the talking, and I will be the shoulder," he said.

When Dominic and Bastian left, Kamara went to Akiri's chamber. She examined the tray on the nightstand; Akiri's breakfast was still untouched. She hadn't even sipped her water.

"Honey, come on, you have to take care of yourself." Kamara was nervous as she approached the Queen. Her eyes were open, but glossed over like she was somewhere else. Kamara was afraid something bad had happened. She sat on the bed next to Akiri and put her finger under her nose. Akiri's breath warmed her finger and she sighed in relief.

"You want me to make you something different to eat?" she asked.

"More tea." Akiri's mouth was muffled against the pillow and she made no effort to move.

"I think you should wake up, maybe take a bath, or get some air?" Kamara urged.

"When I sleep, I dream of Gabe, when I wake up, he's dead. I don't want to wake up. It's all my fault." Akiri turned over, but her shoulders heaved and shook.

"I know, it's hard, but you have to get up or the grief will swallow you whole. Come on, one step at a time, let's try sitting." Kamara tried to help her up, but she groaned and rolled herself into her comforter. "Akiri, please."

"Just leave me alone," she groaned.

"Okay, well, I have something I want to talk to you about and it's pretty important. You are the Queen, so I can't make this decision for you."

"It doesn't matter, there's nothing left for me to rule, my people are gone, their homes are destroyed, and we lost so many good people. It's all my fault, who would want me to be their queen?"

"It's not your fault at all, Nohan was a terrible person and his actions are on him, not you," Kamara argued. Akiri sat up and looked Kamara in the eye.

"You don't understand, when I was captured, he told me all he wanted was half a clutch of pure dragon eggs. He said if I complied, then I could take half our eggs and come back to Ash with future dragons to protect the Kingdom." Akiri wiped tears from her face. "He coerced me into copulating with him by dangling my Kingdom and my husband in front of me like some prize I had to earn. I finally figured out a way to escape and I had only ever seen two of them, Nohan, and the one in the dragon mask. I didn't think he had so many others following him, so I risked it to come home, I put all of you in danger and now Gabe is dead. I've lost him forever because I was selfish, and only thought about getting home." Akiri leaned her head against Kamara's shoulder.

"I know you feel like you can't forgive yourself, but believe me when I tell you, Gabe was ready to go to war to find you, if you hadn't come home, we would have taken the fight to Choddrath. There's no telling if it would have turned out differently, but we can't let the past beat us down, we can only move forward and worry about the future, and right now, there are a lot of people still depending on you to lead them. Now, I know there is nothing left here, but Dominic and I have been thinking you could move your people to Ophay. Dominic and I will have to rule Ledora someday, and we can't possibly be in two places at once, maybe it's time for a fresh start for you and your people and it will be good for you to have friends nearby." Kamara said. Akiri nodded and smiled. This was the first time anyone in her life had called her a friend. She wrapped her arms around Kamara and hugged her tightly.

"I will think about it," she replied.

"Okay. There's one other thing; the funeral of those we lost during the battle. Gabe's body has been prepared, but with the future location of the kingdom in question, we were wondering if you would like for us to prepare a pyre so we might collect Gabe's ashes in an urn so you can take him with you?"

"I do think that is best, but we will need three urns, one for Gabe's mother, one for me, and one for Sophie. She will be mourning too, and I think she should carry a piece of him with her as well." She started to cry again, and Kamara held her in her arms. She couldn't imagine the pain Akiri was feeling, and didn't want to think about ever losing Dominic. Her heart broke for Akiri, there were no words to comfort her or lessen the pain, so they sat in silent despair well into the afternoon. When lunch was delivered to them, Kamara was able to coax Akiri to eat a little. She thought of Sophie, and knew the grief she felt being here with Akiri, would be doubled when Sophie returned.

THIRTY-NINE

THE BEACH ON THE Western shore of Ledora was a little rockier than the beach on the Eastern side. Sophie had not gone to the castle or the Golden City. She stayed on the beach all night, waiting for Bastian to come and tell her the battle was won. He promised he would come back to her. She felt so helpless. She could still cast, and could have helped, but Bastian insisted she go to Ledora.

Sophie spent two days on the ship to get to Ledora, and now had spent the night on the beach, waiting for news, so when she finally saw two dragons soaring her way in the early afternoon, she was overcome with joy. She watched Dominic and Bastian land just off the shore and ran over to greet them as they shifted, but stopped short when she saw their sullen faces.

"What happened?" Sophie asked.

"Maybe you should sit down," Dominic suggested.

"Just tell me, please," she said. Dominic tried to gather himself, to find the right words. No amount of delicacy was going to soften this blow and he knew it was going to be hard news to hear.

"It's Gabe, Sophie..." Dominic's voice cracked as he choked back tears. "He didn't make it out of the battle." he finished.

Sophie stepped away from them with her mouth open and her hands clasped tightly over it. She shook her head in disbelief.

"No, no, please tell me it isn't true." Her hands shook as she spoke.

"I'm sorry, Sophie, I know how much he meant to you." Bastian moved forward to hold her and she collapsed into his arms and cried.

"I'm going to go get dressed then gather Akiri's people and have them go to the ships, are you okay here with Sophie?" Dominic asked as he handed Bastian a change of clothes from the bag he brought with them.

"We'll be okay, we will meet you back at the castle," Bastian said.

Bastian put his trousers on so at least he wasn't completely nude, and then sat down beside Sophie in one of the very few patches of soft sand on the rocky beach. He put his arm around her as she tried to stifle her tears. He didn't speak, and Sophie wasn't ready to talk about it, so they listened only to the ocean waves lapping onto the shore, and the sound of the seagulls overhead. Sophie laid down and rested her head on Bastian's thigh. He stroked her hair, and let her tears dampen his trouser leg.

"Hey, maybe we should go eat something before we go back," Bastian suggested. Sophie agreed and stood up. She had cried out all the tears she had left and now there was a painful throbbing at her temples and behind her eyes which she was sure were puffy and as red as her hair.

Bastian and Sophie walked into the Western gate of The Golden City and found a tavern that was still serving lunch. The smell of seafood chowder greeted them as they walked through the tavern door and Sophie's stomach grumbled. She hadn't even realized how hungry she was. They each ordered a bowl of chowder and a basket of fresh rolls.

Even though she was hungry, Sophie ate a roll, then took one bite of chowder and instantly felt ill. Her skin paled from its normal rosy complexion and she had to push the bowl away so the smell wouldn't be as strong.

"Are you okay?" Bastian asked.

"I'm- nope!" Sophie clutched her mouth as she shot up from her seat and ran to the privy, which was in the garden outside the back door of the tavern. Sophie never ran so fast in her life and barely got her face over the chamber pot before the bread she had eaten made a reappearance, accompanied by an acidic fluid she didn't remember ever ingesting. Sophie drew some water from the well to wash out the chamber pot and cupped her hands bringing the fresh water to her mouth to rinse out the taste. She had almost finished when Bastian came out to check on her.

"How are you feeling?" he asked.

"Not great, but better than I was a minute ago."

"I already paid so we can go back to the castle and rest before we fly back to Ash." Bastian put his arm around her and she leaned into him as they left the tavern.

Dominic was directing groups of people to the caravan of wagons when they arrived at the castle. He carried bags for elderly citizens and helped others who could not walk long distances into the wagon.

"Hi, glad you made it back, we have one more group after this, they're finishing up lunch in the banquet hall right now. Feel free to freshen up or get some rest, I will have Hannah come wake you for dinner and we can fly out just after sunset." Dominic said.

"Okay, we will see you at dinner." Bastian smiled and patted Dominic on the shoulder. This side of Dominic was not one Bastian had ever been here to witness before. He admired his helpful nature and thought about what a great king he was going to make someday.

Sophie's room was just as she had left it the last time she was in Ledora. The dress she had worn to the ball the night she found out Gabe was engaged to Akiri caught her eye as they walked in. It had been freshly laundered and hung on the hook beside the wardrobe. Sophie had purchased many dresses since she started participating in court life, the wardrobe was full of them. She opened the door to the old armoire and slid the dresses one at a time from the right to the left until she found a black one. It was made of lace and silk. Sophie rubbed the material between her fingers as she pulled it from the cabinet and held it up.

"What are you doing?" Bastian asked.

"I need something to wear for the funeral, I should pack it," Sophie said, the sadness on her face was apparent and Bastian wished he could take her grief away, and carry it for her somehow, but he knew it was not possible.

"Kamara told Dominic we would hold the funeral as soon as we got back, maybe instead of packing it, you should wear it." Bastian walked up behind Sophie and wrapped his arms around her. He kissed the top of her head as she continued to examine the dress.

"I think I will wear it, after all, I don't have to worry about ruining it, at least until I can shift again." Sophie yawned, and Bastian took the freshly laundered dress off the hook, hung it inside the wardrobe, and then hung Sophie's funeral dress in its place. He led Sophie to the bed and pulled down the comforter, blanket, and sheet for her to crawl into bed.

"Are you going to lay with me?" Sophie asked.

"If you want me to, but if you need space, I can sleep in the chair," he replied.

"No, I need you to hold me, I feel so lonely, and if you were not here... I don't even want to think about it," she said.

Sophie was laying on her left side and Bastian crawled into bed behind her, wrapping her arm around her middle. He felt her body heaving as she started to cry again, but he continued to hold her and softly kiss her hair now and again until she fell asleep. He thought he should get some rest too, but he couldn't. He was worried about Sophie and wanted to be awake if she needed him.

When Hannah came to tell them it was time for dinner, Bastian got up first and heated some water for the wash basin so Sophie could wash up. He brought her a warm, wet, face towel so she could wash the sleep from her eyes. She stood up and stretched, bending forward to touch her toes, and then to each side to loosen her tense muscles.

Sophie was wearing trousers and a blue tunic and a brown leather belt which she thought was good enough for dinner. "I'll change after dinner," Sophie said as Bastian began laying out her dress to make getting into it easier.

"Okay, It will be ready for you," he said with all the smile he could muster. He could feel her pain, like a blacksmith's vise crushing his chest and he knew she must have felt a thousand times worse.

"I'm ready, let's get this over with," Sophie said.

"We don't have to go, I can ask Hannah to bring our dinner up here if you're not ready."

"No, I need to face this." Sophie took in a deep breath and looked at the door.

"I'll be right beside you."

The table was set when they arrived in the banquet hall. King Haki, Prince Dominic, and Princess Kamara were already seated at one end of the table. Hannah led Sophie and Bastian to the chairs across from them and as soon as they took their seats, a server filled their drinking cups with water.

"I am truly sorry for your loss, Queen Sophie, I know King Gabriel was a very close childhood friend of yours. We don't need to speak anymore on the matter because I know how much it must pain you, but I would like to toast to you, may the Goddess give you strength and safe travels, and I would also like to toast to King Gabriel. From what I hear, his sacrifice, and quick thinking saved Queen Akiri and the people of Ash. To Sophie, and Gabriel." The king raised his cup.

"To Sophie and Gabe," they all repeated.

"Now, on to happy news, Prince Dominic and his lovely bride-to-be, have chosen to wed, here in Ledora on the Summer Solstice, at which time, they will assume the throne as King and Queen, and I will be Dominic's advisor until my end of days."

Sophie was happy for them, but it was difficult to outwardly show it. She congratulated them and went through the motions as everyone toasted. She ate a bite or two of each course, not wanting to re-live the seafood chowder incident. Sophie wasn't listening to the rest of the conversations; she only thought of returning to Ash. She had never been to a funeral or been through the grief of losing someone so important to her. Sophie looked at Kamara, who was smiling and talking to King Haki, ready to get married and become Queen of Ledora. It gave Sophie hope that the grief she felt would not consume the rest life and one day, she too would be happy again.

FORTY

THE ROYAL FAMILIES AND the staff of Castle Ash gathered at dawn on the Northern beach after a procession through the ruins of Ash. White remnants of the wooden houses still floated softly on the breeze and a light fog hung in the distance, waiting for them just off the shore.

Gabe's body was unwrapped and placed on a stone slab. Nadine's assistant rubbed oil all over his body to prepare him for the fire. Everyone was dressed in black, and Akiri wore a veil of mourning as per the tradition of a widowed Queen. Akiri also had a veil made for Sophie. She knew Sophie loved Gabe just as much and deserved to receive condolences as much, if not, more than she did.

Sophie and Akiri stood side by side with their arms linked. Since Sophie couldn't shift, Akiri asked Dominic to breathe fire over the altar. He stood at the head of the altar looking down at Gabe. Even in dragon form, the sadness showed on his face. Kamara linked her arm through Akiri's and Bastian held his out for Sophie. The four of them watched as Dominic drew in a deep breath and exhaled a cone of fire across Gabe's body. The oil fueled the flames and released a fragrant scent covering the smell of the burned flesh. Everyone stood on either side of the altar and watched the fire burn until there was nothing left but ashes. Nadine scooped the ashes into three identical urns. She sealed the lids with wax and then gave one to Akiri, and two to Sophie.

"This one is for King Gabriel's mother, will you please deliver it to her?" Nadine asked. Sophie nodded. Bastian took one of the urns from Sophie to help her as she prepared her bag. She couldn't remember where she'd left her father's leather backpack, so she packed the urns into a cloth messenger bag from Ledora and wrapped them in her spare clothing to protect them.

"I'm ready when you are." Sophie turned to Bastian. He offered to fly her home to Blackwater to see her family, and Gabe's. Sophie hugged Akiri and promised to see her soon. She said goodbye to everyone else and then she and Bastian walked down the beach away from the funeral site. Akiri watched as Bastian flew away with Sophie on his back.

"Come, Your Grace, we will warm you a bath while the builders prepare the funeral rafts." Mister Koffery led Akiri away from the beach. Kamara waited for Dominic to shift and dress before they returned to the castle.

Akiri, Dominic, and Kamara sat together in a small parlor, offering company to one another and sharing their memories of Gabe. Kamara did not doubt all of their memories together could not compare to the memories Sophie held of him and she wished she was there to share some with them. It had been a strange couple of years, but in this time, they all had managed to become friends; a year before, Kamara never would have thought they would be friends with Akiri and she was glad for it but wished their friendship had come because of happier circumstances.

"Can you guys keep a secret?" Akiri asked.

"Sure," Dominic said, and Kamara nodded excitedly.

"Follow me." Akiri led them out the back doors and to her lair. They walked down the stairs and into an empty lair.

"What's the secret?" Kamara asked. Akiri cast light on a stone in the back of the lair and it illuminated from the back wall, toward them in a soft glow. She waved her hand to drop the illusion on the lair. A nest appeared against the wall to the right and Kamara walked forward to look at the eggs inside of it. Six eggs, all dark bluish-green in color.

"Feel this," Akiri walked to the nest and placed her hand on the floor, Kamara and Dominic did the same. The floor was hot, like a fire burned beneath it, but the floor was made of stone and therefore protected the eggs from harm.

"How did you manage to get all of this done?" Kamara asked.

"I asked the builder's guild to make some upgrades before I left to go to Ophay. The morning before the battle, I felt a hard knot in my stomach, it hurt, like I was going to explode. I didn't tell anyone, not even Gabe because I didn't want anyone to know until after the battle. I knew I couldn't handle the pain in my human form, but my dragon form could. I went to the lair and to my surprise, I began laying eggs. I knew they would be safe if no one knew they were here."

"Are these... Gabe's?" Kamara asked.

"No," Akiri said. Her face fell and she looked pained by this.

"I have already decided, raising six baby dragons will be too difficult, there are six eggs, which means two for Ophay, two for Ledora, and two for Lapis Highland."

"Akiri, you don't have to..." Dominic started.

"I know, but I *want* to." Akiri waved her hand and the illusion appeared again, the nest faded away and they were once again standing in a dingy old stone lair.

Kamara hugged Akiri, "I am so happy for you." She said, but Akiri heard the sadness in her voice.

"What's wrong?" Akiri asked.

"I just long to be a mother, Sophie is with child, you have baby dragons on the way, but we have decided to wait until we are married and take the throne, any children we have before then will not be considered eligible for the throne of Ledora.

"As King and Queen couldn't you change the law?" Akiri asked.

"It's not a law, it is a belief of the Ledoran people. The throne must be passed to a legitimate child of the King and Queen only after they assume the throne. A child born before their parents' coronation is not viewed as royal and therefore could not rule after us," Dominic explained, "but it's okay, we will be wed this summer, and we will have as many children as you want," Dominic promised.

"I should get some sleep, there's a lot to do before tomorrow night when the ships arrive," Akiri said as they walked back into the castle. Kamara and Dominic nodded as they headed toward their guest room.

The bed in their room was comfortable and as they settled into it, Kamara and Dominic felt a slight reprieve from the stress of the day. Dominic wrapped her in his arms and held her close to his chest. "I love you," he said as he gazed down at her beautiful dark brown skin and her silver eyes which reminded him of diamonds. Her skin glistened and her cheeks had a slight golden shimmer.

"I love you too. I can't wait until we are married." Kamara reached her hand to the back of his neck and pulled his lips to hers. They fell asleep in each other's embrace, their harts beating in a steady matching rhythm.

After the funeral for the fallen citizens of Ash, everyone boarded the ships to head for Blackwater Bay. They would port one at a time in Torzana and then walk through the forest to their new home, The Kingdom of Ophay. Dominic and Kamara flew back to begin the town's construction before people started arriving.

The next morning, Laughlin brought the entire builders sect of the guild and they got to work. Kamara made them all fresh apple cider and cooked a feast for the builders.

"Where is Juniper?" Kamara asked.

"She's at the cabin with Dusk and Opal, our daughter," Laughlin replied.

"We have been gone for so long it seems, I forgot she was with child the last time we were here. I feel like such a terrible friend now." Kamara said.

"Nonsense, you were dealing with very important things, like rescuing an entire country and defeating an evil dragon. When we finish building here, Juniper and I would love to have you come and visit us," Laughlin said.

"We would be honored," Kamara told him.

FORTY-ONE

SOPHIE DUG A HOLE under the willow tree, poured some of Gabe's ashes into it and emptied the rest of the urn into the creek where he used to wade and throw rocks. The breeze feathered her hair and caressed her cheek. It seemed like his spirit was there with her. Sophie closed her eyes and cried, there was so much she wanted to say to him.

"Gabe, I miss you so much. I'm so sorry we never had a chance to explore the feelings between us and I know it was my fault. I left for the Highland, and you joined the guild, got married, and now here we are. I thought we would have so much more time, I always thought there would be more time. When I left for the wizard's tower right after we got back from Choddrath, I thought when I finished training, I would come home and we would be together. I wonder if the reason nothing ever worked out for us was because you were destined for something greater. I know it was you who softened Akiri's heart, we heard about some of the awful things she did, but you... you could always see the good in people, and you brought it out in her. She has become a friend to me now and I know she grieves for you the same way I do. It seems strange, talking to you here in our spot like I can see you laying in the moss with your hands behind your head listening as I rattle on about anything, or nothing at all. You were always a good listener. Bastian and I are going to have a baby by winter solstice this year, I suppose I ought to introduce him to my dad and mom. Do you think my dad will like him?" The wind kicked up and blew a few leaves from the nearby oak tree into Sophie's hair. "You're right, he will never think anyone is good enough for me, but he will at least be civil, I hope. I suppose at some point we will get married, or not, we haven't really talked about it." Sophie smiled, happy she could feel Gabe's spirit there with her.

"I delivered an urn of your ashes to your mother, that was the second hardest thing I have ever gone through, the first of course, being your funeral. She cried, I cried, it was a whole thing. She's doing okay though, all things considered. I checked on the deed to her house, in the event of your death, ownership was transferred to the guild, which is a smart move if you ask me. They're taking good care of your mom, she even started dating again. Her boyfriend seems nice, he is a lot like you, I think you'd like him. He's good to her too and that's what matters most. Anyway, I should be getting back. Bastian is waiting for me at Blackwater Tavern and we're going to go break the news to my family. Wish me luck." She stood up and when the wind blew again, she felt a warm tingle throughout her body, like someone's hand gently caressed hers. She knew it was Gabe and it made her feel like everything was going to be okay.

Blackwater Tavern was a hole-in-the-wall kind of place only the locals knew about, so when strangers wandered in, it wasn't hard to spot them in the crowd of regulars. Bastian was sitting at a big round table, drinking and playing cards with Old Man Brenner and his normal round of poker players. They were betting coppers and silver pieces. Brenner rarely played for gold, he liked to keep his game friendly, and he found when people lose something as precious as gold, they were the opposite of friendly.

"Hiya Sophie! Your boyfriend was just telling us all about your terrible poker-playing skills, care to lose a few coppers?" Brenner teased. Sophie smiled.

"Boyfriend? Where? I don't remember anyone asking to be my boyfriend." Sophie looked all around and turned in a circle scanning the tavern with her hand on her eyebrows like she was shielding them from the sun." The guys at the table all laughed and nudged Bastian.

"Well, I uh- I thought it was just an unspoken agreement." Bastian winked at her and smiled.

Sophie blushed, Bastian's smile was adorable. He had dimples, which made him even more handsome and his blue eyes sparkled.

"If you don't speak it, how do you know if you agree?" Sophie sat down next to Old Man Brenner.

"Good point there, Sophie," Brenner said. She glanced at Bastian who smiled like a kid who got caught with their hand in the cookie jar.

"Forgive me, please, for my grave error in social etiquette." Bastian got up and walked over to Sophie. He dropped to one knee in front of her and reached for her hand. "My darling, Sophie, will you make me the happiest man in the world and make our courtship official, here in front of these witnesses?" Bastian kissed her hand. His lips were warm and gentle against her skin.

"Well when you put it like that, how could I refuse?" Sophie leaned forward and kissed him. "Now are you ready to lose at poker? I've been practicing, Mr. Brenner, you sure you want me to play?" Sophie joked.

"Deal her in, Lenny," Brenner said. The man with the cards shuffled and then dealt them all two cards, except for himself, He wasn't playing, just dealing. Sophie looked at her hand, she'd been dealt pocket aces. She placed her cards face down in front of her and slid two coppers into the pot to match the big blind. Play circled the table and when the pot was good, the dealer turned three cards face up in the middle of the table; a three of hearts, a Jack of spades, and a three of clubs. Brenner was next to the dealer, Lenny, and he bet a silver on the flop. Sophie matched, Bastian matched, the guy next to Bastian folded, and the guy on the other side of Lenny matched.

"Pot's good," Lenny said and he flipped the next card; ten of diamonds. Brenner threw in two silver, Sophie thought about her hand, two pair was pretty good, but if Brenner had another three, she was out. *Ah, what the hell* Sophie threw in her two silver to match the pot and looked at Bastian who slid his cards toward the dealer.

"Awe, folding? Bastian… tsk tsk," Sophie scolded, jokingly. The guy next to Lenny also folded.

"Okie dokie, pot's good. Lenny said, and laid the river on the table; ace of hearts. It was Brenner's bet. Sophie saw him glance at her, but her face was stone, she wasn't giving anything away. Brenner threw in a silver piece just to bet something, and Sophie raised. She put in three silver pieces. Everyone let out an "ooooooh" in unison as they looked at Brenner for his next move.

Brenner thought about the cards on the table, looked at the cards in his hand one more time, and then threw in his two silver to match Sophie's bet.

"I'm only doing this 'cause I wanna see whachu got in your hand there, Soph," he said as he tossed the coins to the center of the table. Brenner turned his cards first, Sophie was right, he did have another three.

"I got three of a kind," he said proudly.

"Your hand is pretty good, but I got a full house," Sophie said as she laid down her aces. "Three aces and two threes."

"Yep, ya beat me fair n' square, Sophie Rend. Your father will hear about this, young lady." Brenner teased. Sophie laughed as she scooped up the coins in the center of the table.

"In this small town Mr. Brenner, I would be surprised if he hadn't already."

"Ha ha! You got that right!" Brenner laughed heartily. "You playing another hand, Miss Sophie?"

"I would, but Daddy hasn't met my boyfriend yet, and I was hoping we could share the news over supper, we better get going so I can let them know we plan to join them," Sophie said.

"Okay, well, young man, it was nice to meet you, make sure you take good care of this girl right here, I wouldn't want to make an enemy of her father," Brenner joked.

"Yes, Sir," Bastian said as he shook the man's hand.

"You had a good hand back there, I didn't know you knew how to play poker, not many people do, I have only seen a game played twice in my life, once here, just now, and then once on Immernacht," Bastian said as they walked down the cobblestone street toward Sophie's parents' house.

"I imagine there are a lot of things about me you don't know yet, and no one knows how much time we have, so you better start asking some questions." Sophie smiled but kept looking forward.

"Okay, what is your favorite color?"

"Really? All the questions you could ask and you're going with my favorite color?" Sophie teased.

"What am I supposed to ask?"

I don't know, things like what I want to do for a living, or how many kids I want, you know, things to help you get to know me," she said.

"Oh, okay, who is the-" Bastian began, but Sophie cut him off.

"No, you already asked your question, my favorite color is emerald green. It's my turn now. What is your mom like?" Sophie asked.

"Well, my birth mother passed during childbirth, so I don't remember her. I was adopted by the Delacroix, the royal family of Immernacht."

"Is your mother the Queen, are you Prince of Immernacht?" Sophie asked in surprise.

"Sort of. The King and Queen have two children of their own, His Royal Highness, Xander Delacroix, and his sister, Her Royal Highness, Serena Delacroix. My official title is Duke, and I am addressed as 'Your Grace' or 'Your Highness,' but never *Royal Highness*, because I am not in line for the throne, I can only serve the sovereign," Bastian replied.

"We're here," Sophie said as she stepped up to the front door of a modest house made of stone.

"I think I need a kiss for luck first, I'm worried your parents won't like me." Bastian gave her a charming smile and leaned down to meet her lips. He pulled her closer, resting one hand on the back of her neck and his other on the small of her back. They broke apart quickly when they heard someone clear their throat behind them.

"Father, I want you to meet Bastian Delacroix, Bastian, this is my father, Commander Leon Rend," Sophie said.

"It is a pleasure to meet you, Sir." Bastian extended his hand to Leon. It seemed like a long and awkward amount of time before he spoke, or took Bastian's hand, but in the end, he did both.

"Welcome to our home, Bastian. Please, come in." Leon led them through the front door and then sat down to take off his boots. Sophie breathed in the sweet smell of home. Her mother had been baking, it smelled of cinnamon and vanilla. Sophie took Bastian's hand and led him into the kitchen where her mother, Samantha was just taking cinnamon sweet rolls out of the wood fire oven.

"Sophie! Oh, I missed you so much!" Samantha exclaimed. She crossed the kitchen, wiped her hands on her apron, and then wrapped Sophie in her arms. "Who is this handsome gentleman you've brought to meet us today?" Samantha studied Bastian's face as she reached out to greet him.

"I'm Bastian, Ma'am, it's lovely to meet you," he said. Sophie could tell he was nervous because little beads of sweat started appearing on his forehead and he wiped his hands on his trousers more than once before taking Samantha's hand.

"Relax," Sophie whispered.

"Bastian and I would like to join you for dinner tonight if it's okay?"

"You know there's always room at our table for you and guests," Samantha said.

"Hey, uh, Bastian is it?" Leon walked into the kitchen.

"Yes, sir," he replied.

"I was wondering if you would give me a hand with something? I could use some more muscle."

"Happy to help, Mr. Rend," Bastian told him as he followed Leon out of the room.

Samantha watched them walk outside and waited until Bastian closed the door behind them before asking Sophie what she really to ask her.

"How are you, honey? I was so sorry to hear about what happened to Gabe, he was such a nice boy." Sophie nodded.

"This whole year has been a whirlwind, first, Ryul left for Ravenhall, and then I found out Gabe was engaged, I met Bastian, and then what happened with Gabe, It's been hard," she replied.

"You know I am always here for you, any time." Samantha held her daughter in a soft embrace and Sophie loved the way her mother always smelled like the sweet shop. "You look happy, though. Something is different about you, I can't quite put my finger on it." Samantha looked at her daughter suspiciously.

"My hair got longer," Sophie joked.

"That must be it. Now, why don't you go wash up and help me chop some vegetables for dinner?"

Sophie grabbed a pail and walked outside to the well. She could hear her father talking to Bastian on the back side of the house. She knew it was wrong to eavesdrop, but she couldn't help it. She wanted her parents to like him.

"Why are you here?" Leon asked.

"Because Sophie asked me to come," Bastian replied.

"Your father didn't send you?"

"No, Sir. Why would my father send me?" Bastian sounded confused.

"To procure a bargaining chip, perhaps?"

"What do you mean? What would he need a bargaining chip for?"

"I want you to leave. Make something up, and go back to Immernacht. Remind your father the magical protections shrouding your city were part of an agreement, and I've held up my end," Leon said.

"NO!" Sophie screamed. She threw the bucket down on the ground and it clattered as it rolled to Leon's feet. "You don't get to decide the details of MY life anymore. Every time you're afraid someone might love me, you send them away, you did it with Gabe, and now you're doing it with Bastian. I am not your prisoner." Sophie shook with anger.

"Sophie, you don't understand about his family, you don't know what they are, I'm only trying to protect you." Leon pleaded.

"We're leaving, come on, Bastian." Sophie grabbed his hand and began pulling Bastian away from her father. "And to think, we came here to announce your future grandchild, but I guess you don't have to worry about being a grandfather since I want nothing more to do with you." Sophie spat.

Oh no... She's pregnant. Leon's heart sank. He wasn't certain if it was a trick of the light or his imagination, but he could have sworn he saw a smirk of triumph on Bastian's face as he put his arm around Sophie's waist and led her away.

Part Three:

The Chimera of Immernacht

ONE

A DEEP AMBER GLOW illuminated the manicured gardens of Highland Castle in the late afternoon sun. It looked like it would be warm, but the evening breeze brought a chill with it that hinted at the end of autumn and soon the snow would come. Sophie hoped the winter ahead would not be as harsh as the one before—last winter when the frost came early, it killed the crops before the harvest. Sophie used her magic to make what food they had last through the season. The people of Aerulean Lake, Alasia, and Northport were so grateful to her, they pledged their banners to the kingdom of Lapis Highland. Each town sent men to the royal guard, they offered their boys to squire and their girls to serve the Queen.

Sophie stood at the edge of the cliff beside Highland Castle and looked out across the water as the sun reached the horizon. These quiet moments alone were Sophie's favorite, although she was never truly alone anymore. Two of her guards stood a few paces behind her with their backs turned to give her the illusion of privacy. She often thought of her childhood best friend, Gabe, during these times of reflection; remembering how he used to wade in the stream next to the willow tree they both loved so much while she gathered herbs and other components to practice magic. His death had left a gaping hole in her heart. Lucky for her, Bastian was there to ease the pain and make her forget the loneliness consuming her. What began as a whirlwind fling had blossomed into partnership and she had grown to love him. When Sophie and Bastian welcomed their daughter into the world, they named her Willow as a way of honoring Gabe. In fairness, Sophie named her, and Bastian agreed.

The clanging of the dinner bell brought Sophie out of her memories, and she turned toward the castle. Her red hair cascaded down her back in large loose curls and blew forward in the breeze as she turned her back to the water. The guards escorted her to the front steps, but before they reached the door, a rider with a messenger bag approached. The guards stopped the boy and questioned him before accepting the delivery. Sophie's personal guard, Thomas, handed her the envelope. She glanced at the wax seal of The Silver Talons for no more than a moment and then turned back toward the door without so much as opening the letter.

"Wait! I mean- I'm sorry, My Queen, Commander Rend asked me to wait for your reply," the messenger boy fumbled. He looked to be around sixteen and bowed to Sophie to show regret for his outburst.

"You may rise, what is your name?" Sophie descended a few steps so she was almost at eye level with the messenger.

"Beric, Your Grace," he said, wringing his hands together.

"Do you have a quill and a piece of parchment?" Sophie asked.

"Yes, Your Grace." Beric reached into his satchel and pulled out his writing kit. Sophie heard the doors behind her open, but paid no mind to it. She scribbled a quick note onto the paper and handed it back to him.

"Don't you want to seal it?" he asked.

"No, I would like for you to read it, just in case this reply should become lost on the way back, you can still deliver the message. Can you read?" Sophie asked.

"Yes, Your Grace." The boy looked down at the message.

I no longer wish to receive your correspondence. Tell Mother to come and visit, I miss her.

The boy looked back up at Sophie, nodded, placed the parchment into his satchel, and bowed to her once more before running back across the courtyard to his horse. Sophie turned toward the castle and saw Bastian standing in the doorway. As she approached him, he kissed her cheek and guided her inside with a gentle hand on the small of her back. Sophie walked into the parlor and with careless disregard, tossed the unopened letter into the fireplace.

"You should have at least read it. I know you're still angry with him, but it seems like he might be trying to make amends and I'm still here. He didn't scare me away, so perhaps it is time to forgive and forget?" Bastian tried to comfort Sophie with a light touch on the shoulder.

"I will never forgive him. He has tried to control me my whole life, and these letters are no more than an attempt to regain control. I am certain of it. He made Gabe leave and tried to make you leave, too."

"Yet I am still here; he could never convince me to leave you." He took her hands in his and looked into her green eyes lovingly. "Come on, let's go have dinner," Bastian said.

After dinner, Sophie gave Willow a bath with milk and lavender, then once she dried her off and dressed her, Sophie sat in the rocking chair with Willow in her arms, reading her a story. Bastian stood in the doorway listening, and waiting for her to finish so they could tuck Willow in together. They lingered beside the door until she drifted off to sleep.

"I can't believe how quickly she is growing up," Sophie said as she leaned against Bastian.

"I know, It seems like we just met. Do you remember that night?" Bastian turned Sophie around and extended his hand to her. "Would you do me the honor?" Sophie smiled and placed her hand in his. He twirled her around and gracefully pulled her close to him. As they danced cheek to cheek he breathed deep, taking in the scent of her hair.

"I have to work again tonight, but I will be back tomorrow evening," Bastian said softly.

"Are you ever going to tell me what business you are always leaving to conduct?" Sophie asked.

"I will, someday. I promise."

"When can I meet your family? I mean, you've met mine. Even if my father tried to threaten you into leaving. I know your heart, your hopes, your dreams, but nothing of your life. I keep hoping one day you'll share it all with me."

Bastian hated seeing the sadness in her eyes, but the things he kept private, he did so for her safety, and for the safety of their child. "I know, My Love, I know. I'm sorry. One day I will explain everything, but for now, I do what I must to keep you safe and that means keeping this life private from my past. I love you more than life; I will do *anything* to keep you and Willow safe."

Bastian kissed her, and she melted into his embrace. His blue eyes still made her weak at the knees. When he pulled away, he held Sophie's gaze for a moment, then she closed her eyes and when she opened them, he was gone. Bastian moved with such silence, even when he was wearing his boots. Sophie wondered if he might be an assassin, or a spy. Which would explain all the secrecy.

Sophie waited until Willow's night nurse, Emily, arrived and then she went back out to the cliff-side facing the water. She hadn't been able to fly much since Willow was born; it had been too hard to leave her in the beginning, but now Sophie was taking a short flight each night, and working her way up to being able to fly to Leodora again. Dominic and Kamara had wed during the winter solstice and ascended the throne of Ledora as king and queen. Sophie missed the coronation because she was with child. Now Kamara was expecting, and Sophie wanted so badly to be there for her when she gave birth.

Sophie called upon her Draconic power and her fingers stretched, cracking as her talons emerged. Her back bent and her body swelled to an enormous size. Scales formed on her skin, covering her in an almost indestructible natural armor. Her leathery wings expanded, and she flew across the harbor toward Ophay. The town was quiet; the newly paved cobblestone streets looked peaceful in the lantern's glow. The former subjects of Ash were now residents of Ophay, a town, not a kingdom, and Akiri no longer used the title of "Queen." Since King Gabriel died, the residents of Ophay voted and elected a council to represent them, making Akiri the Chairperson, and Roland Koffery the Vice Chairman.

Akiri was still caring for her unhatched clutch of eggs, though, and asked Juniper to be her proxy in the meantime, until the dragons emerged from their shells.

Sophie flew north, and then turned toward the western forest of Blackwater. She saw Laughlin and Juniper's cabin below and a gentle white smoke billowed softly from the chimney. They often came to visit Sophie in Lapis Highland with their daughter, Opal Magnolia; they called her Maggie for short. Sophie was about to circle around and fly back to the castle when she heard shouting from the Blackwater docks. Curious, she flew closer, but not close enough to be discovered. Thankful for the clouds and the cover of night, she tried to hear what they were saying, but she wasn't close enough. She descended into the forest. They hadn't spotted her; she was sure of it. There was something else going on. Sophie landed and crept as close to the docks as she could get without breaking cover. She ducked behind the shipping crates so she could hear what they were saying.

"Are you sure he's dead?" One man inquired.

"Uh'course I'm sure, è just floated over here with his face in the wa'er; unless è's some kinda fish-man, è's dead." The man spoke like a pirate; sarcastic and gruff, with a broken accent from too many years at sea, and too few years among civilized folks.

As the guards stepped away, Sophie spotted her father, Leon Rend. He walked up between the guards to inspect the body, then turned the man over, moving his matted hair away from his neck. Leon pointed to something on the body and the other men leaned forward to look.

"This is the third body my men have found with these marks," Leon explained. The others looked at him with confusion, not knowing what it could mean. Leon pulled a dagger from his belt and ran the blade down the length of the man's arm. The men gasped as the flesh split open, expecting to see blood, but seeing not a single drop.

"How in the- è ain't got no blood!" the pirate exclaimed, backing away as he clutched a pendant around his neck that Sophie could only assume was the holy symbol of whatever deity he served.

"See to it we notify this man's family and give him a proper burial," Leon told the guards. They nodded and got to work. A man dressed in all black stood nearby, surveying the scene with a watchful eye. Those who didn't know to look for him would't see the man, but Sophie recognized him at once; Velen Shrike, Leon's right-hand man. Velen was as quick as a flash, and as quiet as death itself. He was intelligent and tactical. Bastian reminded Sophie a lot of him.

"Immernacht, Sir?" Velen asked Leon. Sophie's ears perked up, and she inched closer, trying to listen, but stopped when Velen's head jerked in her direction as if he heard her take a step. His eyes scanned the perimeter and then turned back to Leon.

"They've broken the treaty. We need to make a plan. If I dispel the barrier, they will know we are coming. We will need a ship that can withstand the worst storm imaginable. As soon as we finish here, contact the hunters." Leon said. Velen nodded in agreement.

Sophie didn't stay to observe more; she had to warn Bastian. She backed away with haste, yet as quietly as she could until she was far enough away to shift. As she flew back to Lapis Highland, she remembered Bastian was not there. Now, more than ever, Sophie wondered what this secret about his family was. He told her he would tell her when the time was right. It seemed now they were out of time.

When Sophie returned to the castle, she went to her bedchamber and grabbed her enchanted notebook from the writing desk. She and Bastian each had one so they could send messages while Bastian was gone. She opened the notebook to the first page, began writing with the special quill which needed no ink, and the words disappeared seconds after she wrote them.

Bastian, body found near Blackwater, my father thinks it has something to do with the treaty. He's coming. Almost immediately, her notebook illuminated. She opened it to read Bastian's reply.

Bring Willow and Emily, meet me here. It's time to explain.

TWO

EVERYTHING FELT LIKE HOME, from the sound of the wind moving through the leaves to the rocks beneath his bandaged feet. Sparrow's year of solitude had been difficult at first, he made a home for himself, planted a garden to grow his food, trapped rabbits and other small game for protein, and built a little shelter beside a stream in the middle of nowhere. His goal was to focus, practice his martial arts, and become a better version of himself. He built training dummies and practiced hand-to-hand combat, meditated by the babbling stream, and spent hours reflecting on his actions which had caused him to take this sabbatical. Now, he was finally going home to the monastery that took him in as a child—a group of peaceful men in service of the deity Gaia. They took pride in using the gifts nature provided, and in return, they protected the forest in which they'd made their home. Their sanctuary was called The Garden Of Life.

Sparrow assessed the sun's location and surveyed the path. It had been a long time since he walked this route. He longed for the comforts of home; the central garden, an actual bed, and the company of his brothers. He had only a few miles left and could barely contain his excitement. The wind howled and blew through the trees like the scream of a spirit; Sparrow knew something was wrong. He dropped the pack he was carrying and ran, jumping over branches and rocks on the path as he doubled his stride. The wind seemed to carry him, urging him to get to the temple faster.

As he rounded the last bend, the stone building came into view. The door was ajar, and Sparrow didn't see anyone outside, which was unusual. During the day, his brothers would be training, meditating, or looking after the animals. Sparrow approached the broken-down door with caution, unsure of what he might find on the other side. He entered the foyer, littered with torn tapestries, broken furniture, and other things that would be meaningless to a looter, but sentimental to his brothers. He tiptoed down the left corridor without making a sound; his hands at the 'ready' position, waiting to find the culprit in action.

When he stepped into the sleeping room, his heart plummeted into the pit of his stomach and he became nauseous. His brothers were dead, murdered in their sleep, and for what? Some tapestries, flowers, a few chickens, goats, cows...? Sparrow couldn't process the possible reason for this attack. He approached one of the men, daring to look for clues. He hovered over his brother, Banyan who had been an agile fighter and bested Sparrow on more than one occasion in their sparring matches. Sparrow knew Banyan would have put up a fight if he saw his attacker coming, but there were no signs of struggle. The only marks he found at all were two small puncture wounds on Banyan's neck. Sparrow knew what did this; it was the work of the undead, evil creatures who feed on human blood in order to live forever. He couldn't deal with this on his own. There were twenty-one members of the monastery, including him, but he only counted seventeen bodies. *Where are the others? I hope they escaped,* Sparrow thought.

After checking the rest of the grounds and finding no one, Sparrow headed away from the temple with purpose. He wished he had a horse; he was a long way from Blackwater, but if anyone could help, it would be the Silver Talons Guild. Sparrow walked hastily down the same path he'd been so excited to see minutes before, now with heavy, pounding steps. After seeing his brothers treated so disrespectfully, their bodies discarded like the core of an apple, he didn't know if he was going to cry, or if he needed to hit something—he might do both. Sparrow couldn't even feel the pain in his feet anymore; his body going numb with fury. *No, snap out of it,* he said to himself, shaking free of the tunnel vision beginning to fill his sight. He ran; it was just the outlet he needed at the time to keep him from spiraling out of control. He did not need to fall into old habits right now, he needed to talk to Commander Leon Rend.

Breathe. Sparrow thought. He focused on nothing but path ahead as he ran. If he could make it to the edge of Alasia by dawn, he might be able to catch the caravan to Blackwater. He swerved through the trees as the forest grew thicker. Even in his shocked and panicked state, he could hear the birds in the trees calling out their warning of his presence. He traversed the terrain with ease, gliding over the fallen branches, rocks, and hills as if his feet barely touched the ground at all.

He startled and fell when he heard a growl from behind him. He looked back but did not see the source of the sound. Then another growl came from the right of him, and a similar noise echoed on the other side. *No, this is not how I die.* He told himself. He got up, brushed the dirt and pine needles off of his white tunic and took off running again. From the rustling of foliage on both sides and the padding of paws on the leaves and sticks littering the forest floor, he came to the conclusion he was being hunted. He suspected a wolf pack and knew his only chance for survival would be to make it across the river. There was no other way to escape them; even then, it might only buy him time. If it had only been one wolf, he might have been able to fight it off, but these animals hunt in packs, and even with his skill and a whole year of nothing but time to practice, he knew better than to take on an entire pack alone.

The river raged several feet below him. The only crossing for miles in either direction was a fallen tree lying across the gap. Sparrow broke into a sprint as he approached it and maintained his speed all the way across, praying to Gaia for protection while being thankful the log was not slippery under his bare feet. When he reached the other side, he dropped to the ground and used the power in his legs to push the enormous trunk toward the water. The wolf jumped onto the tree and growled at Sparrow, stalking closer. He had to scoot forward; give it more oomph. Another push would do it. He extended his legs with as much force as he could, and shoved. The log rolled over the edge of the cliff with the wolf still on it. He heard the animal howl on its descent into the chasm until it plunged into the river below. Three wolves emerged from the tree line on the other side and stared at him. When they saw there was no way to cross, they took off toward the south.

Sparrow had not realized he had been holding his breath. He exhaled a heavy sigh of relief; the wolves were gone for now, but he still had to make it to the caravan and this had cost him a few minutes at least. Sparrow looked around for the quickest path and pushed onward with as much energy as he had left. The adrenaline was wearing off, and he realized his ankle hurt like hell, but stopping to examine it would only give the joint time to swell and it would force him to stay off his feet for a couple of days at least.

He wasn't sure what town these woods surrounded, but once he made it out, he hoped he would be somewhere near the bridge between Aerulean Lake and Alasia Outpost. Sparrow wondered how long it would take the wolves to find a crossing at the river and if they would be able to pick up his scent. He hoped not, but it was possible. Sparrow tried to listen for them as he continued to move quickly through the woods, hearing the river flowing behind him, birds in the trees above him, and his heart beating hard and fast in his chest.

From the top of the hill, and down through the trees, he could see the caravan trail. Sparrow was limping now, the pain in his ankle radiating through his leg and his foot. When he reached the bottom of the hill, just before he emerged from the tree line onto the road, he heard the beating of hooves. Sparrow ducked down to see who the rider was before deciding if he should make himself known or not. The rider was a young man with a messenger bag. He was riding slowly, humming to himself without a care. He didn't seem to be armed from what Sparrow could see, but he knew better than anyone, unarmed did not mean defenseless.

"Wait!" Sparrow called, moving out of the forest with his hands raised above his head. "I came across a pack of wolves in the woods, I'm injured and am in need of a healer. I was hoping you could be so kind as to let me ride with you as far as the caravan in Alasia Outpost?" Sparrow asked.

"Certainly, Sir," the boy said as he moved forward and took his feet out of the stirrups to allow Sparrow to mount behind him. "Do you work with the caravan?" he asked.

"No, I'm just on my way to Blackwater," Sparrow told him.

"I'm headed there myself, I was planning to get a room for the night in Northport and then take Stonehold pass in the morning. A single horse can make it through the mountains faster than the entire caravan with their wagons—if they can make it through at all, sometimes the path is too narrow. You're welcome to travel with me if you like."

"Thank you, That's very kind of you, what's your name?" Sparrow asked.

"I'm Beric. What's yours."

"Sparrow, nice to meet you."

"Sparrow, like the bird?" Beric asked.

"Yep, just like the bird," Sparrow answered.

Sparrow winced from the pain as he put his uninjured foot in the stirrup and lifted his sore ankle over the back of the saddle. He found the bouncing of being on horseback almost as painful as walking. He didn't mean to, but he groaned and alerted the boy to his pain.

"I can give you a little something for the pain, it won't make it better, but it'll make you not care about it." He reached into the pouch tied to his belt and pulled out a flask. It was engraved with a beautiful design that had to have been carved by a skilled engraver. This was no mere trinket, but a gift that would have been specially made for nobility, or someone of extremely high rank, at least. Sparrow did not point this out to the boy as he brought the flask to his lips, not at all surprised it was not filled with cheap pirate's rum, but a high-quality aged whiskey. It was strong, and Sparrow was not a drinker, so it didn't take long, or much, for him to begin feeling the effects.

Sparrow handed the flask back and waited for the alcohol to numb the throbbing in his ankle. The boy continued humming, Sparrow thought for a moment he might have heard the tune before but he couldn't place it. He didn't ask about it, because he was content to just ride to Northport, get some ice for his ankle, maybe some more whiskey, and then sleep. Now that his adrenaline was gone, Sparrow was exhausted and a full night's rest, a warm meal, and a ride to Blackwater all sounded too good to be true.

THREE

SOPHIE ASKED HER GUARDS to bring her dragon saddle to the courtyard. She hastily packed the saddle bags and wondered if it would be safer to leave Willow at Lapis Highland, but Bastian specifically asked Sophie to bring her. Emily, Willow's nanny, was the only person on staff who had been trained to ride on dragonback for such an occasion as this. Sophie strapped Willow to Emily's chest, making sure the child's face would be protected from the wind. Sophie's personal guard, Thomas, secured the saddle to Sophie's back after the transformation was complete, pulling the leather belts as tightly as he could around her dragon form. Then he made sure Emily was strapped into the saddle and waved as the red dragon took off at a sprint toward the cliff's edge.

When they ascended into the sky, Thomas used Sophie's notebook to send word to Bastian that his family was on their way. In her absence from Lapis Highland, Thomas was Regent as per Sophie's command. Thomas was also her apprentice and she made sure to teach him the spell she used to create food and drink. She knew in her absence, at least no one would have to go hungry.

Sophie didn't know what to expect, she had never been to Immernacht, and only knew what little Bastian would tell her about it. The only thing she cared about was the safety of her family; Bastian, Willow, and Emily, too. Her mind raced as she pushed through the night sky. The stars looked like silver glitter sprinkled onto midnight blue silk. Normally,

Sophie could look at the sky for hours when it was like this, but not tonight, she had to get to Bastian. She wished she could see Emily and Willow, to make sure they were okay; Willow wasn't crying, which was a small reassurance.

When she finally got close to Immernacht, the dark clouds covering the island parted for them and Sophie could see Bastian on the shore below. When she landed, he came over to help Emily unhook and step down from the saddle. He uncovered Willow to make sure she was okay and when he saw her sleeping peacefully, he moved to unhook the saddle so Sophie could shift. Sophie's body shrank back down to her human size and the saddle blocked her from the view of the others until she was able to cast an illusion spell to cover her naked body. She grabbed a black dress and her cloak out of the saddle bag, it was colder there than she expected and the illusion spell would not keep her warm. She slipped into the tangible clothing and dropped the spell. Bastian took her in his arms and kissed her on the top of her head.

"I'm sorry, let's get to the castle, my family will want to meet you. I'll send someone to bring the saddle up to the courtyard." Bastian ushered them away from the beach and down a cobblestone street between rows of two-story stone houses. The rooftops were connected by wooden bridges, and the ground level had ropes for hanging the wash stretched across the spaces between the houses. There were only a few lanterns to light their way. Sophie allowed Emily to loop her arm through hers, and she followed closely to Bastian.

"Is it always so dark here?" Emily asked.

"Only at night, it does get light during the day, but the clouds keep the sun out," Bastian answered.

Sophie noted the empty garden boxes and the absence of grass—or anything green for that matter. As they walked through the city streets, Sophie's body tensed and her eyes moved back and forth through the darkness. She could have sworn she saw a shadow move swiftly across the rooftop, but by the time she looked up, there was nothing there. It might have been a breeze flickering the lantern light as they passed, or a trick of her tired mind. The uneasy feeling they were being watched followed her as the road began to incline. At the crest of the hill, Castle

Delacroix came into view. It was an ominous visage reminding Sophie of her first time at Castle Ash, dark spires rose high into the night sky and tall black stone walls ran the perimeter. As they walked closer, Sophie noticed the road was not just an incline, but a bridge towering high above a river below.

Two men stood at the front gate, they were dressed like lords—not guards—and Sophie wondered if they were only there to greet them. When they saw Bastian, they used magic to open the way. The iron emitted a high-pitched scream as the gates swung open slowly and then closed with a loud clank behind them.

"Come on, this way." Bastian turned to his right and led them through the courtyard which contained only dead trees and crumbling stone benches. Sophie wondered if it had once been beautiful back before they blocked out the sun with magic. She was sad to see the absence of life in the place where Bastian grew up and thought if she had grown up here, she would have wanted to escape as well. Bastian led them to a side door of the castle. "We are going to go to the parlor to wait, my parents will join us when they have finished their meal," he told them.

Sophie thought it was late for a meal, but she didn't bring it up. She walked around the parlor admiring the antiques and décor of the space. There were no windows in this particular room, yet long, purple and black curtains hung from rods mounted to the walls where windows might have been, serving no purpose other than aesthetic. A large pipe organ in the center of the room was the most fascinating thing to Sophie. She had never seen such an instrument. When she was young, she played a few instruments, including a new stringed instrument called a cello. This instrument towered to the ceiling in an intricately carved wooden case. Sophie grazed her fingers over the keys and startled when the sound was much louder than she thought it would be. Bastian laughed as she jumped, but walked over to comfort Willow immediately when she began to fuss. The discordant note had woken her and she was not happy about it. Emily unwrapped the baby from her chest and Bastian took her in his arms.

"I think she needs a change, I will take care of it and be right back," Bastian said.

"Oh, I left her bag in the saddle, I will go get it for you, sir." Emily left the room and Sophie was in the parlor by herself.

She hoped Bastian would make it back before his parents found her in there alone. The room was eerily quiet without the others and the same uneasy feeling Sophie felt on the walk through the city washed over her once more. She turned quickly toward the door to see someone watching her. He had dark hair swept to one side like an ocean wave; his bangs grazed his cheekbone and his green eyes pierced into Sophie's. He looked her up and down subtly, If she had not been entranced by his eyes at that moment she might not have noticed it.

"Hi, I'm Sophie, Bastian will be right back," she said nervously.

The young man moved from the doorway and circled her. She wanted to look away, but couldn't. He held her in his gaze and it made her feel excited and scared, like a deer in the aim of a hunter's bow. His lips parted and she thought he might speak, but he exhaled softly and stepped closer. His lips were now next to her ear and he drew in her scent. Sophie waited for a whisper that never came.

"Xander, where are your manners?" A woman's voice startled them and the man turned to face her.

Instantly, Sophie's mind felt clear again, and she stepped away from him quickly to see the female speaker. She wore a dark green satin dress trimmed in black lace, the bouffant skirt bunched up at the hips. Sophie had seen similar dresses on the courtesans at the ball in Ledora. The woman's waist was corseted and tiny, giving her an extreme hourglass figure. She had long black hair, curled and pinned half-up with a pearl comb. Her face seemed so familiar, but Sophie knew she had certainly never met her before.

"Hello, My name is Natalia Delacroix, I am Bastian's mother," she said as she extended her hand delicately to Sophie. "Don't mind my son, we don't receive many visitors, he has forgotten himself." Natalia gave her son a warning glance.

"It's lovely to meet you," Sophie said as she curtsied.

"Please, Dear, you are family, there's no need for formality, but I do have to ask, where is this beautiful daughter of yours we have heard so much about? We've been dying to meet her."

"Bastian took her to get her cleaned up from the trip here. He should be back any—"

"Look who I found!" A man called from the doorway. Sophie turned to see him holding Willow in his arms with Bastian and Emily following behind.

"Oh, Arturo, I am so jealous you got to hold her first," Natalia said as she approached her husband and stretched out her arms for Willow. Arturo turned protectively, blocking Natalia's attempt to relieve him of the baby.

"Ah-ah-ah, I just got her, surely you can wait your turn." He cooed at Willow and then turned his attention toward Sophie who stood awkwardly by the pipe organ, seemingly forgotten by everyone except Xander, who continued to sneak glances at her when he thought no one was looking.

"You must be Queen Sophia Rend." Arturo finally handed Willow to his wife so he could bow and extend his hand for Sophie's.

"It's just Sophie, please," she told him as he kissed her hand. He was wearing a black suit vest over a white ruffle shirt. His vest had a dark green embroidered design and coattails extending to the middle of his thighs. His hair was dirty blond and short with a defined side part; he looked different than Sophie had expected.

Bastian crossed the room and spoke quietly to Xander. Sophie couldn't make out what he was saying because she was trying not to be rude to Arturo, who was asking about her home and her family.

"Oh, the reason we have come, The Silver Talons are on their way, something about a treaty and they're preparing for a fight," Sophie said.

"I heard something about a body? Is that right?" Arturo asked.

"Yes, Sir," she said.

"This means the victim was drained are there more vampires?" Bastian asked as he looked at Arturo.

"There can't be. I mean—unless..." Natalia's voice trailed off as she looked at Arturo, hoping he would be able to calm her fears.

"What is it? What's going on?" Sophie asked.

"We can talk about it later, it seems the little one is getting hungry," Natalia said as she handed Willow back to Sophie. "Tomorrow evening, I would like for Sophie to join us for dinner after Willow goes to bed." She gave Bastian a look of warning. Sophie wondered if she was meant to notice it.

"Where is Serena?" Bastian asked.

"She went out for the evening, but I will make sure your sister is here for dinner."

"Bastian, I need a word with you," Arturo said as he led Bastian out of the parlor.

Sophie looked at Natalia. "Would you mind showing me to our room so I may nurse her in private?"

"Of course," Natalia replied.

As she led them to the door, Sophie glanced back to where Xander had been standing. He was no longer there. She didn't know how he had slipped from the room so quietly. *He's so strange.* Sophie thought.

Their room was more than Sophie could ever want. There was a beautiful wooden cradle for Willow next to the bed lined with soft furs and a changing table stocked with cloth to wrap Willow's bottom. For them coming on such short notice, Sophie was surprised at how prepared they were to receive them. Willow was fussing now and Natalia left them alone, closing the door behind her as she left. Sophie hummed a sweet melody to Willow as she nursed. She curled the baby's strawberry blond ringlets around her finger and let them bounce back into place. Every time Sophie looked at her, she felt abundantly happy. She had never felt so much love in her life, except maybe from her own mother. Sophie wondered what Leon would tell her mother when he went off to war with

Immernacht. She hoped it would not come to that. She wanted this to be a misunderstanding. *What could possibly be so bad about this family that Leon would risk taking the Silver Talons to war?*

Her mind raced until she was too tired from the trip to stay awake any longer. Sophie fell asleep on the edge of the bed with one hand in the cradle so Willow could hold her finger. She slept so soundly she didn't even feel Bastian come to bed, but when early morning came, she woke up to see Willow nestled snugly between two pillows in the middle of their bed. Bastian was still asleep. Sophie smiled; waking up to her perfect family was her favorite moment in life. If she could freeze time, this would be the moment she would stay in forever. She smiled as she dozed off again, clinging to the closeness of her loved ones.

FOUR

THE BLUE LIONESS WAS not the kind of Inn Sparrow had in mind. He had never been to a brothel before, and the abundance of women in low-cut dresses with corsets to push up and accentuate their bosoms made a blush rise to his cheeks. He didn't fault them for using their Goddess-given assets to earn a living, but he did worry for them. The type of men this profession attracted were not always the kindest, or gentlest of creatures.

As promised, the lad he was riding with had paid for his room, which included dinner and all the drinks he wanted. Sparrow did take them up on the offer of alcohol because of the pain he was in, and after he had eaten and was sufficiently numb, he retired to his room for the evening. He left his pack, so he had nothing with him, no extra robes, no bandages, and no coin with which to buy the things he needed. He undressed and looked at his injuries in the looking glass. He was bruised badly on his ribs, and his shins, forearms, and even noticed a few purple patches on his backside. His ankle, although still swollen, didn't hurt as much as it had earlier, but Sparrow credited it to the whiskey. He used the belt of the washroom robe to wrap his ankle and then laid down on the bed and propped his foot up on the second pillow. He knew, from learning to treat wounds, , elevation helped reduce swelling.

When he woke up the next morning, his ankle was nearly normal size again. He didn't know what time it was and he hoped Beric had not left without him. He dressed quickly and ran to the door. He swung it open just in time to see Beric with his knuckle raised to knock. Beric jumped at the sudden movement and clutched his chest.

"Oh, Goddess, you scared me half to death," Beric said laughing.

"Sorry, I was in a hurry, I got nervous at the amount of sunlight peeking through the window and I thought you might have forgotten about me," he admitted.

"Of course not, I just figured you might want to sleep in a little after your trip, it seemed like you had a rough time."

"I did, and I do appreciate the extra time, are you ready to head out now?"

"Yes, Sir," Beric said.

It was a beautiful day, the sky was bright blue and filled with Sparrow's favorite clouds—the big puffy white ones. He could lie in The Garden of Life for hours and find shapes in the sky. He loved watching them slowly morph into other things as they swept by.

"So, Beric, what is it you do?" Sparrow asked.

"I'm a messenger. I work for Commander Rend."

"Perfect because that is just who I need to see." Sparrow hoped Beric would not inquire as to the reason for his urgent need to meet with Commander Rend, and he didn't.

"You have a family in Blackwater?" Sparrow changed the subject.

"Yes, Sir. My Ma and Pa live there. Pa is an armorer, and Ma is a baker, she makes bread and corn muffins and stuff. I began working for the guild because I wasn't very good at baking or making things, and I wanted to travel. Now I get paid to travel," Beric said.

"Well, it sounds to me like you found the perfect job for you."

"I did, for sure. I'm not much for fighting, so being on a strike team was not for me, but riding a horse and delivering letters, well, that's easy-peasy and I like it. Don't get me wrong, I'm not lazy or afraid of some hard work, but I just figure if you don't *have* to, you might as well save your energy, ya know?" Beric chuckled.

Sparrow agreed, but could not relate. He didn't know what else to talk about. Life at the monastery was different than life everywhere else. Sparrow and his brothers had no need of material possessions, coin, or jewels. Out here, men killed for those things and needed to possess them in order to establish their self-worth. Sparrow knew now he was meant for more than jewels and riches, his purpose was to end the blight of whatever undead creature had killed his brothers. The more he thought about it the angrier he became despite the progress he'd made in his seclusion in the last year to free himself of it. Now he was beginning to think he was meant to have this emotion, and he never should have tried to rid himself of it in the first place.

The path through the Stonehold mountains was narrow, it was only wide enough for the horse in a few places. It was cold, but not snowing yet, Sparrow was thankful because he only had his summer robes, he didn't even have any boots or stockings. He would have to work for some in Blackwater when he got there.

When they reached the top of the western peak, Beric stopped and dismounted. He led Sparrow to a small cave with a campfire ring outside of it. Inside the mouth of the cave there was a large pile of wood covered with the hides of what looked like bear, or buffalo, Sparrow wasn't sure. Beric grabbed some wood and began making a fire. He pulled a few packages from his backpack which were wrapped in banana leaves. Once he got the fire going, he placed the packages in the coals and used a shovel to scoop some of the hot coals on top of the packages as well.

Sparrow had never cooked using this method and found it interesting. It was clear Beric spent a lot of time on the road. They sat next to the fire, warming themselves as they waited for their meal to heat up. Beric pulled a small wooden flute from his bag and began to play. Wooden instruments were common at The Garden of Life, they rarely used anything they couldn't make from nature. His brother, Jonah, made pan flutes from hollow reeds, and drums from hollow logs covered with stretched leather. The hunters wasted nothing. They saved the hides, bones, hooves, antlers, and everything. Meat, of course, was given to the kitchen staff who would cook it right away and then seal the meat in jars so it would not spoil. They ate a lot of stew, and a lot of bread, which they baked themselves as well; even the grains for the bread were stone-ground with a mortar and pestle.

Beric was a lovely flutist, Sparrow found himself gazing out across the mountains. The day was so clear, from the mountaintop he could see Castle Highland and Blackwater Bay. He could even see the town of Blackwater below, the people moving about looked like ants from where they were. They were so close. Sparrow didn't know if Commander Rend would be able to help him find the ones responsible for the slaughter of his brothers, but at the very least, the information could protect others.

"You ready to eat?" Beric asked, bringing Sparrow back from his thoughts. Beric handed Sparrow a metal plate with one of the packages on it. He watched Beric snap the string holding the banana leaves closed and he did the same. When Sparrow saw the meal inside he was shocked. There was a nice-sized chunk of meat; rabbit if he had to guess, small potatoes, rosemary, garlic, mushrooms, and spinach.

"This is amazing, where did you get it?" Sparrow asked as he took a bite of potatoes.

"Maureen, the gal who owns the inn, she's kinda like a second mom to me. I have been delivering messages since I was ten years old, and she always told me I was too young to be out here on my own. She used to have this guy follow me around, for the longest time I didn't even know it, but one day I saw him. I didn't say anything then, but I was scared, didn't know Maureen had sent him, so I made sure to hide my coin; in the toe of my boot, in a special inside pocket of my trousers, and even sometimes in my..." Beric pointed to the crotch of his pants. "Bandits rarely want to grab another man's... you know, area, so it's a good hiding spot sometimes."

"Do you deal with bandits often?" Sparrow asked.

"Not often, but more often than I'd like. I think I have been robbed three—no, four times. The first time, they took everything because I didn't know to hide it. The second time they took my backpack, my weapons, my horse, and my coin pouch, but they left me my water skin. After that, I bought an enchanted bag from Alasia Outpost—from the shop selling Queen Sophie's magic items. I had to save up for two full moons to afford it, but it's worth it."

"What does it do?" Sparrow asked. Beric handed him the bag and Sparrow turned it over in his hand. "It's just an empty bag," he remarked. It was old and dingy-looking. It had a patch on the front of it and the leather didn't match. The drawstring was tattered and fraying on the ends. Sparrow handed it back, confused.

"Watch this," Beric said as he reached into the bag and pulled out a handful of gold coins. Sparrow was amazed, he didn't feel any coins in the bag when he held it. Beric reached in again, this time, he reached in deep—deeper than his hand should have been able to go—and pulled out a short sword. Sparrow's eyes rounded in shock.

"How? That's amazing! I didn't feel anything in there, and it's physically impossible to pull a sword from a coin pouch." Sparrow found himself wondering about The Highland Queen, if she could make something like this, surely she could make something to help him win the fight against whatever blood-sucking demons murdered his brothers.

"How far is Lapis Highland from Blackwater?" Sparrow asked.

"About two days if you walk, a day if you ride. It's south of Alasia, up on the high cliff. There is a road leading up there now so it doesn't take as long as it used to. You can take a ship across the bay and make it in a few hours if you get a horse in Northport," Beric said between bites.

When they finished their meal, Beric covered the campfire with sand to smother it and they continued through the mountain pass. It was all downhill from there so it was physically easier for the horse, but by the time they reached the northern gate, the horse refused to walk any further.

"You go ahead, I'm going to give her some water and a bag of oats and camp here tonight. Blackwater is just through that gate, and the guild is the biggest building in the city, you can't miss it."

"Thank you, Beric. If you ever need a hand with anything, come and find me, I'm in your debt," Sparrow said.

"Nonsense, like I said, I was headed here anyway, your company just made the trip less boring," Beric replied.

Sparrow turned to look at his destination. The Northern gate was open and didn't seem to be guarded very well, it looked like he might be able to walk right in. He put one bare foot in front of the other and approached the entrance to the city. On the other side of the gate, there was a small guard station. The guard, who looked to be a teenager, asked him to halt in a shaky voice as if he hadn't expected to see any strangers wandering into the city on his shift.

"What is your business in the city of Blackwater?" He sounded a little more commanding the more he spoke.

"I have urgent news for Commander Leon Rend. I was hoping to catch him before he went home for the night," Sparrow explained.

"Are you alone?"

"Well, I traveled with Beric, the messenger from the guild, but the horse was tired so he's camping about two hundred feet to the north," Sparrow said.

"I know Beric, so I will let you make your way to the guild without an escort, but the city guard is in the area, so keep out of trouble," he warned.

"I will, thank you!"

The Silver Talons Guild was the most magnificent building Sparrow had ever seen. Every stone was perfectly placed and two enormous dragon statues stood guard at the base of the front steps. The entry doors were rounded at the top and intricately carved with the sigil of The Silver Talons. He walked through the entryway into a lobby with white marble floors and a huge red rug in the center of the room perfectly centered in front of a counter behind which stood a man dressed in a black uniform.

"How can I help you, Sir?" the man asked.

"My name is Sparrow, I'm from The Garden of Life, I need to see the Guildmaster, Commander Leon Rend," Sparrow replied.

"One moment, I will see if he is available." The man behind the desk turned away from Sparrow for a moment and then turned to look at him again. "I'm sorry, but he is in a meeting right now. Would you be able to come back later?" he asked.

"No, this is important, I think we are all in danger, there's been an attack and I think it was *vampires*." Sparrow got close to the man's ear to whisper the last bit so he wouldn't raise alarm from passersby. The man turned away from him again, but not for long. When he looked at Sparrow again, his face was filled with fear and he yelled for a nearby squire.

"Take this man to Commander Rend's battle room immediately."

"Yes, Sir," the boy said as he began walking to the grand staircase to the right of the desk.

Sparrow followed the boy to the top of the stairs and down the western corridor. The battle room door was closed when they approached and just as the boy was about to knock, someone opened the door.

"Come in, we have much to discuss," the man said, taking no notice of the squire. Sparrow entered the room and the man closed the door behind him.

"Are you Commander Rend?" Sparrow asked.

"I am Velen Shrike, *that* is Leon Rend." He directed his finger toward a second room which was split from the main area by a magical field. Sparrow could see the men seated around inside peaking, but he couldn't hear them, even though the door was open.

"After you," Mr. Shrike said.

Sparrow moved forward with caution, wary of the magical field surrounding the room. As soon as he was through the doorway, Sparrow could hear everyone perfectly, they weren't even trying to speak in hushed voices, which impressed Sparrow even more as to the effectiveness of the magic.

"We have to be vigilant. The vampires have left Immernacht, we don't know how many there are, or if the dragonshifters are among them." The man turned to face him. "You must be Sparrow, and I hear you have some information about a suspected vampire attack, right? Please, have a seat." It was obvious *this* was Commander Rend.

Sparrow took a seat at the long wooden table. There was a map in the center outlining the entire continent from Blackwater to Braidwood, and the Islands to the south, Immernacht, Ledora, and Ash. "I am from The Garden of Life. We are a small congregation of naturists who practice peace and sustainable living. We never bothered anyone, we kept to ourselves. I came back to the garden after a personal sabbatical to find my brothers murdered, with markings on each which suggest they were bitten. I have heard of vampires, unnatural creatures of the night. I have not put them to rest yet as I thought you might want to investigate the scene yourself, but I came here because I want to help. If you are planning an attack against the vampires, I would like to train to become a hunter. I am already skilled in martial arts. We usually do not use weapons, but I am not opposed to it in order to avenge my brothers." Sparrow said.

"Velen, have you been to The Garden of Life?" Leon asked.

"Yes, Sir."

"Perfect, take Sparrow back there and investigate, confirm the cause of death, and then help him lay them to rest. When you return, I will have a hunter to train him. We can use all the help we can get," Leon said.

Velen nodded and then looked at Sparrow. "Ready?" he asked. Velen led Sparrow to the privacy of Leon's office and closed the door behind them. He grabbed Sparrow by the shoulders and looked him directly in the eye. "Don't let go, and take a deep breath. This might make you nauseous your first time."

"What—" Sparrow began to speak but before he could finish a sentence, he plunged into darkness. Although he couldn't see anything, he felt himself spinning. Sparrow kept his hands firmly clasped to Velen's forearms. The contents of his stomach seemed to be trying to come back up, but Sparrow fought to keep it down. He didn't know how it was possible to feel vertigo without sight, but he felt light-headed and dizzy. His hands began to slip from Velen's arms as his consciousness started to fade, but just before he passed out, the darkness expelled them, dropping them onto the grass in front of the garden.

Sparrow couldn't hold it back any longer, his stomach regurgitated the last meal he ate, the potatoes and rabbit tasted almost the same as they had going in except with the tang of bile which burned his throat as he coughed out the last of it. His stomach continued to heave and contract even after it had emptied.

Velen handed Sparrow his water skin. "Here, rinse your mouth and have a drink, it will help."

Sparrow took the skin and swished the first gulp then spit it on the ground and then drank the rest of it. He looked up at The Garden of Life on the path ahead of them.

"Are you okay? Remember, I am here to help, whatever you need," Velen said.

Sparrow led the way into the temple. Velen was careful not to disturb anything as he followed. Sparrow paused at the doorway to the sleeping room where his brothers all lay lifeless. He drew in a deep breath to prepare himself and then walked into the room. His eyes filled with tears as he looked upon the faces of his family. Velen walked around the room and examined each body. He took notice of the bite marks on their necks, and wrists. Some of them had multiple bites and chunks missing from their skin.

"This looks like the work of a clan. Some of the bites look tidy and singular, whereas others are needful and hungry. This clan has recently sired fledglings. This is not good, this means they are increasing in number. Are any of your brothers missing?" Velen asked.

"There are a few who are not among the dead, but I have not been here for a year, they could have left on their own for sabbatical or other reasons."

"Be wary if you see them after today. It doesn't look like they came here for any reason other than to feed, but you never know. How do you honor your dead?" Velen asked.

"We return them to the earth normally, but they have been spoiled by something unnatural and therefore cannot nourish The Garden of Life," Sparrow said.

"What shall we do then?"

"We have to purify them with fire so their souls are no longer trapped. There are too many of them for the pyre, but this room is filled with wooden beds. We need to fill the room with sage and then we can light the fire in the room. The temple will be left standing because it is stone and the smoke from the sage will cleanse the space."

"Very well. Lead the way," Velen said.

They gathered all of the dried sage hanging in the storage then returned to the room. Velen moved the beds together to form a makeshift pyre. Sparrow covered his brother's bodies with sage. He said a blessing for them before using his flint and steel to start the fire. Their wool blankets caught fire quickly and before the room filled with smoke, Sparrow and Velen had to make it back outside. They moved with haste down the corridor and out of the frame where a door should have been had it not been ripped from its hinges. Sparrow turned and watched the black smoke billow out of the openings in the stone, windows and doorways became nothing more than thick dark clouds. Sparrow let out a scream of despair and crumpled to his knees in front of the burning remains of his family and his home.

FIVE

SOPHIE JOLTED AWAKE FROM a dream she could not remember, but the unsettling feeling lingered. She sat up to look for Willow and found her sleeping soundly in her cradle. Sophie looked to her left and saw Bastian waking up beside her.

"Is everything okay?" Bastian asked.

"Yes, I just startled awake is all. I think it might just be the new room. Willow, however, is having no trouble," Sophie said.

"That's good. While she is sleeping, I should use this opportunity to talk to you about my family before dinner." Bastian's brows turned up with worry and he fidgeted with the bedsheet as he spoke.

"What is it?" Sophie asked.

"My family has a secret. Much like you and I are dragonshifters, they are supernatural as well, only they're *different*. They have special dietary needs because of their affliction, and they are immortal."

"What do you mean by special dietary needs?" Sophie asked.

"They do not eat food, they drink blood," Bastian said quickly and then waited for her response.

"They're *vampires*? I thought all the vampires were gone."

"Our family is the only one left. Do you remember hearing about the Orc Wars that happened back before Orion took over Braidwood?"

"I've heard stories. What do the orcs have to do with vampires?" Sophie asked.

"The orcs were created by vampires to wipe out human settlements. The vampires would take an item from the village and give it to the orcs. Their war dogs would sniff out the settlements and very few survived."

"Why would the vampires want to wipe out humans? Wouldn't they then go hungry?" Sophie asked.

"There are many humans, and very few vampires by comparison. They saw these settlements as a danger to them and their way of life. When a body turns up with bite marks from a careless fledgling, the humans become suspicious. When it happens more than once, they mobilize. These villages recruited the help of hunters to rid them of their vampire problem. Hunters are trained to kill us, and they're good at it. Several clans were wiped out completely at the hands of hunters, so the vampires needed a secret weapon. With the help of an evil sorceress, and elements of the abyss, the orcs emerged from the wet, slimy earth by the thousands. Some say they were created by the blood and bile of human excrement upon their death, and others thought they were some kind of troll hybrid species. The hunters were no match for the orcs, they had not been trained to hunt them, because prior to these events, they didn't exist, at least not in this realm." Bastian paused to gauge Sophie's response, but her vacant stare told him she was still processing what he had told her already. "I can tell you more later, but tonight at dinner, we will feed and for my family, feeding and desire go hand in hand. They don't just drink, they like to *enjoy* their host. I didn't want you to be surprised."

"By '*we*' do you mean to tell me *you* are a vampire, too? Is it even possible?" Sophie asked.

"They call me The Chimera. I am human, dragon, and vampire. I need to feed, but not as often, this is why I leave Lapis Highland and come here; to feed. Part of the treaty your father and our family agreed to says we cannot feed anywhere but on the island of Immernacht. This also means we cannot kill. If the human population dwindles, then we will have no food left. We take care of the people here, because they take care of us. For my family, feeding is not only for nourishment, but entertainment. So anything you see tonight, please don't hold it against me. I am sure they will put on a show tonight, just to see how you react," Bastian explained.

Sophie didn't know how to feel. She was angry Bastian kept this secret from her all this time. She told him everything, they share a child, and he just forgot to mention the fact he drinks human blood. As if sensing her desire to escape the conversation, Willow let out a whimper from her bed. Sophie rushed over to pick her up. She cradled her daughter in her arms.

"Sophie, I—" Bastian began.

"I just need some time. You gave me a lot of information and I can't even begin to process it yet. I need to eat breakfast and drink some water so I can feed Willow," Sophie said as she changed the baby's cloth diaper.

"I'll go make you something," Bastian said. He lowered his gaze to not meet her eyes as he turned to leave the room.

Sophie decided to nurse Willow before breakfast so she could allow Emily to eat first. Then Emily took the baby so Sophie could eat. Bastian made eggs and potatoes with ham. He had his shoulder-length blond hair tied back, and he looked so *normal* to Sophie as she watched him move about the kitchen to prepare her a plate.

"Where is everyone?" Sophie asked.

"They are creatures of the night. They usually sleep during the day. Even though natural sunlight doesn't penetrate the barrier around the island, the internal instincts of the vampire take over and reset their biological rhythm to nocturnal," he explained. Bastian sat Sophie's plate in front of her.

"Makes sense, I guess," Sophie said as she took a big bite of potato. "This is delicious," she commented between bites.

"When I knew you were coming, I had Serena go to the market and pick up a few things."

"Will I finally get to meet her tonight at dinner?" Sophie asked.

"Everyone is supposed to be here tonight, so yes. You're also going to see them feed. I want to warn you, it can be difficult as a human to watch a feeding. There is a sense of loyalty to the human you just do not feel as a vampire. Try not to show your emotion, if you're going to be a part of the family, you have to maintain composure. They want to see you're not frightened of them."

"But I am frightened. I have been scared ever since you told me. I have all of these questions going through my head and I just don't understand."

"What don't you understand? I will answer any questions you have if I can," Bastian said.

"How strong is your craving for human blood? If you had not fed in a long time, would I be in danger? What about Willow? Would *she* be in danger?" Sophie asked.

"No, of course not. I *love* you both so much, I could never do anything to hurt you. If I don't feed for a long time, it suppresses my other powers. After a few weeks without feeding, I cannot fly, and after about a month, I wouldn't be able to shift at all until I feed."

"Oh." Sophie put her fork down and pushed her almost empty plate forward. She looked at Bastian, his face was filled with shame. "Why didn't you tell me before now? You could have mentioned you were a vampire any time, after the first night we spent together, or after you showed up at Lapis Highland, but you kept this secret from me and I told you everything."

"I'm sorry, I know I should have told you, but I thought you would be safer not knowing."

"You mean you thought YOU would be safer. My father tried to warn me about your family and I thought he was being selfish. I haven't spoken to him in more than a year because he tried to keep me away from you and now I find out he had good reason all along." Sophie was almost in tears.

"Please, I can't stand the thought of you being angry with me. We are not the monsters people think we are. Our family has done everything they could to keep the peace with humans. The only reason I was able to leave the island was because no one knew I had been turned. Natalia only turned me to save my life, and she didn't want me to be punished for it, so we kept it a secret from anyone outside the castle," Bastian explained.

"Wait—they can't leave the island?" Sophie asked.

"They agreed to stay on the island, so the spell protecting us from the sunlight also keeps the vampires from leaving."

"How are you able to leave, then?"

"Because I am The Chimera, I am made up of more than two species. I am human, dragon, and vampire, and when I am in my dragon form, it masks the other two forms."

"I need some time to think about all of this. I don't know how I feel. This was such a huge thing to keep from me. Although you are being honest now, just the fact you would keep such a secret makes me wonder if I can trust you moving forward."

"I understand. I'll leave you to your space, but Mother and Father will still expect you to join us for dinner, so I will see you then. After dinner, if you wish to leave, I won't stand in your way. There's something else I should tell you first." Bastian looked at her nervously.

"Tell me later, please, I already have enough to think about," Sophie responded.

Bastian nodded and turned away. He left the kitchen so quickly it was almost like he disappeared. Sophie cleaned her plate and then headed back to her room to relieve Emily.

SIX

THE TRAVEL BACK TO the guild hall was not as physically painful as the trip there had been. Sparrow did still feel nauseous, but was able to fight the urge to throw up. Teleportation was the fastest way to travel, but Sparrow would rather a horse; even saddle sores were preferable to the motion sickness of magical travel. Velen bent down to check on him.

"You okay?" He helped Sparrow return to the upright position and watched as the color returned to his cheeks. Sparrow nodded and drew in a few deep breaths as he regained composure. "I'm sure this has been a difficult day for you, can I buy you a drink?"

"I could definitely use one," Sparrow said as he followed Velen into the guild hall. Sparrow expected a tavern but Velen led him to a members-only club called The Gilded Lily. Instead of the unfinished wooden tables found so often in taverns, this place had cozy corner booths with fancy cushions and round mahogany tables taking up the center of the room with high-backed, studded leather armchairs on either side. This was no tavern, it was a lounge for the town's elite.

"This place is... wow." Sparrow was lost for words.

"It's nice, huh?" Velen asked.

"This is the fanciest place I have ever been," Sparrow admitted as they sat down in a corner booth adorned with decorative pillows.

A barmaid approached the table wearing a very posh black and white uniform. Velen ordered a whiskey on the rocks.

"What does that mean?" Sparrow asked. He had never heard the term 'on the rocks' before.

"They have these special stones, they're smooth and round, but always cold. I think it's an enchantment, but it makes the whiskey more pleasant," Velen explained.

"I'll have the same," Sparrow said.

The server smiled and nodded as she turned around to place their order at the bar. Soft music was playing throughout the space and Sparrow wondered how because he didn't see anyone playing instruments. Velen could tell he was looking for the source of the sound and chuckled a bit.

"It's the harp, over there." He pointed to the far corner of the room behind the bar. Sure enough in an alcove in the corner sat a beautiful black harp trimmed with golden vines. The strings also looked as though they were spun from gold. There was no one playing it, yet he heard the music all the same and could see the strings moving as if invisible fingers were gently plucking them. "It's also enchanted. Almost everything in this guild hall has a magical touch to it. Commander Rend's daughter helped with a lot of it."

"The one who turned the old wizard tower into a kingdom?" Sparrow asked.

"The very same," Velen replied.

Their server returned with their drinks and when Sparrow touched the ceramic cup, it was cold. He took a sip of the whiskey and was pleasantly surprised by the smooth flavor. It still burned, but not as much as it did when he drank it warm. "This is amazing," Sparrow commented.

"I agree, I guess that's why I come here over the Loose Anchor. The company at the Anchor is better if you know what I mean, but the food and drink here cannot be matched. The guild gets only the best for its members."

After a few more drinks and conversation, Sparrow was ready to retire for the evening. Velen showed him to a room and left him to rest. The guest room was just as lavish as the Gilded Lily and filled with comforts like he had never experienced. The bed was twice the size of a normal one and the blankets were not made of the scratchy wool like most inn beds, but a fabric as soft as a cloud looks. The sheets were silk and Sparrow couldn't wait to crawl into bed, but he undressed and bathed himself from the wash basin first.

The silk sheets felt cool on his bare skin as he slid between them. He thought of the people who lived there full-time. He wondered if they appreciated their comforts or if they took them for granted. He fell asleep after that and slept so deeply when he awoke in the morning he had forgotten where he was for a moment until he got his bearings. His feet had barely touched the floor when there was a knock on his door.

"Just a moment," Sparrow called. He wrapped himself in the robe hanging in the washroom. When he opened the door, Velen handed him a box.

"You needed an outfit befitting a vampire hunter," Velen said as Sparrow pulled out the articles inside.

A black vest with iron buckles on the front to connect matching leather straps across the front, a pair of black trousers, stockings, braies, and a black tunic. Next, he pulled out a black hooded cloak with the same iron fasteners as the vest. Underneath the cloak, Sparrow found six weapon holsters. "These look too large for daggers." Sparrow noted.

"They're for stakes. There are many ways to kill a vampire, a wooden stake through the heart is one of the oldest methods, tried and true. The hunter will teach you the rest. You've got a lot of training to do so get dressed and I will take you to her. Oh, here, you'll need these too." Velen opened the door and reached down to grab something. When he turned around he presented a pair of boots. "I'll be waiting outside."

Velen led Sparrow into the western woods, into a seemingly empty clearing. Sparrow walked to the center of the clearing and turned to ask Velen where the trainer was, but Velen was gone. The man had disappeared as quickly and silently as the blink of an eye. A shadow and a gust of wind whipped past Sparrow's back and he whirled around, expecting to see the trainer, but saw nothing. He turned slowly in a circle, scanning the tree line. The shadow kept playing with him, zipping past as his back was turned.

"This isn't funny," Sparrow called. He heard the crack of a twig behind him and quickly faced the sound expecting to see nothing, but this time, he was face-to-face with a young girl. She had snow-white hair and the tops of her ears pointed to the sky. Her black outfit was the same as his, only it was tailored to fit her small frame without slack so her movements were silent. Instead of a vest like Sparrow had on, her stake holsters were attached to an over-bust corset which undoubtedly gave her protection from swords and other piercing weapons.

"Vampires move silently, and quickly. They catch their prey or opponents off-guard by disorienting them. You must learn to use all of your senses, not just your sight. You could not tell where I was until you heard the twig snap behind you. I did it on purpose. If I were a vampire and I wanted you dead, you would be. By the time you turned to face me, it would have already been too late," the girl said.

"Wait—who are you?" Sparrow asked.

"I am Eira. What is your name?"

"Sparrow."

Eira was fast and ducked down to sweep Sparrow's leg, he hit the ground hard and the blow took the breath from him.

"What the hell was that for?" he asked. Sparrow could feel his anger bubbling up inside him, sizzling just beneath the surface. He rocked back and then sprang up from the ground into his fighting stance. Eira rushed forward with a backhanded strike. Sparrow quickly blocked it, but the onslaught did not stop as Eira struck at him again and again. Sparrow did not want to hit her. As feisty as she was, she was still a girl, she looked to be around fourteen and he could not in good conscience strike a child.

"What is wrong with you? Attack me," she said.

"I can't." Sparrow dropped his hands and just as he opened himself up for a strike, Eira spun around, leaned to the side, and kicked him square in the chest. Sparrow flew backward, falling to the ground again. Eira rushed forward and offered her hand to help him up. He grumbled and brushed her hand away as he rolled backward to put space between them so he could get to his feet.

"You're learning not to trust anyone, good," she said. "Now, attack me."

Sparrow lightly bounced around her, looking for a point of weakness. He watched her footwork as he moved forward, she changed her stance to make it more difficult for him to kick her. Her hands were high, and elbows tucked to protect her face. Sparrow quickly rolled on the ground to get close, popped up from his ducking position, and landed a jab to Eira's stomach.

"Agghh!" Sparrow cried in pain as he cradled his hand. He had forgotten about the corset, he wasn't even paying attention. His knuckles felt like he had just punched someone in half-plate armor. "Is this why you weren't blocking your middle?"

"Know where your weaknesses are and protect them. A vampire is a thousand times more perceptive than humans so you have to be one step ahead of them. Anticipate their movements, and never trust they are alone."

Suddenly, Sparrow was surrounded. Four other people emerged from the tree line wearing similar outfits. They all rushed at once, Sparrow was blocking, ducking, and dodging their attacks as best he could. A surprising blow to the back stole his attention and a sucker punch to the gut knocked the air out of him again. He fell to the ground and curled into the fetal position as a fury of kicks battered his body. A sharp whistle rang out and the kicking stopped. Sparrow did not want to cry in front of them, he wouldn't give them the satisfaction, but his body ached. He held his ribs as he climbed to his feet again.

"That's enough for today. Meet me here in two moons and we will continue," Eira told him. She and her friends stepped back out of the clearing and disappeared in a flash of light. Sparrow squinted his eyes to try and see where the flash originated, but when it was gone, the forest looked normal and quiet.

Every step he took sent a shock wave of pain throughout his body. He was pretty sure his ribs were broken. After what he felt might have been thirty paces, Sparrow was overtaken by a coughing fit and blood spattered the ground at his feet. He pushed on through the pain and made it to the entrance to the guild. Leon saw him collapse in the foyer and rushed to him.

"Someone go get Delilah, quickly!" he yelled. A young boy scrambled out the door just as the light of the room around Sparrow faded from his consciousness.

SEVEN

SOPHIE LOOKED DOWN AT the baby, asleep in her cradle. Willow's tiny fingers curled around her mother's and Sophie didn't want to pull away. Emily placed her hand on Sophie's shoulder. "You should get ready for dinner. They're starting to gather in the dining hall."

"I know. I don't know what I'm going to do. Emily, I am so confused," Sophie said.

"What's got you confused, My Queen?"

"If you found out someone you love was keeping a secret that changed your life and separated you from your family, could you forgive them?" Sophie asked.

"I don't know. I guess it would depend on if they did it with intention, or if they were well-meaning." Emily looked thoughtful.

"It's just the kind of thing that should have been mentioned before now, before I spent the last year angry with my father who was just trying to protect me. I can't get that time back now." Tears rolled down Sophie's cheek. "Now my father thinks Bastian's family has broken their agreement and is planning to attack. Only, I've warned them and now they're ready for him. If anything happens to my father, it will be my fault."

"You could maybe warn your father, tell him they know he's coming and ask if they could meet diplomatically instead," Emily suggested.

"Maybe. I have to get through this dinner first. Pack the saddle bags and be ready to fly out with Willow. If nothing else, I want to know she is safe with you in our home at Highland Castle."

"Yes, My Queen," Emily said as she buttoned the back of Sophie's black lace dress.

"Thank you, Emily. You're a great friend," Sophie said.

Sophie entered the dining hall and looked around at the undoubtedly expensive furniture and the exquisitely designed space. The table was long and black with a burgundy runner down the center, with intricately carved acanthus supports. All of the chairs had arms, not just the ones at the ends. It was the most beautiful dining room Sophie had ever seen. It was probably the oldest, too. The sconces on the walls and the chandelier in the center of the room were made of black iron and held dark crimson candles. Arturo sat at the head of the table, and Natalia sat across from him at the other end. Xander sat to the right of Arturo, and the girl Sophie assumed was Serena sat to the right of her mother.

"Come, Sophie, you may sit here." Arturo rose from his seat with grace and speed to pull out the chair to his left for Sophie. Her place was set with three covered silver trays. Based on the smell coming from them, she knew this was her dinner. She sat down and allowed Arturo to gently push in her chair. "You remember Xander, I'm sure. I am sorry he did not remember his manners the first time you met, he had not yet fed. It makes him cranky," Arturo said.

"I apologize for staring when we first met, you reminded me of someone is all and I hope you will not let our first encounter stain your image of me for long," he smiled, and something about his piercing eyes made Sophie feel tranquil.

"It's not a problem at all," Sophie told him.

"Next we have Serena," Arturo gestured to the beautiful blond girl sitting next to Natalia.

"We have not had the pleasure. I am sorry I was out when you arrived, but it is lovely to finally meet you. Every time he is home, you are all Bastian can talk about," she said.

"I apologize for my tardiness. I needed to say goodnight to Willow," Bastian said as he entered the room. His expression seemed sorrowful, and Sophie wondered if he had come across Emily as she was packing.

Arturo picked up a tiny bell and gave it a short ring. The double doors to the kitchen opened and the staff brought out wine and silver platters with roasted meats, potatoes, and fruit displays. They placed the food in the center of the table and handed Sophie the serving utensils.

"Please, help yourself," Arturo said.

"Thank you, Sir," she replied as she placed a bit of everything on her plate, mostly out of politeness. Sophie was taught when you dine with your host, you never refuse the food, for it might offend them.

As she waited for the others to serve themselves, a procession of humans walked into the dining room and Sophie's eyes went wide with shock. They were all naked and varied in appearance, but all were beautiful and young; around the same age as Sophie, give or take a year. There were two males and three females. Arturo slid his chair back so a girl could sit on his lap. She was gorgeously tan with bold brown eyes and long jet-black hair grazing the top of her buttocks.

"Now, Sophie, please do not be afraid." Arturo's eyes dilated and seemed to stare into her soul. Sophie felt herself trusting him and was not afraid, but intrigued.

"Where is Elizandra?" Bastian asked.

"She left around the time you began drinking her from a chalice," Serena told him, gesturing to the cup in front of him. Her voice had a bitter edge to it.

"Who is Elizandra?" Sophie asked.

She watched as the girl next to Bastian opened the vein in her wrist with a thumb ring in the shape of a talon. She dripped her blood into Bastian's cup and didn't cover the puncture until his chalice was full. They all let Sophie's question go unanswered, and she was not sure if she should ask again or wait for Bastian to mention her later.

Arturo caressed the girl on his lap, trailing his fingers from her waist up her torso and to her breasts. He grasped one firmly as he drew in her scent. She moaned with pleasure at his touch and her skin responded with the appearance of a thousand tiny bumps. Sophie looked at Natalia to see if this bothered her, but she was preoccupied. Her human was well-built with gorgeous dark skin and short black curls glistening in the candlelight. He was sitting on the table in front of Natalia with his legs spread open. Sophie couldn't see what was going on in front of him, but from the way he arched his back slightly and supported himself with his hands, Sophie had a pretty good guess. Serena had her human kneel at her side like a pet. He raised his arm to offer his wrist to her, and she drank daintily from it.

The most interesting girl, however, was the one with Xander. She was slender and her body was covered in beautiful, light brown freckles. She had long red hair; it was wavy, not curly like Sophie's, but even she saw the striking resemblance to herself. Xander kissed the girl's lips tenderly and then trailed his kisses down her neck and to her breasts. His eyes rose to meet Sophie's and he stared at her with desire as he sank his fangs into the girl's breast. She moaned as he sipped her. All the while, Xander never broke his gaze on Sophie. He reached down and slid his hand between the girl's legs and she opened to him like a flower to the sun. Sophie watched as he inserted two fingers into the girl's sex and slid them in and out of her. The girl moaned and rolled her hips up to help his leverage. Bastian cleared his throat.

Xander ignored his brother and trailed his tongue down his lover's abdomen to her inner thigh. He bit her again, drinking from the tender flesh of her leg as he massaged her thighs. When he finished drinking, he licked the blood which had dripped from the two small holes. Turning his face from her thigh to her genitalia, Xander kissed her there and then used his fingers to spread her open, flicking his tongue up and down on the button above her entrance. Sophie tried to look away, but it was like she was in a trance; she could *feel* what he was doing to the girl and despite her disgust at the intrusion of her mind, she could also feel the dampness between her legs. He moved his face back and inserted his fingers again. He curled them upward, moving them in a 'come hither' motion. She didn't mean to, but a soft moan escaped Sophie's lips and Bastian flashed with anger.

"Enough, Xander!" Bastian banged his fists on the table and the clattering of the dishes that accompanied his outburst startled Xander and broke his concentration. Sophie shot Xander a spiteful glance as Bastian rose to pull out her chair. She could feel the heat of Bastian's fury radiating off of his usually cool skin as he offered his arm to help her stand.

"You can go check on Willow. I am sorry my brother cannot behave himself. Take your dinner with you." Bastian moved in close to Sophie's ear. "Please wait for me so we can talk before you leave. I won't stop you, but I need to say goodbye to you, and to Willow." Sophie could hear the anguish in his tone and it hurt her heart. He planted a gentle kiss on her cheek before he pulled away to deal with his brother.

EIGHT

"Damn you, Xander, why must you always make a scene?" Bastian accused.

"Oh, lighten up. You have forgotten how to have fun, little brother. I mean, even Sophie seemed to enjoy it." The corners of Xander's mouth snapped up in a grin, enough to send Bastian's anger through the roof. He lunged across the table, knocking over chalices and smashing the leftovers on his way. He grabbed Xander by his collar and jerked him to his feet. The girl in Xander's lap let out a startled cry and scrambled to the side of the room to get away from the impending fray.

"Sophie is mine. She is not your plaything. You always take it too far!" Bastian shouted. He drew back and punched Xander in the mouth.

"You don't know what you're talking about, brother. I saw her future the night she arrived. She will not be yours in the end."

"You lie!" Bastian growled. Xander smirked and Bastian drew back to hit him again.

"Enough, boys. You've ruined dinner with your squabbling. Take it outside or end it," Arturo commanded. Bastian let go of his brother's collar and tried to leave the room. "Not so fast. We need to discuss the information Sophie has given us," Arturo said. Bastian stopped in the doorway and turned back around. "That's all for now, Eve, thank you." Arturo licked a drop of blood from her neck as he dismissed her and all the humans filed out of the dining room. He waited for Serena and Xander to leave as well before he spoke. "Bastian, your mother and I have a theory about the mysterious murderer near Blackwater. Unfortunately, none of us are able to leave the island to see if our theory is correct."

"What is this theory?" Bastian asked.

"We think, somehow, Dmitri is awake and he might be creating fledglings."

"How? I thought the only way Dmitri could wake was by drinking the family blood. You cannot leave the island, and I didn't wake him, so who could have?"

"This is what we need you to find out. I have a map to the location of the tomb, which is deep inside a cave on the mainland in the northern forest region. I hope we are wrong and you find the tomb still sealed. Be vigilant just in case. Take precautions," Arturo warned.

"I will," Bastian said.

"Gather your things. The sooner you check it out, the more time we have to prepare. I will bring you the map. Sophie is welcome to stay here if she wishes, although I think Xander has done his best to ensure her expeditious retreat."

"I wouldn't blame her if she returned to the Highland. I know she would be safe from harm here, but who's going to keep her safe from Xander in my absence?" Bastian shook his head, still furious over the situation.

"I don't know what has come over him. He was always competitive, but he has become so much more aggressive since you left; almost as if he needs to prove he can have anything or anyone he wants. He requested the red-haired girl for dinner only this morning. I know it was intentional and I'm sorry about it. I don't know what to do with him."

"For starters, we could stop making apologies for him and thoroughly kick his ass," Bastian said irritably.

"I know, I think it's only fun for him to get under your skin. If you are not here, his interest in Sophie will disappear, I'm certain of it." Natalia said.

Bastian sighed. She always defended Xander. Her own children could do no wrong. Bastian, however, was given the most responsibility, the least praise for his successes, and the most wrath for his failures. Arturo, on the other hand, treated the children all the same, for they were all bloodbound to their family. A vampire, of course, cannot reproduce in the way humans can. When Natalia married Arturo and expressed a desire for children, he waited to turn his wife so she could conceive. They never spoke of the children's father, so Bastian did not know what became of him. The twins were born nine months after their wedding night, and Natalia nursed them until they were old enough to wean. Once the need for her human body was gone, Arturo made his wife a vampire. Xander and Serena grew as normal children on the island of Immernacht until they, too, were old enough to receive the dark gift. Arturo had made them all—except for Bastian. When Bastian was on his deathbed, Arturo refused to turn him because the treaty dictated they would not make any more vampires. Natalia would not let Bastian die, though. He had saved her life more than once and now, she would save his. She bit her own wrist and held it to his mouth despite her husband's protests. Bastian was still dying, but with her blood in his system, he would return to them. It was her blood—but also Arturo's—which flowed through her veins. The blood of the Delacroix. That was the day he became a member of the family. He was the only dragonshifter to ever be turned. There were four shifters then who were in service to the Delacroix, but now he was the only one left.

Bastian thought about all of these things while he packed a bag. He knew Sophie could not come with him, but he wondered if there was anywhere she would be safe. If she returned to Highland Castle, she had nothing but her magic and a bunch of armored humans to protect her, If she stayed here, he would constantly worry about her proximity to Xander. He didn't think he could trust his absence would be enough to quell Xander's desire for Sophie. When his bag was packed, Bastian walked down the hall to Sophie's room. She was waiting for him as he requested, but she already had Willow dressed for flying.

"Sophie, I am sorry for everything. I don't blame you for being angry with me. You have every right to be. I kept this part of myself hidden from you when I should have trusted you enough to show you all of me from the start. You are the light of my life from the moment I met you. We created this beautiful life together—something I didn't even think was possible because of the blood flowing through my veins. I only want you and Willow to be safe, and I can think of no safer place than with your mother and father. Sophie, I know you were angry at him because he tried to make me leave you, but I want you to know; the only way I will ever leave you is if I am dead. You will have every piece of my heart until that day comes."

Tears rolled down Sophie's cheeks. Bastian cupped the side of her face and wiped her tears with his thumb. His heart ached for her and he longed to embrace her or kiss her, but he waited for her to make the choice for herself. When she stepped away from him instead of closing the gap between them, Bastian's heart shattered. He felt her slipping away, and it was more painful than his death had been.

"May I have some time with our daughter before you go? I am being sent on an errand for my father, and I don't know how long it will be before I return. I will have our message book if you need me."

Sophie nodded, handed Willow to her father, and walked to the hall with tears welling up in her eyes. "I'll be out front. Bring her down when you're ready," she said after she discreetly wiped her eyes.

Bastian held Willow close as he watched Sophie walk away. The tears he had been trying to hold back flowed freely now. Bastian rocked Willow to sleep, admiring her sweet face as he sang to her quietly. He couldn't bring himself to walk downstairs because he knew as soon as he did, Sophie would be gone and there was no telling if she would ever come back. Bastian wiped the tears from his face with the sleeve of his tunic and just as he looked up, a shadow crossed the doorway.

"Sophie?" he asked. Bastian put Willow down in her bed and walked to the door. He looked both directions down the hallway but saw no one. "Well, I guess we should get you to your Mama." Bastian cradled his daughter one last time and kissed the top of her head, hoping this goodbye would not be their last.

NINE

EMILY STRAPPED CLOSED THE last saddle bag as Sophie reached the court-yard. The stone dragons towered over the square and their shadows stretched from corner to corner.

"Oh, I forgot something. I'm almost ready. I'll be right back." Emily hurried off toward the castle doors. Sophie couldn't shift yet, she had to strap in Willow and Emily first. She wondered what was taking Bastian so long and thought briefly about going back inside to get her, but decided in the end, she didn't want to disturb her daughter's last moments with her father before they separated for an unknown amount of time. Sophie sensed someone behind her, although she had not heard them approach.

"Bastian?" Sophie turned around to see Xander. She took a step back and bumped into the dragon saddle. "Xander, sorry. I wasn't expecting you." Sophie tried her best to not look frightened but her heart was pounding so hard and fast she was sure he must have heard it.

Xander reached a hand out and curled a lock of her hair around his finger. He gazed into her eyes. "Take Willow and Emily to your mother's, they will be safe there. Then come back." Xander's eyes seemed to change, his pupils dilated as he spoke and Sophie could only focus on his words, and his lips.

Sophie nodded. "I'll take Willow to my mother's and then come back," she said, almost repeating his command word for word.

Xander moved close to her so his lips gently brushed her ear. "Good girl," he whispered.

A tingling sensation coursed through Sophie's body and she closed her eyes as the feeling washed over her. When she opened her eyes, Xander was gone, but Emily was walking toward her with Willow in her arms.

"I guess Bastian isn't going to see us off?" Sophie asked.

"I guess not, sorry."

Sophie shrugged as she helped Emily strap Willow to her body.

"It's okay, you can strap yourself into the saddle, I just need you to make sure the straps are tight around me after I shift," Sophie said. Emily nodded and backed up to give Sophie enough space to shift under the saddle. When her transformation was complete, Emily walked underneath the enormous standing dragon and pulled the leather straps tight against its body. When each of the four straps were as snug as Emily could pull them, she locked them into position and then stepped out from beneath the dragon to give her the signal.

Sophie stretched out to get her dragon body as flat against the ground as she could. Emily climbed the rope ladder hanging from the left side of the saddle and sat down in the seat. She buckled a strap across each leg and one around her waist just under Willow's lowest position.

"Okay, we're ready," Emily called.

Sophie took off running and when she reached the edge of the courtyard she ascended into the sky, just below the dark clouds shrouding the city in magical disguise. She flew to the edge of the island to the beach where she first arrived. The clouds parted for her like a curtain and she was surprised to see the sky was scattered with stars. Sophie thought of Serena and Xander and wondered if they had ever seen stars. They had lived their whole lives on the island of Immernacht beneath a perpetual storm cloud.

Emily fell asleep on the trip back to the mainland, but Sophie's touch-down jolted her awake. She cradled Willow, taking most of the jarring herself to protect the little princess. Sophie shifted and dressed herself as Emily unbuckled from the saddle. Willow was crying and Sophie rushed over to help Emily untie the sling. When Sophie took the baby in her arms, Willow settled a little but still fussed as she turned her head toward Sophie's chest with an open mouth. Sophie latched the babe onto her breast and held her close. Sophie nursed until Willow was satisfied and then pulled a dress from the saddle bag.

"It's late, my mother will be asleep, we can stay here tonight and get some rest," Sophie said as Emily took the baby.

"What is this place?" Emily asked, staring at the stone temple in the distance.

"This is Ophay. Akiri lives here," Sophie told her as she led Emily through the town to the temple doors. Sophie placed her hand on the door and a bright blue rune circle illuminated against the dark mahogany door. When Sophie removed her hand, the print was still alight on the door. The lock clicked and the door opened to them.

"That was the most amazing thing I have seen today," Emily remarked as they walked into the dimly lit foyer. The light was coming from a magical candle Akiri received as a gift from King Dominic and Queen Kamara of Ledora. When it sensed someone nearby, the candle would light, and when they walked away it would put itself out.

"Our rooms are this way," Sophie said, leading Emily down the eastern corridor. Their rooms were connected by a beautiful archway. In addition to a comfortable bed adorned with small pillows and fancy comforters, Sophie's room had a crib and changing table, and Emily's had a writing desk and a wardrobe.

"I might sneak out to the lair to see if I can visit with Akiri tonight for a bit if you don't mind listening for Willow.

"I don't mind at all, My Queen," She said.

"Thanks. I'll change her and feed her again before I go so she should sleep the whole night," Sophie said as she took Willow to the changing table.

"You must stay here often if you have all this stuff here for you both," Emily commented.

"It's not just for me, it's for us. This room is also for Juniper and her daughter, Maggie, when they stay here. They're here more often than I am, but we got lucky tonight, they must be at their place in Blackwater."

"You know so many people and have so many friends, what is it like?" Emily's voice was just above a whisper. Sophie could see the loneliness in her eyes.

"Honestly, I realize now, I've taken it for granted. I never thought about how exciting it is to be friends with so many people, powerful people at that, Kings and Queens, dragonshifters, trained guild members, and now vampires. It doesn't seem real." Sophie said.

After she nursed Willow, Sophie put her into the crib and let Emily know she was going to the lair. She crept through the temple trying not to wake anyone. The garden behind the temple was lush with fruits and vegetables. Juniper planted flowers around each of the garden beds so it smelled wonderful and Sophie was sure in the light of the day, it looked as beautiful as it was fragrant.

She approached the cliff and the entrance to the lair appeared to her. Sophie felt the heat from the hot springs the second she stepped inside and her clothes clung to her instantly. The air was stagnant and hard to breathe in the tunnel leading to the nest. Sophie heard scraping and movement ahead and became nervous. *What if Akiri wasn't in here and some animal found their way in?* Sophie wondered. It filled her with adrenaline and she ran to the end of the tunnel, expecting to see destruction, which was a sight she had the misfortune of seeing too often in the last few years.

Sophie's jaw dropped when she entered the nesting room. Four baby dragons played happily with each other as Akiri and another woman watched over them. When she saw Sophie, Akiri grabbed a silk robe that hung from a wooden coat rack and covered herself. She looked different, her hips were fuller and her body had a softness to it Sophie thought was so beautiful. She could see why Gabe had fallen in love with her. She approached Sophie and wrapped her in a hug.

"They hatched a few days ago. They're eating chickens from the Miller's farm right now, but they will require something bigger soon. This is Chloe," Akiri introduced the woman beside her. "She is my handmaiden and she helps me with the dragons."

Chloe offered her hand to Sophie.

"It's lovely to meet you," Sophie said. "I thought there were five eggs?" Sophie asked as she looked around the room.

"There were, one of them, unfortunately, didn't make it. I still plan to have one for each of the four regions. One for Ledora, Blackwater, Lapis Highland, and since we are so close to Blackwater, I have contacted the guildmaster of Braidwood and negotiated the employment of one of them. The payments will keep our town comfortable for many years and the council will oversee the monetary distribution based on the needs of our people."

"That's wonderful. I am sorry about the fifth dragon. You are so selfless to not even keep one for yourself." Sophie said.

"I am keeping one, kind of." Akiri walked over to the nest and picked up a shiny golden egg with both hands. "When the fifth dragon didn't hatch, the blacksmith melted some gold in his forge. He had to tap a small hole in the bottom of the egg to let out the liquid inside, but then he filled the hole and dipped the egg in gold so I could keep it forever."

"That's great, it's such a nice memorial to not only the baby dragon, but your first clutch."

"I also made you something, it's inside." Akiri gestured to the temple. "We can go get it, they'll be fine in here for a little while, Chloe can keep an eye on them."

Sophie followed her out of the lair and back into the temple. When they reached Akiri's bedroom, she opened the chest at the foot of her bed and pulled out a small trinket. She held it in her hands at her heart as she brought it over to Sophie.

"Now, before I give you this I want to say something. I am so glad you gave me a chance to be your friend. I know how much Gabe meant to you and so I used a little of my portion of his ashes to make something for both of us. She opened her hand and presented a necklace to Sophie. The circle pendant was clear with a gray heart in the middle.

"I made the pendant from the sap of the willow, It's a bit of a process, but the result is this hardened resin, and the heart inside it is made of Gabe's ashes," Akiri said. "May I?" She held up the necklace and waited for Sophie to nod before moving behind her. She fastened the necklace and then faced Sophie to see it on her.

"It looks beautiful, and now you can always keep him with you. Only... remember to take it off before you shift, the chain isn't long enough for a dragon neck," Akiri said. Sophie lifted the pendant and turned it in the light to admire Akiri's art. The ashes were perfectly placed and it made the heart look like a tangible thing encased in the clear circular pendant. Akiri had layered it and given the heart dimension and shadow.

"This is the best gift I have ever received. Thank you." Sophie's eyes filled with tears and she hugged Akiri tightly.

"Are you staying the night tonight?" Akiri asked.

"Yes, I'm taking Willow and Emily to my mother's in the morning and then I have to get back to Immernacht. I'm sure you haven't heard, but there has been some kind of attack and the victim drifted onto the shore near Blackwater. My father thinks it is Bastian's family and is preparing for something. We are thinking he is going to bring a guild team to attack the Delacroix family."

"So, are you going to defend them against your father and the guild?" Akiri asked in a shocked voice. Sophie knew what it meant. It could mean her expulsion from the guild. It was considered a traitorous act to fight against the guild, but the Delacroixes were her family, too. Attacking without speaking to them first wasn't usually Leon's way, but Sophie hadn't spoken to him in more than a year, it was possible he had become more pugnacious in her absence.

"I don't know what I'm going to do, but I have a feeling my being there at Castle Delacroix might at least encourage peace between them long enough for a conversation. I don't think they did what he is accusing them of."

"What is it he thinks they did?" Akiri asked.

Sophie hesitated, pondering whether or not she should divulge the Delacroix's biggest secret to her. "If I tell you, you can't tell anyone else, and I *mean anyone*," Sophie told her. Akiri nodded and went over to the sofa in the corner of her bedroom to sit down and motioned for her to join. Sophie decided not to mince words. "Bastian and his family are vampires."

Akiri's eyes widened and she put a hand over her mouth which Sophie could tell was open wide. "So they drink human blood?" Akiri asked.

"Yes, and the body my father found was drained of blood. That's why he suspects the Delacroix."

"How do you know it wasn't them?" Akiri asked.

"The island of Immernacht is bound by magic to keep the vampires in, they can't leave the island, it couldn't be them," she said.

"You said *Bastian* and his family were vampires, and Bastian can leave, otherwise you would have never met him, do you think maybe he could have done it?"

"No—I mean, I don't think he would. He can leave the island because his dragon form masks his vampire blood and the barrier can't detect it. He does drink blood on occasion, but…" Sophie's voice trailed off as her thoughts took over. *He could have. Bastian often left for days at a time. He is also very secretive about his activity during these times. Perhaps he has been drinking from strangers all along and this was just the first evidence to be found.* Sophie hoped these things were not true, but she couldn't shake the anger she felt about being kept in the dark.

"I'm sorry, I didn't mean to cause you doubts about him, I know you care for him," Akiri said.

"I do, but he lied to me and it cost me an entire year with my father," Sophie said. "I don't know if I can forgive him."

"Well, whatever you decide, you have my support. Let me know if you need help in Immernacht and I will be there."

"Thank you, it means a lot to me. I should get some sleep though, I want to visit with my mom for a bit tomorrow and then I have to fly back," Sophie said with a yawn.

"I should get back out to the babies anyway. It was good to see you. Come by any time, we have missed you here."

Sophie smiled and squeezed Akiri's hand, then walked back to her room. Willow was still sleeping soundly and so was Emily. Sophie couldn't wait to do the same.

TEN

SPARROW COULD SEE NOTHING but darkness, but he could hear Eira's nimble movements rushing around him. He could also feel the breeze from her body as she zipped past him several times. Sparrow drew in a deep breath and focused on those two senses alone. He readied his position and as soon as he heard the sound of the leaves crunch beneath her feet as she launched forward, his hand shot out in front of him and he gripped her by the neck. Eira tapped Sparrow's arm for him to release her.

"Much better. You're almost ready. Tomorrow morning you will take the oath at sunrise," Eira said as Sparrow removed the piece of cloth she had used to blindfold him.

"How long have you been a hunter?" Sparrow asked.

"You cannot become a hunter until you reach adulthood in my order, so I have been hunting now for twenty-three human years, give or take," Eira said.

"You look so young though, how is it possible you are twenty-three years past the age of adulthood?" Sparrow was amazed. To him, she still looked like a teenager, but if what she said was true, she had to be at least twice his age.

"This is why elves make the best hunters. One look at me and all you see is a child, you would not expect me to be fierce, fast, or know how to fight. Vampires always tend to underestimate me, especially when I am masking."

"Masking, what's that?" Sparrow asked.

"I hide my ears, and I cover my scent with this." She lifted a talisman from her neck and showed it to him. The pendant was the shape of the holy symbol of the Goddess of life. Inside the pendant, Sparrow saw a red cloth. As he came closer to it, he realized the cloth was red because it was soaked in blood.

"It's human blood. When they smell human blood, they can't really smell anything else, it's like tunnel vision, but for their sense of smell," Eira said.

"How do you get the blood?" Sparrow asked.

"From the human hunters. They are willing donors, no one is harmed, and their blood helps me smell human to vampires." Eira sat down on a rock and slid her feet into her boots. "You did well today, get some rest and I will see you here before sunrise." Eira's long silver braid whirled behind her as she turned to run. Sparrow still couldn't understand how she moved so quickly. He needed to head back to the guild and talk to Leon. When morning came his training would be complete and he was ready to get to work.

The Silver Talons Guild Hall was buzzing with activity when Sparrow arrived. He was surprised to see them unloading the carts of weapons and supplies that they should have been putting on a ship. He saw Leon and waved him over.

"What's going on? Are we not going to Immernacht?" Sparrow asked.

"I have decided we need to do some reconnaissance first. I was too brash to suggest an attack on them without giving them a chance to confess or deny my accusations. As far as taking down the barrier is concerned, if I did, then the vampires would be able to leave freely. I know you want to avenge your brothers, and you will, but only when the time is right. My daughter is with the Delacroix dragonshifter, it's possible they are keeping her on Immernacht. If we attack, they will kill her. Vampires feel no attachment like we do, they aren't capable of love, for their hearts no longer beat. I cannot put her in danger," Leon explained, pain filling his eyes at the mention of his daughter.

"I am to take the hunter's oath at sunrise, then I will be ready to hunt. The sooner I find those responsible for the massacre of my brothers, the better. I don't want to wait," Sparrow argued.

"I'll see you after sunrise then and we will make a plan. Ask Eira to come as well." Leon gave Sparrow a quick pat on the shoulder as he hurried off to give directions to the staff once more.

There was no denying Sparrow was a little disappointed. The image of his brothers sprawled lifelessly across their beds kept replaying in his mind and with every thought, his anger intensified. If he didn't find something to do, Sparrow was certain his rage would overcome him. He needed a drink, but the guild members-only lounge was of no interest, so Sparrow went to the Loose Anchor. He pulled a stool up to the bar and ordered a whiskey double. Ladies wearing corsets and short fluffy skirts made from tulle approached him and rubbed his arms. He was never so thankful for the advance Leon had given him to settle into Blackwater.

"Hey there, Stranger," the blonde on his left whispered in his ear.

"You wanna come upstairs with us and we can take your mind off of whatever it is that's bothering you?" asked the brunette.

"What makes you think anything is bothering me?"

"Oh, Honey, I can see the tension in your posture." The woman moved behind him and began massaging his shoulders. Sparrow rolled his eyes and groaned as the knots in his shoulders began to relax.

"Gods that feels good," he said.

"There's plenty more where that came from, for only one gold piece, I'll make you feel good all over," she promised.

The brunette had already moved on to her next client, using the same tactics her colleague was using with him, but he didn't care. It felt good and he had never been with a woman before. *There's a first time for everything,* he thought. Sparrow spun around on the bar stool to face her. She placed her hands on his knees and gently pushed his legs apart so she could move her body between them. Sparrow looked down at her bosom, pushed up by the corset and only an inch from his face. He felt his anger turn to desire and pulled the gold piece out of his coin pouch.

"What's your name?" he asked.

She wagged a slender finger at him and whispered in his ear. "You have to earn it, love." She grabbed his tunic by the ruffled collar and led him upstairs.

When Sparrow returned to the tavern downstairs, he felt refreshed and for now, his anger was masked by the serene feeling of satisfaction he could have only found in a lover's embrace. Polly, the first woman to take him to bed, had cleaned herself up and already moved onto her next patron. The tavern was busier now than it had been earlier and he could see the orange glow of the setting sun peeking through the window on the western wall. He placed a silver piece on the bar and slid it over to the barkeep to pay for the whiskey he had ordered but not drunk.

The walk back to the guild hall was quiet and Sparrow was thankful for the cool breeze from the bay. On a night like this when he was home, he would meditate in the garden with his brothers, cook dinner, and they would eat together by the light of the sunset. Then it would be time for writing and reflection. Sparrow had not written since he left the Garden of Life and reflection was impossible now because all he could think about was the massacre of the only family he had left.

He tried to sleep to no avail. Although comfortable, the bed seemed suffocating, even after Sparrow threw the blankets and pillows to the floor. The room seemed smaller and warmer than it had been earlier. Sparrow went to the window and opened the shutters, hoping to feel the same cool breeze he had felt on the walk back from the tavern, but the air was still. *I need to get out of here,* he thought. He dressed in the hunters' garb Eira had given him and then made his way to the western woods. He listened to all the nocturnal life of the forest as he desperately clung to nature. Life was so important, and vampires cheated these gifts and fed on the lives of others to steal more time. If they feed, they live forever, but at what cost? All of his brothers were gone, drained of their life force by selfish creatures who would rather steal life from others than face their own mortality. The more he thought about it, the angrier he got. Talking to them would not be enough, he would have to kill them. Every last one of them.

Eira arrived just before sunrise and the rest of the order followed. They gathered in a circle as Eira and two other hunters set up an altar with boulders and a stone slab. She poured water into a stone bowl and sat it on the eastern side of the altar.

"Sparrow, I need you to undress your top half and lie down on the altar, facing the sunrise," she instructed. Sparrow did as he was told. The stone was cold against his skin and he shivered. Eira began to whisper, but her voice rose with the sun. She was chanting in a language Sparrow had never heard before.

"Lumina soarelui, dă putere acestui vânător," The other hunters joined her in the cadence and they chanted this phrase until the sun was just above them in the clearing.

"Arise, Hunter Sparrow, and drink the water of the rising sun." Eira handed Sparrow the bowl as he sat up. The water was warm but he drank it all. The liquid immediately activated something in his blood; all his veins illuminated deep orange from under his skin and it seemed as if they were filled with the light of the sun.

"Welcome to the order. No vampire can kill you now unless they too wish to expire. You are filled with light. Your death would turn the one who killed you to ash. You are safe in that regard but do not look a vampire in the eye. They might not be able to kill you themselves, but they can still compel you to do things you don't want to do, like betray a friend or harm yourself," Eira warned.

"I understand. Leon would like for you to join us. I think he wants to try a diplomatic approach because the Delacroixes have his daughter."

"Then he is a fool, you cannot reason with a vampire. Even if you *think* they are giving you what you want, you can't trust them." Sparrow saw a pain in her eyes mirroring his own.

"I promise you, we will rid the world of this plague, and when there are no vampires left, Leon will thank us for it, but the least we can do is try to make sure his daughter is safe first, no one else should have to lose someone they love," he argued. Eira looked at Sparrow, and deep down, she knew he was right.

ELEVEN

THE VISIT WITH HER mother had been short. Sophie wanted to stay longer, but a nagging feeling in her heart told her she needed to get back to Immernacht as soon as possible. She left the saddle with her mother; there was no need to carry the extra weight, but that also meant she had no clothes. When she landed in the courtyard of Castle Delacroix, she shifted back into her human form. A sharp whistle from behind startled her. She snapped her head in the direction of the sound and she saw Xander approaching.

"Mmm, Sophie, looking good." He looked her body up and down and she suddenly felt very self-conscious, remembering she was naked. She quickly cast a spell and gave herself the illusion of a blue dress.

"What do you want, Xander?" Sophie snapped.

"You," he said, giving her a devilish grin.

"Do you have any morals at all?"

"None I recall, why?" Xander stepped closer, breathing deeply, and he seemed to be listening to her heartbeat.

Sophie tried to back away from him, but Xander swiftly grabbed her waist and pulled her in close to him. His fingertips grazed her bare skin, rippling the illusion of clothing covering her body. He lowered his face so his lips were but an inch from hers and for some reason, although she wanted to pull away from him, she didn't, as if they were connected by an invisible tether holding her in place.

"Sophie, I-" Xander began to whisper something but changed his mind.

Just like that, the connection was severed, and she was in control of her own movements again. She drew her hand back and slapped him—hard. He backed away from her with impossible quickness, his cheek reddening in the shape of her palm. He didn't say another word, and she found herself wondering if he had been trying to apologize. She hurried past him and into the castle, hoping to escape the awkward feeling inside her. In the hall outside the parlor entrance, Natalia and Arturo spoke in hushed voices and looked up at her as she entered the hall. Silence filled the air and the look of concern on their faces made Sophie's heart leap into her throat.

"What's happened?" Sophie asked.

"We were just saying we need to have a family meeting. I'm glad you came back," Natalia said as she extended a hand to Sophie and escorted her to the parlor. "Arturo, Darling, will you invite the children to join us?"

Sophie thought it was funny how Natalia still called them "the children" although they were both fully grown adult vampires. It warmed her heart to know a mother's love was eternal. She thought about her mother and Willow. She wondered if her father knew Willow was with Samantha yet, or if he was still plotting against Immernacht.

"Can we make this quick? I have plans," Serena asked as she huffed into the room and sat down on the organ bench with her arms crossed in front of her.

"We have reason to believe Dmitri is awake. A body was found near Blackwater drained of blood. Was that quick enough for you?" Arturo's voice boomed. Sophie glanced at Serena. She no longer seemed interested in going through with whatever plans she had, and her mouth fell open in shock as she stared at Arturo. Sophie didn't know who Dmitri was, but from the expressions on the various faces in the room, she knew he was feared.

"It had to be Bastian; no one else can leave the island," Xander said with a shrug. If Sophie's eyes could set people on fire, Xander would surely be ash with the look she gave him.

"No, Bastian wouldn't hurt anyone. It couldn't have been him," Sophie shouted.

"Xander is not talking about the body. He is talking about my maker, an ancient vampire by the name of Dmitri. We drained him of his blood and left him in a tomb many years ago to protect humans from his lust for power. There was only one way to awaken him, with the blood of the Delacroix family. Think about it, Sophie. If we were all stuck here, and Dmitri's tomb is on the mainland, it couldn't have been us. There is one person with Delacroix blood who *can* leave the island," Arturo explained.

"Darling, why would he? Dmitri wants Bastian dead as much as he wants to kill the rest of us. I hope for Bastian's sake Dmitri is still asleep," Natalia said.

"Where did you ask Bastian to go?" Sophie couldn't contain her worry and was certain she wore it on her face for all to see.

"We sent him to Dmitri's tomb." Arturo's voice was filled with what sounded like regret.

"What will happen if he's awake?"

"Bastian better hope Dmitri is already far away, if that is the case," Xander said.

Sophie hated the way Xander's voice seemed to lack concern for his brother. She wanted to redden his other cheek, but turned her anger toward Arturo instead. "I can't believe you made him go alone. You could have very well sent him to his death!" Sophie's anger exploded. "Where is this tomb?"

"Bastian took the map with him, but I know the general location. Write to your father, ask him to drop the barrier, and we can go after him together," Arturo said.

"There is no way my father will let you go free now with the bodies he's found. He said it was the third one." Sophie's eyes searched the faces in the room for any hint of another idea, and when none appeared, she relented. "I will ask him to come and meet with you. We will ask him together. He was never able to tell me no when I was young; let's hope I haven't lost my touch."

TWELVE

BASTIAN MADE IT TO Aerulean Lake before he needed to rest. He carried a small cross-body satchel with some clothes, torches, a couple of wooden stakes—just in case—along with his notebook and quill Sophie had given him, and a coin pouch so he could rent a room for the night. He thought it would be safer to visit the tomb during the day. If there was one thing growing up in a family of vampires on a magically darkened island taught him, it was that the sun was not kind. He never had a problem with the sun because, although he did need blood once in a while, his dragon heritage absorbed some of the ill effects of vampirism.

The cabin he rented was just a small wooden room with a bed, which was all he needed for the night. Bastian locked the door and slept until the sun shined in through the window and woke him. He was only a few miles from the location of the tomb. He thought about getting breakfast before he left the lake, but fish sounded less than appealing, so he followed the map into the forest. The path on the map led him between two old oak trees, and to the right of a rushing river. The most frightening part of the trip, so far, was crossing the rope bridge. It swayed side to side, threatening to tip Bastian into the deep canyon below. The boards creaked under the weight of his step.

As he neared the end of the bridge, he heard a snap and looked toward the noise. The rope frayed and strands of it were breaking as he made his way across. He wished he had gone further north and taken the other bridge, but he was already halfway to the other side. With every step he took, he heard another pop, and the bridge dropped half an inch with each sound. He ran now, desperate to make it across before the rope gave out completely. He would have to jump, but he needed to get closer. The last strand of rope on the left side broke and the end of the bridge tipped to one side, Bastian leaped with all his might and barely grasped the earth on the other side; he clawed his way up the edge of the cliff and was able to take hold of a root. He pulled himself up and collapsed onto the ground, thankful he did not need to shift mid-fall, a skill he had never quite mastered.

Bastian heard rustling in the foliage around him and instantly went on high alert. He scanned the tree line, but saw nothing. It didn't matter. He was faster than most, and where speed failed him, his dragon form would not. Bastian pushed himself up and tried to brush some of the dirt off his hands. He could feel the caked earth beneath his fingernails and, for some reason, he hated the feeling more than the cut of parchment or a sliver of wood in his palm. He pushed his fingertips down the legs of his trousers in an effort to push the dirt out from under his nails.

□Another sound caught his attention and Bastian quickly moved through the trees for cover. He didn't have time to delay. Bastian used his speed to put as much distance between him and the bridge. There was a nagging feeling in his chest making him dread going to the tomb. He knew the tomb was west of the river, but he couldn't tell from the map exactly how far. He took wide paths when he could, and continued west through the thick brush when he could not, looking for the cave. Deep within it, Dmitri's body should still have been encased in the iron maiden sarcophagus which drained him of his blood twenty years ago. It was Dmitri's lust for power that brought about his imprisonment, but he hated The Delacroix especially, for many reasons, his punishment no doubt being the biggest. *There it is!* The cave came into view and Bastian felt more nervous than ever as he approached the entrance and paused to light a torch before continuing. Wiping the sweat from his forehead as he stepped cautiously into the mouth of the cave, Bastian grimaced at the sudden change in air quality. The stench of bat guano and damp earth filled his nostrils, and he coughed as his torch flickered in the darkness. The sound of dripping water and falling debris echoed throughout the cavern. A high-pitched screech made Bastian jump as a swarm of bats swooped from their location above. He had to duck to avoid being battered by their tiny wings as they flew past him.

The path was becoming narrow and the rocks beneath Bastian's feet crumbled away and plunged into the deep recess of the cavern. He dared to look down, but he could only see to the edge of his torchlight. As soon as the path became wide enough for him to shift, he did. Bastian could see into the darkness a little further in his dragon form, but he would need the torch again when he reached the bottom. Bastian grabbed his satchel off the ground and carried it in his teeth as he descended into the depths of the tomb.

When he finally reached the bottom, Bastian shifted back into his human form, dressed, and lit a torch. Dmitri's sarcophagus was just ahead, and the pit in his stomach felt like it had a boulder in it now. He crept into the slender opening between two walls. He had to turn and take sidesteps to get through the passage, which made him thankful for his vampiric metabolism. He was certain a human at his age would have a hard time squeezing between the rocks in a few places. The passage opened up into a circular area with nothing but the old iron sarcophagus in the center of a pool of dark and murky water. There were several tunnels around the space, leading in opposite directions, but Bastian was only interested in the sarcophagus which stood open, and empty.

"What is this..." his voice trailed off as he walked closer to the device and looked closely at the hollow spikes on the inside. The blood on them was sticky and almost completely dry. Bastian's inspection was interrupted as he felt something brush his ear. It was almost like a whisper. He whirled around and his mouth fell open in shock when he saw who was behind him.

"You—" he started to say, but before he could get out another word, his attacker grabbed his head and he could feel the invasion of his mind. His memories played like a theater skit. He saw Sophie and then Leon telling him to leave her, and then the scene flashed to them, dancing at the ball in Ledora, and then they were kissing. He tried to push those thoughts away because he knew his attacker was in his head watching these memories, too. Suddenly, a wail louder than the shriek of a banshee rang out in his ears and he covered them as a forceful blast knocked him backward, into the iron maiden. A deep blue smoke surrounded his head and made his mind feel fuzzy and he wanted to sleep, but he fought the effects. Bastian cried out in pain as the spikes of the sarcophagus impaled him, and his blood began trickling out into the pool behind him. The door slammed closed and darkness enveloped him.

"Let me out. Don't do this, please. You don't have to do this!" Bastian screamed as he heard the iron padlocks click. Bastian sighed in defeat as he listened to the footsteps retreating from the area. As his consciousness faded, he thought of Sophie and hoped, for her sake, she would not come looking for him.

THIRTEEN

Thwack! Eira's bo staff cracked against Sparrow's back. "Ow!" he cried. "It's not fair you get to use weapons and I can't."

"You need to prepare for any situation. What if you are attacked while bathing, the only sword you'd have then is between your legs." Eira smacked him again, lightly this time on his leg. "I could sweep you off your feet right now if I wanted to," she boasted.

"Don't take it personal, honey, but you're not my type."

"Why?" Eria feigned offence."

"I prefer certain guarantees," he replied.

"Like what?" Eira asked, striking at him again. This time, Sparrow ducked the bo, maneuvering himself behind her and earned a point against Eira with a backfist to her head. He pulled the strike before it made contact, showcasing his control and speed.

"Ooh, very good, nice move," Eira complimented.

"No strings."

"What?" Eira stopped and looked at Sparrow, pondering what he meant.

"I don't want to fall in love, or have a woman getting ideas in their head that we could have a future. I don't want to be tied down to anyone, so no one will be sad when I don't come back," he said.

"I see." Her voice had a slight twinge of disappointment in it.

"Hey, I hate to break up the training session, but Commander Rend wants to see you—both of you." Beric looked at Eira and Sparrow.

Eira leaned her bo staff against a tree and followed Beric without question. Everyone who worked for Commander Rend followed orders without question. He inspired a type of loyalty which, in Sparrows opinion, bordered on unhealthy. It had been days since the last time Sparrow had spoken with Leon and he was no closer to eliminating the vampires than he was the day he arrived and with every passing day he grew more impatient.

"I received a letter from my daughter. She says they have a plan to end the vampire problem once and for all, but we need to meet her there to discuss it. I would like you two to come with me just in case negotiations go south," Leon told them.

"What if it is a trap? You can't trust them," Eira argued.

"If they betray me, then you will have my full support to deal with them however you like, but I promised Sparrow we would find the ones responsible for the massacre of his brothers and if they can deliver that person to me, then I have to try," he explained. Eira looked at Sparrow and saw the desperation in his eyes.

"Fine, when do we leave?" Eira asked.

Sailing to Immernacht was scheduled to take five days. Sparrow had never sailed before, but on the first day of the trip, he discovered he enjoyed it more than he thought he would. Eira had sailed many times, however, and Sparrow noticed how she stared longingly across the sea. They set sail in the early morning aboard the Crimson Wyrm, which was the second fastest ship in the Blackwater fleet, just behind the Red Dragon. The ship glided effortlessly across the gentle waves and the sails billowed softly in the breeze; it was not at all what Sparrow had expected. The ship's captain stood at the helm with a distant gaze, the map to Immernacht rolled up and wedged between his belt and waist. The deck crew busied themselves doing what they had to do to keep the ship on course. Sparrow knew nothing of sailing, ropes here, sails there, big wheel steers the ship... which was the extent of his knowledge.

"Do you like to sail?" Sparrow asked as he moved next to Eira.

"I used to when I was younger. We sailed from the original elven city of Aranor to Braidwood all the time back then. When Aranor was destroyed, the surviving families built the new city in the forest south of Braidwood, which is now called Ravenhall. It never felt like home to me though. I miss Aranor. Our homes were nestled in the treetops of the Sequoia Forest, high above the ground where most predators could not reach us. We used nature's gifts and the magic it bestowed upon us to make the city of Aranor an oasis where all the creatures of the Fae Forest would be safe and happy. I've not seen a faerie, a nymph, or even a pixie since Aranor was destroyed. There are no more centaurs or fauns. The existence of the Fae world is dwindling because of vampires, and the orcs they created to ravage not only human settlements but ours as well." Eira wiped a tear from her cheek with the back of her hand.

"I know how you feel, vampires killed all of my brothers at The Garden of Life and then just left their bodies there like garbage. I am so sorry you had to experience the loss of your home and loved ones. I promise you, we will avenge them." Sparrow put his arm around Eira and she leaned into his shoulder, sniffling softly as she fought against more tears.

They spent the rest of the day watching the water. Whales breached and dove back down into the ocean, otters drifted by, holding hands so the current couldn't separate them. Seagulls sang overhead in melody with the percussion of the waves lapping against the sides of the ship.

Eira pulled her hat down a little, and glided effortlessly to a cargo trunk strapped to the mast. She sat down on it, but her eyes barely left the water. "The ocean is so beautiful," she remarked.

"It is, think of all the beautiful things beneath the surface. How amazing would it be to dive into the deep and see the world's hidden wonders?" Sparrow asked. Eira nodded in agreement. She knew it was not a true question, but a spoken dream; something he wanted but would likely never attain.

The clanging of a bell broke the serenity and a large gruff crew member alerted them it was chow time. The ship's galley was larger than most, but it was still hot and stuffy from the wood-burning iron stove on which they cooked. Most of the heat traveled through the pipe of the stove and out the top of the ship, but the residual warmth was still enough to heighten the body odors of everyone in the space. *Maybe a long period at sea isn't for me after all,* he thought scrunching his nose. Sparrow grabbed a tray and slid it down the metal bars in front of the serving line. The first server scooped a pile of mashed potatoes directly onto his tray. He moved down the counter to the next pot and the server plopped two sausages right on top of his mashed potatoes. When he reached the final server, he realized the smell he thought was the odor of the crew, was coming from the pot.

"What's in there?" Sparrow asked.

"Cabbage, you never had cabbage before?" the man asked as he scooped a heaping spoonful and plopped it beside Sparrow's potatoes and sausage.

Sparrow carried his tray of food up the wooden stairs and sat down at the base of the forecastle deck. He stabbed a sausage with his fork and took a bite off of the end of it.

"Is there room for me over here?" Eira asked. Sparrow looked up at her and smiled. He was surprised to see she was still wearing the knit cap she had worn all day, even after being in the heat of the galley.

"Aren't you hot wearing that?" he asked, gesturing to it.

"Of course, but ears like mine draw attention, there are still those who think they can collect on old bounties," Eira replied.

"No one has hunted elves to my knowledge for a decade or more now."

"Maybe so, but you can never be too careful when you're in a group this size headed to an island filled with vampires," she said.

Eira sat down beside Sparrow and watched as he moved the cabbage to the edge of his tray so it wasn't touching his potatoes. He poked the middle of his sausage with his fork, picked it up, and bit the end off. He looked at Eira as she cut her sausage into tiny pieces and then mixed it into her potatoes. Sparrow dipped his sausage into his potatoes, pulling up a heaping bite. He was surprised at the flavor and texture combination of such a simple meal. When only his cabbage was left, Sparrow scraped it to the edge of his plate and then emptied it over the side of the ship.

"You don't like it huh?" Eira asked.

"Not really, it smells like dirty unwashed armpit," he replied.

Eira laughed. "I suppose it does, and the gas of it doesn't smell any better on its way out. I'm already expecting the sleeping quarters to smell rancid tonight. I'm thinking about laying my bedroll out on the upper deck. I don't want to be closed in below deck with the flatulence of all these men," Eira said it jokingly, but Sparrow knew she was serious about sleeping on the upper deck. He noticed she wasn't eating her cabbage either.

They talked for hours as the ship gently swayed back and forth, until finally, a man came along to collect their trays so they could close the galley. When the sun had set, Sparrow bid Eira goodnight. He hadn't thought to bring a bedroll, so Sparrow slept below deck with the crew. Eira had been right about the smell and he listened to the rumbling of bellies all night until he finally fell asleep with his tunic pulled over his nose.

The next day was a little cloudier, and not as warm; they had a different meal and Sparrow was thankful it was rice and a hearty stew made of beef, carrots, celery, and potato. The sleeping area smelled much better too. On the fifth morning, the last of their journey, Sparrow jolted awake to the sounds of shouting and the roar of thunder, the ship rocked to one side and Sparrow fell out of his hammock and onto the floor with a thud. The rain pounded the upper deck and the ship rocked and creaked as it battled against the raging storm. Wind howled like a vengeful beast, tearing through the sails with a force threatening to rip them to shreds. The once softly billowing canvas now flapped violently, the sound akin to thunderous applause.

The bow plunged into towering waves rising over the sides of the ship like mountains, their peaks lost in a dense fog. Each crest sent the vessel hurtling forward, only to plummet downward with stomach-churning velocity. The timbers strained and wailed under immense pressure, groaning with a protest echoing the fear pulsating through the crew. The sailors fought against the maelstrom, their bodies swaying synchronously with the tempest's wrath. Each surge threatened to sweep them overboard, but they clung to the ship's lifelines, their knuckles white with strain. The very air seemed electrified with a potent mix of adrenaline and trepidation; they knew a single misstep could send them tumbling into the abyss below.

Thunder cracked overhead, shaking the ship to its core. The rain-soaked deck became a treacherous slope, and every step demanded unwavering focus and balance. Fear gnawed at their hearts, but the sailors were driven by a fierce loyalty to their captain and a shared desire for survival. Leon, who had been sequestered away in the captain's quarters for most of the trip, now bravely worked alongside the crew to secure the sails and against all odds, keep the ship from capsizing.

The storm ended suddenly and the ship came to a slow stop as it ran aground. Sparrow looked around to see the violent weather they had just faced was part of the magical barrier of Immernacht. He could still see the lightning and the crashing of turbulent waves behind them, but not a single drop of rain penetrated the dome of magic covering the island in darkness. Sparrow looked around at the faces of the crew members, angry and confused about having narrowly escaped death to reach the island with little to no warning of how dangerous the trip would actually be. Leon grabbed a large bag, slung it over his shoulder, and set it down beside the captain.

"Sparrow, Eira, I need you two to accompany me. There will be no quarrel today, we are here at my daughter's request to solve our problem with diplomacy. In the event a peace cannot be reached, Sophie is to leave with us. I have a sneaking suspicion if we bring weapons we will be relieved of them upon entry to the castle. Do not hide anything or try to be deceptive, they will see right through it," Leon said.

Eira and Sparrow put their weapons down on the deck and exchanged a glance. Eira's eyes seemed to say 'told you so' to him as he thought back to their last day of training. The crew dropped the gangplank and an old woman emerged from the captain's quarters and joined Leon. She grasped his elbow as he led her to the ramp. Her eyes were pure white. They had no iris, and no pupil, yet still when she looked at Sparrow, he knew she saw him before she even spoke. "I'm sorry about your brothers," she said.

"Thank you," Sparrow replied. *Leon must have mentioned it to her*, he thought.

Sparrow's legs felt weak when they stepped onto land. He stumbled slightly as they buckled beneath his weight for the first few steps. The beach was rocky, with a disappointing amount of sand and very few shells. He looked back at the ship. The crew waited there, not daring to leave the boat. The tales of Immernacht reached the ears of every sailor, and they were all too eager to repeat the stories to anyone who would listen, especially after a few mugs of ale. Very few Sailors were willing to deliver here, even though the ones who did got paid handsomely.

The rocky cliffs in front of them gave the beach an eerie vibe, like a death omen. Howls in the distance caught Sparrow's attention and a chill in the air made the hairs on the back of his neck prickle. A mist rolled in, spilling from the path between the two cliffs. Sparrow took a step back, reaching for a stake. His hand fell against the flat leather of the empty holster and then he remembered they'd left their weapons on the ship.

Two shadows of humanoid figures emerged from the mist. Sparrow eased when what little light there was revealed the two men. They dressed in fine clothing, befitting of noblemen, and as far as Sparrow could tell, they were unarmed. The men approached with their hands clasped in front of them.

"Are you Leon Rend?" one of them asked.

"I am, nice to meet you." Leon extended his hand to the man but he only looked at it and kept his hands firmly clasped in front of him.

"We have come to escort your party to the castle, I'm Harris, and this is Garridan," he said, "Follow us, please."

FOURTEEN

"WE NEED TO SEE Queen Sophia Rend," Leon said with authority.

"We know, and we're here to escort you to Castle Delacroix. That is where Miss Sophie is," Alexi said.

Leon wanted to tell him Sophie was a queen and he should address her by title, but this was not the mainland, this was their kingdom. All Leon cared about was his daughter's safety. He thought only of Sophie as they walked through town toward the castle. She had not spoken to him in over a year and he wondered what she would say. He wanted to be a part of her life again and hoped they could repair their relationship. He grew more anxious with every step, the uncertainty weighing on him like he was swimming in full-plate armor.

The castle courtyard was a wasteland of old crumbling stones and two gargantuan dragon statues stood sentry on each side of the entrance. Alexi opened the front doors and the hinges creaked loudly, echoing through the hall. The foyer flickered with light from the chandelier. Red candle wax dripped from the overflowing bobeches and cooled before it could fall, forming stalactites of wax.

The stone walls held paintings of lush landscapes, tropical paradises, and fields of daisies. *Seems a little off-brand for vampires.* Leon thought as they moved in two-by-two formation down the corridor. The torchlight danced shadows through the hall and gave Leon and uneasy feeling; he could not recall the last time he'd been face to face with Arturo Delacroix.

The council chamber was a small private room branching off from the great hall. Maids and servants scurried about their duties, and several guards moved about the castle on patrol. Arturo, Natalia, and Sophie sat at a small round table awaiting their arrival and stood at once to greet them as they entered. Leon had aged considerably since last they met, his brown hair had turned a salt and pepper gray, and now was more salt than pepper. Arturo had not aged a day, and despite the knowledge that this was how immortality worked, Leon was still taken aback by his youthful vigor.

"Commander Rend, how lovely to see you again, thank you for making the difficult journey to our home to speak with us. I have heard about the troubles on the mainland, but I assure you, it has nothing to do with us. We are still here on this island living by the terms we agreed upon after we helped you defeat Orion and liberate Braidwood from his tyranny." Arturo's voice was charming.

"Sophie indicated in her letter you might have an explanation for the nature of the deaths that occurred at both the temple of life and near Blackwater?" Leon asked. "I'm so sorry, how rude of me; this is Eira, and this is Sparrow. They are part of an elite vampire-hunting organization funded by the Silver Talons Guild. We seem to have a fledgling problem and they are specially trained to handle such vampires. They have come to offer their services."

"We have heard nothing of the temple you speak of—how do you know this is a fledgling problem?" Arturo asked.

Leon looked at Sparrow and nodded, giving him the floor to tell his story.

"I was a member of The Garden of Life, a temple sanctuary of peace and reflection. We had many members, until recently. I returned home after a year in solitude to reflect on my anger and gain inner peace. When I came home, there was nothing to return to—all of my brothers had been drained of blood and were discarded like garbage, thrown about the room without care. We saw the bite marks and torn flesh. This was not the work of an older vampire with self-control, or even one fledgling alone, this had to be a group of them feeding en-masse," Sparrow said.

Arturo seemed to be digesting the information as he looked at his wife and then to Sophie. "Go on, Sophie, you can ask your father what you need to ask."

Arturo spoke to Leon's daughter in such a kind and caring way, the same way Leon would speak to her himself. It hurt to see Sophie more a part of the Delacroix family than her own. "Father, I asked you to come here because this problem is going to require vampire assistance. You are facing an enemy you cannot handle alone. I am sure the hunters are very skilled, but to take on an army of newly turned vampires would be a suicide mission. I am asking for you to dispel the barrier trapping the Delacroixes here on this island, and let them help you win this fight."

"First of all, who is this enemy we are up against? I thought the Delacroix was the last of the vampire line?" Leon asked.

"We were, however, I am not sure if you know this, but my maker, Dmitri has been in a state of hibernation since the liberation of Braidwood. When Orion took over the city, Dmitri was his right hand. He was obsessed with power and thought if he had dragons of his own, *and* immortality, he could rule the world. He would have killed everyone—human, vampire, and everything in between to make it happen. So we tricked him into following us into a deep underground cavern. We told him we found a lair and a nest filled with dragon eggs. When we got there, a sorceress awaited with a spell prepared to trap him in an iron maiden sarcophagus designed to drain him of his blood. He can't die, so for more than twenty years he has been desiccating in the tomb. The only way to wake him is with immortal blood, the blood of the Delacroix. But we are here, and he is—or was—deep beneath the northern forest on the mainland. It was not any of us who woke him. There is no doubt he wants us dead for what we did to him and now he is building an army to take back this castle and maybe even the mainland, too. If we allow him to get strong and keep making more vampires, we will never be able to defeat him. Please, I beg you, dispel the magic keeping us here and let us help you trap him once more." Arturo pleaded.

"Why would we keep him alive?" Leon asked.

"If you kill him, you're also condemning me to die. When a vampire is killed, any vampire they have made also dies. It could happen instantly, or it might take a week, a month, maybe even up to a year, but I will die. I pledge my service to the guild if you allow us to deal with Dmitri our way. The hunters can take care of the fledglings," Arturo pleaded which was unlike him.

"You make quite a case, service to the guild is vowed until death which for you could be a very long time," Leon pointed out. "I don't know what I was expecting when I agreed to come meet with you, but how do you know it is Dmitri? Like you said he needs *your* blood and you're all here. Only Bastian is able to leave, but it's because he is a dragon and not a vampire, so how would Dmitri get your blood?" Leon asked.

Arturo and Natalia shared a glance and Sophie looked at them with a flash of fear in her eyes and she shook her head.

"What am I missing here?" Leon asked.

"Twenty-three years ago, Bastian was fatally wounded. I did what any mother would do and I saved his life. He is part vampire as well, although his dragon form masks his vampiric nature," Natalia admitted.

"So you have broken the agreement and made another vampire, and tell me, where is Bastian now?" Leon demanded.

"We sent him to investigate the tomb to see if Dmitri was still inside it. He's not made it back yet and we are concerned for his well-being," Arturo said.

"How do you know it wasn't him all along? How do you know for certain Bastian didn't wake Dmitri?"

"Father, Bastian wouldn't—couldn't, he hadn't. He has been with me at Lapis Highland, and when he wasn't there, he was here, the only place he is allowed to feed. They have followed the rules of their prison for years, why do you think they should remain imprisoned here? They're not monsters, they're my family, and Willow's too because she is Bastian's daughter. Please, father, let them help make this right and put Dmitri back in the tomb," Sophie begged her father, looking at him with those sad green eyes he'd never been able to resist. He would do anything to have the respect of his daughter back.

"Fine, I will dispel the barrier and once we have dealt with Dmitri, you can return to the island and live by the same agreement. No new vampires, and no killing humans."

"What of the barrier, will this still be our prison, or will you trust us to attend your Solstice gathering, attend court in Ledora, or maybe even finally visit my niece who has been ruling Ash alone since my sister died?" Natalia asked.

Sophie looked at Natalia, realizing why she looked so much like Akiri. Luciana was her sister. The features they shared were now so obvious, Sophie had no idea how she'd missed it. Natalia's long black hair flowed in waves to the middle of her back and her red lipstick stood out against the pallor of her skin. Her brown eyes contained the same amber flecks as her niece's and Natalia wore the same stern face as Luciana—at least in the portrait Akiri kept in the storage room. They had so much to talk about but now was not the time.

"You will be free to come and go as you please," Leon said.

"You can't allow that, are you serious?" Eira looked at Leon in shock. "Releasing vampires willingly into the human population? Do you even know how many enemies you will invite to your doorstep?

"I'm sorry, I have no reason not to trust them; they have first-hand knowledge and experience with Dmitri, and we need their help. You can trust if they so much as bend the agreement again, this privilege will be revoked." Leon looked back at Arturo who nodded his agreement to the terms. Then he glanced at the old woman. She sat so quietly in the corner of the room, everyone else had forgotten she was there. He motioned for her to join them at the table. "This is Agatha, she is a sorceress with wild magic. She draws energy from elementals, like the storm surrounding the island. She can take in the power and the barrier will fall. She will need to go to the center of the island to do the spell," Leon told them.

"Very well, Alexi will show her the way. In the meantime, you are all welcome to stay. If you need to rest, any of the staff can show you to a room," Arturo said.

"Thank you, Sophie, could we please speak in private?" Leon looked at his daughter, then to Arturo, and back again. Sophie nodded as she stood to leave the conference room with her father.

FIFTEEN

SOPHIE LED LEON TO her chamber. She wanted him to see the kindness she saw in Arturo and Natalia. Her father looked surprised to see how well taken care of she was here with this family of vampires. Her room was fit for a queen. The bed was twice the size of the one he shared with Samantha. Willow's crib and matching changing table looked like they were hand carved with love and care. Leon sat down on the bench at the foot of her bed and Sophie moved the rocking chair to sit near him.

"Father, I wanted you to know I'm—"

"No, Sophie, you do not need to apologize, I do," Leon interrupted. "I was a fool. When I tried to send Bastian away, I thought I was protecting you, but I see now you can take care of yourself, and these people love you."

Sophie's eyes welled with tears. She didn't realize until just now how much she had longed to hear her father apologize. She stood up and walked over to Leon, prompting him to stand as well. Sophie rushed into his open arms the way she had when she was little. "I'm so happy you came, and you understand. We will take care of this and everything will be great. You'll see."

"Sophie, I don't want you anywhere near this fight. I need you to please go home and be with your mother and Willow; keep them safe. I will request Dominic, Kamara, and Akiri to come and help us with the fledglings," Leon said.

"Okay, I will. I do agree they need me there more than you guys will in battle. I miss Willow so much. I have never been away from her for more than a few hours, I'll leave as soon as the sun has set."

"I have to get back to Eira and Sparrow and see how they're doing; I can't imagine it was easy for them to hear what I have just agreed to, and no doubt they are making plans of their own, which I must now abolish." Leon looked at Sophie with a sense of pride, then he turned and walked out the door.

Sophie listened to the sound of his footsteps grow quieter as he moved down the hall. She stretched out across her bed, wishing it were not empty. She stretched her hand across the bed, clutching the sheets in her fist. Sophie closed her eyes, holding back the tears threatening to spill. A knock on the door interrupted the nap she'd hoped to have and with a groan, Sophie got up and opened the door. Serena held a bottle of wine and two stemmed cups. Sophie was really not in the mood, but she was curious about the purpose of her visit. She moved aside and allowed Serena to enter.

"I wanted to apologize to you," she said, setting the wine cups down on the mantle above the fireplace. She pulled the cork and poured the wine before continuing. "You must think we are monsters, and through all of this, I never asked how you were doing."

"Do you really care?" Sophie asked.

"Of course I care, you will someday be my brother's wife, and you're the mother of my niece," she said, handing me one of the wine cups. "When I was young, I thought I wanted this life; immortality, wealth, and all the pretty things. My mother made it look so divine. I have to admit, I'm jealous of you. I've never left the island. Bastian used to tell me about Ledoran court, and the places he would travel. He'd bring back gifts from all over—he was being nice, but his gifts made me long for freedom all the more."

"So, you wish you'd been left mortal?"

"Sometimes, but I can't change it, so I have to make the best of it." Serena paused to finish her cup of wine. "I want to thank you for talking to your father. I'm going to get to leave here for the first time because of you and I really appreciate it. Elizandra promised to take me to see the world one day, but then she never came back." Serena looked longingly out the window.

Sophie remembered the conversation about Elizandra at dinner and she couldn't help wondering who she'd been to Bastian. "Did Bastian and Elizandra used to be together?" She regretted asking as soon as the words left her mouth, did she really want to know the answer?

"I argued back and forth with myself about whether or not it was my place to say anything," Serena paused to gauge Sophie's reaction. "Please don't be angry with me if I tell you, you are the closest thing I have to a sister and I'm sorry my stupid brother didn't tell you himself. Elizandra is Bastian's wife." Serena placed a gentle hand on Sophie's shoulder. The scene at dinner replayed through her mind and she thought of Bastian doing to Elizandra all the things Xander had done to the red-haired girl. Her face grew hot and she knew she might not be able to hold her temper back for long.

"I think I need to be alone right now, I have a lot to process." Sophie clenched her fists as she stood to escort Serena to the door.

"I hope you aren't mad at me, I just thought you deserved to know," she told her.

Sophie waited for Serena to descend the staircase before she rushed to the bed, grabbed the pillow, buried her face in it and screamed. Pacing the floor, she still couldn't wrap her head around it, Bastian had a *wife*? She felt so stupid. He was living an entirely separate life, coming here and drinking from his wife's neck while his mistress was at home taking care of their child. She had never pressured Bastian to marry her, even though a child out of wedlock, by most kingdom's standards, was a bastard with no right to their parent's throne. Sophie's thoughts sent her into a rage and she grabbed the nearest item and threw it without caution toward the wall by the open doorway. She expected to hear the vase shatter, but Xander caught it before it made contact.

"Sophie, Darling. What's got you so upset?" He sat the vase down gently on top of the chest of drawers.

"Serena just told me the man I love and share a child with has a *wife* he just forgot to mention, is it true? He also never mentioned he was a vampire so I guess I knew nothing about him at all. My father knew and he tried to make Bastian leave me, but I got angry at him instead and didn't speak to my father for more than a year. Bastian watched me go through this and still said nothing. How can I continue believing he is a good person?" Sophie wiped the tears from her face as she looked up at Xander who flashed across the room to her in the blink of an eye. He slowly reached up and cradled her cheek in his palm. He gently wiped away the next tear that fell and wrapped his arms around her.

"No, I'm still angry with you, too." Sophie said, pushing him away."

"I would be lying if I said there wasn't a part of me that wanted to let you hate Bastian, but you mustn't be too hard on him. From the moment he met you at the ball, he began drinking Elizandra's blood from a chalice, never touching her in a way a husband would touch his wife. Their relationship was never truly romantic. She was in a bad situation with her drunk of a father who was going to marry her off to a man just as equally horrid. Bastian, being the bleeding heart he is, offered his hand instead, and a dowry her father could not refuse. Once the ceremony was complete, I went to her father and suggested he name his daughter heir to his fortune. Once his legacy was filed with the citadel, he took his own life."

"Was that a result of your *suggestion* as well?" Sophie asked.

"He was an awful man, he's lucky I didn't kill him myself, but I must honor the peace between us and The Silver Talons Guild and it means we cannot take a human life."

"Why would you speak on behalf of Bastian now, after you have accused him of waking Dmitri?" Sophie asked.

"He's my brother."

"If you care so much about your brother, how could you accuse him of waking Dmitri? Not only that, but you go out of your way to intentionally anger him."

"Every vampire receives special gifts when they complete the transition, I have speed, the power of suggestion, and future sight. I can't see everything all the time, but when I first saw you in the parlor, I had a vision. I saw us together, I saw your heart and your soul and their connection to my own. We are fated to be together."

"I don't believe in fate. What about the night at dinner? What power made me feel what you were doing without touching me?" Sophie asked, remembering the way it felt when his eyes locked onto hers as he pleasured the red-haired girl. It was as if she were the one on the table in front of him, bared for all to see, claimed in such a primal way. Even now, thinking about it made her feel things... things she didn't want to feel for Xander. The thought of him touching, kissing, and caressing her sex with his tongue excited her.

"It was part of the *suggestion* ability," he replied. "I can make people feel things without touching them, or give them false memories, make them dream what I want them to dream or do things I want them to do," Xander's voice was hardly more than a whisper and his face was so close to hers she could feel his breath on her skin as he spoke.

"And if you suggested I kiss you now...?" Sophie moved closer to him.

"Then you would do so without hesitation." He swallowed hard, not backing away.

"What if you suggested we do more than kiss?" Sophie asked, placing her hand on his chest and gliding it upward.

"I could make you do anything I wanted." Xander's heart began to beat faster, he never felt it do that before.

"What else have you made me do?" Sophie asked.

Xander pulled away from her and looked at her in surprise. "This was not the reason I came in here," he said, trying to change the subject.

"Tell me, what else has not been my choice?"

"I asked you to take Willow to your mother's and come back," he admitted.

"Why, so you could get me alone now with Bastian gone?"

"Sophie, I- no... we *are* fated so I can't help this connection I feel to you, but I want *you* to want it too, I would never force you to be with me if Bastian is really your choice," he told her.

"Did you think I wanted to feel what you made me experience at dinner? In front of Bastian no less. Do you know how much guilt I was filled with for enjoying it?"

"I know, I'm sorry. The truth is; I felt guilty for the vision I had and I thought it would be easier if you hated me because then you and my brother could be happy and I would find a way to deal, but then when you were leaving, it felt like you were ripping out my heart and taking it with you. I regret taking your choice away from you and I swear I will never do it to you again." Xander turned and left the room.

Deep down, a part of her was attracted to him and the thought of his hands roaming her body as he removed her clothing sent a thrill straight between her thighs. She had secretly hoped for him to be as inhuman as she thought him to be. Sophie recognized what this behavior was… When she felt sad, betrayed, or heartbroken, physical intimacy was the only way to take her mind off the pain. Xander could have let her hate Bastian for all he withheld, but he had explained away the doubt she felt and told her why he had kept the biggest secret of all from her. He didn't want to be married, he just wanted to save Elizandra from her abusive father. Bastian has a good heart and despite the secrets, Sophie knew he loved her, and he loved Willow. *She deserves to have her mother and her father.* Sophie thought. She pushed the thoughts of Xander away. They would find Bastian, she would forgive him, and then everything would go back to normal, they would work everything out, rule Lapis Highland and raise Willow together, just like they planned.

Sophie spent the evening preparing to fly home to be with Willow and her mother. Leon worked with Agatha to dispel the barrier imprisoning the vampires. When the magic field was gone, Agatha cast a spell on the Delacroix family to protect them from the sun during the day. They loaded the ship with stakes, bows and arrows, and meat—a generous gift of thanks from Arturo for freeing his family from their prison.

"Can we talk?" Sophie turned to see Xander. He pointed to an area away from the others where they could speak privately. Sophie nodded and followed him over there. "I want to be able to communicate with you, so I can let you know when we find Bastian, but the only way I can is to create a blood bond. You don't have to, I'm not compelling you—"

"Fine," Sophie cut him off before he could finish. "How do we do it?"

"Let me see your finger." Sophie extended her pointer to him. Xander gripped it gently and raised it to his mouth. She started to pull away, but she thought about Bastian. She needed to know he was okay. Xander pricked her fingertip on his incisor and gently licked the drop of blood from it he let the red linger on the tip of his tongue before closing his mouth, clearly savoring the taste of her. Sophie groaned in disgust and pulled her finger away, wiping it on her dress. Xander pricked his own finger and offered it to her.

"I won't turn into a vampire will I?" Sophie asked warily as she looked at the almost burgundy droplet on his finger.

"No, bond will only link our minds. If you are in trouble I will be able to sense it and vice versa. If I close my eyes and imagine you standing before me, I will be able to speak to you in your mind. I can let you know when we get to the tomb," Xander said. Sophie nodded and accepted his offering.

"Stay safe," Sophie told him.

"Watch out, I might get the impression you care," he grinned and gave her a wink as she took his finger into her mouth. His blood tasted bitter and metallic, but Sophie did her best not to make a face. A groan escaped his lips as her tongue caressed the tip of his finger. Her green eyes sparkled in the setting sun and stared into his as she sucked the droplet of blood. He looked at her with desire, his pants growing tight against his stiffening cock. *Gods how he wanted her.* Sophie felt her heart skip a beat. *No, I'm not supposed to feel this way,* she thought.

I should go, Sophie heard Xander say, although it was not out loud. Sophie closed her eyes and pictured Xander in her mind, she could see him staring back at her; his dark brown hair swept back and to the side. He was close enough she could feel his breath.

Please, find him, she thought. His lips were so close to hers and she found herself longing to taste them. She wanted to be angry at him, but instead, she was drawn to him in ways she couldn't understand. She should hate him; after all, he was vile and rude, but, he had told her the truth about Bastian and Elizandra, so maybe there was good in him after all. When she opened her eyes, he smiled at her and nodded. The touch of his hand lingered on hers as he backed away.

Sophie walked to the loading dock and watched as the men carried bags and supplies on board. Leon stopped in front of Sophie and smiled warmly. "I love you, kiddo. Get home to your mom and Willow, they're probably missing you. I'll do my best to help find Bastian."

She threw her arms around his neck and hugged him the way she had when she was a child. "I love you too, Dad. I'm sorry I went so long without speaking to you. I really did miss you and I took Willow's time with you too."

"Hey, like I said before, you don't need to apologize. I should have trusted your judgement. I'll see you at home after we find Bastian." Leon boarded the ship and turned back to wave to her as they lifted the gangplank and set sail.

SIXTEEN

DRIP...DRIP...DRIP. THREE FORTY-ONE, THREE *forty-two, three forty-three...* Bastian counted the only sound he could hear. It was the only way he could tell time was still passing and he was still alive. Bastian hadn't started counting until he caught himself nodding off, but he needed to stay awake. He had to be able to call out for help when Sophie inevitably came looking for him. He hoped she wouldn't. He didn't remember how he ended up inside the iron maiden sarcophagus and the more he tried to remember, the stronger the pounding in his head became. Memory or not, there he was, locked inside the contraption and impaled by more than twenty blood-leeching spikes.

Was it Dmitri? Bastian thought. He tried to recall, but it was as if his attacker had filled his mind with a fog lingering over that one tiny memory. Bastian felt himself growing weaker as the blood drained from his body a few drops at a time. Glimpses of Sophie and Willow entered his mind and he felt himself drifting into unconsciousness again. *Three forty-four, three forty-five,* he counted. He wished, now more than ever, for the telepathic abilities of his brother. If he had Xander's gift he could make Sophie dream of him, he could fill her mind with the memories of the route he took to get here and then she would know where he was, but even then he didn't know if he would use it unless he were truly desperate. Sophie knowing his whereabouts would only endanger her.

A sudden noise other than the dripping of his blood startled him back to full alert. Footsteps—lots of them—were headed his way. "Help! I'm here!" Bastian called, but his voice came out raspy and dry. He was too dehydrated to scream. The footsteps entered the area and then he heard voices.

"The bloodstone should be charged now," said a feminine voice. She sounded familiar, but Bastian couldn't picture the face to which the voice belonged. He heard the splashing of water as someone walked into the blood pool behind the sarcophagus. The female began chanting in a language he did not know, and the low hum of magic reverberated off of the walls of the iron maiden. Bastian wished to see what was happening in the room around him, but he was consumed by the darkness of his entombment.

"It's not working!" the deep, gravelly voice of a frustrated man echoed through the chamber as the clattering of what sounded like a large rock bouncing across a stone floor and then plopping into a body of water confirmed his anger.

"If you break the stone, you can ensure it will not work. Perhaps it is because his blood is not pure, it is tainted with vampire blood—no offense." The way she added the words 'no offense' told Bastian the man she was speaking to was a vampire. *It has to be Dmitri*, Bastian thought.

"What do you suggest?" He asked.

"Well, there are four other dragonshifters—one of which is of particular interest to me and could be the key to your survival should they try to employ the hunters. Lucky for us, I know just how to get her here. With Sophie Rend under your control, you will have power over The Silver Talons Guild, Lapis Highland, Ophay, and Ledora. No one would dream of killing you if it meant she would die, too. Now, find the stone while I invite our guest to join us." Bastian heard someone empty out a bag—his bag—and he knew this sorceress could sense the magic in the notebook and knew how to use it.

"No! Leave her alone, please," Bastian pleaded weakly. If they heard him, they pretended not to, and his consciousness faded.

When he woke again, Bastian tried to call out for help again, but his voice was even less than a whisper now. His lips were cracked and dry. Rubbing his fingertips together felt like crumbling dried mud. This must be what it's like to die. The sounds around him reminded him of the mines of Stonehold Keep, the hammering and clanging of metal on stone kept Bastian awake. *What are they doing?* Bastian wondered. When the pounding stopped, Bastian's mind once again drifted off to sleep. He couldn't tell how long he was out, but every time he was awakened, it was by the sound of metal tools striking stone. He wouldn't have thought it possible, but Bastian was longing for the day his mind would stay asleep through the noise because at least then he would not have to hear the constant noise which made his head throb in sync with every strike.

After days of constant noise, it was finally quieter. Bastian was almost in a deep sleep when a conversation woke him.

"Sir, we have not found any more. That was the only stone."

"Impossible, keep digging. You there, did you find the one in the blood?" Dmitri barked orders and questions back to back, the impatience in his tone apparent. Bastian heard the clattering of tools again—the sound of a tantrum in progress. Dmitri had an infamous temper.

"No Sir, I'm sorry, I've lifted every stone I felt under the crimson water and none of them were the stone you seek."

"Well, KEEP LOOKING!" he shouted. Moments later, Bastian heard splashing in the pool behind him. What did they want with a rock? He didn't understand how it could possibly be of importance, or why there was only one of that specific rock.

"I told you not to throw it, and now it lies somewhere beneath this disgusting pool of tainted blood. You will never find it. We have to go before they send the hunters here to kill us all," the female voice scolded. Why did she sound so familiar? Bastian couldn't remember—his mind felt fuzzy and like it was missing time between sleep and wakefulness.

"Very well. We will find another way. Chain up our guest and take him with you, since I did promise him to you. I will wait here for Sophie." Bastian perked up at the mention of Sophie's name.

"Don't bring her with you, do what you must, then leave her here. I won't have her knowing where loverboy is until I'm finished with him." The smoke once again made his eyelids heavy and although the iron maiden was open now, Bastian could not see what was going on. The woman cut off a chunk of his hair. "I'll leave a piece of him for her to find. I know she will use a location spell; I would." The golden lock fell to the floor in front of the open sarcophagus.

Please, Sophie, whatever you do, don't come for me. Just let me go, Bastian pleaded silently. He only wanted to keep his family safe, and now she was going to be in danger because of him.

When Bastian woke again, he was in a sealed coffin made of pine—a scent he knew well. The bouncing motion, creaking wheels, and the clopping hooves told him the coffin was in a carriage. No matter how hard he tried to stay awake, sleep always came for him. He wondered if help was near and the woman was just keeping him quiet. A recurring thought passed through Bastian's every waking moment; *I'll make it home to you, Sophie. I promise.*

SEVENTEEN

SAMANTHA REND WAS OVERJOYED to have her girls at home with her. It had been too long since Sophie stayed the night, and Samantha had missed her daughter terribly. They sat on the floor in the living room surrounded by a fort of pillows and furs to keep the baby safe. Willow cooed and babbled with glee in Samantha's arms as she looked at the child and gasped, mouth open, and her eyes wide.

"Peek-a-boo!" Samantha exclaimed. Willow giggled and Samantha's normal expression resumed. She waited a few moments and then repeated the surprised emote again with the same result. "I could listen to this sound forever," Samantha said. "I remember when you were this little, you used to sing. It was the strangest thing to hear an infant singing—well actually, it was more like humming. You didn't know any words yet, but you had a beautiful melody. Once you sang in front of a seer and she called it a heartsong. She said only those with a deep connection to magical power can sing a heartsong at such an age." Samantha hummed what she could remember of the tune and Sophie recognized it.

"You used to hum it to me all the time, you never told me that story though," Sophie said.

"It was so long ago, you were so little then and I didn't want to influence you one way or another. If you came into magic, I wanted it to be your choice." Samantha reached over and gently squeezed Sophie's hand.

"If you wouldn't mind keeping an eye on Willow, I would love to lie down for a bit and get some rest. I'm exhausted."

"Of course I don't mind, dear." Samantha smiled as Sophie bent down to kiss Willow on the top of her head, then leaned over and kissed her mother's cheek.

In her childhood bedroom, Sophie stretched across her bed and closed her eyes. She thought of Xander and pictured him in her mind. *Where are you?* She thought.

We are still on the ship. Two more days and we should reach North-port, he replied. Sophie heard his voice in her mind and his face appeared clearly to her despite the distance between them. She groaned at his response. She forgot how long travel took when you couldn't turn into a dragon at will. Before she could respond, the low hum of magic took her away from the conversation. She launched up from the bed and raced across the room to her bag, upended it, and allowed the contents to scatter across her comforter. She grabbed the notebook which was aglow and hastily opened it to read word from Bastian.

Bastian is dying; his blood is slowly draining from his body. If you want to save him, you need to get here quickly. Sophie had no idea who wrote this message in Bastian's notebook. The Delacroix family was still on the ship, Xander said they still had two more days before they would reach Northport, but no matter who it was, she couldn't just leave Bastian to die.

"Mama!" Sophie ran down the stairs calling for Samantha.

"What is it? What's happened?" Samantha asked breathlessly.

"It's Bastian, I have to go. Please, go to the guild and hire a wet nurse for Willow and tell her I love her every day until I return." Sophie hugged her mother and then kissed Willow on the forehead. "I love you both." Sophie's eyes filled with tears as she rushed out the door.

In her dragon form, she flew straight to Highland Castle and rushed to her bedchamber. She grabbed one of Bastian's tunics and headed for the study. A locator spell would lead her directly to him, she only hoped she would make it in time. Sophie cut a piece of the tunic and grabbed the most complete map of the land she had. She took it to the spell altar where her pendulum hung. She placed the cloth into a stone bowl beside the pendulum and then poured in a sparkling blue liquid until the cloth was covered. Sophie submerged a white crystal into the bowl and began to chant. Nothing happened at first, but she kept chanting. She'd never used this particular spell to find anything farther away than the castle gardens, but she knew it would work. After a couple of minutes, the shutters on the window blew open and a gust of wind whistled through the room and put out the candles. The pendulum swung wildly in a circle around the map. Sophie chanted louder. The crystal seemed to suck up the swirling blue liquid and glowed a bright light blue. The stone illuminated the map and the chain of the pendulum stretched taut and the bob pointed to an exact location on it. Sophie marked the spot and then took the crystal out of the bowl. The candles re-ignited and the pendulum swung loosely once again. Sophie packed the crystal and the map into a small bag with some provisions and a change of clothes. She found Ezra in the library with a group of tinkers. They were discussing plans to make tasks like cleaning, travel, and combat more efficient.

"I'm so sorry to interrupt, Ezra," Sophie began as she walked into the room. Everyone stood and bowed to her.

"How can we be of service, Your Grace?" Ezra asked.

"Bastian is in trouble and he needs me. I must be away a little while longer. I might need backup, but I do not have time to contact the Dragon Council. I need you to contact them and let them know where I am headed. If I am not back in three days it means I need help." Sophie unrolled the map and showed Ezra the location she marked on it.

"Yes, My Queen. Let me make a copy of this location." Ezra walked across the room to a shelf containing a stack of maps. He found one that matched and brought it back to the table. Ezra laid the two maps next to each other and followed his fingers from Lapis Highland to the 'x' Sophie marked. He measured the distance on his map and marked it in the same place.

"I will contact them now and have them ready to deploy, if we do not see you by sundown on the third day, I will have them mobilize in that direction." He bowed to her.

"Thank you, Ezra. Hopefully, I will see you again in three days."

Sophie flew to the northern forest where the mark on her map indicated. The trees were thick and made it difficult to see any landmarks from overhead, so she landed in the first clearing she came to. The view from above told Sophie she was just south of the mark so she slipped on a dress and a pair of bloomers. The northern path from the clearing was not as trodden down as she expected. The sinking feeling she was walking into a trap returned as she neared a dark opening in the cliff ahead. She pulled out the blue crystal and pointed the end of it toward the cave. A beam of light shot out from the end of the stone and pointed directly into the mouth of the cave.

"Of course, I have to go in there," she groaned.

Sophie proceeded with caution, stepping carefully and quietly as she moved into the darkness. The beam of light from the crystal wound down the circular path to the bottom of the deep cavern. Sophie didn't have time to walk all the way down. She stepped off the ledge and plummeted through the darkness, counted to five and then muttered an incantation. She felt her weight leave her body as she floated like a feather to the floor of the cave.

She pointed the end of the gemstone around looking for a path forward. Moving in a circle, Sophie shined it toward every wall until finally, the light bent around a corner and revealed the narrow passageway. She squeezed through the best she could, the walls of the passage scraped against the skin on her buttocks and left it raw. Wincing from the pain, Sophie forced herself to keep moving forward. When she reached the opening, she couldn't believe what she saw; a pool of blood and a sar-cophagus.

"Bastian!" Sophie screamed rushing over to the circle. She thought she heard the faint sound of moaning coming from the sarcophagus, but it was the lock of golden hair lying in front of it that made her certain it was him inside. Sophie stepped to the side and inspected the lock. It required a key. She wasn't much of a lock-pick, but she might be able to spell it open. Sophie took the metal box in her hands and whispered an incantation. The familiar sound of magic, like a gust of wind, startled her. She looked at the lock; it was still closed tightly. She was about to start the incantation again when someone grabbed her from behind and an intense pain coursed through her body as the creature sunk its teeth into the side of her neck and drank deeply. Sophie became lightheaded and the tomb around her grew dark.

EIGHTEEN

THE HAIR ON THE back of Xander's neck stood on end. He closed his eyes and focused on Sophie. He saw the tomb, the blood, and Dmitri clearly before the scene faded into oblivion. Xander rushed to the captain.

"Can't you make this damned thing go faster?" he growled.

"We can only go as quickly as the wind will blow us, Sir," he replied.

Xander turned away from him with a huff and ran to the captain's quarters where Leon was sequestered with Agatha. "Commander Rend, Sophie is in trouble, we need to get to the tomb NOW!" Xander shouted as he banged on the captain's door.

Leon walked out onto the deck with a stern look on his face. "How could you possibly know Sophie is in trouble? She is supposed to be at home with her mother and daughter."

"I saw it. I had a vision of Dmitri. He has her. I don't know how, but we need to get there now, can't your witch conjure up the wind or something?"

"You will mind your tongue. Agatha is an elemental sorceress, not a 'witch' and she would be disinclined to grant your request should she hear you refer to her in such a manner," Leon stated gruffly. "I will speak to her about giving us a tailwind, but I have just received word that Blackwater is under attack—fledglings. My wife and Sophie's daughter are there. I need to trust you to do whatever it takes to keep Sophie safe, I need Sparrow and Eira with me to help with the fledglings. We will dock shortly in Blackwater and then you and your family will continue to Northport. I have sent word to have a horse and wagon waiting for you at the docks there. I'm counting on you." Leon clapped Xander on the shoulder. It was a gesture he did not expect.

"I will do everything in my power to bring her home." Xander watched as Leon walked back into the captain's room and closed the door behind him. Moments later, large white clouds gathered in the sky and a strong breeze blew from the south. It caught in the sails and the ship picked up speed.

"I'm coming, Sophie. Please be okay," Xander pleaded.

"So Mother and Father were right, it's Dmitri?" Serena startled him as she came up behind him.

"Yeah, but what I don't understand is *how*? If there's no way Bastian would wake him, especially now with Willow to protect. None of us could have done it because we were all stuck on the island until now. So how could our blood have made it to him?" Xander asked.

"Oh no..."Serena began to speak but her voice trailed off, the weight of realization on her face.

"What?"

"I think it's my fault," she whispered.

"How could it possibly be?"

"Remember how Elizandra and I dated after Bastian left?"

"Yeah, but what's—

"As a gift on our one-year anniversary, we exchanged vials of blood. It was supposed to be a token of our undying love," Serena interrupted. "Right after, she was gone. She said she was going to find a way to end the curse on the island so we could travel the world together..." Xander watched the sadness on his sister's face turn to anger. "Who knew all she wanted was to get back at Bastian?" Serena finished.

"So you think Elizandra used your blood to wake Dmitri in order to frame Bastian?" Xander asked.

"What else could it be? There's something else you should know about her." Serena looked at Xander nervously.

"What is it?"

"The whole time she was on the island of Immernacht, she was learning magic. She mostly studied necromancy," Serena told him.

"Like bringing dead people back to life?" Xander asked.

"Just communicating with the dead from what I saw, but what if she has been talking to Dmitri this whole time?"

"Dmitri wasn't dead though, but I guess maybe she could still learn to communicate with the undead just as easily. So, he uses her to get back at us, but I don't understand what she gets out of it."

"Isn't it obvious? She gets Bastian. I think we need to tell Mother and Father," Serena said.

"We? Oh no… that's a conversation I do not wish to be inserted into, but let me know how it goes."

"Really, Xander? You're an ass. Are you really going to make me do it alone?"

"Dear sister, how else will you learn?" Xander cracked a smile and he could tell Serena wanted to punch him, but she sighed and nodded to him before making her way to the bow of the ship where Arturo and Natalia stood gazing out over the ocean waves. Xander sat down and focused on Sophie. He couldn't see her, but he could hear soft whimpers as if she were having a nightmare. *Hang in there, Sophie, I'm on my way. I wish you could let me know you're alright.* Xander thought.

After everyone else but the captain and the lookout were asleep, Xander walked to the bow of the ship and looked up at the stars. Immernacht was covered in perpetual storm so it was very rare the stars peeked through. Here, the sky was clear and the stars looked like diamonds scattered across black velvet. One star shined bigger and brighter than all the rest and Xander recalled the songs Natalia would sing to them, and the fairy tales she read them when he and Serena were young. He gazed at the star and whispered a wish to the celestial beings above, should they see fit to grant him this one wish, he didn't care about his own fate. "Please let Sophie be okay," he whispered.

"You couldn't sleep either?" Xander startled and turned to see Natalia gracefully gliding up behind him.

"I don't think I will ever get the hang of sleeping on a ship. It looks like you have quite a pair of sea legs though, so what is it keeping you awake?" Xander asked.

"Serena told us about Elizandra. I never thought she would betray our family like this. We were so good to her, we didn't turn her away, or make her live on the streets. Goddess knows we didn't even feed on her after Bastian left, we just let her stay and enjoy the life of a princess at court." Natalia recalled. "Anyway, I just came to tell you the captain says we should make it to Blackwater by sunrise, and Northport is only another hour or two more. Your father has decided if we get the opportunity to kill Dmitri, we should take it. He said he has lived almost three lifetimes and he will gladly take the eternal rest to ensure our safety."

Xander looked at her in shock. "No, he can't, we'll find another way," he objected.

"I feel the same way, but you know your father, I can only hope reason takes over his madness when we arrive at the tomb. I'll keep bending his ear about it."

"Thank you, mother," Xander said, unable to hide his fear. Natalia placed a hand on his shoulder.

"Do not let this infatuation with Sophie cloud your judgment. Bastian is your brother and If he is down there with Dmitri we have to do all we can to save him. We will need you," Natalia warned.

"Bastian will have you, Father, and Serena. Sophie will have no one. If we all have to make a choice then I will save Sophie knowing Bastian will be okay."

"Family should be your priority, how would you feel if Bastian died while you were rescuing Sophie?"

"How would Bastian feel about me if he lives, knowing I could have saved Sophie and didn't?" Xander asked. Natalia gave him a disappointed look and walked away without another word. Xander decided he would forgive her for this conversation, surely the stress was affecting his mother as much as it was himself. He stood there at the bow for a few moments longer and finally decided he should try to get some sleep.

Xander was awakened by a loud thud as the ship docked in Blackwater. Leon, the hunters, Agatha, and some of the crew disembarked, leaving them with half a crew and the captain. Xander and Commander Rend exchanged a glance; an unspoken acknowledgment of their agreement. When the ship departed again, Xander kept his eyes fixed to the north, counting the seconds until they docked again. Every moment felt like an hour on the last leg of the trip. It seemed the faster he wanted time to pass, the slower it did. His heart twisted and ached with not only worry but a longing for Sophie he couldn't describe. *Rescue Sophie, make sure Bastian is safe, then go somewhere far away*, Xander thought. His plan would only hurt himself, but he could live with his choice if it meant Sophie would be happy.

As soon as the gangplank dropped in Northport, Xander wanted to run to the tomb, but he didn't know the exact location so he closed his eyes and focused on Sophie. He pictured her beautiful smile, and the way her freckles glittered like golden stars across her nose in the candlelight. Her flame-red curls appeared vividly, contrasted against a dark green dress. The thought of her made his heart feel like it was going to explode. Xander felt their blood connection pulling him toward her like a magnet. He kept her at the front of his mind as he broke into a sprint. He was moving so quickly that to anyone else, he might look like no more than a gust of wind or a shadow moving through the trees. He didn't know how long it would take the others to catch up, Natalia and Serena were not blessed with vampiric speed and he knew Arturo would not leave them alone.

Xander's connection to Sophie did not lead him to the cave, but rather, a small cabin in the middle of nowhere. It was mostly reclaimed by nature; covered in a thick moss and shrouded by trailing ivy. Without care, Xander shouldered open the door to see Sophie on her knees, hovering over an old woman's body. Sophie's shoulders heaved as she sobbed quietly.

"Sophie," Xander called to her as he stepped inside and when she looked up at him, he saw blood spilling down her chin and all over the woman's neck. "Oh no, no no no..." Xander's voice trailed off as he rushed over to kneel beside her. He put his arm around Sophie's shoulders and held her, not knowing what to say. He expected Dmitri to use her against them, but he didn't expect him to *turn* her. He thought of what his mother told him on the ship about Arturo saying they should kill Dmitri if given the chance. *I hope Dmitri is far away. If he dies now, so does Sophie, her life tied to his through the maker's bond.* The thought made the familiar heat of fury rise into his face.

"They locked me in here with her. Dmitri looked at both of us and told us not to leave until my transition was complete. I didn't know what he meant, she and I were here all night together, but this morning I was so hungry. It was such an intense hunger and when she came near me all I could hear was the beating of her heart. I told her I was hungry and she must have seen the way I looked at her because she seemed frightened." Sophie looked at the woman she had cradled in her arms and tears fell from her cheeks. "I killed her. I ripped open her throat and drank her blood."

Xander stood and then reached down and helped Sophie to her feet. "Hey, it's going to be okay. I can help you. I am so sorry this happened to you and he left you here alone, but I'm here now." He took her hand in his and gripped it firmly, reassuring her she would be safe. "Did you see Bastian?" he asked.

"I'm not sure. I thought there was someone in the sarcophagus but it was locked and before I could spell it open I was attacked," she said.

"We need to get back to the tomb. Do you know how to get there?"

"I think I can find it again." Sophie moved toward the door but as soon as she stepped into the beam of sunlight peeking through the crack, her skin began to burn and sizzle. She screamed in pain and before she could take a step back, Xander covered her with a blanket and pulled her backward out of the rays.

"I'm spelled to be immune to the sun, but you aren't. You can't leave until nightfall. Even under this blanket, the rays can still penetrate your skin. I'll stay with you." Xander removed the blanket from Sophie's face, but left it over her shoulders as he looked into her eyes. *Gods why did she have to be so beautiful? Even now, with the woman's dark red blood staining her face and hair, to him, she looked like a celestial from the stars above.*

Sophie reached up and tenderly swept a lock of his dark brown hair away from his face so she could see his eyes. He shivered at her touch. She gently ran her fingertips down his jawbone. He groaned with equal parts pleasure and guilt as Sophie's fingers traveled behind his neck and she pulled his head forward and pressed her lips to his passionately. His willpower broke in the heat of the moment and he kissed her back. Their lips only parted when Sophie reached her hands under his tunic and pulled it up over his head. She quickly pulled off the blood-stained dress she had on and pressed her body against his as her hands roamed up his back holding him tightly. He groaned as his body responded to her touch, showing her how much he wanted her. *I'm going to regret this,* he thought as he took a step back.

"Stop, we can't. Bastian... You—I mean," he fumbled his words. "Your emotions are heightened, you just fed, it's like being drunk and Bastian is still out there, we need to make a plan." Xander broke away from her and grabbed his tunic. He handed it to Sophie and then picked up her dress. "Put this on, I'm going to rinse this out for you and fetch some water to clean up in here. I'll be right back," he said. Sophie nodded as her eyes moved over Xander's bare chest.

Making sure Sophie was away from the door, Xander stepped outside and walked to the left side of the cabin to an old stone well with a little wooden roof over it. He peered down into the darkness, and then turned the crank to draw up the bucket, the whole time, berating himself for stopping Sophie. She wanted him right now because she was high on the blood of her first kill. The feeling could last for days, even weeks sometimes for new vampires. With blood lust, comes primal lust. Feeding and fucking were often one and the same. He pushed the needful thoughts deep down and buried them beneath the nagging sense of loyalty he felt to his brother. Finally, the windlass stopped turning.

The water in the bucket looked clean enough, he'd been afraid the well would be dry or full of algae, but neither was the case. Liquid sloshed from the bucket as Xander carried it inside, he plugged the sink with a dish rag the previous occupant left hanging across the side of the washtub. After putting Sophie's dress in the sink to soak, he carried the body of the old woman outside and laid her to the right of the house out of sight. Next, he washed up the drops of blood on the floor, scrubbed the stain from Sophie's dress, and hung it to dry outside. When he was finished it was like nothing had happened at all.

"Thank you for helping me," Sophie said. She sat down on the old sofa and motioned for Xander to come sit beside her. "What am I going to do?" she asked.

"What do you mean?" I can't go home to Willow like this." Sophie leaned over and rested her head on Xander's shoulder.

"Of course you can. You'll just have to feed more often than Bastian does because you're so new to it. I mean, Bastian manages just fine around Willow, I have faith you can too," Xander said.

"He's had years of practice being a vampire. He can control his hunger, it doesn't control him. I tried my best not to kill this woman, but once the warm blood pulsed into my mouth with every beat of her heart it became sweeter and I couldn't stop. What happens if I wake up hungry and I'm alone with Willow? I couldn't live with myself if I hurt her."

Xander cupped Sophie's face with the palm of his hand. "We will NOT let that happen. I promise you can fight this urge and control it." Xander relaxed once more, letting Sophie lay her head back on his shoulder. He draped his arm around her and comforted her as best he could.

"What was it like growing up on Immernacht, and wat does the name mean? It seems like such a strange name for a town." Sophie asked.

"Immernacht means 'always night'. It was almost always dark there because of the storm. Even when the sun shined brightly in your sky, ours was gray and completely covered by clouds. As a child, my mom insisted we eat a lot of mushrooms. The health benefits the sun provides, can also be found in the fungus. I love them, but Bastian *hated* mushrooms. I guess it was a good thing he could leave the island and the sun didn't affect him the way it did us." Xander smiled as his fingertips lightly brushed up and down Sophie's arm. "Serena, Bastian, and I used to play outside all the time. We had friends for a number of years, until the whispers began.

One parent would tell another who we were and then one by one, our friends were no longer allowed to play with us."

"How awful. I'm sorry."

"It's okay, I guess. At least we had each other. What about you, did you have any childhood friends?" Xander asked.

"I did. His name was Gabe," she replied.

"Was?"

"He died in battle. We grew up together. He and I used to climb this old willow tree in the woods by his house. He liked to play in the creek and fish as I leaned against the trunk of the tree reading. He was my best friend and my first kiss, but by the time I realized my feelings for him were deeper than friendship, it was too late, he was engaged to someone else," she said.

"I can't imagine, it must have broken your heart."

"It did. I met Bastian the night I found out about the engagement and I drank too much, used him to make Gabe jealous, then woke up in Bastian's bed the next morning. Not the best thing a girl can do for her reputation, but I am queen of Lapis Highland, and those who serve me, do so because they want to, not because they believe I have some divine right to rule, so my virtue is never questioned."

"I guess it worked out in the end, you and Bastian stayed together and now you have Willow."

"Yes, but he also lied to me. He didn't tell me he had a wife."

"It wasn't really a *lie*," Xander disagreed.

"A lie of omission is still dishonesty."

Xander sighed. "While he may not be an open book, Bastian loves you, and even though you're upset with him right now, I know you love him too."

Sophie rolled her eyes. *Why does he have to be right?*

When it was dark enough for Sophie to leave the cabin, Xander retrieved her dress from outside. She looked so good wearing only his white tunic, he thought about hanging onto the dress a little longer. He stood in the doorway watching her walk about the living room, picking up the woman's old knick-knacks to inspect them. When she reached for something on the shelf, his tunic raised and he admired the curve of her hips, and when her firm round cheeks peeked out from beneath his shirt it made his breath stop. *Why did she have to be so perfect?* He hated he'd been stuck on Immernacht and unable to meet her first. Fate was cruel to have his brother fall for her, too. What were the odds, of all the girls Bastian could have met at the ball, it had to be *his fated mate.*

"Is that my dress?" Sophie asked as her eyes landed on him.

"Yes, sorry, I was just–"

"Staring? I know." She walked over and stood so close to him their bodies almost touched. Sophie took the dress from his hand, letting her fingers linger on his as she looked up at him.

"Mind turning around so I can change?" Sophie asked playfully.

He was about to tell her he would rather watch, but he bit his tongue as he turned his back to her instead to remind himself the flirtation wasn't real. Although seeing women in their natural form was as normal to him as breathing, he obliged only because she asked him to. Besides, he was pretty sure Sophie couldn't stand him at all before. To act on his desire now would be taking advantage of her in a vulnerable state and she would surely go back to hating him for it later. Sophie handed back his tunic and he could feel her eyes on him as he slipped it over his head. He decided it best not to acknowledge her obvious desire as he knew it had more to do with her newly acquired vampire drive than it had to do with him.

"You ready?" he asked.

"Yes, I'm ready." Sophie responded and together, they stepped outside into the night. Her eyes suddenly snapped to the trees above and then to one path through the forest, then another. Xander knew she was taking in the overload of her heightened senses. He too heard the hoot of the owl and smelled the various creatures hiding in the foliage nearby.

"It can be a little overwhelming your first time. You okay?" he asked. Xander offered his hand to her and she took it as they began walking down a path through the woods.

Sophie led him in the direction she thought was northeast, but without the crystal, or the map she wasn't certain of anything. It seemed they had been walking for miles when they finally reached the cavern just on the other side of the clearing. Sophie was thankful vampires could see in the dark, otherwise she would have never found her way out of the woods.

"Sophie, wai-" Xander tried to call for her to wait as she rushed into the clearing without caution, but someone grabbed his shoulder and he froze mid-sentence.

NINETEEN

Sophie was about to make her way to the mouth of the cave when she heard Xander begin to call for her, but an eerie moment of silence interrupted and it put her on edge. Sophie whirled around and let out a sigh of relief as she watched Arturo pull Xander into a hug.

"Thank goodness you found Sophie!" Arturo said.

"Yeah, we have a problem though," Xander said. Arturo and Natalia both looked at Sophie taking note of the changes in her; the contrast of her hair which was now a richer, darker, red against her skin, the way her eyes had a new glow about them, and the glint of two elongated incisors becoming visible when she smiled nervously.

"Tell me you weren't this stupid after the agreement we just reached for our freedom from the dreadful island." Arturo's eyes flashed in anger at Xander.

"No! I mean, it wasn't him. It was Dmitri," Sophie said rushing over to them.

"Why would he turn you and let you go?"

"He said it was to ensure his survival," Sophie explained. Natalia stepped forward; the bottom of her dress red with blood, as was her right arm from her elbow to her fingertips. Sophie was about to ask what happened when Arturo reached a realization.

"Unfortunately, he might be right. No one cares about my life, I have lived a long time. He was likely informed of the guild's involvement with the hunters and knew Leon wouldn't hesitate to kill him, even if it meant killing me; but if it would mean killing *you*, well, there are at least a dozen people who would stand in his way."

"Arturo, don't think for one second you would have no one in your corner. You have your family, which includes me, and If I can help it, nothing will happen to you either. We will find a way to stop Dmitri that doesn't involve killing anyone."

Arturo moved toward Sophie and reached for a lock of her hair. There was sadness in his eyes as he inspected her face. *Was he searching for a hint of emotion?* Sophie wondered. He opened his arms for her, letting Sophie close the distance. "I'm so sorry he did this to you. Just know, we are here for you—anything you need."

"Thank you," Sophie replied.

"Have you been inside the tomb yet? Was Bastian there?" Xander interrupted. His eyes moved between Arturo and Natalia.

"It was empty. Except for this." Natalia held up a green rock with red cracks running through it.

"What is that?" Sophie asked.

"I'm not sure, but one of my gifts is the ability to detect magical items. I saw it shimmering beneath the pool of blood. The walls of the tomb looked like miners had been digging for something important. I'm guessing this is what they were after." Natalia placed the stone into a pouch on her belt.

"I hate to cut the reunion short, but we need to get to Blackwater to help with the fledgling attack." Arturo said.

"The what attack?" Sophie's eyes widened as she looked from Arturo to Xander.

"Blackwater was under attack by fledglings, newly-turned vampires that have been allowed to feast to their hearts' content, trapped in perpetual blood lust. It's the reason Leon isn't with us," Arturo explained.

"Xander, why didn't you tell me?" Sophie demanded.

"Because when you tried to leave, the sun hurt you. I knew you'd risk your life to get there if I told you of the danger, but we can go now. I have vampiric speed, I can carry you. The others can catch up."

"No need. I can take all of you; get ready for a crash course in dragon riding," Sophie said. She took a few steps back and shifted into her dragon form. Her dress ripped as her body grew larger and covered in fiery red scales. The vampires climbed onto Sophie's back when the transition was complete and held on tightly to whatever scale or horn they could grab. Sophie backed up to the tree line to ascend from the clearing without smacking into every tree branch on the way up. She nervously looked down every now and then. With little feeling in her scales, she had to make sure no one was plummeting to the ground as she flew.

Sophie landed on the beach of Blackwater less than an hour later. She shifted back to her human form and cast her clothing spell. It was the best she could do for now. They took off toward the western gate of the city but before they got inside, Sophie stopped and looked around, sniffing the air, her eyes grew bloodshot and a deep growl escaped her throat.

"It's the scent of blood, It's too much for her," Xander said.

"Maybe we should—Sophie, no!" Serena said, but it was too late. Sophie was no longer thinking of anything but the satisfaction of warm life fluid flowing across her lips like cream. The man she had spotted was nursing a bloody nose as he stumbled out of the Loose Anchor. Sophie was on him in an instant. She sank her teeth deep into his neck and drank from him, savoring the spicy whiskey-flavored nectar. A feeling of euphoria washed over her as she gasped, coming up for a breath of air. Suddenly, she felt herself being jerked backward as Xander grabbed her by the shoulder and tried to pull her off of the man, but her grip on him was iron-tight.

"You're going to kill him, Stop!" When Xander was finally able to break Sophie's hold on him, the man crumpled lifelessly to the ground. Sophie's eyes, which had been scarlet with frenzy, were now beginning to resume their normal green hue.

She looked down at the man as her breathing slowed. No, *not again.* Sophie thought as she dropped to the ground beside him. She placed her hand on the man's chest waiting for it to rise and fall, but it remained still. "I killed him, he's dead." Sophie stared at him in horror as the realization hit. Sorrow weighed her down like a boulder on her chest. The thought of her mother looking at her with disappointment filled her with shame, but when she thought about Willow, Sophie's heart broke. She was a monster, and Willow would be terrified of her—and with good reason. Would she ever be able to see them again? What about her father, what would he think? She wondered if Leon would have left her trapped on Immernacht if this had happened sooner. Maybe imprisonment was what she deserved.

"I can't go with you, I need to go to Ophay. Akiri can help me, she can lock me in her dungeon. I can't be near my family like this, not yet. Just make sure Willow is safe, and my mom and dad," Sophie pleaded.

"Serena, go with her, please. We will find Leon and make sure everyone is okay here," Xander promised.

Sophie turned and led Serena through the forest, south toward the town of Ophay. It was taking them so much longer than Sophie expected because she had to keep stopping to wait for Serena to catch up.

"I see you got vampire speed, what else did you get?" Serena asked with a hint of jealousy in her voice.

"Vampire hunger," Sophie joked. She thought she heard Serena chuckle but she couldn't be sure. She recalled their conversation about Elizandra and anger bubbled up inside her. If there was any chance she and Serena were going to be friends, she needed to get something off her chest. Sophie stopped and put out her hand to halt Serena. "I need to ask you something." Serena's eyes widened upon hearing Sophie's tone. "Why did you not tell me the whole truth about Elizandra; how Bastian only married the girl to save her from her horrible father? Instead, you let me think he was just unfaithful."

Serena let out a sigh and shook her head. "I can't believe Xander told you when it's so obvious he's in love with you himself."

"He is not *in love* with me. He—" Sophie wondered if she should share the fact Xander believed they were fated to be together. He didn't know her well enough to love her, but then what was it?

"He what?" Serena urged.

"Never mind, he's just not," Sophie replied, trudging forward with slow careful steps so Serena could keep up.

"I'm angry with Bastian. I thought if you were angry at him too then I wouldn't be alone in my misery. If I could make you hate him, I thought we could, I don't know... bond over our anger and I would have a friend. I can't share anything with anyone at home because they all *love* Bastian. He can do no wrong. But he DID! He married Elizandra and then just left her. He went to the masquerade ball in Ledora, met you, and then it was like his wife didn't exist. She was heartbroken. She always thought maybe he would love her eventually. It wasn't Bastian who loved her though—it was me." Serena wiped a tear from her face. "Anyway, she left and might be the reason Dmitri is awake and Bastian is gone. I feel really guilty."

"Wait, would she hurt Bastian?"

"She was angry, but she loved him. I doubt she could do it herself, but Dmitri would have no problem hurting him...or worse," Serena replied.

"She's probably keeping him alive, we need to find him, but first, I have to learn to control this urge or I'll end up murdering everyone along the way." Sophie dashed forward again and didn't stop until she reached the tree line at the edge of Ophay.

The road was blocked off to deter wagons from getting too close to town and two guards waited near the entrance with blood-covered stakes firmly in their grasp. Two dragons stood at their backs scanning the perimeter and the bodies of several fledglings lay piled to the side of the path. Sophie and Serena approached with caution. The dragons were already taller than the guards, Sophie was shocked by how much they had grown since the last time she saw them. The dragons let out a roar and breathed fire in their direction as they neared. Serena shrieked and backed away, but Sophie stood her ground.

"Whoa, hey..." She spoke calmly to the dragons as she put her hands up. Then she looked at the guards. "I'm Queen Sophie of Lapis Highland, I'm here to see Akiri; she's my friend."

"I don't care who you are, because of the recent attack in Blackwater, Akiri said to kill all vampires on sight. The other ones didn't talk though," one of the guards said, jerking his head toward the pile of bodies, "so I'm giving you the chance to turn around and go back where you came from."

"I'm afraid I can't. I need to see Akiri," Sophie insisted.

"Come on, ladies, you're both real pretty and I'd hate to have to stake ya, or feed you to these guys," he jabbed his thumb in the direction of the dragons. "Just go back to Blackwater."

Serena walked closer with her hands raised. She looked directly at the guard who was doing all the talking and their eyes met. The man looked as if he were suddenly unable to form words. She looked at the other guard and he did the same.

"You are going to let us in," she said to the one in charge, "and *you* are going to take us to Akiri," she told the other.

The head guard moved to the side and his partner turned and motioned for them to follow him through the barricade.

"How?" Sophie whispered.

"Maybe I'll teach you once we get you settled."

They walked to the edge of the town almost to the temple. Sophie could feel the eyes of the townsfolk following them as they passed by. When Sophie finally saw Akiri, a flood of relief washed over her as she called her name and waved her over. Akiri stopped short when she saw the state of her friend. She stepped forward with caution and Sophie saw the sadness in her eyes, or was it pity? She couldn't tell.

"Oh Sophie, who did this to you?" Akiri asked, looking at the blood covering her chin and part of her chest.

"It's a long story. I need your help. Do you have a free cell in the dungeon?" Sophie asked.

"Yeah, why?"

"I need you to lock me in for a while," Sophie told her.

"Sophie, lock you up? What do you mean, why?"

"The smell of blood sends me into some kind of frenzy and I can't stop, when I'm near a human, all I can hear is the pumping of their heart." Sophie's eyes wandered to Akiri's chest, the rhythmic thumping called to her like a siren's song. "I need to learn to control my hunger," Sophie looked down at the ground in shame. She hated she couldn't trust herself around her friends, or her family, and she knew the only reason she could right now was because she'd just fed on that poor man leaving the Loose Anchor.

"I'm going to head back and see how things are going, I'll bring Xander once we are finished in Blackwater." Serena looked at Akiri, "Are you going to be okay to take her from here?"

"Yes, we'll be okay," Akiri replied.

The cell inside the lair was not what Sophie expected. It looked like a room at the guild inn. Against the southern wall stood a large bed with a fluffy goose-down comforter and pillows dressed with the softest fabric covers Sophie had ever felt. On the floor beside the bed was a large fur to keep her feet warm from the cold stone floor. Sophie had been in the cell for hours and would have enjoyed the room more if not for the intense hunger gnawing at her from the inside. Her stomach was in knots. Sophie wanted to yell for Akiri, or someone, to let her out but that was the opposite of control. She looked up at the cavern ceiling and the stalactites hanging from it like icicles. She groaned in frustration as she paced across the room. No one came to visit or brought her a meal until the next day.

Ugh, finally! Sophie thought as she rushed over to the bars. Akiri came into view with a small chalice of blood on a baker's peel. She stretched the handle out so the chalice was in front of the food service slide in the cell door. Sophie knew Akiri was afraid to get close to her, knowing the smell from the cup could set off a bloodlust within her. Sophie opened the serving window and took the chalice from the wooden paddle. It was nearly empty, filled only a third of the way.

"This isn't enough. I am so hungry," Sophie complained.

"You need to learn moderation. We will start with this amount, three times a day, and then increase it to half a cup twice a day. When you are ready for one full cup we should be able to stretch it to one cup every two days. Xander made a schedule for me to follow."

"Wait, so how long do I have to be locked up in here?" Sophie asked.

"I'm not sure. The schedule Xander gave me goes until the new moon," Akiri replied.

"A whole moon cycle? Are you kidding me? I can't stay in here that long!" Sophie objected.

"I'm sorry, the alternative is: you kill people, maybe your mother, or Willow. This is the safer option, wouldn't you agree?"

"We have to track down Dmitri, and find Bastian, I don't have time for moderation."

"Those things are going to have to wait, or you can work harder to fight your urges and then maybe it won't take a full moon cycle."

Sophie didn't want to admit it, but Akiri was right. She thought about the man she attacked outside the Loose Anchor. She caught herself wondering if he had a family. Did his children expect him to stumble home to tuck them in, and plant his whiskey-scented kisses on their foreheads? Did his wife stay awake waiting for his safe return? Sophie tried to push the sorrow away, but a final thought intruded; *What if the fledglings got to his children before they even realized their father wasn't coming home?* She tried her best to block out the ramblings racing through her mind and eventually, she drifted off to sleep.

"Sophie, it's time to eat." The voice that roused her was almost a seductive whisper. She rubbed her eyes as she sat up and looked toward the sound. Xander held her chalice out to her through the serving window. Sophie got out of bed and crossed the room in the blink of an eye. She gulped the blood down eagerly as she looked back to Xander; a lock of his dark brown hair curled softly in front of his eye. Sophie tried to reach through the bars to sweep it to the side, but her arm touched the iron and began to sizzle. Searing pain coursed through her.

"What the hell?" Sophie jerked her arm back, cradling it to her chest. The iron left a raw and blistering wound on her skin and as she looked at it, the blisters closed, and her raw skin faded to pink and healed on its own.

"Akiri infused the iron with sunlight using a spell, if any vampire touches it, they burn as they would in the sun," Xander explained.

"Wow." Sophie turned her arm over still in a state of disbelief.

"Yeah, we weren't sure if you would get vampire strength, we couldn't risk you tearing the door off the hinges."

"I thought you would have gone after Dmitri by now," Sophie said.

"We have a plan to trap him on Immernacht. Your father has agreed to put the barrier back up over the island so Dmitri will never escape. We stayed here to help Commander Rend dispose of the dead and clean up the city. Quid pro quo."

Sophie nodded. "I wish I could touch you right now," she admitted as she looked into his eyes.

"I don't know what to say. Part of me wishes we could just run away together, but you have Willow, and the rational part of me knows I would lose my brother. We *are* fated, but maybe it just means I will always be in your life no matter what." Xander turned his eyes away as if it hurt to look at her. "I have to go, I'll come back before we leave to say goodbye."

Sophie wanted to ask him to stay, but she had the feeling he would refuse even if she weren't locked in a cell.

"Before I go, close your eyes," Xander said. Sophie did as he asked. A soft light grew brighter as a dream-like vision began. They were in a strange place, it seemed like a new world with magic like she had never seen. Storefront signs flashed and glowed, demanding the attention of passersby as they made their way down the walking paths made of lightly colored stone. Oddly shaped metal carriages moved down the smooth flat streets without the need for horses. Sophie and Xander held hands as they strolled through the busy square. Their clothing was peculiar; Sophie wore tightly fitted trousers tapered at the ankle and bearing a small pocket on each side of her bottom, her top was ill-fitted and cut off to expose her midriff. Her hair was darker now, but the reddish brown ringlets still hung to the middle of her back. Xander's trousers were similar to hers but looked more comfortable and loosely fit than hers. He wore a strange tunic with short sleeves. His dark brown hair made his green eyes shine through the darkness.

New and different music filled the air and people dressed in strange costumes passed them on their way through the city. It was like a masquerade ball, but instead of keeping to the castle, the guests roamed the streets singing and dancing. Xander swept her off her feet and twirled around. She looked into his eyes as he lowered her to his chest until their lips met. She felt his fingers slide up her neck to the back of her head as he kissed her passionately. Just like that, the dream began to fade. When she opened her eyes the cell reappeared and she was sad to see the iron bars standing between her and Xander.

"We *will* be happy. This is proof. I see visions of us every day, we will have a long and happy future as the world changes in unimaginable ways. We will survive long after this world is gone, but for now, we need to focus on finding Bastian and stopping Dmitri," he said.

Xander's gaze lingered as he backed away from the cell and then turned down the dark corridor and disappeared. She crawled back into her bed, replaying Xander's vision in her mind. She thought about his strong hand on the back of her head, pulling her into a kiss; his fingers gently tangled in her hair. She imagined them making their way to a dark alley as the music and party in the streets continued. She dreamed about his other hand reaching down and lifting her thigh to his hip as he pushed against her. Sophie wondered what it would be like to slip her hand down his trousers and free the hard erection pressing against her so firmly and what it would feel like when Xander slid it inside of her. She longed for him to hold her against his bare skin and feel his heart beat in time with hers.

Sophie moaned Xander's name as she slid two fingers inside her wet center and worked them in and out. She put the tip of her middle finger on the other hand into her mouth then swirled the moist fingertip across the nipple of her breast trying to emulate her daydream. Her nipple hardened at the wet touch and she squeezed it to give it the sensation of a nibble. Her hips moved up and down as her fingers danced inside her; in and out, and deeper until she felt an explosion of satisfaction and bliss. When it was over, Sophie dreaded opening her eyes, because she knew Xander would be gone and she would still be locked in a cell alone.

TWENTY

A HOWLING WIND SHOOK the trees violently, and torrential rain battered the ground. Lightning ripped through the sky, illuminating the darkness for only a moment. "Which way?" Two paths; one to the right, and one to the left, gave him pause. The sound of hooves neared from behind. He had to choose. Bastian quickly darted left because the path seemed to curve downhill and he thought it would, no doubt, allow him to run faster. He made it halfway down the hill before the toe of his boot caught under a raised root and his legs seemed to tangle beneath him. A searing pain shot up to his hip as the hoofbeats drew near.

"You thought you could escape?" Dmitri's voice boomed, followed by a wicked laugh. The vampire dismounted his horse and took careful steps down the hill. Looming over him, Dmitri shook his head. "What a waste." He drew his sword and raised it high above his shoulder, and striking it down on Bastian's neck.

Bastian's eyes snapped open, and he gasped for breath inside the wooden box. He wanted to bring his hands to his neck just to make sure it had been a dream, but the space was too confined for him to lift his hands.

He was drenched in sweat, smelled like death, and the urge to urinate weighed on his bladder. How long had he been in the box? He wasn't sure because moments of consciousness came and went and time blurred together like old memories.

He knew he was now on a ship because the gentle rocking of ocean waves made the need to relieve himself greater. At least the travel was smooth now. The wagon had not been kind, and he was certain his entire body was bruised from being jostled around inside the hard wooden box. Bastian balled his fist and banged on the side of the box as hard as he could.

"HELP!" He tried to yell, but his voice came out raspy and quiet from lack of water. He heard no sound other than the lapping of the waves, not even footsteps on the deck. He wondered if it was nighttime, which would mean the crew was asleep. Usually, some of the crew slept in the cargo hold and surely they would hear him. He banged louder and tried to scream again. This time, he heard footsteps coming toward the box.

"We're almost home. Sleep now," cooed a female voice. The smell of sweet violets surrounded him and the box filled with smoke too dark to see. Bastian drifted off once more.

Bastian waited patiently at the altar next to Xander. The musician playing the harp paused briefly as the double doors to the ballroom opened. A beautiful woman in a white gown appeared in the doorway and the musician began playing the traditional wedding song as she took the first step onto the aisle. One step at a time, she glided to the altar. Bastian could not take his eyes off of her. The bride handed her bouquet to Serena so she could join hands with Bastian.

He lifted her veil and marveled at her beautiful, deep brown eyes and her chestnut skin. Tendrils of her long black hair framed her face in springy curls where normally her hair was straight. Her lips were the color of raspberries in the summer. 'No, this is wrong. Why am I dreaming of Elizandra?

I love Sophie.' Bastian's conscious mind tried to fight the dream. He tried to picture Sophie's face. It was her he wanted to marry. SHE should be his wife. The dream was strong and persisted through the fight from Bastian's heart.

Bastian carried her in his arms, across the threshold of Castle Delacroix. When he set her on her feet, Elizandra wrapped her arms around his neck and pulled him into a passionate kiss. Her smile beamed as she looked up at him with stars in her eyes. Their friends and family were waiting for them, gathered in the ballroom they barely ever used.

They drank, feasted, and danced the night away, celebrating the beginning of their great love story. 'No, this isn't how it happened. Stop.' The voice was disembodied, almost like a whisper from the Gods. Bastian looked around the ballroom. He pushed through the crowd from one side to the other and back again, searching for something—no, someone; but who was he searching for? His mind couldn't remember. Maybe he would know when he saw her. The crowd parted, and he saw fiery red curls hanging down the back of a form-fitted green dress. 'It's her,' Bastian thought. He tried to walk toward her but it seemed every step he took he was farther away than before until the image of her slipped away entirely. 'No, Sophie...' Sophie, that was her name. How did he know her?

Elizandra appeared in front of him and placed her hands on his shoulders. He looked down to see his hands were on her waist. They were dancing. All his thoughts melted away as he looked at his wife. They were married.

"I am yours, and you are mine," she said. Bastian twirled her and leaned her back into a dip, brushing his lips against hers as he guided her back up. "I love you, and you love only me," she said.

"Only you," Bastian repeated.

TWENTY-ONE

SNOW... IT WAS STARTING to snow and the sky was a depressing gray. Sparrow grumbled complaints under his breath as they made it out of the Stonehold Mountains. Eira seemed unbothered by the change in temperature. Their search began in the south by the cliffside, then Torzana, Ophay, and Blackwater. They found a few stray fledglings they had to deal with, but no sign of Dmitri, or Bastian. Velen Shrike, Leon's right hand, and Beric also accompanied them. Sparrow knew it was to make sure Dmitri was not harmed, and he didn't know how he felt about it.

Sparrow tried not to let his anger about it show. If he got the chance to take out the vampire responsible for the death of his brothers, he was going to take it. He knew what it meant, though. Not only would he make a lifelong enemy of Leon, but the Delacroix as well. Sparrow wanted to kill all the vampires, and he suspected Eira felt the same.

"We can stop here in Northport for some warmer gear," Velen said, pulling back on the reins of his horse.

"It's okay, I'm fine, really," Sparrow said.

"I don't believe you. Come on, they have wool socks, cloaks, and even gloves here at this store. We'll get you all bundled up," Velen told him.

They dismounted and walked to the shop, leaving Beric and Eira in charge of the horses. A bell jingled as they opened the door to the shop and a frail-looking old man greeted them from behind the counter. Sparrow found a pair of stockings, gloves, and a warm hat. He heard the bell overhead jingle again and peeked over the racks to see who had come in. An old woman with a bulbous nose and milky-white eyes felt her way around. She tripped over her own feet and fell, her face hurdling toward the hardwood floor. Sparrow dropped all of the items he was holding and lunged forward to catch her before she hit the hard stone floor. She grabbed his arm, her hands as cold as ice, and looked up at him as though she could see him. She pulled him down to her level and whispered in his ear.

"Heart of coal meets hair of fire, only then will he expire. If the fire is snuffed out, the world will end without a doubt." She let go of Sparrow's wrist and hobbled back toward the door.

He listened to the bell ring and the door close behind her. What could she mean? *Heart of coal meets hair of fire.*

"Ready to check out?" Velen asked.

"Yeah, did you see that woman?" Sparrow asked, still touching the place on his wrist where she grabbed him.

"What woman?" Velen asked.

Sparrow knew he hadn't imagined her, but he let it go. They paid for their things and Sparrow changed into his warmer clothes, while Beric picked up some food from Maureen at the Blue Lioness Inn. They took the bridge from Alasia Outpost into the northern woods. The snow accumulated on the trees, weighing down their branches. The forest gave off a melancholy vibe. Sparrow blew a hot breath into his cupped hands and a white cloud escaped through the spaces between his fingers.

"It's going to be another cold winter, I'm afraid," Beric said.

"It gets colder every year, earlier and earlier, too. I remember the first time I ever saw snow, it was well after the winter solstice. I was just a girl then, maybe four and twenty years. Every year after, the snow has come sooner. We still have two moons until the solstice." Eira looked around at the trees, their branches drooping under the weight of the blanket of white.

"How are you spending the holiday?" Beric asked. Sparrow followed Beric's gaze to Eira.

"I'm not sure. I haven't celebrated since I left Aranor," she replied.

"You should join us for the tree decorating ceremony in Blackwater. There's always a festival with musicians and warm cider. We also make paper lanterns to light the paths through town, it's fun."

Goddess above, this kid has such innocence about him. Sparrow thought.

"We will see." Eira's lips hinted at a smile.

Through the trees ahead, Sparrow saw the large dark opening in the hillside. He dismounted his horse and inspected the ground in front of them as they moved forward but could not tell if anyone had passed this way recently because of the freshly fallen snow.

"I think this is the place Commander Rend told us about. We have to check it out. I know Arturo said it was empty last time they were here, but you never know." Sparrow go back on his horse and they rode to the mouth of the cave. The others followed Velen inside, weapons at the ready. When the path began to curve around the wall, Velen pulled out a torch and lit it. The ground beneath them cracked and crumbled. Sparrow's heart pounded as he listened for the falling rocks to hit the bottom. Sparrow side-stepped with his back pressed to the wall, testing the strength of every space before stepping to it.

"You guys go back. Wait for me by the entrance. I'll check it out."

"We can't let you go alone, are you crazy?" Eira asked.

"The path is broken and unless you can fly or climb the walls it will be too dangerous."

"Which of those things are you able to do?" Eira raised an eyebrow at him.

"That's for me to know. Please, go back. I don't want you to get hurt."

"Come on, Eira. We can check out the nearby woods," Sparrow suggested, sensing she would not give in unless she could otherwise be useful.

"Fine. I really wanted to see what's down there, though."

"I know you did." Sparrow patted her on the back and they walked out with Beric. The snow was still coming down and Sparrow was sure it had gotten colder. They took a path through the woods toward the west and fanned out twenty paces apart. Sparrow listened for the wolves he knew inhabited these woods and kept his guard up. He was about to give the command to turn around when he spotted a cabin in the distance.

He crept up to the tree line and watched for a few minutes to make sure the house was devoid of activity, then crept to the door to peer inside. No one moved about the kitchen or sitting room, and no fire burned in the hearth. Sparrow walked to the side of the house and stopped in his tracks. The body of a woman lay dusted with snow. He rushed over to inspect her and when he saw the hole in her throat and the blood frozen to her face, Sparrow called out for the others. "This was definitely a vampire. We need to burn her body to give it back to the earth. The ground will be too frozen for us to dig a hole to bury her in at least until spring, so that's our only option. I'm going to check out the house, can you two get the fire going?"

"Sure thing, I think I saw some dry wood on the other side of the house." Eira motioned for Beric to follow her.

Sparrow waited for them to be around the corner before he pushed open the splintered and broken door. It looked fairly normal; shelves of trinkets, a fireplace, and a small sofa made up the living space. The dining room only had room for a two-top table, but the thick layer of dust on the back of one of the chairs told Sparrow this woman lived alone. *How sad. I'm sorry this happened to you,* Sparrow thought of the woman laying outside in the snow, discarded just as his brothers were, left for the wolves or worse. The wash tub sink had residue of bloody water and the rag in the bucket was still damp. Sparrow stared at the area as thoughts danced through his mind. He wiped his palms which were damp with nervous sweat, on his trousers then he turned and ran out the front door to where Beric and Eira stood stoking a small fire.

"This wasn't the work of fledglings, someone cleaned up the mess after they killed her; I don't know who it was, but we should make this quick. Beric can you help me grab all the wooden furniture from inside, we need to make this fire a little bigger."

"Couldn't we just put her inside the cabin and set it on fire?" Beric asked.

"Sure, if our goal is to attract every vampire in the area to our location. We'd be over-run with a signal like that, it would be best to keep it small."

Beric followed him inside. They each grabbed a side of the coffee table and carried it out to the fire, then went back for whatever other dry wood they could grab. The two men lifted the old woman's body and placed it on the coffee table over the fire, covered her with a wool blanket they found on her bed, and then tented her body with the remaining wood. The blanket caught quickly and helped to get the rest of the wood burning. Sparrow contemplated saying a few words, but silently watched the flames engulf the woman instead. The popping and crackling of the fire was drowned out by the sizzling of flesh as it melted from bone. Sparrow pulled his tunic up over his nose to block the smell. Beric and Eira backed away from the fire just as Beric's horse reared up on it's hind legs and let out a high pitched roar. He ran to grab the reins before the horse could bolt.

"Woah, hey girl what is it? What's got you spooked?" Beric asked, rubbing the animal's neck.

As if in response to his question, a scream rang out in the air from the direction of the cave which caused the three of them to snap to attention.

"Velen!" Sparrow took off running without further hesitation and he could hear the light footfalls of the others leading the horses behind him. "Velen, We're coming!" he yelled. As his horse neared, Sparrow grabbed the saddle horn, caught the stirrup with one foot and swung his leg over the saddle without pause. He tapped the sides of the horse with his heels and leaned forward willing it to run faster.

When they reached the cave, Velen was locked in battle with a group of fledglings. Sparrow dismounted and rushed forward into the fray. He pulled two stakes from his vest, one for each hand. Stabbing one vampire with his left, he sent the stake from his right hand sailing through the air at the one trying to flank Velen. Sparrow quickly grabbed another stake and kept one in each hand as he sprinted back to the horses to grab the bo staff he had strapped to the side of his saddle. When Sparrow reached the horse he put the stakes back in his vest holsters and took his other weapon in hand. Both ends of the wooden pole were filed to a point. It was nearly as tall as Sparrow but he twirled it through the air with ease. He lunged forward, skewering one of the fledglings. He kicked the vampire off the end of his bo with his foot and twirled the weapon around as a blue dome of magic surrounded him. "What the hell?" Sparrow wondered. Searching the scene, he saw Eira and Beric fighting back to back, circling and protecting each other inside a dome of blue light of their own, but Sparrow's eyes searched for Velen.

A high-pitched squeal erupted from the cave. He rushed toward the sound stopping at the chasm in the center. He lit a torch and pointed it toward his feet. *Oh no*, Sparrow thought as he saw several more fledglings crawling up the walls of the pit. He ran back to warn the others.

"Where's Velen?" Sparrow shouted. "We have more—a *lot* more coming, we're going to be overrun." As if summoned, a swirling vortex ripped sideways through the veil of reality and Velen appeared with Akiri.

"I thought we could use more help," Velen said with an apologetic tone.

Sparrow didn't have time to be angry, the first wave of fledglings came running out of the cave at them.

"Stand back," Akiri commanded as she shifted into her beast form. Her green scales shimmered even in the pale light and it was the most magnificent thing Sparrow ever witnessed. The ground shook as the great dragon stomped out in front of them and unleashed her fiery breath at the mouth of the cave. Even from behind her, the heat was intense. She moved forward toward the cave's entrance and with another breath, took out a second wave. As the vampires burned, their screeching voices sounded like the cry of a hot kettle.

Akiri disappeared into the cavern, but the sounds of flame and dying creatures persisted. With the threat outside gone, Sparrow turned to Velen. "You *left* us? We could have died! I mean, thankfully you made it back in time, but what if you hadn't? Not all of us can just teleport away. Next time take us with you or something."

"I can only bring up to three others, if I had taken you, we would have not been able to bring Akiri back with us. I knew you would be okay," Velen said.

"How could you possibly know?"

"Because I shielded you all before I left and the shield lasts for at least ten minutes. I knew if I was quick we could win this fight. I was right."

The cave was now quiet and Sparrow watched to see if Akiri or another horde of fledglings would emerge; and to his relief, Akiri emerged from the cave as a human, but she had no clothing on. Sparrow cleared his throat and looked away. Twirling her hands, a green wisp of light encircled her hands and then enveloped her body. When the light dimmed and then went out completely, Akiri was wearing a green dress.

"It's okay, you can look now," she said.

"Thank you for your help, Akiri. We wouldn't have survived this without you," Velen said.

"Well, if not for all your visits during my nesting period I would have surely died of boredom so the way I see it, I owed you one," she replied. Velen looked at Akiri with adoration.

"We could use your help if you would like to stay with us, if not I can teleport you home."

"I can fly home. I would go with you, but the dragons are big enough to leave now, so I have to travel with each of them to their new homes. It's going to be a busy week."

"I understand." Velen nodded.

Akiri embraced him and he leaned down to kiss her cheek. She laced her fingers through his and for a few moments it seemed they were the only two people there.

"I'll see you soon." Akiri said with a smile as she moved away from him. When she was far enough away, Akiri dropped to all fours. Her fingers stretched and clawed into the snow and dirt beneath them as they became long black talons. Her hips bulged and swelled as the body of a dragon grew in her place. The illusion spell flickered as the green dress disappeared and only scales remained. She let out a thunderous roar as her spine stretched and the final stage of her transformation completed.

Sparrow would never get used to this.

TWENTY-TWO

MOMENTS OF DARKNESS AND light intertwined as Bastian blinked, trying desperately to stay conscious this time. He didn't know how they kept putting him out, but he knew the fog in his memory was magical in nature. Bastian tried to rub his eyes but discovered his wrists were bound to the headboard of a bed. He looked around the room; it looked vaguely familiar. Dark stone walls and a floor to match, a hearth with a small crackling fire, and a window with iron bars. He'd been in a room like this before, in Ash right before the kingdom was destroyed.

"How do you like our new place? I couldn't believe my luck when I found a whole island kingdom abandoned. Then I heard the story of what happened here from a couple of the shifters, and well, if I'm being honest, it only made it much more appealing." Elizandra sauntered over to the bed and crawled in next to Bastian. Why was she here? Was he still dreaming? "Don't you remember the fun we used to have?" she asked as she laid her head on his chest and trailed her fingers down his abdomen.

Bastian quickly realized he was naked, and he groaned in frustration. "Elizandra, let me go, please," he begged.

"Why? So you can abandon your wife a second time and go running back to your red-headed mistress?" Elizandra growled angrily.

"Don't call her that."

"What else do you call a woman who sleeps with a married man and breaks up a family?"

"We were never—"

"What? Never married, or never a *family*? You're wrong. I loved you. I would have done *anything* to make you happy, but you threw it all away the second you met her."

"El, please."

"You will eventually be happy with me again, you'll see I can be a good wife, I can be the wife you deserve." Elizandra wiped her tears and stood up, "I brought you breakfast," she said as she moved her long dark hair to one side revealing her neck. He turned his head away. He was hungry, but the thought of touching Elizandra, let alone drinking from her, made him ill. "You either drink from me or not at all," she sneered.

"I'd rather desiccate."

"Which can be arranged. You know, I thought you would be happy to be alive after I got you out of the sarcophagus."

"How did you even find out about Dmitri?" Bastian asked, changing the subject.

"When I was learning magic, I was really bad at it—I mean *really* bad. So I struck a deal with someone in exchange for magic. He told me all I had to do was wake his servant, I'm guessing that's who Dmitri is, anyway, in exchange, he gave me all this great new power, I can do amazing things with it, like for instance, this—" She reached out and touched his arm, he felt his mind being taken over. "You will drink from me," she said, putting her neck to his lips. His teeth sank into her skin and as he drank her blood, she moaned with pleasure. When she pulled away, he tried to grab her, but quickly realized his hands were still bound. "Enough for now." Elizandra got up from the bed and moved toward the door. She obviously enjoyed toying with him. He wasn't going to drink, but then he did, almost like he was compelled. *That's impossible, isn't it?*

He had to get out of there before she came back. Bastian pulled on the bonds securing him to the bed, but they held tight. Whoever tied the knots did a fantastic job, and if he weren't in danger, Bastian might have been impressed. He rubbed his wrists raw trying to loosen the ropes before he remembered he was a dragonshifter. Surely the knots would not be able to withstand the transition. He focused first on his legs, which were not bound. He stretched his toes and tried to force the shift to happen, but the stretching and straining only made him feel sleepy. *Why isn't it working?* Bastian tried to form a talon with his finger. He pushed his pointer out as far as he could and bent it into the shape of a claw. He tried to push a talon out of the end of it. "Come on, just one talon," he pleaded to his own body.

Then he heard Elizandra's laughter from the doorway. She looked at him with excitement. "It worked! I mean, I didn't think it would. I told Dmitri he was crazy and there was no way you could steal a dragon's magic, but here you are, unable to shift. Awe..." Elizandra puckered her bottom lip to feign pity. "Looks like you're stuck here with me!" Elizandra couldn't hide her glee as her fake pout turned into a joyous grin.

"Did you come back just to gloat?" Bastian asked.

"Of course not. I thought we could spend some quality time together. I brought some books, we can read, or we can play a game, or..." She set the books down on the bedside table and took off her dress. Her copper skin was flawless and Bastian recalled how smooth it felt from the days when he would drink from her. Despite the protest of his mind, other parts of his body betrayed him at the sight of the unarguably beautiful woman standing in front of him. She saw the response, too. It was hard to miss, although he was trying to fight it. Elizandra slowly crawled from the end of the bed to straddle him and he felt his erection stiffen even more as she moved her hips back and forth, rubbing her wet, hot sex up and down his shaft, though not allowing it to penetrate her. She leaned forward and whispered in his ear. "You are mine, and I am yours. You will forget everyone you ever loved except for me. Now, make love to me, Husband."

Elizandra reached up to the ropes inhibiting Bastian's hands from caressing her body and spoke an incantation. The ropes glowed with a soft yellow light and then released. Bastian was unable to refuse her request, and the strangest part was, he didn't feel like he even *wanted* to refuse. The softness of her skin mesmerized him. She looked like a goddess. He cupped her backside as she continued to tease him. Elizandra leaned forward and kissed him. He gasped as their bodies touched. Her body was so warm, she was like a summer day. Bastian ran his hands up her back and held her to him as she rolled her hips again, this time allowing him to enter her. She moved on top of him so seductively he couldn't keep his hands off of her. They roamed from her back to her stomach and up to her perfectly round breasts. Passion overcame him and he couldn't let her lead any longer. Bastian grabbed her by the hips and flipped her over onto her back. He looked her in the eye as he guided himself into her. He quickened the pace with deep thrusts seeming almost primal and angry. She cried out his name as this brought her to climax, and then Bastian felt her walls constrict around his erection. The ecstasy was too much for him and he let out a deep growl as he tried to pull out.

"No," Elizandra said firmly, as she grabbed his hips and pulled him deep inside. Bastian felt his warm fluid fill her and he throbbed inside of her until the orgasm was over. She looked at him with her hands on his chest. "I am yours, and you are mine. You love only me." Purple smoke lightly swirled around her and her eyes flashed as she looked down into his eyes.

"I love only you," he repeated. Bastian looked back at his wife. *How did I ever get so lucky?* he thought.

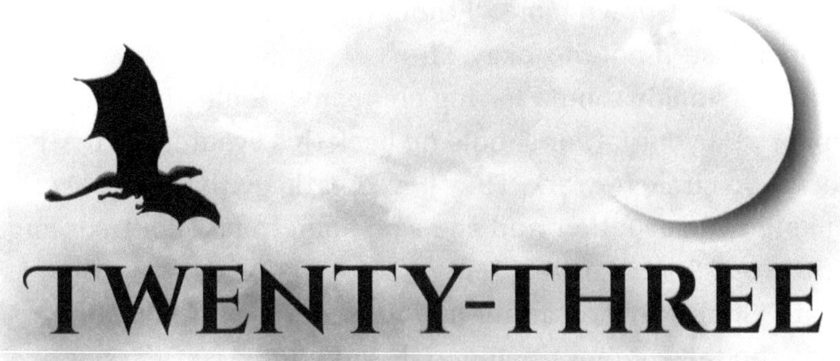

TWENTY-THREE

SHE WOKE TO THE sound of scraping iron as the serving window in her cell door slid open. Sophie rubbed her eyes and squinted through the darkness to see who was delivering her meal. She moved forward to accept the chalice from the window and met Chloe's eyes.

"Serena is bringing you some food, she will be here in a moment," she smiled. Sophie took the half-full cup and drank it down. Chloe took a lantern from the hook behind her and hung it on the hook outside the cell to give Sophie some light.

"Is Xander back yet?" Sophie's mind was clearer than it had been in days, months if she were being honest with herself, and now since it had been a couple of days since she had seen him, she felt perhaps she had been giving him the wrong impression. She wasn't in love with him, she barely knew him. Now that her hormones seemed to be balancing out, she was only interested in finding Bastian and being able to go back to Lapis Highland with him and Willow. She missed her normal life. Even the day-to-day duties of being queen she used to loathe seemed to be preferable to her current situation.

"Are you ready to have some breakfast? I brought you flapjacks and sausage." Sophie could smell the food before Serena even rounded the corner. It reminded her of the morning with her mother when she was little. When Sophie looked up at Serena, she saw two plates in her hands. She waited for Chloe to open the door to the cell and then set the two plates on the fold-down table. "I thought you might like some company for breakfast. If not, it's okay, I'll—"

"It's fine, I wouldn't mind having company," Sophie interrupted.

"Xander and your father should be back this evening. If they get the teleportation circle to work. They have Agatha with them. I overheard her talking to your father and she said something about passing her power to you," Serena said.

"What?" Sophie looked at her and waited for her to elaborate.

"Yeah, she talked about dying and said you were the only one she would trust to wield her power. I shouldn't have listened as long as I did because I don't think I was supposed to hear what Agatha can do—what you will be able to do." She looked at Sophie with genuine worry on her face.

"What is it?" Sophie had forgotten all about her food, "what was so startling about Agatha's power?"

"She said you will have the power to walk between worlds. She said there is a fabric between this world and all the others, unimaginable places where you could be safe. If it's true, and you can go somewhere safe, I want to go with you. My family although we are free, will never be accepted for what we are, but if we could go to a world where maybe they didn't know..." Serena got lost in thought.

"Even if Agatha *can* transfer her power to me, there's no guarantee I will know how to even do the spell, I could mess it up, and then what? We end up in a world worse than this one, or we could actually die. This isn't something I can agree to before I know the possible outcomes." Sophie thought about the vision Xander showed her, the strange world seeming so different from this one. His gift was future sight so maybe she could take them somewhere safe. "If I can learn how to do it, go somewhere safe, I promise I won't leave you behind," she said.

Sophie turned to take a bite of her nearly forgotten breakfast. The eggs were cold now so she took a few bites and drank the water Serena brought for her. The visits with her mom and Willow were not frequent enough. Sophie missed her daughter and couldn't wait until Akiri could see she was not a danger to her. There was so much she needed to do before she could go back to her normal life. She took a few more bites of her breakfast; it helped suppress her appetite for blood for short periods of time.

"I know you haven't been outside for a few days, but it has started to snow. The ground is covered. I've never seen snow until now, it's pretty amazing. Chloe wants to go for a sleigh ride through the city tonight; maybe if Xander is back by then you can come with us? If you want to."

"A night out sounds lovely, I used to all the time around the winter solstice," Sophie told her. She wondered why Serena had stipulated *if Xander was back*. Sophie pushed her tray away and stood up.

Serena gathered up the breakfast dishes and carried them to the door. Chloe opened it as Serena approached and closed it behind her. Serena looked back at Sophie through the bars, "I'll see you tonight," she said.

"What's going on tonight?" Akiri asked.

"I thought maybe Sophie might like to go on a sleigh ride with us tonight, you know, get out of her cell for a while," Serena said.

"It sounds nice, but I don't know if she's is ready," Akiri said.

"Xander and I will take responsibility for her. We will go right after her evening meal so she won't be hungry." Serena looked hopeful, like a child asking to stay up past bedtime.

"Okay. Be careful," Akiri relented.

"We will." Serena smiled and hurried off with Chloe.

Akiri entered Sophie's cell and sat down at the table. "I delivered your dragon to Lapis Highland. Ezra seemed a little scared. Thomas stepped right up, though, and the dragon seemed to really like him. Have you thought of a name yet?"

"I honestly haven't had time. Things have been so crazy lately. I mean, first, there were the bodies near Blackwater, then I found out Bastian and his family are vampires, then Dmitri turned me, and now here I am. There is always something going on, always some crisis, I don't know how much more I can take," Sophie admitted.

"I get it," Akiri said. "So, what was Dmitri like? Did he look like a corpse?"

"Actually, no. If he wasn't pure evil, he might even be handsome. He was more muscular than I expected him to be. When you hear a vampire has been rotting in a tomb for twenty years you kind of expect him to look like a zombie, but he didn't. He had short brown hair and brown eyes, and looked pretty normal, all things considered."

"So how did he turn you? I mean, how does it work?"

"First, he drank my blood. I am sure I passed out because when I woke up again his wrist was to my mouth and I was drinking his blood. Then, he locked me in a cabin with a woman and compelled us to stay there until my transition was complete. I didn't know what he meant until—" The words caught in Sophie's throat, she hadn't thought about it since the day it happened. "Until I killed her. I didn't mean to, I was just so hungry, she offered to make me breakfast and turned her back to me, and the next thing I knew I was on top of her, drinking her blood. I couldn't stop." Sophie choked back her emotion.

"I'm sorry, it must have been awful. I noticed Xander seems quite infatuated with you, what's going on there?" Akiri raised an eyebrow and grinned at Sophie.

"I don't like what you're insinuating," Sophie joked, smiling for the first time since Akiri got there. "He thinks we are fated. He has visions of the future and he said we are together and happy in the visions he has of us. Even when my thoughts and emotions were going crazy after I turned, he never actually made a move. I basically threw myself at him—a symptom of the transition and proximity, I'm sure. He could have taken advantage of me, but he didn't."

"What about Bastian, do you think he is still the one? What do you think will happen when you find him?"

"I don't know, honestly. There is definitely a lot we need to talk about. He kept so many secrets from me and I didn't talk to my father for a year because of it. On one hand, Bastian is charming, handsome, and fun." Sophie wanted to add he was amazing in bed, too, but didn't want to be crass. Just thinking about it made a heat rise to her cheeks.

"He can also still make you blush apparently, so that's a good thing, right?"

"Yeah, I guess so."

"Well, I hope whatever you choose makes you happy. I know it seems unlikely given how our relationship began, but you are one of my closest friends. Which reminds me, Dominic and Kamara will be coming to the solstice celebration and Kamara asked me to tell you she can't wait to see you."

"I can't wait either. It will be so nice for us all to be together again." Sophie smiled.

"Well, I have to get going, I have duties to attend to. Since I am finished taking care of the dragons, I have to catch up on council business." Akiri stood up and hugged Sophie. "I'll see you at dinner. Oh, by the way, I brought you this," Akiri handed Sophie a piece of parchment.

She unfolded it and read the spell written on it. "The sunlight protection spell? Thank you, Akiri."

"It won't work against the bars because they also have a spell on them, but when you're able to leave you'll be able to live as normally as a vampire can." Akiri hugged her before exiting the cell and locking it behind her. She waved as she walked away, and Sophie watched until Akiri disappeared around the bend.

When she was alone again, Sophie thought of Bastian. She missed him more and more every day. It was like being separated from him was slowly tearing her heart in two. The longer they waited to go after him, the less likely they were to find him. He could be anywhere now. Sophie closed her eyes and tried to focus on his face. His bright blue eyes haunted her as the image of him inside her mind called out for her to help him. *Sophie, Help me! Please...* The image of him faded away.

He needed her. *I'm coming, Bastian,* she thought.

Hours passed and finally, Sophie heard footsteps nearing. She was hungry again, although, not as hungry as she had been the first week of her confinement. Akiri and Serena rounded the corner, both empty-handed.

"I thought we would try something and see how this goes. You need to learn control." Akiri came into the cell and sat down at the table. She pulled a knife from her pocket.

"No, wait, what are you doing?" Sophie asked, backing away from her.

"I trust you." Akiri pressed the blade to her wrist and made the smallest cut. Crimson fluid began to bead up at the incision site and Sophie backed away. She could feel the urge starting to take over. The smell of Akiri's blood filled the space and enthralled Sophie's senses. It smelled better than any scent she had ever experienced. She thought she felt herself moving closer, as if she were not in control of her own body, but her back was against the wall. She wasn't moving, Akiri was coming closer.

"Stop, please, I don't want to hurt you," Sophie pleaded.

"You won't, I trust you."

"Famous last words," Sophie grumbled.

"You're not going to hurt me, you're going to drink, and then you will stop. It's all about control. You can do this." Akiri held her wrist up and Sophie watched as the blood began to run down the side of her arm. She couldn't resist anymore. Sophie latched onto the wound like a babe to the nipple, sinking her fangs into the soft tissue of Akiri's wrist. It was so warm, and delicious. Sophie sucked the thick life-sustaining fluid in greedy gulps. "Stop. Enough," Akiri said, but Sophie couldn't hear her. All she could hear was the pumping of Akiri's heart and the sound of the liquid as it flowed from her vein. "I said STOP!"

Sophie's senses came flooding back to her and she pulled away. Akiri cradled her wrist and dropped to one knee. Sophie gasped. "I'm sorry, I told you not to do it, I wasn't ready, I didn't mean to hurt you, I—"

"No, you stopped. You *are* ready. Your human mind can and will over-rule your hunger. I'm okay, just weak now. I will rest and replenish, you're free to go on the sleigh ride tonight. Xander and your father have just come back, too, so I imagine tomorrow you'll be pretty busy." Akiri gave Sophie a quick pat on the shoulder and smiled. "I'll see you soon."

Sophie was so happy to be released from the cell. Akiri's maids drew her a bath in the guest suite inside the temple and bathed Sophie in milk and lavender. They washed her hair with scented oils reminiscent of the women of the Ledoran court. It was so much easier to comb through her curls with the oil in her hair, she needed to remember to get some for later.

When she stepped out of the tub, the maids wrapped her in a bath sheet. Her reflection in the looking glass was not as she remembered it. Features which had seemed dull before were now more vibrant, her eyes, once dark green were now like shining emeralds. Her hair grazed the top of her buttocks, hanging in luscious ringlets. It grew so quickly now, it was strange. She expected with vampirism her body would be frozen, in stasis almost. She found that to not be true as she marveled at how long her hair had gotten even since she came to Ophay.

"Do you think you could cut my hair?" Sophie asked one of the maids.

"Of course, Your Majesty," she said and curtsied as she hurried out to find something to cut it with. She returned a moment later with a straight razor. "How short would you like it cut?"

"To about right here." Sophie touched the side of her shoulder almost to her bicep. She closed her eyes as the maid worked taking piece by piece and cutting it off with the razor. When the girl was finished, Sophie dared to open her eyes. Her mouth fell open in shock. "It looks amazing. You have a real talent. It's not easy to cut curly hair, I have had many bad haircuts in my life, but this one..." Sophie scrunched her curls up gently and watched them bounce right back to the middle of her shoulder. "It's perfect, thank you." So much hair now lay at her feet, if she had looked at the floor first, she would have been surprised she had hair left on her head but her curls still hung past her shoulders just like she wanted. The maid pulled back the front of Sophie's hair, braided it loosely, and secured it at her crown with a pearl comb.

"I have your dress ready for you," the other maid said as she moved aside to show her the beautiful green dress with long bell sleeves and two rows of buttons down the front. The dress was tapered at the waist and trimmed in black fur. Next to it was a black knit cowl and black fur hand muff. "Do you like it? If not I can go and find something else," the maid told her.

"It is very beautiful, but I do prefer trousers if I can be honest," Sophie said.

"Ah, yes, Akiri did mention this and that is why we also brought these to wear underneath. In case you need to ditch the dress and make a getaway on horseback." The maid reached under the dress and pulled out a pair of warm-looking trousers.

"These are perfect, thank you."

"Would you like for us to help you dress, My Queen?"

"No, thank you. As long as I don't have to wear a corset, I can manage." Sophie smiled. She realized this was the first time she had been trusted alone with humans since she was turned. She was quite proud of herself.

Xander was waiting for her outside of the guest room and when their eyes met in the hall, he looked too stunned to speak. He smiled and offered her his arm. She accepted, gently sliding her arm through his.

"You look beautiful, as always. I like your hair."

"Thank you, I must say you clean up rather nicely as well." Xander was wearing a black velvet swallowtail jacket accented with a dark green silk handkerchief in the chest pocket. This was also the first time Sophie had seen him wear a hat. He looked good in the black top hat which was trimmed in the same green silk as his handkerchief. She looked down at the dress she was wearing and noticed the color was very similar, although the material was different. *Does he think this is a date?* Sophie wondered.

Serena and Chloe were already in the sleigh when Sophie and Xander stepped outside. The small town of Ophay was beautiful covered in the fresh-fallen snow. White smoke rose from the chimney tops, billowing softly into the night sky. Xander approached the sleigh and extended his hand to Sophie. "My Queen," he said with a slight bow.

She accepted his hand as she stepped into the sleigh and he climbed in after her. They settled onto the cushioned seats rivaling even those of a Ledoran carriage. The coachman commanded the two horses forward and the sleigh began to glide smoothly over the snow. The world seemed more vivid through Sophie's Vampire eyes. She saw through the darkness perfectly now and she could hear sounds which would have been impossible for her to hear before, like a bird high in the tree ruffling its feathers to sleep, or a shrew burrowing beneath the snow. She couldn't feel the bitter bite of the cold like she used to when she was human. Although she was dressed for the weather, Sophie had a feeling she would be fine even if she weren't.

As they neared the edge of the forest separating Ophay from Blackwater, Sophie looked at Xander. "Where are we going," she asked.

"I have a little surprise for you," Xander told her.

They continued through the southern gate which was usually unguarded since Ophay and Torzana were both peaceful towns to Blackwater, but tonight, there were two guards posted and the coachman brought the horses to a halt as they stepped together to block the path.

"Who are your passengers?" one of the guards asked.

"Well, for starters, I have Queen Sophie Rend of Lapis Highland, daughter of Leon Rend, and Wizard of Highland Tower," The coachman retorted with authority. The other guard scoffed as he walked back to the sleigh, torch in hand. He pointed the torch in their direction as he looked at their faces.

"Looks good, Kade, no feral vamps in this sleigh, just regular vampires." He looked closely at each of them. "Don't try anything funny while you're in our city, guards are working triple and if I'm honest, they're a little jumpy." He turned and walked back to his post as the other guard moved aside for them to pass. The horses pulled them slowly toward the town center.

"It looks so beautiful!" Sophie's eyes filled with excitement and joy as she took in the sight of the snow-covered rooftops, lantern-lit pathways, and tree branches glittering with hoarfrost.

"Yes, the most beautiful thing I've ever seen," Xander said. Sophie turned to see what Xander was looking at and she was startled to discover he was looking directly at her. She wasn't sure if he had said it out loud or if she was hearing his thoughts. Sophie wanted to talk to him about whatever was going on between them. As if sensing her discomfort, Xander looked up at the sky. "I wish we could see the stars tonight."

"Me, too! When we were on the ship, the stars were so bright and they twinkled like millions of tiny diamonds. I never thought the sky could be so beautiful," Serena mused.

"From Northport you can see the northern lights this time of year, brilliant wisps of green, blue, pink, and purple dance throughout the night sky. it's incredible. Maybe I could take you some time?" Chole asked, looking at Serena, her eyes twinkling at the prospect of friendship or maybe something more. The horse slowed from a canter to a trot as they glided through the residential neighborhood. The sleigh pulled up in front of Sophie's childhood home.

"Xander, What are we doing here?" Sophie asked.

"This is your surprise," he replied. Samantha came out the front door, holding Willow.

"Mama!" Willow shouted when she saw her mother. Sophie had to choke back tears as she climbed out of the sleigh. Just hearing Willow's little voice calling her 'Mama' made her heart leap for joy. She took her daughter in her arms and hugged her tightly. She put Willow back down so she could hug her mother too. Willow ran to the sleigh and tried to climb in. Samantha let go of her daughter and called to Willow.

"Wait for your mom, honey!" Samantha said. They walked back to the sleigh and Sophie climbed in, Samantha lifted Willow to her and Sophie sat her on

"Are you coming with us?" Sophie asked.

"No, I'm going to get some cleaning done while you're spending time with Willow. I'll see you in a little while," she smiled at Sophie and then she and Xander shared a look. It was unspoken, but Sophie knew Xander had promised to keep Willow safe. Sophie pretended not to notice, but it hurt her heart to know her own mother didn't even trust her to be around Willow alone.

The sleigh pulled away from Samantha as she waved farewell. Sophie looked at Willow's face. She had grown so much. Her hair was strawberry blonde and her eyes were blue, like Bastian's. She had his nose, too. Willow reached for Xander with her eyes fixed on his hat. He smiled at her, took the hat off, and handed it to her. Willow immediately put her head inside and the brim rested on her shoulders. Everyone chuckled and

Willow raised the hat to look at them, then promptly pulled the hat back down, held it there for a few seconds, raised it again, and yelled "Boo!"

Sophie smiled. "I love you, Willow!" Her daughter said something similar back. Sophie hugged Willow to her chest, wishing all was right with the world and she didn't have to go find Bastian, and trap Dmitri. Sophie wished she and her daughter could just go home to Lapis Highland and find Bastian waiting for them. Sophie gazed off into the distance, holding her daughter close to her. She hated she couldn't do anything to help Bastian, she didn't even know where he was. Now was not the time for thoughts of what she couldn't do, though. Willow was there with her, and they were gliding over the snow in a beautiful sleigh. Xander watched the two of them with a smile on his face and Sophie couldn't help wondering what he was thinking.

The stars twinkled and smoke rose softly from the chimneys, filling the air with a woody scent reminding her of home. Not Highland Castle, but *home*. Willow nestled in beside her and drifted off to sleep and Sophie's mind wandered to Gabe. Did they ever have a chance? If only she had stayed in Blackwater, and had not left to learn magic with Ryul. She and Gabe could have gotten married, had kids, and lived a happy life together. She *had* left though, and as a result, Gabe had no one but Leon to turn to when his mother gambled away their home. If she had been there, Sophie would have found him another way to save his mother's house; a way which didn't involve him marrying Akiri and giving his life to save her kingdom—a kingdom that fell anyway, despite him.

Sophie felt Xander's arm around her shoulder. He rubbed her arm gently as she sat in silent contemplation, gazing into the night. She expected him to start talking and ruin the moment, but he didn't, he held her close, and let her lean on his shoulder as Willow slept, none the wiser.

TWENTY-FOUR

BRAIDWOOD WAS AS BUSY as ever. Sparrow remembered being there as a young boy, back before his parents left him at the Garden of Life. That was such a long time ago, just before Orion took over the city with his thunder of dragons and their riders. Sparrow was too small to remember the events first-hand, but he heard the stories growing up about how Leon Rend defeated Orion by stealing the orb from the top of his scepter which broke the spell keeping the dragons hypnotized. Once the scepter was destroyed, Orion's dragons turned against him. Many bards sang about his dragon swallowing him whole. Sparrow would have liked to witness it.

Velen led them to a large dockside tavern. Fire from a large stone hearth in the center of the room illuminated the tavern in a deep orange glow dancing shadows throughout the crowded bar. The Blackwater flag and the crest of the Silver Talons hung down from the wood beams above, and the head of a dragon-like sea monster stared down over the dining area. "Pirates are great for gossip if you supply them with enough alcohol," Velen said to Sparrow. Eira and Beric followed closely behind them. "We should split up though, so we can hear more. Make sure you ask around about any vampire attacks, missing people, or dragonshifters, maybe we can get a lead on one of the people we're looking for."

They spread out, mingling and talking to patrons, serving wenches, and bartenders. When it seemed like they were getting nowhere, Sparrow suggested they sit down and just listen to the conversations around them. He and Velen sat at a table on one side of the room, and Beric and Eira took a table on the other. The windows were wide open so the whole place was filled with fresh sea air and natural light. It was cool, but at least it wasn't snowing there like it was back in Blackwater. Velen turned to the group of men next to him. To Sparrow, they looked like they had just made port after months at sea. They were dirty and sweaty, playing dice and drinking ale from large metal tavern mugs.

"You guys look like you have some stories. How long ya been here?" Velen asked, trying his best to sound less refined than he actually was.

No, Velen, I said listen, not chat. Sparrow thought.

"What's it to ya?" One of the men grumbled.

"We're just a couple of monster hunters, looking for our next adventure, I didn't mean to bother ya, I've just heard stories about the kinds of monsters you can encounter on a ship. Mermaids, sirens, maybe even vampires, although, I doubt you've seen one of those—they usually stick to land," Velen said dismissively.

"I 'ave too seen a vampire. I delivered a load to one just a few days ago, we got to that island, you know the one the dragons burned down not too long ago?"

"You mean, Ash?" Velen asked.

"Yeah, that's the one. Anyway, we got there during the day and some lady came out and told us we were early and we couldn't be unloaded before nightfall. When night came, so did he. Now I never told him this because I feared for my life if he knew, but I thought they were dealing in fancy rum or something and I cracked open the lid of one of the barrels, only it wasn't filled with rum, it was *blood*. I pretended like I didn't know anything at all because I didn't wanna be his next meal. He gave me a sack of gold and we sailed away as quickly as we could."

"Wow, fascinating. Will you excuse us?" Velen turned to Sparrow. "Let's go, they're in Ash. We have to get back to Blackwater." Velen rushed over to Beric and Eira and ushered them toward the door. He led the three of them to a back alley.

"Huddle in," Velen said. They gathered around him and in a flash they were back in Blackwater, standing in the middle of the rune circle inside the guild hall. Eira and Beric were both queasy and looked as if they might vomit. Sparrow was thankful he felt fine this time, maybe he was getting used to teleportation after all.

"How did you do that? I thought you could only teleport if you have a rune circle matching where you want to go?" Sparrow asked. Velen smiled, took off his shoe, and reached inside it, pulling out a piece of leather with the rune circle of the Silver Talons Guild burned into it.

"Brilliant," Sparrow said, marveling at Velen's quick thinking. He'd managed to get the pirate tell him all about the vampire he met without making their inquiry obvious, and then the rune circle in his shoe... Sparrow had to hand it to him, he was impressed.

"Where is Commander Rend?" Velen was now speaking to Hank, the human man who worked for the guild as the receptionist.

"He is with Miss Sophie in Agatha's study, but they cannot be disturbed right now. Agatha is transferring her memories to Sophie, in preparation for the transfer of Agatha's power; they've been in there since before sunrise. I will let Commander Rend know you wish to speak with him when he is done in there," Hank said.

Velen sat down in the lobby. "We have to wait, we can't interrupt them, Leon would end us if something happened to Sophie because of us."

Sparrow nodded. Velen was right. Sparrow then paced the floor. He was aching to find Dmitri. He knew killing him would result in Sophie's death too, and therefore his own life was forfeit, but how could he live with himself knowing Dmitri was living comfortably as King of his own Island? No, imprisonment on Immernacht was not enough, and if he got the chance to kill the vampire who took his family from him, he was going to take it. They waited there for hours until finally, Leon and Sophie entered the foyer.

"Sir, we think we have located Dmitri. He has taken over the Castle on the Island of Ash," Sparrow blurted as they approached. "I would like to go after him."

"No, we must make him come to us, we need him in the rune circle. I know why he waits," Leon said.

"Why?" Velen asked.

"He is waiting for the solstice celebration. We have invited everyone, all the high-ranking officials from Braidwood, Ledora, Ravenhall, Northport, and Ophay. All of the dragonshifters will be here in Blackwater. He craves power and there is no greater show of force than to take out all of your enemies at once. I have no doubt he will bring his sorceress, but she will be no match for Sophie. As soon as she is trained the power transfer will be complete and she will have no trouble taking down his witch then." Leon looked at Sophie with pride. She, however, looked nervous.

"So we just wait here and allow him to raise an army of feral undead?" Sparrow argued.

"Not quite, Juniper Moonshadow, a decorated member of the Silver Soldiers, is going to take Willow to the hidden Fae lands to keep her safe. I have invited every cleric from here to Braidwood and they are mass-producing holy water as we speak. You will train every day as will Sophie and everyone else who wishes to help us fight. When Dmitri comes, we will be ready to defeat him, his witch, and any undead they bring with them!" Leon declared.

Sparrow stormed away. Velen started to follow him, but Leon called him back. Sparrow was halfway across the guild courtyard when he heard Sophie calling after him. He stopped and turned to face her, trying hard to keep his anger from showing. She paused at the door apprehensively and reached her hand out into the first sun rays she'd seen since the first time it burned her. The golden light kissed her skin and she knew she would be safe. She caught up with Sparrow and placed a hand on his shoulder.

"I know how you feel. I don't want to wait, either. I was told today what the price of absorbing Agatha's magic will be. I'm going to lose the ability to shift into dragon form. I think they have Bastian imprisoned on Ash. We need to go now if we're going to save him." Sophie said.

"What about Dmitri?" Sparrow asked.

"I have thought of a way to solve our situation to both our satisfaction."

"How? I want him dead and if he dies so do you, how could you possibly be satisfied with that outcome?"

"With this." Sophie opened her hand and revealed a small vial of dark blue powder glittering with magical dust. "It's a sleeping curse."

"No one has been able to make one since the days before dragons. It's said they're a myth. How do you know this will work?" Sparrow asked.

"Because this one *was* made in the days before dragons. Agatha is very old. She made this when she was seventeen; over three hundred years ago," Sophie told him.

"Where did you get it?"

"Agatha gave it to me," she replied.

"No way, I've heard you can cut off people's limbs and everything while they are under this curse and they won't wake up even for the most painful torture. The only way to wake them is with the antidote—"

"Which no longer exists," Sophie interrupted. "So you can torture him as much as you like, forever," Sophie said.

"What are we waiting for? Let's go!" Sparrow said.

TWENTY-FIVE

"You're not going anywhere without me." Sophie and Sparrow both whipped around to the sound of a third voice entering their conversation as Xander approached them from behind.

"I don't need you to protect me. I'm going to go get Bastian back, We're going to put Dmitri to sleep with Agatha's sleeping dust and If Elizandra has hurt Bastian, I'll kill her myself." Sophie said.

"You don't have Agatha's power yet—you can't just go into a war without caution, hoping *your* magic will save you; what if Elizandra decides she doesn't mind sacrificing Dmitri now since she has what she wants? She could kill Dmitri herself with a flick of her wrist, therefore killing you, too."

"I never thought of that," Sophie admitted.

"I know you didn't." He sounded angry.

"I'm sorry, I—"

"I know, you only care about saving Bastian, and damn it all, I want to save him too, but Sophie..." His face showed frustration as his words trailed off as if he was afraid to say what he really wanted to say. "We will save Bastian, but we have to be smart about it."

"What's your plan then, if you think mine is so dumb?" Sophie growled.

"I didn't say that, and what plan? You were just going to fly off to Ash and take on Elizandra, Dmitri, and goddess knows how many fledglings with just the two of you, it's not a plan, it's a death wish. I heard your father say something about the solstice, what is happening then?"

"He has invited everyone with power to the tree-lighting, he thinks Dmitri will not be able to resist. All the dragonshifters will be here... That's it!" Sophie exclaimed. "All the dragonshifters will be here, except perhaps Kamara, she's having a baby this month. If Dmitri and Elizandra both show up to the solstice celebration with an army of fledglings, then Bastian would be left alone on Ash."

"Kamara can't rescue Bastian herself either still pregnant or having just given birth, Sophie it won't work," Xander said.

"Which is why you will go with her. I can take you there now so we can tell her and Dominic the plan, and then Akiri can take you back before the Solstice. I've been meaning to see Kamara for a while now."

Xander nodded. "Sure, let's see what they say. I'm certain the King will not allow Kamara to put herself at risk but I'll let you do *this part* your way," he said, following Sophie's lead.

The flight to Ledora took a few hours. The kingdom shimmered in the afternoon sun, the white stone archways trimmed in gold luster When they landed on the beach, Xander looked away so Sophie could conjure herself some clothing. Illusion or not, the beautiful black dress she created clung to her curves and would be sure to be the height of fashion at court. She had not been here in so long, she wondered if King Dominic still held the Ledoran Ball every weekend like his father had. They walked from the beach to the western entrance to the city, the path to the right led to the shops and homes of the Ledoran subjects, but Sophie led Xander left toward the castle.

As soon as the guards spotted Sophie they moved aside and the next set of guards opened the heavy metal doors for them. It was just as she remembered; the white marble floors trimmed in gold tile, the grand staircase to the guest rooms, and beautiful arches lining the ballroom.

The King and Queen were seated on their thrones. Sophie made her way through the crowd leading Xander by the wrist. As soon as Kamara spotted them she stood up and stepped down from the platform. The crowd parted for her as if they were afraid to touch her. Kamara's gown glittered under the flickering candlelight from the chandeliers and her matching crown stood tall on her head with spikes resembling the rays of the sun. She looked like a goddess. Sophie started to kneel in front of the queen, but Kamara's hand shot out to stop her.

"My friends do not bow to me in this court." Kamara wrapped her arms around Sophie and held her tightly.

"You look so beautiful!" Sophie gushed. Kamara's blue and purple hair was braided in small, tight braids hanging to her waist. Half of her braids were pulled up in a bun and nestled inside the golden crown of Ledora. Kamara's belly was perfectly round and small compared to how big Sophie's had been.

"Me? No, look at you! You cut your hair! It looks good!" Kamara exclaimed. Sophie ran her fingers through her curls. She'd forgotten how short they were now. Dominic approached and stood next to his wife, waiting for his turn to pull Sophie into a hug.

"It's so good to see you, Sophie! I wasn't expecting to see you until the solstice celebration," Dominic said.

"This is actually why we have come. Is there somewhere more private we can speak?" Sophie asked. Dominic looked over at Xander.

"Who's this?" he asked.

"This is Bastian's brother, Xander. Xander, this is Queen Kamara and King Dominic of Ledora." Sophie introduced them as they walked to the library. Dominic closed the door behind them.

"So what is this reason you have come, I mean, if it couldn't wait until solstice it must be important," Dominic said as he pulled out chairs at the large study table in the center of the library.

"To keep it brief, there is an ancient vampire who has woken up and he's creating an army of feral bloodsuckers to help him seize power. They kidnapped Bastian and turned me into a vampire."

" We did hear there might be some conflict at the Winter Solstice Celebration—What about him?" Dominic asked, nodding to Xander.

"He's been a vampire since I met him, oh, and apparently Bastian is too, but his dragon blood masks the vampirism," Sophie said. "We think Dmitri is going to attack at the solstice celebration, which means Bastian will be alone in the castle on Ash. I was hoping while we are all fighting Dmitri in Blackwater, Xander could fly with Kamara to rescue Bastian. She could stay on the beach, she doesn't even have to go in, we just need to get Xander there."

"I don't know if I'm okay with that, how about this: bring him back here five days before the solstice and I will send him with a Ledoran army by ship. I don't want Kamara near any of this."

"I understand," Sophie nodded. "I agree to your terms."

"Wonderful. Now, you both are more than welcome to spend the night, I know it's not a quick trip here and it's already getting late. Unfortunately, because of the ball we only have one guest room left, will that be okay?"

Xander looked at Sophie and shrugged. "It's fine," Sophie said. "I need to feed though, perhaps we should leave."

"No need, I will have a maid sent up for you, just don't make a mess and be gentle. This is only because we are friends and I trust Sophie," Dominic said looking at Xander. "Will you be needing one as well?"

"A kind offer, but I can wait until we get back. Don't worry about the maid you send for Sophie, I can compel her to forget the entire incident." Xander told him. Dominic nodded.

"Very well then, Someone will show you to your room and after you've eaten, please come join us for a bit at the ball. We will have Kamara's mistress of robes bring you both some formal attire." Dominic rapped on the library doors and someone opened it from the outside. Dominic tapped the shoulder of a nearby chambermaid and asked her to guide Sophie and Xander to the vacant room. She curtsied to him and motioned for them to follow.

Their room didn't have a fireplace. It must have been one of the only rooms in the entire castle without one. Xander inspected the bed. There was a fitted sheet, a flat sheet, a thin quilt, a wool blanket, a large fur pelt made of several skins sewn together, and four pillows. Xander took one of the pillows and the wool blanket and placed them on the floor. "I'll sleep down here, you can take the bed."

"So chivalrous." Sophie grinned.

"It's not that, the bed just looks way too soft. I'd feel like a princess if I slept in it. I have to maintain my manly image," Xander joked.

"Mmmhmm," Sophie hummed through pursed lips. A quiet knock interrupted their banter and Xander jumped up to answer the door. A maiden entered nervously, looking at the two of them.

"Do not be afraid, and do not scream," Xander looked into her eyes and she nodded slowly as the fear left her expression. He led her over to the bed where Sophie was sitting and moved her hair away from her neck. Sophie could smell the girl's pheromones seeping from her skin, the artery in her neck throbbed with life and she could not resist. Sophie's lips brushed the maid's skin and she licked the saltiness from them as she tried to savor the taste. Sophie slid her fingers to the back of the girl's neck and felt the maiden's skin pop as her fangs punctured her skin. The flavor of spices and honey danced across Sophie's tongue as she pulled the blood through the two small holes in long drags.

"Enough, let her go now," Xander said. Sophie pulled away and drew in a deep breath. Xander turned the girl to face him. "You felt a bit under the weather while performing your duties and King Dominic gave you the rest of the night off. You will go back to your chamber and go to sleep. When you wake up, you won't remember us or anything about what happened here." Sophie watched the girl's brown eyes dilate and she walked away in a trance. Xander turned back to Sophie, his eyes widened and he gasped, unable to look away for a moment until he was able to organize his thoughts. "Sophie, I think you lost focus on your clothing spell," he said, quickly turning around.

Sophie looked down at her bare skin and with a momentary panic, muttered a quick incantation. The illusion spell flickered back into existence. "You can look now," she said. He turned back to face her and stood silently. It looked as if he wanted to speak, but another knock on the door interrupted the awkward silence. "That's probably Kamara's mistress with dresses. I'll go with her and get dressed. I'll see you down there." Xander nodded as Sophie turned walked out the door.

Sophie and Kamara were already in the ballroom, deep in conversation at the wine and refreshment table when Xander entered the room. He had an aura about him that commanded attention. He glided effortlessly through the crowd, bowing to ladies and shaking hands with Noblemen as he passed by them. Sophie had a feeling he was going to ask her to dance, but he didn't. Instead, he bowed to Kamara and extended his hand with his palm facing the vaulted ceiling.

"Would Her Majesty care to honor me with a dance?" Xander asked.

"Wow, he does have manners after all." Sophie joked.

"When he wants to." Xander replied with a smirk. Kamara nodded to Xander and put her hand in his. Sophie watched them as he gently waltzed Kamara around the ballroom. Sophie couldn't help thinking about Gabe. It had been in that very room she had found out about his engagement to Akiri. It was also where she had met Bastian for the first time. He had asked her to dance and was very observant, noting her eyes had been fixed on Gabe and Akiri. He did his best to not only take Sophie's mind off of her heartbreak but to show Gabe what he was missing. Sophie's eyes snapped to the pillar on the right side of the ballroom, which had been where she and Bastian, after too many drinks, shared their first passionate kiss. She was still deep in thought when Kamara and Xander returned from their dance.

"Sophie!" Kamara shouted her name.

"Huh? Oh, sorry. I got lost on memory lane. How was it?" Sophie asked.

"Why don't you find out for yourself, you would honor me greatly, Queen Sophie," Xander said, extending his hand to her.

"I uh—" she started to object, but she couldn't think of a reason and Kamara nudged her. "Okay, sure." Sophie gave Xander her hand and let him lead her to the floor. The music started; it was a song Sophie had never heard before.

"I don't know this dance," she admitted.

"It's okay, hardly anyone does anymore. It's very old, it tells a story about fate," Xander placed his hand on the small of her back and held her body close to his as he guided her leg backward with his own. A woman began singing in a high key reminding Sophie of a nightingale's song. Xander twirled her away from him and they circled each other with one hand raised, palms facing each other but not touching.

"I can't understand the words," Sophie said as Xander pulled her in close again.

"It's the first language of Immernacht. This song is about two Gods who were enemies to each other, one had a son, and the other a daughter. One day, the boy's father was told his son was fated to the daughter of his enemy so he did all he could to keep them apart. The girl grew up to be the Goddess of the sun, and despite his father's efforts, the boy still fell in love with her." Xander's lips were next to Sophie's ear and the tickle of his breath against her skin sent a shiver through her body. "His father was so angry he asked a sorceress to curse his son with an affliction that would make him burn in the sun should he ever look upon the Goddess again. So she did, she cursed him with vampirism. He wandered the darkness for years, trying to break the curse so he could be with his beloved again, and after much time had passed, the misery of being without her became too much." Xander's lips were ever so close to hers but she didn't pull away.

"What did he do?" Sophie asked.

"He waited for the sun to rise just so he could look upon her one last time."

"What a sad story."

"It is. When two are fated, but kept apart, their hearts are never whole. Fate is strange, one in the pair usually feels it more strongly than the other. He couldn't live without her, but she seemed fine without him." The music ended and Sophie was face to face with Xander.

"It's a beautiful, tragic story, but I still don't believe in fate." Sophie turned from him and retreated from the ballroom before her emotions could get the best of her. The farther she got from the ballroom, the stronger the ache in her chest became. Why had his story affected her so? *I need to leave, now*, she thought. The clicking of her heels echoed down the hall as she walked toward the front door. Dominic stood in the grand foyer conversing with a pair of noble women. Foregoing formalities, Sophie walked up to King Dominic. "May we speak, privately?" Sophie asked looking at the other two women. Dominic nodded and both women glided back toward the ballroom.

"What's wrong, are you okay?" Dominic asked.

Sense was beginning to return to her and the need to escape was now not as strong as it had been a moment ago. "I think I just need to go for a flight to clear my head. Please tell Xander I will return." Dominic nodded in response and Sophie headed for Kamara's room to change out of her dress. She would feel awful for tearing such a stunning garment to shreds.

Sophie went to the beach and let the dragon within her take over. Flying was different now that she was also part vampire. She couldn't feel the cool wind on her face like she used to, it was almost as if her dragon skin was numbed. The feeling in her chest grew from a dull ache to a stabbing pain. She didn't want to feel this, she wanted to love Bastian, and go back to being a family in Lapis Highland, but the more time they spent apart, the less hope she had they could rekindle their romance. It was possible her feelings for Xander were complicating things, she didn't loathe him anymore, and if she was being honest with herself, she only hated the attraction to him she felt when he was near.

Sophie made a tight turn and circled back toward the castle. She felt the weight in her chest growing lighter the closer she got. *Damn him*, she thought as she landed at the edge of the Golden City. When she appeared dressed, Sophie took off through the city looking for the White Raven Mystic Shop.

She saw the shop the last time she was there, it was on the same street where she had bought her dress for the ball where she met Bastian. She didn't know if the store was open at night, but she hoped it was. She had to know the truth. She walked down three streets before she found the right one. Relief washed over her as the White Raven sign came into view. She ran to the door and knocked loudly, hoping the owner by chance lived above her shop. Sophie was about to walk away when she heard a shuffle behind the door.

"What do you need at this hour, child?" The woman asked as she opened the door a crack.

"I am so sorry to bother you, but I have some matters of the heart and I need answers. I'm afraid I didn't plan very well, and I didn't bring any gold with me but—"

"I don't require gold from a magical creature such as yourself. You have a strange aura about you."

"What is it you require?" Sophie asked.

"No more than a pinprick, a drop or two of blood, I can absorb some of your magic and give you the answers you seek."

"Okay," Sophie agreed as she followed the seer into her shop.

"My name is Madame Moira, follow me to the back and we can begin." She led Sophie to a room behind a beaded curtain and tapestries depicting the phases of the moon. Candles flickered as they entered and Sophie swore the shadows moving along the walls did not belong to them. She had an eerie feeling as the woman sat down on the floor and motioned for Sophie to sit across from her with the table between them. Madame Moira put a candle and a metal bowl in the center of the table, took several jars of herbs from the shelf beside her, and set them on the table. "Now Dear, you said this was a matter of the heart, what question does your heart need to be answered?"

"Do you believe in fate?" Sophie asked.

"Why yes, child. The Fates assign each mortal being a destiny at birth and then it is the duty of the Fates to ensure each destiny is followed. If a prophecy is not fulfilled, the results can be catastrophic."

"What do you mean?"

"Well, for example, It was the destiny of King Haki to have a son anointed in the blood of the golden dragon. It was the fate of his son, Prince Dominic to become king after him, and for his son, who is yet to be born, to rule after him. If his destiny does not come to pass, then Ledora could fall into war. Sweaty soldiers will swing their swords at each other without care and race to the throne to claim power for themselves. Without the balance of the Fates, our world would not exist."

"What about fated mates, or fated love?"

"I see the true heart of the matter now, is there someone you like, or perhaps it is someone you do not like..." Moira looked at Sophie with one eyebrow raised.

"I just need to know who is my fated mate, who am I destined to spend my life with?"

"Okay, I have just the spell you need." Moira opened one of the herb jars and sprinkled some of the contents into the bowl, she did the same thing with several other jars and then added a reddish-brown stick. It smelled sweet but spicy. She used it to mix the ingredients in the bowl and then picked up a bunch of dried leaves wrapped with string and held the end of the bundle over the candle until it took the flame. When she pulled the herbs away, white smoke continued to rise from the leaves and Sophie recognized the smell of sage. Taking Sophie's hand in hers, Moira separated Sophie's pointer finger and gripped the tip of it. She pricked the finger with a sewing needle and squeezed a few drops of blood into the bowl. Moira placed the smoldering end of the sage bundle into the bowl and let the smoke and ember spread to the other herbs. Moira reached for Sophie's hands and laid her palms on top of her own. Moira's eyes turned milky white as the smoke seemed to fill them. "I see a man, very handsome indeed. Black of hair, brave, with a bit of darkness in him. He is destined to be yours, but... I knew you had a strange aura about you. This has never happened that I know of, but I see another with golden hair. They are both your destiny."

"How can they both be fated to me and who am I supposed to choose? I don't understand."

"I'm telling you, child, they will both love you for eternity no matter if you choose them or not," Moira said.

"I don't have to choose?"

"They are both fated to you, they will love no one else, but be careful, for two who love the same woman can grow to hate one another."

"How can I stop it from happening?"

"What is fated to be, will be and there is no stopping it."

TWENTY-SIX

SALTY DROPS OF SWEAT dripped down Sparrow's face and clung to his bottom lip as he struck the training dummy with the bottom of his bo staff. He twirled it around as he stepped to the left and struck again. Next, he unleashed a fury of blows as he worked out the anger building up inside him. The thought of waiting for Dmitri to attack seemed stupid. Velen stood behind him, watching. Sparrow guessed that Leon had tasked him with babysitting, making sure Sparrow wasn't sneaking off to kill Dmitri. It was all Sparrow could think about though. Killing Dmitri would eliminate all the fledglings and then his work would be done. Eira and the hunters could deal with Arturo's children—or not, if they so choose.

Sparrow wiped his face with the bottom of his white tunic, which was now stained with dirt and sweat and had more of a yellow hue. He pulled it off over his head and balled it up beneath his arm. He left the training yard without a word to Velen and didn't have to look over his shoulder to know he was being followed. When Sparrow reached his room at the guild, he turned to face his shadow. "Do you think I can bathe alone, or do you need to watch me do that too?"

"I know this isn't ideal, I don't like this assignment, but I have to follow my orders from Commander Rend. I would like to think we have become friends, so this isn't easy for me. Of course, you can bathe alone, but I'm going to have to stay close to make sure you don't go sneaking out the window. Miss Sophie is not just important to Leon, she is loved by so many, the cost for your vengeance is too great," Velen explained.

"Have you ever been close enough to anyone to experience true loss? Do you know what it feels like? The anger, the emptiness, the hole left in your heart from the removal of everyone you ever loved or cared for?"

"No. I have not had the experience, but killing Dmitri won't bring them back. It will only cause dozens of people to feel the same loss you feel right now," Velen countered

"I made a promise to my brothers; I vowed to avenge them."

"The mercy of a quick death is not deserved by all." Sparrow saw the darkness behind Velen's eyes as he said this.

"Perhaps you are right."

After he took a bath, Sparrow's energy waned. He crawled into bed but his mind could not rest. Instead of sleeping, he thought of all the ways he could make Dmitri suffer without killing him. Imprisonment was not enough. *Maybe taking a pound of his flesh every day would make me feel better.* Sparrow thought. *If the sleeping spell put Dmitri in a sleep from which he could not wake, would he be able to feel the torture being inflicted on his body?* Sparrow hoped he would, he wanted him to feel every plunge of his dagger, and every broken bone. He'd leave him in the pillory when not inflicting torture, so even in sleep, Dmitri's body could not rest. When sleep did finally come, it was deep and dreamless. The night passed uneventfully and and too quickly. Sunlight poured in through the open curtains and Sparrow woke up to the sound of a knock on his door.

"Just a minute!" he called as he grabbed his trousers from the back of the chair beside the bed. He stumbled as he tried to get his second leg in and fell backward onto the bed. Once both legs were in his trousers, he quickly shimmied them up over his hips and opened the door. Eira stood before him, her eyes trailing to his bare chest before she cleared her throat and took a step inside.

"How was your night?" Eira asked as her eyes moved from his half-dressed body to the bed which looked as though he'd fought with the covers and lost.

"Um, fine. Is everything okay? Do you have news on Dmitri?"

"No, I'm sorry. I just received word from Ravenhall and I'm afraid I have to leave. It's not a vampire thing—it's family."

"You're leaving? Will you be back in time for the Solstice celebration?"

"It's a long trip, I doubt it," she replied. Sparrow moved close to her and raised a hand to her cheek. He'd been so consumed with revenge, he had not given thought to how much he'd grown to care for Eira. He leaned in and brushed his lips against hers, hoping he had not terribly misjudged the moment. Eira placed her hands on his bare chest and for a second, he thought she might push him away, but her hands slid up to his neck and she deepened the kiss.

"I hope you'll come back soon." Sparrow said breathlessly when Eira pulled away.

"Me too," she replied.

He walked Eira to the door and as he watched her walk away, he noticed Velen still standing outside. "Did you even sleep last night?" Sparrow asked. Velen shook his head.

"I don't require sleep. Just a few hours of quiet meditation and Commander Rend and I switched out for a little while last night so I could. What do you have planned today? Wanna grab some breakfast?"

"Sure, but I'm not getting paid if I'm not working, so it's on you today." Sparrow said, clapping Velen on the shoulder.

"Fair enough," he replied.

The Gilded Lily was busy when they arrived, but they had no trouble getting a table. As they walked through the place, several of the patrons waved to Velen and he smiled and greeted them all. Sparrow hoped someday he would have this again, a happy community with friends and not this overwhelming burden of hatred and anger. Velen ordered scrambled eggs, over-easy with fresh bread and jam, ham, potatoes, and a morning mimosa. Sparrow decided on the sausage croissant with a fried egg on it over-hard and a horn of mead.

"Solstice is next week. We need to prepare. We have the rune circle set up already, so we just have to lure Dmitri to the spot and speak the incantation. It will send him directly to the rune circle at Castle Delacroix. Agatha will be waiting there to weaken him and get him into the sarcophagus—an extra security measure should the barrier spell ever be broken," Velen explained.

"What do you need me to do?"

"I'm expecting chaos when the fighting begins. There will be fledglings everywhere, but our focus is on Dmitri. We need to give him a reason to pursue us."

"I don't mean to interrupt, but I overheard you talking and I think I can help." Natalia approached their table and gestured to one of the two empty chairs at their four-top table. Velen nodded and seemed as interested in what Natalia had to say as Sparrow was. She sat down and reached into the small handbag she was carrying and pulled out a small green stone with lightning streaks of red magic swirling through it.

"What is it?" Velen asked.

"I'm not sure, but it contains magic, and Dmitri was looking for it. The walls of the cavern had deep grooves suggesting it had been mined. I spotted this beneath the pool of blood behind the sarcophagus, I'm guessing he lost it and was looking for another."

"We might be able to lure him to us. He is power hungry and if he wanted the stone as badly as you say, its magic must be very powerful." Velen put his hand out to accept the stone, but Natalia pulled it back.

"First, I need you to promise me you will not kill Dmitri. Both of my sons are desperately in love with Sophie. Xander can deny it all he wants, but a mother can see these things. Not only will they both lose Sophie, but I will lose Arturo. I know you have no love for our kind," She was now looking at Sparrow. "I'm no stranger to hunters. I heard about your family and I'm awfully sorry about what happened to them—and you, but we had nothing to do with it; we were still trapped on Immernacht. If my boys lose Sophie, they will not want to go on living without her, and if I lose Arturo *and* my boys, this cycle of senseless violence will continue because I will do *anything* for my children." Natalia's eyes were ice cold and Sparrow believed she was a woman of her word.

"I have already agreed to this. Killing Dmitri now would make far more enemies for me than I care to have. I will settle for trapping him for eternity as long as we can take out all the fledglings," Sparrow said.

"Works for me." Natalia handed the stone to Velen and left them to their breakfast.

Velen turned the stone over in his hand and inspected it closely. "I think I know what this is; it's a bloodstone. Witches and sorcerers were once a lot alike—both believing certain gemstones held power and energy which could be harnessed during different moon phases. Legends my mother used to tell me spoke of a stone pendant capable of giving it's wearer the ability to shift into dragon form. She described it to me a few times, and from what she told me, I think this is it," Velen said.

"How do you wear it? It's just a rock," Sparrow remarked.

"I'm not saying I would wear it, the stone is similar is all, I should give it to Commander Rend, just in case." Velen opened his leather coin pouch and dropped the stone into it.

They finished their breakfast while making light conversation, avoiding all work related topics.

TWENTY-SEVEN

FATED TO BOTH? MADAME Moira's words turned over in Sophie's mind the whole way back to the castle. She was fated to Bastian *and* Xander. She debated with herself about whether or not she should tell Xander about her visit to the White Raven. On one hand, he was right, they were fated. On the other, they still needed to rescue Bastian, and admitting her attraction to Xander would only distract them from their task. Sophie stepped lightly as she walked down the hall to her room, she didn't want to wake Xander if he was already asleep. She opened the door and light from the hallway torches filtered into the room enough for her to see Xander lying on the floor with a pillow and the thin blanket from the bed. Sophie took no pleasure in his discomfort, so she approached to wake him. He opened his eyes before she reached his side.

"Hey, are you okay?" he asked.

"Yes, I'm fine, why don't you sleep up here in the bed? I hate to see you looking so uncomfortable on the hard floor like an animal. Please, I insist."

"I'm not letting *you* sleep down here," he replied.

"Who said I was going to sleep on the floor?" She waited for Xander to catch her meaning and when he did he stood up a little too eagerly. "We're *just* sleeping," Sophie warned him.

Xander nodded, grabbing his pillow and blanket and putting them on the bed. Sophie walked around to the right, which was the side she slept on anyway, even when alone. She crawled into bed beside him, but not touching and closed her eyes.

"Where did you go?" Xander whispered.

"I flew around for a little while, got some fresh air."

"I just wanted to say, I'm sorry you didn't get a choice in your immortality, but I'm curious. If say perhaps Bastian had presented you with all the facts, and asked you if you wanted to turn, would you have chosen this for yourself?"

Sophie rolled over to face him. Xander was lying on his back, staring at the canopy with his head resting on his hands like a pillow. "I don't know what I would have chosen. Forever is a long time to live and you would be forced to watch everyone you love die while you're stuck in your grief for all eternity."

"It sounds awful when you put it like that," he replied.

"Why did you choose it?"

"It was my father's legacy. Some day he would go into a willing hibernation—the long rest—we call it, and I would take his place as Lord of Immernacht. It was my birthright. Since we might not ever have to go back there, it seems it was for nothing, but I won't complain about having eternity with the people I care about." He looked over at her, not moving his soft gaze from her eyes.

"Have you ever loved anyone who wasn't a vampire?" Sophie inquired.

"Once," he replied, but didn't elaborate.

"What was her name?" she asked.

"Sophie."

She pushed him playfully. "Stop, I'm serious."

"Okay, the truth is, I have never been in love before. I've been with women, sure, but I've had no lasting or meaningful relationships. It always felt...wrong."

"Wrong how?"

"I don't know, almost like... have you ever put your shoes on the wrong feet by accident? They're the right size, but uncomfortable."

Sophie thought about her first love and how it never seemed like the right time for them. The one kiss they shared still lingered in the forefront of her mind. It was through the pain of his rejection Sophie had met

Bastian and although she had grown to love him, their relationship began as a string of secret rendezvous. She never expected it to last, even after she found out she was with child. The first time she saw Bastian cradling Willow in his arms was when she knew she loved and wanted to make a home with him.

"What are you thinking about?" Xander rolled over and brushed a red curl behind Sophie's ear.

"Life, love... fate," She replied softly. Xander looked at ease in the dim moonlight coming in through the window. He gently twirled the locks of her hair around his finger and let them go, it felt relaxing in a way she never knew it could. She closed her eyes and fell into a dreamless slumber.

Sophie woke in the middle of the night—or the early morning, she wasn't sure which—with Xander's body pressed to her back and his arm around her middle. She could feel his skin against hers and suddenly remembered she was naked. She had never put on clothes after flying and the illusion spell had long since worn off. If she moved, she would risk waking Xander, but she was still sleepy and didn't want to get up. *I'll worry about it in the morning.* Sophie thought as she drifted back to sleep. When morning light poured in through the barred window, she awoke to find herself wrapped in Xander's arms and looked up to see he was already awake. He kissed her forehead.

"Good morning, beautiful," he whispered. The way he looked at her sent a thrill through her. It was the same way Bastian had looked at her in the beginning. Quickly realizing she was still naked, Sophie cast the illusion spell to get out of bed. If Kamara was awake, maybe she could borrow a tunic and a pair of trousers.

Sophie opened the door and was surprised to see not only were people awake, but something was happening. Maids rushed from place to place, carrying buckets of water, blankets, and more wood for the hearth.

Sophie rushed down the hall to Kamara's room but when she tried to enter, The Queen's Mistress halted her.

"No one is allowed in right now except attendants, the wet nurse, and the midwife," she said with an authoritative tone.

"I am an attendant," she lied, trying to use the power of suggestion like she'd seen both Xander and Serena do.

"No, you're not, attendants wear white and are hand-picked by me. Now, you can stand back, or I'll have the guards remove you from the castle."

She backed away slightly, but craned her neck to see inside the room from the hall. There were too many people in the way, she could only hear what was going on.

"Breathe, My Queen, short breaths, good. Okay... you can do this. Trust your body. Thousands of women have been right where you are." the midwife said in a soothing voice. Sophie saw Xander approaching and hurried over to talk to him before he got close enough for the mistress to hear.

"Kamara is having her baby. I want to be in there with her, but the woman at the door won't let me in. Do you think maybe you could convince her to?"

"I thought you didn't like it when I used my compelling gift?" Xander teased.

"I don't like when you use it on *me*," Sophie clarified.

"Okay, but it means you'll owe me." Xander extended his hand to seal the deal.

"Ugh, fine, but nothing which would impugn my honor." Sophie took his hand and his lips curved up in a charming smile. He strolled over to the mistress and they exchanged a few words. Sophie watched as the woman's eyes dilated and returned to normal. She moved aside and allowed both Xander and Sophie to enter the room. Kamara was standing, bent over the side of the bed with her head buried in her arms and her hips moving slowly from side to side. Her dressing gown was drenched with sweat.

"Who are you and who let you two in here?" The midwife asked in a hushed but not silent tone.

"I'm Sophie Rend, I'm—"

"Stay," was all Kamara could say through labored breaths as she looked up at Sophie.

"Fine, but keep out of the way and remain silent, do you understand?"

"Yes Ma'am," Sophie agreed. giving Kamara a gesture of luck. Two maids stacked more wood on top of the red-hot coals in the bottom of the fireplace, and another folded towels and placed them in a cast-iron pot, covering it with the lid. She set it next to the fire to warm them. Kamara climbed up onto the bed and arched her back with her head down, took a few breaths, and then stretched her back in the opposite direction looking toward the ceiling.

"Good, just breathe through. I'm going to check you now to see if I can see the baby." The midwife said. Two of the attendants held up a white linen to obstruct the view of anyone but the midwife. "Okay, you need to slow down, Your Majesty. Rosie, please hand me the surgical knife, I need to make a small cut, nothing major, I don't want you to worry, but I need to move the cord."

Sophie couldn't see what was happening behind the sheet, but the smell in the room changed. It went from a sweet-smelling nectar, to the coppery tang of blood. The room began to spin and Sophie felt an ache in her stomach. She stood and tried to take a few steps back but darkness overcame her.

When Sophie opened her eyes, Xander hovered over her, pressing a cool, damp rag to her forehead.

"Kamara...what happened? Last thing I remember, Kamara was delivering her baby, and...Oh no, please tell me I didn't hurt her or the baby."

"They're fine, you just passed out. I brought you back here and Dominic sent breakfast." Xander opened the door and a maid walked in carrying a tray of food. She set it down on the bedside table and then sat next to Sophie. "Have some fruit," Xander instructed, looking at the maid. She picked up a strawberry and brought it to her lips. She bit into the middle of it and Sophie stared at her pink lips around the red berry and caught herself wondering what the girl's mouth would taste like. She had the urge to bite her lower lip and taste the sweet berry as its juice collided with blood.

"Just wait, Sophie. Trust me." Xander held up a finger and Sophie obeyed. "Have some more, try a bit of everything," Xander told the maid. She did as Xander said, taking piece after piece from the pile. She ate pineapple, grapes, shaved coconut, mango, strawberries, raspberries and dates. *Okay, now Sophie, I want you to look at her, and tell her to not be afraid.* Sophie heard Xander's words in her mind, but his lips did not move. She turned to the girl and stared deep into her brown eyes.

"Do not be afraid."

"Why would I be afraid?" the girl asked.

"I guess suggestion isn't one of your gifts," Xander said kneeling down in front of the girl. "Do not be afraid, Sophie and I are going to drink from you, and when we are done, you will leave and forget ever meeting us." She nodded in response and when Xander looked away, her eyes seemed smaller than they were before.

Sophie leaned over, unable to curb her appetite any longer, and sank her fangs into the girl's neck and Xander bit into her neck on the other side. They drank until her skin began to pale and the rosiness had left her cheeks. Sophie let her go without instruction from Xander.

"What did you think?" Xander asked.

"Her blood was so sweet, it was like the berry wine from Ravenhall they used to serve at The Gilded Lily," she recalled.

"Okay, you may leave. Thank you," Xander said to the maid. She nodded and left the room without another word.

Sophie stared off into a far corner, unable to focus on anything in particular.

"What's on your mind?" Xander asked.

"You should know, can't you hear my thoughts?" she asked.

"No, I can implant thoughts into the minds of others, change their perception, even make them do things they don't want to do, but I can't hear anyone's thoughts, unfortunately, not even yours. I would love to know what you truly think though—about me," he clarified.

Sophie swallowed hard as she gazed at him, his emerald eyes sparkled when he looked back at her. His lips, still stained red from blood, looked so inviting and she longed to feel them against hers, but there was no way she could tell him. "You're my friend; I hope, for now, this answer will suffice," she said. His face fell and she knew he hoped for more, but until Bastian was safe, she couldn't allow herself to explore any other possibility. "I want to see Kamara and the baby, and then we should be getting back," Sophie said as she rose from the bed. As she started to cross the room, the illusion of clothing on her body shimmered outward, then disappeared completely and she was left standing naked. *How long was I passed out?* She wondered. Xander's eyes grew as wide as dinner plates and when she shot him a stern look he quickly turned his gaze from her. "Maybe there's a robe in here." She ran to the washroom and thankfully, beside the washtub, there were two robes. She slipped one on and tied the belt around her waist to secure it. "Okay, I'm ready now." Xander looked back at her with more desire now than ever, but with a hint of pain. "What's wrong?"

"Nothing. I'm just... If you only knew." He let out a barely audible groan as he stood up and moved toward the door. He was trying so hard to respect her boundaries. He was different now than he had been when they first met. At the time he was actively trying to make her hate him. He'd said he thought it would be easier, but she wondered who he thought it would be easier for—him, or her?

Kamara was sitting up, cradling her new bundle of joy when Sophie entered her bed chamber. She had never seen Kamara look happier, or more beautiful than she did in this moment. Her brown skin was glowing with love and radiating her happiness throughout the room. Her purple and blue braids hung loose over her shoulder.

"Sophie, come, meet our son. I have named him Asante, it means gratitude so he may be thankful for his blessings and give blessings to our people," Kamara said as she gazed lovingly at her son.

"It is a beautiful name." Sophie smiled as she approached and sat in the chair next to Kamara.

"Would you like to hold him?"

"I would love to," Sophie said, standing to accept the child from his mother's arms. She looked down at the sleeping baby and her heart filled with pain as a realization crossed her mind. She was a vampire, and would never have another child. It's not as if she'd given thought to having more children, but now that the possibility had been stolen from her, she wondered if she would have wanted them. Questions raced through Sophie's mind as she cradled Asante. He was so tiny and new; his fingers wrapped around Sophie's and made her heart ache in a way she'd felt only once before—when Willow was born. He began to fuss and Sophie handed him back to his mother. "He is perfect."

"I am glad you think so. Dominic and I wanted to talk to you about a betrothal. We are already family in our hearts, we could join our kingdoms, and this way, when Dominic and I pass on, we know Asante and Willow will rule after us. What do you think?"

"Our children ruling together does sound lovely, but do you remember what happened with Gabe? He was my best friend and by the time I realized I loved him he was betrothed to Akiri, what if they fall in love with another, or worse, they resent us for making this choice for them?"

"I see your point, we could raise them together, they could spend the winters here in the south, and in the spring and summer, they could stay with you and Bastian in Lapis Highland, they will grow up to be best friends just as you and Gabe did and we can see if love blooms. If not, then no marriage is required, but if it does, then Willow shall be the next Queen of Ledora *and* Lapis Highland."

Sophie knew it was a gracious deal, one benefitting them both. "I can accept this. At least I know Willow will have a lifelong friend, if not more." She smiled and leaned down to hug Kamara. "I need to get back, the Solstice celebration is in a few weeks and I need to get ready. I'll return a few days before the holiday to bring Xander back so he can travel by ship to Ash and retrieve Bastian. I can't wait to see you again. I love you, my friend."

"I love you too, Sophie, safe travels."

Xander was waiting in the hall when Sophie left Kamara's room. He didn't say anything, but the way he looked at Sophie made her feel strange. He really was in love with her, and she wondered how long he would be able to refrain from acting on his feelings. Sophie cast clothing for herself and then took off the robe, handing it to a passing maid. "Can you please take care of this for me, I'm so sorry, but I have to go."

The maid nodded and bowed to her as she and Xander made their way to the door. The Ledoran courtyard was the most beautiful Sophie had ever seen; tall golden fountains sprinkled water down into pools filled with spotted colorful fish, lily pads, and four-leaf clovers floating above them. Sophie and Xander walked to the beach in silence. He seemed to be struggling with his thoughts, and Sophie wasn't sure what to say either. The flight back seemed to go by quicker than the flight there had been. Sophie wondered if it was because she dreaded going to Blackwater instead of Ash. She desperately wanted to know if Bastian was okay and hated she would not see for herself until Xander brought him home.

Instead of returning to Blackwater, Sophie flew to Lapis Highland. The castle looked as it had since the day it was built and the sight of home put Sophie at ease. She descended into the courtyard and once Xander was safely on the ground, she shifted back to human form. Quickly casting an illusion of clothing, Sophie and Xander made their way toward the castle. When the guards saw them approaching the front steps, they rushed to announce her arrival. Everyone bowed to their queen as they walked through the front doors and into the grand foyer.

Thomas, her personal guard approached rapidly and bowed to her, his face flooded with relief. "My apologies Your Majesty, we haven't heard from you in some time and I'm afraid we feared the worst. We did request word from your father, and he told us you were safe, but I can't tell you how happy I am to see you, My Queen."

"Is everything okay here?" she asked.

"Oh yes, everything is just fine, we harvested our first crop already and planted the second, this year we should have plenty of food without needing magic. The tavern in town started hosting a potluck, everyone makes a dish to bring and we all feast, so it's been fun. Have you any word on Sir Bastian yet?" Thomas asked.

"We know where he is, we just have to find the right moment to go and get him," she replied.

"Who is your handsome friend?" Thomas looked back at Xander.

"This is Bastian's brother, Xander. He is helping us get Bastian back," she explained. The kingdom was doing fine without her, it should have made her happy, but it didn't. She walked up the stairs and down the hallway to her study. Thomas and Xander followed behind her. When she opened the door and stepped inside, Thomas stopped in the hall.

"Shall I wait out here?" he asked, looking from Sophie to Xander.

"No, it's not like that," she replied.

"What are we doing in here?" Xander asked.

"I'm going to look through some of Ryul's old spell books and see if there's one that can help us. Here, you look through this stack, Thomas—you can take those books over there. I'm going to start with the ones in the cabinet," Sophie instructed.

"Is there anything specific we should be looking for?" Xander asked.

"A long-range message spell, or some way to just let Bastian know we are coming. Immunity spells would be helpful too if you can find one for resistance against being stabbed or burned with fire—you know, useful spells." Sophie went behind a folding room divider and dressed herself, then crossed the room to sit down at the desk with as many books as she could carry from the top shelf of the cabinet. "This could take us a while, you boys might want to get cozy."

TWENTY-EIGHT

THE RED-HAIRED GIRL KEPT appearing in his dreams. Was he supposed to help her? Were they related? The recurring dreams consumed his waking thoughts as well and seemed to be causing discourse in his marriage.

"Bastian! Hellllooooo," Elizandra waved her hand in front of his face as she drew out the last word to get his attention. Shaking his head to brush away the thoughts of his dream girl, his vision returned to the breakfast table. They were dining on the balcony outside their bedroom where they so often ate. It had been weeks since the dreams began. He often suffered headaches these days and wondered if he might be coming down with something. He looked at Elizandra, the scowl on her face made it clear her patience was thin.

"I told you I have to leave tomorrow, did you even hear me?" she asked.

"I'm sorry, where are you headed, would you like for me to come with you?"

"No," she said gruffly. "It's business. Dmitri needs me to take care of a few things."

"I still think it's strange you're working for Dmitri, you know it was not so many years ago he wanted me and my whole family dead." Bastian told her.

"Darling, I told you he's over your silly little feud. His new plan is much bigger than the issues with your family. Besides, there was no way I was going to allow him to harm you, my love." She flashed him a brilliant smile and gave him a wink as she rubbed her foot up the side of his leg. "Wanna head back to bed?" She raised a perfectly manicured eyebrow at him.

"Again? You're insatiable, woman."

"I can't help it, I'm just so happy to be your wife and I want to please you every day, multiple times a day, can you blame me?"

"I'm not feeling well right now, I'm afraid. My head... it's hurting again," he admitted.

"I'll make you a tonic." Elizandra left the room and came back a few minutes later with a small cup. Bastian raised it to his nose and gave the herbs a whiff. He gagged as the smell violated his senses.

"It smells awful, what's in it?"

"It's mostly wild lettuce extract for pain, but I put some cinnamon and honey in it to make it more appealing. It might not taste great, but it will cure your aches and pains," she said. Bastian drank it down in one quick gulp and had to clasp his hand to his mouth as if it would stop the tonic from coming back up. He gagged but kept down the awful mixture.

"Why don't you lay back down until you feel better? I need to pack anyway." She crossed the room and began picking clothing from the wardrobe to fold and place into her trunk. Bastian curled back into bed. The concoction worked fast and he entered the land of dreams once more.

'Come back to me...' The melody of an angel called to him through the darkness. He moved toward the sound of her voice, desperate to find out who she was. She stood on a cliff over the ocean with a large castle looming behind her. It almost looked haunted. Her red curls blew softly about her shoulders as the breeze kissed her skin.

"Who are you?" he asked as he reached out to touch her shoulder. She turned to face him, her red hair dancing in the wind. He startled as he looked upon the featureless burred oval where her face should have been. Why did his dream obscure her from him? Why couldn't he stop dreaming *about her, and thinking about her? There was a reason she kept appearing, he knew it.*

"What's your name?" Bastian asked.

"It's me, Sophie. Come back to me." She started to fade away as a thick purple smoke swirled out from behind her.

"No, wait!" Bastian cried. He reached out to grasp her but his hand cut through the and it swirled away, taking Sophie with it.

"SOPHIE!" he shouted as he woke up. The minutes seemed like hours as he tried to pull the image of her to the front of his mind. Images of the ball in Ledora came instead, the gowns, the golden ballroom, and Sophie. He remembered dancing with her and then moment from their courtship came back to him. He remembered. Suddenly the urge to escape was stronger than it had ever been. The memories, both false and real fought for domination over his mind. He wasn't sure what was real.

The room was dark and empty, a few embers of a dying fire glowed faintly in the hearth. Bastian got out of bed and tiptoed to the door. He listened for footsteps before stepping into the hallway. He recognized the black stone arches lining one side of the hall and was sure he remembered how to get to the front door. He navigated the hallways of the upper level and found his way to the stairs. He moved as silently as he could to the door, hoping it was both unlocked and well-oiled. He grasped the handle and pulled. The door creaked loudly as it opened and Bastian cringed, looking around for signs he'd been discovered. From the west wing came arguing voices, one male and the other female. Though he wanted to leave and was about to, he heard the mention of *her* name. He stopped, frozen in place. They were talking about Sophie. Bastian abandoned the door as he crept toward the voices.

"I just don't understand what spell that little witch has over everyone. You promised me I could peel her skin from her bones and now you're saying *you need* her?"

"I have someone on the inside informing me of their plans. She is the key to fulfilling your pact with Apollyon, I thought you would be desperate to cling to your power."

"I am, but I don't understand why we can't just find another way to open the portal?"

"I already told you, it will require too much magical energy. We need the power of the shifters *and Sophie.* She is going to absorb the power of the old hag, Agatha, and then Sophie will be the most powerful witch in every dimension, even more powerful than you."

"Then we should go get the witch, make her give her power to me, and then I can open the portal for Apollyon."

"We don't have time. Besides, once she opens the portal, this world will be gone. Apollyon will see to it, and don't worry, he will take us to a new world where we can have everything we ever wanted."

Bastian didn't wait to hear more, he tiptoed back to the door and slipped out, not bothering to pull it closed. He ran toward the rocky shore without stopping or looking back for fear he would be captured. The sharp rocks cut the soles of his feet leaving a trail of blood, but he didn't care. He would make it back to Sophie or die trying.

Bastian tried to shift, stretching his limbs and urging from his soul for the dragon to take over. No matter how far he stretched or how hard he pushed the dragon would not come. He didn't know how, but they'd stripped him of his magic, maybe it was the draining of his blood—dragon blood that caused it. He collapsed at the coastline and cried, waiting for the waves to claim him.

A loud screeching brought Bastian back from the pit of despair as his survival instinct kicked in. *It's swim or be dragged back to the castle*, Bastian thought. He ran into the water until it reached his waist and then plunged beneath the waves, paddling wildly to distance himself from the jagged shoals and the dragon he thought was almost certainly looking for him. Of course one of Baelfire's misplaced minions would have fallen into Elizandra's service. There was no time to wonder who the shifter was, he had to keep swimming. When he tried to come up for air, the waves crashed into his face and pushed him back under. He desperately tried to breach the surface as the sea fought equally hard to send him to the depths. Finally, he gave in; letting his arms and legs go limp, he floated on his back. He drew breath as soon as the breeze caressed his face, filling his lungs with air before another wave rose up behind him and pushed him beneath the surface again.

Bastian fought his way back up and looked back at the island of Ash, a brown dragon surveyed the beach. At any moment the beast would pick up his blood trail and spot him out here in the ocean. Bastian turned back toward the mainland and gasped. A fishing boat bobbed across the sea in his direction. He thought about waving his arms to flag it down but he was too far from it, and too close to the dragon. Propelling himself toward the fisherman, Bastian cut through the water now at a quicker pace As he neared the vessel he waved his arms, the sailor threw him a line and pulled him in.

"I didn't think anyone lived on the island of Ash anymore, what were you, and *that* doing out here?" he asked, motioning toward the shore where the dragon flew back and forth.

"You need to go, sail as quickly as you can toward the mainland, it may have spotted us," Bastian said.

The dragon roared and launched toward the sea. It unleashed its fiery breath. *This is it*, Bastian thought as he braced himself for death. When death did not come he dared to open his eyes and saw a blue shimmering shield surrounding the boat. He glanced at the very old and frail-looking fisherman, his long bony fingers clutching a wooden staff. The focus on the end of it was a glowing orb, much like the one he'd heard trapped the draconic magic. It glowed the same blue as the dome surrounding the boat and, somehow, Bastian knew he would make it to shore. He collapsed to the floor of the boat, relieved his fight with the sea was over.

"Rest now, Bastian. I'll see you home."

Bastian didn't have enough consciousness left to ask how the man knew his name.

When he came to, the old man was tying the boat to a small dock leading to a beach Bastian had never seen before. "Where are we?" He managed to choke out the words even though his throat was dry and sore from all of the salt water he had swallowed.

"We are on the southern shore of Ravenhall," the man replied.

"Are we going to see the elves?"

"We will likely see them, yes, but they are not the reason for our docking here. We are going to my study, Bastian."

"Who are you? How do you know my name?" he asked.

"I know a great deal of things, but the one thing I am certain of, is Sophie needs you."

"You know Sophie, too? How?"

"My name is Ryul. I was—"

"You're the wizard Sophie learned from. She thought you died and she mourned you. Why didn't you come back?"

"I tried, but she changed the rune circle and it no longer matched the one I had here. I figured she didn't want to see me," he replied.

"She wrote you letters, though," Bastian argued.

"The humans are expanding their territories, they're trying to run us out of Ravenhall by intercepting our messages—both sent and received—and cutting off our supply lines, the only problem is: we don't rely on anyone else and they weren't expecting that, yet still they shoot down any messenger birds."

Ryul led Bastian through the winding paths of the elven forest. Butterflies fluttered about and Bastian could have sworn he heard the sound of a child's laughter. The trees were taller than anywhere else he had ever been and bridges made of wood and rope connected the treetops. The grand castle came into view; white towers in every corner guarded spires reaching the top of the northern cliffs—or so it seemed from the ground. Beautiful flowers grew wildly around the castle, they made no effort to manage them or box them in.

They made their way through the front doors of the castle and up a winding staircase of the southeast tower. Ryul's study was modest, two shelves filled with potions lined the southern wall beside the door and the twine stretched from one side of the room to the other had bunches of herbs and flowers clipped to it for drying. He didn't have many books or even many possessions of personal nature. He had a single-sized bed pushed into the northeastern corner of the room, a writing desk in the middle, and a makeshift brewing station with a small wood stove along the western wall.

"We can stay here tonight, you can sleep in the bed, I only need to meditate for a few hours and I'll be good to go. We can get a couple of horses and ride to the tower tomorrow," Ryul said.

In the middle of the room on the floor, Bastian saw symbols he recognized drawn with chalk into a rune circle. "I see the changes Sophie made in the spacing of these markings, and I think I can get this rune circle to match again if you still remember the incantation to activate it," Bastian said, kneeling to inspect the runes.

"I do, and I would appreciate your help, I would love to see Sophie again. Let me find you a rag and some chalk." Ryul walked over to his writing desk and rummaged through the drawer on the right-hand side. He returned with the required items and handed them over.

Bastian studied the runes. For each location, Sophie used a different formula of runes. The spell was always the same but Blackwater was abbreviated 'BW' and Lapis Highland was 'LH'. The only problem was; Bastian couldn't read Ryul's writing and wasn't sure which markings to change. "Where is the location? You can read this, right?" Bastian asked.

"The spell begins here," he pointed to the left side of the circle. "It goes across the top and ends here, so these two runes here would be the location if that's how she does it. She might have written the spell across the bottom and placed the location at the top, or she could have even written it backward. I know some wizards who do just to make their work unreadable to the untrained eye."

Bastian worked on his hands and knees for hours trying different combinations to make the rune circle work. He'd write the incantation, the location, and then Ryul would speak the words. They worked well into the evening until Ryul stopped him. "Let's have some dinner and get some rest, I'm sure fresh eyes will help."

That night was the first Bastian's mind felt clear. The purple smoke Elizandra was poisoning him with seemed to be mostly out of his system. He tossed and turned as he thought of getting back to Sophie and his heart, which should have been filled with relief and joy, was instead heavy with guilt. Thoughts of playing house with Elizandra and making love to her turned his stomach. The worst part was, he had enjoyed it, not knowing he was not in control of his own mind. *How could I have done this to Sophie, my mind wasn't even strong enough not to forget her. I don't deserve her.* Bastian berated himself in his thoughts. He pictured her face, her creamy pink skin, and light brown freckles scattered like the stars of the heavens across her body. He dreamed of her perfect green eyes and the feel of her full lips against his. He longed to twirl the locks of her red hair around his finger as he watched her sleep in his arms. Not only had he forgotten Sophie under Elizandra's mind control, but he forgot about his child. How could a father forget his own daughter? In the midst of his self-loathing, sleep finally came for him.

The sun dipped low on the horizon silhouetting Highland Castle against the dark red sky. Finally, he was home. Bastian ran to the front doors, anxious to see his love and hold his daughter in his arms. The guards at the door let him in without a word and he went straight to Willow's room. She was so much bigger than he remembered. How long had he been gone? Willow was a baby the last time he saw her and now she was a child, out of the crib and tucked snugly into a bed with no rails. He ran to the queen's chamber which he had shared with Sophie. Thomas stood at the door.

When Bastian tried to enter, Thomas blocked his path, his face solemn. "You don't want to do this to yourself. You've been gone a long time, a lot has changed," he warned.

"I need to see her," Bastian pleaded.

"She's not alone."

Thomas's words pierced his heart. "I don't care," he insisted. Bastian pushed the guard aside and crept into the room, his eyes confirming his worst fear. Sophie's head rested comfortably in the nook of Xander's shoulder as his fingers gently stroked her hair. They were not covered up and Bastian's eyes flashed with envy to see their bodies tangled together in post-coital bliss. He was going to be sick. He ran from the room desperate for escape, dying to erase the image of the woman he loved and his brother.

Bastian's eyes snapped open as his stomach turned. He shot up from the bed and darted to the chamber pot. The contents of his stomach made a violent reappearance.

TWENTY-NINE

The courtyard of Highland Castle lay buried beneath a mesmerizing blanket of sparkling white snow. The gardens, once bursting with color and life, now slept in quiet slumber awaiting the breath of spring. The towering walls of the castle were adorned with frosty icicles glistening like diamonds. The serenity of the snow-covered ground was broken only by the occasional footprints of a lone wanderer, leaving behind evidence of their passage. The winter chill did not affect Sophie as it once had. She could detect the cold, but there was no longer a need for her to retreat to the warmth inside the castle walls as she had when she was human. In this frozen oasis, time seemed to stand still. Sophie wondered if this kind of peace would ever be sustainable. Ever since that day on the top of Dragon Peak when she claimed the Red Dragon Throne, her life and the lives of those around her had been in constant peril. At least Willow would be safe. By now she would be with Juniper and the Druids of the Forgotten Grove, in a protected land where no vampire could step foot.

Sophie and Xander stayed in Lapis Highland for almost a week. With Xander there, Sophie allowed Thomas to focus on training the Highland Dragon, which she'd told him he could name. Sophie caught up on her royal duties while Xander trained everyone to protect themselves against feral vampires. He helped them make weapons and build more defenses. Sophie was surprised at how readily he pitched in. She watched him as he played with the children in the training yard, fending off the attacks of their wooden swords with one of his own. His side-swept bangs hung loosely over his forehead on one side and he raked his fingers through his hair, clearing his line of sight. His green eyes shined vibrantly and he flashed Sophie a smile as he whirled around to parry the strike from another play sword.

"My Queen! My Queen!" Thomas burst through the doors and into the courtyard. "It's Bastian!" he yelled rushing over to her.

"What about Bastian?" Sophie asked.

"He is here with some old guy; they came through a teleportation circle in the old part of the tower!"

Thomas barely came to a stop before Sophie bolted for the door, calling for Xander to follow in a panicked tone. He dropped his wooden sword and ran after her. Sophie's wet shoes slipped on the tile floor as soon as she entered the foyer so she kicked them off and kept running. She took the stairs two at a time, ignoring the stitch in her side. Sophie threw open the door to her study and her eyes darted to the only part of the old tower left and the two men struggled to stand.￿

"Bastian?" *Was it really him? Has he found his way back to me?* she thought. He looked up at her briefly as he helped his companion to his feet. Sophie screamed when the man's face came into view. "Ryul? I thought you were dead!" Sophie darted across the room to wrap both of them in her arms.

"I thought I was too, but as it turns out, the enchanted forest is restorative," Ryul replied.

"Bastian, I can't believe it's you, I was so worried. I tried to come to rescue you but—"

Bastian's expression turned dark as his eyes left her. The vision from his nightmare resurfaced and images of his brother and Sophie haunted him. He stared with fury burning in his eyes. Sophie turned around and followed his gaze to see Xander in the doorway. There was almost something inhuman about the deep growl that escaped Bastian as he lunged across the room at Xander.

"What the hell?" Xander managed to shout before Bastian grabbed him by the collar. Bastian's fist connected with Xander's jaw. He picked him up by his lapels and launched him across the hall and through a decorative table. Shattered glass clacked across the tile floor as the debris exploded away from the force.

"What is wrong with you?" Sophie demanded of Bastian as she rushed over to pick Xander up off the floor.

"Oh sure, take his side. You wasted no time moving on with him. Were you even the least bit concerned for me?" Bastian's face contorted in anger as his rage turned to Sophie. His eyes were still darkened, and lacked his usual kindness. She cowered away from him. Xander immediately moved in between them, diverting Bastian's focus to him. "You can be pissed off at me all you want, but this whole time she has thought of nothing but finding you. Dmitri turned her, and we had to lock her in a cell so she wouldn't kill her mother, Willow, or random strangers in the street, we taught her to control the bloodlust and even going through all of that, *you* have been her priority, even at the expense of herself. Don't you *ever* speak to her like that again, or I'll kill you myself." Xander stood nose to nose with Bastian.

"I can see it, don't patronize me; you've had your eyes on her since the first day we arrived on Immernacht. The way she rushed over to you just now... you slept with her didn't you? It's okay, you can admit it, your lust for each other is all over your faces," he said, pointing his finger back and forth between them.

"You're wrong," Xander said quietly.

"What was that? Speak up and tell me you're not fucking her!" Bastian screamed.

"I love her, but she loves *you*. Although, the way you're acting, Gods knows why."

"You *love* her? So you have fucked her then?"

"Bastian no, we haven't—I mean..." Sophie couldn't think of the right words. Bastian looked at both of them with disgust, huffed and shoved past them.

"I should go talk to him," Sophie said, looking at Xander.

"No, I don't want you to be alone with him, he's not himself right now," he replied.

"Don't worry, I can handle it." Sophie gave him a reassuring pat on the shoulder as she tiptoed between the pieces of broken glass to follow Bastian.

Sophie took a moment to find her shoes when she reached the foyer. The front doors stood open and Sophie stepped out into the cool night air. She spotted Bastian standing by the edge of the cliff on the other side of the courtyard. The snow crunched softly beneath her feet, warning him of her approach. He turned to look at her, but did not speak. He looked back across the water.

"I feel like this reunion could have gone better," Sophie said as she stepped up behind him. "Want to talk about it?" She thought about placing a hand on his shoulder but caution gave her pause. He had been so angry with her, and why had he assumed she and Xander were together? Sophie needed answers but she wasn't sure she would be able to coax them from his lips this night. "Want to fly with me?" she asked. They always used to feel better after soaring through the stars. He stayed silent for a long time as if considering her request.

"I can't shift," he said finally.

"Maybe after a rest you—"

"No, they drained me of my power. I don't know how; some spell," Bastian said as he kicked the toe of his boot through the snow. "Dmitri and Elizandra held me captive at Akiri's old castle. She filled my head with false memories and erased everything good, she… she kept me chained to the b-bed," he stuttered and choked as he recalled the events. "Oh, Gods, Sophie." Bastian wailed as he covered his face to hide his shame. Sophie reached for his shoulder and turned him to face her.

"What did she do to you, Bastian?" Sophie cupped his face to bring his eyes to hers.

"She kept dosing me with this purple smoke that made me forget. I didn't remember you, or Willow. All she allowed me to remember was being married to her. Sophie, I swear I didn't want to… I would *never*," his eyes welled with tears and his lips pursed in anger. Beads of perspiration glistened on his brow and he clenched and opened his hand several times as he tried to tell her what he'd been through.

"Did she *rape* you?" Sophie asked, her voice barely more than a whisper.

Bastian broke down. Loud sobs escaped his throat and he kept sniffling. Sophie wrapped her arms around him and let his tears dampen her shoulder as he nodded. "I'm so sorry, Sophie. I betrayed you."

The way he said it broke Sophie's heart. She had been angry at his outburst when he thought she had been unfaithful to him but now the truth of the matter, and the whirlwind of emotion he must have been fighting in that moment when he saw them, was evident. Sophie guided Bastian to take a step back and she brought his face to hers once more. "What happened to you is not your fault. I think you need to rest, come on, you're safe now," she said firmly, urging him to believe it.

Sophie took his hand and walked beside him, allowing him to set the pace as they made their way back to the castle. She led him to their bedchamber. It was just as it had been the last time they shared this room. Sophie watched Bastian's eyes dart around the space taking in the familiar scene. His grip on Sophie's arm tightened as they reached the bed. "I think I would like to just sit by the fire for a while," Bastian said as he crossed the room and lowered himself into the armchair. "Where is Willow?"

"Juniper took her to the Forgotten Grove. Dmitri plans to attack Blackwater at the Solstice celebration, Juniper will bring her back as soon as the battle is over." Sophie put a few logs in the fireplace and grabbed a handful of kindling to stuff into the crevices. She ignited the kindling with the whisper of a word and watched as the crackle turned to flame and spread throughout the hearth. "Can I bring you anything?"

Sophie asked, kneeling in front of Bastian. He shook his head. Sophie reached for his hand to give him a comforting pat and he jerked away from her. "I'm sorry, Sophie, I don't mean to be jumpy. I think I just need some time, why don't you check on Xander, and tell him I'm sorry? I'm sure Ryul will also be waiting to see you," he said. Sophie tried to hide her sadness as she nodded and left Bastian in front of the fire as requested.

She found the others sitting in the parlor, mingling with Thomas, Emily, and Ezra. Sophie watched as Ryul regaled them with a tale about the elves of Ravenhall and all manner of magical creatures he had encountered since he left the tower. Sophie smiled. She missed his stories and the way he performed all the parts when he retold them. He looked different than the last time she saw him. He had been old and frail, barely able to get himself into bed on his own, now he was full of life and seemed as if he were aging in reverse. Sophie wondered if his aged appearance back then had anything to do with the cost of wielding magic.

Xander spotted Sophie watching from the doorway and smiled. He moved silently to her so he wouldn't interrupt the story. Sophie raised her hand to the unmistakable mark of his recent altercation with Bastian. She hovered her fingers over the blended hues of purple and red on his cheek and marveled at how quickly the bruise changed color, by the time he went to sleep it would likely be gone. His split lip had already scabbed over but was still twice its normal size and Sophie wondered; if this was partially healed already, how had it looked earlier?

"I'm so sorry, I won't make excuses for his behavior. He's not okay, it might take him a while to recover from the trauma he's experienced. He did tell me to pass on his apologies to you though," Sophie said. Sophie had an inexplicable urge to embrace him, maybe it was how close he was standing, or how fearlessly he had put himself between her and Bastian.

"Are you okay?" He gently stroked the side of her cheek with his thumb. She leaned her face into his palm, savoring his caress.

"I'm okay." She tried to smile, but the corners of her mouth resisted and her brows remained furrowed with worry.

Xander pulled her to him and held her until he felt her tension ease. "He'll be okay. I mean, he's come back from much worse. I watched him die and be reborn as a vampire," he said.

Sophie pulled away and looked back at Ryul. He was just finishing up his story and flashed her a smile. Sophie rushed over to him and wrapped her arms around him. "I missed you so much! I wrote you many letters, did they never reach you?" she asked.

"I'm sorry to say, I didn't get any messages, but I missed you very much, too."

"How did you age in reverse? You look amazing." Sophie took a step back to examine him closer.

"Apparently, living in the human world for so long and using human magic, I aged like them, too. It was a curse I didn't even know I had. In Ravenhall, the healer had the ability to remove the curse and I began to lose some of the wrinkles and the pain. Oh goodness, the pain was the worst part about growing old. My back hurt, I could barely stand, and for some reason, I got shorter," he let out a hearty chuckle.

They sat in the parlor talking for hours, Ryul told them about his life with the elves and asked Sophie about her role as queen of Lapis Highland. One by one the castle staff slipped away to bed and when Sophie too let out a yawn, Ryul stood up to leave.

"You can stay the night if you want," she said.

"I do need to be getting back. If I'm away from the forest for too long, the pain creeps back in," he replied.

"Want me to walk with you back to the runes?" Sophie asked.

"No, I'll be fine. You have more important matters to attend to. I hope Bastian will be okay. Your circle leads to my study now, so feel free to visit any time. I'll miss you," Ryul said.

"I'll miss you too. Don't be a stranger, okay?"

"I'll do my best. Xander, it was lovely to meet you. Take care." Ryul called as he exited the parlor.

"I'm going to go check on Bastian," Sophie said, turning to Xander. He nodded in response and she walked back up the stairs. The maids had already cleaned up the broken glass and debris from the table. She paused and took a deep breath, hoping Bastian was feeling better. When she opened the door, Bastian was stuffing some of his clothing into a bag. "Where are you going?" Sophie tried to keep the panic out of her voice, but the lump in her throat fell like a boulder to the pit of her stomach.

"I need some time. I'm going to rally some more support for Blackwater, between these visions I can't shake, and everything Elizandra's magic made me forget, I can not be the partner you need right now. My hope is that we win this war, and then maybe when life slows down again, and I've recovered from this fog I feel like I'm in, maybe I can still be the man you fell in love with. I am so afraid of these visions and the anger they make me feel, and if I hurt you—I mean physically hurt you... I would never forgive myself."

"Bastian, what are you saying?"

"I'm not sure, but until I figure it out, move on. Don't wait for me. I don't know how deep this madness goes, or how long it will last." Bastian's eyes were red where they should have been white and glistened with tears.

"Here, take this," she said as she lifted the skirt of her dress and fished a strange silver coin from her pocket.

"What is it?" Bastian turned it over in his hand and examined the runes stamped into the metal.

"This will allow you to cross into the Fae Lands. Willow will be with the Druids in the Forgotten Grove—you can visit her there, maybe seeing our daughter will help you find yourself again. The druids might also be able to help you heal." Sophie couldn't hold back the tears any longer; they flowed like rivers from her eyes, streaking her face.

"I will visit Willow, then I will see you again on the solstice. I'm sorry, Sophie. Please try to be happy, even if it's with Xander. I know at the very least, you will be safe with him." Bastian's expression was now stone, the moisture threatening to spill from his eyes a moment ago was gone.

"I'll wait for you to find your way back to me," she whispered.

Bastian shook his head. "No, if you can have happiness now, take it. Life, even eternal life, can end at any moment. It only takes a stake, or dragon's breath, and then it's all over. Don't waste a moment of your life, Sophie Rend." Bastian walked out of the bedroom with his bag of clothing slung over his shoulder.

Sophie waited until she heard the front door of the castle close before she let her sadness engulf her. She slammed her bedroom door and let out a wail of frustration and sorrow. She sobbed as she crossed the room to her chest of drawers—an altar of little trinkets and gifts she'd received from Bastian over the course of their courtship. She swiped everything off the top of it with one swift motion. Everything clattered to the floor.

"Are you okay, My Queen?" Thomas asked, bursting into the room. He took one look at her and rushed to her side. He helped her to the bed and when she sat down, he removed her shoes and lifted her feet. "You should get some rest, Your Majesty. Can I bring you anything?"

"No, just leave me," she said.

Thomas bowed to her and crossed the room. Sophie turned over, bringing the covers over her head and cried, unable to sleep.

THIRTY

AGATHA'S MILKY EYES SEEMED to stare right through him as Sparrow placed the stone in her hand. She felt the magic within it beating like a pair of giant wings. He looked at her with curiosity as she brought the stone to her ear and listened. Sparrow hadn't heard the stone make noise and didn't know how much of Agatha's craft was performance. Oracles, seers, fortune-tellers, or whatever they called themselves, were as much of a game of chance as dice or cards. For every forty people who claimed they could see your future, only one would have real magic, the rest were charlatans whose talents included little more than an ability to pay attention to detail. Sparrow cleared his throat quietly, hoping not to disturb her concentration.

"There was another artifact containing magic like this, it was called the Orb of Dragonkind. This stone contains the magic of a dragonshifter. Without it, their power to morph into their beast form is gone," she told him.

"Who's magic is it?" Sparrow asked.

"I would have no way of knowing. I see many things, but I do not see all," she said handing the stone back to him. Sparrow slipped it back into the leather pouch he wore on his belt.

"Thank you, Agatha," he said as he stood up to leave.

"Be careful with that stone, whoever sealed the magic into it, will be looking for it."

"I will," he nodded as he crossed the room. The scent of sage and clove followed him as he opened the door and a cloud of smoke puffed out around him. Velen was waiting by the door when Sparrow stepped out into the hall.

"What did Aggie have to say?" Velen finally asked.

"The stone contains the magic of a dragonshifter," Sparrow repeated her words.

"Bastian?" Velen asked.

"That's what I'm thinking."

"We should have listened to Sophie. I received word a few days ago she is still at Lapis Highland," Velen said.

"Did Akiri tell you?" Sparrow jokingly waggled his eyebrows.

"No, we didn't really work out. We're still friends, though." Velen shrugged.

"Hey, I'm sorry, I didn't know."

"It's okay, we kept things quiet. Anyway, what are we going to do about the stone?" Velen asked, changing the subject.

The guild hall was busy with preparations for solstice, and the foyer was crowded with guild members, maids, merchants, and Silver Soldiers. Sparrow looked around for Commander Rend, but did not see him among those in the foyer.

"There's Beric," Sparrow said. "He can take a message to Lapis Highland for us." He raised his arm and waved the young man over as Sparrow made his way through the crowd to talk to him.

"Sparrow, good to see you," Beric said.

"It's good to see you too, we are in a bit of a situation, and we were hoping you could help. Are you busy right now?" Sparrow asked.

"Not really, I was asking Commander Rend if there was anything I could do, but he doesn't have anything for me yet," Beric replied.

"How would you like to take a message to Sophie for us?" Sparrow asked. "We'll pay you," he added.

"Alright, what's the message?"

"Tell her Bastian can't fly, they've taken his magic, but don't worry, we're going to come up with a plan to get him out of there," Velen told him, handing him a small pouch of gold. Beric pocketed the coin pouch, nodded quickly, and took off running through the guild hall.

"That's probably the best messenger we've ever had," Velen said.

"He's a pretty good cook, too." Sparrow thought back to the meals they made in the campfire on his way to Blackwater. "He's a good kid. I enjoyed his company," he said.

Leon emerged from the crowd. "Just the two I wanted to see," he said. "We need to make this place look festive. The goal is to carry on as if we suspect nothing of this possible attack. What do you say? Help us decorate?"

Sparrow and Velen spent the day hanging dried oranges, cranberries, cinnamon sticks, clay sculptures of the sun, and boughs of pine. They lit lanterns along the paths in town and wrapped the lantern hooks with pine garland and strings of cranberries. People sang beautiful songs of the season as they worked and even though he knew this celebration was doomed to end in war, Sparrow couldn't help feeling the warmth creep into his heart and fill him with joy. His brothers didn't celebrate the solstice and he hardly remembered anything from his life with his mother. This was his first solstice and he didn't know how long he would be able to enjoy it.

When the work was done, Sparrow returned to his room still under Velen's watchful eye. He bathed and got dressed up to go out. It wasn't that Velen wasn't good company, Sparrow had come to consider him a good friend, but he wanted female companionship tonight. Maybe it was the warm and fuzzy feeling that hit him while they were decorating, or maybe it had just been too long. He wondered if Polly might be working as he opened the door, to see Velen still standing guard.

"I'm going to the Loose Anchor, wanna come?" Sparrow asked, knowing Velen would have no choice but to follow him, it was, after all, still his duty from Commander Rend to make sure Sparrow didn't go rogue.

They walked in silence through the lantern-lit square, the only sound was the crunching of the snow beneath their feet. Plumes of chimney smoke swirled up into the night sky and disappeared among the gray winter clouds. Sparrow figured it might snow again because he couldn't see the stars, and clouds usually brought inclement weather with them. It didn't matter what the conditions were outside, soon he would be wrapped in the arms of a beautiful girl. This was not the life he envisioned for himself, but it wasn't a bad way to pass the time, he had to admit. Velen broke the silence, whistling a tune that sounded much like the songs the townspeople sang as they decorated. They strolled out the western gate, to the docks of Blackwater Bay.

Every dock was occupied and people came to and from the ships at a steady pace. The Loose Anchor Tavern sat nestled in the few trees left in the area and the merriment met their ears before they reached the door. Inside, it was shoulder to shoulder and much warmer than outside. There was a barrage of chaotic energy; the deafening sound of laughter, clinking tankards, and the clacking of dice across wooden tables. Sparrow squeezed through the crowd and sidled up to the bar. Declan, the owner of the establishment was busy at the other end, but worked his way down as quickly as he could, passing drinks and taking coin from patron after patron. Sparrow looked back to ask Velen what he wanted to drink but didn't see him. *Maybe I lost him in the crowd.* Sparrow thought.

"What can I get you?" Declan's voice brought Sparrow's attention back to the bar.

"Hey Declan, busy tonight huh?" Sparrow asked.

"Yeah, The inn's all filled up and I'm guessing the Blackwater Inn is full too because we have quite a few people sleeping on the ships. You want your usual whiskey double?" he asked.

"Actually, can you give me two of those?" Sparrow asked and handed him two silver pieces. Declan took his coin and slid a few coppers back across the bar but Sparrow waved it away. It wasn't much of a tip, but Sparrow figured by the end of the night it would be.

His eyes searched the crowded tavern, the working girls slipped through the sea of people with ease, running their fingers down the arms of lonely pirates or dancing on the laps of the men who looked like they had deep pockets. Sparrow didn't see Polly anywhere. He pounded his two-finger glasses like shots and ordered two more as he shuddered at the thought of taking anyone but Polly to bed. She was his first and she had made him comfortable.

"Hey there, you look like you could use some company."

Sparrow turned as a smooth and soft female voice whispered in his ear. She was pretty, but she wasn't Polly. Her eyes were gray like the storm clouds in spring and her auburn hair was pinned half up, the other half hanging in ringlets to the middle of her back. Her dress was barely clothing at all, the corseted top pushed her bosom up and accentuated the shape of her waist. "I'm looking for Polly, actually," Sparrow told her.

"It's her night off, but I promise I can please you, sir." She slid her hand up his thigh, resting it on his hip as she slid between his legs. Sparrow cleared his throat and put his hands up in front of him to quell her advances. She scoffed loudly as she twirled away from him and pushed through the crowd. Sparrow finished his whiskey and twirled his finger in the air to signal to Declan he wanted another round. He spotted Velen a few tables away playing dice and glancing occasionally in his direction.

As Sparrow brought his metal whiskey tumbler to his lips, the hair on the back of his neck prickled and he had the feeling he was being watched by someone other than Velen. He set the cup down and looked from one side of the tavern to the other and then he spotted her; the auburn-haired girl pointed him out to a large man with broad shoulders and an unmannerly expression. He downed the last of his whiskey and prepared for confrontation as they pushed through the tavern toward him.

"What's this I hear about you asking around for Polly?" The man's gruff voice was supposed to sound intimidating, but Sparrow didn't flinch.

"What can I say? When you've had the king's feast, it's hard to go back to eating gruel."

"Geo, did he just call me gruel?" The woman lurched forward and landed a hard smack against Sparrow's cheek.

"Now, Cynthia, calm down, I'm sure he didn't mean it, let's give him a chance to explain." Geo stepped forward, towering over Sparrow, his hot stinking breath violating his nose. Sparrow groaned in disgust as he took a step back from the stench.

"Actually, I said exactly what I meant," he sneered.

"Polly belongs to me, and you don't get to come in here and disrespect my girls. I think it's time for you to leave." The man reached out to grab Sparrow by the collar.

Sparrow grabbed his hand, pressing his thumb into the tender webbing between Geo's thumb and pointer finger. He suppressed a cry of pain, but Sparrow was able to easily manipulate Geo's stance all the same. Bending his arm at the elbow, Sparrow twisted Geo's arm behind his back. He had him right where he wanted him until a tankard filled with ale collided with the back of his head. He whipped around to look at Cynthia. She backed out of his reach and the diversion of Sparrow's attention was all the other guy needed. He turned back just in time to see the man's fist plowing toward his face. Blood and spittle flew from his mouth and nose. A searing pain blurred his vision, there was a flash of bright white, and then the darkness consumed him. Everything looked far away, like he was watching the scene from a tunnel rather than participating in it. Sparrow assumed his fighting stance and prepared for the next blow. Catching his assailant's arm between his, Sparrow applied the right amount of pressure to make the man double over. He kicked him three times in the stomach, and Geo tumbled backward. Sparrow waited. His attacker rushed him again, this time, Sparrow slid to the floor, trapping Geo's leg as he moved. Geo face-planted through a table. Everyone in the tavern scrambled out of the way, but pushed each other around to get a better view. Declan rang the bell over the clamoring of the crowd to put a stop to the fight, but no one seemed to notice. Sparrow picked the man up off the floor and looked into his bloody face.

"I trust this will be the last time you lay a hand on me," he spat, shoving Geo away from him. "By the way, happy solstice." Sparrow would get no love there tonight, but perhaps it wasn't sex he had been craving after all. He wiped the blood from his nose onto the back of his hand, pulled out his coin pouch, and tossed the whole thing to Declan. "Sorry about the mess," he said as he headed for the door.

THIRTY-ONE

BASTIAN WALKED OUT THE door without saying goodbye, not surprising given their recent quarrel, but so soon after arriving? Had Sophie sent him to get Willow, or was he leaving to help Commander Rend? Xander couldn't fight the urge to go to her. He went upstairs to Sophie's chamber, her guard, Thomas, stood in front of her door and shook his head at Xander as he approached.

"The Queen is not taking it well," he whispered.

"Please, let me talk to her," Xander said.

Thomas moved aside and allowed him to knock. He could hear Sophie's heartbreak through the door. Even though she had not given him permission to enter, Xander slid the door open and called her name softly. She was bundled in her blankets, sniffling as her body heaved in quiet sobs He crossed the room with soft steps and dropped to his knees at her bedside. He gently rubbed her back, coaxing her to uncover her face. She moved the blanket down to look at him; her eyes were puffy and bloodshot and her face was splotchy and damp.

"Hey, there's my beautiful queen," he said. "Wanna talk about it?" Sophie shook her head. "That's okay, you don't have to say anything." He took her hand in his and held it to his lips. "What can I do for you?"

"Will you just hold me?" Her voice broke as the words left her lips and she started to cry again.

"Of course," he said.

She picked up the blankets and scooted back for Xander to crawl into bed with her. She cried into his chest as he hugged her firmly and gently tangled his fingers in the back of her hair. He hated to see her so upset, and he hated Bastian for upsetting her. "He's so broken from all he went through. He said he can't be the partner I need right now. He told me to move on, but he's the father of my child and I love him, even when I try to let him go, I can't," Sophie said.

"He actually told you to move on? After the punch in the face I took because he thought we were together, he ended your courtship?" Xander's jaw clenched as he thought about Bastian's erratic behavior. "I'm sorry he hurt you, Sophie. I wish I could make the hurt go away," he said.

"You can. You can compel me to forget the pain, compel me to not be sad anymore," she said, looking up at him.

"Sophie, I can't do that to you, that kind of mental manipulation..." Xander stroked her hair back away from her face. "I care too much about you," he admitted.

"Then help me forget another way." She caressed the back of his neck then traced her fingers upward to his head, pulling his face to hers. She pushed him onto his back and rolled on top of him. Sophie pressed her lips to his and tasted him eagerly, only breaking their connection long enough to pull her shift off over her head. Xander felt the stiffening of desire in his trousers as she guided him up to a sitting position and pulled off his tunic. He wrapped his arm around her waist and pulled her closer to him. How long had he been dreaming of this moment? Her soft skin pressed against his, and the heat between them was undeniable. Xander rolled her onto her back and got lost in the way she gazed up at him. Why did he have this nagging feeling and voice in his head telling him it was wrong?

"Sophie, I'm not sure about this." He wanted to take the words back as soon as he said them. He didn't want to cause her more pain than she was already feeling, but he didn't want to be a tool she used to forget his brother either.

"Why?" Sophie asked, gazing up at him with her eyes which were still red from crying.

"I just don't think you're ready, I mean, I want this—*you*. I want you, but I need the feeling to be mutual. I'm just afraid you'll regret it later," he admitted.

"I won't. Xander, there has been this force between us, pulling me closer to you since the day we met. I didn't want to admit it, and I didn't want to believe we are fated, but I went to the White Raven and asked Madame Moira of my fate and she said..." Sophie looked at him apprehensively.

"What did she say?" Xander asked.

"She said we *are* fated, you were right, our souls are connected," she said.

Xander couldn't read her thoughts but it seemed like she was holding something back. "Is *that* what she said?" He rolled over and laid down beside her. If this was going to happen, he wasn't going to be the one to start it. He wanted it to be her choice.

"Mmhm," Sophie forced a smile, nodding as she leaned over him, pressing her lips to his. She kissed her way down his chest and her fingers trailed down his stomach, pulling loose the string of his trousers. He couldn't take his eyes off of her; she was mesmerizing, an absolute Goddess. Who wouldn't fall in love with her? Sophie pulled his trousers off and his undergarments came with them. She kissed his abdomen just beneath his belly button and slowly worked her way up his chiseled abs and then to his chest, lightly kissing his neck and then his jaw, making him wait for it. Sophie slid her hips back and forth at a teasing pace and the lips of her sex rubbed up and down his erection. She was so wet. Xander groaned as the desire became almost too painful to bear.

"Are you sure you want me? I'm not my brother, nor am I a gentle lover. The things I want to do to you right now..." he growled in her ear.

"I'm sure, and don't worry, there's no need to be gentle. I'm a vampire," she reminded him.

Here she was, giving him permission to ravish her and oh, gods, how he'd wanted to do just that since the day they met. Xander gripped her by the hips, flipped her around, and pulled her backward onto his erection. His fingers dug into the meaty flesh of her hips as he rammed into her again and again with a pace and force that made her cry out his name.

Xander let go with one hand and smacked her ass; she let out a moan. The sound sent a thrill throughout his body, so he did it again and watched as her skin reddened in the shape of his hand. Xander tangled his fingers in the back of her hair and gripped a handful of it, thrusting into her even harder.

"My Queen, are you okay?" Thomas called from the hall. Xander withdrew from her and flashed across the room to barricade the door. Sophie groaned with frustration at his absence from her.

"She's fine," Xander replied with a grin. He liked the worry in Tomas' voice, this meant he had never heard these sounds coming from behind her door before and it filled him with a sense of pride. He walked back over to the bed. Sophie was on her hands and knees, waiting for him. "Good girl," he praised, rubbing the red handprint on her backside. He turned her around and positioned himself in front of her, rubbing the tip of his sex on her lips. She took him into her mouth, swirling her tongue around the head and squeezing her lips around the shaft. "Your mouth feels so damn good, Sophie," he groaned as he pumped his hips faster with his hands on the back of her head. Xander's climax tried to make an early appearance and he wasn't about to let that happen. He pushed Sophie onto her back and grabbed her legs, pulling her to the edge of the bed. He folded her legs up as high as they would go and rubbed his sex around the outside of her entrance, teasing her as she had done to him.

"Mmmm, Xander, I need you inside me, now." Her tone was commanding, but she was forgetting who was in charge. He continued teasing her and she grew more needful with every passing moment.

"Stand up," he told her. She did, although her legs were wobbly already. Xander gripped her throat and dropped his voice to a whisper as he moved his mouth next to her ear. "Tell me how badly you want me."

"If I don't have you inside me soon, I shall perish, please," she said.

"I like it when you beg for me," he whispered as he pushed her back against the wall. "Keep your arms up like this," he said, raising them above her head and crossing her wrists. Xander kissed her hard and took his lips away too quickly, and knew she craved more. He kissed her neck, her collarbone, and then moved to her breasts. He sucked her nipple until it hardened and lengthened in his mouth and then bit down on it just enough to get a reaction. Sophie gasped and dropped her arms to tangle her fingers in his hair.

"No, you will follow directions, or you get no more." He backed away from her, stroking himself in front of her. She quickly put her hands back up resuming the position he'd put her in, begging for him to touch her. "You learn quickly. I like that." He pricked the tip of his finger with his fang and squeezed it until a drop of dark red blood beaded on it. He put his finger in her mouth and as she licked the fluid from his fingertip, he felt the pulsing of her desire like a single heartbeat shared between them. Xander grabbed a handful of her hair and gently, but firmly pulled her head to the side bearing her neck to him. He kissed her soft flesh before sinking his teeth into it. As he drank from her, he could feel their souls becoming one, enveloping one another like twisted roots fighting to reach the sun. He wiped a droplet of blood from his lip as he lifted her leg with one hand then used his other to guide his cock back to her hot, wet center. He moved his hand to her throat, holding her firmly against the wall, and waited for her to beg for him again before pushing into her with a long, deep thrust. He pulled out to the tip, and paused, delaying her satisfaction until she couldn't stand it.

"Now, I want to feel you climax for me." He lifted her other leg so he was holding her up off the floor and pulled her into him as he drove his cock into her, quickening the pace with every pump. Sophie moaned and called out his name. He leaned forward and growled in her ear. "Scream my name, tell everyone here who you belong to." He twirled her away from the wall and carried her back to the bed. He pulled out long enough to turn her around and bend her over. He pulled her hips back hard and fast, the slapping sound of their bodies colliding, filling the room. She obeyed, screaming his name in ecstasy. Warm fluid exploded from him and filled Sophie as her walls tightened around his throbbing cock. His useless seed dripped out of her as her red and swollen sex pulsed.

"I hope I didn't hurt you," he commented as she turned around. His hand instantly moved to touch the red fingerprints around her neck. He kissed the parts of her he'd marked.

"I'm okay, you didn't hurt me. In fact, it was amazing. I'm glad you didn't hold back," Sophie told him as she grabbed a washcloth to clean herself up.

"Actually, that *was* me holding back." His eyes darkened.

"Oh," was all Sophie could say. He detected a hint of fear behind her eyes and it excited him. She sauntered over to him and gently caressed his cock. Her touch sent a chill through him and he stiffened again. "Next time, I won't let you go easy on me," she said.

Xander picked her up, threw her back onto the bed, and straddled her. "Challenge accepted," he grinned. Xander covered her mouth with his, parting her lips with his tongue. He squeezed her breast and groaned against her lips as he felt his shaft harden even more. He'd never been happier to be a vampire than in this moment, the wait time for humans was excruciating. He sat up and gripped his cock, stroking it while looking down at the constellations of freckles covering Sophie's skin. "Turn over," he commanded. She flipped onto her stomach, craving his touch. He grabbed her hips and jerked them up so she was bent over; fluids still dripping from her. "I love how you're still wet for me," he said as he teased her with his cock.

She wriggled against him, trying to force him to enter her, so he smacked her thick, round ass. He furiously rubbed his cock against her vulva, never entering her, and every time she flexed her hips or pushed back against him, he gave her a good smack. Both ass cheeks now bared the red print of his hand. Xander slapped his cock on her sex and she begged him for it. *Fuck, I love hearing her beg*, he thought. He leaned over her and wrapped his fingers around her throat, pulling her to him so her back was against his chest. "I like you on your knees for me," he growled. Holding her by the throat with one hand, he reached between her legs and caressed her dripping sex with his first two fingers. Her moan came out raspy and deep which made him loosen his grip. He kissed her shoulder and trailed his lips up the back of her neck.

"You've not even *started* to beg yet—but you will," he whispered in her ear. "Turn around and stay on your knees."

She did as he asked.

"Good girl." Xander presented his cock to her, and when she put her lips around it he raked his hands through his hair, keeping his fingers interlaced behind his head until he finished in her mouth. He watched her swallow his fluid and she waited to see if she had pleased him. He stood up, guiding her to her feet as well. He kissed her deeply and when he let go of her she looked woozy.

"Is it my turn now?" she asked.

"Not today. You're *really* going to beg me for it, but trust me, the waiting makes it better," he said, kissing her on the forehead.

THIRTY-TWO

LAVENDER AND CLOVE FILLED the air as Leon entered Agatha's dimly lit room. She was still in bed—not a good sign. He was hoping she would be well enough to help them send Dmitri through the teleportation circle, but it was looking like it would have to be Sophie. Agatha's wrinkled hand reached up from her bed weakly as he entered her room. Taking her hand in his, Leon sat in the chair beside her bed. "Oh, Aggie, how can I help?" he asked. She had grown weaker in the last few days. Leon brought her meals, made sure she'd eaten, and kept her water cup full. He cared for her as he would have cared for his own mother had she lived that long.

"I need... Sophie," she managed to choke out.

"I'm not ready for this. I'm scared. What if your power is too much for her? I know what you're capable of." Leon bowed his head to her hand.

"She will be just fine. I am leaving her my grimoire. Please, I won't make it to solstice, we need to do this now," Agatha pleaded.

"Very well, send her a message for me, please, tell her to take the teleportation circle. It will be faster than flying. In the meantime, I will see about your breakfast and have the maids give you a sponge bath," Leon said. Agatha nodded and began whispering incantations before he could even stand up. Shadows danced around the room as he stepped out into the hallway.

Leon paced the floor, waiting for Sophie. He didn't know how long Agatha's message spell would take, but it had been hours already and he was getting nervous. *What if it didn't work, or what if Sophie didn't want to come because they wouldn't invade Ash for Bastian?* All manner of thoughts went through his mind, none of them good. When at long last the circle lit up and hummed with magical activity, he let out a deep sigh of relief; Sophie appeared in the circle with two others, Xander and Beric.

"Thank goodness, I'm glad you're here, Agatha says she won't make it until solstice and we need to do the transfer soon. She's dying, Sophie." His daughter ran into his arms the way she had when she was little. It brought him a peace and comfort he couldn't explain.

"Wait, is it dangerous?" Xander asked, stepping up behind Sophie.

"All magic is dangerous," Leon replied.

"I mean, isn't Sophie powerful enough? What happens if the transfer hurts her?" Xander argued. Leon looked from Sophie to Xander; something between them had changed, he was more protective of her than he was before.

"Sophie, I'm sorry about Bastian. We can't go to Ash, not kno—"

"Bastian escaped," Sophie interrupted. "He found his way to Ryul in Ravenhall and they teleported back to Lapis Highland."

"Where is he now? We will need all the help we can get," Leon asked.

"He said he was going to see Willow, and then try to rally more troops for Blackwater. He promised he would be here for the celebration," she replied. "Now, about Agatha, I'm ready."

"Meet us in the temple by next bell," Leon told her. It would take him at least that long to get Agatha to the altar. He walked with purpose to Agatha's door and knocked twice before gently easing it open. She was sitting up now and trying to stand. He offered her the crook of his arm to steady her as she rose from the bed. Leon guided her steps as they made their way to the hall. He was thankful Agatha was on the first floor, it looked like walking was difficult for her and he imagined stairs would be nearly impossible. Her slippers scuffed across the stone as she took heavy steps, one louder than the other, indicating she was favoring one leg. When they reached a bench, Leon helped her sit down for a rest.

"Would you like for me to get you a wheeled chair?" he asked. Agatha nodded, rubbing her knees. "Sit here for a moment. I'll be right back," he told her. Leon hurried away to the clinic wing. He signed out a chair and wheeled it back to Agatha. "Here, this will make you more comfortable."

Agatha took Leon's arm and turned around, easing herself down into the chair. Leon pulled it backward and turned it in the direction they needed to go.

"Would you like for me to push you, or do you want to try to use the wheels?" he asked.

"I'm too tired," she replied.

Leon gripped the handles on the back of the chair and wheeled Agatha to the temple just as the bell rang. The enormous room looked even bigger without the pews and usual décor. Two braziers burned at each end of a stone slab altar, warming the area and bathing it in a flickering light. The altar looked more like the forest floor layered with flowers and herbs; a bed of black alder leaves with angelica flowers, purple and brown echinacea peeking out from under a scattering of lady's mantle and tarragon. Sophie and Xander waited near the altar as they approached. He gazed into Sophie's eyes and whispered something to her. Leon watched their exchange and noted the furrow in Xander's brow and the tenderness when he touched his daughter's cheek. Sophie walked over to meet them.

"What are all of these herbs for?" Sophie asked, looking at Agatha as Leon brought her to the altar.

"Some for protection, some for divination and dragon magic. All are necessary for what comes next. First, if you are using any magic right now, I need you to drop concentration on the spell. Your mind needs to be clear." Agatha said.

Sophie looked nervously at Xander and turned away from Leon as she dropped the illusion spell. Faint red fingerprints appeared on her neck. Leon placed a hand on her shoulder and she turned around reluctantly. Leon's eyes snapped to the marks on her skin and rage boiled inside him, but he tried his best to hold it in. He hoped Sophie couldn't see his anger bubbling beneath the surface, it was not toward her. He hugged his daughter and kissed her cheek with a clenched jaw. Xander looked as if he too were waiting for another moment with Sophie. Leon crossed in front of her, blocking Xander from her path, and gestured to the door.

"I'll be right here, Sophie," he called to her as Leon ushered him away. Leon's posture was rigid and stiff as they exited the temple. His jaw hurt from clenching it so tightly. He rarely got this angry, but when it came to his family, Leon couldn't control himself. As soon as the heavy wooden doors of the temple closed behind them, Leon's anger exploded to the surface. He grabbed Xander by the lapels and shoved him into the wall. "I saw the marks on my daughter's neck, she never had marks like that before. What have you done to her?" The heat from his anger turned Leon's face a deep shade of crimson as he drew back to punch Xander but stopped when his voice came floating on the breeze like dandelion seeds in the summer. "Any marks you see on Sophie's neck are only freckles, nothing more."

Leon's eyes dilated. He relaxed for a moment, his brow unfurrowed and his shoulders slumped back down and he rested his hands at his sides. When Leon's eyes returned to normal, the anger was replaced with worry as he thought of Sophie and Agatha transferring so *much* power. He paced back and forth in front of the door. *What is taking so long?* he thought. Xander seemed just as worried, he sat down on the bench, watching the door while wringing his hands and picking at his nails. Leon didn't hear any sounds coming from the temple, no chanting, whispering, or anything. He wondered if it meant they were done, or maybe they hadn't even begun. He wished he could open the door just to check in and make sure Sophie was okay.

"Why don't you come have a seat over here? You're making me nervous," Xander said, gesturing to the bench.

"You're right, I'm sorry, I'm just so worried about her. Agatha has more power than I have ever seen and it's a heavy, dark magic, but Agatha saw the future of our world and Sophie will be the one to save it. A darkness is coming the kind which swallows the light whole and destroys everything in its path. Light magic can't defeat it. I fear for Sophie."

"How long have you known?" Xander asked.

"Six full moons have come and gone. So much has happened in that time and we didn't intend to wait so long, but with Sophie just having Willow, we couldn't do the power transfer then."

A scream rang out from the temple, not just a scream—Sophie's. Xander jumped up and raced back to the temple doors. He was just about to pull them open when Leon's hand clamped onto his wrist and pulled him back. "Sophie is hurt, we have to help her!" he pleaded.

"We can't disrupt the transfer, it could kill her," Leon said. Both of Xander's hands rested on the heavy wooden doors. He lowered his head, pressing his forehead against it. Leon put a hand on his shoulder. "What is going on between you and Sophie?" Leon knew it was more than friendship, Xander's behavior was fierce and protective. Leon had seen the same look many times on the faces of his Silver Soldiers before every deployment. Their faces all heavy and glum as they said goodbye to their sweethearts, not knowing if they would ever make it home. It was the same look he was sure he had every time he had to leave Samantha.

"I love her." Xander didn't lift his head or look at Leon. His voice was barely more than a whisper. Leon bent down, trying to see his face. Xander turned away from him, choking back his emotion before looking back. "I don't just love her, I *need* her. We are fated to be together and I can't tear myself away. Even if she chooses Bastian, I will love and protect her with every last unnecessary breath I take," he said as he leaned his back against the wall and slid to the floor.

Leon had tried so hard for so long to protect Sophie from this world, even before she was born. He still had nightmares about fighting the aquahydra. Sophie's blood father, Baelfire, had been aboard his ship. The monster occupying the depths of Blackwater Bay had the upper hand and Leon couldn't figure out why for every head he cut off, another grew in its place. Baelfire stood chanting on the bow of the ship, looking directly at the many-headed dragon. Leon watched as the aquahydra attacked everyone *except* Baelfire. The whole guild was going down in flames and that bastard was the accelerant. The choice to put him to the sword had not been easy. Leon knew of Baelfire's wife and also knew she was with a child. Striking down a man and simultaneously making his wife a widowed single mother was not something he ever wanted, but it was that, or lose the entire Blackwater army, countless magic wielders, and perhaps even his own life.

He charged Baelfire, striking him in the leg with his sword and hurling him overboard. Leon's intention was to stop him from muttering his incantations, not to kill him, but when Baelfire disappeared beneath the dark and treacherous waves, Leon felt a pang of guilt. He had no time to dwell on it when the sea dragon crashed one of its heads into the water right beside the ship. Fire and electricity struck the dragon at regular intervals from all directions as the wizards and sorcerers on the other ships cast their spells without Baelfire's interference. Just as one of the dragon's heads rose out of the water, Leon jumped on its neck and sliced through it with a heavy, two-handed swing of his vorpal greatsword he called Destiny.

Three heads of the dragon remained. Leon dipped and dodged in the valleys between the creature's several necks and waited for a clear strike. Too many things were hitting the dragon for it to focus on Leon who was no more than the size of a flea to the great beast, but his sword struck hard and true. Another head dropped into the water and the beast roared in pain and anger. Leon finally had its attention. The dragon bucked wildly, flipping its two remaining heads into its own body trying to crush Leon. His sword wouldn't fail, she couldn't; that is after all why he named her Destiny. Leon kept climbing around, dodging spells, and dragon heads until he was finally steady enough to bring his sword down on yet another neck. They were no longer growing back, Leon didn't know why, nothing was different, except for the fact Baelfire was gone. When he finally sliced through the last of the dragon's heads, the entire bay erupted in cheers and applause. They did it, the beast in the bay was dead. Leon swam back to the ship as the body of the monster sank to the depths of the water.

Another scream from Sophie chased the memory away and Leon was reminded of his biggest fear. It wasn't the seven-headed dragon, the vampires, or the tyrant, Orion; it was losing the ones he loved so dearly that frightened him more than anything else in this world. Leon, much like Xander, was also contemplating breaking down the doors every time Sophie screamed. His heart softened as he watched the younger man's relentless march. He could see the same pain he felt, reflected in his eyes and he believed his feelings were true.

Why did Sophie attract vampires? Leon's thoughts turned to Sophie's friend, Gabe. They had grown up together and he was a good kid, responsible and compassionate. If only he had not sent him to marry Akiri, perhaps Gabe and Sophie would be happily married and none of this would be happening. Or maybe it would have happened all the same, fate was funny sometimes.

Finally, the doors burst open and both Leon and Xander ran in to find the altar empty. Agatha was gone, but behind the altar, a great dragon stood tall and majestic. Its wings were like dark leather and when she stretched them out, they spanned across the entire temple. Her scales had an almost celestial glow as the shades of red and blue blended to create a dark purple hue. Leon's jaw dropped open. It was the biggest dragon he had ever seen. The beast reached out its silver talons, stepping toward them. Leon and Xander took a step back and the dragon roared. Leon closed his eyes and bent forward, holding his ears. With a swish of its tail, the dragon sent the altar flying across the room, the stone slab broke into a thousand pieces as it hit the wall. The dragon roared again and took another step in their direction.

THIRTY-THREE

'HEART OF COAL MEETS hair of fire, only then will he expire. If the fire is snuffed out, the world will end without a doubt.' Sparrow woke up with the words of the doomsayer repeating in his mind. *What the hell did she mean by that? Was she talking about Sophie? Who was Heart of Coal?* Sparrow's body ached, and his lower back seized as he tried to stand. He thought back to the tavern brawl the night before; the knuckles striking him, the blunt force of a table's edge colliding with his spine, and the tankard he took to the back of the head. No wonder he was so sore. He dressed himself slower than usual then opened his door to find Velen standing there waiting for him, as usual. "You know, this is pretty creepy right?"

"What is?" Velen asked.

"You, standing by my door just staring at it like some kind of night stalker," Sparrow said in a joking tone.

"Well, if anyone had to stalk you—you're lucky it's me, Leon's other informant, Ivy, would have watched you bathe, sleep, and... well... other things." His eyes went wide as if he were giving Sparrow a warning. Sparrow didn't want him to elaborate.

"Breakfast?" he asked, eager for a subject change.

"Of course," Velen replied.

Sparrow turned to lock his door and then they walked across the square to the Blackwater Inn, which had the best and cheapest breakfast in town. Two coppers could buy three eggs, pork of choice, homemade biscuits, freshly churned butter, a pint of milk, and a stack of flapjacks with maple syrup. The inn was busy with the usual crowd, some of them left over from the night before. One man at the end of the bar was dozing off and kept nearly falling off his stool. Sparrow still felt a little groggy as well. His dreams must have bothered him last night. A cheerful hostess walked them to a table and handed them a menu then left. When she returned, she brought back a kettle, turned up two mugs on the table, and filled them with coffee.

As they placed their orders, Sparrow noticed the waitress's accent and it reminded him of his time in south Braidwood—what he could remember of it anyway. It was where he was born and where he and his mother had lived before she left him at the Garden of Life.

"Ever since the day in Northport, when I saw the woman no one else could see, I can't stop thinking about what she told me. 'Heart of coal meets hair of fire, only then will he expire. If the fire is snuffed out, the world will end without a doubt.' What could it mean?" Sparrow asked.

"Well, hair of fire could be Sophie, or maybe even Samantha or perhaps it's no one we know at all, but heart of coal means what? A black heart full of corruption and evil, or a heart which perhaps no longer beats, one like a lump of coal, it could mean the new vampire guy—Bastian's brother, maybe a heart burning like coal, a dragon perhaps." Velen replied.

"Maybe, but the woman made it sound dire. This morning I woke up from a nightmare I couldn't remember all the details of, but her words have been stuck in my head ever since. It's important, I know it is."

"Or it could just be a woman reciting nonsense to get people riled up, we have doomsayers from here to Braidwood, they're not so uncommon."

Their server arrived with a tray of food and water. Sparrow's stomach growled as soon as the aroma wafted to his nose. Their conversation halted as they ate breakfast except for the occasional comment about the taste. Sparrow still could not stop thinking about the old woman, was she a true seer or another charlatan? Solstice was four days from now, and if there was going to be a war between the dragons and vampires, it very well *could* all go down in flames.

As they approached the guild hall, a sea of residents surrounded the building. It was a curious sight for the otherwise usually empty courtyard as people pushed and huddled together trying to get a better view of something near the front doors. Sparrow and Velen shoved through, headed for the entrance. "What are all these people doing here?" Sparrow asked.

"Excuse me," Velen tapped the lady in front of him. "What's going on here?"

"I'm not sure, something about Queen Sophie and some witch lady. Leon had us all evacuate the building," she replied.

Velen took off running, leaving Sparrow behind. Figures, the only time Velen left him alone was in a sea of witnesses. He didn't know any of them, but if Velen was half the informant Sparrow thought him to be, then surely a few of them would know *him*. He pushed his way through the square and into the front doors of the guild. The grand foyer was empty but voices came from the north wing. Sparrow headed toward the hallway when an ear-splitting screech rooted him to the spot. *Is there a dragon inside the guild hall?* he wondered. Running, Sparrow's boots skidded around the corner and led him to the temple doors. A great purple dragon with huge leathery wings and shimmering scales appeared to be writhing in pain. Its talons scraped and cracked the tile as it tried to pull itself across the floor. From its nose to the tip of its tail, Sparrow guessed the dragon was as long as at least eight caravan wagons, maybe even more. The tail alone was three times as long as Sparrow.

"What's happening?" he asked. Leon, Velen, Beric, Xander, and several members of the Silver Talons Guard watched from the doorway.

"I think she's trying to shift back into her human form," Leon replied.

"Is it Sophie?"

"I'm not sure. If so, Agatha is gone and I don't know what happened to her because we weren't allowed in the room. They started the transfer last night and it took until now to get this far, we have already tried everything we can to help her, we even called on a cleric and a wizard from the caravan, they both said we just have to let the transformation happen. We couldn't leave her, and she won't fit through the door, so we have to just hope for the best" Leon said, looking at Sparrow with red eyes. The dragon roared and thrashed about, inhaling a deep breath.

"Close the door!" Leon commanded while pushing as many people away from the doors as he could. Two of the guards moved to grab the handles, but as soon as they stepped over the threshold, the dragon exhaled in frustration and the result was something Sparrow had never seen before. The dragon didn't breathe fire like most, what came out of her mouth instead, was a purple shimmering ball of darkness. The energy inside it erupted and everything in the room except the dragon disappeared, including the guards. Sparrow looked around, thankful Leon had recognized the signs and moved them to safety. He felt sorry for the guards who gave their lives to pull the doors almost closed, containing most of the blast.

"What *happened*?" Sparrow asked.

"Agatha's power... complete erasure, a void, a black hole swallowing everything in its path, and she can cast it in both forms." Leon's eyes were frozen wide as he looked at the dragon still struggling to shift. "Beric, go tell the apothecary we need tranquilizer bolts. Velen, grab your crossbow, we need to knock this dragon out to force the transformation." They nodded and took off in opposite directions.

When it was safe to reach for the doors, Leon darted forward and closed them quickly. The last thing they needed was for one of Agatha's black hole bombs to explode into the hallway. The dragon whined and panted from behind the door. Xander paced, clenching his fists with every agonizing sound from the temple. Sparrow watched as they waited impatiently. He'd never seen Commander Rend so worried before, it was strange, he was usually so calm and collected, with a plan ready.

Velen and Beric came barreling into the hallway with Velen's crossbow, two quivers of bolts, and a jar of sleeping serum. Beric dipped the tip of the bolt into the serum and handed it to Velen for him to load.

"Aim for the soft tissue, like under the arm," Leon directed. Velen steadied his aim and let the bolt fly. It bounced off of the dragon's scales.

Beric handed him another prepared bolt and yet again it ricocheted off the beast's natural armor. "This isn't working, give me the jar," Leon said, unscrewing the top. He unsheathed his dagger, cut a strip of cloth from his silver cloak, and stuffed it into the hole. He grabbed a torch from the wall and lit the piece of cloth. The material took the flame quickly and he knew he only had a moment before the fire would reach the liquid inside. "Stand back," he said, grabbing the door handle and throwing the jar at the dragon's feet. The glass shattered into a thousand pieces and the liquid accelerated the fire, blue smoke rising from the oily substance. The dragon yawned and Leon closed the door to keep the fumes inside the room. "Now we just have to wait."

They listened as the beating of wings, screeching, and banging slowed and then eventually stopped. Sparrow watched from the hall as Leon cautiously opened the door and peered into the temple. Spotting someone on the floor in the middle of the room, he stepped inside. Sparrow followed, glancing around at the hollow space where a temple used to be. Now it was nothing but cracked stone walls and a floor covered in gouges from the dragon's talons.

"Sophie?" Leon whispered as he approached, stepping quietly on the tips of his toes. He needed to see her face to be sure. This girl had curly hair, but it was a deep auburn—darker than Sophie's had been. Leon reached out and placed his hand on her shoulder, rolling her to her back.

"Sophie!" Xander's voice startled him, Sparrow hadn't heard him enter the room. Xander zipped to Sophie's side, and in one swift movement, took Leon's cloak from around his neck and covered her body as he scooped her into his arms. She stirred and he kissed the top of her head with such relief. Sparrow had never seen anyone move so quickly.

"Where should I take her?" Xander asked.

"You can ask Hank for a room here at the guild hall. I'm not sure it's safe for her to go home to Samantha just yet," Leon replied.

Xander nodded and carried Sophie away. Sparrow looked around the empty room. The pews, the statues of deities—everything was gone. Where did it go? The black orb of Sophie's new magic left no trace or residue, it just sucked everything into it and then blinked out of existence. He caught himself wondering if a *person* could survive being blinked from existence or if the swirling black hole was more like a teleportation circle and simply moved things from one place to another. More importantly, could Sophie use her magic to get rid of Dmitri without it killing her, too? If it were possible, Sparrow could live with it, knowing the love he saw in this room would live on, and the creature responsible for the death of his brothers would get what he deserved.

THIRTY-FOUR

THE ROOM HANK ASSIGNED them was dark, but Xander's eyes had no trouble seeing the layout of the space. He requested clothing for Sophie, and a human willing to feed her. Xander didn't care about himself, he just needed Sophie to be okay. Tucking her into bed, he swept her hair from her face and fanned her curls out over the pillow. He moved across the room to the hearth and placed several pieces of wood into it. Grabbing the flint and steel from the top of the mantle, he lit the fire, not because he was cold, but because he wanted Sophie to wake up to a safe and cozy room, dimly lit by firelight.

He sat beside her on the bed and stroked her hair, willing her to wake up. He admired the way her hair had changed but hoped it was the only thing about her that had. She was the kindest, most intelligent person he had ever met and of all the visions he ever had, did her no justice, for she was far greater than he could ever dream. His attention snapped toward the hall at the sound of approaching footsteps. Xander waited for the knock and then opened the door to invite the maid inside. Xander took the clothing from her arms and laid them flat on the other side of the bed. Sophie stirred, and Xander moved around the bed to kneel at her side.

"Sophie," he called her name softly, stroking her cheek with his thumb. Her eyes fluttered open, and she smiled at the sight of him. Relief flooded him as he bent down to kiss her forehead. "I was so worried about you, but let's get you fed and then we can talk." Xander motioned the maid to approach. "Have no fear. She will not harm you," he said, looking into the girl's eyes. She nodded in response as Xander gently lifted her arm and placed her wrist in front of Sophie. She looked at the maid, with her blond hair and soft skin. Sophie shook her head.

"She's so young," Sophie said.

"It's okay, you're not going to hurt her, and I'll make sure she doesn't remember a thing," Xander insisted.

"Sophie looked down at the girl's wrist again. She could hear the blood pumping through her veins, and with every beat, she grew hungrier. Finally, unable to resist, Sophie brought the girl's wrist to her mouth and sank her fangs into the soft pink flesh. The girl did not flinch as Sophie bit her and when she was finished, Xander compelled the maid to forget the incident and sent her on her way.

"How are you feeling?" Xander asked.

"Incredible, and powerful. My head hurts, though. Agatha's memories and abilities are still embedding themselves in my mind."

"Do you remember what happened in the temple?" Xander asked.

"Agatha asked me to lie down on the altar. She propped me up with bundles of herbs. Then she took a knife and opened her wrist. She told me to drink until she was unconscious. When I did, it was like my blood started to boil, and it seemed as though my heart turned to coal and burst into flames. It was excruciating. I remember screaming as her blood fused with my own, and her magic, this dark energy...I could hear these voices—infernal voices—screaming things I couldn't understand. I started to wonder if taking Agatha's magic was a mistake. My body began to shift and I couldn't stop it, like it was reacting to my fear. My power was different, I tried to shift back but this ball of energy like the night sky blasted out from me and took everything in the room away. I was afraid it got you and my father. It might have been my fear keeping me trapped inside the dragon. It isn't like my power before where I am the dragon and I still think and act like me, it's like the dragon has a mind of its own and I am fighting for control from the inside."

"Wow, I'm sorry you went through that—I heard some of your agony. If you only knew how many times I almost crashed through the doors to rescue you." Xander drooped his face into his hands. He knew Leon had been right, if he'd gone into the room, he would likely not be here now. The black hole would have swallowed him up with everything else. "Can I get you anything?" he asked.

"I could use a pitcher of water. I am so thirsty," Sophie said.

"Coming right up." He patted her leg and kissed her forehead as he crossed the room to grab the pitcher. It was empty; he looked back at Sophie. "I have to go get some from the well."

"No, it's okay, bring it to me," she said. Sophie took the pitcher, pointed a finger into it, and whispered: *imple aqua* and the pitcher filled with water. Sophie drank all of it straight from the container and when she was finished, she sat it on the bedside table.

"There are some clothes here for you if you'd like to get dressed," Xander said, gesturing to the neat stack of clothing laid out at the end of the bed.

"Honestly, I was hoping to have my turn now," she said, lifting an eyebrow with a seductive gaze.

"Sophie, you're insatiable, but I think we should give you a day or two to rest and make sure you're okay," he said.

She got out of bed and stood in front of him, her green eyes staring into his. He tried to keep his gaze from wandering, but he couldn't help admiring her beautiful form and he couldn't resist the pull between them. His lips met hers and she pulled him closer. She lifted his tunic up over his head. He could have insisted she rest, but he didn't, because no matter what role they played in the bedchamber, *she* was the one in charge; though he would likely never admit it to her. She continued undressing him, tossing his clothing to the floor as their lips crashed together in furious need. Xander picked her up, and she wrapped her legs around him as he carried her to the bed. He loved the sensation of her skin against his. It filled him with a kind of energy that made him think of lightning streaking across a night sky. Why was she so gods damned irresistible?

"I love you, Sophie." He didn't know why he said that. He couldn't help it, he was caught up in the moment and even if it were true—which it was—Sophie had been through a lot and a declaration of his love was the last thing she needed to hear.

"You *love* me?" she asked playfully. She didn't seem appalled, in fact, it seemed like it turned her on. "Say it again," she coaxed.

"No, see now you've ruined the moment," he teased. She feigned offense and pushed him off of her.

"Fine." Sophie crossed her arms and tried to scowl at him but Xander crawled back to her and kissed her pressed lips. She relaxed, uncrossed her arms, and reached up to pull him to her. Sophie's fingertips pressed into his shoulder blades as they kissed. He rolled over to his back and pulled Sophie on top of him. If she wanted control, who was he to deny her? He could see the excitement in her eyes and, just as things were heating up, Sophie let out a chilling scream.

"What is it Sophie, what's wrong?" Xander asked.

She didn't answer; he back arched and her muscles seized. She groaned in agony as a cracking sound shot from her body. Sophie grabbed a sheet from the bed, quickly wrapped herself, and ran from the room. Xander fumbled getting back into his trousers and had no time to grab any more clothing than that as he followed after her. She ran until she reached the stadium, and by the time they got there, she was already transforming.

"I can't control it!" She screamed as her bones cracked and her body shifted before him. She wailed and writhed in pain as the gigantic dragon form battled its way out. Sophie dropped to her hands and knees as her fingers dug into the dry earth and became shining silver talons. The screech of a beast came out of her mouth as her neck stretched and grew until the shape took over her beautiful face. It was killing him to watch her in so much pain with no way to help. Finally, the transformation was over, Sophie was gone and in her place stood the purple dragon she'd been in the temple. The dragon took a stance Xander recognized as the pre-flight acceleration, and fear gripped him. He dashed forward, grabbing onto one of the long tendrils coming from the dragon's back. He quickly found something else to hold on to as she began picking up speed and then lifted into the sky. There was no way he was going to leave Sophie, but he hoped for his sake, her mind was still in control.

THIRTY-FIVE

DANCING THE SILVER COIN across his fingers, Bastian paced the barrier between their world and the Fae lands. "How in the hell does it open?" he wondered aloud. He tried walking forward, but his feet rooted in place just before the invisible line and he could go no further. He walked west along the border, hoping the entrance would reveal itself, but so far, no luck. If he could shift, perhaps he could get in, just the same as he was able to leave Immernacht, but those pricks had taken his dragon magic.

He walked for hours until finally a shimmering black door with millions of feathers carved into the wood appeared before him. Where the handle should have been was a small circle, the same size as the coin he'd been holding in his hand. Bastian placed the coin into the circle and heard a click as it opened slightly. As Bastian stepped through the mystical threshold, his senses were immediately overwhelmed by a breathtaking display of otherworldly beauty and enchantment. The air shimmered with a subtle iridescence, casting a soft, ethereal glow on everything it touched. Towering trees with leaves glowing like precious gemstones stretched toward the heavens, their branches swaying in the breeze with delicate flowers which emitted a gentle light, and ripe, plump fruit, inviting him to eat. He looked around for a path or a hint of which way he was supposed to go. How in the world was he going to locate Juniper, or the forgotten grove having never explored the fae lands himself? He moved through the forest, and as he did, tiny creatures fluttered from the foliage and zipped through the air too quickly to see.

"I wish I knew where to go." He groaned out loud to no one in particular.

"Where you should go, depends on your purpose here," a childlike voice called. Bastian whirled around.

"Who's there?" his eyes darted around trying to see the creature the voice belonged to but saw nothing. It giggled and Bastian turned again toward the sound but still, saw nothing. "I only want to find my daughter, she was brought here a few days ago by a druid named Juniper, have you seen them?"

The creature appeared to Bastian on the branch of a tree. She was a tiny, humanoid creature with transparent pastel wings. She looked at him with a sad expression on her tiny round face.

"I did see them, but I'm afraid they have been captured by the Fae King—King Cirros," she said.

"Where did he take them?" Bastian asked.

"All prisoners go to the castle," she replied.

"Can you show me the way?"

The creature's wings fluttered with excitement. "Sure I can!" She exclaimed, flying off the log and zipping through the air.

"Hey, wait, I can't go as quickly as you can fly!" Bastian called. The tiny creature flew back.

"Oh yeah, I forget sometimes, you big humans so are slow," she said, landing on his shoulder.

"Hey, that was mildly offensive, I'm not completely human," he said with a grin.

"Sensitive too, I see," she joked.

"So are you like a pixie or something?" Bastian had heard a lot about the creatures of the fae lands, but he'd never seen any for himself.

"Close, it's a common mistake, I'm actually a sprite. We are similar in a lot of ways. While pixies like to play pranks and trick those lost in the forest, sprites are helpful." She stuck her tongue out at one of the other creatures, but before Bastian could turn to look at it, he heard the tiny faerie flutter away.

"I'm Bastian, what can I call you?"

"My name is Lumen," she said proudly, "I go by Lu for short."

"Nice to meet you, Lu, now, which way to the castle?"

Lumen sat on Bastian's shoulder, directing him through the massive forest which seemed strangely lonesome. He'd expected to see all manner of fae creatures he'd heard stories about over the years, dryads, faeries, satyrs, maybe a brownie or two, although he probably wouldn't be able to tell the difference between them, but Lumen led them through the quietest parts of the forest.

"Where are all the other creatures?" he asked.

"They can sense you are not fully human; lucky for you, otherwise, they would be dragging you to King Cirros, too."

"Why?"

"King Cirros doesn't allow humans in the fae lands. If they are discovered they're either imprisoned or kept as slaves for the rest of their very short lives. Time moves faster here for humans so they don't last very long anyway."

Bastian's heart started beating out of his chest, "How much faster?" He and Sophie had assumed Willow was a dragonshifter like them, but they wouldn't know for sure until she turned sixteen.

"They grow years older every day," Lumen replied.

"Is there a faster way to the castle?" he asked.

"Can you fly?" Lu asked. The question stung.

"Not anymore," he replied sadly, still angry his dragon form had been stolen from him.

"Then I'm afraid there's no faster—wait, there is!" Lu said flitting off into the air. She was out of sight for a few minutes and as she returned, the sound of hoofbeats followed. A centaur followed behind her. Bastian looked nervously at the half-human, half-horse warrior. His chest and abs were nothing but pure muscle and his shoulders were twice as wide as he was. From his waist down, he was a brown horse, even bigger than a war horse. "This is Dane, he owes me a favor. Dane, we need a ride to see King Cirros."

Dane scooped Bastian up with one arm and put him on his back. "Okay, but after this, we're even Lu. Hold on," he called as he galloped away toward the gates. Lumen flew beside them until even she got tired and then she nestled down in Bastian's shirt pocket. They rode for what seemed like hours through the forest until finally, Bastian could see their destination just beyond an enormous bridge. The dark aesthetic reminded him of Ash. It was a looming black fortress with four spires stretching into the sky and it did not look like a friendly place to visit. He kept hoping Willow and Juniper were okay.

The centaur came to a halt at the edge of the bridge and reached back to help Bastian dismount.

"I thought you—

"This is as close as I like to get to the ancient ones, so this is where I will leave you, but good luck, traveler," Dane interrupted.

"Thank you, I appreciate your help." Bastian extended his hand. Dane shook it firmly, but briefly then he galloped away in the direction from which they'd come. Lumen waved from Bastian's pocket.

"Well, this is it, Lu, are you coming with me?" Bastian asked.

"Can I stay in your pocket?" she asked.

"Of course you can," Bastian smiled. The tiny creature was cute after all.

The gates which had looked small from afar stood almost as tall as the first tower of the castle itself. Two guards, both of them at least twice as tall as Bastian and three times as muscular, stood sentry with spears in hand. Huge black feathery wings shot out from the backs of the two Fae as they moved closer to each other to block his entry.

"What is your purpose here, Vampire?" one said in a booming voice.

"I'm here to see the king about my daughter," Bastian said.

"The king only meets with other Fae. Be gone," the man said.

"I will not leave here until I speak with the king!" Bastian shouted.

"Oh, this little creature has a big sack, coming to *our castle* making demands of *our ruler.* Maybe we should take him to the king. I bet he will get a kick out of the mouth on this one, King Cirros could always use another slave."

The two guards grabbed Bastian and dragged him through the front doors, he didn't have time to notice much more than the exquisite stone architecture and the black marble floor as the guards dragged him directly to the throne room at the end of the main hall. One guard let him go long enough to pull open the black double doors resembling the one at the barrier. King Cirros sat on an enormous chair made of shining black rock. To the king's left, Bastian spotted Juniper chained to the floor. She had red cuffs around her wrists and her expression was hopeless. *They're suppressing her magic*, he thought.

The guards stopped Bastian right at the Fae king's feet and kicked the backs of his knees, forcing him to kneel. King Cirros stood, his form hulking over Bastian. Even if he were still standing, he would have had to crane his neck to meet the King's eyes. Protruding from each side of his crown were two massive curling horns, he was dressed in all black with a leather strap across his chest. Bastian felt Lu trembling from the pocket of his tunic. He was scared too. The fae were known for their power, even Arturo showed fear when he recounted witnessing the strength and magic of the ancient ones. They were no more than tales to Bastian until now, the fae lands had been closed off to outsiders for as long as he could remember.

"You smell different, bloodsucker. How have you been able to retain your humanity through the vampire's curse?" King Cirros lifted Bastian's chin to look into his eyes and inspect his face. His nails were long, black, sharpened to a point, and looked like they could serve as a dagger if the need arose.

"Because of my dragon blood," Bastian replied.

"Dragon? You don't look like a dragonshifter to me," King Cirros said coldly.

"I'm not now. Someone took my magic," he admitted. Bastian dared to sneak a look at Juniper. Her eyes were filled with sorrow. Was she trying to tell him something about Willow without saying it out loud? "I just want my daughter, and Juniper, then we will leave and never return," Bastian said.

"Ah, I see, you've come for the druid elf and the human girl, but you can't have them. They were caught trespassing in our lands. Everyone knows humans are forbidden here, and yet the elf still carried the child across our borders. The druid will be my servant for the period of one hundred years, as per her sentence, and the human, well, she was kind of cute at first, like a puppy, and I thought I might like to keep her as a pet, but she aged so quickly and developed quite the sailor's vocabulary."

"Please, Your Majesty, can I see my daughter?" Bastian asked desperately.

"Majesty? You say that word as if I am some mere mortal king of a human realm, we do not use such words and titles here, but I will forgive your lack of etiquette because I believe we can come to an arrangement."

"I will do anything for my daughter," Bastian said.

"I'm so glad to hear you say it because I have heard whispers of four dragons born in the human lands. We both know where they belong. Humans are a blight on this world, they destroy everything they touch. They hunted the dragons to near extinction not so long ago. The human realm is no place for such creatures," King Cirros said.

"You want the dragons here in the Faelands." It wasn't a question. "I'll get the dragons for you, but you have to release Willow and Juniper first. If what you say is true about Willow aging rapidly, her life is in more danger every moment she stays here," Bastian argued.

"You'd better hurry then," King Cirros said. "I will, however, grant your request to see your daughter, just so you have a reminder of what's at stake. I'll give you five minutes." The king unleashed his enormous wings, grabbed Bastian's arms, and flew through the skylight above the throne. Bastian shouted in surprise at the sudden ascent and frantically thrashed to wrap his legs around the enormous fae. King Cirros landed, but Bastian's eyes were still closed. He didn't know why he was expecting the king to drop him, he couldn't deliver the dragons if he was dead.

Bastian opened his eyes and saw they were standing atop one of the towers, in front of a door. He didn't know what to expect, Willow had been a baby the last time he saw her. He opened the door slowly, and as he peeked his head inside, a pitcher flew in his direction and shattered against the wall next to his face.

"Willow?" Bastian called as he entered. His daughter stood facing the doorway, no longer the infant he had so recently held in his arms, but a young girl with wavy strawberry blond hair. She appeared to be well kempt and well fed. At least they were not mistreating her. She had a comfortable bed, books, clothing, and even dolls to play with. "Willow,

I am so sorry I wasn't there for you." He wanted to hug her, but her expression was one of fear, not love or even recognition.

"Who are you and how do you know my name?" she asked, her brows furrowed as she searched his features.

"I'm your father. I'll be back for you. There is something the king needs for me to do and then he will let me take you home. Your mother misses you just as much as I have."

"Then why isn't she here?" Willow demanded.

"Time is running out," King Cirros reminded him from the doorway.

"I'll be back for you, I promise." Bastian turned and walked out of Willow's room clenching his jaw. He had missed so much of his daughter's life—time he could never get back.

"I can't fly anymore. How am I supposed to get to all the dragons and get back here?"

"You'll have to fly the dragons back. You'll be able to cross the veil anywhere as long as you are wearing this," King Cirros said, pulling a pendant from the pouch hooked on the leather strap across his chest. "You will also be able to teleport anywhere except this castle, just by thinking of the location. Which should make it easy enough for even a half-human," he said.

"If I had time, I would be offended," Bastian said dryly, "thank you, though."

"Thank me by delivering the dragons. You can teleport out now." The pendant glowed as if it heard the King's command. He stayed there in front of Willow's door, waiting for him to leave. It was clear he was not going to give him the chance to teleport away with her. Bastian held the pendant between his fingers and thought of Lapis Highland.

When Bastian opened his eyes, he was standing in the courtyard of the castle he had once called home. He could see the dragon flying around the courtyard. He didn't know how Sophie trusted it to roam free without worrying it would take off. There were only a few days left until solstice, he had to gather four dragons and make it back with Willow and Juniper before then to help ensure their victory. The only thing he wanted almost as much as Willow's freedom, was to see Dmitri and Elizandra burn for what they did to him.

He followed the dragon with his eyes, wondering how he was going to get it to come down to meet him. He let out a long, loud whistle and waited. The dragon paid him no attention. Several guards patrolled the courtyard. They bowed to him as they walked by and continued their rounds. Bastian didn't know why he felt out of place or why he expected to be treated as such, but relief flooded him as the guards walked away. Finally, the dragon landed in the middle of the courtyard and Bastian reached his hand out to it as he neared, touching its snout and willing it to trust him. The small beast snorted a few times but didn't turn away.

"I think he likes you." Bastian whirled around at the sound of a voice. Thomas stood behind him, peering up at the young dragon.

"What's his name?"

"Custos," Thomas replied.

"Has he been trained for riding yet?" Bastian asked. He was certain Thomas sensed something was off because it took him a long time to answer.

"I have ridden him bareback, but he's not saddle trained yet, the saddle is still much too large," Thomas replied.

"Do you think maybe I could ride him? I have been missing flying. I can't shift anymore, Dmitri and Elizandra did something to me and stole by magic." Bastian explained. Thomas nodded, his eyes filled with empathy.

"Of course you can. Custos, kneel." As soon as Thomas gave the command, the dragon bowed his head and shoulders to allow Bastian to climb up. He grabbed the spines on either side of the dragon's head and held on as Thomas gave the command to fly.

Bastian pulled back on the spines and the dragon went up. He leaned to the right, and the beast turned. When he was far enough away from the castle to be out of view, Bastian pulled the necklace out of his tunic, keeping the leather rope around his neck, he held the dragon pendant in his hand and thought of the bridge in the Fae lands. He closed his eyes and hoped the Fae magic was strong enough to bring the dragon with him. This time, he kept his eyes open. Everything went black, and he was overcome with a sensation of falling. He could still feel the dragon beneath him, so he held on tighter.

When the world blinked back into existence, Bastian was at the bridge once more. He flew the dragon to the front doors of the castle and heard the sounds of cheering from the Fae below. King Cirros stood on the parapet above the doors and nodded to Bastian as he dismounted the dragon. He nodded to the king and then grabbed the pendant. *Three dragons to go*, he thought.

Thinking of Ophay and picturing Akiri, Bastian rubbed his thumb across the embossed dragon. He blinked, one second he was standing in front of the Fae king's castle and the next, he was in the field in front of Temple Ophay. He spotted Akiri near the chicken coop, gathering eggs in a large woven basket. Akiri turned toward him and when she recognized him, she set the basket of eggs down and ran over to hug him. Her long dark hair was tied up in a messy bun and she wore a long-sleeved blue dress with a dirt-stained apron he was sure used to be white. It was a modest look, vastly different from the queenly appearance she used to keep. She was pretty, even without the fancy dresses and glittering jewels.

"Bastian, are you okay? I heard you were kidnapped, how did you escape? You don't know how relieved I am. Sophie had a whole plan ready to send in troops from Ledora to rescue you, or so I heard from Kamara," she rambled as she pushed him back a step so she could look him over. "We suspect Dmitri is planning to attack Blackwater on solstice, Braidwood offered their dragon back to us for the battle, we've been trying to prepare.

"That's actually why I'm here, Juniper took Willow to the Fae lands, but they were captured by the Fae king. Willow is apparently not a shifter like Sophie, and because of this she is aging very quickly, she looks to be about ten. King Cirros will only allow Juniper and Willow to go free if I bring all the dragons to the Fae lands." Bastian tapped his legs with his fingertips as he awaited her response.

"How awful, Sophie will be devastated. Of course we have to get Willow back, but what am I supposed to tell Commander Archdale? He was nice enough to loan the dragon back to us for the battle, but he has already contracted the dragon's service for a year at least," Akiri said. "Isn't there some other way?

"Honestly, with Willow's rapid aging, we don't have time to come up with another plan. She has been there for a couple days our time and she has aged ten years. If I don't bring Cirros the dragons, Willow will die in the Fae lands, and Juniper will be forced to serve the king for a period of one hundred years. That's the penalty for bringing a human across their borders," Bastian told her. "Please, Akiri, I promise I will find a way to return to Commander Archdale whatever fee he paid to contract the service of your dragon, but I need to save my daughter." he pleaded.

"Why does he want them?" Akiri asked.

"To give them freedom they can't have here in the human realm. Akiri, you know it's true, there will always be some power-hungry tyrant who thinks controlling the dragons will make them reign supreme. The Fae have no interest in human land or politics and their borders are sealed. The dragons would be safe there, and we will be safe from them."

Akiri let out a sigh and relented. "Fine, but I want to go with you to meet this Fae King."

"Akiri, no, he is honestly quite frightening. I don't want to endanger anyone else. I just want to get Juniper and Willow and leave as soon as possible."

"I'm going and you can't stop me. If my dragons are going to live there, I should get to meet the Fae responsible for their survival. Now give me some time to change my clothes and grab a cloak." Akiri hurried away and disappeared inside the temple. Several minutes passed and Bastian began to think Akiri was stalling. He paced back and forth, watching the front door. Finally, Akiri led two dragons around the side of the temple.

"Here, you can ride this one. Her name is Ember." Akiri handed him the leather lead. They took off from the garden and flew northwest toward the barrier; Bastian was getting tired already, and he still had to go to Ledora. *One more dragon, though, and Willow will be free.* Bastian thought.

THIRTY-SIX

THE PURPLE DRAGON BARRELED out of control, screeching in pain as the magic inside bubbled beneath her scales. Xander desperately clung to anything he could grasp to stay on the dragon's back. They dipped low, flying through the trees. Branches and leaves smacked Xander in the face and scratched his arms.

"Sophie, slow down, let's land, please, I can't hold on much longer," he pleaded. Sophie screamed in her own voice through the dragon's mouth. Her body began to reshape itself, first an arm, and then a leg. She screamed again as the transformation took her concentration. "We're going to fall, you need to land, NOW!" Xander shouted.

The huge body of the dragon grew smaller and Sophie's form returned. They were both dropping through the treetops, crashing through the branches on their descent. Xander reached out for Sophie's hand but it slipped through his grasp and they tumbled to the ground. He groaned as he tried to roll over, every muscle in his body ached and reminded him he could not die, but in that moment, he wished he could. He put his pain aside and rolled over, searching for Sophie.

Her body lay battered and bruised from the fall and Xander had to crawl through the broken branches to reach her. Ignoring his own pain, Xander crawled to her and removed the debris from her body, to reveal her chest. Thankful no piece of splintered branch had pierced her heart, Xander pulled her into his arms. He stroked the hair away from her dirt-covered face as he tried to gently rouse her. Her body, covered in lacerations, seeped the tiniest amount of dark crimson blood.

□"Sophie, wake up, I don't know which way to go." Xander looked around for anything he recognized from the last few weeks, but found nothing he knew. They were in the middle of nowhere, Sophie was injured, and he was too sore to carry her very far even if he did know where they were. With nothing more to do than wait for her vampire blood to heal her, Xander curled up beside her to offer her what little warmth he could, wishing he had grabbed a cloak or at least a tunic to cover her. He held her in his arms to protect her body from the snow. He did not know why she would not wake, perhaps it was some lingering effect of the potion they had used to force her back into human form. He closed his eyes and focused on the slow rise and fall of her chest. In the calm of the forest, and with the comfort of her in his arms, Xander drifted off.

The full moon was shining through the trees, bathing them in a cool blue light. He didn't remember falling asleep. When he felt her squirm, Xander opened his eyes to see she had rolled over to face him. The visible side of Sophie's body was tinted pink from contact with the cold. *Damn, you had one job, and you had to go and fall asleep,* he berated himself. Xander didn't know what time it was, but from the position of the moon he was guessing they had about five or six hours until sunrise.

"How are you feeling?" Xander asked.

"Sore, but I'll manage, you?" she replied.

"I think unfortunately you broke my fall; it might be why you seem a little worse for wear," he said as they sat up, brushing off the snow and debris from their fall. "We should be heading back. We only have a couple more days until solstice and Blackwater won't stand a chance without you," he said as he kissed the top of her head.

□"Do we *have* to go back?" Sophie asked as she snuggled against him.

"Are you sure you're feeling okay? I think you might have injured your head," Xander teased, touching her forehead with the back of his hand. "Unfortunately we can't run away together yet, duties and all; nothing would make me happier than to have you all to myself, but your family needs you," he said, getting up and reaching out his hand to pull Sophie to her feet. She looked happy for a moment, but the joy faded as a storm cloud brewed behind her eyes. *Would Bastian make it back in time for the battle? Would Willow remain safe in the Fae Lands? What about the dragon? She couldn't control Agatha's magic and it had put Xander in danger. All it would have taken for either of them to die was for a piece of that tree to pierce their heart.*

"What are you thinking about?"

"What if I hurt someone? I can't control Agatha's magic. Maybe I shouldn't have accepted it," she replied. Xander wished he knew how to reassure her.

"I'll be right beside you," he held her close. "I'll never leave you. We will figure out a way..." he whispered, resting his cheek against the top of her head. "Now, any idea where we are?"

Sophie looked around, given how far they'd flown and the direction she remembered going, she had a good guess. "It looks like we are in the forest south of Aerulean Lake. If we head north, we can catch the morning caravan. Maybe they have a cabin left we can stay in for the rest of the night." Sophie looked up, searching the spaces between the tops of the evergreens for the northern star.

"Um, Sophie?" Xander watched her from the small clearing where they had slept. She turned back to look at him. "I'm not complaining, I love looking at you like this, but you might want to spell yourself some clothing before we get into town."

She looked down at her naked body and then back up at Xander with a smile. She looked like she was going to say something, but changed her mind and took his advice. "We need to go this way," Sophie walked off in a direction he wasn't certain was north.

"Are you sure?"

"Positive. There's the north star, right there," she pointed her finger in the direction of a bright white star twinkling between the branches. They were lucky it wasn't cloudy. They followed the path for a while, she hadn't been counting the minutes but Sophie guessed they'd walked for about an hour. Her aches and pains dulled as time passed and the scrapes and bruises faded. She was amazed at how quickly her vampire body healed.

"What is your favorite color?" Xander asked.

"What?"

"Your favorite color; I just realized I never asked." The path twisted to one side and inclined, making the walk more strenuous.

"Green, I guess, it's the color of new grass and leaves in spring and the soft moss on the forest floor," Sophie replied.

"Spring is nice, I can see why you like it."

"What's yours?" Sophie asked, keeping her eyes on the path ahead.

"Black, like my soul," he said with a mischievous laugh. "No, I'm kidding, it is a very nice color, but I'm partial to purple."

"I think you would look very handsome in purple," Sophie remarked. "What job did you want when you were a kid?"

"You mean besides being Lord of Immernacht?" Xander asked in an amusing tone.

"Yes, that's exactly what I mean."

"I guess I always wanted to be an artist, or a musician," Xander replied thoughtfully.

"Do you play an instrument?"

"Regrettably, I never learned. I have listened to and enjoyed many composers, but duty was always my first priority."

"It's never too late to learn, especially for us. I can teach you to play cello. I have played since I was a young girl," Sophie said.

"I never knew you played cello, who taught you to play?"

"Lord Amati provided me lessons as a personal favor to my father. They had been good friends during the battle of Braidwood, and we hosted him in Blackwater a number of times."

When the trees cleared and the lake came into view, Sophie let out a sigh of relief. A row of cabins on the northern side of the lake caught her eye. Those were usually reserved for royalty and nobles, but on busy nights such as these, they sometimes rented the cabins to the wealthier merchants as well. The camp was buzzing with activity, people cooking over campfires shared food and drink with others; a few people strummed their lutes, and played drums or pipes while others sang and danced. Each site had at least one covered wagon occupying it, some had two or three. Sophie and Xander crossed the grounds, keeping to the right side of the water. They entered the office and the man behind the counter jumped from his seat and bowed quickly to Sophie.

"Queen Sophie, how can I help you this evening?" he asked.

"We need a cabin for the night and we would like to travel back to Blackwater with the caravan in the morning."

"Right away, My Queen," he scrambled to grab the last remaining key from its hook. "We always keep this one off the books for situations just like this. I'm sorry, it only has one bed, but I can give you a bedroll for your... um... guard?" His eyes moved to Xander who was still topless.

"We would love a bedroll, thank you." Sophie glanced at Xander who said nothing and waited for the man to return with a bundle.

"The cabin is two doors down on the left side. I'll let the caravan leader know to expect you in the morning," he told them.

Sophie thanked him and they made their way to the cabin. Xander carried the bedroll and Sophie led the way. She opened the door to reveal one large room with a double-size bed and a small wood stove. In the front left corner, sat two armchairs, one on each wall with a table in between them. Xander laid the bedroll on the floor and unrolled it.

"You know you don't have to sleep down there right? I just haven't had time to announce Bastian and I have separated. I want to control the rumors until I can make an official statement." Sophie explained.

"I wasn't planning on sleeping, but at least this way it will look like I did." Xander grinned.

"If not sleep, what did you have in mind?" she asked, moving close to him and dropping the illusion spell. His pants tightened as she drew near.

"I have a lot of things on my mind, but I still haven't heard you beg," he said, running his fingertips down her back.

"Maybe I'd rather hear you beg for *me*," she told him.

"As long as you promise to tell me if you start to feel strange, like perhaps the dragon might make a reappearance."

"Don't worry. I can feel the absence of the magic, I think it is depleted for the moment. There is only so much energy I can conjure before it needs to be restored. My rest in the woods helped a little, but I think I will need a good night's sleep before my body can shift again whether I control it or not," she said. Sophie's heart pounded faster, her humanity taking over and revealing her desire to both of them. She looked up at him, beckoning for him to kiss her, yet she didn't say the words out loud. He brought his lips to her ear and growled softly as Sophie rubbed her hands up his smooth, chiseled form. She felt his breath on her neck, but he denied her the feel of his lips against her skin. He cupped her breast, moving his finger gently over her peaked nipple. Her eyes rolled back at the sensation of his touch and she let out an almost inaudible moan.

"Ask me for what you want," Xander told her.

"I want you," she replied.

"I'm right here, I'm afraid you'll have to be more specific."

"Kiss me," she told him.

"I didn't hear you say 'please' in your request." He walked forward, gently pushing Sophie with his body so her back was against the wall.

Her heart felt like it was going to pound out of her chest as Xander rested his hand on her collarbone with his thumb against her throat. He hovered his lips over hers, teasing her with his hot slow breath. She tried to move her mouth to his, but he held her back against the wall. Why did she find it so sexy? His green eyes stared into hers and she couldn't take the torture anymore. "Please, kiss me," she said, finally.

"There's my good girl," he smiled as he closed the gap between them and claimed her mouth with his. She grabbed for the string on his trousers and undressed him with desperate need. "On your knees, My Queen," he commanded.

She loved it when he called her 'My Queen'. Bastian had called her that sometimes too, but it was mostly in tender moments. It was different when Xander said it; it affected her differently, excited her more. Xander grabbed a pillow from the bed and tossed it to the floor for her to kneel on. She dropped to her knees on the pillow in front of Xander and took him into her mouth. He groaned as she moved her tongue up and down his shaft and then closed her lips around his cock and sucked. When it was harder than she had ever felt it, he lifted her from the pillow and crashed his lips to hers. He turned her around, bent her over and rubbed the length of his cock over the top of her ass.

"Tell me how badly you want me to fuck you," he said.

◻"Please, Xander, don't make me wait any longer, I can't. I *need* to feel you right now," she said. He groaned and took his cock in his hand, guiding it to her entrance. He rubbed the tip of it up and down, not penetrating her yet. Every nerve went crazy, sending pulses of tingling energy throughout her body. Her nipples hardened in response and moisture pooled between her legs. She squirmed against his cock, her body filled with need for him.

◻"I still need to hear you beg, I need to hear the words; *Xander, I want you to fuck me, please.*" She followed his instructions, repeating the words he gave her, and without further hesitation he fulfilled her craving, slowly at first, working his way up to a steady rhythm. She loved the way his cock filled her and she moaned as he pulled her back by her hips, slamming into her so deeply his balls slapped her clit and filled her with a sensation she couldn't describe. She screamed as his hand made contact with her ass in a loud smack. It made her cheek feel tingly and warm.

◻Xander pulled out and turned her around, kissing her again. He picked her up and she wrapped he legs around his waist as he carried her to the bed. He laid her on her back and pushed her legs up firmly, burying his face between them. He licked her wetness, savoring the taste, dipping his tongue into her core, and then sliding it up and down the crevice of her intimate parts. Sophie balled the blankets in her fists as he sucked her clit and grazed it with his teeth.

◻"Oh gods, yes!" Sophie cried as she felt her nerves exploding, she was more sensitive to his touch now and she tried to squirm away, but Xander backed off the bed and stood, pulling her to the edge. He hooked one arm under her leg and guided his cock back inside her, driving it in deep and slow. He leaned down and kissed her, gripping the base of her neck. He looked into her eyes and Sophie felt his passion, and a hunger for him which resonated in her soul. Leaning forward, Xander growled softly in her ear and she could feel the low rumble in his chest and his breath on her skin.

Sophie pushed him back and stood up, guiding him to the bed. Having traded places with him, Sophie pushed him onto his back. She crawled toward his face, kissing every inch of him on her way. She straddled him, rubbing against his erection. The way he looked up at her in awe made her feel like a goddess. Rolling her hips and sliding onto his throbbing cock, Sophie moaned as she rode him. His hand trailed up her thighs to her hips and he held her in place as he thrust into her. Her skin prickled with goosebumps as Xander throbbed inside her, pumping faster and harder by the second and when he let out a loud, throaty moan and called out her name Sophie was driven over the edge again. Every part of her body electrified as they reached orgasm together and her legs shook uncontrollably and gave out, and she collapsed on top of him. She rolled to one side and curled into the nook of his arm with her head on his chest, waiting for her heart to slow. Xander rolled to his side to gaze at her, tracing the constellations of her freckles with his finger. She shivered from his touch and he smiled as if he knew it tickled and kept doing it anyway.

□"I love you, Sophie," he whispered.

Her feelings for him were so deep, and strong. There was no denying she felt the same way, but somehow admitting it seemed like a betrayal to Bastian. She didn't even know how she felt about him now, she had loved him. He'd had been there for her when Gabe broke her heart, and stayed by her side throughout Gabe's funeral; they created life together. He had secrets, sure, but he was a good man, despite the parts of himself he hid from her. Bastian leaving still hurt to think about, but he'd *told* her to move on, and not to wait for him, so why did she feel so guilty about her feelings for Xander?

□"It's okay, Sophie, you don't have to say it back. I know it's only been a few days since Bastian left and I have forever to love you, so I can wait." Xander smiled as he pulled her in close to him.

They were still awake when the first rays of the morning sun peeked in through the window. Sophie got up first and dressed herself in her magical clothing. Xander put on his trousers and looked outside.

"Do you suppose the caravan has a clothing salesman?" he asked.

□"I don't know, but we should head out there and find out. If not, we will be back in Blackwater by this evening, we will just have to manage until then."

□"We don't have to go all the way to Blackwater, we can take the rune circle from Lapis Highland," Sophie remembered.

None of the wagons were in the caravan line, just horses with fully loaded saddle bags. Sophie had forgotten the path through the Stonehold Mountains was too narrow for wagons, especially in the snow. Everyone who needed travel found a vendor to double with. Sophie had hoped she and Xander would get a horse of their own, but no such luck. Sophie was paired with a farrier, his stallion was neatly groomed and a bag of tools hung from the its right side. After she and Xander found a clothing vendor and purchased a tunic for him, and a dress for her, they quickly put on the items and mounted their steeds. The farrier helped Sophie up and then mounted behind her.

□"Hey, do you think we could stop in Lapis Highland, it's only about an hour from here and it's on the way?" Sophie asked. The farrier agreed and snapped the reins. The animal took off, trotting east toward Alasia, following the other riders on the well-traveled trail.

When they neared Alasia, the caravan went on high alert. The smoke rising upward from the town was not the soft, white, billowing smoke as from a chimney, but instead it was thick and black, pouring into the sky and covering the town in a gray haze of ash. Sophie's hands grew clammy and she wiped them on her trousers, a scream from the front of the caravan made the hair on her neck and arms stand on end. The horses all began to buck and neigh, desperate to turn and run from whatever this threat lay ahead.

□"Run, ride as far and fast as you can away from the east," Sophie said as she dismounted.

She ran to the front of the line to see what was going on, Xander following closely behind. The town had been overrun. Fledglings feasted on people and discarded the bodies without care. Sophie spotted a woman moving through the houses, each one erupting in flames as she passed by. Sophie knew it had to be Dmitri's sorceress, Bastian's *wife*, Elizandra. Fury filled her and she couldn't contain her anger, the dragon took over faster than it ever had before and she flew toward the burning buildings. The thick smoke made it hard to see, but wisps of the woman's shadow caught Sophie's eye. Sophie flew in front of the woman and landed facing her. Elizandra stopped and stared into the dragon's eyes without fear. Sophie roared and stormed toward her, but still, Elizandra did not flinch. She blinked out of sight before Sophie could reach her. The smoke from the fire obscured her view. She squinted through the haze in search of Elizandra. The dragon form was too slow, she would have to look in human form.

Sophie shifted back, thankful she could control it this time. A shadow stepped up behind her and Sophie whirled around to face a monster. She stared at Elizandra with hatred in her eyes; this woman had hurt Bastian. She held him prisoner and made him forget her and even his own daughter. Worst of all, she'd taken him against his will. Sophie made a movement with her hand and produced a ball of flame. She hurled it at Elizandra. The sorceress disappeared and reappeared to Sophie's right.

"Where is Bastian? I know he came back to you, I've been to your castle, what's left of it anyway. They told me he wasn't there anymore, where did he go?" Elizandra asked. "Don't make me go to Blackwater, I would hate to have to kill your whole family just to get back what belongs to me," Elizandra threatened. Sophie moved toward her.

"Bastian will never be yours," Sophie spat.

"I suppose as long as you're alive how could he be? We can fix that though." Elizandra's lips spread into a sickening grin as she cast a spell. The magic shot out from her hand like a vine and wrapped around Sophie's throat.

It tightened around her neck as Elizandra raised her hand and lifted Sophie off the ground. She kicked her legs and thrashed, desperately trying to escape. Just as the edges of her vision started to turn white she saw Xander move at a speed faster than she thought possible. He grabbed Elizandra's head and turned it hard and fast. It made a sickening crack and her body hung limp in his hands. Sophie dropped to the ground as the vines dissipated. Xander let go of Elizandra's lifeless body and it crumpled to the ground; he ran over to Sophie and cradled her in his arms.

◻"I'm so sorry, I couldn't keep up after you transformed. I was so scared I wasn't going to make it to you in time," he said.

"I'm okay," Sophie said as she stood up and turned toward the spot where Elizandra's body had been. "Where did she go? I thought she was dead."

◻"So did I," Xander replied, bitterly. "Come on, we can't stay here, we have to get to Blackwater before they return." He took Sophie by the hand and they ran back to the caravan. Several of the horses lay dead, chewed to pieces by the fledgling horde. They saw the last of the feral vampires retreating to the south. A lone surviving horse ran frantically back and forth, neighing and bucking. Sophie walked up to it and started to hum, a green light emanated from her entire body and enveloped the animal. He slowed to a halt as he felt her calming energy. When he was relaxed, Sophie mounted him and Xander got on behind her. He wrapped his arm around her and placed his hand over her heart holding her tightly. She could feel his relief flooding over her. Had she ever felt this strength of emotion from Bastian? She couldn't remember.

Sophie shouted the command to make the horse run and they rode up the sloped road, back to the castle on top of the Highland cliff. Elizandra had not been lying. Parts of the castle looked as if it had exploded. Bricks and debris lay scattered over the entire courtyard. Ezra and Thomas were moving bodies of the murdered to the funeral pyres. Some of them were squires and lady's maids from the bannermen's homes.

◻"I want you to evacuate the castle, tell all of the surrounding towns to leave as well, go to Braidwood, or Ashenport, or even the plains, wherever you can find shelter in the west. We need to prepare for war. The guards can travel to Blackwater, but everyone else needs to flee to safety," Sophie commanded as she dismounted. No one commented on her lack of clothing and her men were decent enough to avert their eyes from her body. She would have spelled herself some clothing, but she needed to conserve her magic. "Is the rune circle still intact?"

"Yes, My Queen, your study had a dome of protection over it, no debris made it into those rooms," Ezra said.

"Perfect, Thank you, Ezra. I'll see you in Blackwater tomorrow?" she asked. He nodded and bowed to her as she and Xander passed him and headed for the study.

THIRTY-SEVEN

Akiri and Bastian crossed the veil just north of the Stonehold Mountains. As they passed, Akiri glanced down at the snow capped peaks. She could barely tell that pine trees grew along the trails as the boughs were heavy with snow. The veil shimmered and just on the other side of it, the snow was gone. The trees were dark green and the air was as warm as a summer day. Bastian directed her to the castle and they dismounted in the courtyard.

"What are you doing? You can't just walk in," Bastian called.

"Why not? I don't see any guards," she replied.

Akiri took quick and heavy steps toward the black double doors. Bastian waited apprehensively, tapping his foot as she gripped the large knocker and crashed it against the wood. A large Fae guard appeared as the door swung open. He glanced at the dragons in the field and then looked back at them. "King Cirros would like to speak with you."

They stepped inside, and then the guard closed the entrance and led them to a small council chamber. The guard opened the door and Akiri walked in with confidence. Bastian tried to follow but the guard put his hand on Bastian's chest to stop him. "Not you, just her," he said. Akiri looked back at Bastian as the door closed.

King Cirros crossed the room and towered over her, gently gripping her shoulders, he turned her body to face the door. "Do not be afraid,

I won't harm you," he said. The King pulled the back of her tunic up to inspect her back.

"What are you doing?" she demanded.

"You're a shifter, I knew you were coming as soon as you crossed the border and we have been waiting for you for a long time," he said as he withdrew his hand. "You have the markings."

"What markings, and why?" Akiri asked, turning around to face him.

"Your name is Akiri," King Cirros asked, although it was more of a statement.

"Yes, why have you been waiting for me?"

"Your name was promised to my father many years ago by a Fae female who wanted to choose a mortal life. In order to give up her Fae magic and live as a human, she had to promise one of her descendants to the fae to serve as queen. Have you ever felt out of place, like you don't belong?"

"Yes, but what do you mean I *was promised to the Fae?*"

"You were promised to me, to be my wife. That's why you came, your destiny pulled you here."

"No. I came here to meet the people who will be caring for my dragons, that's it."

"Tell me why it is I do not sense your fear? You were about to walk right through the front doors of this castle as if you owned it. I sense no caution in you, only curiosity."

Akiri looked over the Fae king's features. His long, dark hair fell to the middle of his back, and his horns twisted upward and nearly grazed the chandelier. He was so much taller than she was. His face was handsome in a dark and rugged sort of way with a chiseled jaw and eyes as black as coal. "I have to go, my friends need my help."

"I am still owed one more dragon. You could stay and I would consider the debt paid, your friend could take the prisoners and go home."

Akiri thought about his offer, it would take them so long to go to Ledora, convince Kamara to give up her dragon, and get back here before Solstice. She looked up at King Cirros. Her mind was swirling with thoughts and they had no time to waste. "Their town will be under attack on solstice, please, allow me to help them win the battle, and then I will return."

"Will you swear the blood oath?" he asked.

She was caught off-guard. Akiri was bluffing when she said she would return, knowing that the Fae usually did not leave their lands.

"What is a blood oath?" she asked.

"It is your promise, signed with a drop of your blood on an enchanted parchment. If you break the contract, you die. It will simply say; you will return here, by sunset the day after the battle ends, or your life is forfeit."

"I want to amend the contract," Akiri said.

"What amendments would you make?"

"I want you to swear the blood oath saying you will never intentionally cause harm to me or anyone I care about to include the dragons, either yourself or by proxy. I want my own room. We will not wed until I am ready, and you will not force me to share your bed. I also want to be granted the right to visit my friends in the human realm as I please."

"Those are some steep terms, I would expect no less from a Queen, and I accept." King Cirros grabbed a piece of parchment and wrote their agreement. He unsheathed his dagger, pricked his finger, wiped the dagger clean, and then handed it to her. Akiri pricked her finger and squeezed a drop of her blood onto the agreement. Golden magic shimmered over the entire document and sealed the words into the blood oath. King Cirros crossed the room and opened the door. □

"Release the human girl and the elf," he said to the guard. "You two can wait out front, we will bring them to you."

Bastian looked at Akiri and then to King Cirros. She "I told him he would have the dragon the day after the battle. He made me sign an agreement," she said. Her words were not outright lies, and barely omissions, but Bastian needed to keep his mind on his family, and the the battle.

Two guards escorted Juniper and Willow out and then closed the doors behind them. Bastian rushed to Willow and Juniper. He stared at Willow as Akiri approached. She could see the pain in his eyes as he looked at his daughter's face. No longer the baby she was when Akiri had last visited them. Her hair was the perfect blend of her mother and father, wavy and strawberry blond. She had Sophie's freckles, and Bastian's blue eyes. She was a teenager now, probably nearer adulthood than childhood.

Akiri glanced from Willow to Bastian. "I'm not sure I can carry the three of you the whole way," she said.

"No need," Bastian said reaching into his pocket. His hand touched something warm and moving. He pulled it out quickly with the tiny sprite in his palm. "Lu, I'm so sorry, I forgot you were in my pocket."

Lu rubbed her eyes and looked around. "I'm pretty sure I passed out when the king grabbed you and started flying. I woke up as we were crossing the border a couple of times, but flying, or however you were traveling makes me woozy. From what I remember, it was a fun trip, but I think I'll stay home this time, though," Lu said.

"It was so very nice to meet you, thank you for all your help," Bastian replied. Willow walked up beside him to see the tiny creature.

"Take care of your family, and good luck!" The sprite smiled as she flitted away.

Bastian pulled the dragon pendant out of his pocket and motioned for them all to link hands. He closed his eyes and thought of Blackwater and the Fae lands faded from their sight.

THIRTY-EIGHT

"My Queen!" Thomas called from the bottom of the stairs. Sophie turned to look at him as he took the steps two at a time. "I'm afraid I have some bad news. Bastian took Custos and never returned," he said.

"He did say he was going to gather an army for Blackwater, maybe he is bringing all the dragons to the arena. I'll see what's going on when I get there. Thank you for letting me know." Sophie turned and went to her room first. She threw on a dress because it was quick and easy, then packed a bag of clothes to take with her. She grabbed one of Bastian's shirts and a pair of boots for Xander. "Ready to go?" she asked.

Xander nodded and stepped into the center of the circle. Sophie followed him and spoke the incantation. The runes around the outer ring lit up and their surroundings changed in an instant. They were no longer in Lapis Highland, but in Agatha's old room. Sophie didn't know the sorceress had a rune circle in her room. She wondered why her runes brought her to this one? It was exactly the same as the one she usually came to. Could it detect Agatha's magic? She didn't have time to think about it right now, Sophie needed to find her father. She led the way through the guild hall, checking all of his usual places. She was about to ask Hank where he was when Bastian barreled through the front doors.

"Sophie!" He ran to her and wrapped her in his embrace.

"What is it?" Sophie asked.

"I have some... news. Willow looks a little different than the last time you saw her. Don't get upset, it's not Juniper's fault, humans age quickly in the Fae lands." Bastian moved to one side, Juniper to the other, and stepping out from behind them was a girl who looked only four or five years younger than herself. Sophie gasped and her hands shot to her mouth to cover it as she looked her over. She had a mix of Sophie and Bastian's features; wavy strawberry blond hair, hazel eyes, and the faintest sprinkling of freckles just across her nose and cheekbones. She looked just how Sophie imagined she would as a teenager.

"My baby? Willow..." Sophie's eyes filled with tears and when Willow wrapped her arms around her, they fell like rain.

"Why didn't you bring her back sooner?" Sophie asked, looking at Juniper.

"It's illegal to take humans to the Fae lands, we were captured before we reached the forgotten grove and the Fae king held us captive, otherwise I would have brought her back the first night when she aged three years before my eyes. Sophie, I'm so sorry." Juniper's face expressed the same worry as her voice.

"I'm not," Willow said. "I can defend myself now and it's not on you to protect me. It's really for the best." She gave Sophie a smile.

"I don't want you anywhere near the fighting, have you ever used a sword, or magic?" Sophie asked.

"Well, no, but King Cirros gave me a lot of books so I could learn things, the hours there seemed like years to me."

"Book learning is not the same as application, but if you want, after we win this battle, you can begin training with a sword," Sophie said. "I hope we can make up for lost time when all this is over."

"Are you hungry?" Juniper asked Willow.

"Yes, I'm starved, how did you know?"

"Because I am, too. Let's go to the Gilded Lily and get some food, let your mom and dad talk. Is that okay?" Juniper looked at Sophie.

"Yes, it's a good idea," Sophie said.

Xander looked at her awkwardly. "I'm going to go see if I can help Commander Rend with anything," he said, leaving them to talk.

"Bastian, I'm sorry. I didn't know the Fae lands would have this effect on her; otherwise, I never would have let Juniper take Willow there. I also thought she would be a shifter like us," Sophie said.

"I know, you don't have to apologize, you just wanted to keep her safe, that is all I want for the both of you," he said. "I can tell you and Xander are closer, you seem happy and so does he," Bastian said, not meeting her gaze. "I want to be with you and Willow when this is over, even if it means I move into another room in the castle and I am only there as Willow's father, and your protector. I want you to be happy, but I can't see that for myself without the two of you."

Sophie extended her arms to Bastian, letting him be the one to close the space between them. She held him firmly, comforting him. "You, Xander, Willow, and I will have to talk when this is over," she said, releasing him from her embrace. "Elizandra attacked Alasia and Highland Castle; I had everyone evacuate. The fighters will all be here by tomorrow morning so they can rest up before the battle. Thomas said you took Custos, did you bring him here?" Sophie asked. Bastian looked down, once again avoiding eye contact. "Bastian, where's my dragon?"

"I had to give the dragons to King Cirros for Willow and Juniper. I'm sorry." Bastian hung his head.

"I probably would have done the same thing. I would give the world for our daughter, but we really could have used the dragons for the battle ahead." Sophie sighed and looked at Bastian, thinking of the past and the nights they spent dancing in Ledora. He had mended her broken heart, or at the very least, distracted her from the pain. Bastian caressed her cheek as he kissed her forehead. Why did she feel so guilty? He told her to move on, and she did, yet she still did not want to let Bastian go. "Bastian, I have to tell you, Xander and I... we..." her voice trailed off as she searched for the right words. She and Xander had never discussed what they were to each other. He told her he loved her and she hadn't known what to say.

"I think I knew the moment I saw you guys together after Ryul brought me back. I could tell by the way he looked at you. He loves you, Sophie."

"What about you? How do you feel?" She asked.

"About you and him?" Bastian asked.

"How do you feel about me?" she clarified. Bastian lifted her chin to meet his eyes. Her heart fluttered. Why was she so afraid of his answer? His pause was killing her.

"Would knowing how I feel change your heart?" he asked. The sadness in his voice matched the sorrow she felt. He could say he loved her, but it wouldn't change the way she felt about Xander. Madame Moira had been right, fate was ripping her heart in half, she was equally drawn to both of them.

"Sophie, Bastian, I'm glad I found you!" Sparrow called. He approached them and pulled something from his pocket; a green rock with glowing red lines akin to molten lava. "I think this contains your magic. Natalia found it in the blood pool behind the sarcophagus." Sparrow handed it to Bastian.

"Do you think you can find out how to give me my magic back?" he asked Sophie.

"Let's go check Agatha's grimoire. Maybe we can find a spell that will work. Sparrow, can you tell Juniper where we are going? She's having lunch with Willow at the Lily." Sophie asked.

After Sparrow agreed, Sophie and Bastian headed for Agatha's study. The room had a lonely kind of air about it now since Agatha was gone. Sophie wondered if all sorcerers ended up so lonely. She had never thought of herself as a sorceress, she was the wizard's apprentice, the red dragon, a queen, and a wizard—only they didn't call females wizards, they were witches, and being a witch was still frowned upon.

"Look around for a large old book," she said to Bastian. They searched the room, sifting through old stacks of parchment and box after box of crystals, and candles.

"Maybe your father has it? Surely a book like that would be dangerous to just keep lying around. Besides, we have more important things to worry about right now," Bastian said.

"You having your draconic power is just as important, I wish we had more time."

"It's okay. We will have you, Akiri, Dominic, and Ledora's dragon. We're going to stop him. Don't worry." Bastian took her hands in his. "I will always protect you because I love you, and love is the greatest power in the world."

She wanted to tell him she loved him too, but her heart was so confused. How was it possible to love them both at the same time?

"We should get back to Willow," Sophie said as she slipped her hands away from his. Someone cleared their throat from the doorway and startled them. Bastian and Sophie turned toward the sound and saw Xander waiting there.

"Leon is holding a feast tonight for all of us to raise morale before the battle tomorrow. I've been tasked with letting everyone know." Xander said.

"In the great hall?" Sophie asked.

Xander nodded. "Sophie, would you mind if I talked to my brother for a minute?" he asked.

"No problem, I was going to go spend some time with Willow. I'll see you guys at dinner." Sophie crossed the room and glanced back briefly before leaving them alone in the room together. She listened outside the door for a moment, hoping they would not fight again, but her morals took over and she decided it was best not to eavesdrop. She walked down the corridor to the Silver Talons foyer. The entrance hall buzzed with the voices of early arrivals—soldiers and bannermen from other regions. Sophie spotted Natalia and Arturo among the sea of faces and squeezed through the crowd to get to them.

"You were gone for a long time, how are things?" Sophie asked.

"We packed up all of our things from the castle while we were there. The cargo will be here in a couple of days," Natalia said.

"I'm sorry you had to leave your home. You know you guys are always welcome at Highland Castle."

"We appreciate you saying so, Sophie," Arturo said.

"Bastian is back, by the way, he's over there, talking to Xander," Sophie pointed toward Agatha's room.

"Oh thank goodness!" Natalia let out a sigh of relief and looked down the hall.

"Also, my father is having a feast in the great hall tonight. One more night of peace."

"We will see you there," Arturo told her.

A feast on the eve of battle was never one of pomp and circumstance, everyone arrived wearing their battle garb instead of formal clothing. Sophie was most comfortable like this. She had gotten used to wearing dresses as Queen, but would much rather wear trousers and boots than skirts and heels. Sophie had special armor she wore for these occasions, although she would not wear it into battle. Her dragon form was far more effective than the decorative scale mail breastplate and epaulettes she planned to wear for dinner. Sophie braided her auburn hair back and secured the end of it with a ribbon. Willow dressed in a similar set of armor and Sophie braided her hair as well.

Her heart fluttered as she looked at her daughter. "For me, you left only a week or so ago, but now you're nearly a woman. It must have seemed like we abandoned you, or forgot about you, but it's not true. We just wanted to keep you safe from the war. We are about to face a horde of feral vampires, an evil sorceress, and an ancient vampire we can't kill."

"Why can't you kill him?" Willow asked.

"He turned me into a vampire. If he dies, any vampire he has sired also dies. He knew those who hunted him, loved me, that's why I was targeted."

"So if he lives, you will live forever and never grow older?"

"My life can still be ended by external forces, a stake to the heart, maybe fire, of course, I'm also a dragonshifter so fire might not have the same effect on me as it would other vampires," Sophie told her.

"You have to drink human blood?" Willow furrowed her brow and scrunched her nose.

"Not as often as I used to, because I am part dragon, my human side did not completely die when I transitioned. My heart stopped beating, and then started beating again at a much slower rate. Your father was the same, dragon, vampire, and human."

"Could you turn me, too?" Willow looked ashamed to ask it by the way she glanced down, refusing to meet her mother's eyes. Sophie's heart ached. She would give anything to freeze time with her daughter. She had missed so much of her life already, but turning her would go against the treaty with the guild.

"We can talk about it after all this, when we go home to Highland Castle, and once you've had more time to think about it." Sophie kissed Willow's forehead. "I love you so much," she said.

Sophie had not seen so many people packed into this dining room since she was a child. Each of the four banners had their own table; The Silver Talons, Highland Castle, Braidwood, and Ledora. Sophie looked around for Natalia and Arturo, wondering where they might sit since Immernacht did not have a banner. She spotted them sitting with Akiri, Serena, and Chloe at the end of the Silver Talons Table. Serena and Chloe couldn't tear their eyes away from each other. *Good for her.* Sophie thought as she saw the smile spread across Serena's lips.

"Come Willow, you should officially meet your grandparents." Sophie led her first to Leon who sat in the chair at the center of the table on the raised platform at the back of the room. Next to him, Samantha looked at the girl she had cared for as an infant just weeks before and her eyes welled with tears, she stroked Willow's hair and held her in her arms. Leon hugged her next and then held his wife's hand, giving her comfort and strength.

After reintroducing Willow to *her* parents, Sophie took her to speak with Bastian's parents who were equally surprised and emotional.

"She looks so much like you both," Natalia commented to Sophie. "Willow, darling, you have grown up beautifully."

"Thank you," she said.

"Willow, you can sit wherever you like; either this table, or you can join us at the Highland Castle table just over there," Sophie pointed to the next banner over. She left Willow to mingle and become acquainted with her family and as she approached her seat, Bastian and Xander both stood up and reached for the chair between them, but it was Bastian who pulled it out for her. When she sat down, Xander was the one to push her in. It was a strange kind of teamwork and as odd as it was, it pleased her because at least they weren't fighting. Madame Moira's warning still echoed in her ears and the last thing she wanted was for Bastian and Xander to hate each other.

Xander poured her a glass of wine, and Bastian made her a plate of food. Each table had the same spread; bread, cheese, turkey, ham, greens, fresh fruit, salads, and mini tarts with lemon, strawberry, and orange. Bastian put a little of each on her plate. Although she knew she would not be able to finish it all, she thanked him just the same. They ate together and talked about anything they could think of to distract them from tomorrow's tasks.

With all the voices and bodies in the room, the temperature increased at a rapid rate and Sophie needed some fresh air. Bastian and Xander both sprang to their feet to either assist or accompany her, but their strange behavior only added to the anxiety she was experiencing.

"I need some time alone," Sophie told them as she stepped away from the table. She hurried across the crowded great hall and to the front doors of the guild hall. She walked to the gardens, enjoying the cool breeze on her skin. It had not snowed in days and as a result, the snow was packed down and mixed with dirt. The trees and lantern posts still looked beautiful with the strings of cranberries and garland, dried orange slices and bunches of cinnamon sticks tied together with festive string. The clouds parted and an unsettling red hue spread across the snow. Sophie looked up to see the moon red and full hanging low in the night sky. *The blood moon.* Ryul told her of the blood moon long ago, he said when it came it would signify the end of the world. Sophie had never hoped for Ryul to be wrong before, but she sure hoped he wasn't right about this.

THIRTY-NINE

ARMORED IN HALF-PLATE FROM The Silver Talons guard stock, Bastian stood next to Leon with a sword in his hand. It had been a long time since he fought with a sword but he tried to keep his nerves at ease. All of the willing fighters stood in rows with shields, swords, axes, and other weapons held in defensive positions. On the parapet of the guild hall, archers held their bows with flaming arrows nocked and ready to fire. The mages used spells to produce the sound of singing. Songs of holiday cheer filled the air around them and it would have been soothing if only its sole purpose was not to make Dmitri think he had caught them unaware. Bastian gripped his sword tighter as a bright green light flashed into the sky and danced above them, mesmerizing those who dared to look up.

"Look away! Don't look at the sky!" Bastian shouted. It was too late for some, they stood frozen, staring up at the rippling illumination. A rumble like violent thunder came from behind them as the guild hall erupted in screams. Their eyes had been fixed to the north, Stonehold Pass was the only way to get to Blackwater unless you took a boat or could fly.

Bastian whirled around just as the guild hall doors burst open and a sea of fledglings flooded out. The mages, who usually assisted from the back of the formation were now on the frontlines of the battle and caught completely off guard. Howling screams as the fledglings tore into their flesh haunted him as he rushed forward with his sword. How were they coming from inside the guild hall? Bastian could only think of Willow in the catacombs below the guild with the other women and children. Had they found the entrance and attacked them first? Bastian heard the dragons roar behind him as he swung his sword at several of the feral creatures making way to the guild hall doors. Fledglings gnashed their teeth at his armor as the crowd of enemies grew thicker. He kicked one away as he swung his sword at another. The creature's head hit the ground with a thud and thick black ooze bubbled from the corpse as it crumpled at Bastian's feet.

He jumped over the body and barreled his way through the other fledglings. The Silver Talons Guild teleportation circle glowed with the same eerie green light Bastian saw in the sky. Dmitri and Elizandra appeared in the circle and fear took over Bastian's body, rooting him to the spot. Elizandra's lips curled up in a sinister smirk at the sight of him. Bastian hadn't thought about how it would feel to see her again. It both disgusted him and filled him with anxiety. She sauntered up to him and grabbed his face with one hand, holding it in place with what seemed like vampire strength.

"Did you miss me, lover?" she asked as she brushed her tongue from his bottom lip to his top. He shuddered, still unable to move away.

A loud screeching sound from the doorway made Elizandra toss Bastian to the side. A massive purple dragon crashed through the door frame. Bastian looked at Dmitri and Elizandra, why didn't they look scared? The purple dragon unleashed a strange weapon, a black ball of sludge. Elizandra caught it in her hands and threw it back at the dragon.

"That's not the right one, and I think you can do better," she teased. As the ball of sludge hit the dragon, her beast form melted away and Bastian saw Sophie standing in front of them.

"Are you too afraid to fight me without your magic?" Sophie asked.

"Why would I fight anyone without magic?" she scoffed.

Dmitri kicked the back of Bastian's knees, buckling him to the floor, and held a dagger to his throat. Sophie's face betrayed her and she gasped, almost playing into their hand.

"You're right, we wouldn't want for you to have to admit I'm just better than you and that's why you couldn't get Bastian to love you," Sophie spat.

It was a touch too far. Elizandra's face turned brick red and any trace of amusement was gone. The sorceress reached for the daggers at her hip.

"I don't need magic to gut you like a pig," She said as she rushed forward.

Sophie had only a moment to save Bastian and she had to take it. She shot a bolt of fire from her hand, over Bastian, and it hit Dmitri directly in the head. By this time Elizandra had reached her and she stabbed at Sophie's shoulder with one dagger while simultaneously slashing low with the other. Sophie had not been prepared and could only block one attack. She howled in pain as Elizandra's dagger sank into the muscle of her shoulder. Sophie punched her in the nose and blood trickled from it as she backed away. Sophie used the opportunity to strike. She grabbed a handful of Elizandra's hair and drove her face downward into her knee. She heard the bones crack as Elizandra screamed. "You bitch!"

"You will never touch Bastian again, and I mean NEVER!" Sophie growled. Elizandra scrambled away and used her magic to teleport to the front of the hall. Bastian caught a glimpse of her running out the door just before Sophie bent down in front of him. "Are you okay?" she asked, her eyes searching for Dmitri.

"Yeah, I'm okay. They were using the teleportation circle though, how is it possible? I thought each location had unique runes and they had to match in order for someone to use it."

"They had a little help," Sophie and Bastian turned toward the sound of the voice to see Beric near the east corridor clutching a book in his arms.

"Why would you help them?" Sophie asked. Beric looked her up and down with an approving grin. She let out a groan of disgust and dressed herself in illusion.

"Easy, my loyalties lie with those who have the most power. He's the oldest vampire in the world, and she is a powerful warlock."

"I'm a powerful witch, a dragon, and a vampire, with a family of vampires, a thunder of dragons, and The Silver Talons Guild on my side, this can't be about power," Sophie said.

"You see, the problem with your power is; it's too easily manipulated," Beric said as he pointed to the hole where the front door used to be.

Dmitri had his fingers curled around Willow's neck. He brushed her hair to the side revealing her pulsing neck.

"No! Don't!" Sophie shouted. Her body jerked uncontrollably and she screamed in pain as she tried to force the dragon to emerge from her.

"Don't what?" Dmitri asked, bringing his lips to Willow's neck. She whimpered and tears fell from her eyes. "Her fear smells so lovely," he said as he drew in her scent.

Beric dashed to Elizandra's side and handed her the book. Bastian cursed him under his breath as the young boy looked up at the sorceress with stars in his eyes. *Such a fucking apple polisher, a gods damned teacher's pet,* he thought. Another scream from Sophie stole his attention.

"I can't control it," she cried. Her body was only partially shifted, scaly and enlarged only in patches.

"Yes you can, Sophie, you're the strongest woman I have ever met, you can do anything," Bastian encouraged her, although he wasn't sure if she was trying to complete or stop the transformation. Elizandra leafed through the old book.

Dmitri and Elizandra disappeared with Willow before their eyes. Leaving Beric standing in the doorway. Bastian used all his speed to flash across the room behind him before he could process the danger.

"Looks like they left you all alone, pity," Bastian said wrapping his arm around his neck. Beric flailed and pulled at Bastian's arm, clawing for freedom. Bastian held tighter, pulling the boy backward as his consciousness faded. Sophie was breathing heavily but reverted to her human form. Bastian dragged Beric's body to her.

"Here, Sophie," Bastian said as he held Beric up for her. "Drink him dry." She needed the strength and did not hesitate to sink her teeth into his flesh. She drank until his heart stopped beating and then stepped over his body with careless haste.

"Willow!" She screamed as she made her way out of the hole her dragon form had left behind. Bastian followed her with his sword in hand. Bodies lay strewn about the battlefield on top of the blood-soaked snow. Her daughter's scream rang out across the courtyard and Sophie ran in the direction of the sound. She realized Dmitri was standing right on top of the teleportation circle, the one matching Immernacht's design. She had to get Willow away from him. "What is it you want Dmitri?" Sophie asked.

"The same thing I have wanted every day since my maker died. I want to be with her."

"That can be arranged, all you had to do was ask," Sophie said as she shot fire from her hand in his direction. Dmitri waved the bolt of magic away with a flick of his wrist.

"Do you really think I haven't tried?" He pushed Willow aside and ripped open his tunic. His chest was covered in scars right around where his heart should have been. "This world is my prison. I have lived for almost two thousand years without the love of my life, without my fated. We committed terrible crimes, we feasted on entire villages together, we crumbled empires, toppled regimes, and the fates saw fit to punish us. They took away our link to each other, killed her, and forced me to stay in this world forever, and never die—never to reunite with *her*." Dmitri picked up a stake and tossed it to Sophie. "Don't believe me? Take your best shot." Sophie held the stake in her hand. If he died then she would die, too. Was this some kind of trick? Was he only playing on her sympathies?

"If you can't die... You turned me into a vampire for nothing! Why let everyone believe if you died, I would die too? " Sophie shouted.

"Do you really think I would reveal my greatest weakness before I ensured my victory?"

"Say it, Sophie!" Bastian yelled from behind her. Sophie's eyes sparked with understanding as she saw what he did; Dmitri standing alone in the rune circle that would trap him on Immernacht. He watched Sophie speak the incantation to activate the teleportation circle and Dmitri disappeared as the last word was spoken. Bastian rushed to the circle with a handful of snow and washed some of the runes away.

"Do you really think I needed him?" Elizandra asked. The green light in the sky ripped like a piece of fabric and the hole spread from the sky to the ground. Elizandra tossed the grimoire aside and stepped back to admire her work. A loud hissing sound erupted from the darkness of the rift and black leathery creatures with wings like giant bats clawed their way out.

"Grab your weapons!" Sophie yelled. Bastian raised his sword and prepared to strike. Dominic, in his golden dragon form, flew above them and unleashed his breath weapon. Electricity surged into the void and the resulting sound was like the whistling of a hundred kettles at once as some of the demons tumbled back into the darkness. Elizandra's attention snapped to the gold dragon and she extended her hand shooting a beam of frost at it. He barrel rolled out of the way, circled around, and flew straight for Elizandra. She fell prone in time to avoid being snatched up by his massive talons, but they slashed her back. leaving gouges in her skin. She stood up, wincing in pain, and began casting a spell in the direction of the rift.

Bastian spotted Willow cowering behind what was left of a garden wall. "Come on, Willow, let's get you out of here." Bastian put his arm around his daughter and ushered her toward the guild hall. A beam of magic flowed from Elizandra's hand and encircled Willow like a lasso. The magic wrapped around Willow's neck and Elizandra dragged her back.

Sophie screamed in fury and tried to blast Elizandra with her magic, but something went wrong, a dark energy burst from her; a swirling orb of endless black, deep purple, and a sprinkling of glittering stars exploded into a vortex. It siphoned the magic from the rift Elizandra had opened, foiling her plan to unleash the creatures of the abyss. The garland and strings of cranberries flew off the trees and into the void. It was swallowing everything whole. Elizandra still had Willow by the throat. She looked at the twisting mass and her lips turned up in an evil grin as she looked at Sophie. Before she could act, Xander emerged behind her, beaten and bloody from fighting off the fledglings. He stumbled as he pointed his sword, and plunged the steel into Elizandra's back. Her face contorted in anger. There was no blood. *Why is there no blood?* Bastian thought.

Elizandra let out a sound akin to a wailing banshee and in the blink of an eye, Dmitri appeared, grabbed Willow, and launched himself into the black hole with her in his grasp. Bastian hardly had time to process what happened, he thought they'd been successful at trapping Dmitri on the island of Immernacht, how was he here?

"No! Willow!" Sophie cried as she propelled herself forward, running faster than she ever had before, and dove into the endless dark after them. Bastian looked at the void in horror as his family disappeared. Elizandra pulled herself off of Xander's sword and turned to face him.

"Go, go find them! I love you, brother." Xander yelled to Bastian as he took another swing at Elizandra.

He had to do it; he couldn't leave Sophie and Willow. He didn't know if they would still exist on the other side, but the small chance they did was all he needed. Bastian ran toward the anomaly. Elizandra tried to follow but Xander pulled her back and held her until the rift was too small for anyone else to go through it. The circle grew smaller as Bastian fell further into the swirling night.

FORTY

A CHURNING GRAY CLOUD circulated above. Lightning streaked through the sky but no thunder followed. A golden dragon soared over the battlefield with two others, searching the area for remaining enemies. Xander dug his fingers into Elizandra's throat and cursed her under his breath as his chance to be with Sophie slipped away. She twirled her fingers and flicked her wrist, muttering against the crushing force of his hand. When nothing happened she clawed at him, desperate for air.

"What's wrong? You failed at your task and now your power is gone?" Xander asked in a mocking tone as he watched the blood spread out from the sword wound. "I'm really going to enjoy this..." He jerked her head to the side and sank his fangs into her neck. He didn't bother telling her not to scream. In fact, her screams made her blood that much sweeter. Xander drank until her heart stopped beating, and then he plunged his hand through her chest and ripped out her heart for good measure. "I'm just sorry Bastian wasn't here to see it."

Xander turned toward the rift. Was the way still open? Xander watched the last speck of Sophie's magic flash from existence. He fell to his knees in defeat. How could he go on in this world without them? Sophie, and his brother. A hand on his shoulder startled him, and he turned to see Dominic.

"There aren't many survivors, we need to start preparing the pyres, there are too many bodies to bury," Dominic said. Xander nodded and stood to follow him across the battlefield.

"What about the catacombs?" Xander asked. Dominic shook his head. *Sophie's mother had been down there.* "Commander Rend?" Dominic's face filled with sorrow again, and he turned his head from side to side.

"A mercy at least; had he survived, he would have to live without his entire family. It's a fate I wouldn't wish on anyone."

The soldiers from Ledora and Lapis Highland helped them build the pyres and carry the bodies. They removed all the weapons and salvageable armor before they laid their corpses upon the stacks. Samantha, Leon, Thomas, and so many others. Part of him was thankful Sophie did not have to see this, but the other part wanted to crawl onto the pyre so he wouldn't have to live without her.

"Can you guys bring around some wagons so we can get all the armor and weapons gathered up?" Xander asked. No one else seemed to be taking charge and staying busy was the only thing keeping him from shutting down completely. He walked to the edge of the garden where he had last seen Sophie, picking up broken swords, spears, dented armor, and arrows as he walked. When his arms were full he put the debris in a pile and started over again.

Along the southern perimeter of the garden wall, Xander spotted a familiar item and a discarded leather-bound book. He picked up the magic stone Natalia had found in the blood pool behind Dmitri's sarcophagus. He turned it over, studying the bright red markings flowing like rivers through the green rock then slipped it into his pocket. The book was lying open; its pages crumpled and spattered with blood. He grabbed it next and flipped page after page, glancing at the hand-written spells and pictures when one in particular caught his eye. *This is it. This is the spell Sophie used by accident.* "Dimension Gateway" he read aloud.

"Whatcha got there?"

Xander looked up from the grimoire to see Arturo. He closed the book, tucking it under his arm. "It was Sophie's spell book from Agatha," he replied.

"Was? I didn't see her on the pyre…" Arturo was confused. How could he possibly know what had happened to Sophie? He was on the other side of the battlefield when it happened.

"Willow, Sophie, and Bastian were pulled into a dimension gateway. It's a spell in this book. I'm going to find someone who can cast it and I'm going to try to bring them back," he vowed. This sliver of hope filled Xander with determination. The visions of their future replayed in his mind and brought a smile to his lips. One lingering thought dominated: *this is not the end.*

Acknowledgement

Becoming an author has been my dream ever since I began reading Stephen King novels in fourth grade. I loved both horror and fantasy books throughout my teenage years and my adult life. I wrote a lot throughout my youth; mostly poetry and journaling, but I always dreamed of becoming an author. I began my journey to publication in 2020, during the height of COVID, school closings, and business closures. I honestly didn't know how things would turn out in the end, but I was determined to see it through. A few people made achieving my dreams easier, and I honestly cannot thank them enough.

Firstly, my husband, my rock, my best friend, and my love. While I was writing my first book, we were both working full-time, caring for the children and the house, and were often tired and sometimes cranky when we got home. He cooked, helped with homework, and always made sure that I had time to write. He pushed me to keep going when I wanted to quit, wiped away my tears of frustration while I learned to format, edit, and publish my own book. He believed in me, and cheered me on. Now He has started his own business and made it possible for me to not only write as my hobby, but make it my full-time profession. I know that I chose the right partner for life and I love you more every single day!

Next, I have to thank my wonderful friends in The Author's Pub! The countless hours you have spent with me during my writing, editing, cover designing, marketing, and publishing phases made such a huge difference in determination and morale. One member of the Author's Pub gets special mention: G.T. Gretz, Thank you for helping me edit and giving such great feedback!

Most importantly, I can't forget to thank you, dear reader. Without you this is all for nothing. You make stories worth telling and It is such a pleasure to share my imaginary world with you! I hope you look forward to the rest of this series as much as I do and know that I am forever grateful for you!

ABOUT THE AUTHOR

C.L. Carner is a bestselling and award-winning author, a U.S. Army veteran, and former teacher. She studied at Pickaway-Ross Career and Technology Center and Ohio University-Chillicothe. She wrote and published her first book; My Fair Verona in 2020 and is currently working on The Silver Talons Guild Series. Due to her wandering spirit, she has lived in many states, including Alaska, Georgia, and Ohio. Mrs. Carner currently resides in Texas with her husband, two children, her golden retriever, Malcolm, and two black cats, Poe and Loki.